More praise for the
DREAM OF EAGLES series

"With historical detail that rivals any textbook and a genius for description and characterization that defies myth and fiction, Whyte's series has recreated a post-Roman Britain that could have created a once and future king."
—*The Globe and Mail*

"Dazzling ... perhaps not since the early 1970s, with Mary Stewart's *The Crystal Cave* and *The Hollow Hills,* have the Roman Empire and the Arthurian legends been intertwined with as much skill and authenticity."
—*Publishers Weekly* (starred review)

"Whyte succeeds brilliantly in bringing to life a period of British history rich in myth but scant with historical details. [One can] almost feel the brutality and harshness that dominated the lives of people struggling to survive the chaos that swept Britain in the wake of hundreds of years of Roman order."
—*Calgary Herald*

"If you have even a passing interest in Arthurian legend or the history of ancient Britain, you must read these books. You will not be disappointed."
—*The Telegram* (St. John's)

"Whyte weaves historical fact and folklore together with an accomplished and bardic verve."
—*Edmonton Journal*

"To read Jack Whyte is to surrender to a storyteller of the old school. His writing is firmly rooted in the basics of good storytelling: strong characterization, effective plotting, and excellent writing."
—*Quill & Quire*

"Whyte makes the reader think, Yes, this is the way it could have been. ... [He] has taken the time to build the Arthurian legend piece by piece and make it come alive."
—*The Leader-Post* (Regina)

"Whyte's descriptions, astonishingly vivid, of this ancient mystical era ring true, as do his characters, who include a number of strong women. Whyte shows why Camulod was such a wonder, demonstrating time and again how persistence, knowledge, and empathy can help push back the darkness of ignorance to build a shining future."

—*Publishers Weekly*

"Rich in historical detail, especially where warfare and the use of cavalry are concerned. . . . We are not just dipped, we are plunged into the minutiae of life in post-Roman Britain."   —*The Hamilton Spectator*

Praise for the TEMPLAR trilogy

"This is Jack Whyte at better than his best."

—Diana Gabaldon, on *Knights of the Black and White*

"Whyte's found the key to refreshing the legend and making it live again. . . . The wealth and richness of the historical detail are fascinating."

—*Calgary Herald*

"Taut and gripping."   —*The Vancouver Sun*

"Whyte's Templar trilogy . . . finds the author in his top form. Few authors can match Whyte when it comes to epic battle scenes involving blazing heat, choking dust, rearing horses and thousands of sword-wielding knights and Saracens locked in mortal combat."

—*Publishers Weekly*

"Whyte brings his Templar trilogy to a rousing conclusion. . . . Readers are in for a thrilling, exhilarating ride."   —*Booklist*

Praise for the GUARDIANS trilogy

"William Wallace shines forth not just as an Achilles of the late 1200s, but as a reluctant outlaw, a Latin-speaking kingmaker and a sword-wielding patriot. . . . Whyte opens the novel brilliantly [and] succeeds in weaving history into the story as it crackles along."

—*The Globe and Mail*

"Whyte's prose is punctuated with moments of tension that contrast perfectly with the book's somber tone."   —*Winnipeg Free Press*

"Whyte [is] a master at painting pictures on an epic-sized canvas."

—*Booklist*

"Whyte writes with a clear sense of history as an ongoing chess game. . . . [*The Guardian*] is both captivating and transporting, plunging the reader into an utterly alien world of conflict, the repercussions of which are being felt to the present day."   —*The Vancouver Sun*

Also by Jack Whyte

The Burning Stone (prequel to the *Dream of Eagles* series)

A DREAM OF EAGLES

The Skystone

The Singing Sword

The Eagles' Brood

The Saxon Shore

The Sorcerer, Volume I: The Fort at River's Bend

The Sorcerer, Volume II: Metamorphosis

~

Uther

~

The Golden Eagle, Volume I: Clothar the Frank

The Golden Eagle, Volume II: The Eagle

~

THE TEMPLAR TRILOGY

Knights of the Black and White

Standard of Honor

Order in Chaos

~

THE GUARDIANS TRILOGY

The Forest Laird

The Renegade

The Guardian

The Eagles' Brood

Jack Whyte

PENGUIN

an imprint of Penguin Canada,
a division of Penguin Random House Canada Limited

Penguin Canada
320 Front Street West, Suite 1400, Toronto, Ontario M5V 3B6, Canada

First published in Viking Canada hardcover by Penguin Group (Canada),
a division of Pearson Canada Inc., 1994
Published in Penguin Canada paperback by Penguin Group (Canada),
a division of Pearson Canada Inc., 1995
Published in this edition, 2018

1 2 3 4 5 6 7 8 9 10

Text design: Jennifer Lum
Cover art: Greg Banning

Printed and bound in Canada.

Library and Archives Canada Cataloguing in Publication data available upon request.

ISBN 978-0-735-23740-7
eBook ISBN 978-0-14-319766-9

Publisher's note: The Eagles' Brood *is based in part on actual events,*
but all the principal characters are fictional.

www.penguinrandomhouse.ca

Penguin
Random House
PENGUIN CANADA

To my wife Beverley

ACKNOWLEDGMENTS

I have dedicated each book in this cycle to my wife, Beverley, because she has been the one who has lived with the writing of it—one single, huge chronicle—since its inception in 1978, in a condition that too frequently verged upon what used to be known as "grass widowhood." To this point, however, I have made no other attempt to acknowledge any other contributions or contributors, irrespective of, or perhaps because of, the fact that there have been so many.

Few things can be more daunting than the contemplation of the task of writing, then refining and eventually finding a publisher for a first book, let alone a quartet of books, when you are a complete unknown. There are legions of people who rush to warn you of the impossibility of what you hope to achieve. Heartfelt thanks and appreciation, therefore, to all my friends who didn't. So many people have endeared themselves to me over the years by *not* saying "Are you still slugging away at *that?*" that it would be impossible to name them. Some, however, have been even more supportive.

Bob Sharp of Calgary, Alberta, is the man who got me started on this whole thing, the only man I have ever met whose reading tastes and mine coincide absolutely. We sat together one day, fifteen years ago, wondering how the sword got into that stone and how the boy was able to pull it out. Suddenly I remembered something from my boyhood, a lightning succession of synapses triggered immediately, and I knew how it had been done!

Robert A. Willson of Calgary demonstrated early on that he could recognize a winner in Caius Britannicus, and Peter C. Newman steadied and readied me on my first public appearance as a bona fide Author. Ray Addington of Vancouver, B.C., went digging in the antique shops of Colchester to find five Roman pennies that Publius Varrus might have handled. My friend Bill McKay demonstrated to me most effectively that a creative artist is seldom truly effective as a pragmatic businessman, and then shook his head ruefully as he held me aloft to drip dry. Alma Lee of the Vancouver Writers' Festival and Ann Cowan of Simon Fraser University guided my feet towards succour in the form of Marian Hebb, literary lawyer *extraordinaire*. Joyce Elliott, a friend for many years, read the original manuscript before anyone else and thereafter kept me on the straight and narrow path of fidelity to my tale.

Professor Jim Russell of the Department of Classical Archaeology at the University of British Columbia advised me on where to dig for information on Roman Britain. I should state here, however, that any errors of authenticity in my work are attributable only to my fiction, and not to Jim's guidance. My friend Michael McCrodan read the first manuscript in draft and refrained from discouraging me.

There are many more, but most specifically I wish to thank my editors, Kirsten Hanson and Catherine Marjoribanks. These ladies, between them, taught me what objective professionalism can achieve when allied with fervent enthusiasm. To each, and to all, my thanks.

Jack Whyte
Vancouver, British Columbia
November 1993

The Journey To
and From Verulamium

Showing the Main Places and Events of the Story

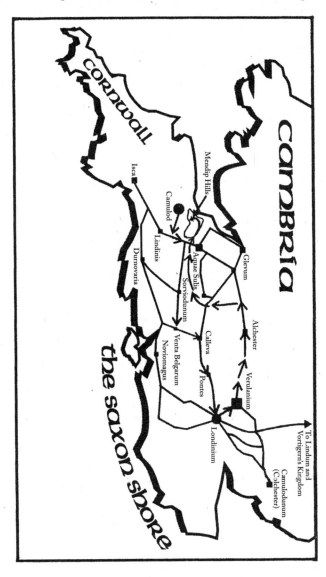

Merlyn's Pursuit of
Uther into Lot's Country

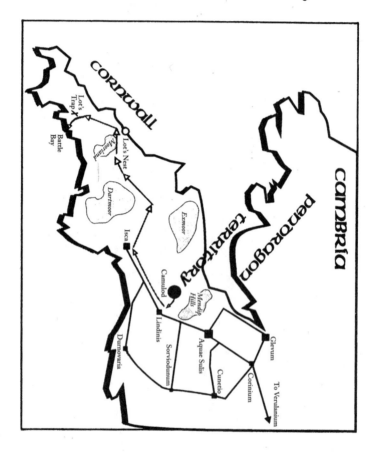

The Legend of the Skystone

Out of the night sky there will fall a stone
That hides a maiden born of murky deeps,
A maid whose fire-fed, female mysteries
Shall give life to a lambent, gleaming blade,
A blazing, shining sword whose potency
Breeds warriors. More than that,
This weapon will contain a woman's wiles
And draw dire deeds of men; shall name an age;
Shall crown a king, called of a mountain clan
Who dream of being spawned from dragon's seed;
Fell, forceful men, heroic, proud and strong,
With greatness in their souls.
This king, this monarch, mighty beyond ken,
Fashioned of glory, singing a song of swords,
Misting with magic madness mortal men,
Shall sire a legend, yet leave none to lead
His host to triumph after he be lost.
But death shall ne'er demean his destiny who,
Dying not, shall ever live and wait to be recalled.

PROLOGUE

I cannot think of Camulod without thinking of horses. They were everywhere and they dominated my boyhood. The life of the place revolved completely around them—them and the men who rode them—and the earliest sights and smells I can remember are those of the stables. Almost half of the entire hilltop on which the fort was built was given over to stables and exercise yards, and a huge, barren *campus*, or drilling ground, had been created on the plain at the bottom of the hill. At any hour of the day, you would find up to a dozen separate groups of horsemen there, wheeling and manoeuvring at the walk, the canter or the gallop, and sometimes charging in great, massed formations, so that in the summer months a pall of dust hung over the plain and never settled. Horses, and the noises and the smells of horses, were a constant and unchanging fact of life in Camulod, and every generation of them bred there was bigger than the one that had produced it.

I did not know that at the time, of course, because I was a boy, and to my eyes they grew ever smaller. As a very small child I was dwarfed by the horses of the mounted troopers I admired as gods. As a boy of eight, they still made me feel small until I mounted one of them. But as a youth, approaching man's stature, I found that they had become reasonably sized.

Throughout my boyhood, Publius Varrus, who was my great-uncle and my guardian in the absence of my father, kept entire crews of smiths working in revolving shifts in six separate smithies, four within the fort itself and two more in our villa on the plain beneath the hill. The fort smithies were completely dedicated to the needs of the cavalry. Two of them made nothing but horseshoes and harness and armour. A third made nothing but nails, thousands upon thousands of them: nails for horseshoes and nails for building barracks and stables and stalls; small nails and studs for boots; and rivets for leather and armour. In later years, this manufactory also produced the bronze and iron wire for the tiny loops that we joined to make the chain link armour our horsemen used. The fourth smithy in the fort produced weapons for the riders: spears, swords and daggers, fitting products for the largest and the noisiest forge of all.

On the plain below, the villa smithies supplied the rest of our Colony, producing all of the farming tools and implements and the thousands of utensils required for their daily working needs by a population of upwards of four thousand people.

In Camulod today, the fort, the smithies and the great, barren drill field below the hill lie empty and unpeopled. The villas that it guarded are no more. They are burned, torn down, despoiled, defaced, their glorious mosaics ruptured and destroyed. The Colonists who lived there are dead for the most part, the few, forlorn survivors scattered on the winds. I alone remain, ancient in years but filled with youthful memories, living hidden in the hills close by the Colony, in solitary sanctuary, railing at the heavens by night, and thanking them by day for leaving me with my hands, and my mind, sufficiently intact to allow me to set down my tale.

I have no sense of faith that men will read the words I write. None live whom I would wish to read this tale, and only few who could. The men who roam this land at will today are brutal, fierce in their savagery and awful in their pagan ignorance. They know no gods but Lust and Gluttony, no love but Satiety, and their women match their baseness. The art of reading and writing is dead in Britain. And yet I write, because I must. Mine is the only voice left, though muted to scratchings on parchment, to tell this tale of what once was and what might—could—have been.

All of the treasures that filled Camulod are shrunk to four, and they are lodged with me here in this small stone hut. One is a window of glass, so clear and fine as to be almost transparent. One is a mirror of lustrous, polished silver, owned by my aunt Luceiia long ago—I retain it in memory of her beauty, keeping it clear and untarnished, but have not dared to look into it these thirty years. Another is the wondrous, shining sword that is my sacred trust. It lies securely hidden in the pit concealed at the rear of my dwelling.

The fourth of these treasures has value to my eyes and mind alone. It is a tiny mountain of papyrus and fine parchment, covered in the writing of four clear, separate hands, one of them my own.

Now that I am old and toothless, I am driven to continue and complete the chronicle begun by my grandfather Caius Britannicus almost a century ago, and carried on by his friend, my great-uncle Publius Varrus. Even my father, Picus Britannicus contributed a few of his personal evaluations and followed this family's tradition of struggling to find words to write down to describe the lives we have led.

I have been a scribbler since childhood, aping Uncle Varrus, who would spend hours each day writing in his parchment books. But I could frighten myself, I think, were I to give way to the awe I feel when I open my chests of parchments and papyrus and look at the sheer bulk of what still remains of all I have collected. For years now, I have been winnowing these writings, burning the major part, the trivia, and setting aside those elements essential to the telling of my tale. The first part is done, and ashes lie mounded in a shrunken, rain-sodden hillock in front of my house, here in my hidden valley in the hills. My sole remaining task is to arrange the remnants in sequence and provide sufficient additional details to bridge the few gaps that yet persist. All I require to achieve that end is time, and time I have—time in abundance. Longevity is my penance; fidelity to my tale, my burden.

This tale is mine, to a great extent, since mine was the living of it. Much of what I have written, however—the parts I did not experience directly—I discovered simply because I am Merlyn and men feared to lie to me, believing me magical. I did not care to disillusion them, since it suited my purpose later in life to be both magical and feared. Those attributes ensured my solitude, and therefore my freedom to do what I must do, and I taught myself well to be uncaring of what men thought of me.

I taught myself well, I say, but it was far from easy. I was not always lonely, nor feared and shunned by men. As a boy, my name was Cay, short for Caius Merlyn Britannicus, and I had a sunny childhood, unmarred by pain or sorrow. As a young man, I enjoyed my status as a leader in our Colony and my life was filled with laughter, with adventures, and with friends. Later still, I learned the joys and the grief of love—and lived beyond them, filling my days with duty as men did at that time, until my forty-second year. Only then did I learn the awful secret that divorced me forever from the lives of other, ordinary men and brought to me the status of Sorcerer and all the allied pains of solitude.

I was born in the year that brought catastrophe to Britain: the first year of the new, fifth century from the birth of The Christ, the year the Christians call 401 Anno Domini. The world our fathers had known disappeared forever in the course of that fateful year, when the great change began, and yet the awful significance of the change itself was slow in penetrating our world.

It was not that the word spread slowly—the speed of calamitous news is always swift—but this cataclysm was so huge, so overwhelming in its implications, that it defied credence, so that people, hearing the news and passing it along to others, remained themselves unwilling to countenance the truth of it. It was so appalling, so terrifying in its ramifications, that people would not talk of it. They could not digest it. They could not believe it. Yet neither could they long avoid it, for the emptiness of the roads, stretching unmarched for mile after silent mile, bore witness to the truth of it. The brashness of thoughtless children playing noisily in the streets of the deserted camps bore witness to the truth of it. The keening of abandoned women, deserted in thousands throughout the land, bore witness to the truth of it. And the terror of the people of the eastern and south-eastern coasts and of the northern reaches below the great wall Hadrian had built bore witness to the truth of it.

The Eagles had departed, flown away. The Legions had been called home. The Armies were gone, leaving only a skeleton presence to maintain a show of strength while the Empire struggled for its life elsewhere. Within six years, even the few legions left behind had followed that first exodus, and after four hundred years of *Pax Romana*—Roman peace, protection and prosperity in Britain—the country lay soft and undefended, at the mercy of her enemies.

BOOK ONE

Hatchlings

I

I was six years old by the final year of the great evacuation, awakening to my life in the colony we called Camulod, which, like Rome itself, had been built on a hill and dedicated to the high ideals that built the great Republic. It was Publius Varrus's wife, my great-aunt Luceiia, who had thought of naming the Colony Camulod, in honour of Camulodunum, her brother's—my grandfather's—birthplace, an ancient place sacred to Lod, war god of the tribe of Celts the Romans had named the Trinovantes. Today men call it simply Colchester, meaning the fort on the hill, but her brother had refused to use that new, brash, graceless name. By modifying the ancient name to fit a new location, Luceiia Britannicus had honoured both her brother and his monument.

One of the first lessons I learned in extreme youth was that things had not always been as they were. Camulod had not always been rich in horses, nor had its economy been purely equestrian. It had been my own father who had changed everything, I learned, the year that I was born.

My father was Picus Britannicus, and his title was Legate, or General. He was Supreme Cavalry Commander and Deputy in Britain for the great Flavius Stilicho, Commander-in-Chief of the Armies of the Emperor Honorius. In the year of my birth, 401 in the Year of Our Lord and the eleven hundred and fifty-fifth year of Rome, Alaric, war chief of the barbarian Visigoths, had threatened invasion of the Roman heartland itself. He had penetrated as far as Stilicho's home city of Milan before Stilicho was able to assemble an army by means of an emergency summons for all uncommitted Legions to return to Italia to combat the threat. My father, a close personal friend of Stilicho as well as a trusted colleague and confidant, had answered that summons, embarking immediately with most of his troops and as many horses as he could transport in the time and the vessels available to him. The remaining stock, no less than six hundred and eighty prime animals, he had left in the care of his father, my grandfather, the *proconsul* Caius Britannicus, who had been named by Stilicho *Legatus Emeritus*— Supreme Commander—of the Irregular Armies of South-west Britain. The charge implicit in my grandfather's title was the interim governance of the south-west, and the protection of its territories against invasion, pending the return of the Imperial Legions following the defeat of Alaric and his Visigoths.

By the time word arrived of my father's departure, however, my grandfather was dead, murdered by a madman, and my great-uncle Publius Varrus had assumed command of our Colony. Uncle Varrus knew what Caius Britannicus would have wanted him to do, and so he used my grandfather's seal and sent out soldiers to accept the consignment of horseflesh. This immediate quintupling of the Colony's herds had a revolutionary and permanent effect on the Colony. Victorex, the stablemaster, had to increase his staff of grooms and stablemen tenfold, and farms that had been under the plough had to be given over completely and immediately to the keeping of livestock. But the concerns voiced over the loss of arable land in this exercise were quickly stifled by the realization that this great influx of mounts gave us the capability to reclaim previously abandoned lands, and even to break new ground, since our corps of mounted troopers quickly became large enough to permit constant patrols in strength, and continuous protection for all the workers employed on these lands.

The biggest impact of all, however, was upon our foot-soldiers. Now that we had the livestock, every man who wanted to ride was able to do so, at least for part of their duty. Very soon infantry patrols of our territories were a thing of the past. Our central core of infantry was reduced from fifteen hundred to eight hundred men, who were distributed as semi-permanent garrison troops to three of our major outlying villa farms, and to the fort of Camulod itself.

As I have said, mine was a happy childhood and I grew in sunshine, shaped into the man I was to be by two stern and loving guardians: my two great-uncles, Ullic, King of the Pendragon, and Publius Varrus, Master of Camulod. My youth was divided equally between the rugged, lovely hills and mountains of the Pendragon strongholds to the north-west, in south Cambria, and the calm beauty of the wooded plains and forests that, seen from the hilltop, spread like a carpet around Camulod.

Ullic's Celtic hill people taught me to hunt with a sling and to trap with snares. They taught me to shoot with a bow and to fish for trout in the brooks with my bare hands. They taught me to sing and to pluck the harp and to love the history in their glorious songs, so that even before my voice broke from boyhood I was revered as a bard of great promise and had I not been who I was, the Druids would have claimed me as their own. As it was, I spent much time among Druid teachers, learning their sacred mysteries and the lore of their ancient ways, for they respected who I was and dreamed great dreams of fame for me. And while I was among them, they taught me to do all of the other things a boy must do: to run like the wind, mile after mile without respite; to wrestle and fight with my bare hands and feet; and to seek out the nests of the upland birds—the curlew and the plover and the wild ducks and geese—for the succulent eggs they held. They bred in my impatient, questing soul the patience to stalk deer and the strength to ignore the timid, placid gentleness and see only the walking food. They broke me young to the mastery of their wild mountain ponies, so that by the time I was seven there was nothing on four legs that could throw me from its back once I was mounted.

There in that lovely, wild and sometimes savage land, I was always at peace, but Uther, the brother of my soul, was in his element. Uther Pendragon and I were cousins, born, by some strange conjunction of the stars, on the same day, less than an hour apart. From our youngest days we thought as one in many things, and this was something we took for granted. We were alike all our lives, as long as Uther lived, two sides of a medallion—different, perhaps, in appearance, but faces of the same piece.

He was the dearest friend I ever had—warm, loving, generous and kind, and yet possessed of a wild man's temper and a wellspring of savage, primitive violence that could frighten me when it came into view, for it was utterly implacable. Those who knew him as a friend worshipped the ground he trod. His enemies went in terror of his name, for his strength was lethal and his enmity absolute. He chose to have no living enemies and worked hard to deprive them all of life, for only then, he said, could he trust them and know what they were doing. In his own way Uther Pendragon, King among his Celts, was far more savage than the hordes who sought to overrun this land of ours. It was my fate to love him as a brother and to be in fear of him throughout my adult life until he died.

Violence, as I have said, Uther knew and loved, but treachery was a trait that no man, even his greatest enemy, would think of in connection with his name. No man but I, and I only suspected, nor was I ever able to divine the truth, whether for or against him. Forty years and more have gone since Uther's death and I still wonder whether or not he did the deeds my mind tells me he did, the deeds my soul curses me for even thinking he could do. I have sworn to myself that, lacking any kind of proof, I have a duty to admit I might be wrong. But still, inside my heart, I know that Uther had a black and fearsome devil strongly chained, deep at the bottom of his soul. And still I ask myself, did he control it at all times, or did it sometimes control him?

Somehow Uther did not belong in Camulod. He bore it stoically, but his heart was always back in the hills of his home, where he had been born the son of Uric the King and his wife Veronica, daughter of Publius Varrus, and thus the grandson of King Ullic Pendragon. Unlike me, he was a poor student, with no interest in books of any kind. He never became literate and was content to leave the esoterica of texts and records to me. The only excitement he ever found in Camulod was in the fort itself and in our cavalry.

Uther was a born warrior and every spare minute he had was spent on the drill field or in the stables.

My happiest hours in Camulod, on the other hand, were spent in Publius Varrus's private rooms. The room he called his Armoury was a boy's paradise filled with weapons and armour of every description, gathered from all over the Empire and beyond. Uther enjoyed that room too, at one time, but he soon grew bored with it when he found we were not allowed to handle any of its treasures. For my part, I could sit there and gaze at those exotic shapes and dream for hours on end. I even had a special chair there that only I could sit in. It was a saddle of some kind, although a strange, ungainly one with a high, wooden back and dangling appendages, made to fit a boy and found on a horse belonging to a party of defeated Frankish raiders. Its young rider had worn rich clothing and a chieftain's golden torc. Our people reasoned that he must have been a cripple, the strange device fashioned to support his malformed body astride the horse. My uncle had kept the thing as a memento, an oddity of the kind that had attracted him throughout his lifetime, and it had sat unremarked in the Armoury for years until I grew tall enough to pull myself up and bestride it.

The Armoury had great, wooden doors covered with beaten, hand-worked bronze crafted by Uncle Varrus himself. I had watched them being hung in place when I was just an infant, as I had watched the laying of the solid, wooden floor. That was the only wooden floor I ever really noticed, and my uncle loved it. He said it kept the room warm. I thought he must be mad when he said that, for even I could see that the room was kept warm by a massive brazier housed in an open fireplace, and by the central heating hypocausts that warmed the entire household. I remember asking him one night how the smoke going up the chimney stopped the rain from coming down and I remember how he laughed at me and showed me the trick his stonemasons had used in building the great fireplace. They had built the flue at an angle, opening into an upright vent so that no rain could enter.

It was on another such occasion that I asked him which weapon in the room was his most valued treasure. He looked at me in silence for what seemed the longest time that anyone had ever looked at me and then he stood up and towered above me.

"Cay," he asked me, "do you know what a secret is?"

"Yes, Uncle," I answered him. "A special thing that you must never tell to anyone else, no matter how hard it is, or how much you want to tell it."

He smiled at me then. "That's exactly what a secret is, Cay. Exactly. Because the moment you give in and tell the secret to another living soul, no matter who it is, you have destroyed the secret. It is a secret no longer."

"I know, Uncle."

"I know you know, Cay. That's why I am going to share a secret with you. A secret between us only. Are you ready?"

I nodded, my breath suspended in anticipation. He looked at me, narrowing his eyes, and then went on. "I have one secret, Cay, that I share only with my partner Equus. Now I shall have another that I share only with you, and it is this: my most valued treasure in this room is one that cannot be seen. It is hidden from men's eyes."

My eyes darted all around the room, peering into every dark corner. "Where, Uncle?"

"That is the second secret, the one I share with Equus, but I will share it with you, too, some day. Some day soon, I promise. That will make you the third person in the whole world who knows that secret. But before that happens, you and I have some things to talk about." *Some day. Soon. Not today.* My disappointment must have been written on my face, because he smiled at me again and tousled my hair. "One day soon, I promise. How old are you now, Cay?"

"Seven, Uncle Varrus," I said, knowing he knew.

"And when did you learn to read?"

"When I was five."

"In truth, you were only four. Do you like to read?"

"Yes, Uncle." Why was he asking these questions? He knew how I loved to read.

"And what do you like to read most?"

"Grandfather Caius's books."

"Would you like to read my books?"

I felt my eyes grow wide. What a silly question. I had been asking for months if I could read his books! "Yes, Uncle. Please."

"Very well, then. I'll make you another promise, here and now, man to man, between the two of us. You can start reading my books tomorrow. As you do, we'll talk about them and you can ask me anything you like. I'll answer all your questions. D'you understand?" I nodded, not daring to speak. "Good. Now, this is very important, so listen carefully. There is one question, one very important question, that I'll be waiting for you to ask me, and when you are old enough . . . No! Let me put that in a different way, for this is really important . . . When you *understand* enough to ask me that one question, I'll show you my most valued treasure. Does that sound just?"

I nodded again, almost sick with disappointment. That "when you're old enough" had rung in my ears like a death knell, but I did my best to hide my feelings. A seven-year-old boy's best. "Is there a lot to learn in your books, Uncle?"

He laughed out loud, his big, deep, booming laugh. "Aye, Cay, I think there is," he said. "But I'm sure you'll learn it all quickly, won't you?"

"Yes, Uncle. I will."

"Good lad! Now, come and kiss me good night. It's time you were abed, and tomorrow you start to read my books."

I slid down and hooked my left foot into the loop in the strange chair, swung my right leg over its high back and stepped down to the floor. Uncle Varrus hoisted me high into the air and kissed me on both cheeks the way he did every night at this time. Then he took my hand in his own hard-skinned palm and walked with me to find Uther and Occa, the servant who slept in our room with us.

I have many such memories of Uncle Varrus. He would talk to me, and with me, which is not at all the same thing, for hours on end. He taught me all he knew of weaponry and armour and war-fare, including siegecraft. He told me of Alexander, whom men called The Great, and of Alexander's father, Philip of Macedon, and how the two of them conquered their world. And he enthralled me with tales of ancient Rome and the great Republic where, for the only time in history, a man could make of himself what he wished, secure in his right to be what he desired to be, and free to bear arms to protect that right. He used all his wiles to teach me how the Republic had been warped by men and twisted to suit the designs and desires of a privileged few, and how the resultant Empire had become cancerous, doomed by its own wasting sick-nesses. He also taught me the lore of iron and of what he himself referred to as "the other, lesser, metals," including gold and silver, and I spent one entire winter in his forge, when I was nine, learn-ing to handle iron and to make the metal work for me, since that, he convinced me, was the secret of the master smiths. And because he was my uncle Varrus and my god, I listened avidly to his words, absorbed his lessons and devoured his writings.

I never knew my grandfather Caius Britannicus, but I grew up seeing this land of Britain through his eyes, thanks to his skills in writing down his thoughts. From him and from Uncle Varrus, I learned the reasons for the destruction of the Empire before I even knew what the Empire was. I was aware of Armageddon long before I knew that I dwelt in Armageddon, and I saw the High King's destiny before his parents ever saw each other. And through all of this, through all the years of being a sponge, soaking up every scrap of lore that came my way, absorbing the essence of the great Dream dreamed by my grandfather and his friend Publius Varrus, I was protected from the world by the life I led and by the self-contained society that had been built around me. We in Camulod thought of ourselves as *Britons*, rather than Romano-British or Celtic people, and in my youth, because of Publius Varrus, I imbued the word with a unique, metallic significance, imagining a *Briton* to be a carefully crafted alloy, a tempered fusion of the strongest prop-erties of Roman and Celtic greatness.

Beyond our Colony, however, outside the sanctuary of Camulod, in the separate, other world of Britain and beyond its shores, the disintegration of Rome's Empire hurtled on.

Our land never recovered from the loss of the legions Stilicho recalled in 401. Five years later, the few legions that remained, feeling forgotten and abandoned there, elected a man called Marcus as their emperor, but he was murdered by a rival faction who elected another, Gratian by name, to lead them. Short months later, he too was dead, and a third prospect, Constantine III, was proclaimed Emperor in Britain. This was the man who dealt the final blow to Roman Britain. Mustering all the troops that he could find, he assembled a fleet of ships from all the ports of the land and crossed with his army to the continent, leaving Britain abandoned at last. We in the Colony called Camulod, the only place in Britain prepared for this development, remained unaware of the event for several months, and when we did hear of it, we were thrown onto the verge of panic, expecting to be victims any day of massive invasion forces.

For a long time, however—almost four years—there was no great increase in the raids, for there were few who really believed that the Romans would not return. But then weeds began to grow on the great roads, and the camps began to show the wear and tear of time and neglect, and as they crumbled, the predators stepped up their raids. The word was passed that the way to Britain lay safely open. The Jutes, the Danes, the Angles, the Saxons, the Picts and the Scots came in ever swelling numbers, and Britain knew pillage on a scale hitherto undreamed of.

II

I was eight years old when I first knew real terror and real awe. Both of these new experiences came on the same day, within moments of each other, and both left indelible impressions upon me.

Uther and I had spent the spring and summer as usual with his father's people in the hills, and we were on our way back down to Camulod to spend the autumn and the winter in the Colony. We were escorted by a strong party of King Ullic's people, all mounted on the small, shaggy ponies that they breed among their hills. We were making leisurely progress, since the weather was fine, still high summer with never a hint of autumn to be seen. We had come down onto the plain that morning, out of the hills at last, and were no more than twenty miles from Camulod when we made a stop to eat.

Some of the men had fished successfully in a mountain-fed stream a few miles back, and now they lit fires to cook their catch. As boys and princes, neither Uther nor I was expected to take part in the cooking, and we had ridden some way away from the fires, playing a game of throwing a rag weighted with a stone for the other to catch, when we came across a tarn of some kind that cried out to be explored. It was a deep, black pool, set where no pool should be, upon a level stretch of open ground in firm, springy turf. We decided that it was a magic tarn set there by some goddess to receive the offerings of the people who had once lived nearby. It had been the custom in this land since time began to throw sacrificial offerings into pools and lakes, to propitiate the goddesses who lived in them. But now Uther decided he was going to dive down to the bottom of this pool to find some of the treasures offered to the goddess.

The mere suggestion made me uncomfortable. Even to talk that way smacked of blasphemy, although I did not know the word at that time. Respect, however, I knew all about, and the water looked deep and very black. But even as I sat there, staring at it, Uther had slipped from his pony and begun to strip.

"Uther! Don't!" I said. "It looks too deep. It's dangerous."

"Don't be stupid, Cay. It's just a pool, and I'm hot, anyway. Aren't you coming?"

I shook my head.

"What's the matter? Are you afraid? Don't be stupid." By this time he was naked and he jumped right in, disappearing with a mighty splash. As the ripples settled, I could see him diving down, deeper and deeper, his body pale and insubstantial, and I realized that the water was not black at all, but crystal clear, and I knew that its blackness came from its great depth. I watched him climbing back up from those depths towards me until he broke the surface and flicked his hair out of his eyes, gulping for breath.

"It's deep, deep, deep, Cay, and it's cold, but it's wonderful! Come on in!"

Still I shook my head, watching him as he grinned at me, sucking in air and preparing to go down again. "Uther," I said, "you'll never reach the bottom. It's too deep. Come out."

Instead of answering me, he dived again, and I watched him dwindle smaller and smaller, until he turned and came up again, fast as a cork, to splash back to the surface. This time, however, he swam to the side and held up his hand and I pulled him out. He sat there for a while, shivering, his entire body blue and covered with goose-flesh.

"Well?" I taunted him. "Did you find any treasure?"

He shook his head, his teeth chattering.

"How deep did you go?"

He began to chafe himself with his hands, scrubbing at the goose-flesh, then he leaped to his feet and took off at top speed, running around the perimeter of the pool, screaming gleefully at the top of his voice. I decided that he was mad, but happy mad, and

I took off my own clothes and leaped into the water. It was ice cold! Even today, long decades afterwards, I can recall the shock of it. As I regained the surface, gasping, Uther splashed in beside me, pulling me down again. I fought him off and regained the surface, catching my breath and looking for him below me, but he grabbed me from behind and dragged me down again, and by the time the cold finally defeated us, we were both exhausted and had to help each other up onto the bank, where we collapsed, shivering.

"It's like a well," said Uther.

"What d'you mean?"

"Deep. With stone walls. Straight down."

"Probably is a well. That'll be why the water's so clear." By this time we had stopped shivering and were beginning to enjoy the warmth of the sun.

"Want to try to reach the bottom?"

"No," I remember saying. "We'd never—"

Uther cut me short, his hand raised, his body tensing. "What's that?"

He sat erect and twisted to look behind us. "Whoreson!" he spat. "Saxons!"

I spun and looked towards the camp. There was a battle raging there and our people were heavily outnumbered, and even as I looked I saw four blond-haired strangers running towards us, naked iron in their hands, their mouths open in yells of battle lust.

Uther was already on his feet. "Quick, Cay! Get out of here!" I scrambled for my clothes.

"Forget your clothes, grab your knife!" He was already running for his pony.

I snatched up my knife and ran for my own mount, grasping its mane and swinging myself hard up onto its sun-hot, dusty back. Both animals were galloping almost from a standing start.

"Split up," yelled Uther. "You go right!" He swung away to the left and I wheeled my pony in the opposite direction, looking back over my shoulder to see what our pursuers would do. It was obvious that they were surprised to see only two small, naked boys. It must have been our ponies that attracted them in the first place, for they could not have seen us lying by the water's edge. They had stopped running as we split up, and they stood staring after us, having no hope of catching us on foot and no great desire to tire themselves out chasing naked children. I pulled my pony to a halt and sat watching them, feeling safely distant, as they approached the tarn and found our clothes and our torcs, the heavy, decorative gold collars that marked us as chief's sons.

That discovery made them decide we might be worth pursuing after all. One of them, the tallest, dropped his axe and shield, threw off his helmet and fur tunic, and came after me at a run. I sat and watched him, knowing that he could never catch my fleet-footed pony. When he was about twenty-five paces from me I swung my mount again and kicked him to a dead run. Only then did I look around for Uther, but he was nowhere to be seen. The fringe of the forest was about two hundred paces ahead of me and I aimed my pony at it like an arrow, easily outdistancing my pursuer. Then, fifty paces short of the sheltering trees, my mount tripped and fell, hurling me over his head, the distinct sound of his snapping foreleg in my ears.

I landed on my back and knocked myself out of breath completely. When I regained my senses, the pony's screaming ringing through my head, the big Saxon was close, not even breathing hard, an evil grin on his face. I watched him approach me as I struggled for breath. The pony had thrown me about eight paces. The man stopped by the screaming animal, drew a knife, and then bent over to saw at the creature's throat. The sight triggered all my survival instincts, and I came to my feet running as fast as my legs could pump. He must have been absorbed in what he was doing, because I had covered about half the distance to the trees before I heard his shout, and then I heard the sounds of his running feet, gaining on me with every stride of his long legs. Still ahead of him, I came to the edge of the trees, dodging to my left as I passed the first of them, and then swerving again, and again as I passed each successive tree, changing direction sharply all the way. I knew that I was running for my life.

I was lucky that the forest was thick, even here on the fringe, and that I was so small, for I was able to burrow at a dead run into places where my pursuer could not follow. Slowly and surely I gained distance on him, fighting my way into the thickest clumps of underbrush and worming through, until eventually I knew that he was thrashing far enough behind me to give me a breathing space.

I dove under the roots of a great, lightning-split tree and crouched there in terror, hearing the thundering of my own heart over the approaching noise of my pursuer. And then he stopped moving and I knew that he was listening for me, searching the woods around him carefully with his eyes and ears, but I did not know how close he was. The silence grew and lengthened until I could stand it no longer and I eased myself upright and cautiously raised my head. He was nowhere in sight. Then, being only eight, I did a very foolish thing. I climbed higher in order to see further, believing him gone, and there he was, looking at me from less than thirty paces away, across the top of the last thicket I had dived through. He saw me as I saw him and he plunged into the bushes towards me as I launched myself away from him, running with wings on my heels after the few moments' rest I had gained. I ran and ran, choosing the densest thickets again, unmindful of the stinging slash of brambles and nettles and springy twigs, until suddenly I broke from a screen of bushes to find myself in an open, grassy glade of huge old oak trees, their branches choked with mistletoe, the sacred berries of the Druids. I could hear him crashing too close behind me, and in panic, gathering the last of my strength, I threw myself at the biggest oak and scrambled up high into its branches, seeking to hide among the tangled mistletoe. Up and up I went until I could climb no higher, and there I crouched, hugging a branch, and watched him enter the glade.

He stopped on the edge of the clearing, out on the open grass, and looked all around him, peering and listening. Then he began to walk towards the tree in which I was hiding. I was almost sick with dread and terrified that I would lose my hold and tumble from my perch to land at his feet, and in my fear I hiccoughed. He heard me. Dumb with terror, I watched his head come up as he searched the tree until his eyes found me. I can still remember the expression on his face as he smiled an awful smile and beckoned to me to come down, talking to me in his heathen tongue, although we both knew, he and I, that he was going to have to come up and get me.

He had to try three times to get his first purchase on a low branch, but after that he began to climb surely, and more and more quickly, towards my perch. I was saying all my small boy's prayers as he came, willing him to trust a too weak branch and fall, to be too big to come higher—anything to stop him coming closer.

And then I heard the thump of heavy hooves and I saw him freeze and look down. I could see nothing, for the bole of the tree was between me and the sounds, but the Saxon forgot me immediately and began to drop, hand over hand, almost falling from branch to branch in his haste to regain the ground, and then he jumped and landed sprawling, rolling forward and over like a cat and coming to his feet on the run, dagger in hand. The clump of hooves was below me now and suddenly there was a man on a huge, running red horse that bowled the Saxon over by striking him with its shoulder. Before his sprawling form could even come to rest, the rider pinned him to the ground with a spear between his shoulders, and the Saxon squirmed and kicked for long moments before he finally was still. The horseman left his spear sticking up into the air and turned to look up at me, twisting his body sideways so that he could see up to where I was.

"What are you? A Druid god?"

I said nothing, swallowing hard, trying to control my terror.

"Can you get down from there by yourself?"

I tried to say yes, but nothing came out.

"Well? Come on down. He's dead. You're safe enough, now. I have no cause to hurt you."

Still I did not move. My rescuer dismounted and pulled his spear free from the body of the man he had killed, bracing his foot on the corpse to give him purchase. This done, he wiped the blade clean on the dead man's tunic and then stepped back to his horse, stroking its muzzle and talking softly to it, although loudly enough for me to overhear what he was saying.

"Now, Horse," he said, "there is a boy, a boy with no clothes on, hiding up in the tree above your head. I'm telling you this so that you won't be frightened when he comes down, for he looks ferocious. I promise you that he won't hurt you, Horse, if you don't hurt him." He stopped and looked back up at me again. "Are you coming down, boy? You're keeping me from my meal. I've been riding all night long and have not broken fast today, and there's a tasty rabbit stew simmering on my fire, not half a mile from here. Now you may not be hungry, but I am starved, so it will please me greatly if you will come down and let me get back to my food."

Slowly, feeling my way with care, I climbed down from my refuge, suddenly feeling all the cuts and scrapes that I had gathered in my flight, and all at once aware of the abrasive bark of the great oak that had sheltered me. As I reached the last branch above the ground, my rescuer leaped nimbly up onto his horse's back and ambled over to me. I was perched now about three feet above him. He smiled at me and I knew I was really safe.

"What was all that about? Who was this fellow?" He indicated the dead man.

"A Saxon. A raider. They caught us away from our camp, swimming. He chased me and I ran."

"He must have chased you a long way. Why did he do that? I would have let you go."

"He found my torc."

"He what?"

"He found my torc. My gold collar. He knew I am the son of a chief, and he meant to kill me."

"So, you're the son of a chief, are you? Not just a chieftain, eh? A full chief! I'm impressed. What do you call yourself? And how does a Celtic chief's son come to speak Latin so well?"

I drew myself erect and spoke with all the dignity I could muster, determined, naked and bruised as I was, to impress this stranger. "I am of Roman blood. My name is Caius. Caius Merlinus Britannicus. My father is a Legate of Rome. He rides with Stilicho."

The effect of my pronouncement upon him was salutary. He choked. As he spluttered and coughed, his horse pranced nervously, skittering around so that I lost sight of the rider's face, but eventually he regained control both of himself and of his horse and came to a stop, facing me again, his eyes wide and red with coughing.

"Pardon me," he said. "I swallowed some spit the wrong way. So, your father is a Legate? Well, he ought to be, to have burdened you with a name like that. Merlinus? That's not a Roman name. At least, I've never heard of it before."

"No," I admitted. "You are right, it's not. It's really Merlyn. That's Celtic."

"I see." He shook his head, now wearing a grin of open disbelief that even I could decipher, and held up his right hand to me. "Here, take my hand and swing yourself down here in front of me. A man with a name like that should ride in front." I did as he bade me and he held me in place with his left arm. "Can you ride, boy?"

"Yes, sir."

"Good, then hold my spear and hang on to the horse's mane. We'll be at my camp very quickly."

He did not lie. I barely had time to tell him about Uther and our flight from the well before I smelled wood-smoke, and we broke from the trees again to find a well-ordered camp where five other men lay resting. They all looked at us curiously as we rode up to the fire.

"General," my rescuer said, "I think this young man should meet you. He tells me his name is Caius Merlyn Britannicus." He lowered me gently to the ground in front of the fire where a giant of a man in black leather armour stood up to tower over me, a strange expression on his face.

"Caius Merlyn Britannicus," said my rescuer, "this is the Legate Caius Picus Britannicus."

My father had come home.

III

How does a boy find out about his father? About the man himself, I mean? The fact is, he does not. At least, not the truth about the things the world holds to be important, for when a boy is still a boy, such things truly do not matter. I only discovered my father after I became a man myself, and much of what I have discovered since his death has been made available to me, as I have already said, simply because I am Merlyn. As a boy, I found my father to be a mystical, almost mythical presence on the periphery of my life. He was constantly at war throughout my childhood and my boyhood and I saw him only briefly and occasionally, on his infrequent visits home.

Broad-shouldered, deep-chested and heavily muscled, Picus Britannicus was more than simply a big man. In a world where normal men were five and a half feet tall, he towered more than six. Fully half a head taller than his tallest subordinate, he was a soldier from head to toe, inside and out. He was magnificent to look at, with his unusual golden hair, a splendid tunic of white wool bordered with a thick, black stripe, and his gleaming, highly polished black leather armour and equipment. Even the crest on his helmet was striking, composed of alternate clumps of black and white horsehair. The only part of his dress that did not fit his strict colour scheme was the bronze hilt of the short-sword that hung by his right side, the sword given to him by Uncle Varrus when he first joined the legions. His horses, too—always jet black—were specially selected for their height, so that he was prominent no matter where he went, drawing men's eyes by his size, and by the flashing whiteness of the soft, white wool that lined his great black war cloak. My father was every man's vision of a Commander, and his soldiers loved him.

To his small son, however, he was a daunting, intimidating figure. He spoke little, for an arrow had torn his throat before I was born and had left him with a terrible affliction, so that when he did speak his words were laboured and guttural. He was determined to overcome this failing, however, and as he grew older he did defeat it to a very great extent. He wore his golden hair long, an affectation to cover the hideous scar where the arrow that pierced his mouth had emerged through the back of his neck, and that also marked him as singular among the short-haired Romans whom he led.

On that first day I met him, he awed me completely. The first thing he did after looking me over in silent, wide-eyed surprise was to pick me up by the elbows and lift me like a feather, up into the air until I came eye to eye with him. Then he grinned a huge grin, full of white teeth, and shook me, gently, and placed me back on the ground, growling something I couldn't understand. His men all stepped to meet me, shaking hands with me solemnly, as though I were a man, while the one who had saved me recounted my adventure almost word for word the way I had told him it happened.

This man was Titus, it turned out, one of my father's friends of whom I had heard and read. Another, Quintus Flavius, knelt by the fire, tending the rabbit stew Titus had been savouring on his scouting patrol around the camp before he found me.

As soon as Titus had finished recounting my story, my father looked at me. "Uther?" he growled. "Where is he?"

I shrugged, aware of my own confusion. "I don't know where he went, sir."

"Was he followed?"

Again I shrugged. "I don't know."

"Right. Mount up!"

We left the fire burning. Flavius upended the cooking pot into the coals and a hissing cloud of smoke and ashes whirled into the air. In a matter of seconds we were all mounted and heading back the way Titus and I had come. I rode in front of my father this time, my nakedness covered by his long cloak, and I felt fine, although I was worried about what we might discover on reaching the scene of the attack.

We emerged from the forest almost at the point where I had entered it, and the first person I saw was Uther, fully dressed, riding towards us with four of his father's men. He saw us at the same time and hauled his pony back in a rearing stop, but even as he prepared to run from this new threat, he saw me mounted in front of my father, and I heard the gladness in his voice as he yelled my name and waved my tunic above his head.

"That's Uther!" I said. "He has my clothes."

Two of the men with Uther recognized my father and they came with us as we approached the rest of the survivors. One of my father's men let out a low whistle of wonder. "Will you look at that!"

For the first time, we saw the effect of Ullic Pendragon's long, yew bows when they were wielded by trained and determined men. There were Saxon bodies everywhere. I tallied fourteen before losing count. Some of our Celts were out among them, pulling their arrows from the dead and wounded bodies. It turned out that our party had lost four men, killed in the first attack, which had caught them by surprise. Not one had been lost after the bowmen began to fight, and the surviving Saxons had fled in terror from the arrows against which they had no defence.

One of the hillmen laughed as he described what had happened. "They thought they were safe, you know, inside their fancy ring shirts, until they started falling, pierced through, fancy shirts and all. They've fought against bowmen before, but they've never come up against anything that bites as hard as our new arrows do. Huw, there, hit one of them smack in the head and pierced him through, helmet and all!"

"How far away was he?" my father asked.

"No more than twenty paces. These arrows will go through an oaken board a handsbreadth thick at a hundred and sixty."

My father grunted, an impatient sound, and looked around at the corpses littering the grass. By this time, all of them had been stripped of weapons and of armour, and these had been dumped into a pile close to one of the cooking fires. Huw, the leader of our party of Celts, noticed the Legate's seeming lack of patience and shouted to his men in their native tongue, telling them to get ready to move out, and ordering that the bodies of our four slain men be thrown across their horses for burial later.

Titus nodded towards the pile of weapons and armour. "What will you do with those? Do you have a wagon to load them into?"

"No," growled Huw. "And we can't carry them. I'd thought to bury them. Can't leave them lying around."

Uther interrupted, his voice sounding out of place among the men. "Offer them to the goddess of the tarn, there, where Caius and I went swimming. It's very deep."

"Now there's an idea, boy!" Huw took him up on it and immediately detailed four men to carry the booty over and throw it into the pool. "Breaks my heart to see such waste, but a proper sacrifice in thanks for victory never hurt anyone nor went amiss."

"What about the bodies? The Saxons?" This was Titus again.

Huw's look of contempt was eloquent as he answered. "What about them then? Let the whoresons rot where they lie. The wolves and crows will not take long to clean them up." Something had caught his attention and he raised his voice to a yell. "Come on, you people! Get a move on, will you? It's twenty miles to Camulod from here! We want to get there during damn daylight! Move your arses!"

Flavius was frowning slightly, his face showing puzzlement. "Camulod? Where's that?"

"That's what we call the fort, sir," I answered him. "Camulod."

He looked at my father, who raised one eyebrow and shrugged, saying nothing.

We left the body-strewn field as it was and set a good pace for the Colony. I had pulled on my clothes again and my body was a mass of pain from all the welts, bruises, scratches and cuts I had taken. My right eye was swollen shut and I wanted to cry, but I dared not show myself to be so weak.

Titus reined close to me. "How are you feeling, young Merlyn? Tired?" I tried to smile at him, nodding my head. "I thought so," he continued. "You had a long run there." I nodded again. "Why don't you come and ride with me? Then, if you fall asleep, at least you won't fall off the horse."

He must have read the gratitude in my face, for he brought his horse right alongside my pony and lifted me up in front of him. I looked around me to see if any of the others were laughing at me, but no one was paying any attention at all, and I fell asleep almost immediately, cradled in the grip of Titus, my protector.

I awoke a long time later to the sound of horns, and there in the distance were the walls of Camulod, crowning their hill and overlooking all the valley below. I was a very stiff and sore little boy by then, and I remember it took all of my determination not to cry out in pain as Titus handed me down to the willing hands that reached for me in the courtyard of my uncle's villa. I had a hot bath, and my tiredness overcame me in the course of it. I have no memory of being put to bed. The next morning, however, I awoke with all my normal vigour, remembering that my father, the Legate Picus, had come home, and hoping that he would stay. He did. He was home this time for good.

Stilicho, my father's Commander-in-Chief, had been recalled from campaigning against the Ostrogoths by his former ward, the Emperor Honorius, and had returned to do his master's bidding, only to be summarily executed for an alleged plot to usurp the Empire for himself. My father had remained behind, facing the Ostrogoths with Stilicho's army, completely unaware that the same schemers who had brought down Stilicho had condemned him, too, so that Picus Britannicus was a Legate one day and a hunted outlaw the next.

Thanks only to a timely warning and the loyalty of his own veterans, he had been able to make his escape ahead of the men sent to kill him. He had then crossed the continent with a small band of officers and men, and returned to Britain, where he was now safe from the displeasure of the Imperial Court.

Any hopes I had in my small boy's heart of being with my father from that time on were doomed, however. From the time he returned to Camulod, the military activities of the entire Colony increased. Uncle Varrus gave up supreme command of our forces to my father, who immediately set out to upgrade and improve the standard of everything we were involved in, from strengthening the Colony's defences and intensifying the ongoing building activity on the walls, to a major increase in the frequency, and the thoroughness, of mounted patrols around our outlying territories.

In the spring of that year of 409, the realities of large-scale invasion were becoming inescapable. All parts of the coast around our Colony were reporting heavy raids, and rumours abounded of strong parties of raiders—armies composed of many shiploads of warriors—pillaging towns, killing the men and keeping the women for their casual use, and then fortifying the towns themselves as bases for sorties into other parts of the country. Word came that one such base camp had been established to the south-east of us, in a village protected from surprise attack by its location on the upper rise of a low hill. According to the report that reached us via a wandering priest, three raiding groups had combined their strength and had occupied and fortified this place. Now, from the security it offered, they were terrorizing the land for miles around.

I was in the Armoury, listening to a conversation between my father and my uncle, when this news arrived. My father had been talking in his slow, laborious way of the need to build turrets in the walls of the fort to hold *ballista*, scorpions and other artillery pieces of the kind used by Stilicho's armies. Siege warfare had progressed considerably since the days of Caesar's campaigns in Gaul and Iberia, he said, but most of the brilliant innovations were being developed in defence against siege engines. Castellations at intervals along a wall, jutting out in front of the main line, allowed defenders to pour down murderous fire on their attackers, and the effectiveness of these castellations increased with the concentration of them in any stretch of wall.

Look at the forts of the Saxon Shore, he was saying. They were impregnable simply because of the way they were built. Siege engines could not get near them. That was what we needed to do with Camulod. We must add towers to jut out—far out—along the front, where they could protect the weakest spots in our defences; towers that would allow our soldiers to maintain supremacy, no matter what an attacker might bring up against them; towers that were strategically placed at the salient peaks of the hill of Camulod, and from which defenders could look down and in, towards the shallower gradients.

It was at this point in the discourse that Titus interrupted the meeting, bringing in a messenger with news of the raiders and their fortified base to the south-east. I knew as soon as I saw him that he was one of the wandering priests who spread the Gospel of the Christ throughout the countryside to all who would listen. He was a tall, skinny, bearded man dressed in a simple homespun robe and clutching a shepherd's crook, the symbol of his calling. He stared in awe at the splendour of the room as he came forward to greet the two occupants, for he was unaware of my tiny presence on the floor behind my father's chair. Both Uncle Varrus and my father listened without interrupting while he told his tale. My father had only two questions: "How far to this place? And how many Saxons?"

The man was unsure of the distance, estimating it at between twenty and thirty miles, but he had himself counted no less than two hundred men in and around the village in the space of two days. My father thanked him and nodded to Titus, who took the priest to find someone who could show him the way to the kitchens. When the doors had closed behind them Uncle Varrus spoke.

"Twenty to thirty miles. That's not too close. They're nowhere near our lands."

"No, Publius, you're wrong. They're far too close. A hundred miles would be too close."

"How do you mean? That's three days' march for that rabble, maybe four or five! A boatload landing to the north or south of us tomorrow could get here sooner."

My father shrugged. "Granted. But they wouldn't. Not unless they were desperate. They'd be too far from their ship, their base.

Don't you see it? That's what's important, Publius! These animals have made themselves a base camp on solid ground. You heard the priest. It's fortified. That means it's solid. They don't have to worry about somebody finding it and sinking it. And they have women, too. With enough food and sex, they'll be in no hurry to go back to where they came from. Enough time to relax and enjoy it, and they might decide to stay. Enough time to grow strong and plunder all the countryside around them, and they'll start striking out for new hunting grounds." He stopped and shook his head, then continued. "I don't like this at all. Not one little bit of it."

The door opened and Titus came back into the room.

"Well, what do you think, Titus?"

Titus nodded and spoke.

"Alaric's Visigoths, General. I was thinking of the time they jumped us in Thrace. Once burned, I tend to be wary of fires."

"Good man. Exactly what occurred to me. Tell Publius. Sit down."

Titus turned to my uncle, seating himself as he did so. "The Visigoths were doing the same thing in Thrace, Commander. They'd storm a town, kill the men, keep the women, and keep them in order by threatening the children. Then they'd pretend to be citizens—changed their clothes and their weapons. We rode right through one of those towns without suspecting a damned thing. Two days later, we met Alaric head on, and just when we needed and expected it least, these people hit us from behind. Damn near cost us the battle and it could have cost us a lot more in men and horses than it did. We thought we had cleaned out all the lands behind us, but they were there all the time. An expensive error."

My father spoke up again, his voice very guttural and almost unintelligible. "Safe base, Publius. Never had one there before. Used it like a catapult. Almost destroyed us."

"So what are you suggesting?" Uncle Varrus asked.

"An expedition. Burn the whoresons out!"

My uncle looked upset. "That's easy to suggest, but how would we go about it? The village is fortified, the priest says. What can your cavalry do against fortified positions?"

"Bowmen."

"What bowmen?"

My father nodded emphatically. "Ullic's people. Those bows of theirs. Pick these people off like pigeons."

"But how, Picus? I don't follow your logic."

Uncle Varrus was at a loss and I could see my father becoming more and more frustrated by his inability to speak clearly. Finally, however, he spat out one word. "Trickery!"

"Trickery? Trick them, you mean? The Saxons? How?"

"Get them out into the open. Alexander's tactics. Surprise them. Draw them out. Damn this throat! Get me a drink, Titus. Something to write with, too."

He wrote for what seemed to me to be hours, with the others reading over his shoulders, and I could see the excitement growing in them as they read. Uncle Varrus clapped him on the shoulder at one point, his voice pitched high with excitement.

"By God, Picus, that might just work! It'll frighten them to death at first and then tempt them to death afterwards! It's brilliant! We have to get word to Ullic and Uric immediately. I wonder how many bowmen they have now? Well, we'll soon find out. This will be our first chance to try both sets of troops together."

My father spoke again, his voice much clearer now. "Tell them, lots of arrows."

King Ullic himself came, with my uncle Uric and fifty-four bowmen. It took them ten days to reach us, for they had to be summoned, and then they had preparations to make before they could set out. Titus was the messenger who rode to them with word of what was afoot. He took three horses and rode practically without rest, covering the journey of four days in three, over mountainous terrain all the way, and then he rode straight back again with the word that my grandfather's people were coming at his back. By the time they arrived, the plan of campaign had been made and all the arrangements were in place. A council of war was held on the night of their arrival, from which Uther and I were banned, and the expedition set out early the next morning.

Two hundred and eighty men rode out from Camulod that day, mounted on the pick of our herds. Uther and I watched them go, the first formal military expedition to be sent out from Camulod; the first manifestation of a new force in the land of Britain.

My father rode at their head with Uther's father and Titus. King Ullic rode further back, with his contingent of bowmen, who were mounted for this expedition on our large horses. Used as they were to their small mountain ponies, many of them would be suffering by the end of the forty-mile ride. Each of them carried two quivers of arrows, with the exception of their king himself, who was now too old to pull his own mighty bow.

At the very back of the contingent rode a party of men who looked very different from the others. Uncle Varrus had spent much time experimenting with a new shield suitable for mounted men to carry, ever since the weight of his own shield had bruised his thigh in the charge at Vegetius Sulla's villa years before. Now most of our cavalry carried circular or oval shields slung across their shoulders as they rode. The men at the back of the column, however, all carried the great, heavy *scutum* of the Roman legionary, and each *scutum* had a selection of throwing spears and javelins fitted into the leather slings at the back. They made an incongruous addition to the group, but they were there for a purpose.

Uther and I climbed to the top of the walls and watched them until they disappeared among the trees in the distance. We were sick with disappointment at being left behind, but we assured each other that the day would come when we would not only ride out, but would ride out at the head of such parties.

IV

Camulod seemed dead and deserted after the departure of the troops. They took with them even the pleasure of the games that normally filled our free time, so Uther and I went our separate ways, he to the stables and I to my uncle's Armoury, where I perched myself on my cross-chair and gave myself up to imagining the outcome of their expedition according to the little I knew of the plan drawn up by my father and the others. It was to be two weeks before they came riding home again, battered and bloodied, but jubilant and victorious.

Uther and I tried our best to stay close to the leaders that homecoming night as they recounted all that had happened to Uncle Varrus and the other council members who had gathered to hear their news, but it was very late by the time the gathering had assembled and Occa found us and dragged us off to bed. We scrambled to hide from her, but succeeded only in attracting the attention of my father, who had neither the time nor the patience to accommodate small boys that night. We were dispatched to bed in a disgust so profound that neither one of us as much as thought of spying on Occa, which we usually did as she prepared herself for bed.

We found out about the battle the next evening from Titus, who had become the best friend Uther and I had among the grown men of Camulod—with the exception, of course, of Uncle Varrus, Uther's grandfather. Titus approached us as we fought each other with wooden swords and shields, and stood watching until I found an opening in Uther's guard and smacked him soundly on the top of his head with the flat of my blade, far harder than I intended to. With a roar of rage, Uther threw down his weapons and came for me with his bare hands, murder and tears in his outraged eyes, and in a second we were rolling on the ground in mortal struggle. Titus pulled us apart and held us, struggling and kicking, one at the end of each of his strong arms.

"Hey!" He roared at us. "What good is there in training you to fight and be leaders if you are going to try to kill each other? There's no room for fighting between you two!" Abruptly, he bent his elbows, pulling us both against him, our faces cheek to cheek close to his own, which looked ferocious, glaring at us both. "I thought you might have preferred to hear the tale of how we fought the Saxons, but if you'd rather waste your time fighting each other, I'll leave you to it and go and dally with a woman, instead."

Our quarrel was immediately forgotten. "Tell us, Titus, tell us, please! We weren't really fighting," we squealed, almost in unison.

"Well, are you sure you want to hear? The tale might bore you." We protested immunity to boredom. "Very well then, come with me. It's getting late and this story needs a fire."

We followed him out of the gates onto the open hillside, where he stopped and looked to left and right. "Over there." He nodded to a spot that had been used as a campsite. "There's a fire pit, and logs to sit on, but no wood. Scatter, infants, and find fuel for our flames."

We were gone in a flash, returning with armloads of firewood from the great heap piled against the walls. Titus had found some kindling in the time we were gone and had crossed to borrow a burning log from another fire close by. We watched him, breathless with anticipation, as he fed dried grass and twigs to the glowing ember, blew it into flames and slowly built the fire until it could live on its own. Finally he was satisfied: he piled some good-sized logs onto the fire and straightened up to his full height, looking out across the plain below us in the growing dusk. He hitched at the armoured kilt of leather straps around his waist and turned to us. Neither of us had spoken in a long time. We sat there staring at him, waiting for his story.

"Where can I start? Two stalwart warriors like you should be told everything. Someday it will be up to you to lead our troops." He was half joking—we could see it in his eyes—but then his face grew serious and he seated himself on a log across the fire from us. The flames were dancing high now and the logs sparked crisply.

We sat there listening to the crackling of the dry wood for long moments and then Uther cleared his throat. "The Saxon fight, Titus."

"Ah, yes. The Saxon fight! That's why we came out here, isn't it?" He paused yet again, remembering, and we hung on his silence, our eyes never leaving his face. "Those Saxons had a real stronghold there," he finally said. "We watched them from a small wood on the opposite side of the valley, and believe me, we were impressed. The priest who brought us the news of these people told us they were quartered in a fortified village on a hill. We had been hoping he was wrong, or just being an inaccurate civilian, and he was. The place was actually built on the end of a long ridge that stuck out into the marsh beneath it like a finger. That made a big difference. Can you tell me why?"

Uther was quicker than I to answer. "A hill is easier to defend than a ridge—against us, anyway."

"Why?" Titus was deadly serious, not a note of condescension in his tone.

"Because our horses can attack along the ridge better than they can from below."

"Good man. So we had one problem solved. Caius, what was our other problem?"

I thought hard, just to be sure that my first reaction had been the right one. "The marsh. If it was too wet, you wouldn't be able to cross it."

"For what purpose? You're right, but why would we want to cross the marsh?"

"To get to the bottom of the hill, to get the Saxons to come down against you and take their attention away from the ridge and our cavalry."

His eyes went wide with mock admiration. "Splendid! You should make a great general some day, my lad."

"Not as great as his father," Uther grumbled, ill-naturedly, I thought, until he went on, "He hasn't got the legions."

Titus grinned. "Well, perhaps not, but neither does his father now, yet what he planned, and the way he made it work, was brilliant. It was more than that; it was sheer, absolute genius."

He shifted to a more comfortable position on his log and threw some more wood onto the fire, watching it catch and blaze until I had to ask, in an agony of frustration, "What *did* he do, Titus?"

"Forgive me," he grinned, "I was remembering. We watched from the woods for an hour or so and then fell back to where we had set up camp, about two miles back in a valley that was secure. Ullic's people spent the rest of that day and night making their own preparations. About an hour after it got dark, your father dispatched me with a dozen men down into the valley to test the firmness of the ground. Remember, it had been raining hard for days."

"How did you test it?" I asked.

"By walking on it. Is there a better way?"

"But didn't anyone see you?"

"In the dark? Remember our cloaks are black."

"But white inside."

"Not all of them. Only the officers'. I exchanged mine with a trooper. We blackened our faces, went barefoot, and crossed the entire valley floor to the bottom of the ridge."

"And?"

"The ground was wet, but firm. Our eyes were used to the darkness and we had no trouble. We went back to camp and I made my report. Then it started to rain, and it poured without let-up for the rest of the night, thunder and lightning frightening the horses, and everything glopped up with mud and impossible to fight in. We had planned to attack at dawn, but it was hopeless. We had to sit tight in our hidden camp and wait for the weather."

"How long did you have to wait?" This was Uther, as avid for details as I was.

"Only a day. The clouds broke up in the middle of the morning and the sun blazed for the rest of the day. Late again that afternoon, the General, Uric, King Ullic and I went back to the wood on the valley side. Our timing was perfect. We had estimated about eighty men in the enemy camp the day before, but no sooner had we got into position in the woods that second day than we saw a large party—at least a hundred men—approaching from the east. They had obviously been raiding. They had loaded wagons with them, and lines of women, all tied together. We watched them climb the hill and enter the camp, and we stayed to watch the celebrations that started immediately afterward. We were glad we had waited, for we knew there would be a lot of thick, aching heads in that camp, come morning."

"So? What happened next?" I was growing more and more impatient of his introspective pauses.

"Oh ... We returned to camp and reviewed our plans, and then we slept for a few hours. Then, just before midnight, General Picus left with his cavalry, to make a great, circular sweep that would position them on the ridge to the west of the stronghold well before dawn. He had sent out scouts the night before to mark their way while I was down in the valley with my men."

He glanced at Uther. "Two hours later, King Ullic and your father, Uric, left with their bowmen, and shortly after that the others left, leaving me with a reserve of twenty mounted men, to take my place on the hillside we had been using as an observation post. And after that, it was simply a matter of waiting for daylight." Titus chuckled aloud and shook his head.

"What are you laughing at?" I asked him.

"Oh, I was just remembering. I've never seen anything so beautiful, and I had the best view, among all the people there. It was truly magnificent." He shook his head again, grinning.

"Well?" Uther sounded as impatient as I was. "Tell us!"

"All right. What happened eight years ago and then again two years ago that all the Saxons know about?"

"The legions left."

"Correct. The legions left. So, imagine dawn on a summer morning, just as the birds begin to sing, and here's a camp of Saxon raiders, safe behind walls of stone on the top of a hill, and suddenly there's a sound in the distance that they don't expect, or want, to hear—a drumbeat. And along the valley comes a sight that none of them had ever thought to see again in Britain. A troop of Roman soldiers. Legionaries, marching in full armour, shields and spears and cloaks and helmets, three centurions on horseback at their head. A full maniple, a hundred and ten men, marching along the valley. Suddenly the trumpeter blasts a call and they all break into double time. I'll wager my best parade armour there wasn't a single Saxon still asleep within three minutes of the sound of that first drumbeat.

"But then, unexpectedly, and suddenly, the senior centurion notices the camp on the hill and gives the command to stop. Everything stops. The soldiers are almost at the bottom of the hill. The centurion sends a trooper forward to survey the camp. Most of the Saxons are hidden along the walls. The trooper approaches, hesitates, goes forward again, stops, sees something suspicious and turns to wave his maniple away. As he does so, someone in the camp fires an arrow at him. It misses, and he begins to run back down the hill. The senior centurion shouts a command, his men turn around, and he begins to double time them back the way they came. Romans, running away!

"Those Saxons came over their walls and down that hillside in a solid wave, along the entire length of it, and the Roman retreat broke into a rout, the legionaries running as fast as their legs would carry them, out into the marshes. And as they ran, the Saxons followed them, right down the pathway they had taken between two lines of bowmen who lay hidden beneath the covers they had made for themselves from grass and rushes two nights before. When the legionaries had run far enough, the trumpet sounded again and the bowmen threw off their covers and stood up for the slaughter. The Saxons were caught between two lines of them, twenty-seven on each side. The Celts were firing as fast as they could draw their bows and the closest Saxon to any of them had to run fifty paces *into* their fire before he could engage."

Uther and I were spellbound.

"In the meantime," Titus went on, "the cavalry had begun their attack along the ridge as soon as the enemy was committed to chasing the running legionaries. They had no opposition. Took the place on the first charge and didn't lose a man.

"The trumpet call that brought the bowmen out was also the signal for the maniple to reform. By the time the bowmen began to run low on arrows, the Saxons who were left had a perfectly disciplined diamond infantry formation coming down their throats. They ran, back to their camp, until they saw our horsemen on the hilltop. After that, those that still kept their senses could only run towards my position, through the hole that the bowmen had conveniently left open for them on one side. There were no more than thirty of them left when I broke cover with my squadron and went to clean them up. I didn't even bloody my sword."

"Were they all killed?" My voice was strained.

"Every last one of them. Those bowmen of your uncle's are wild men. No prisoners."

"What about the women in the camp?" Uther's question surprised me. I had completely forgotten about the women.

"What about them? We gave them food and let them go back to their homes."

"What about the camp?" To me, this was far more important than women.

"We destroyed it completely. Toppled the walls. They weren't high like ours—no more than stone fences. We scattered the stones. No one will use it as a camp again. And that was it. Except for one more thing, your father's idea, Caius. We piled the Saxon dead in one great pile, making sure they still wore their helmets and held their weapons. In days to come, any who find that pile of bleaching bones will know that these were Saxons and that they died in battle against a force far mightier than they."

"How many were there, Titus?" Uther asked. "Did you count?"

"Aye, a score more than three hundred. We had to assume that another large party had come in the night before, after the group we had watched arriving."

Uther was impressed. "And you left three hundred dead men piled in one heap?"

"A mountain of dead men, Uther Pendragon. That place will stench for the coming five years. But it will show any who look that there is no place for living Saxons in this land."

I sat there, staring into the fire and trying to imagine a pile of three hundred dead men. How many bones would that make?

Change was afoot in our land in those years, and in the eyes of the leaders of our Colony, it was centred upon two increasingly urgent needs, food and weaponry. That first punitive expedition, coupled with one more, almost simultaneous event, marked the beginning of a new phase in the life of Camulod just as surely as had the other key events referred to in the chronicles of Caius Britannicus and Publius Varrus: the wedding of Varrus and Luceiia, which started the whole thing, the decision to fortify the hill behind the villa, the first meeting with King Ullic Pendragon, and the decision to mount our troops.

The other crucial event passed largely unnoticed by the common people of Britain. Only the Council of Bishops and the few remaining centres of government knew of it. A delegation of bishops, acting as messengers of the Church, had been dispatched early in the year in one of the last available fortified galleys to implore the Emperor Honorius to intercede on the Church's behalf and send some regular troops to Britain to serve as a rallying point for the island's defensive forces. The delegation returned the following spring, just about the time of our raid on the Saxon settlement, with the word of Honorius: Britain should arrange its own defences and not look to the Imperial Armies for help.

That message combined with the destruction of the Saxon settlement—Picus's Raid, as it came to be known—forced the councillors of Camulod to recognize that they could no longer maintain a policy of insularity in matters of defence. We had discovered the existence of the new Saxon base almost by accident and had dispatched an expedition to deal with a band of about one hundred and fifty hostiles. They had encountered a force of more than three hundred and had been almost too late to thwart the enemy presence on our threshold.

The lesson was obvious: in order to prevent the emergence of any similar threat so close to us, the colonists of Camulod would have to extend their patrol activities beyond the Colony's present perimeter. That meant an immense increase in the territory to be covered, for if Camulod was the centre of a circle, every mile pushed outward vastly increased the area contained within the protective circle. It was a grim predicament, but one that had to be accommodated; there was no other option. So the name of Camulod echoed through the land, as towns and villages that had never heard of the Colony were visited by patrols of disciplined troops. In this way the people learned that they were no longer alone and defenceless. They were warned to keep watch, and told how to find Camulod if they were in grave need of armed help.

One of the first results of this increase in people's awareness of us was a dramatic influx of would-be colonists, most of whom were totally lacking in the qualifications we demanded for admission to the Colony. They came in hundreds, seeking shelter, and in their hundreds we had to turn them away, not from callousness, but from necessity. Since we had started our Colony, we had developed an economy that centred upon food supply. We could eat only what we could produce and we were faced immediately with the impossibility of feeding everyone who came to us. Philanthropy and survival were not compatible for us. We threw up a cordon of guard posts around our lands for the sole purpose of turning away people whom we could not use. It was a terrible responsibility to place upon the men who staffed the posts, for it endowed them, in effect, with the power of life and death over everyone seeking entry to Camulod. I fear there were many who abused it, too: any woman will give her body in return for her life, and rare is the common soldier who can resist the sexual wiles of determined and desperate women, especially young, ripe women. We began to notice large numbers of nubile young women appearing in the Colony very soon after we threw up our cordon, and we had to take firm disciplinary steps to stop the flood, or at least slow it to a trickle.

The young men who came our way were all judged on their

suitability as soldiers, for our increased commitments placed a greater strain on our military resources than on any other. My father was inexorable in his demands regarding these. Only the strongest were accepted right from the start, for he presumed, and was quickly proved correct, that we would have ample choice. The foot-soldier came back into his own very quickly in the new Camulod, for we soon ran out of horses for our new recruits. Within a year of the beginnings of this new policy, sub-garrisons had been established in half a dozen outlying camps at various distances from Camulod itself. These camps, as had the Roman camps four hundred years before, began to attract their own groups of colonists dependent on the safety and the promise of life and strength the camps afforded them. Consequently, new fields were broken and sowed with new crops, and we were glad of the surplus supply. There were also many artisans who came to our gates carrying their tools and the secrets of their trades, and none of these were ever turned away. They had a demonstrable value and were happy to work for the common welfare in return for a secure home.

To my mind, however, the most significant change effected by Picus's Raid was in the attitude of Ullic's people to our ways. The action had been their first real taste of the concerted power of their mighty new longbows used in conjunction with disciplined infantry and cavalry, and they wanted more. But the fifty-four bowmen that Ullic had been able to provide for that expedition were the only ones he had, and any increase in their numbers depended upon the availability of suitable wood for new bows. The making of the great bows was handled by the ageing master bowyer Cymric, who had created the first of them, and by his two sons, and each bow was a unique work of art. The importance of the weapon, and of the tree that was its source, rapidly became the dominant force in Ullic's whole kingdom. As his warriors learned its power, there was no need to tell them not to speak the name of the yew tree to others. It became sacrosanct almost overnight, from the day the first bow was completed, and this sacred inviolability contributed to the growth of the legend that sprang up around it.

As a tree, the yew fell within the religious provenance of the Druids, and within a short space of time every Druid who walked the land did so with the assistance of a seven-foot staff. Had anyone been curious enough to look, he might have noticed that all of these staves were remarkable in their similarity: all were of a length and thickness, and all were of yew. But no one did notice, and the Druids roamed the land, cutting their yew staves wherever they could find them, while in the hidden paths among the woods and hills, coverts of seedling yews grew untended, save that each would receive a passing Druid's glance from time to time.

Ullic and Uric made a new law among their people. No man could own a bow. Each was custodian of one for a time, charged with its welfare and responsible for its condition while it was in his charge, and all men were required to be trained in its use, just as all men were required to be constantly on the lookout for straight ash saplings from which arrows could be made.

By the end of the second year after the Raid, Uric had a hundred and four longbows and five hundred trained bowmen, but he still could take no significant part in our military affairs. He had to keep his bows close to home, where they were needed for training, since the short bows his men had used in the past were no longer adequate. Just as the change to long-swords had required us to change our training techniques, so had the change to the new longbow dictated new terms of training to Ullic's people. They were determined, however, to be ready for any emergency that might arise, so a chain of beacon towers, modelled upon the Roman watch towers, was set up to pass word quickly between our two communities.

In Camulod, Varrus and Equus kept their armourers at work constantly, forging the new long-swords for our mounted men and the old short-swords for the infantry, and once again apprentices were set to work turning out heavy shields for foot-soldiers. The whole of Camulod rang with the hammering of the armourers and the clashing sounds of drilling soldiers until people grew accustomed to the noise and oblivious to the constant clamour of military preparations.

Meanwhile, Uther and I grew older and stronger, and I combed my uncle's books in vain for the question that would entitle me to learn his great secret.

V

As those months grew into years there were times when I despaired of ever asking the correct question of my great-uncle. For three years I read and reread his notes and chronicles, and asked him every question that occurred to me. I learned a great deal about warfare and strategy and about history and the lessons of the past, and I learned even more about the character, wisdom and personality of my guardian. But I did not find the question that was the key to his greatest secret.

Then one day I noticed an inconsistency that had previously escaped me. In the beginning, it was no more than a niggling little doubt at the back of my mind, but its formless persistence annoyed me, and I worried at it for days before I went searching for the cause of it.

One cardinal rule governed Uther and me when we were in Uncle's Armoury: we were welcome there, but we were forbidden to touch any of the treasures he kept there and forbidden under pain of banishment to indulge our boyishness in any form of horse-play. The rest of Camulod was open to us for high fun. That room was for study only. Most of the time, we had no trouble conform-ing to this rule, since there was always an adult around, but on one frightening occasion, Uther tripped me, just for fun, while I was carrying a heavy book. I fell, naturally, but I fell against the small table that held Grandfather Caius's statue, the one that Uncle Varrus called the Lady. The table overturned and the statue hit the floor with an awful clang and clatter that appalled us both, since the great wooden doors to the Armoury stood open. Uther cursed and scrambled to set the table upright again, and I righted the statue, aware of its great weight—I had to really grunt to get it up high enough and Uther had to help me get it back onto the table—and aware also of the great gouge it had made in the polished wooden surface of Uncle Varrus's precious floor. It seemed as big and as deep as a ravine, that gouge. I knew it would be seen, and there was no way it could be hidden. I thought of moving the entire table over to cover it, but the mark was a full stride away from where the table normally stood, too far for any casual relocation to pass unnoticed. We left everything as it was. I replaced the book I had been carrying and we scampered out of there as quickly as we could, expecting to hear adult voices challenging us at every step.

As it turned out, no one had heard the noise, and as the day passed, no one seemed to notice the mark on the floor. After our initial fright, we giggled together about the event, dramatizing our shock and the risk of Uncle's displeasure that we had incurred. Only that night, before I fell asleep, did I become aware of a tiny uncertainty, an anomaly, an infuriating, unidentifiable inconsistency in the back of my mind.

I was a pragmatic boy with an enquiring, logical mind. I did not like mysteries and I could not tolerate unresolved mysteries, so the next day I went over the entire scene in my mind, time and time again, just as it had happened. I had been carrying the book, Uther had tripped me, I had fallen against the table, then Uther righted the table, I wrestled the statue upright and together we lifted it and put it back in its place on the table. Then I had noticed the hole in the floor and panicked because it was so obvious. I had picked up the book, which had fallen open but was luckily undamaged, and replaced it where I had found it, and then we had both fled the room. So what was wrong? Why this uncertainty? The only thing that came to me, eventually, was the terrifying thought that the book had been damaged in falling and that I had not really taken note of the extent of the damage, dismissing it as insignificant beside the damage done to the floor. The more I thought about it, the more chilling the thought became. I knew how highly Uncle Varrus prized his books. To Uther they were unimportant, but I knew better. In truth, it was the gouge in the floor that was insignificant. If Uncle Varrus discovered that I had ruined, or even marred, one of his precious books because of a foolish boy's irreverence, he might bar me forever from using them.

Filled with anger at Uther for his thoughtless stupidity and lack of respect, I ran from my own room to the Armoury. As I approached it, my uncle came striding out, his face white and pinched and angry looking, followed by an equally white-faced servant. I skidded to a halt as he came sweeping towards me and hung my head in shame to receive his wrath, but he ignored me, hurrying past as though I was not there. Hardly daring to believe my good fortune, I went into the empty Armoury and straight to the table that held the precious books. They were all still there, including the one I was looking for. It was one of Grandfather Caius's books and I remembered thinking that day that I had not dipped into it in years, although I knew the entire text almost by rote. I reached for it and examined it minutely. It was absolutely unmarred; not a mark or a blemish anywhere.

Conscious of a feeling of great relief that I had been wrong and that nothing was amiss, I pulled over a stool, made myself comfortable, and opened the book at random, folding the heavy parchment sheets over the bindings that held them in place, and began to read of Grandfather's doubts about the skystones and how they could have fallen from the sky in flames. And then my memory gave a leap and I closed the book with a bang and searched among the others until I found what I was looking for, and there were the words, written as I remembered them in Grandfather's broad script:

". . . I reached to pick her up. 'Careful, Caius! She's heavier than you think,' warned Publius. 'Here, let me help you.'

"Between the two of us we picked her up and carried her, with some difficulty, across the yard into the house and placed her in my day-room on a table by the window . . ."

There was the source of my mystery, the anomaly that had been plaguing me! I had no recollection of my grandfather, but Uncle Varrus was massively strong, and yet it had taken their combined strength to carry the statue "with some difficulty" from the forge to the house. But Uther and I had picked it up from the floor, although admittedly not easily, and replaced it on the table. I knew I could carry it alone for some distance, given a strong first grip on it, and I had not the slightest doubt that Uther and I together could carry it as far as we wanted to. But Uther and I were three months short of twelve years old. Uncle Varrus and my grandfather had been grown men, big men, strong men, at the time my grandfather had been writing of. Even today, old as he was, Uncle Varrus had more strength than both Uther and me combined.

I rose slowly from my seat and crossed to the table where the statue stood and, reaching out my hand, I traced my fingertips across her cold surface, seeing in my mind other phrases that spoke of "generous curves" and "ample" breasts and buttocks. I thought of Occa and her large breasts, belly and buttocks. They were ample. But the word did not apply, as I understood it, to the Lady's shape.

I heard a movement behind me and turned to see Uncle Varrus staring at me, an odd expression on his face that made me afraid again.

"Uncle?"

He ignored me, turning slowly to walk from the room, and as he did so, I saw a streak of wetness on his cheek. The sight shocked me and I stood there gaping as I watched him walk away. I knew something bad had happened, and as soon as he had gone I went running myself to find out what was wrong. I met Uther in one of the corridors, running to find me and tell me the news. Equus, my uncle's closest friend, had been found dead in the forge. He had been working alone, it seemed, when he died, and had fallen at his anvil. By the time they found him, the blade he had been working on was cold, but it had burned through his thighs to the bone before it cooled.

Uther turned and ran towards the stables as soon as he had blurted out his news, assuming that I would be at his heels, as keen as he to see whatever was to be seen, but I made no move to follow him. His excited words had immediately plunged me into a state of complete terror and overwhelming nausea, and I sank to the floor to huddle with my knees gripped tightly between my arms and the cold sweat of sickening fear fouling my hot skin.

I had dreamed Equus's death two nights before, but his agony had been mine! My mind quaked with horror as I remembered, in awful detail, the excruciating pain that had consumed me and brought me screaming to wakefulness in the darkness of my room. A glowing, white-hot band of pain had fallen across my legs, searing my thighs and groin, and I had seen the smoke belching from the awful wound it caused and smelled the charring stench of my own cooking flesh.

I had long been plagued by such dreams. Indeed, I could not remember a time when I had not been disturbed by the formless memory of some nocturnal terror. They did not come often, but when they did, I awoke in horror, sickened to the point of vomiting and drenched with the sweat of abject fear. I seldom remembered any details, but invariably I suffered for hours afterward, wracked with chills and cramps and painful nausea. And always, it seemed, formless as the dreams had been, they returned in splintered fragments to haunt me during my waking hours, unexpectedly recalled by some detail or incident that seemed to waken echoes in my soul and frightened me unreasonably.

Now it had happened again, but this time I could not deny the reality. Equus, the gentle, friendly giant, lifelong companion of Uncle Varrus, had died in just the manner I had dreamed! A series of images of Equus flashed through my mind, all of them portraying him as I had always known him, working alone with his beloved iron amid the smoke-hazed half-light of his smithy. Sparks showered upward from his hammer as he lovingly crafted the furnace-heated metal of sword and spearhead and ploughshare, and suddenly I saw him fall, dropping his pincers and their glowing contents, and again I felt the pain and smelled the stink of burning.

I do not know how long I crouched there in terrified solitude, but I arose at length and went out into the bright afternoon. No one sought to stop me, and I ran for miles, vainly trying to escape the terror I bore inside me. When I stopped at last, I sat beneath a tree and wept, shuddering with formless guilt, until the trembling in my limbs died down. And for a while I slept.

On my return to Camulod, however, I told no one what I thought, or what I felt, or what I had dreamed. People would have thought me mad. At times—on those few occasions when I could overcome my inner fears enough to think about my terrors for a brief spell—I, too, feared I might be mad. And so I made myself forget the entire incident. Only once more, when Uncle Varrus mentioned that Equus could have felt no pain, since his apoplexy would have rendered him unconscious, did I feel guilt and fear.

That episode marked the beginning of a tragic time in our household. The Druids say that deaths occur in threes and I must admit now, in my old age, that three has always seemed to me to be a potent number, endowed with mystical proclivities, and never more so than in this strangeness of deaths. Old Bishop Alaric, close and longtime friend of both my grandfather and Uncle Varrus, died in his sleep within three days of Equus and was found at the third hour of the morning. My great-uncle Ullic, Uther's grandfather, also died within the month, his back broken in a fall from a rock. Throughout his life he had often sat on this rock, a boulder on a bare hillside from which he swore he could overlook his entire kingdom. I heard that he had risen to climb down from his seat and simply pitched over backwards as though his heel had caught on some projection, although none was there.

There was no gaiety in our house that winter and for a long, long time I had no other opportunity to speak to my uncle about the mystery of the statue. It was not until the springtime that I found myself alone with him again, and him in the frame of mind that might at last make allowance for my curiosity. It had been the kind of afternoon I had grown used to in the long winter months. Uncle Varrus had done no writing since the day Equus died, seeming content to sit unmoving by the fire, his eyes far off as though he were living elsewhere. His hair, even his beard, had turned white and he looked very old. I was reading that day, and Uther was about his own affairs, probably in the woods below with some girl. Aunt

Luceiia had come into the room and I had half heard her fussing over my uncle. There had been a mention of "the boy" and then I had been aware of her leaving.

Sometime after that, my uncle spoke. "What are you doing, Caius?"

"Reading, Uncle." This was the first time he had spoken directly to me in months.

"I can see that, boy. What are you reading? That's what I want to know."

"Your books, Uncle. I was reading about your forge in Colchester." With a sinking feeling, I realized he would think immediately of Equus and feared he might withdraw into his thoughts again, but he surprised me.

"And what about it? Why does that interest you?"

"Well, I was reading again about how you found the dagger that your grandfather had made for you."

"Ah! The skystone dagger." He fell silent for a spell, thinking of it, then, just as I was thinking he had forgotten me, he spoke again. "It was beautiful, Caius, the most beautiful thing I had ever seen. Equus had hidden it, along with all the other treasures my grandfather had left for me. Poor Equus! I miss him, Cay. You never saw the dagger, did you?"

"No. You buried it with Grandfather, when I was still a baby."

"Aye, that I did. It seemed fitting."

"Uncle?"

"Aye? What is it?"

"Why did you bury the dagger with Grandfather? It must have been very valuable." I was looking directly at him and was happy to see the fond, real smile that had been absent for so long from that beloved face.

"You think it was wrong of me to bury the thing I had loved most in this world with the man I had loved most?" He paused and considered that for a few moments. "Well, there are probably others who would agree with you." Again he paused. "I wonder if I can explain that to you. The dagger was a dream, Cay. A dream come true for my grandfather and for me. But Caius Britannicus had had a dream that came true, too."

"Camulod," I said.

"Aye, Camulod. His Colony. That dagger of mine, with its mirror-bright blade, seemed to me to embody whatever it was that drove both your grandfather and me to make our dreams real. It was a shining proof that great and wondrous things, things miraculous, can spring from the minds of men. It pointed the way for both of us and led us to satisfaction. So, when he died, it seemed to me fitting that he should take it with him, wherever he might go. I buried it and him together and I have never regretted the impulse." He looked straight at me. "Does that make any sense to you at all?"

"Yes, Uncle, it does, but I have a question to ask. May I ask it now?"

"Of course! Since when do you need permission to ask questions?"

I made no comment on that, but pressed ahead with the question that had been puzzling me for months. "You know the statue? The Lady?"

"The Lady of the Lake. What about her?"

"Is she really made from a skystone?"

"What do you think?"

"I think she is. Your books, both yours and Grandfather's, say that she is."

"So? Was that your question?"

"No, not really, but . . ." I grappled for the right words, now that I had my chance. "Do you remember the first night Grandfather Caius saw the statue in the forge?"

"Very well. Why?" He was lounging in his chair, watching me curiously, with one eyebrow raised.

"Well, Grandfather Caius says in his book that it took both of you to carry it to the house that night."

"It did. She's a heavy lady."

"She's not that heavy now, Uncle." He sat up straighter, his expression changing, the blanket that had been around his shoulders slipping away unheeded. I gulped and charged ahead. "I knocked her over, one day, and picked her up and put her back on the table. She made a gouge in the floor, over there." I pointed to the spot, but he did not even glance that way.

"So? What are you saying, boy?"

"Just that if she's . . . if the statue's as heavy as Grandfather said it was, I shouldn't be able to lift it."

"Perhaps he exaggerated a little. Is that all?"

"No, Uncle, not all. Several times, in both of your books, each of you talks about the Lady as if she were much . . . fatter . . . bigger, somehow. That would have made her heavier." I fell silent and he looked at me very seriously.

"I'll ask you again, Caius. What are you saying to me?"

I felt a kind of panic. "I don't know, Uncle Varrus. It just seems strange to me, that's all. She should be bigger."

His voice was very soft. "Caius, do you remember the day a few years ago when I told you I would be waiting for a certain question from you?" I nodded, staring. "Well, you have almost asked me that question. Would you like to try to rephrase it?"

Suddenly I knew! The question lay in *Grandfather's* book, not Uncle Varrus's! My mouth was dry and my thoughts were racing. A thousand possible questions flashed through my mind and I rejected all of them, all save one, which I knew had to be exactly the right question. Yet I reviewed what I knew before committing myself to the asking of it. He had buried the skystone dagger with Grandfather Caius because, he said, his own dream had come true. He had smelted the skystone into the metal statue because, he said, he had not yet discovered the proper use for it. And now the statue was lighter, much lighter, if I could pick it up, and his greatest treasure was hidden in this room.

"Uncle?" His eyes snapped open, wide and alert. "What did you do with the rest of the skystone metal after you melted the Lady down again?"

There was a long silence before he rose to his feet and placed a hand on each of my shoulders. "Caius," he said, deep voiced, "there were times when I thought you would never ask me. I had begun to fear you would never see it, that I had covered my tracks too well. Bring me the wooden hammers."

Mystified, but extremely excited, I went immediately to the far wall and took down the two wooden hammers he referred to. Of all the wonderful things in this great room, these were the most innocuous and I had asked about them long before. He had told me then that they were no more than mementos carved for him by an old friend, replicas of the hammers that he used in beating silver. As I retrieved them he strode across the room and closed the great doors, dropping the bar in place to lock them.

"Bring them here." I crossed to where he stood in the middle of the floor. "Give me one of them." I did so. "Now stand there, opposite me. Move back, further. Now look down. What do you see?"

"The floor. The end of a board. Like the one at your feet. The same board."

"What else?"

"The studs that hold it in place."

"Put the end of your handle on the left stud." I did. It fitted perfectly. "Now push down, hard and steady." I felt my eyes grow wide as the stud sank into the floor and its neighbour in the opposite corner of the board rose out of its hole. "That's enough! Now, take hold of the raised stud and lift."

The board came out of the floor easily, revealing a long case of highly polished wood in the recess beneath. Carved into the lid of this box, about two-thirds of the way up its length from where I stood, a star was inlaid in silver, trailing long, arcing streamers of gold behind it. I stood gazing at it, seeing the significance of the symbol immediately and wondering what miracle might be contained beneath it.

My uncle interrupted my trance by leaning over to grasp the ends of a leather strap that lay on top of the case at his end. "Hcy," he said, "this is only the case. Lift it out." I fumbled for the strap at my end and we lifted it together. It was not heavy. Balancing it between us, we carried it to the light and placed it reverently on a

table top. I ran my fingertips through the dust that coated it, mar-
velling at the silken smoothness of the polished wood. "Hold the
ridge on the bottom at your end."

My fingers sought and found the ridge and then held it firm
while he twisted something and pulled the cover free. A rush of
blood to my head almost deprived me of my senses as I saw what
lay inside. Of course, it was the Sword.

It lies here beside me as I write. Men have talked of it for years
now, even the men who own this land today. Many search for it,
and there are already people living in this land who doubt it ever
was. No such Sword existed, they say, save in the minds of dream-
ers and minstrels. I could have told them that they were wrong, but
they did not even know I was nearby, and had they seen me they
would have killed me instantly, so I left them to their ignorance
and their doubts.

Many eyes have seen this Sword, but none lives today, save
only myself, who ever held it. It came into the lives of ordinary men
in one moment of pure magic, and from that day forward, all men
believed it to be truly magical, and I suppose it is, if the word magical means not of this earth.

I write of ordinary men and how the Sword came into their
lives in a summer moment, so I must now, I suppose, think of
myself as being extraordinary, since it came into my life fully thirty
years and more before any other saw it. Mine were among the first
eyes ever to gaze upon its beauty, and I was shown it by the man
who made it, and I, myself, became the eventual Keeper of the
Sword. That, I know, would make me extraordinary if nothing else
did. My name is whispered in fear and awe today. Magician, they
call me; sorcerer. That makes me extraordinary.

I have heard seven tales of my own death, and that, too, makes
me extraordinary, for they were seven different tales of seven deaths
and I sit here alive and alone, an aged man filled with the melancholy
of long, friendless years, the fugitive guardian of the greatest treasure
in the world. And I know that, should a band of raiders invade my
refuge now, this instant, the sight of my old man's face would send

them screaming, fleeing from my sight. That makes me truly, in the worst way I could imagine, extraordinary. But on that day, I had no thought in my boy's head of being extraordinary. I stood weak-kneed, gazing in slack-mouthed awe at the magnificence of the weapon that lay before me, cradled in a sculpted bed of brushed, unborn calfskin. I watched my uncle's hand reach out and pluck it from its bed and I saw the reflections race along its blade as he raised it.

"Sit. By the fire."

I groped my way back to my chair, not daring to take my eyes away from the lethal beauty of that blade lest it should disappear. My uncle came and sat in his own chair across from me. He placed the point on the wooden floor between us and held the Sword upright, with the tip of his index finger pressing on the very top of the pommel so that I could admire all the lines of it.

"Well?" he asked me. I shook my head, for I had no words to say. My eyes could not comprehend the purity of that blade. It was almost colourless, and yet it was polished silver, smooth and unmarked and flawless. The light from the fire blazed from it in a way I had never seen. Not even the finest mirror of polished metal could reflect colour with such astonishing perfection.

"Take it," my uncle said. "It won't bite you, although it could. Be careful of the edge. It's sharper than anything you've ever felt before. Go on, take it." I reached out and closed my hand around the hilt, feeling the texture of it against my palm as I drew the Sword towards me. My uncle's face was split by an enormous smile, which I knew later to be the satisfied, ecstatic smile of the sublime artist and creator. "You like it?"

Again I could only shake my head. Gradually, I began to test it. It took the strength of both my arms to lift the point free of the floor, seated as I was, but then I reached the balance point and I felt its weight settle back into my grasp like a living thing.

"It's alive!" I whispered. "What have you named it, Uncle?"

"It's called Excalibur."

"Excalibur?" I repeated it, still whispering. "Excalibur! It is a beautiful name. And it is a beautiful sword."

He laughed. "Aye, look at the hilt. You see that grey-black stuff covering the grip? That is the belly skin of a mighty fish. A shark. I had it sent to me years before you were born. A fisherman in Africa used to use it to wrap the handles of his knives. That skin will never slip in a man's grasp, no matter how he sweats. It's constantly firm and hard and never slippery. I bound it into place, as you can see, with wires of gold and silver intertwined into a net. It took me five months just to bind that hilt the way I wanted to."

"And this?" I asked. "This cross-piece? How was it made? Is it silver? It's different from the blade. How did you do it?"

"It's one piece, lad. A secret I learned from my own grandfather. Give it to me, let me show you." I handed the Sword back to him, and he held it up in front of him, admiring the lines of it as he continued speaking. "You know the making of a blade, any blade. What's the main difficulty?"

That was easy. "Binding the hilt to the tang."

"And why is that?"

"Because they're two different pieces. If the blade is short and broad, you can rivet the sides of the handle together through the tang. That's the best way. But the bigger the sword, the harder it becomes to fasten the hilt securely. You can rivet it, and then bind it with wire, or you can drill a hole lengthwise through the hilt piece, insert the tang, and then bind the whole thing together with a weighted pommel at the end against the heel of the hand, flattening the end of the tang against that, like a rivet."

He smiled at me again, pleased with my knowledge. "Good! But there is another way, Caius, and that's what you are seeing here. Can you guess how this was done?"

I looked closely at the Sword again, trying this time to ignore its beauty and see only its construction. It had a wide cross-hilt stretching almost the entire span of my twelve-year-old hand on either side of the hilt itself, and the arms of this cross were intricately worked in flowing designs of thorn branches and leaves. The hilt itself was slightly more than double the length of a normal short-sword's hilt and was wrapped in the manner described, sharkskin held in place by a net of golden and silver wires. The pommel, the endmost piece of the Sword, was a full cockleshell, perfect in shape and detail, the tracery of the scalloped shell perfectly symmetrical. There was no sign of the tang ever having protruded through the pommel. The entire construction, cross-piece and all, was, as my uncle had said, of one solid piece. I stared at it, racking my brain for an explanation and then shook my head.

"No, Uncle," I said eventually. "I can see that it's one piece, as you said, but I can't see how you were able to do it. How did you do it?"

His smile was still one of great pride. "My grandfather left me a parchment outlining a method used by a friend of his who had discovered it in North Africa. It is a little-known way of pouring whole metal figures that was once widely used by the Parthians and the Medes—"

I interrupted him. "You mean for making statues?"

"Yes, something like that."

"They use that method in Rome today, don't they?"

"Almost. As I say, something like it. In that method, the Roman one, the metal is melted in a crucible and then poured into a series of moulds to cool, and when the pieces are assembled, you are left with a hollow metal replica of what you set out to duplicate."

He had caught my interest. "How do you make the mould in the first place?" I asked him.

He stood up and crossed to one of the many tables in the room to pick up a small box-like object I had seen so many times that I had lost awareness of it. He threw it to me and I caught it like a ball, almost dropping it because of its unexpected weight.

"That's a mould. If you look closely, you'll see how to open it." It opened into two halves and protruding from one of the two pieces was a brass hemisphere that looked familiar. I shook it free and a brass apple fell into my hand. "Do you remember that?" I did. I had played with it as a young child. I nodded. "Now look inside the mould. Each half is a perfect replica of the outside of half the apple, even to the stem."

He took it from me and placed the two pieces together, pointing out a blocked hole in the top and a number of smaller holes all around the shape. "If I were to pour molten lead, silver or gold into this, and leave it to cool, I would open it to find a metal apple. A little cleaning and polishing and it would be as perfect as that one you're holding."

"And that's how you made the Sword?"

"No, of course not! Only the hilt."

"I'm sorry, that's what I meant."

"I know it was, but you must learn to say precisely what you mean."

"Yes, Uncle. But, if that's all there is to this secret, why haven't we been using it all the time?"

"I didn't say that's all there is to it. I said it was almost the same thing as the method generally used. The method I have learned is a different one. It uses different techniques. Most people today pour into clay moulds, and it is almost impossible to keep air bubbles out of the molten metal. That's why most of the moulded forms we have are hollow. That one, the apple you are holding, is solid, and so is the hilt of the sword. I had Father Andros carve me a hilt in wood. I made a clay mould of it and then I moulded the shape itself in wax, so that I ended up with a perfect wax replica of the wooden hilt, d'you follow me?" I nodded my understanding. "Good. Well, then I packed the wax in sand, tightly, and poured molten bronze into the mould. The bronze melted the wax and replaced it, perfectly, although not the first time I attempted it. When I was convinced I had the method perfected, I repeated it, this time with the tang of the sword inserted into the wax in the mould. It did work, eventually, but it took me five months and ten attempts to get it right. That hilt is absolutely solid; metal bonded to metal."

"Bronze? But it's silver."

"No, Caius. It is beaten silver over bronze."

I held out my hand and he returned the Sword to me. I held the hilt up to my face and looked at it again, closely and carefully.

There was no sign of any seam or joint. "How did you say this is named, Uncle?"

"What? The technique? It has no name that I know of, but my grandfather wrote that the people of Africa and Asia Minor who deal in such things apparently call their moulds 'qalibr.'"

The word sounded strange and exotic in my ears and the small hairs on my arms stirred. "*Qalibr*," I said. "The hilt came out of a mould. *Ex-qalibr*. That's where you got the name!" I tested it with my tongue, knowing by the goose-flesh on my arms and neck that it was the perfect name. "*Ex-qalibr!*"

"Excalibur." My uncle smiled, humouring me. "I'm glad you approve, Caius."

VI

Once I had seen Excalibur, it was never out of my mind. The other swords I had admired and wanted for so long became dull and clumsy in my sight. I had a long-bladed wooden sword that was my own treasure, and I carried it with me everywhere I went that summer, slung over my shoulder in the style that had been adopted by our horsemen. I was holding it in my hand, I remember, when the cry went up announcing the return of my father and his men from another of their endless patrols. I ran to watch them clatter up the road and into the fort, admiring again the sheer size and bulk of my father, their General. Titus rode with him, as did Flavius and several others I had come to know among his officers, and as soon as I had seen that they were all there, I ran to my uncle's Armoury, hiding my wooden sword among his books and pretending to read, for I knew that my father and his officers would come here to make their first report to Uncle Varrus before going to the baths.

Uncle Varrus himself arrived shortly after I did and busied himself at his writing table, paying no heed to my silent presence. Minutes later came the sound of nailed boots approaching, and my father strode into the room accompanied by Titus and Flavius. They were accompanied by three troopers, each of whom carried a burden which, at a nod from my father, they placed on the floor and then left.

"Greetings, Publius," said my father, pointing to the objects on the floor. "Look at these. Familiar?"

I watched from lowered brows as my uncle approached the three items on the floor, his eyes wide with surprise. "The boy's saddle-chair!" There was wonder in his voice. "These are the same device, but larger. Where did you find them?"

"Under three Franks. They strap them to their horses' backs and ride in them. Tried them ourselves. Useless. No sense in them."

"How so? What do you mean?"

"You have to climb onto them! Not possible to mount them any other way. You put your foot in the device—that hanging loop there—and swing your leg across the horse's back. We thought that might be so when we got the first one years ago, remember? We assumed the boy rider was crippled. Never occurred to any of us that whole men might need steps to get on a horse. Once you're up there on the thing, the raised part at the back sits strangely against your rump. Uncomfortable, and you can't grasp a horse's barrel through it. The thing's too thick."

My uncle appeared perplexed, his face furrowed in thought. "And yet you say these people all ride in these things?"

My father sat down heavily in a chair, his leathers creaking. "Aye, it appears so. Saw seven of them, but only caught three. With Uric's bowmen, we could have had all seven."

My uncle was shaking his head, an expression of incomprehension on his face. He crossed and touched one of the cumbersome saddles. "This is strange, Picus. I wonder what the benefit of using these things is? There must be some. Benefits, I mean. Wouldn't you think so?"

"Aye, you would think so," my father agreed, speaking slowly and clearly. "But whatever they might be, none of us could guess at them. We tried, but we were no more successful in divining their usefulness than we were at mastering them. We decided that these Franks are just poor horsemen. But I suspect that's far from the truth."

"Did you ask the prisoners to show you?"

"No prisoners. Fought like wild men and all died. Brought these back for your collection. No use for them, throw them out."

My uncle shook his head. "They're of no use to me, Picus. I already have one, small as it is. I've no need for the larger ones." He knelt by one of the strange devices, running the flat of his hand across its seat, his brow knitted in thought as he tried to make sense of the thing's purpose. Finally, however, he gave up and rose to his feet again. "How did the remainder of your patrol go?"

My father was pouring wine for himself and his officers. He shook his head as though dismissing the question. "Smoothly enough. Nothing except those Franks. Four got away, as I said. Apart from that, a long, peaceful and uneventful sweep. I'm ready for a hot bath. Feel I've got half the lice in Britain mating in my hair."

"Go then, all three of you, and wash the travel off. Welcome back. I will tell the cooks to roast a deer tonight."

"Do that," my father said, smiling one of his rare smiles. "Tell them to cook something for the others, too!" All four of them left the room, carrying their wine and laughing among themselves, leaving me alone. I crossed to the strange "chairs" that had been left on the floor and examined them. They were exactly like mine, but bigger, man-sized.

On a balmy afternoon in the following spring Uncle Varrus came into the Armoury to find me perched upon my sideways chair, swinging my wooden sword at imaginary foes who swarmed around me. Since I had discovered that the chair was really a riding harness of some kind, I had attached a rope to serve as a bridle, looping it around one end of the saw-horse on which my chair was mounted. I heard my uncle say "Great Mithras!" in a shocked voice before I was aware that he had entered the room and I scrambled from my chair in alarm, prepared to be punished for indulging in levity here in this hallowed room.

"Go back, Caius! Back onto your chair." There was no anger in his voice, merely an urgency I could not define. Surprised, I clambered back to my seat again as he continued speaking. "Do what you were doing when I came in." I gazed at him in confusion, but I could see from his face he meant what he said, so feeling peculiarly foolish I began to wave my wooden sword around half-heartedly. "No, no, no! Not like that! You were fighting, killing men. One of them was down by your left foot. Kill him again, as savagely as you did before."

Deciding that I would never understand the inconsistencies of adults, I did as he bade me. My feet were firm in their two supports, and I was almost standing upright, my "reins" in my left hand. Tightening my grasp on them for balance, I swung my sword with all my strength down across my front to the left, where I had imagined an enemy grasping my ankle.

"There! That's it!" he said in a strained voice. "When did you start to stand upright like that?"

I blinked at him. "I don't know, Uncle. I never could, before. I couldn't reach the supports with my feet. I must have grown tall enough to reach them."

"Aye, lad. To reach them and to stand upright in them! And standing upright like that, you're standing on a platform!" His last words meant nothing to me, but he spun on his heel and almost ran into the passageway outside the doors, shouting for attention at the top of his lungs. A wide-eyed servant came running to see what was amiss, followed by an equally alarmed soldier. My uncle pointed an accusatory finger at the soldier. "You! You're the man I want! Find General Picus and get him here immediately, and be sure he comes alone! No one else! Quick now, or I'll have the hide off your back!" The man left at the run and my uncle turned to the gaping servant. "What's the matter with you? The General will be here shortly. Bring wine! Move!" He turned back to where I still sat dumfounded in my chair, looking at me with narrowed eyes and then shifting his gaze to sweep his eyes around the walls of the room until they came to rest on a light, but metal-headed club. He crossed to where it hung and removed it from the wall, bringing it back to where I sat watching him.

"Try that. Is it too heavy? Swing it." He took my wooden sword out of my hand and replaced it with the war club. I swung it tentatively, finding it top heavy but not too cumbersome for me. I swung it again, a little harder. "Wait, Caius!" He moved to a table and took an earthen vase full of flowers and placed it on the ground to my left, removing the flowers as he did so, letting the water from the stems puddle unheeded on his precious floor. "Now," he said, his voice thick with excitement, "this vase is a man's head. He's wearing a heavy helmet. Let's see how big a dent you can put in it." He noticed my eyes and smiled. "I'm not crazed, Cay. Just do as I ask."

I indicated the club. "With this?"

"Of course."

"But I'll break it."

"It's only a vase, and I want you to break it. Stand up in those pedal things and smash it, hard as you can. Go ahead."

I missed it with my first and second swings because I was not trying hard enough and I saw displeasure in his face, so my third try was a real one. I settled my rump in my seat, gripped my "reins" tightly, rocked myself slightly to get the required motion of a horse, and then swung myself up and onto the balls of my feet and swung at the vase with every ounce of strength I had, pulling the reins tight in my left hand for leverage. Shards of the shattered vase flew in every direction and the water exploded in a great, splattered puddle across the polished wood of the floor.

"Great Jupiter!" Uncle Varrus's voice was hushed in awe and I was afraid I had done too well. He went to another table and brought a second vase to the same spot, throwing the flowers carelessly on the floor. This was his sacred Armoury! I had never seen an item out of place in here and I really began to think that he was beginning to lose his mind, but he spoke to me again. "Just like that, Cay. When your father arrives, I want you to shatter this vase just the way you did the first one. Even harder, if you can. Use all the force you can muster. Here he comes now." We heard my father's hurried stride in the passageway outside and then he strode into the room, almost skidding to a halt as his eyes took in the carnage on the normally spotless floor.

"What in the name of . . . ?" He saw me then with the club and his face flared in anger. "What have you done, boy?" His voice was terrible and I quailed before the fury that had sprung into his eyes.

"Quiet, Picus!" My uncle's voice was impatient. "The boy has done no harm. This was my doing. Now, just be quiet and watch, and learn. Learn about the chair saddles of the Frankish horsemen that we dismissed as useless. The boy is on a horse, enemies all around him. The vase on the floor is the head of an enemy grasping his foot. Show him, Cay."

Knowing somehow that this was a very important moment, although still having no idea of how or why, I drew myself together, collected my energies and then swung the club once around my head, tensed my legs, pulled hard on my reins, lifted myself to my full height, my backside clear of the seat and smashed the vase into a thousand pieces, splashing water clear across the room to splatter against the walls. As the sounds of the falling fragments died away, I looked at my father. His jaw had fallen open and his eyes were stunned and I still did not know what was happening here.

"Well, Picus?" My uncle's voice held a smiling note of pride.

"Do it again," my father rasped. We did it again, and by this time I was really enjoying the sensation I was causing. The entire Armoury was a littered shambles.

After the third vase, my father groped his way to a chair and sat, never taking his eyes from me. My uncle spoke again. "A twelve-year-old boy, Picus! Think what that thing could do for a mounted man."

"His whole body," my father said, his voice hushed as my uncle's had been earlier. "Used his whole body! All his force and strength. From the back of a horse! Standing up, braced, on the back of a horse!"

"Exactly, Picus! And we dismissed it. I have had this thing—this . . . seat—here in this room for fourteen years and I never saw it!"

Listening to them, I was still half afraid and totally mystified. Something momentous had happened, but what it was remained unknown to me.

"It's the leg braces," my uncle said. "They are exactly the right length for his feet to reach comfortably, now. They never were before—he literally grew into them. And every man's legs are a different length."

My father continued from there, his voice a deep rumble as though he were talking to himself. "Adjust each man's equipment to suit his own leg length . . . and we have a squadron of riders who can stand up and smite from a horse's back! A new cavalry force like nothing that has ever been seen before!"

"The Franks have seen it, Picus. This is theirs."

My father barked his sharp, unique laugh, "Aye, Varrus, but the Franks have no long swords like ours. And no discipline, no training. This could make us invincible."

"It *will* make us invincible, Picus. But, once again, it will mean teaching everyone to ride in a new and different way."

"So?" My father's tone of voice said that was a mere technicality. "The Franks can do it. It can't be all that difficult. How fast can you make these things? What are they called, anyway?"

My uncle shrugged his shoulders. "Saddles, I suppose. There's no other word for them in any tongue I know of. To make them? I don't know. I threw the large ones out."

I cleared my throat and spoke out. "I know where they are." Both men looked at me.

"Where?" asked Uncle Varrus.

"Uther and I use them as chairs in our secret place."

"Good," said my uncle. "Bring them back here. We'll take them apart and see exactly how they are put together and then we'll make our own."

The servant who had been sent for wine had returned and now stood staring in stupefaction at the condition of the room. My uncle finally noticed him and rounded on him. "What are you gaping at? Have you never seen water spilt before? Bring young master Caius's chair there and follow us, and then come back here and clean this place up. Cay, you come with us to the stables. Let's see how it feels for you to sit on your chair on your pony's back."

I was the first person in Camulod to ride a horse with what eventually came to be known as a saddle with stirrups. Uther was mad with jealousy at first, but I taught him first how to relax and master this strange new chair and before the first man in Camulod knew how to ride in one, we two were experts, and it fell to us to be instructors general.

I have already mentioned my belief that the number three has a mystical power. I spoke of deaths occurring in threes, but the potency of the triune conjunction is not confined to death alone; the triad appears to hold equal prominence in the grouping of the signal events of life. The great dramatists all wrote in the belief that a tripartite relationship between people is the essential element of heroic human conflict. Confined between two people, conflict, no matter how violent, is the mere pettiness of rivals; it requires the interaction of a third person to expand the conflict into tragedy. In retrospect it is now clear to me that my own life, and the fate of our Colony, was influenced at that time by a triad of events, which, combined, changed the lives of all of us forever. The discovery of the secret of the saddle and the adoption of the bracings we called stirrups was the first of these; my discovery of the Sword, the second.

The third fateful event was very different in nature from the two that went before it. Camulod had a visitor from the land in the far south-west, that place our people call Cornwall because it sticks out far into the sea like a great *cornua*, or horn. Emrys, the king of the people there, called himself Duke of Cornwall, after the old Roman title of Dux, or Leader. He had heard tales of Camulod and had come north to gauge the truth of them for himself. He was a loudmouthed, far from amiable man who did nothing to endear himself to Uncle Varrus, and he had a hulking, loudmouthed, even less amiable son called Lot, Gulrhys Lot, who did still less to endear himself to me or to Uther. Our relationship was based on hatred almost at first sight.

Lot was two years our senior and big for his age, and from the moment when Uncle Varrus told us to look after him, he set out to let us know who was the master and who the servants among us three. We led him from the Council Hall out into the courtyard where, mindful of my uncle's strict laws of hospitality, I offered to show him around the fort. He ignored me and stopped, wide legged, clenched fists on his hips, and looked around at everything with a wide sneer upon his face.

"Fort?" he said. "You call this hole a fort? It's like the kennels we use at home to keep our dogs in." I looked at Uther and said nothing. My cousin had a look upon his face that I had come to know very well, and it always announced trouble.

"You keep your dogs in a place like this?" he asked, his voice filled with what sounded like wonderment, "your *dogs?*"

"Aye. We do."

Uther nodded his head deeply then, as though accepting the straightforward explanation of a concern. "Then that explains the stink that hangs about you. You've given up your quarters to the dogs. Laudable, Lot, but stupid. You obviously inhabit the sty now, with your swine."

Lot was not to be provoked into immediate action, however. He smiled an evil smile and moved forward onto the balls of his feet. "What would you know about healthy swine, you little shit? Pigs are too clean for the likes of a gutter-dropped pile of Roman dung like you to know. I hear tell that your mother was a Roman whore who sold herself to beggars before she really disgraced herself by stooping even lower, to your father Uric."

I was appalled. I had never in my life heard a more extreme insult. Uther went white. "Whoreson," he said in a calm voice. "You are dead. You'll never grow a beard. Stay here and don't move. Cay, don't let him sneak away." He began to back away and then he turned and ran towards Uncle Varrus's house.

"Where are you going, dungheap? To tell your grandfather?" Lot yelled after him.

"Just you stay there!" Uther yelled back, and disappeared round the corner of a building.

"Well," sniggered Lot, turning his eye on me. "He threatens death and then he runs away. Are all your men so brave?"

I looked at him with loathing, almost unable to speak. "He'll be back," was all I was able to say at first, and then I added, "and when he comes, you are the one who had better run. Uther will kill you."

"Kill me? Truly? Stone dead? I'm terrified. Perhaps I'd better leave now."

I longed to wipe the sneer off his face but I knew that if I moved towards him he would give me the beating of my life.

"You don't like me, do you, small boy? I can see it in your pasty Roman face."

"No," I said, shaking my head in agreement with him, "I don't like you. Not at all."

"But why not? We've just met. We could be good friends. You could hold my pizzle for me when I pee, and if you were really nice, I'd even let you wipe me."

I could not believe what I was hearing. Uther and I used language that would earn us both a whipping if Uncle Varrus were ever to hear us, but neither of us ever was as foul-mouthed as this uncouth outsider. Looking back on it now, I can see that it was his way of thinking that offended me even then, not his choice of words.

He took a swift step towards me and I drew back involuntarily as he snarled, "Wipe that look off your face, pretty boy, before I wipe your face off your skull!"

I don't know what I might have done then had not Uther come back around the corner at that very moment, clutching a bundle to his chest. I didn't know what that bundle contained, although I suspected the worst, and my stomach turned over. He walked right up to Lot and looked him in the eye.

"All right, Mouth, come with me." He turned and walked into the nearest building, which I knew was empty, for it was unfinished and the thatch not yet in place. Lot swaggered in after him and I followed, casting my eyes right and left in the hope of seeing someone I could appeal to, but there was no one there. By the time I got inside, Uther had already unwrapped the bundle, exposing two of Uncle Varrus's short, lethal swords. He took one and kicked the other to Lot's feet. "I hope you know how to use that, you foul turd. It's the only thing that might be able to keep you alive." As he said this, he swung his sword in a short, hissing arc. My mouth was dry. I knew Uther and I knew he meant every word he said. There was death in the very look of him. Both he and I were trained in the use of swords, well trained, and he was more than capable of killing. I stepped between them.

"No, Uther! This is bad. Fight him, with your fists. I'll help you, if you need help, but don't do this. Uncle will flog us both."

Uther looked at me as if I were mad. "Have you looked at the whoreson? At the size of him? He'd cripple both of us. Besides, you heard what he said. Stand aside, Cay."

In the event, I had no choice, although I did not stand aside. I felt Lot's weight slamming between my shoulders and I was cata-pulted towards Uther as I heard the whistling hiss of a hard-swung sword blade close to my head. I landed sprawling on my hands and knees and my head hit hard against the wall, stunning me for a time so that my vision darkened. When it began to return, it was accom-panied by a loud roaring in my ears, inside my head, as well as by a ringing, external sound as blade clashed loudly on blade. I looked up incredulously, my head still swirling with dizziness, to see them cir-cling each other in the crouching stance of fighters. Lot looked twice as big as Uther and he obviously knew the feeling of a sword in his hand. As I stared at them, before I had time to move, they swung again, and again the clang of meeting blades shattered the silence.

They went at it hard and furiously, their swords striking sparks from each other. Lot pressed forward, using his weight and height to force Uther backwards, and then there was a scramble and a deep grunt and I saw Lot's sword edge embedded in Uther's thigh. Still kneeling where I had fallen, dizzy and wide-eyed, I saw the blood begin to well and my gorge rose into my throat as they both stood there, frozen, until Uther hissed and lunged, stabbing his blade into Lot's breast.

"Sweet Christ in Heaven! What's going on in here?" I heard the roar and saw my father's huge shape blocking the doorway and I saw Lot sway and start to fall, and then everything went black.

Unfortunately, I was unable to remain unconscious for long enough to evade my father's wrath, or that of Uncle Varrus. It made no difference to either of them that I was not personally involved in the real fighting; as far as they were concerned, I was a party to it and had not tried to stop it. I had, in fact, but I knew that I had not tried hard enough, so there was no point in protesting innocence. Uther and Lot were both carried off to receive medical attention and I was hauled in to face my father, Lot's father Duke Emrys and Uncle Varrus. They sat side by side at my uncle's long writing table and I had to stand facing them on the other side. About an hour had elapsed since the time of the fight, an hour in which I had been confined to my room under guard, I suppose because they feared I might try to run away. Aunt Luceiia had been forbidden to approach me beforehand. I was escorted into the room like a military prisoner going to a court martial. All three men sat there and glowered at me, the Duke Emrys the most malevolent of all.

My father still looked furious, but was now in control of his fury—more visibly, tenaciously in control than I had ever seen him. I had the feeling that he might come leaping across the table at me at any time. Uncle Varrus looked more troubled and hurt than angry. He gazed at me with great solemnity and it was he who spoke.

"Caius Britannicus, a great wrong has been done here this day and you have been part of it. Two boys lie injured and bleeding, gravely hurt, perhaps close to death. You are the only one who can throw light on this. The laws of hospitality have been violated in my home. Those laws are sacrosanct, as you well know. The Duke of Cornwall here, under my roof, is guarded by those laws while he is here. So is his son who came here with him. And now his son lies wounded, stabbed by my own grandson like a Saxon savage. You had better tell us why this has happened, bearing in mind that the penalty for such flagrant outrage should be death."

This long speech, delivered to me in such unnatural tones by Uncle Varrus frightened me to the point of sickness. My stomach heaved up into my throat and I had to swallow hard to keep from vomiting. I still remember the appalling feeling of inadequacy that overwhelmed me. I could not speak, although my mouth moved.

My father spoke into my silence. "Hear me, boy, and hear me well. We want the truth behind this outrage." His voice was more of a growl than anything else, hampered as it was by his wounded throat, but I had been around him long enough by then to hear the words beneath the guttural effects clearly as he continued. "No excuses. No interpretations. And no lies! Tell us exactly what happened: what was said and done, and by whom to whom." My flesh crawled. How could I repeat the words I had heard to these ears?

That was when Duke Emrys spoke for the first time, and his words were ill timed for his purposes, because the jeering, sneering tones of his harsh voice dispelled my terror and my doubts like a douche of cold water. "We'll get no truth from this whelp! See the terror on his face. My son lies dying and you ask to hear the truth from one of the two who killed him?"

He had barely stopped talking when I answered him, my own voice loud and angry, which surprised even me. "I am no liar! I will tell you what happened." I looked at Uncle Varrus, appealing to him alone, and my great anger lent me an eloquence beyond my years. "You have trained me to recall words exactly, Uncle Varrus, whether they be written or spoken. The Druids have trained me also, the same way. Lot provoked this fight. Uther was bound to kill him for the things he said. I should have killed him, too, had I been Uther, but I am not."

It was my father who responded to my outburst, and his tone was far less angry than it had been before. "Tell us what happened, boy," he said. I collected my thoughts and started at the beginning, relating the events and the conversation word for word as it had happened. I missed nothing, left out no insult, added nothing.

When I had done, there was silence for a while until my father spoke again. "This was bad work."

Duke Emrys agreed with him. "Aye, General, foul work indeed. Murder done on a boy for spouting boy's words. Foul work indeed."

"There has been no murder done, Emrys." This was my uncle, who had finally found his normal voice. "The boys are both alive, no thanks to themselves, and thank your gods that they are boys, for had those words been spoken between men then death would have been the end, beyond a shade of doubt."

"Pah! You make too much of words!" Emrys's voice was rich with disgust.

My father had risen and walked away from the table, but now he swung round and approached the Cornwall duke, and when he spoke his voice was menacing, the more so for the care he took to speak quietly and clearly through his injured throat. "Look you here, Duke of Cornwall. This boy is my son. Young Uther is my nephew. Uther's mother, the victim of your disgraceful son's foul slander, was Publius Varrus's daughter. My wife was sister to young Uther's father. I do not know your son, but I know he is no fit company for any son of mine. If he were here, instead of lying bleeding for his foul-mouthed sins, I would take my boot to his ill-mannered arse. Now, the laws of hospitality be damned! If you desire to defend your uncouth brat's honour as Uther did his mother's, I will be glad to step outside the walls with you. I have listened to your sneers and insults long enough. I find you boorish, bullying, envious and not in the least amiable. Our doctors will soon heal your sewer-tongued son. When they have done so, I'll show you the gates myself. You are not welcome here, neither you nor your son. Is that clearly spoken? Do you understand me? Do you doubt *my* words?"

Through all of this, Duke Emrys sat purple-faced, gaping at my father. In the silence that followed, I watched him as I would an insect. I knew without doubt that he would not accept my father's challenge, but I wondered what he would do. My eyes never left his. I saw him fight to hide fear and then struggle to draw what dignity he had to aid him. Finally he turned to my uncle and tried to speak disdainfully. "I thought you were the master here. Is this a sample of your mastery? Allowing your guests to be maltreated at your board?"

My uncle heaved a deep sigh. "Too late, Emrys. You forget that the lady impugned, Uther's mother, was my daughter. Besides, I am the senior here, not the master. We have no need of such distinctions. Picus has said what I myself should say, were I not your host. Now that it has been said, I find that I cannot, in conscience, disagree with it. You may leave any time you wish. Please do not come back." He stood up and left the table and my father walked with him. He beckoned to me in passing and we left Emrys alone in the Armoury.

Lot's wound healed quickly. It was not deep and had touched nothing vital. He and his father were gone within four days. Uther limped for a month. And the enmity created on that day lived on for years and blighted a thousand lives.

VII

I was enjoying a meal of cold sausage, cheese, bread and home-brewed beer when I heard my name being shouted in the street outside. The woman of the house looked at me curiously as a fist hammered on the door. I nodded to her and she opened it to admit one of my squad leaders who stepped into the room and snapped to attention as he saw me sitting at the table.

"Commander Caius, sir, I thought you'd be asleep."

"I was, but now I'm eating, as you see. What is it?"

The man's eyes were wide with the portent of his message as he snapped out, "Courier, sir, from Camulod. You are to return at once. The Lord Varrus lies dying."

I was on my feet before he finished, my chair clattering over backwards. "Where's Commander Uther?"

He shrugged, his eyes admitting that he had already tried to find that out. "Nobody seems to know, sir."

"Damn the man! He's never—" I cut myself short, regretting the words as I allowed them to slip out. "Send out some men to search the wine shops. He's off duty. Find him, and quickly!"

"Yes, Commander." He saluted and withdrew and I righted my chair and sat down again, all thought of food forgotten.

Publius Varrus was a constant in my life. The thought of his being ill was alien to me and yet, if he were ill enough to cause our recall, he must really be close to death. I tried to think of how old he was, but I had no real idea. Uncle Varrus was ageless. Other men grew old, but not he. The only time I had seen him ailing was when Ullic and Equus and Bishop Alaric had all died close together. But the joy of showing me Excalibur had brought him back to health, back to himself, back to living again. And now he was sick.

Suddenly, for no real reason at all, I knew where Uther would be. We had stopped at a house on the way into town, a place that had once been a *mansio*, an official hostelry for travellers and soldiers before the legions left. It still survived, catering to those travellers yet brave enough or desperate enough to dare the roads between Glevum and Aquae Sulis. The fellow who kept it now had been well supplied with sluttish serving maids and a couple of them had caught Uther's roving eye. I knew that was where he would be. We had just ended the northern sweep of our patrol in Glevum and were to remain here three days to rest our horses and allow our quartermaster to buy up the list of items he would not be able to find in Aquae Sulis. The second leg of our patrol would take us back to Camulod through that town, and this was our first full day of relaxation. And to Uther, relaxation required women.

Uther had always been ahead of me in matters concerning women and sex. We were born within the same hour of the same day, but it was he who led the way to physical, sexual maturity at every step. His was the first erection, the first pubic hair, the first ejaculation and, of course, the first penetration of a female body. I lagged behind always, learning from him, letting him show me how. In almost every other field save war, it was I who led the way while Uther followed, but to a growing boy there is no area of life more crucial than the sexual one and I felt constantly betrayed, condemned by my own body to be forever second best. Even well into manhood, I would have a dream in which I was with Uther in a grand debauch. This dream was different from those I thought of as my terror dreams: it never varied and was always clear. We would be surrounded by voluptuous, wanton beauties, Uther lying back, laughing in sensual pleasure, displaying his jutting, arrogant maleness to their admiring looks and caresses, and always one woman, her fingers hooked into a rake, would comb the hairs on his bared belly and clasp his phallus. The blood by this time would be hammering behind my eyes and I would feel hands tugging at my clothes as my own seed threatened to spill, and then would come the laughter, and the shame of looking down to see my own hairless body and the smallness of a little boy's pizzle. Our minds can do strange things to us. I was never less than a month or so behind Uther in development at any stage and I was no less well equipped than he, nor did I have any problem in performance or in gratifying any woman's desire and yet, somewhere in my mind, that deep-seated fear persisted.

I thanked the woman who had fed me and left some silver coins on the table. My horse was tethered right outside the door and as I swung into the saddle I scanned the empty street, looking vainly for one of my men. Two streets further south, I met a party of them on foot, all reasonably sober.

"Quintus," I called to the biggest of them. "I am recalled to Camulod with Commander Uther. Extreme emergency. Illness in the family. Find Dedalus, give him my apologies for not taking the time to contact him personally, and tell him he is now in command. Commander Uther and I will ride alone. Dedalus is to finish the patrol as planned. Tell him Commander Varrus is dying and we must ride on ahead. There are search parties out looking for Commander Uther, but I think I know where he is, and they won't find him. If I am wrong, and he is still here in Glevum, I will be waiting for him at the hostelry ten miles south of the town. I will have extra horses with me, so tell him he need not waste time with that. Do you understand?" I waited while he repeated it back to me verbatim, then I returned his salute and kicked my horse into a gallop to our depot where I picked up two extra horses and some food before heading out of town.

I remember riding those first ten miles trying to think of anything that would take my mind away from Uncle Varrus and what his death would mean. I was eighteen years old and although this was my fourth patrol, it was the first that Uther and I had commanded jointly without overt supervision. It crossed my mind that our first responsibility should be to the patrol before all else, but I dismissed the thought very quickly. Dedalus was a senior centurion and my father had charged him with the authority to override our orders if he believed Uther and I were acting foolishly or rashly at any time.

It had hurt my pride at the time to think that we were only nominal commanders, but my intellect had reassured me that this last patrol with Dedalus was to have been our final test. Now it turned out that we could not complete it.

It was late afternoon by the time I drew near to the hostelry, and as I did so I began to get a bad feeling in my gut, a feeling that my boyhood Druid teachers had taught me to respect, since they believed that what we call intuition is a natural gift that man has allowed to grow rusty. I have always been glad of the emphasis they placed on that teaching. It almost certainly saved my life that day.

I drew rein about a hundred paces from the place and sat there looking at it, remembering that I had not liked the looks of some of the characters who had been there when we arrived two days previously. If Uther had gone in there alone, and I reasoned that he would have, because of who and what he was, he could have bought himself trouble along with a jug of beer. If, on the other hand, he was not there at all and I rode in alone, mounted on one horse and leading two more, I would be buying myself trouble of the same kind. My uniform would not save me, nor would any air of authority I might command. I was a man alone who could be dealt with quickly and disposed of cleanly. Any search for me later would produce nothing. I looked around for signs of Uther's horse, but there was nothing to see. It would have been stabled in one of the outhouses at the back or at the side of the main building.

I almost talked myself into believing that I was being foolish. Thank God I didn't believe myself. I left the road and made my way through the trees and around the place without being seen, and tethered the horses safely off the road on the south side, and then I walked back. I left my war cloak, my shield and my long-sword with the horses and carried only my short-sword and dagger. My helmet felt heavy on my head and my nailed boots rang loudly on the cobbled surface as I walked. I stepped right to the centre of the main courtyard entrance and stopped there, looking around the interior of the yard with care. It was empty. There were no signs of life at all. I crossed the yard quickly, making my way to the main door, and as

I did so I heard shouting and commotion from inside. I knew what I would find even before I entered, and I wished I had not left my shield back there with the horses. I paused on the threshold, took a deep breath, then swung the door open and stepped inside, moving immediately to bring my back against the inside wall.

The place was more like a barn than anything else, one huge, communal room with dried rushes on the floor and trestle tables scattered here and there for the clientele's eating needs, if not their drinking. A long table standing against the wall to my right held amphorae and casks of ale. A massive, open fireplace in the opposite wall held spits for roasting meat. Directly across from where I stood, a wide, open flight of wooden steps led to a second level, like a loft, which served as sleeping quarters and business premises for the women.

Uther had thrown a table of some kind lengthwise across the top of this stairway and was hard set defending it, sword in one hand, dagger in the other, against a mob of eight or nine desperate-looking rogues. I didn't know how long he had been there, but I had the distinct feeling that the fun had only just begun, there was not enough evidence of violent action lying around for the fracas to have been older, and he could not have hoped to hold out for long against so many. They were crowded together at the top of the stairs, hampering themselves, but all they would have to do was take their time and they would overwhelm him sooner or later. As I took all of this in, one of the girls up in the loft with him leaped onto Uther's back, wrapping her legs around his waist and attempting to pin his arms to his sides and render him defenceless. There was a concerted roar from his assailants and from him as he broke the grip of her arms, wrenched her free and threw her over his shoulders and down towards his attackers. She screamed as she landed among the men, sweeping one of them with her off the open edge of the stairs to crash to the stone floor beneath. The scattered rushes did nothing to break their fall, and they both lay still. I glanced around me, looking for something I could use as a better weapon than my short-sword and dagger and there, on the floor beside me, lay a spear that I recognized as Uther's. I picked it up, hefting it for balance, and then I was across the floor and up the stairs, feeling the blade of it bite deep between the shoulders of the first man I could reach. I jerked the spearpoint free and pierced the kidney of another man before the first fell back and past me down the stairs. This time I jerked to my left, pushing and guiding my victim off the edge of the stairs, almost losing my balance as the weight of his body fell free of the spear's blade. They still did not know I was there behind them.

"Caius! What kept you?" Uther's welcoming roar told everyone I had arrived and they swung round as one to face me. As they did so Uther's long blade decapitated the rearmost of them and he kicked the headless, spouting corpse to fall among the legs of the others. The man who owned the hostelry, a one-eyed misanthrope who clutched a Roman sword, was right in front of me. I jammed the spear into his belly, just below the ribs and saw death come into his eyes as he dropped the sword and grasped at the shaft of the spear, stopping me from pulling it out. I gave it a vicious twist to lock the barbs and jerked him down towards me, stepping to my left to avoid his fall and almost plunging myself over the edge of the stairs. I hung there, my arms waving in the air, while they all had time to get over their surprise. I saw Uther plant his sword in another's back, but there were still three of them facing me with Uther's sword embedded and me defenseless.

One of them came at me with a roar just as I found my balance. I saw an axe whistling towards me and I jumped, out and backwards, flexing my knees and hoping to land without breaking a leg. In midair, I saw the axe bite deep into the step where I had been standing, and I saw Uther pick up the table that had sheltered him and rush the others on the stairs, sweeping all three of them off balance into a fall. By sheer good luck, I landed like a cat, easily, on all fours, and I was on the whoreson who had swung the axe before he landed at the bottom of the stairs. I had no thought of mercy in my head. The point of my sword grated on the stone floor beneath him and I had to plant my foot on his chest to pull my blade free. I heard a grunt, a chop and a death rattle as Uther clove another of them, and then came scuffling footsteps and the slam of a door. It was over. I collapsed onto the stairs, my head hanging between my knees as I fought for breath, and I heard the sound of the door again.

When I looked up, Uther was standing in the middle of the floor, grinning at me, his chest heaving as he gulped in great breaths. "One of them got away," he wheezed.

"Good riddance. Let him go." I was too exhausted to care.

He crossed the floor and sat on the steps beside me, hooking his right elbow around my neck and squeezing tightly, to my very great discomfort. I was too tired even to struggle and so I just sat there, pulled across him, seeing the curling hair on his thighs that were within inches of my face, smelling the well-known smell of him and thanking God I had arrived when I did.

Eventually he released me and lay back against the stairs and our breathing slowed down and began to return to normal. After the pressure and the tensions of the fight—the first real, life and death struggle in which I had ever been personally involved—I felt as weak as a baby, and I began to tremble all over. I sat erect and clasped my hands together tightly in an effort to control the shaking, and as I did so I became aware of the blood for the first time. It was everywhere. Wherever I looked I saw blood. It lay in puddles and gouts and rope-like streaks on the rushes of the floor. The man who had tried to kill me with the axe lay less than three feet from me, across the legs of the owner of the place whose upper body reared freakishly erect, impaled on Uther's broken spear. He had obviously landed on it as he fell, breaking the shaft and forcing the point clean through himself. Everything misted over and I vomited where I sat, choking and retching on the bitter gall of victory. When my vision cleared again, I was kneeling on the floor and Uther was removing my helmet, letting the cool, fresh air reach my heated forehead and my sweat-matted hair.

"Feeling better?" I nodded, wiping my lips and chin and spitting to clear the sourness from my mouth. "Good," he went on. "I've just decided I do not ever want you to be angry with me. You are a wild man, Cousin, when you are angry. You killed four of these people."

I looked around me at the slaughterhouse. "So did you."

He grinned. "Ah, but I killed them all from behind, while they were watching you."

"I was behind them too, remember. Lucky I found your spear on the floor over there." My voice was shaking. "And lucky you had them all involved at the top of the staircase. If things had been different, we would be dead now, you and I."

"Foolish talk. They weren't and we aren't."

I spat again. "My mouth tastes foul. I need a drink." I rose and crossed to the table with the casks and poured myself a cup of ale. It was flat and stale, bitter and sickening. Unable to swallow it, I rinsed my mouth and gargled and spat the stuff on the floor, feeling better with every second that passed. I looked around me then and nodded at the carnage. "What do we do about this?" As I spoke, I heard a sound above me and my head snapped up to see two women looking down at us from the loft, large-eyed and very frightened. I nodded towards them. "Some more friends of yours?"

Uther looked up and saw them. "Come down here, quickly!" When they had reached us, cowering with terror, their eyes flickering wildly from one to the other of us, he drew his sword again. "Take off those clothes!" They did as he said, and when they stood naked he shook his head slowly from side to side, looking at them in rueful amusement. "Caius, can you believe I almost got killed for this? *We* almost got killed for this, and I know *you* wouldn't stick *mine* into either of these, let alone your own!" The women stood close together, staring at him in fear, not knowing whether they were to live or die, but knowing completely that they were looking at Death himself in my cousin. "You!" he said, pointing his sword at the larger of them. "Turn around. Look at my friend." She turned to face me, her large breasts hanging heavy against her ribs, her belly sagging sadly over her pubic hair. "You almost got him killed, you slut, and he's a prince! He almost died because you teased my lust with your great, squeezy teats!" He slapped her hard across the buttocks with the flat of his sword and she leaped in fright and pain, tears springing from her eyes. "Get out of my sight, both of you," he roared. "Out! Out, out, out, out!" The smaller one started to reach for her clothes, but he swung his sword again, catching her on the flank with the flat of it. "No!" he roared. "Take your thieving, murderous lives and let that be enough! No clothes. Be born again, as the Christians say. Go naked into a new life as you entered this one and think twice before you dare to tempt another witless reveller to his death! Out!" They ran, scampering in terror across the body-littered floor and out into the gathering dusk.

He watched them go, with that half-crazed grin of his that I loved, and then he slid his sword into the ring in the belt across his shoulders so that the blade hung down his back. "Should I have let them go, Cousin? They did try to kill me."

"No they didn't, Uther. They merely enticed you. All three of them together could hardly have raped you, but only one of them attacked you, and she suffered for it."

He was watching me closely, a half smile still lingering around his mouth.

"You think I was too hard on them?"

"No, not too hard. They deserved some chastisement, I suppose. You let them off lightly."

"But?"

I shook my head. "But nothing. It merely occurred to me to wonder what they'll do now to feed themselves, now that their livelihood is gone."

He grunted. "They'll find a way. What would you have me do, take them with us?" He picked up my helmet and mounted the stairs to the loft, where he gathered his cloak, put on his own helmet and picked up his shield before returning to where I stood watching. As he handed me my helmet he asked, "Did I tell you how glad I was to see you?" I nodded, and he crossed to pick up a lamp that burned by the ale casks. "I'm always glad to see you, Cay, but today you looked beautiful. Usually you are unimpressive. In fact, most of the time, you're almost ugly. Today, however, you were magnificent. Mad, but magnificent." As he prattled on, he was kicking the rushes into a pile at the bottom of the wooden stairs. He decided finally that he had enough of them and dropped the oil-filled lamp so that it broke on the flagstones. As we watched, the flames spread quickly.

"This is no fit place for decent people, anyway." He glanced again at each of the bodies on the floor. "May they rest in peace, as the Christians say. Let's get out of here. Why did you come here, anyway?"

I felt as though I had been doused with icy water. I had forgotten! "Varrus is dying, Uther. We are called back to Camulod."

His face went blank with shock. "No ... You can't mean that, Cay. Not Grandfather!"

I could only shake my head. His disbelief mirrored my own so closely, it threatened to unman me. "We have to hurry. I brought extra horses."

We left the hostelry and its silent crew to the leaping flames. Uther's horse was safely stabled in one of the buildings at the rear and I held it steady as he threw the saddle over its back and tightened the cinches, kneeing the horse in the belly as he did so to make sure it wasn't playing tricks on him by distending its gut. In the early days of using the device, we had often found ourselves falling sideways because the harness had not been properly secured. He swung into the saddle and I leaped up behind him and directed him to where I had hidden the other animals. He took the lead rein of one of the extra horses and we headed south, keeping off the road surface to save our horses' hooves.

Neither of us had spoken since we left the hostelry, except for a few grunted directions from me, and the silence lasted until we had ridden for three or four miles at a steady canter. It was Uther who spoke first, breaking into my thoughts and showing me a different, more serious side of himself than he had shown earlier.

"That was foolery, that nonsense back there. I could have been killed ... would have been if you hadn't arrived. That would have been no great loss, but I can see now that you and the others would have wasted time and effort turning the country upside-down looking for me. It was criminal and stupid. Forgive me, Cay. I'll never take off again without letting someone know where I can be found. But how in the name of all the Roman gods did you know where to find me?"

"Bodies," I said. "Willing, female bodies. You saw them there when we passed through the first time, and you didn't get to use them, and then you found yourself with three days off within ten miles of them. It wasn't difficult. I know you, Cousin. But you are right. It was stupidity, although had you been killed, I doubt that it would pass as no great loss. Not from your grandfather's viewpoint. In his eyes, you were bred and trained for a purpose, and it wasn't to get yourself killed in a den of thieves and whores."

He said no more for a while, then, "How bad is he? How much time have we lost because of this?"

"I don't know how bad he is, but he must be really ill, or they wouldn't recall us from patrol. It'll take us about three days to reach Camulod at this speed—less if we cut down on sleep. As to time lost, no more than an hour, all told. I had to come this way and I wasted no time looking for you in Glevum. The fight was brief, long as it seemed."

I stood upright in my stirrups and looked back the way we had come. We were in a stretch of open grassland, cleared of trees years earlier by a farmer whose time had long since passed and now showing signs of reverting to forest. I saw a pall of black smoke above the trees in the far distance. We fell back into silence and rode each with his own thoughts.

We changed horses regularly and the miles dropped away behind us. When darkness fell, we took our horses onto the road-bed, riding between the trees on either side, seeing our way by moonlight. We stopped and slept for a brief spell after the moon went down, and were back on our way before the first flush of dawn, stopping only to void our bladders and bowels on that second day. Each time I got down from the saddle for such a purpose, I felt that I would never be able to walk properly again, and the thought of hauling my aching body back up into the saddle daunted me. But we had no trouble on the road and by mid-afternoon of the third day we came in sight of Camulod.

We had been riding through our own home territories for some time by then and had learned from our own outposts only that Varrus had fallen, breaking both legs and several ribs in rolling down the hillside. He had become congested in his lungs and had been spitting blood for the past eight days. Grim-faced, we travelled on, to be met by Aunt Luceiia at the entrance to the villa. She looked fragile, yet somehow indomitable, as she smiled at us through her tears.

When we had kissed her, Uther spoke. "How is he, Grandmother?"

"In great pain. But he's a stubborn man and will not die before he speaks to both of you."

There it was. We both knew there was no point in uttering stupidities about his not dying.

"Can we go to him now?" I asked.

"Of course you can. He is in his day-room." We left her and walked rapidly towards the room that had been my own grandfather's day-room. Both of our fathers were there already, one on either side of the bed. Patricus, head of the Colony's Council, was there too, white-haired and solemn. I could have wept when I saw what had happened to my great-uncle since we had left, just two short weeks before. He was a different man, a stranger to my sight. Only the eyes, set in the sunken, withered, pain-racked face showed me the Publius Varrus that I loved, and even they were misted with pain.

"Uther," he said. "And Caius. Welcome home." His voice was a hoarse whisper. He held out a clawlike, shrunken hand to each of us, and as I took his hand in my own I saw how the skin of his once-mighty wrist hung in folds and wrinkles from the bones. I pressed his hand to my cheek, feeling the wetness of my tears between the two surfaces. "What are the tears for, boy? This is the way of all men. We all have to die. I have lived far longer than I ought to have, and I have lived well. Have you ridden far?" I nodded my head, unable to speak. "I thought so." The parchment whisper held a trace of the old humour. "You smell like horses, both of you. Caius, this was your grandfather's bed. He enjoyed it for years before he died. I've had it only for days. I do not intend to die in it with the smell of rancid horse sweat in my nostrils." His fingers squeezed my hand gently. "Go you and bathe, both of you. I'll still be here when you are clean. Then I shall speak with each of you alone." His hand pushed gently against mine. "Go. I will not die before I speak with you, I promise. Picus, are the baths prepared?"

"Of course they are, Varrus. Have you ever known them not to be?"

"Aye, I have. Once. The hypocausts were blocked. But you were not here then."

My father spoke to us. "Do as he says. You'll feel better. And find something to eat. Publius Varrus should have some rest." Unwillingly, we rose to do as we were bidden.

When we returned, clean smelling and refreshed, we found Aunt Luceiia sitting by the bedside, holding one of her husband's wrinkled hands between her own. His eyes were closed, but he opened them as he heard our footsteps crossing the room and he smiled at us. "Ah," he whispered. "That's better. These are the boys I know. Cay, go with your Aunt Luceiia and keep her company while I speak with Uther. Uther, come here and sit where I can see you."

Aunt Luceiia and I left the two of them alone and I closed the doors behind me as we left the room. She led me through the house into the family room, her own domain, and nodded for me to sit on one of the couches. "Well, Caius," she said, "Publius Varrus will not be here with us much longer, now." I swallowed the painful lump in my throat and managed to ask her what had happened. She shrugged her shoulders in a gesture remarkably like the one I had seen her husband use a thousand times. "Nobody knows, Cay. He won't tell us, and nobody saw it. He had been down here at the villa all that afternoon and was on his way home to the fort when it happened. It was after dark, we know that much, for if it had been earlier, he would have been seen." Her face crumpled and she began to weep. I crossed to where she sat and held her as she spoke through her grief. "He always was a strong and stubborn man. Too stubborn to grow old as others do. Too stubborn to admit a loss of strength or youth. I believe he put his horse to the hillside, rather than take the long route up the road. I think he lost his balance and fell from the horse. He never could abide to use a saddle, said he had ridden bareback too long to change his ways.

"Anyway, a pedlar found him at the bottom of the hill early the following morning. His horse was grazing, unhurt, not far away. He had been lying there for hours and was soaked to the skin and chilled with dew." She paused, and then shook her head violently, scattering teardrops. "I hadn't even noticed he had not come home. I had noticed, I mean, but I had not been concerned. He used to sleep here in the villa, sometimes, if he had worked late. I thought that was where he was. How could I think the old fool would try to scramble up the hill like a boy of twelve? And now he's going to die and I'll have all my life to wonder if I might have found him earlier."

I hugged her tightly and tried to reassure her that there was nothing she could have done, but she was not to be consoled so easily.

"Oh, Cay," she sobbed. "I can't believe what this has done to him. All of his flesh has melted! There's nothing left of the man I love but skin and bone and pain and the inner strength that won't let him die!"

"I know," I said into her hair through my own tears. "I know. His strength is fierce. He will not go until he wants to."

"And when he does, I'll be alone." Her own words shocked her, for I felt her stiffen in my arms, and then she spread her own arms, breaking my gentle hold on her and rising to her feet. She wiped away her tears with an edge of her *stola* and I watched the strength flow into her so that she seemed to grow before my eyes. When she spoke again her voice was firm and steady. "Well," she declared abruptly. "That's enough foolish weakness and tears for one day. My husband would be shamed had he heard that last remark." She turned her eyes on me and I saw the warmth in them. "Your uncle is one of the finest men who ever walked this world. All that I have, all the happiness I've ever known, has come directly from him. Now that his life is ending, it will be left to you and me, Caius, and to Uther, and to your children and grandchildren, to make sure that the life he lived and the wonders that he performed are not forgotten."

Excalibur was in my mind as she said these words, for therein, I knew, lay Varrus's immortality. The name trembled on the tip of my tongue, but I did not give it voice, for I remembered that only five pairs of eyes had seen and known it that I knew of, apart from my own. Those eyes belonged to Varrus himself, to his friends Equus and Plautus, to Father Andros—the man who designed the moulded hilt—and to my grandfather. I wondered now if Aunt Luceiia also knew of it, but I dared not ask. Incredible as it seemed to me then, Uncle Varrus might have kept all knowledge of it from her. She was a woman after all, above all else, and might have seen in it only a device for killing men, disapproving of it, for all her pride in her husband's creation. And so I could not ask her, fearing I might wound her with sudden knowledge of her husband's secrecy. I held my peace.

Seeing and misreading the anguished indecision in my eyes, she reached out and grasped my arm. "Your uncle will be finished soon with Uther. I know he has words for you. Go to him, Caius. Wait outside until Uther leaves and then send him here to me."

Uther was closing the door to my uncle's room as I turned into the passageway. He stood there and watched me sombrely as I approached. "He wants to see you now."

"How is he?"

"Bad, Cay. Very, very bad."

"Aunt Luceiia's waiting for you in the family room." He nodded and left. I stood there for a moment with my hand on the handle of the door and then I drew a deep breath and went inside. This time, as I approached the bed, I saw what it was that had made my first sight of the old man so shocking to me, so different.

His beard was gone, and its absence had changed the entire appearance of his face.

"Uncle? Are you awake?" I was whispering.

"Yes, Caius, I'm awake. Come close."

I went and sat on the chair close by his head. "Uncle? You've shaved your beard off."

His smile was ghostly, like his voice. "Not I, lad. The damned medics. Couldn't keep it clean when I was fevered. Feels strange, as though I'm naked." He looked at me sidelong. "You're a fine man, Caius, or you will be, in a few years. Now listen. I've much to say and little time. But I know what I have to say and you don't, so don't interrupt me. Agreed?" I nodded my head and he looked up at the ceiling, gathering his strength.

"Excalibur is yours. A sacred trust. No other knows it exists, now. Leave it beneath the floor where it is. It's safe there. Guard it with your life, Cay. That blade will cut iron chains. It's that strong. It's a king's sword, an Emperor's. Keep it in trust for the Emperor of Britain. Not Uther. Boy's too rash, too wild. He knows nothing about it."

"Does Aunt Luceiia?"

He lay silent, thinking, collecting himself, and then resumed in a slightly stronger voice. "No. The greatest thing I ever made, and I kept it from her. The knowledge would have been too dangerous for her. Men would fight wars to own Excalibur, Cay. Don't let them. Guard it in secrecy. One day, a time will come. You'll know the day, and you'll know the man. If he hasn't come before you die, pass the sword to someone you can trust. Your own son. You'll know. You've been well taught. And you have learned well. You found the secret of the Lady, Cay, and then the secret of the saddle. You'll find the secret of the King, someday. You'll know him as soon as you set eyes on him." I was holding my breath with the effort of listening, and each word he spoke burned its way into my brain. "Your grandfather Caius was my greatest friend. You know that. He was a dreamer, Cay, but a grand dreamer. He dared majestically in his dreams, and he had the courage and the strength to make his dreams come true . . ." I waited for him until he continued. "He started a process, Cay, a progression that you and your future sons will continue. He dreamed of—and he initiated—the rebirth of the greatness of Rome here in this Britain. He wanted to mix his blood, the blood of his people, with the blood of Ullic's people. Uther is the seed of his plan. So are you. Keep watch for Uther, Cay; he hasn't your long head. He lacks your sense of rightness. Hold him in restraint. He will be King of the Pendragon when his father, Uric, dies, when . . ." His voice trailed away and then rallied. "Make him a good king, Cay. Advise him. He'll listen to you. He has great love for you."

Again a pause, this time a long one, before the feathery voice resumed, "Use the horses, Cay, and breed more. More and more horses. The Saxons cannot withstand a charge of horsemen. The horses, and the long-swords. Use them hard, and build an army to follow where they lead. You will need legions. Build them. You know how. And Ullic's longbows, Uther's people's weapons. Don't let them go. They stand for power, lad. They can win battles for you from far away. Use them. That's all I have to say. Now call your aunt and go with God."

I rose to leave, but his fingers tightened on mine and pulled me down to him again. "I had forgotten. The Armoury and all its treasures are for you. Uther knows this. There is much in there still to profit from." His eyes closed again and this time I was sure he slept, but he stopped me again as I rose to go and find Aunt Luceiia. I had to lean close to his mouth to hear, so faint was his voice. "Your grandfather Caius wants you to use the name your mother gave you . . ." The short hairs on the nape of my neck stirred at the tense he used, but his fingers dropped from my hand, and suddenly afraid, I hurried to the door to fetch my aunt. She and Uther were standing outside in the passageway. I beckoned, and as she hurried to his side, Uther and I looked at each other, sharing each other's grief without speaking.

We buried Publius Varrus two days later, beside his friend Caius Britannicus. That night Uther and I got drunk together, each telling the other as much as he could about what Varrus had said to him. Uther was to be King. I was to be his Councillor. From that day on, I became known to everyone except my closest family as Merlyn. Caius, the boy, had died with his uncle Publius Varrus.

BOOK TWO

Fledglings

VIII

I have spent years considering the events that shape the destinies of men and have often come close to accepting the evidence of my own experiences, for all their despair, which indicate that the zenith and the nadir of each man's life, all the grandeur and all the absurdity of life in general, are dictated by sheer chance and blind coincidence. The image that taunts me most when I think such thoughts is of a woman's mouth. It is a remembered image, not an imaginary one.

The integrity of this chronicle now demands that I write of the events that gave rise to that particular image, and to the tortuous and convoluted pathways that radiated outward, from one central set of circumstances, to confuse the footsteps of an entire people. I am not sure, however, that I can do so with detachment, even after five decades, for my emotions are as raw today as they were then. Let me therefore begin slowly and try to reconstruct those circumstances and the foolish, youthful hubris that led to the death of my youth.

Four years had elapsed since the death of Publius Varrus, and in the interim the two hesitant, neophyte captains recalled from that initial, probationary patrol had evolved into brash, confident but effective and competent commanders of the cavalry troops of Camulod, tried and tested in battle. Uther and I had emerged from the crucible of harsh experiences transformed into professional soldiers—warriors in the true sense of the word. We had become men, and in the pursuit of that status we had progressed far along the road to building the legions Publius Varrus had told us we would need in the days ahead.

Uther was a voluptuary, a lecher and a hedonist. So was I. But neither of us thought of ourselves in such terms. Why should we? In the days of our youth the notion of carnal sin was confined to incestuous relationships with immediate family members. It was only much later that the new, monastic churchmen introduced to our beautiful island the idea of the sinfulness of casual lust, and then, I am convinced, they used it callously, as a tool to prime the minds of men to accept the idea that women were inferior beings and vessels of sin.

Their efforts were to no avail, thank God, but in the attempt to force their will upon our people they caused great hardship and much grief in every corner of our land, where men of God and men of goodwill struggled with the incompatible desires to serve God by heeding the edicts of His Church—which now demanded no less than the disenfranchisement and subjugation of one-half of our society—and to please Him by continuing to love, honour and respect the proud women of Britain who had been the equals of their men since time immemorial.

None of this, however, affected us as young men. As I have said, we were voluptuaries and, as to carnal sin, completely innocent. Equally innocent were the young women who shared our lives and our carnal pleasures. For the most part, they were attractive and sometimes even beautiful outsiders who had few or no family ties within our Colony. They worked for their keep, as did everyone else, performing by day whatever tasks best suited their individual natures and abilities, and spending their evenings and nights enjoying the pleasures available to them. In effect, they were the camp followers of Camulod, and in the way of camp followers, many of them found permanent mates among the soldiers of the Colony. Invariably, in the way of youth everywhere, they considered themselves Immortals—fit, healthy and full of life and love and admiration for the equally young, healthy soldiers who ensured their safety and prosperity in a time when safety and prosperity were undreamed of luxuries the length and breadth of Britain.

And so we shared each other's pleasures. As we were insatiable without being satyrs, they were concupiscent without being concubines; as we were riotous without brutality, they were acquisitive without venality. None criticized our conduct with one another, or felt or betrayed any censure or surprise. Why should they? Uther and I, living to the full with all our friends, were the Princes of Camulod, the wonders of all our Tribe. We were at the flood tide of our rutting youth, and we were invincible in war. And when we had no wars to fight, we patrolled long and hard, trained long and hard, and worked long and hard at the onerous duties of the administrative Council, set up by our own grandfathers to govern our Colony, on which we both served as members. What could have been more natural than that we spent our evenings and our nights in Camulod and elsewhere filling our bellies and emptying our loins at every opportunity? Food and sex ruled our off-duty existence, with food taking only as much precedence over sexual pleasure as was required to maintain the strength we needed to generate new seed. My own early dreams of inadequacy in the face of Uther's lusts had long ceased to bother me. I was his equal in size, endurance and instant readiness at any time. In those days, impotence was a temporary phenomenon engendered only by over-indulgence and was easily and quickly cured by rest and titillation.

I was in just such a state when I first noticed Cassandra. I had seen her previously, but there is a vast difference between merely seeing a woman and really noticing her. We had returned that same day from a long, tedious patrol, and she had been part of the baggage we had collected in the course of our sweep. Uther, riding apart from our main body, had found her in an open glade, deep in the forest, hidden from the road, and crouching by the corpses of two people we had to assume were her parents. There was no encampment, only a rough shelter of green boughs and dead wood thrown together so that it barely remained upright around the supine corpses. There was no evidence of struggle or violence surrounding the deaths, nor was there any means of telling how the two had died. Uther had had to drag the girl by the wrist to get her

to go with him, and had lifted her onto his horse and ridden with
his arms around her for the remaining days of the patrol. She was
a skinny, lacklustre little thing with great grey eyes and a wide
mouth that dominated her small, pointed face. And she was utterly
silent. She had not spoken a word from the time he found her. She
reminded me of a frightened little rabbit, looking at no one, and
walking, when not on horseback, as though she held herself close
within her own arms. On our return to Camulod, she had refused
to quit Uther. No one could talk to her, none could penetrate her
total silence, and she steadfastly refused to leave Uther's side all
that day, even when his fancies led him where she should not be.

That evening found the three of us in what Uther called the
games room, where I was reclining like an emperor on a bed of
thick furs. I had just been thoroughly serviced by two of our willing
and nubile hero-worshippers and I had that empty, sated feeling in
my belly that told me I would not be ready for any more play for
some time. I lay back, my hands clasped comfortably behind my
head, as I watched my two companions try in vain to raise my dead
to life, their heads together, nibbling lips and tongues and teasing
fingers willing the impossible.

A series of deep, determined grunts from Uther, over on my
left, told me that he was rapidly approaching his destination and I
turned indolently to look, finding myself pleasantly positioned to
observe his phallus being engulfed and regurgitated by the wench
who rode him like the stallion he was. Her buttocks quivered and
shuddered with the effort of receiving him, presenting quite a sight
to my clinical and rather cynical gaze. Uther liked his women big.
And then it was that I noticed the girl, Cassandra, as Uther had
named her. She was sitting there on the edge of his pile of furs,
watching the goings-on in front of her as casually as though she
were watching him at dinner. I hitched myself up on one elbow to
see her better, dislodging myself in the process from my own atten-
dants, who resumed their activities as soon as I was resettled.

Like me, Uther had two companions, the one who was impaling
herself so determinedly upon his spike, and another who knelt behind

him, supporting his shoulders on her lap while her large breasts fell
on his face and supplied him with the handholds he needed for
leverage in his exertions. Her associate, who faced her across his
body, gripped her firmly by the shoulders for balance as she rode.

Cassandra's face was empty of expression. No lust showed there,
no interest. Her eyes moved over the heaving, grunting tableau in
front of her emotionlessly. I saw her glance downward at the junction of the two slapping bellies and then up again at the other woman's breasts and the hands that gripped them and as I looked, the
woman supporting Uther's shoulders opened her mouth and lolled
out her tongue like a thick, pink snake glistening with saliva. The
sight of it must have triggered the peaking lust of her companion,
for she went into a paroxysm, jerking the other toward her and sucking the jutting tongue into her mouth. But the movement pulled her
free of the meat that pierced her just at the wrong time and there
was a frantic scramble to reinsert the already spitting object before
the moment was lost forever. I found myself laughing at the unconscious buffoonery of the sight as my eyes returned to Cassandra.

Her expression had not changed, but this time I noticed how
her seated posture drew the rough, grey fabric of her plain smock
into tension against her thigh, outlining the sweep of it, and my loins
gave an involuntary twitch, which did not go unnoticed by my two
friends, who redoubled their efforts and found life where none had
been. The reaction, unwilled and unexpected, surprised me, so that I
looked more closely at this strange young woman. She had none of
the attributes that I normally found attractive. In fact, I decided, she
was almost ugly. And she was definitely not right in the head.

Uther and his rider had collapsed, and I could feel my own
resurgence progressing. I left Cassandra to her vacant observations
and returned to what was going on below my waist.

I lost track of the time that elapsed between then and when
Uther called my name, but when he did I was preoccupied. My companions and I had achieved a happy state of closeness that allowed
me to move from one to the other with great ease and speed, and
so I ignored him and concentrated upon not concentrating too

much on anything. But he was not to be ignored, and his insistence finally distracted me.

"What is it, Uther? What do you want?"

"Come here! Come over here and look at this."

"I'm busy! Look at what?"

"Come and see. Look what I have!"

I tried again to ignore him, snuggling my face into a plenitude of flesh, but he became even more insistent and I finally had to respond to him, merely to quiet him. "I don't care what you have," I told him, "I have things of my own to see to here."

"You can finish that later. Come and look at this."

I rose with a sigh and crossed the room to where he lay, aware of the cool night air on the moist parts of my body. "What?"

"Look at this. Have you ever seen the like?" I had, but I was looking at the wrong thing. One of his two companions was working at his erect phallus with her mouth, enjoying in her turn the mouth of her companion who suckled noisily between her lazily spread thighs. "Not that! This, this, this!" Uther drew my attention to Cassandra's face, which he held in his right hand, pinching her cheeks between finger and thumb so that her lips were pouted out of shape into a formless mass of soft flesh. Above her puckered lips, her eyes still gazed at him with that same, almost mindless docility. "Look at that mouth, Caius. Does it remind you of anything?" I looked. It did.

"I think so," I said, "but I don't know what. Let go of it." He released her and her mouth went back to normal. It was an astonishing mouth, taking up more than half the width of her face, with full, fleshy lips. The mouth, and those eyes which never strayed from his, eclipsed the rest of her entirely. I found myself wishing she would look at me.

"That's quite a mouth," I said, as he squeezed it again from both sides, not enough to hurt the girl, but just to crush the lips back into the shape they had been in before. "What does it look like to you, Uther?"

He gave a great shout of laughter and released the girl, twisting his body around to grasp the hips of the wench who was being tongued by her friend. "This!" he shouted, pulling her body towards him with one hand and slapping her worshipper away with the other. Ignoring the disgruntled protests of both of them, he pulled and hauled at the one he wanted, twisting her around and lifting her legs over in front of him until she lay face down, diagonally across him, her nakedness turned up towards his face and her head down by his feet. "Come round here and look at this!"

Grinning, I moved around to his right shoulder. The girl on his lap began to squirm in protest and he slapped her a stinging blow on the buttocks. "Lie still, woman, and spread your legs!" He reached with his left hand and pinched the lips of her vulva between his thumb and forefinger, hard enough and with enough downward pressure to pout them open. "There! You see? It's wetter, but it's the same."

"Hairier, too," I agreed, smiling, "but there is a resemblance."

He reached out again with his right hand and pinched Cassandra's mouth once more, his eyes going from those lips to the ones he held pinched in his other hand.

"Uther! You're hurting me!" This came from the region of his feet.

He slapped her again. "Then get your great wet arse out of my face, woman!" Finding herself released, the woman scrambled away from him, pouting reproachfully over her shoulder at him, but he was oblivious to her. Her friend, on the other hand, leaned towards her and pulled her lazily over to where she could resume her interrupted activity. Uther, in the meantime, continued to stare at Cassandra's mouth. Slowly, without relinquishing his hold on her chin, he got to his feet and stood in front of her, the tip of his phallus poised about an inch from her pouted lips. Her eyes had moved upwards, following him as he rose, so that her head was now tilted back to see his face. He twined the fingers of his left hand, gently enough, in her hair, and pulled her face downward.

"Now," he said, pushing himself gently forward, finding the space between those lips and inserting himself minutely. She did not respond in any way and he withdrew and did it again, a little more firmly. Still no response, although it was obvious that her teeth were together, barring his entrance. My own tumescence had shrunk to a bud and my two bedmates were watching the proceedings with bored interest. I began to feel some misgivings at what he was doing, although I could not have said why. She was here of her own free will and he was not harming her in any way. Nevertheless, I felt ill at ease.

"Uther—"

"Sssh, Caius! Watch! Come on, beauty, open it." He pinched harder, forcing her teeth apart. "That's better. That's good . . ." I watched him penetrate her mouth, sliding in slowly and then withdrawing, then sliding again as he released her chin and placed his hand on her head, and then she bit down on him. I knew she was going to do it a full second before she did it, for I was watching her eyes.

He roared like a wounded bull and jerked himself away from her, his hands flying to cradle his injury. In the instant that I had to look, I saw no sign of blood or of tooth marks on him, but any injury would have been too new to have had time to bleed. Cassandra jumped to her feet, her great grey eyes gleaming, but whether in fear, anger or in satisfaction I have no idea. Uther roared again and went for her, his big arm raised to smash her to the ground. One blow he landed, hurling her across the room before I could stop him, and then I hooked an elbow behind one of his and threw my other arm around his neck and wrestled him to the floor. It was all I could do to bring him down. He was in a monstrous anger and I knew him to be capable of killing her there and then. I got my chest across him, pinning him, and exerted all my strength to keep him there. He bucked and thrashed beneath me like a demented thing and then quite suddenly stopped and lay passive. I took that for a ruse and continued to press down on him, but when he spoke, I knew the danger was past.

"It's all right, Cay. You can let me go. I won't harm her. Get up."

I heard the truth in his voice and let him up. I looked for the girl, but she was gone. The other four sat staring wide-eyed at the two of us.

"Where did she go?"

The one with the long tongue shrugged her big shoulders. "Don't know, she just ran."

I rose and went to the door and looked out into the night-filled courtyard. There was no sign of Cassandra. I heard the approaching pacing of a guard and realized I was naked, so I turned back into the room and closed the door.

"The bitch. I'll find her later and teach her a lesson she won't soon forget." Uther was sitting hunched over, examining the shrunken thing he cradled in his fingers. "She almost bit me in two! I'll kill the bitch."

"No, Uther," I said, with a smile. "You won't kill her. Not now. But for a moment there, I thought you would have. Is it bleeding?"

He checked again. "No. But it might have been. The bitch!"

I grinned at him. "Come on, Uther! She didn't even bite hard. I was watching. You were more shocked than hurt, admit it. Your pride suffered more than your cock."

He glowered at me. "What do you know about it? You didn't feel her teeth!"

"Let's have a look at it, then. Is it marked?" I stepped towards him, but he cupped himself in a protective hand and I laughed outright in my relief, forgetting about his pride. "From the size of it now, it looks as though she bit three-quarters of it off!" Only then did I notice how upset he still was and realize that I should not be baiting him. I continued, however, to make light of it, hoping to make him see the humour in the situation. There is no more effective poultice for wounded pride than the ability to laugh at oneself. "Hey!" I said. "That was a jest! It'll probably work just as well as ever once you stop thinking about it. Girls, why don't you try to see if Uther's staff is still strong enough to lean on?"

They were willing enough and clustered round him in glowing, warm-fleshed nudity, but he would have none of it. He slapped them away and got to his feet with a scowl, grabbing his tunic and pulling it on as he did so. "I'll see you in the morning," he snapped on the way out, and left the five of us sitting there staring at the closed door.

I got up and poured myself some wine from the jug on the table. "Well, ladies," I said. "He'll be back when he's cooled off." I toasted the four of them silently. "In the meantime, why don't we try to see how many times one will go into four?" The fire had burned low and there was only one lamp left burning in the room by this time. One of them, the one with the long, pink tongue, blew it out as I approached them.

IX

I was wrong. Uther did not come back that night, and to this day I know of only two people who might have seen him in the course of the next week. The first of these was the guard on duty in the courtyard when Uther stormed out of the games room; the other, the girl, Cassandra.

I awoke just after dawn the following morning and left my four bedmates asleep in a tangle of limbs. I had had no more than two hours of sleep, and when I finally dropped off, at least two of the girls were still pleasing each other. As I dressed, I noticed that Uther had not returned, but I thought nothing of it at the time. I went to the stables and saddled my horse and galloped down to the villa, letting the crisp, cold air of the frosty morning clear my head, and anticipating the humid, seductive warmth of the bath house, where I could steam and soak the previous night's excesses out of my body.

There was a regular Council session scheduled for noon that day, and I had nothing to do until then, so I spent an hour or so rooting around in the villa. For many years the focal point of the Britannicus family, it was an empty, echoing place nowadays, barely used since the entire family had moved up to live in the hilltop fort years before, although servants still kept it in first-class condition as guest quarters and maintained its magnificent bath house. The fort had baths of its own, of course, but they were utilitarian, make-shift and barely functional—primitive beside the luxury offered by the facilities at the Villa Britannicus.

It was mid-morning by the time I finally went back up the hill to the fort, where I changed into more formal clothes and began to make my way to the kitchens to eat before getting ready for the

Council meeting. On the way there, I heard my name being called and I turned to see Lucanus, the head of our medical staff, looking towards me and waving. I stopped to let him approach me, wondering what he could want. He was an able surgeon, our best in fact, but I chose to think he was not himself an amiable man. He asked me whether I had seen Uther.

"No, Lucanus, I haven't. Not since last night. Is there a problem? Can I help you?"

He frowned and nibbled at his lower lip. "Yes, Commander, there is a problem, but I don't know ..."

"You don't know if I can help. Well, neither of us will know the answer to that until you tell me what the problem is." He still looked unsure of himself.

"Well? Come on, man, spit it out!"

He grimaced. "It's the girl, Commander."

I frowned at him, not knowing what he meant. "What girl, Lucanus? I'm not a mind reader."

"The woman, sir. The one Commander Uther brought back yesterday."

My mind clicked. "Cassandra. What about her?"

"I have her in my quarters, Commander."

"Do you, indeed?" I grinned at him. "You'll get little co-operation out of that one, Lucanus. Be careful of her teeth."

The man had no sense of humour. He frowned, heavy browed with displeasure. "She has been badly beaten, Commander. Brutally beaten, almost to death." My breath stopped as he went on. "Some soldiers found her this morning, in the stables against the west wall. They brought her to me. I thought that since Commander Uther is her protector, he should be told immediately, but I have been unable to find him. When I saw you, I thought you might be able to tell me where he is."

I had a sick sourness in the pit of my gut, but the lie came to my lips of its own volition. "No, I can't tell you. He rode out of the fort last night on a private matter. I have no idea when he will be back. Bring me to the girl." I followed him back to his quarters, stopping only to tell one of the men heading towards the Council Hall that I might be detained and that the session should proceed without me and without Uther.

Lucanus had not exaggerated. The girl lay naked on a cot, hidden from view by folding screens. She had been beaten without mercy with a club of some kind, and the contusions on her white skin would take weeks to heal. Most of the blood had been washed away, and several of the angrier-looking cuts had been stitched together. Her eyes were puffed and bruised completely shut and her startling mouth, which I was immediately sure had been the cause of this, was a shattered, bloody mass. *"I'll find her later and teach her a lesson she won't soon forget!"* I could hear Uther's voice and my skin crawled in loathing. How could he have done this to a skinny little girl? My mind could not accept it, but there was the evidence, lying naked and smashed in front of me.

"Has she been violated?"

"I think you could say that."

I heard the sarcasm in his voice and rounded on him in a fury. "Sexually, I mean, you fool! Has she been raped?"

His eyes were glacial. I had made an enemy. "Yes, Commander. She has been brutalized and sodomized. Both by extreme force. Her vagina and her anus are both badly torn."

I felt the room swaying around me. "Will she live?"

"I think so, if she wants to."

"What do you mean by that?"

He shrugged his shoulders and ducked his head in a curious manner, pursing his lips as he did so. "Just what I say. If she wishes to live, she will live. People can die by simply choosing not to live. This young woman has had a terrible experience. Is it true she is mute?"

I looked down at her again. "We don't know. She hasn't spoken since we found her, but we found her beside the bodies of two people who might have been her parents. Commander Uther thought at first that she might be in some kind of trance brought about by witnessing their deaths."

"How did they die?"

"We don't know that, either. There were no signs of violence, and we saw no indications that they had been sick. They were just dead, and the girl knelt beside them."

He made that peculiar gesture again. "I suppose that could be true. She might have been in what we call shock. The body's defensive systems are a wonder we know practically nothing of. How long has it been since she was found?"

I did a quick calculation. "Six days."

"Hmm! Well, even if she was not in shock then, she certainly is now."

I was looking down at her body as it lay there on the couch in front of me. Her skin was white and her body small, but she was not as emaciated as I had suspected. Her thighs were rounded and full, and her breasts small, but firm and plump. I felt another stirring of desire and was filled with disgust at myself.

"Are there any bones broken?"

"No. No fractures. Only contusions, as you can see, both front and rear. And perhaps internal bleeding. Whoever did this is an animal."

"Aye, there's no doubt of that. How can you tell about the internal bleeding? *Do* people bleed internally?" I had never really thought about that before. His raised eyebrow was an eloquent mockery.

"Aye, Commander, that is what causes bruising. At times, however, a severe blow will rupture a major blood vessel and cause heavy bleeding into the body's cavities."

"And what does that mean?"

Again the shrugged shoulders and the peculiar gesture. "It means the person will probably die."

I squeezed my temples with my left hand, feeling as though my head might burst apart. "What time did this happen, do you know?"

"Sometime in the night. We do not know when. But the blood was congealed when they found her."

"What about the guards?" I was speaking to myself, more than to him. "Didn't anyone hear anything? Surely to God she must have screamed?"

"Not if she's truly mute, Commander."

I heaved a sigh that was part sob and jerked my eyes away from the girl's ruined body, fighting to bring my anger and revulsion under restraint and keeping my back to Lucanus until I could control the muscles of my face. Finally, I calmed down enough to hide the roiling sickness in my soul and to speak evenly.

"Thank you, Lucanus. You have done well. Where are the men who found her?"

"I sent them back to their duties."

"Hmm! So word of this will be all over the fort by now. Whoever is responsible for this will know she is still alive. I want guards posted outside every door to this place. I'll see to it myself. As soon as you know whether she will live or not, I wish to be informed. In the meantime, you will stay here with her. Don't leave her alone for a moment. That's an order." He nodded his head and I made myself go on, "If Commander Uther should return today I'll send him over. Do what you can for her, Lucanus. She did nothing to deserve this." *Not if she'd bitten it off,* I added to myself.

He stopped me at the door. "Commander?"

"Yes? What is it?"

"How do you know her name?"

I frowned at him and then realized what he meant. "We don't," I told him. "It's our name, not hers. She seemed tragic enough, even then, to be Cassandra of Troy. Uther named her."

"I see."

I grimaced, deciding in mid gesture that I had no smiles in me. "No, Lucanus, you don't see." *Because you did not see what I saw,* my mind added.

Outside again, in the bright sunlight, the image of that bruised body still tore at my eyes. I started to walk towards the Council Hall, but when I saw my fellow councillors thronging in that direction and thought of the dry, bloodless, boring trivia on that day's agenda I knew I couldn't cope with it in my present frame of mind.

I turned aside and walked off, fighting to keep my face blank and my mind empty, and nodding to the people who greeted me at every step. I ended up beneath the scaffolding against the inner wall, where the masons were at work adding new quarters abutting the main defences of the fort. I sat there in the shadows undisturbed for a long time, thinking this whole mess through.

Had I been the only one who knew the circumstances of this affair, I would have sat on my knowledge until I could face Uther with it privately, but I was not the only one who knew. Our four consorts of the previous night had witnessed the whole thing and would lose no time in airing their knowledge. Struck by a sudden thought, I stood up quickly and made my way back to the games room. It was not yet noon.

As I approached the door, it opened and two of the girls came out. I stopped them with a stiff, insincere smile on my face, and open arms, and asked where they were going. To eat, they told me. They had not yet broken fast? No, they had just arisen. And where were the other girls? Still abed. In my relief, I almost betrayed myself, but managed to guard my features like a hardened liar. I turned them both around, led them back inside, told them to take their clothes off again and promised to bring food, wine, a masseur and Uther back with me shortly. They were surprised, but complacent. I fondled the one with the long tongue— I never could remember her name, but I never forgot her—and asked her if she had tasted the other two as she had the one with whom she had shared Uther. She had not, she said, but was willing to, if they were.

My two erstwhile companions looked at each other uncertainly, wondering what I was up to, but I clinched it by offering a golden *aureus* to the one who seemed to enjoy it most when I returned with Uther. Even in a society where money is not used, gold is a powerful persuader. I left them settling down to experiment and made my way directly to Titus's quarters.

He was working on his records and looked up at me in surprise as I entered. "Shouldn't you be in Council?"

"I should, but something came up. Is anyone else around? I need to speak with you alone."

"Right now?"

"Immediately."

"Speak then. There's nobody here. What's going on?"

"I'll tell you everything later, Titus. For the moment, I can only ask you if you trust me enough to do something for me at once, without explanation."

"That's a silly question, Cay. What's up? What do you need?"

"A squad of men you can trust completely. I want you to come with me to the games room and help me abduct four women."

"Only four?" He was smiling.

"I'm serious, Titus. I'll tell you what it's all about later. Have you seen Uther today?"

"No. Why?"

"Never mind, it's not important now. Will you do what I ask?"

He looked at me appraisingly for three long counts and then rose to his feet. "It'll take me a little while to round up some men I can rely on. I presume you want men who can keep silent?"

"Yes, I do, above all else. I've got some things to round up myself. I'll meet you in the courtyard in a few moments."

When I opened the door and stepped inside with Titus in tow, the looks on the four girls' faces ranged all the way from lively interest to disappointment.

"Where's Uther? And where's our food?" the long-tongued one asked.

"The food is coming, girls. Uther's left the fort on emergency business. Now, sit up, all of you, and listen carefully to what I have to say. This is important." They sat up and stared at me, beginning to wonder what was going on. I perched with one buttock on the edge of the table and looked at them, considering what I was going to say, how I was going to phrase it. These young women were creatures of pleasure. I reached into my tunic and brought out a leather bag, heavy and rich-looking, and dropped it onto the table top with a solid, metallic thud.

"Gold," I said. "Uther and I have a proposition for you ladies." I opened the drawstring of the bag and poured a stream of gold coins onto the table. "There are eighty gold *aurei* here—twenty for each of you. That's enough money to see all of you set for life. At current value, you are looking at about forty thousand silver *denarii*." All four pairs of eyes were fastened on the pile of gleaming coins. I produced another bag and poured a second stream. "Twenty more for each of you. But there are conditions. You have to earn it." All four of them together could not have earned twenty *aurei* if they had serviced an entire legion on their backs for five years.

The Tongue licked her lips. "What . . . conditions?"

"You leave Camulod now, immediately, saying goodbye to no one. I'll provide an escort for you as far as Glevum." That was more than sixty miles. "Once in Glevum, you will buy a house, set it up for . . . your own purposes, shall we say? . . . and keep it warm and welcoming for Commander Uther and myself and the Legate Titus, here. As you know, we returned yesterday from a long patrol. We found no entertainment in Glevum. For a while there, in fact, we were beginning to look attractive to each other."

None of them smiled at my attempt at humour. One of them, one of the two who had been mine, asked in a husky voice, "When do we get the money?"

"Now. It's yours as soon as you agree to the terms."

"Why would we have to leave right now? What's going on here?" This one's voice was sullen with suspicion.

"Going on?" My mind was racing. "That's an easy question to answer. I'll tell you what's going on, if you really want to know."

"Well? We really want to know."

I cleared my throat and charged ahead with the lie that had come to me. "Uther and I decided to do this when we were in Glevum. To set up a house there, I mean. This morning, at breakfast, we decided that if we are to do it at all, we have to do it quickly, today, in fact. General Picus, my father, is due back today. He would forbid it, totally. He spends much time now with the Christian priests and talks of the pleasures of the afterlife. He disapproves of our casual ways with women, and he would have apoplexy if he thought we were dispatching soldiers on such escort duty. If you leave now, immediately, you will be gone by the time he arrives and he will never know. But you must leave now, and you must go secretly, for if anyone suspects what we are doing, and the word gets back to General Picus, he'll have us court-martialled and our lives won't be worth living. Neither will yours."

The sullen one was still not convinced.

"Of course," I went on, bluffing with all my power, "if you don't like the idea, you can all stay here and there's no harm done. I'll return the money to the treasury and we'll forget the whole thing." I picked up a handful of coins and let some of them slip through my fingers back to the table top. That did it.

"How do we get there?" one of them asked. "I can't ride."

"Don't be silly, girl. We'll send you in comfort, in a wagon with seats and an awning. You'll go in haste, but in style, too."

"What about your soldier boys?" asked the Tongue. "Aren't you afraid they'll blab?"

"No," I smiled. "Not until they get back. After that, when they know they stand to lose their visiting privileges in Glevum *and* be in trouble with the General, I don't think they'll say too much. And I'm sure they'll have a pleasant journey, at least one way." It was her turn to smile.

They were aboard the wagon within half an hour, their money in their hands, with enough rations to feed an army. Titus had instructed his men on their duties as escort, and together we watched the party proceeding through the gates and down the hill road. Uther's games room was empty. Every skin and fur and cushion had gone aboard the wagon.

When they were safely out of sight, Titus turned to me with a slight smile. "Aren't you amazed at my patience? What is going on, Cay? You just gave away an emperor's ransom. What's it all about?"

"Rumours and reputations, Titus, that's what it's all about. Let's take a walk where we can't be overheard and I'll tell you the whole sorry tale."

He was gazing closely at me now, his mind working quickly. "Where's Uther, Cay? There's something here I can't grasp."

"Huh," I grunted. "There's something here that will stink in the nostrils of God, my friend."

We walked down the hill and I talked for half an hour, telling him everything I knew. He was as shocked and profoundly disturbed as I had been. When I had finished talking he stopped and caught my elbow, turning me so that he looked me in the eye.

"You don't really think it was Uther, do you?"

I turned away and started walking again, letting my words drift back over my shoulder. "What else can I think, Titus? I've told you what I saw and heard. It all adds up to Uther, and Uther is nowhere to be found. Am I wrong?"

He caught up to me. "You must be, Cay. You have to be. Uther couldn't be capable of the bestial savagery you're talking about."

"I know, Titus. That's what I would have said, until today. But you have to admit he is capable of savagery. You've seen him enraged; we both have. He can be a killer."

"Of course he can, in battle. We're all killers then." He shook his head. "No, I can't see it. He might have beaten her after she bit him, while he was so angry, but not like this! Not in cold blood." His face cleared suddenly, and hope gleamed in his eyes. "But you said she was raped, front and rear. He couldn't have done that, with a bitten cock."

I shook my head then, too. "I don't know, Titus. I don't know. That had occurred to me as well, but I really don't know how badly she bit him. I thought at the time he had been more shocked than hurt, but I don't know with certainty. He might still have been capable of that. And there's another thing that crossed my mind, too, although I think I'm leaping at shadows."

"What?"

"She had been beaten with a stick of some kind. No one could find it, apparently." I had to stop and think again about what I was suggesting, before I went on. "It occurred to me that he might have used whatever he beat her with to penetrate her, too, so it would appear she had been raped when we knew him to be incapable of rape because of his injury."

"Sweet Christ, Cay! You're making him into a ravening beast!"

"You haven't seen that girl, Titus. Whoever did that to her *is* a ravening beast!"

"But that's simply not Uther!"

I rounded on him at that. "Then who is it, Titus? Is it you? Is it me? My father? Somebody did it! Somebody right here in Camulod. I'm not making this up out of my head. It happened!" I realized that I was almost shouting and dropped my voice. "That girl is lying over in Lucanus's quarters, Titus. She is not a figment of my imagination and neither is what happened to her. Someone in this fort savaged her like a wild animal—worse than a wild animal would have—and left her there for dead. It's a marvel that she is alive at all, and she may very well be dead as we speak. I hope not. If she lives, she'll be able to identify her attacker."

"How? I thought she was deaf and dumb?"

"Come on, Titus! She can point a finger."

"Oh, of course. Stupid of me."

"She has to live, Titus, because I can't function properly with these suspicions in my mind and no proof one way or the other. She has to live to look Uther in the face, and I have to be there when it happens, so I have to make sure she stays alive if and when she starts to recover."

Titus frowned at me. "I don't understand. You're not making sense. Surely, if she starts to recover, she'll stay alive?"

I bit down on my impatience and managed not to snap at him. "Think about it, Titus. Think it through. We are not dealing with the normal here. Suppose it was you who had done this thing, and you thought the girl dead and your secret safe. And then you found out she's alive and recovering, and that she'll be able to identify you. What would you do?"

"Run." There was absolutely no hesitation in his voice.

"Right. That's a good answer, and exactly what I'd expect of you, although you'd have to run fast and far to be sure of safety from Picus's justice. But suppose that for any one of a thousand reasons, you couldn't, or didn't want to run away from Camulod? What then? What would your next move be? Remember, we're talking about a small, sick, deaf and mute girl who is the only witness who might condemn you. What might you try to do then?" I was putting words into his mouth, but I had to.

"Try to kill her. You're right, Cay. We'll have to guard her day and night."

"How, Titus?"

"What d'you mean, how?" His brow was creased in perplexity.

"Who will you set to guard her? It was someone in this fort who did it to her, don't forget."

His face clouded. "We'll set a double guard."

"To guard the guards? What if there were two or more men involved? We don't know, and we can't afford to take that risk."

He stopped walking and looked straight at me. "You frighten me, Caius. You're telling me that I can't trust my own men."

I put my hand on his shoulder. "It's even worse than that, Titus. We can trust no one in this. That's the crime that has really been committed here. The only person in this fort whose innocence I can be absolutely sure of is myself. I *know* I didn't do this thing. The medic, Lucanus, I can be sure of, too, since he is the one keeping her alive. And you, my friend, are simply yourself incapable of such bestiality. My father and his men are on patrol. When they return, they'll guard her. Until then, it's up to us." I paused. "She is the only one who can clear Uther of suspicion, or condemn him."

"Damnation! This stinks like the sewers of Rome!" His voice was choked with disgust. "So what are we to do? How do we handle this? Have you any ideas?"

I only half heard his last question, for we had just reentered the fort and in the distance, disappearing in the direction of the kitchens, I had seen the unmistakable figure of Daffyd, my best friend among the Druids. The sight of him brought an associated image wholly formed into my mind and I suddenly felt a great surge in my chest as though something heavy had been lifted from me, and all at once I felt much better. I spoke to Titus over my shoulder.

"I've just had an idea, Titus. Leave me alone now and let me chew on it for a while."

He shrugged and shook his head, then raised his hands, palms outward. "I hope it's a good one, Cay. Take care of it because God knows we need it. I'll be in my *cubiculum*."

I watched him walk away, then I retraced my steps to the secluded masons' scaffolding against the wall. There, secure in the knowledge that none of the masons would consider approaching or disturbing me, I made myself comfortable and began to consider the idea that had flashed into my mind, considering it and adapting it until I had transformed it into a feasible plan of action.

The safety of the girl Cassandra was paramount. Upon it depended the end to my doubts, slight as they were, concerning my cousin's guilt. The two must be confronted with each other, were I to continue living in sanity. Her initial reaction to Uther would, I was convinced, establish his innocence or his guilt immediately, and either outcome would relieve me of these agonizing suspicions. In the interim, however, until the return of my father's patrol, I had the pressing problem I had shared with Titus: *Who would guard the guards?*

I do not know when the idea of a mysterious disappearance had first occurred to me, but it had crystallized in my mind the moment I saw Daffyd in the distance, for my next thought had been that Mod, one of Daffyd's two apprentices, a slim, adolescent, almost androgynous boy, would have come with him. Somehow, I had known immediately, I would substitute Mod for the girl Cassandra, and arrange the exchange in such a way that no one would be aware of it.

That was the basis of my plan. The plan and its implementation, however, had remained disjointed and undefined beyond the fact that their formlessness lay heavy and solid in the pit of my gut like a mass of undigested food. Now, as I thought the matter through, plotting my course of action in my head, the whole mosaic came together and my enthusiasm grew stronger as the final pieces fell convincingly into place. I could achieve little alone, but I had staunch friends whom I could trust to aid me, and Lucanus the physician, on whom I could rely concerning the welfare of his charge. I knew my plan would work.

Less than an hour after my arrival beneath the scaffolding, I began putting my stratagem into effect. I sought out my friends and assembled them in Lucanus's infirmary, where I explained the situation, told them what I proposed to do and enlisted their support.

Ludo, one of my oldest friends in Camulod and head of the kitchens of the fort's Commissariat, would play a crucial part in our abduction. Uther had often warned me about Ludo, during our boyhood, citing the man's notorious fondness for youngsters of his own sex, but Ludo had never made any improper advances to me, nor had I ever given him cause to resent me. Now his commitment to this endeavour of mine was absolute and instant. He agreed to empty one of his secure storerooms close to the infirmary within the hour and put it at my disposal. Lucanus undertook to remove Cassandra from his quarters and conceal her safely in the storeroom as soon as it was empty. Mod would immediately take Cassandra's place, his identity disguised with the same kind of dressings in which Lucanus had swathed the girl. Some of the girl's original dressings, stained with her blood, would amplify the effect. When all these arrangements were completed, in a matter of an hour or so, I would mount a strong guard, night and day, over the infirmary, first making sure that every guard had verified Mod's presence and his battered condition—believing him to be Cassandra—for himself. At dusk, Ludo would load a wagon with "supplies" for the villa kitchens, and would transport the injured girl to the bottom of the hill, where Daffyd would be waiting to lead her to a sanctuary where she would be safe from all harm. Later, Mod would "disappear" in safety in the dead of night, crossing in the darkness from the rear door of Lucanus's quarters to the rear door of the kitchens. The guards would be seeking to prevent an intrusion to the physician's quarters; they would never think to look for an escape. The only criticism of my plan came from

Lucanus, who demanded to know where we would take the girl. He was extremely unwilling to allow her to be moved at all, doubting her capability to survive such an ordeal, and he was incensed when I refused, claiming the need for secrecy even among ourselves, to divulge Daffyd's destination. In the absence of alternatives, however, he had no choice but to accede, grudgingly, to the urgency facing us all.

And so it was done. Cassandra was moved safely and without mishap and Lucanus installed Mod in her place, swathing him so convincingly in blood-stained bandages and sheets that the mere sight of his slight, featureless form inspired pity. I spent the afternoon spreading the word widely, first to the Council, which I interrupted in session, that the girl had survived the outrage to which she had been subjected and that she would be protected thenceforth, under heavy guard, until she grew well enough to identify her attacker. By dusk, everyone in the fort was aware of the girl's situation, and a steady stream of curiosity-seekers passed the infirmary to view the impassive guards at their posts.

The girl was transported safely out of Camulod at nightfall, surrounded by crates and baskets in a sheepskin-piled cart, and Titus and I together provided sufficient distraction for the guards during the second watch of the night to allow Mod to make his own escape from the infirmary.

Several hours later, during the fourth and last watch of the night when the darkness was absolute, I presented myself once more at the main entrance to the infirmary and questioned the Guard Commander on his charge. He was one of my father's ablest and most trusted veterans, our senior centurion and therefore Camulod's equivalent of the noble and ancient rank of *primus pilus*. I felt a strong twinge of guilt at deluding him this way, but I had determined that something more—some final touch—was necessary at this point to solidify and seal the mysterious element of what we had done and what I hoped to achieve. I asked him to inspect the guard with me and when we had done so, I stood talking to him for a few moments.

"A bad business, this, Popilius."

"Aye, Commander," he grunted. "Bad through and through, but the lass is safe enough now. No more harm will reach her, and if she recovers, she'll point the finger at the whoreson who did this. If he's one of mine, I'll have the balls off him before he dies."

I believed him implicitly but made no response, allowing a silence to grow between us before asking my next question. "Do you believe in dreams, Popilius?"

He was an old soldier, too old to respond without thought to such a question. "Dreams, Commander?" he mused, eventually. "I believe they exist, 'cause I have them. But that's not what you're asking, is it? I don't believe they have any significance. I don't believe in that witchcraft stuff. I have dreams, sometimes, as I said, but I can't often remember what they're about. Why do you ask?"

His response surprised me, for I, too, had dreams I could seldom remember afterwards, and it was the memory of those, their incompleteness, that had prompted me to take this present step. I turned to face him in the flickering light of the wall torches by the door to the building, forcing myself to smile a rueful, self-deprecating smile.

"Because that's why I'm here. I had one tonight that woke me completely, and it was vivid in my memory."

"A nightmare?" There was a rough sympathy in his voice, as though he were familiar with nightmares.

"No, no, it wasn't a nightmare. There was no fear. I dreamed of a storm, high, howling winds and harsh, red light. Through it walked a figure in a long, black cloak with a high, pointed hood. He—it—was carrying the girl, out through the main gates. Ridiculous, of course, but this damned mess has been on my mind all day, and when I sprang awake the way I did, that dream seemed very real. So real, in fact, that I had to get up and satisfy myself all is well."

Popilius smiled and nodded. "All's well, Commander, but I know how you felt. As I said, I sometimes dream myself. Strange things, dreams. But the girl hasn't gone anywhere, and no one's entered the building. Lucanus sleeps in the room with her."

"Hmm. You're right, of course. I suppose I'm being over cautious. Anyway, I'm going back to try to sleep again. If anything strange or untoward occurs, send for me immediately, understand?"

"I will, Commander. Good night to you."

"Good night, Popilius."

And so was born the first tale of Merlyn's strange and magical powers, for when the empty cot was found, Popilius was there to remember our conversation, and he lost no time in letting everyone know. To this day I have no idea what prompted me to do what I did that night, for in those days I had no thought of ever being more than what I was then, a soldier. But there it is, something inside me told me what to do and I did it.

We conducted an investigation, naturally, into the girl's disappearance, but no disciplinary action was taken against the very worried guards. I had taken care to arrange matters so that there were enough men on guard at any given moment of the night to preclude any charges of negligence, collusion or subornment. The girl had disappeared from heavily guarded premises while her physician slept within reach of her. She had not left by any of the infirmary doors and no one had passed into the infirmary since the last time she had been seen by her guards during the third watch, when Titus and I inspected her ourselves.

Lucanus swore that when he had last seen her she was incapable of locomotion. Popilius swore that she had not been abducted during his watch, even though Commander Merlyn had told him personally of his dream that she had been abducted by a cloaked, storm-racked figure. He had been vigilant at his post prior to that, he declared—and none doubted him or his men—but afterward, he had been even more attentive to his charge. The disappearance of the injured girl was, and remained, a mystery. It became part of the legend of the Colony, and none of those involved ever told the truth of it until now. It was our secret.

As a Druid, Daffyd was familiar with the place I thought of as my secret valley; it was, and had always been, sacred to him and to his kind, who saw trees, tree-crowned hills, and tree-filled hollows as the natural habitat of their ancient gods. Uther, on the other hand, had no knowledge of the valley's existence, even though there had been times when I was sorely tempted to share my secret with him. That I had never done so was the result of a promise made to Uncle Varrus, who had first shown the place to me. He had taken me to the valley one day and made me a gift of it, telling me that every man had need of a secret place where he could be himself, by himself. There would be times, he assured me, when I would be glad to escape from my public life and rest in solitude, gathering my strength and my thoughts. Here alone, he told me, I would be safe from Uther. I had not understood what he meant by "safe," so he explained then that Uther would be a king one day, and that kings and emperors are cruel taskmasters, believing their own concerns give them the right to dictate the lives of others at all times.

This place, he told me, this valley, might come to be my only sanctuary in the whole world, but only if I kept its secret close. Here I might find some peace from time to time and let Uther rant and rave until I should return. It would do him good, his grandfather said, to realize that there was at least one man in his kingdom who could maintain some independence of his king. Uther was not yet king, but his grandfather had already been proven right.

I had thought my secret to be mine alone after my uncle's death, until the day I opened my eyes from sleep and found my father looking down at me. He had come there to fish as a boy, he told me. We fished together that day, and I told him what Uncle Varrus had told me. His only comment was that Varrus had been a wise man, and from that day my father had never come near the place again. He, too, had given it to me for my own. Over the years, I had built a strong stone hut at the water's edge, with a fine, weatherproof roof of red clay tiles that I had salvaged, a few at a time, from a great pile of the things that had lain for years behind one of the outhouses of the Villa Britannicus. I loved to sleep there beside the little lake, lulled by the gentle sound of the sliding waterfall. I had also, over those same years, varied my approach to the only entrance so that no tell-tale path would betray my sanctuary to the eyes of others.

Now I stood outside the door of the hut with Mod, gazing at the yellow lamp light that shone through the translucent glass of the window I had built into the wall. It had taken me a long time to make that window, ten pieces of thick glass joined by lead and carefully fastened into a wooden frame. It was a good window, letting in light and keeping the weather out. I stood with my left hand on young Mod's shoulder, reluctant, for some reason I could not identify, to enter the hut.

He finally twisted his head and looked up at me. "Are we going in?"

"Aye, Mod, we are." I stepped forward and pushed the door open.

The room was small, and now it seemed crowded with three people in it. Tumac, the younger of Daffyd's two apprentices, was asleep on a pile of furs against the wall, and Daffyd sat by the side of the cot, feeding the girl Cassandra with a spoon. He turned when he heard us enter and smiled at us. The girl gave no sign of knowing we were there. She did not hear us enter and her eyes were covered by a strip of white cloth. I crossed the room and looked down at her. Her mouth was still a mess, but some of the swelling seemed to have abated.

"How is she?" I asked him.

"On the mend. She has a lot of pain ahead of her, but it is the pain of healing."

"How long will it take her to mend completely?"

"A week, two weeks, perhaps three."

"Why are her eyes covered?"

He reached forward and tucked an edge of the covering more securely into place before he answered me. "Protection. They are badly swollen. There is an unguent on the cloth."

"Why? Has her sight been damaged?"

"I don't think so, although I cannot be sure." He looked back at me. "But how are you, Merlyn? You look frayed."

"I'm well enough, Daffyd. I just need some sleep. I have not had much these past few nights."

"Has Uther returned?"

"No."

"And you have no idea where he might have gone?"

"None at all." Daffyd shook his head and continued spooning a broth of some kind into the girl's mouth. "What are you feeding her?" I asked him.

"Only the boiled juice of some herbs. She is too weak to take anything stronger. Perhaps tomorrow I will stew a rabbit and start her on broth." He paused in his feeding and turned to me. "You really believe Uther did this?"

I seated myself on the wooden chair beside the table. "I don't know, Daffyd. I don't know what to think. And the more I think about it the more confused I become." I looked at the girl and felt a surge of anger and resentment towards her. Her sudden intrusion into our lives had upset everything. She had appeared from nowhere, unannounced, and her mere presence had undone the pattern of my life. Because of this girl, my dearest friend had turned into a monster in my mind and the entire Colony had been thrown into upheaval. She had been aptly named Cassandra, the harbinger of doom. And then, as suddenly as it had come, the feeling passed and I was left looking at a tragic little girl who had had no control over the blows that fate had dealt her. From anger and revulsion my feelings changed directly to pity and concern. I realized that I was overtired. Suddenly the idea of lying down and closing my eyes was irresistible. "Daffyd," I said, "I have to sleep. This minute."

"I know that, my young friend. I was hoping you might realize it, too." He nodded towards an empty corner. "Lie down there."

I went to where Tumac lay and took one of the furs from his pile, but before I yielded completely to temptation, I spoke to Daffyd again. "How long can you stay with her, Daffyd?"

"As long as she needs my care. Why? Did you think I would leave her unattended?"

"No, but I thought you might be expecting me to stay with her, and I can't. I have to be back in Camulod early tomorrow. My father is expected and I don't want him to hear this from anyone's lips but my own."

"That is understandable. Sleep, and don't worry. The girl will be well cared for."

"Thank you, my friend." I spread my fur on the floor, lowered myself onto it and fell asleep before I had time to wrap it around me.

X

As I entered Camulod the following morning I met Titus crossing the main courtyard, looking tired and uncharacteristically irritable. He wasted no time in telling me that my father had returned from patrol just after dawn and had been looking for me, and there was a tone in his voice that fell just short of censure. I thanked him and made no comment on his unusual demeanour, having a shrewd idea of the reason for it. I stabled my horse and went looking for my father immediately, finding him, as I knew I would, working on some records in his day office. He glanced up at me as I entered and nodded towards a chair. I sat down and waited for him to finish what he was doing.

He finally finished a document, sealed it and took it to the door, where he gave it to the guard and told him to have it delivered to the Legate Titus.

"Titus?" I asked him. "Couldn't you just tell him what you want?"

He closed the door carefully before answering me. "Some things must be written . . . have to be, for the sake of order . . . and for future reference." Having said this, he crossed slowly back to his table and seated himself. "Now. Please, in as few words as possible . . . what in Hades has been going on here in my absence?" He was speaking very slowly, forcing himself to articulate his words clearly, fighting the tendency to slur forced upon him by his damaged throat.

"What have you heard?"

"Nothing I could believe. Rumours . . . murder and witchcraft. Titus was . . . unwontedly silent. Told me to my face I should wait for you. I have waited. I am waiting."

I began at the beginning and told him the whole story of

finding the girl in the first place and bringing her back to Camulod, and then of the assault and of her disappearance. I did not lie to him. I merely made no mention of the scene in the games room or of the real abduction from the infirmary.

When I had finished he sat looking at me for a long time. "Fine," he said finally, rasping the word. "That's what the common soldier knows. Now . . . What really happened? Where is Uther? How did the girl vanish . . . from the infirmary? Why—" He stopped and cleared his throat, then continued very carefully. "Why all this concern . . . in the first place . . . over a mute found-ling who gets herself into trouble? There's . . . There is more to this tale than you are . . . telling."

I sighed and began again, telling him this time what really happened and leaving out no detail. As I spoke, he got up and began to pace the tiny room, gnawing on the inside of his lower lip. When I had finished my tale this time his comments and questions were terse and to the point.

"You have the girl in your valley?"

"Yes. It's the only safe place I know of."

"Safe from Uther, you mean."

"Yes."

"You're convinced he did this." It was not a question. I said nothing. "Why?" Again I said nothing. "Why are you so prepared to believe that Uther . . . your blood cousin . . . your best friend . . . whom you have known literally all your life, could do . . . these things you describe? I want an answer, Caius."

I shrugged helplessly. "What choice do I have, Father? I don't want to believe it, but all the evidence points to Uther. There isn't even another suspicious-looking person in the place!"

"Have you verified that?"

"What? That there are no other suspects? Of course I have, Father. Everyone who was on duty that night, everyone who was awake or astir or abroad at all has been questioned thoroughly and his story checked. There is no person other than Uther whose movements and activities cannot be accounted for."

"Where is Uther?"

"You tell me, Father. Where is he? Why has he disappeared now? Earlier or later would have been acceptable, but he left minutes after the girl and he has not been seen or heard from since."

"What is this girl to you?"

"To me?" I was surprised. "Nothing. Nothing at all. I have had no dealings with her, other than to have her removed from Lucanus's quarters that night."

"Is she pretty? Attractive?"

"What does that have to do with anything? Attractive? No, she is not attractive. She is plain, thin, unappealing. Singularly unattractive, as a matter of fact."

"You are angry with her. Why?"

"What?" I thought about it and realized that I was angry at the girl. "I don't know why I'm angry at her. It's not her fault, really. I resent her because if she hadn't been where she was, when she was—at any point—none of this would have happened."

"Perhaps, perhaps not." He was silent for a moment, and I wondered what he had meant by that. Then he crossed to the table he had been writing at and picked up a knife that lay there. He balanced it in his hand and then threw it hard at the closed door, where it stood thrumming in the solid wood. He went to it, pulled it out and examined the point, all the while evidently thinking deeply. Finally he turned back to me. "Here," he said, lobbing the knife to me, hilt first. "I brought this back for you. It's balanced for throwing . . . cleverly. One complete turnover every twenty paces, if you loft it correctly." He was silent as I examined the knife closely, and then he asked, "Have you ever heard of giving anyone the benefit of the doubt?"

"You mean Uther?" I looked him straight in the eye. "I've already done that by getting rid of the four women. I've also done it by keeping my suspicions to myself, except in the case of Titus. He had to know if I was to have his help. My problem with the benefit of the doubt, Father, my only problem, is defining the doubt. I'm not sure I have any."

"Of course you have. If you had none, you would not be so upset."

I nodded, accepting the truth. "You're right. Of course I have. But my doubts are all emotional. The evidence I have to consider is not. The hard facts destroy all room for doubt."

"What hard facts? You have none." He left me gaping at that while he sat down again at his table. "The only facts you have are these." He raised one finger for each of the points as he made them. "The girl was assaulted. You moved thereafter to protect her. Those are the only facts. Explanations of what happened between the girl's quitting the room and being found next morning are guesses . . . pure conjecture. You have no facts there."

"But the evidence—"

"What evidence? None of that, either, except the girl's injuries. Nothing to indicate who, when or why."

"Yes I have! Uther—"

"Uther . . ." He cleared his throat again, his frustration with his own voice more apparent than I had seen it in a long time. "Uther left shortly after the girl. That's all you know. Everything else you feel . . . or believe . . . is based upon your own interpretation of the circumstances."

I dropped my eyes to the knife in my hand and flung it hard at the door. It hit flat and rebounded almost to my feet and I sat staring down at it unseeingly.

When my father spoke again, his voice was gentle. "As I said, you have to loft it correctly. A matter of balance, Cay. Everything else is, too. Admit it. All you have to point towards Uther is your own interpretation of the circumstances that surrounded this event. It was an awful event . . . not condoning it in any way, shape or form. The perpetrator will be punished. If it was Uther, he will find no leniency in me. But you are a long way from proving complicity, let alone guilt, in my eyes. Your interpretation is no more than that . . . not provable fact. You can only prove that Uther left the room after the girl left, and by your own admission he did not seem to be in pursuit of her."

I picked up the knife and weighed it in my hand, giving myself time to digest what he had said, fighting against an urge to scream to him that he had not been there, had not seen what I had seen. As frustration welled up in me I threw the knife again at the door, this time hammering the point into the wood a good half-inch. I went then and worked the point free, making myself calm down before I faced my father again.

"Very well, Father. I admit the truth of what you say. I have only my own interpretation of what I saw and heard. So? Help me, then! How would you interpret the evidence as you see it?"

"In a total absence of witnesses, I would not." He saw my retort taking shape and forestalled it with a raised hand. "Total, I said, Caius, total! We have a witness. We can prove the truth. The girl will know. She may not know, perhaps, who attacked her . . . if it wasn't Uther . . . but she *will* know whether or not it *was* Uther!" I stood there with my back to the door, feeling the tension roiling in my stomach.

"You did the right thing, Caius, in removing her." A long pause. "As a matter of fact, you seem to have done all the right things. You did well." He nodded towards the chair I had been sitting in. "Sit down. I want to tell you a story. Might prove the point I am trying to make." He got up again and went to tell the guard outside his door that he did not wish to be interrupted, then he came back and seated himself at the table where he pressed the heels of his hands together and examined his open palms minutely. He sat that way for a few moments and then pursed his lips and looked at me quizzically, a crease that was not quite a frown between his brows. I sat unmoving, waiting for him to begin, and when he did, there was something new in his voice. I cannot explain what it was, and at the time I was almost unaware of it, except that I found myself hanging on his every word, having lost all awareness of his speaking difficulties.

"Caius . . . ?" he began. His voice tailed away uncertainly, then he cleared his throat abruptly and grinned at me. "The story I'm going to tell you may shock you . . . but only because it happened to me and I am your father. Had it happened to another man, you might be able to accept his version of it without comment or judgment, although I doubt you would. I know that if I were to hear it . . . my instinct would be to disbelieve. But I am your father, and it did happen to me. I want you to have no doubt of that. It happened."

I wondered what was coming, but he did not keep me waiting. "I took this wound in the throat the year you were born. Did you know that?" I nodded, and he went on, "I almost died from it . . . I should have. It was a bad one. I can remember that, as a boy, you were afraid of me, frightened by my voice. I used to see it in your eyes . . . Over the course of the years, however, you have grown accustomed to the sound of it until now you hardly notice its strangeness. Am I correct?" Again I nodded and he smiled a small, thin smile. "Then again, perhaps I am simply speaking better as I grow older, I don't really know and have no way of judging. But for the first three years after I took that arrow in the mouth, Cay, I did not speak a word. I wrote . . . everything. And I developed hand signals so that eventually my officers and men could understand and obey any order instantly. But that's beside the point. What I am getting at is this: During my convalescence from that wound, I strangled a man to death with my bare hands. He tried to kill me, was trying to kill me when I finished him." I shifted in my chair. I had read a reference to this in my uncle's books, but I knew nothing of the story.

"I was wounded in a skirmish with the northern Picts who had come down over the Wall when it fell for the last time that year. They had penetrated further south than we had expected and we ran into them sooner than we had thought to. One of them put an arrow into my mouth. It was open at the time. I was shouting orders . . . Anyway, that was the end of the fight as far as I was concerned, and it should have been the end of me, too. Titus took over from me and broke them and sent them back to the north licking some deep wounds. We were in north Britain, as I've said, close to the town of Lindum . . . between there and Danum, as a matter of fact. No one expected me to live, but I surprised them all and they finally left me at the villa of one Marcus Aurelius Ambrosianus, a noble Roman of ancient family who had retired from public life in Rome itself to live in his villa here in Britain. He was an old and noble man in the way that few of his compatriots were noble in those days."

He broke his narrative at that point to rise and open a small chest, from which he withdrew a flask of mead and two horn cups. "It's early," he said, "but talking this much makes my throat dry and sore." He poured for both of us and handed one cup to me before sitting down again and sipping at his mead, holding it in his mouth and allowing it to trickle slowly down his throat. "That's good," he murmured, taking another sip. "Well, as you know, our own lineage is not petty. Ambrosianus made me welcome in his house and had his people aid my own in caring for me. I knew nothing of his kindness, for I was at death's door and lay that way for more than a month. They fed me on liquids, through tubes of animal intestine that our sawbones inserted in my throat by way of my nostrils. Everyone looked on me as a living miracle. I should have died immediately. I survived. I should have died later, of starvation, since I could not eat. I survived again, thanks only to that mad physician! And do you know I can't even remember his name today?"

"Did you lose much weight? You must have."

"Aye, I did, of course, but not as much as you might think. He kept feeding me almost constantly—strong broths, milk and honey, even ale! I was no Hercules by the time I finally started eating slops of mushed bread in hot milk, but neither was I skeletal. Anyway, my story . . . One night, in the middle of the night, I awoke, or half awoke, to find that there was someone in the room with me. I saw a shape in the dimness at the bottom of my cot and I saw a sword being swung at me. I rolled somehow, I don't know where I found the strength or the speed, and the blade only caught me in the side. My attacker fell on me and I grabbed him by the throat and began to choke him with all the strength I had. The effort brought on pain the like of which I had never felt, but I hung on to him and squeezed until I could bear no more and fainted.

"A short time later, I was told, someone looked into my room to check on me as they did every night, twice a night, and found me with my hands locked around the neck of my host, Marcus Aurelius Ambrosianus."

I felt my chest tighten in horror. "Ambrosianus? But why? He was an old man, you said!"

"He was sixty-nine, and feeble."

"But why would he do such a thing?"

"Good question, and one that everyone was asking, including me."

"Had he gone mad? Insane? Just like that?"

My father shrugged, his face expressionless. "You tell me. That's what the verdict was. I had never met the man, not while I was conscious at any rate. I had been a guest in his house for more than three months and in all that time I had not stirred from my bed. He had dropped in to visit me a few times during the first month of my stay with him, but I was always asleep or unconscious and so he stopped coming.

"The previous day, it seems, he had been seen sharpening his sword. And he had been behaving strangely, avoiding his family and his servants and hiding in his rooms for several days before that. There was never any question of my innocence in the affair, you understand. When they found me I was still all tangled up in my bedclothes and bleeding from the slash in my side. They found a lamp burning on the floor of the passageway around the corner from my room, and the scabbard of his sword where he had left it in his own room ... The evidence was conclusive. He had lost his sanity and plotted my death far enough in advance to have taken his sword from where it hung in his day-room, making sure the edge was sharp enough to kill with. Then he had waited until the middle of the night, unsheathed the sword, left the scabbard on his bed and crept to my room, leaving his lamp behind him in the corridor so that its light would not awaken me, and so that he could make his way back quickly to his own room after killing me."

I felt stunned. "But it makes no sense, Father? Why you?"

"It made no sense to anyone, Cay, but insanity has its own sense. I was congratulated on my reflexes, ill as I was, and the whole matter was hushed up. I began to regain my strength very quickly after that and was out of bed within fifteen days. Fifteen days after that I was back on duty. Garrison duty, of course. I was still too weak to ride and I could not talk."

"Why didn't they retire you?"

"They tried. I wouldn't let them. Remember, I had no superiors. I was Stilicho's deputy in Britain, and Stilicho was Regent of the Empire. By the time they complained to him it was too late. We were recalled to fight against Alaric and his Visigoths and they needed every available man, even mute officers."

I was nonplussed and dissatisfied with the inconclusiveness of his tale. And I was disappointed. If there were any parallel with our present situation, it had escaped me. "That's quite a story, Father, but what has it to do with Uther's case?"

He smiled at me, a slow, humourless smile. "Nothing, on the surface, Caius. Everything underneath. We were talking of evidence and of circumstances. In Uther's case the circumstances point to his guilt. If it were not for the circumstances that sent him out of that room with a motive to hurt the girl, there would be no question of suspecting his involvement in such filth."

"So?" I said, tentatively. "That's a big circumstance."

"Aye. It is. So be it. Marcus Ambrosianus made the attempt on my life and died for it. He was convicted *post mortem* of insanity because the circumstances surrounding his actions dictated that he had to be insane. I had done him no wrong. But consider this, if you will. How can I put this?" He plucked at his lower lip, then continued. "I had been in his house for more than three months. He was an old man. He had a beautiful young daughter of perhaps thirteen, fourteen, no more. I had heard my physicians speak of her in wonder. Apparently her hair was so white it appeared to be silver. They told me she was a real beauty, the type that men fight over. Now, you have to understand that, although I was badly wounded, I was not out of action in other respects. My wound was to my mouth and neck. The rest of my body was functioning normally by the end of a month. I wasn't much older then than you are now. You understand me?"

I nodded. "Did you ever see the girl?"

"No, but she had been in my room, and I had heard her voice. She came with her servants on a couple of occasions. Anyway, I had been having dreams . . . recurrent dreams. Always the same, and always very . . . pleasant. I slept very heavily every night, but one night I dreamed that I awoke to find myself being, well, ridden's the best word to describe it, I suppose, by a woman. I couldn't see her through my bandages and I couldn't move. She took me to completion and was gone, without a sound. I slept again and when I woke, I remembered and checked myself to see if it had really happened, but there was no sign of anything having occurred. It had been pleasant, extremely so, as I said, but it was a normal enough dream, and I dismissed it . . . Several nights later it happened again, and again there was no sign of anything having taken place; in fact, this second time, I wasn't sure if I had had the dream or not. It happened again about a week later, and in case you are beginning to think I am wasting your time, let me reassure you that I am not. Thereafter, it happened every night for a week and then every second night for another week. On some of these occasions I was barely aware of the dream, on others it was quite vivid. And on one particular night, when my bandages had been removed, there was a moon and I saw my dream mistress."

"His daughter!"

"No, and I was quite disappointed, because I had convinced myself she was the dream mistress. But this was a stranger. A true dream-woman. I had never seen her before. I didn't see her clearly, but I saw enough to know that I did not know her. She was merely a woman in a dream."

"And the dream never changed?"

"Never. I would struggle awake to find myself sheathed in her. I never remembered going to sleep again."

"Did you tell anyone?"

He smiled at me ironically. "What? That I was having erotic dreams?"

"So? What happened?"

A brief headshake, then, "Nothing. The dreams stopped, and I forgot them. About a week or so later, my host attacked me."

I blinked at him, frowning. "You never dreamed that dream again?"

"Never. From the night of the attack, I started sleeping more lightly, as you might imagine. I heard every sound in that house. My strength started to come back to me more and more quickly and, as I've told you, I was out of there in a matter of weeks."

"What happened to the daughter?"

"She left, after the funeral, to live with relatives in Danum. I never saw her again."

"So what is the point of the story? How did the old man find out you were dreaming of his daughter? Was it witchcraft?"

He snorted. "Aye, it was, of a kind. He never did find out I dreamed of his daughter. He never knew I dreamed." My father sucked in a great breath through his nostrils. "There is, however, a sequel to the tale. Many months later, shortly before I left Lindum to return to Londinium prior to setting sail for Italia, I saw a woman who resembled my dream-woman so much that it astounded me. We were in a crowded market-place and I saw her over the heads of the crowd between us. I tried to reach her but could not. I then tried to follow her, at least, but I lost her among the throngs of people in the street, so I went back to the market and found the merchant at whose stall she had been buying trinkets. I wrote him a note, asking him who she was." He looked me in the eye. "The fellow couldn't read. And I could not speak. I had to find someone who could do both. It turned out she was the young widow of Marcus Ambrosianus. She was pregnant."

I felt the small hairs on my arms and at the back of my neck prickle in horror and it must have showed on my face, for he barked his short, abrupt laugh. "That shakes you, eh? It shook me, too, at the time. That woman was black with the guilt of murder and I was the instrument she used, and yet the circumstances did not include her at all. The old man may have been mad with grief and wounded pride, but he was no more insane than I was.

"I told you they fed me with tubes. I had been drugged, through my food, every night and used like a stud bull, but Ambrosianus could not have known that ... Somehow, he found out that his wife was amusing herself with me, and under the circumstances he had no other option than to believe that I was her willing partner." He paused for a moment, looking at me keenly before continuing in a clipped, emphatic voice. "You must understand I am not denying that I might have been perfectly willing, had I had any say in the matter, but the old man interpreted the evidence of his own senses and concluded that I was putting horns on him in his own house while enjoying his hospitality. Had I been him, I might have handled it a little differently, but the whoreson in that bed would have been dead!" He leaned over the table and took the knife from my hand. "How would you have interpreted the 'hard facts' had you been him, Caius?"

I was chagrined, my voice reduced to a whisper by the enormity of what I was only now realizing and appreciating. "I see what you mean, Father."

"I hope so. And don't lose sight of the fact that I said I might have been her willing partner, given the chance. The point is I didn't have the chance—or the choice. In spite of all the evidence to the contrary, in the final analysis I was not guilty of the sin for which he condemned me."

I dropped my face into my hands and combed my fingers across my scalp, heaving a deep breath. "So where does that leave us with Uther?"

The voice that answered me was gentler than I had ever known it. "Waiting to see how the girl reacts when she is well again and you confront him with her."

"And if he is guilty?"

"Then he pays the price."

"And?"

My father tossed back the remnants of his mead and stood up, reaching for his helmet, and indicating that our conversation was over. "And nothing, Caius. You know as well as I do, the price for violation of a woman in my command is death."

XI

To this day, I find it hard to believe that the confrontation between Uther and Cassandra never did occur. I have no explanation that a rational judge could accept as perfectly plausible. It simply worked out that, for one reason after another, the two were never brought face to face in my presence.

The first and most important of these reasons was that I was provided with genuine grounds for more than reasonable doubt of Uther's guilt by no less a person than my Aunt Luceiia, who had no suspicion of any suggestion of Uther's involvement in the matter.

I was summoned to her quarters on the afternoon of the day my father told me his story, and I went to meet her feeling guilty over my recent neglect of her. Aunt Luceiia was a very old woman by this time and she seldom ventured beyond "the family rooms," as she called her living quarters. From the age of six or seven, through the descriptions in my uncle's books, I had known another Luceiia. Therein I had met her when she was twenty-five, before she became wife to Publius Varrus, and thus she had remained in his writings over the years, unmarred and unimpeded by their passage. In reality, however, more than forty-five years had passed since then, and although the Luceiia Britannicus who lived today showed more than a slight resemblance to the raven-haired beauty of those writings, her hair was now snowy white and her face, still beautiful with its high-cheeked, sculpted lines, was deeply etched by the passage of time. I had not seen her since the day we returned from patrol, when I had stopped by to pay her the obligatory call to mark our safe return. I found her this afternoon, sitting in the light from the glazed window that was her greatest pride, a far more splendid aperture than the one in my hut, being made from four large and carefully fitted sheets of glass so fine that it was almost fully transparent.

As soon as she heard my footsteps, she turned to me and waited with upraised arms for her kiss. I embraced her and she squeezed me fondly. "Oh, you feel good when you're not all wrapped up in armour! I forbid you ever again to wear armour when you visit me, although I suppose that means I'll never see you at all, now that I've given you an excuse."

I took the rebuke as it was intended, gently. "I'm sorry, Auntie. I know I've been neglecting you, but I've been really busy. There's much happening."

She released me from her embrace but continued to hold my upper arms, leaning back slightly to gaze up into my face. "God, how those words sound familiar! That was Publius Varrus's favourite song! But at least he did come home to me, from time to time. He was not like you, staying away and breaking an old woman's heart while he tried to break a young one's hymen."

"Aunt Luceiia!"

"Don't Aunt Luceiia me! I've heard all about you, young man. And you needn't pretend to be shocked, either. One of the few privileges of being an old woman is that you don't have to worry about what people think of you, and another is that you can still remember what it's like to be young. Would you rather have me pretend that I don't recall what life is like? Or that I have never known passion or a man's love? That would dishonour me, as it would Publius Varrus. Here!" She grasped me by the wrist and pulled me down towards her. "Kneel down, boy, I have things to say to you."

Smiling, I knelt in front of her and she leaned close to me, directing her words straight into my eyes. "I—am—*alive!* Do you believe that, Nephew?"

I laughed aloud. "Of course I believe it, Auntie. What's the matter? Don't you?"

"Oh yes, Nephew, I believe it, but there are too many people around here who do not seem to. They all tippy-toe around me as if I'm not here, or as if I'm asleep, or dangerously ill, and they are afraid of disturbing me. Even worse, some of them seem to think I am a piece of furniture that remains in the spot where it is placed and is not supposed to communicate anything other than its presence—and that mutely! Hmm!" She nodded her head and stamped her foot emphatically. "But I know what goes on around here," she continued. "More than most people think I know. For one thing, I know about that poor girl in the stables."

My heart almost stopped at the unexpectedness of this. I looked at her for several heartbeats, trying to mask my dismay while she grinned at me with a look of pure triumph. How had she found out? And how much? I forced my voice to remain calm, as I asked, "What do you know, Auntie? What about her?"

"I know who did it."

I swallowed the sudden lump in my throat. "Then you know more than anyone else. Who was it?"

"Remus."

"Who?" The name meant absolutely nothing to me.

"Remus. The priest."

"What priest, Auntie?"

"The strange one. You know! Remus, the one with the cold eyes. He is an evil man, that one."

I took a deep breath. "Aunt Luceiia, I have no idea of who, or what, you're talking about."

"Of course you do, Caius, or you've simply forgotten him. I am talking about the priest, the Christian priest they call Remus. At least, he calls himself a priest. You met him here, the day you got back from your last patrol."

I remembered then that there had been a priest in the room when I had last called, but I had paid no more attention to him than I would to any other cleric, which is to say I had ignored him. Aunt Luceiia was always being visited by ecclesiastics on the search for alms and charity, and I had long since stopped paying attention to any of them. They were simply a fact of Aunt Luceiia's life. She was a very religious woman. I swallowed again, hard.

"You called him evil. Why would you say that about him?"

"Because he hates women."

I began to relax, feeling a superior smile invade my face. "Come now, Auntie! How does that make him evil? I can think of a dozen men I know who have no liking for women." Ludo's face had popped into my mind immediately.

"Caius, listen to me," she snapped, utterly impatient with my male obtuseness. "Listen to what I am saying. I know men, and what they like and dislike. That one hates women. He cannot conceal his hatred. He tries to dissemble it, but it comes out. I am not suggesting the man is effeminate; I am saying he is depraved."

I was frowning by this time. "Auntie, I remember seeing him, but I don't remember anything about him. Who is he? Where will I find him? And why would you think he could do such a thing? I mean, disliking women, even hating them, is one thing, but beating a girl almost to death for no reason other than that is another matter altogether. Particularly if the man is a Christian priest."

Aunt Luceiia sat erect and began to pleat a fold in her gown, looking down at her hands almost primly. "You know Bishop Patricius?" I nodded, and she continued. "He is a pleasant man, and well-meaning, but he is not half the man his predecessor, Bishop Alaric, was." Alaric had been a dear and lifelong friend to my great-aunt and all her family and I knew him well from their writings. "I saw that the first time I met him, but I could not condemn him for that. God makes very few Alarics. Patricius will be an able enough bishop, but not an inspiring one. He lacks the human insight Alaric had.

"Anyway, Patricius came here to visit me, and he brought this Remus with him. I did not like him then. He disturbed me, but I said nothing to Patricius. Remus returned that same day you and Uther did, and I sent him away. I am not normally discourteous or inhospitable, but he offended me deeply and so I banished him. I told him to leave my house and this fort immediately and never to return. I threatened to call the guards and have him escorted from the main gates, but he left before I could do so."

I was impressed. The man must have been a boor indeed to

have such an effect on my aunt, who was the most gentle-natured person I had ever known.

"What did he do to offend you so deeply?"

"He was himself, that is all. He refused to accept a drink from the hands of one of my serving girls. He dashed the cup from her hands and told her to stay away from him, that she was unclean! Unclean, Caius! In my house!"

"I see. So what did you do then?"

"I threw him out. Told him to leave immediately, not just my house, but Camulod itself. He was unwelcome here and would remain so."

"And you threatened to call the guards?"

"Yes."

"But you didn't?"

"No." She shook her head. "I told you, there was no need to. He left."

"And? That was all of it?"

"No, not quite. That was all that happened, but there was something else that I dismissed at the time because it was unimportant: He walked with a slight limp, and instead of a staff, he leaned on a curious stick, strongly made and shaped to fit his hand."

"Sweet Jesus! Why have you waited so long to tell anyone this?"

She threw up her head, in mute protest at my outraged tone, her face betraying a strange mixture of resentment and guilt, and the asperity of her immediate response showed me how deeply conscious she was of having said nothing about this earlier. "Because I did not know until this afternoon that the girl had been beaten with a stick. When I heard that, I sent for you at once. It was late in the afternoon when this man Remus left here. Almost dusk. I think now he might have lingered in the fort and spent the night in the stables."

"Might have!" I was on my feet. "Auntie, you did well to make the association with the stick and tell me this. How well, you may never know. But I wish you had screamed for your guards at the time this happened. Excuse me now, I have to find this man." I kissed her on the cheek and almost ran out of there.

A search of the entire fort, backed up with intensive questioning, produced only five people who had seen this priest, and all of
them had seen him on the way to Aunt Luceiia's quarters. No one
had seen him leave again, and no one had seen any sign of him
after that. I sent out patrols to scour our entire territory in search
of him, but it was hopeless. He had had three days and three nights
to remove himself and we found no trace of him, nor was anyone
resembling him ever seen again in our lands. Proof of his existence
had, however, established reasonable doubts of Uther's guilt in my
mind, and I was glad of them. There was another suspect, the only
one, as far as Aunt Luceiia was concerned, and I did not under-
value her judgment.

Notwithstanding all of that, a secondary reason for my failure
to confront Uther with Cassandra was the fact that life in Camulod
quickly returned to normal, which meant that a messenger arrived,
begging our help against a raiding party of Saxons to the south-east.
My father had just returned from a patrol sweep, and so I was sent out
with a flying column to do what I could against the raiders. They were
long departed, safely back at sea by the time we arrived, however,
so after remaining for a day with the villagers, doing what we could
to help put their lives together again, we headed back to the fort.

Uther had returned during my absence, offering no explanation of where he had been, but accompanied by twenty of his
father's bowmen, and had already left again, this time on a routine
sweep of our territories in the south-west. I was glad to have missed
him by several hours, for even with my reasonable doubts established, I still did not relish the thought of meeting him face to face
with my remaining concerns unresolved.

"How was he?" I asked my father.

"The same as ever, just Uther. No guilt in evidence, if that's
what you mean."

"That's what I mean. Did you tell him the story?"

"I did, yes."

"How did he react?"

"Shock, and concern. Both, I felt, quite genuine. But he didn't believe the story of her magical disappearance. He knew you had something to do with it."

"How could he know that?"

"He didn't *know* anything, Cay. He merely said it smelled like one of your tricks."

"What tricks?" I remember the injured innocence in my voice before the next thought occurred to me. "You didn't tell him how we did it, Father? Did you?"

"No, I did not, nor did he ask me."

"I wonder if he asked Titus?"

"I asked Titus that. He didn't."

"So," I shrugged my shoulders, hitching my armour so it hung more comfortably, "shock, concern and no guilt. Good for Uther." I shook my head. "I'll be glad when this affair is over, one way or the other."

The next day I rode out to the valley to check on Cassandra, hoping to find her much improved. She was. I could see that the moment I opened the door of the hut. She was sitting up against the wall, feeding herself with a spoon from a bowl that Daffyd held for her. I looked around the interior of the tiny room.

"Hello, Daffyd. Where are the boys?"

"Hello, yourself, Princeling. They are gone. I sent them home days ago. They were driving me mad, cooped up in here like a couple of randy weasels."

"How is she?" She was staring at me over Daffyd's shoulder and her eyes were enormous, far bigger than I remembered. The bruising had begun to heal, and her whole face was now a mottled, yellow colour, tinged with blue in places. There were a couple of small scabs on her eyebrows, and around her mouth where her lips had been split open.

"She is recovering. Don't you think she looks better?"

"Aye, she does. How are her teeth?" I did not know what had prompted me to ask that.

"Oh, she'll bite again. They are all still there. Two were a little loose, but they are stiffening. She's young and she's healthy and mending fast."

"Good. Any broken bones?"

"No, and her eyes are fine, before you ask. But she is deaf, and mute, as we suspected. Here, come over here and hold this bowl for her. I have to make water."

I took the bowl and he went outside and I heard the gush of his urine against the wall of the hut. Up close, the girl's face was a sight to marvel at: it was one enormous bruise, from brow to chin. Her eyes were fixed on mine, and she made no move to resume eating from the bowl. I moved it slightly towards her, indicating that she should continue to eat, but she just stared at me and her eyes filled with tears, throwing me into a state of consternation. Women's tears had always unnerved me and, with this woman in particular, I was totally at a loss as to what I should do. I stared, appalled at the great drops of liquid that seemed to hang forever on her lashes before plummeting down her yellowed cheeks, and then, looking around frantically for something to dry them with, I found a cloth of some kind lying beside me and snatched it up, moving clumsily to pat the wetness from her face. She flinched at the contact and, as I realized how painful her face must be, I flinched, too, in sympathy, and then she smiled at me through her tears and my stomach turned right over.

I had never seen her smile before, nor had I ever seen a smile to equal this. It transformed her whole face, lighting it up from within, bruised and discoloured as it was, and changing it into a thing of ethereal beauty. I was undone on the spot. Even today, decades later, I can remember realizing that that tremulous, slow, painful smile had ensured that I would never seek a smile from any other woman. Even the fact that the movement stretched her tender, healing lips and made her wince again in pain did nothing to disenchant me. I was already lost. She dropped her eyes to the bowl I had abandoned, and I picked it up again and held it out to her. She began to eat again, or sip, as delicately as a fawn drinking from a pool. I lost all track of time and sat there, rapt, until the bowl was empty, when she tapped it with her spoon and smiled again, bringing me back to awareness.

"I thought you thought her ugly, boyo?" Daffyd's voice came from right behind me, but I didn't take my eyes from her yellow face.

"I did, Daffyd, but I had never seen her smile. I must have been blind."

"Aye, or preoccupied, perhaps. Anyway, from the way she's looking at you, she doesn't find your face too frightening."

"Hmm." I was gazing at her face. "Daffyd, how . . . How are her . . . other injuries?"

"Her body openings? They're healing. She will be fine, in her body, at least. In her mind . . . I just don't know, Merlyn. I've seen women who have been violated in war, some of them brutally. They've taken it in their stride, for the most part. But I have only ever seen two women who were treated like this before, outraged for no apparent reason with what had to be a mindless violence. Neither of them was ever the same afterward."

I felt a chill in the pit of my belly. "What do you mean? In what way? Who did it to them? Was it the same man?"

"No, no, the two were years apart." He moved away from the table and gave his attention to the fire in the small, open hearth, blowing carefully on the embers and then feeding in sticks one at a time until the fire was blazing heartily again. In the meantime, I sat staring at Cassandra, who stared right back. Finally satisfied, Daffyd straightened up and turned back to me.

"The first man was really insane. Completely possessed. Threw himself over a cliff and killed himself and good riddance. The other one, years later, was never caught. Never knew who he was."

"How long ago was this, Daffyd?"

"The last one? Oh, must be ten years gone, now."

"You said the first one was possessed. Do you believe in possession?"

He looked at me severely, quirking one eyebrow. "Anyone who doesn't is a fool."

"Then you believe in evil." Aunt Luceiia had used the word to describe the priest Remus.

"Of course I do. If you believe in good, boyo, you've got to believe in evil."

I was uncomfortable with that, with his loose definition of the idea I was grappling with. I looked again at Cassandra. She was the antithesis of everything with which I was trying to come to grips. I shook my head in a qualified denial of what Daffyd had just said. "No," I said, "the opposite of good is bad, Daffyd. Evil seems to me to be far beyond mere badness. It's something else altogether."

Daffyd was looking at me strangely. "What are you trying to say, Merlyn?"

I could only shake my head. "I don't know, Daffyd. But this . . ." I nodded towards the silent girl on the bed. "It seems to me that anyone who is truly evil must be unfit to live."

"How many such people, truly evil people, do you think there are in this world, boy?"

"Truly evil? I don't know that, either, but there can't be that many. I've never met one." Something ticked in my memory. "Wait, though! I'm wrong. I have met one. One person." My memory was churning now, spinning out a long, connected series of images. "When Uther and I were boys, we met Lot, the son of the Duke of Cornwall. He and Uther fought, and tried to kill each other. I mean, it was no boys' fight, Daffyd. They went at each other with swords and both were wounded. My father dragged them apart before they could kill each other. Thinking of it now, I remember Lot as evil . . . profoundly, unbelievably wicked, through and through, for the sheer pleasure of it . . . almost mindlessly bad, but not endowed with the saving grace of mindlessness, for he knew exactly what he was doing."

"Hmph! Do you feel the same way about Uther?"

"Uther? Gods, no!" I was genuinely shocked.

Daffyd smiled slightly. "I'm glad to hear that, boyo. Lot of Cornwall, eh? Funny, now, you should pick him. You're not the first I've heard say such things about him. He's a bad one, all right. Calls himself King Lot now, he does. Rules out of that fort that his old father built himself after he saw your Camulod. Quite a place, they tell me."

I was intrigued by the tone of his voice at the mention of this fort of Lot's. "Have you seen it? The fort?"

He hunched in scornful dismissal of the suggestion. "No, never been down that way. Better things to do with my time, haven't I? But they built it right on the edge of the sea, I'm told, on the top of an island that's cliffs on all sides. No way to capture it, they say. It's a stronghold, no doubt about that."

"Does it have a name, this stronghold?"

He shook his head. "Not that I know of, but then I don't care, do I, boyo? But by all accounts, it's an unusual place. Perhaps you'll see it for yourself one day."

"Perhaps I will, Daffyd, although I hope not. I should not be welcome there."

"Aye," he grunted, "I dare say you're right. Conquerors are seldom made welcome any place they go."

"Conquerors? Why would you say that? You've just told me the place is impregnable."

"No, boyo," he responded. "You're starting to forget all the lessons I taught you. You've forgotten already how to use your ears. What I said was, "they say there's no way to capture it," but who are *they?* And yet, if people want to pay attention to them, whoever they are, then nobody will even try and the place might never be taken at all, so it would be proved impregnable, wouldn't it? You see?" He was staring at me.

I nodded. "I think so."

"That's good, then, for what I said, and what you thought I said, were not the same thing at all. But I'll tell you one thing, and you should hear me clearly: there's not much good farming land down that way, and if Lot of Cornwall is as big a swine, or a king, as they say he is, he is going to come your way, sooner or later. He has people to feed, so I would say sooner is closer to reason than later. And when he does—notice I'm not saying *if* he does—you are going to have to teach him his place, you mark my words."

XII

Few struggles can be more fruitless than the bitter, silent battles that a man in love will fight with his own meagre store of words. The odes that I wrote in praise of Cassandra and the new view of life she brought to me were pitiful, but I struggled on, blind to the truth: there are no adequate words to describe what I was feeling. Cassandra, on the other hand, had no need of words at all. Hers was a world without words, a world of total simplicity in which her feelings shone clearly through her eyes and permeated her whole being.

After that first occasion when she smiled at me, I made myself stay away from the valley for a whole week. I had to be strict with myself, for each day I seemed to find a hundred and one good reasons for going there. For seven days I was haunted by a vision of those great, grey eyes. By the time I did return, the bruising had faded entirely from her face and I again found myself staring unashamedly at her, wondering how I could ever have thought her plain or unattractive. I stayed for three days on that occasion, and the happiest times of the three days were her mealtimes, when I fed her because she was still too weak to sit up on her pile of skins and eat her food unaided. She seldom looked directly at me and seemed unaware of my constant scrutiny of her face, which had now become the most beautiful thing in my world.

When I returned again, a week later, she was able to walk, although still very weak. From that time on she improved daily until soon there was no sign at all of the injuries she had sustained. Nor was there any sign of the extreme melancholy that had marked her when we first found her crouched by what we could only assume to be the bodies of her parents. She was a complete delight to me.

It was obvious that Daffyd had been her saviour. He alone had brought her back, not merely from the abyss of the injuries she had sustained, but from the mourning that had cloaked her when we found her.

And then, riding towards the valley one morning, eight weeks to the day from the time we had found her, I received the surprise of my life. I was always at pains to vary my approach to the valley. This time I had used the longest route available to me, heading out north from Camulod and swinging east and then southward in a long arc once I was safely out of sight of the walls. This roundabout approach required two more hours in transit than the shortest alternative, and I tended to use it only in fine weather, since it followed no path and called for careful passage through several stretches of low, boggy ground that could be well nigh impassable during or after bad weather. Once started on this particular route, however, I never had to worry about being seen, since my way lay far from the borders of our closest farm, and its inhospitable terrain held no attraction for casual visitors. The greater part of the path I took, apart from the low-lying, boggy areas, was heavily wooded and strewn with huge, fragmented rocks. Only as I began to approach the low hills that contained my valley and its precious secret did the swell of the land begin to breast upward through the covering of trees until I finally found myself riding among grassy slopes above shallow, tree-filled vales.

The early morning sun had grown warm on my shoulders and on my horse's back that day, lulling me until I drifted mindlessly along, paying no attention to the scene around me and allowing my mount to pick his way at his own pace. I was jerked back to awareness, however, by a sudden, half-seen flash of whiteness moving quickly in the valley below me to my right.

My reaction was instinctive, in spite of the instant chaos of my thoughts. I reined in immediately, every muscle tensed to hold myself and my mount immobile as I scanned the area in which I had seen, or sensed, the movement. Exposed as I was on the side of the hill, I found myself on the edge of blind panic, unable to decide what I should do next. I could discern no further movement in the valley below and, aware all at once of the rhythm of my heartbeat pounding in my ears, and struggling against an unreasoning terror of discovery, I fought to control my breathing and my fears. Even had I been seen, I reasoned, no harm had been done and I was still more than a mile, almost two miles, from my destination, so that I yet had a choice of three directions ahead of me, any of which would lead me well away from the hidden valley.

And then, as I hung there, agonizing, the movement flashed again and I saw a human form, white clad, in the valley bottom, running away from me, its passage masked by dense foliage. I caught only a glimpse of the runner, and it may have been the speed with which he disappeared from sight that sent me plunging downhill in pursuit, reins loose, allowing my horse to pick his own way across the sloping hillside. We were quickly down, and I pointed him in the direction of the runner, leaving him free thereafter to choose his own route swiftly and easily among the trees while I concentrated on avoiding low-hanging branches. A swing to the left around a thick-boled oak took us to the lip of a narrow, steep-sided depression that fell away rapidly beneath us as my willing horse launched himself up the sloping edge, his great muscles bunching and thrusting easily until he had driven us upward twenty paces and more above the floor of the depression. There the ground leveled again and I drew rein, searching the cleft below for any sign of my quarry. After the thunderous clatter of my horse's heavy hooves on the rocky, sparsely turfed ground, I could at first hear nothing other than his blowing breath and the creaking of my own saddle and equipment. Gradually I became aware of the deep silence. No bird-song disturbed the stillness and nothing moved anywhere. I was on the point of swinging around to ride down again to look elsewhere when I heard a distant, grunting sound that seemed to come from the only large tree in the small gorge, some hundred or so paces to my left. I looked that way and saw the most astonishing sight.

I had read in my uncle's books of creatures he had seen in Africa that lived in trees and had the ability to climb so swiftly that they seemed to fly among the branches. Now one such creature met my sight, dressed in human clothing, a brief tunic of spotless, brilliant white. Of course, as soon as I had recovered from my initial surprise and adjusted to the distance separating us I realized it was a boy, but never had I seen a boy who climbed in such a manner. As I gazed in amazement, he pulled himself up effortlessly to stand on a stout branch far above the ground, then crouched there, gathering himself, gazing upward and balancing on all fours, before launching himself in a flying leap to grasp another bough above him and swing himself nimbly onto it, spreading his legs and scissoring them to grasp the limb, then gliding fluidly, with no sign of effort, to where he sat astride the branch, at a dizzying height above the rock-strewn forest floor. There, without pausing to look around him, he repeated the entire sequence and so continued, seeming indeed to fly upward, until the limbs of the huge tree grew so closely together that he was able to use them simply as a stepladder, practically running upward to disappear completely among the thick foliage at the apex of the tree.

Although my reason told me that this was simply a boy, when I lost sight of him at last I had to suppress a shiver of superstitious dread, an old and formless fear stirred by remembered tales of dryads and forest sprites. And then as I sat there unmoving, he descended again, dropping from branch to branch and limb to limb as though falling wildly, yet every move and every leap timed and controlled to perfection so that again I felt the stirring of gooseflesh, this time caused by incredulous admiration.

He leaped nimbly to the ground from the lowest fork of the tree and disappeared again among the bushes before I thought to rouse myself and swing my horse around to give chase.

Down and around we thundered, my horse and I, gaining the valley floor and swinging back hard to cover the ground between us and the fleeing boy, and as I rode I wondered who he might be. We emerged at full gallop from the cover of a thick clump of bushes and yet again I hauled my mount to a halt, so that he slid, stiff-legged, his haunches almost on the ground while I stood in my

stirrups in amazement. Before us, the far wall of the ravine in
which we rode rose sheer for thirty paces and more, and on the flat
sward at its feet the boy stood staring upward, his eyes fastened on
the cliff above him. Before I could move, he sprang forward and
began to swarm up the stony, grass-covered face. No more than
thirty paces and a thin screen of leaves parted us, but I knew that
he was unaware of me, having neither seen nor heard my approach.
I kicked my heels into my horse and then, just as it began to move
forward, the boy stopped climbing and looked sideways, allowing
me to see his face for the first time.

It was Cassandra! The realization stunned me. Her name
sprang to my lips and I kicked my horse harder, urging him forward, but she had already made her choice of direction and now her
total concentration was on the cliff face and her climb. I shouted
again, knowing as I did so that she could not hear me. I waved
wildly, but her concentration was absolute. In almost less time than
it takes to describe, she had reached the rim of the cliff and disappeared beyond it without once looking back. But I had had ample
time to look at her, and wonder how I could ever, even from a
hundred paces, have erred in thinking she could be a boy.

Bitterly disappointed by her disappearance—she had vanished beyond the rim of the cliff so quickly that I knew I had no
hope of catching her—yet filled with a glorious elation, I sat there
beneath the stony face of that cliff and thought on her: the clear-
etched muscles of her long, lithe legs below the shortened, tucked-
in skirts of her white tunic, and the shape of her body as she had
paused at several points in her ascent, her weight distributed perfectly, her eyes scanning the rock above her for her next handhold,
had brought an ache to my throat. What kind of girl was this? I
asked myself. How and where had she learned to perform such
feats? Where had she come from? And where might she disappear
to, once she had fully recovered from her injuries? One thing was
frighteningly clear to me. Her body had fully recovered already,
and today I had seen little evidence of any other damage, either to
mind or spirit.

I made my way eventually to the hidden valley, my thoughts and my heartbeat still in turmoil, and found it strangely difficult to approach the small stone hut. She was there, as was Daffyd. When I entered, she looked up at me and nodded, then continued what she had been doing, scraping and curing what I took to be a rabbit skin. She had discarded the white tunic and now wore the simple homespun shift that was her normal dress. Daffyd mumbled at me, and then he, too, continued working on whatever had demanded his full attention that afternoon.

I felt uncomfortable there, even though the concentration shown by both of them left me free to stare at Cassandra as much as I might wish. Her hair, unbound, fell down before her face, obscuring all but the line of her cheekbone on one side. The fullness of a soft breast was a mere suggestion to interfere with my breathing. The line of her thigh beneath her shift was as clean and pure as the arc of a rainbow. I felt guilty and miserable, although to this day I have no idea why that should be so, and soon I took my leave and rode home in a mood that was half misery and half unbearable excitement. I knew she had recovered. I knew that I loved her. And I knew I had no way of telling her, of wooing her, or of keeping her beside me.

Heading back to my quarters one morning, however, on the way from a dawn parade, I was shocked to see Daffyd coming towards me. I gazed at him, wondering what he was doing here in Camulod, so far away from his ward.

"Daffyd," I said, hearing the incredulity in my voice. "What are you doing here? Where's Cassandra?"

"At home, boyo! In the valley."

"Alone? What are you thinking of?"

"I'm thinking of the work I have to do, and the tasks I have been neglecting."

"What? What d'you mean?"

He winked at me and shook his head in reproof. "Merlyn, I said I'd stay with the girl as long as she needed me. She doesn't need me now and there are others, I hope, who do. Mod and Tumac, for a start. Their education has been sadly neglected these past weeks. They'll be wild as the heather by the time I see them again. Probably have to beat them, I will, to get them back into harness."

I was still gaping at him, aware of the movement of people around me and the clatter of hobnailed sandalled boots on the cobbles as the men dispersed from the parade. The sky was cloudless; the day would be hot. A blackbird was singing somewhere close by, and I was almost whispering in my urgency to chastise Daffyd without anyone hearing what I was saying. "But you left her all alone out there?"

He looked at me as though I had lost my wits, and made no attempt to lower his voice. "Out where, boy? She's not 'out' anywhere. She's safe and snug in a stone hut with a fireplace and a strong roof in a valley that's as secret as this place isn't."

Almost panicked by the loudness of his voice, I grasped him by the arm and pulled him aside, to where we could stand in an angle of the walls of a building without being jostled or overheard. "For the love of Jesus, Daffyd, keep your voice down. Remember the girl's life is at stake!"

He freed his arm from my grasp and adjusted the folds of his long cape, glancing casually at the passers-by as he chastised me for my unthinking use of my aunt's prayer which had, on my lips, become an oath. "For the love of Jesus, is it?" he murmured, out of the corner of his mouth. "I am a Druid, boyo. What would I know about the love of your Jesus? But the girl is safe hidden. Nobody is going to bother her there, except perhaps you." He cleared his throat and continued, "She's a strong girl, your Cassandra, and healthy as a horse now, too. No need to look after that one. Not anymore." His expression changed and he smiled at me, stepping close to grip my shoulder with his free hand. "She's happy there in your valley, Merlyn. Perhaps happier than she's been in a long time. Who knows? She has food and a clear pool for fish and for water and she can snare rabbits better than I can. She's happy there. No threats, you see.

"She'll be waiting for you to go and see her. Now the rest is up to you. Remember, though, what she has been through. She trusts

you now, but who knows what she thinks of men in her mind? You
know what I mean? If you can treat her gently, kindly, you might
make a fine, full woman out of her, but run at her like one of your
great, rutting stallions, and I won't be responsible for what you'll
do to her, or she to you. Remember that, Merlyn. There is a young
woman who has been hurt in ways that you and I can't even begin
to imagine, let alone understand. Do you hear me?"

"Aye, Daffyd, I hear you. I know what you mean. Are you sure
she has enough food?"

"Food? That one? She'd charm honey out of the bees! She will
be fine. Next time you pass that way, take her some flour and some
salt. That's all she'll need. And don't worry about her. She has a home
and it's the perfect place for her. Leave her to enjoy it for a while
and then go and see her. But be careful, Merlyn. Don't hurt her, boy."

That hurt me. "Do you think I could?"

"I know you could, without intending any harm at all, so be
careful with her. Now I have to go, and so, by the dress of you,
do you."

"No, I'm done. I've been on parade. Now I have some free time
before I have to meet with my father."

"Then go your way, boyo, and let me go on mine."

I thanked him again and watched him depart, then returned to
my quarters, my mind full of one single truth: the woman who had
become the centre of my existence was alone in my valley, unknown
to anyone else in the world except Daffyd, Mod, Tumac and my
father, and she was waiting there for me.

I had loved that tiny, secret valley all my life, and now it had
become the home of my love and nothing could have been more
appropriate. During the course of that morning, the people I dealt
with must have wondered if I was ill, for I was oblivious of where
I was and what I was doing. My valley and its precious secret stole
the whole of my concentration. It never left my mind for a moment,
and a whimsy that I had been toying with for more than a week
became a reality. It was *my* valley, my secret, sacred place, with its
silent, sliding waterfall and its deep pool, its moss-covered cliffs,

rich grass and stately, screening trees, nestled in the central bowl of the hill there, and I felt that it should have a name that reflected its peaceful solitude and its mystical seclusion. I named it Avalon, after the fabulous place of legend.

That same day, shortly after noon, filled with an almost painful anticipation that left me unable to bear the tedium of my daily duties any longer, I delegated the last of my tasks to a subordinate and left Camulod, riding far south before doubling back and around, away from curious eyes, to the valley and Cassandra.

My intestines seemed to have tied themselves in knots as I approached the entrance to the valley and began to descend between the high banks of bushes that lined the path all the way to the bottom. I had spent the entire journey trying to visualize the expression that would come into her eyes when she saw me. Would they show pleasure or anger—or indifference, which would be even worse? The doubts that assailed me left me feeling sick. In vain I tried to reassure myself that I was merely being foolish, acting like a callow, lovesick boy. But reason had no place among my hopes and fears. At times I would imagine her face lighting up with pleasure at my approach, and then I felt light-headed and elated, but for the most part, I saw her face within my mind registering an endless range of frowns, bleak looks and glances of displeasure and resentment.

All of my agonizing was as nothing, however, beside the despair that swept over me when I reached the valley bottom, because the vale lay empty and abandoned-looking. No smoke rose from the fireplace to spread out above the water, and the entire scene had that air of emptiness that bespeaks an utter lack of human presence. Stunned with disbelief, I felt a massive emptiness within me that resonated with bereavement. My horse, sensing no guidance from my slackened muscles, moved forward slowly towards the tiny building and came to a halt some paces from the door, where he stooped his head and began to crop while I sat gazing hopelessly at the mossy red roof tiles of the hut. The sound of tearing grass was loud in my ears, amplified by the silence that lay heavily around me.

Stiff-legged, I kicked my feet free of the stirrups and dismounted, resting my full weight against my horse's shoulder before straightening up and moving to the door of the hut. It swung open slowly at my touch and I stepped into the dimly lit, shadow-filled interior, so sure of finding it barren that I almost missed seeing the cloth that lay upon the small table, tented and mounded by the shapes it covered. A half-pace took me within reach of the table and I leaned across it to remove the cloth, uncovering a wooden platter, a small, sharp knife, an earthen cup, a squat, covered jug of wine, a partial loaf of bread and a crescent of dried sausage. Uncomprehending, I asked myself why, having prepared a meal, she would have left the valley without eating it. It took some time for the realization to filter through my confusion that she had not run off, and that this meal was awaiting her return. Instantly my despair turned to elation, so that I startled my poor horse as I burst through the door of the hut again, throwing it back on its hinges with a crash. She was here, somewhere! Giddy with relief, I reeled around like a drunkard, looking upward to the summit of the hills that hemmed me in, as though I could divine her presence from the air that separated us.

Behind me, I heard a fish jump in the lake, a heavy, clean, plopping sound, and I spun to watch the ripples spreading outward from the spot where it had breached. Then as I watched, another splash occurred mere paces from the first, although this time my gaze was close enough to see that nothing had preceded the sudden, singular sound of the splash—no swirl in the water, no flash of colour, nothing but that solitary, unheralded, plummeting impact upon the water. Alert now, I watched and waited, although for what I could not have said. And then I caught a blur of movement and my eye adjusted to it in time to see the water split again, sundered by a falling stone! Someone was hurling pebbles high into the air from the deep brush on the other side of the water. Keen-eyed now, I watched carefully and saw a movement, and another stone arced high into the air and seemed to hover against the sky before beginning its fall.

I was running along the edge of the water before the stone hit the surface, uncaring that I wore breastplate and greaves. She was there, across the lake, and she was making sport of me. As I rounded the far end of the lake, just before I plunged into the dense greenery of the trees and bushes, I caught another glimpse of movement high on the hillside above me and heard what I took to be a whoop of delight and excitement. Grimly, yet wanting to sing aloud in exultation, I charged onward and up, knowing that she would hear the noise and speed of my approach, and then suddenly becoming crushingly aware that she would not. In mere moments, it seemed, I was close to the top of the steep bank, pulling myself at every step by the stems of the saplings that grew thick among the larger trees, aspen and birch. I stopped and listened carefully, but heard nothing. The silence was profound. I began to move forward more cautiously now, feeling the need to be more circumspect. A pheasant exploded almost from beneath my feet, startling me so that I slipped, lost my balance and sat down heavily, rolling legs over shoulders backward until I came to rest against the bole of a birch tree. This time I distinctly heard a feminine giggle from somewhere above and ahead of me.

Again I gave chase, but that was the last I saw or heard of my quarry, save for the impact of one hard-shot, well-aimed stone that clanged against the back of my armour, pulling me back from the edge of the hilltop surrounding the valley and directing me towards the dense bushes on the hillside at my back. An hour later, frustrated and angry, I gave up the search and made my way back to the hut. My horse was still grazing by the door, but his saddle and blanket had been removed, and now a thin haze of smoke drifted upward from the chimney hole in the roof. Mastering my offended pride and dignity, I drew a deep breath and slowly opened the door.

The hut was still empty. A small fire blazed in the brazier in the hearth. Cassandra had eaten. Now the platter, knife, cup and jug were arranged for my use on the side of the table closest to me, along with the remnants of the bread and sausage.

I ate slowly, smothering my resentment, resolved to wait her

out in patience. But she did not come. Eventually, as the day began
to turn to evening, I gave up and went outside to saddle my horse.
A small posy of yellow flowers lay, bound in a sprig of grass, in the
centre of my saddle's seat. I picked it up and sniffed at it, breathing
deeply of its fragile, sweet aroma, then laid it aside as I resaddled
my mount. I picked it up again before climbing into the saddle and
then sat there for a short time, rubbing the silken petals against my
upper lip. By the time I nudged my horse forward to make my way
home, I felt at peace, satisfied on a number of points, though without proof of any of them: Cassandra was nearby, watching me; she
was self-sufficient and it would be pointless to make any further
attempt to find her; she would appear to me when she was ready to
do so, irrespective of my desires; she was not unkindly disposed
towards me; and she had no intention of leaving the valley. I whistled all the way home to Camulod.

Nothing I have to say will begin to do justice to the love, the
joy or the private splendour of the short years that followed. In the
earliest days, Cassandra became my life and all I wanted out of life,
and I was hers and all she seemed to need. Responsibility, however,
is an inescapable burden of manhood and I had mine, which my
conscience would not let me ignore. Although she and Avalon
comprised my secret life and all my private world, there was also
the world of Camulod, which I could not neglect. Cassandra knew
each time when I must return and she never tried to detain me, but
each time I had to leave her in our valley of Avalon, the parting
grew more difficult for me.

I tried to take her with me only once. I mounted my horse and
lifted her up in front of me and as I placed my arm around her waist
to keep her safe, a vision of Uther holding her just so made me
cringe. This was the day I had sworn to myself I would find out the
truth, for Uther was at home in Camulod and I had come to Avalon
to see this confrontation effected. She leaned back into my arms as
my mount climbed the narrow, tree-lined path from the valley floor,
and there she remained content until we were clear of the bushes
and mounting the rim of the hollow that concealed her home. But

when she saw the distant towers of Camulod on its hilltop, miles away across the valley, and realized that I was bound that way, she stiffened and grasped the reins, bringing my horse to a stop. Gently, she prised my arm from around her waist, and then slipped smoothly to the ground, where she stood gazing up at me. Surprised, and slightly put out, I gestured to her to climb up again, trying to indicate that this was important to me, but it took only one look into the calm, slightly stubborn resolve of her gaze to convince me of what I should have known. Cassandra had no wish to go to Camulod, or even to see it on a distant hill. My heart was filled with love for her, and shame for what our Camulod had come to mean to her.

I decided then and there that Uther's guilt or innocence was not important. It had happened in another lifetime. If I were to face her with him now, and he were guilty, I might be ripping the scab from a barely healing wound. If, on the other hand, he were not the one, I would only have put her in needless mind of what she had endured, and possibly even have placed her in danger once again from the true culprit. She had no need of any of this. I dismounted and left my horse to graze by the side of the path and I held her close as we walked back down the winding, hidden path to Avalon, where she was content to be alone.

And yet, as we walked back down that sheltered path, another thought squirmed, guilty and fully formed, in my mind. If, as I had now come almost fully to believe, Uther was in fact innocent of any violence upon her, I had no wish to expose her to him, or him to her. When I had thought her ugly, she had been fascinated by my gallant cousin and I had been uncaring. Now that I was lost in her beauty, I could not bear the thought of seeing her look at Uther as she had before.

As was my invariable habit on leaving the valley, I turned my horse to leave by the back of the hill, keeping its bulk between me and the fort, making my way around to the south-east. This added another hour to a one-hour journey, but I was more determined now than ever that no eye should ever follow me to Avalon or mark me coming from it. On that particular day I had completed my detour and was approaching the last copse of trees between me and the open valley when I heard a noise that shocked me and made me kick my horse to a gallop within paces.

My father always knew where I was, whenever I was not in Camulod, and we had devised a signal by which he could summon me immediately, if the need arose. There were three high hills around the plain of Camulod. Both he and I knew that there was only one of them that interested me, but we had no wish to betray the fact that I could always be found close to the same spot, so the plan was that in emergency he would send riders to the tops of all three hills, each one carrying one of the shrill screaming stones on a string that Vegetius Sulla had used to silence a noisy Council long before I was born, the singing or screaming stones the barbarians beyond the Rhine used as missiles.

The signal had never been used before, and it was never used again, but when it sounded this time I was already more than two-thirds of the way back to the fort. I put my heels to my horse and was soon galloping up the hillside road, and as I rode up, soldiers came pouring down past me to join the ranks of the army already assembling on the great campus, or training ground, at the foot of the hill. They came in squads and troops, already in formation from the courtyard of the fort, and so I knew that whatever had caused this tumult was momentous. I turned my horse and put it to the hillside, leaving the road to the descending squads, and as I climbed I looked off to my right and saw cavalry approaching from the villa and from the direction of the outlying farms.

My father was already in council with Uther, Titus, Flavius, Popilius the senior infantry centurion, and several others, among whom I recognized Gwynn, the captain of Uric's bowmen from the hills. They all looked up as I strode into the Armoury and I saw that every one of them was in full battle armour. Even in the tension of the moment, I saw that Uther, who stood with his back to me and turned as I approached, wore a new red cloak with a great dragon in embroidered gold on the back of it, and I knew at once who owned the big new standard I had seen out in the courtyard.

"What's going on?" I asked as I crossed the room.

"Merlyn!" Uther's smile was the one I knew and had always loved. "You return by magic! Where have you been?"

"Riding," I snapped. "Father?"

My father nodded an abrupt greeting. "We're being attacked . . . in double force, it seems. Our breeding stock has been raided. Horses stolen. One attack out of the north, from the river estuary—Gwynn brought news of a fleet coming upstream—and one from the south and west."

"The south and west?" I looked at Uther. "But that's . . ."

"Aye, Cousin." He finished it off for me. "Our boyhood friend, Lot of Cornwall. It seems Cornwall is no longer big enough for him."

I remembered Daffyd's words of only months earlier. "What's he after?"

"What he is after and what he will find are two very different things."

My father cut both of us short by slapping the flat of his sword blade on the table. "Gentlemen! We have work to do here and no time for idle chatter. Caius, we know from Gwynn here that a fleet of more than a hundred galleys is landed to the north."

"A hundred!" I was stunned. "That's more than three thousand men!"

"Thank you, that had occurred to us." I subsided, and he went on, "Gwynn thinks they are Hibernian. Whoever they are, they could not have chosen a worse time to hit us. We have already sustained heavy losses in the south-west. The hostile force there is at least four hundred strong—cavalry strong enough to have overrun our outlying farms and to have stolen the herd of horses that was gathered there."

"How do we know this?" I was hoping not to hear what I heard next.

"Because two of our men got away and brought us the news."

"Two? That's all?"

"That is all. The others are all dead."

I could not believe what I had heard. "Father, we had more than two hundred men stationed there!"

"That was yesterday, Caius. Today we have none. However he did it, Lot managed a complete surprise attack in the darkness before dawn. From what the survivors tell me, our men were slaughtered before they could react."

"How did the two survivors escape?"

"They didn't escape. One of them was on his way to the main camp there with dispatches from me. The other was returning from a visit to his dying mother. They met going west and travelled together. They arrived in sight of the camp just after daybreak and saw what had happened."

"How many of the enemy did they count?"

"Approximately four hundred that they could see, all mounted and preparing to move out again, coming this way."

"Were they seen, our men?"

"They don't think so."

I glanced around at the faces of my companions. "What's our plan?"

"We haven't time to do anything too elaborate. Uther and Flavius are riding to meet them with five hundred horsemen. They'll take Lot's people as and when they meet them. It will be our disciplined horse against their lack of discipline."

I grimaced. "We hope! I would think it required some strongly disciplined manoeuvring to surprise our camp there. Who was in charge?"

"Lucius Sato."

"That's what I thought. He was a good man." My mind was fully occupied in grappling with the logistics of what faced us. Finally I nodded, satisfied that I knew what to do. "So Uther and Flavius will tackle Lot's men to the south-west. What about the others? To the north? How much time do we have there?"

My father answered me by looking to Gwynn.

The big Celt shrugged. "We rode hard to get here, and when we left, the fleet was still on the water. They couldn't have landed before yesterday afternoon. That means they can't get here until tomorrow."

I frowned at him. "You mean you didn't see them land? Then how do we know they are attacking us? They may have landed on the northern coast of the estuary. They may be looking for the gold-mines again."

"No." Gwynn shook his head emphatically. "We thought of that. The beacon fires were to be lit if the Scots were coming this way. The fires passed us on the way this morning."

I turned back to my father. "What, then?"

"We leave immediately. If all three thousand of them come this way, we'll stop them in the valley fifteen miles north of here, the one with the bog. It's a natural trap. We'll let them walk in and then spring it shut on them." He turned to Uther and Flavius. "You two can be on your way. Good luck and may Mithras the god of soldiers ride with you."

"Hold!" I stopped them before they could even salute. Both of them turned to stare at me. "Father, why are you only sending five hundred men?"

"Against four hundred? Because it is enough."

"I disagree. And if Uther thinks about it honestly, he will, too. They have four hundred and they're coming this way quickly. Their morale is high, remember, they've already slaughtered one contingent of our people."

My father frowned at me. "What are you trying to say, Caius?"

"I'm not *trying* to say anything. I think we should send Titus's two hundred with Uther and Flavius, too. Seven hundred against four. Give Lot's people a taste of numerical weakness. Then let them try to fight against our tactics in the field. Smash them now, while we have an early opportunity. They don't know we know they are coming. Let's teach them not to invade our Colony. Smash them, Father, now!"

Uther intervened, his face clouded. "We can do that with the troops we have. We need no more."

"Be sensible, Uther," I snapped. "Forget about the glory, and see the perils! These people are dangerous. If Gulrhys Lot has made alliance with the Hibernian Scots we can't afford to let a man of his escape. Take the extra two hundred and hammer him flat."

He looked at my father, who was frowning at me and who now spoke for Uther. "I see your point, but what about the north? We'll need those two hundred horsemen there."

"No we won't, Father. Between your men and mine, we will still have four hundred cavalry. If you want to trap the Scots in the valley, we can bring our four hundred horse behind them and chase them into our hidden infantry. The Scots have no horses. We can hide two thousand infantry and more along the sides of the road out of that valley, among the trees, and have another thousand waiting for them when they crest the hill on the far side. We can hit them front, rear and flanks all at the same time. *If* we arrive there soon enough!"

My father's eyes flashed. "You're right, Caius!" The decision made, he swung to Titus. "Titus, take your command with Uther and Flavius. Among you, wipe Lot from your path. We will take the others in the valley to the north. Now let's move, gentlemen, we have no time to waste." The trumpets started blaring immediately in the courtyard outside as the party began to stream from the room. My father had hold of big Gwynn by the arm and was talking urgently to him.

I stopped beside them. "Father, I have to arm myself. I'll join you in the yard." He nodded and I turned on my heel to walk from the room, and then I hesitated and looked down at my feet. I was standing on the shortest floor board, the one that hid Excalibur. I felt a sudden thrill at the thought of carrying that burnished blade into battle.

"What's wrong, Caius?" My father's voice was impatient.

"Nothing, Father." I started walking again. "I just had a thought, that's all. It's not important."

By the time I emerged at the run from my quarters, trying to fasten my war cloak around my neck, my father and our senior officers were all mounted. I ran to my fresh horse, a huge black, and had my foot in the stirrup when my father called my name. I turned to look at him.

"One moment, Caius." He kneed his horse over to where I stood, so he looked directly down on me. "I meant to mention it at the time, but I was distracted and forgot. One day, about a month ago, while we were standing face to face, discussing something, I noticed that I was almost looking up into your eyes . . ." He smiled, and I saw love and pride in his face. "Almost, I said. Bear that in mind. I don't think I've ever had to look up into anyone's eyes since I was a child, but the fact is, my son, you are now as tall, and every bit as big, as I am." He beckoned to someone, and I turned to see a soldier approaching me with a great black war cloak held across his arms. "We were to have had a ceremony tomorrow," my father continued, "but now is as good a time as any. New standards for yourself and Uther. His is a golden dragon, yours is this." The soldier carrying the cloak swirled it open and presented it to me. The inner lining was white, like my father's own, but across the shoulders of the black exterior a great, rearing bear was depicted in heavy, silver embroidery, its arms flung wide to show its massive claws. It was magnificent. I was speechless, for my father and I had almost quarrelled a short time before over such a creature— he, angry that I had endangered myself rashly by fighting it, and I that he should belittle my single-handed victory over the monster. This was an olive branch.

"Wear it," my father shouted. "Our enemies should grow to fear it as soon as possible." There was a shout of laughter as I unclasped my own plain cloak and the soldier helped me to don my new one. As I fastened it, the soldiers in the courtyard gave a mighty cheer and I felt grand. I stepped up into my saddle and another soldier appeared by my side bearing a shield decorated with a silver bear, and a long, black-shafted spear. I took them and sat very tall and proud on my great, black horse. My father raised his arm again and there was a clatter of hooves as yet another soldier drew near, this one carrying my new standard of black and silver. General Picus dropped his arm, the trumpets blasted, and we rode out through the gates of Camulod, on our way to war again.

From the road outside the gates, we could look down on the

plain beneath us, where our three thousand infantry were already moving out in cohorts of five hundred men each. Dust shrouded our view, but we all knew that we were looking at a phenomenon: the largest armed force our Colony had ever assembled for an aggressive strike. We had two hundred men to avenge, and we meant to succeed.

BOOK THREE

Raptors

XIII

From my lookout at the edge of the little wood I saw the distant figure of my decurion scout emerge from a clump of bushes and wave to me. I spoke over my shoulder.

"There's the signal. They've passed. Let's move up." I kicked my horse to a walk and began to move along the floor of the little ravine-like valley that had hidden us between two ridges. Behind me, four hundred mounted men rode in double file. I crossed the wide, beaten path of the Hibernian Scots who had passed us transversely and counted one hundred more paces before reining in and turning my horse to the left to face the steeply rising ridge. A glance to my left showed my men lined up and waiting for my command. I looked to the top of the ridge before me and made myself count again to one hundred, slowly. I knew what lay on the other side of the ridge and I did not want to commit us too soon. Finally, I gave the signal and we put our horses to the slope and soon arrived at the crest overlooking the valley below. Four hundred of us, a double line of men and horses, two hundred to a line, now straddled the road that the Hibernians had followed down to the valley bottom. I sat there, gentling my horse with my hand on its neck and looking at the scene before me.

Most of the valleys in this part of the country stretched from east to west, widening to the coast. We were now facing south across a valley that was different, deepening as it fell inland away from the coast. It was almost two miles wide from where we sat to the top of the opposite ridge. Thick forest blocked it inland to the east and covered the hillside opposite us, but the hill on our side was bare and green, as was the floor of the valley, which rose gradually towards the sea on our right until the valley itself tapered out among high crags. It was the valley floor that had made us choose this spot for our action; a deathtrap of a place, as my father had said. The roadway ran directly south across the centre of it, from crest to crest, and more than half a mile of it lay on the flat valley floor, flanked on each side by innocent-looking grass that covered deep and treacherous bogs capable of swallowing a troop of horsemen and their mounts and leaving no sign of them thereafter. On the other side of this flat stretch, the road began to rise again to the south, through thickening trees that encroached on it from both sides until the road itself resembled a tunnel. From where I sat, I could see no signs of the two thousand men we had hidden among the trees.

Timing was crucial now. The enemy had to be beyond the point of no return before we moved. They had to be hemmed in by the bogs, so that when we began our charge at their backs, they could not spread out defensively to meet us. We wanted to panic them. But the bogs were as much our enemy as theirs. We had to pull up short of them, and before we did that, we had to make these Hibernians run—up the road ahead of them and through the trees with their two thousand hidden men, and out of the valley to where my father waited with another thousand to receive those who escaped the trap.

I raised my shield arm high, holding it there, gauging my moment and enjoying the strain on the muscles of my arm and shoulder. The enemy force was a great black caterpillar on the road below us, more than half of them already on the road through the bogs. I dropped my arm, our trumpets sounded, and we began to advance at a walk. The effect was instantaneous: those in the rear who heard our trumpets looked back and saw us coming, and even above the noise of our own advance we could hear their shouted warnings to the men in front of them, and could see the worm of panic start to squirm. We broke into a canter, our rear line moving up between the men in front, forming a solid line. The first signs of real disorder below appeared in the rear ranks as the men there began to increase their pace, crowding in on those in front of them. Not all were panicked, however. A number of figures broke from the column and began to organize lines of defence, but they were too late. My timing had been right. The bogs had them. The lines they tried to throw out on their flanks floundered in mud as men slipped and fell helplessly in the sucking muck. And then the rout began in earnest. I had ordered my trumpeters to sound without let-up, and now my men began screaming. Our pace had been increasing steadily and we were now less than three hundred paces from the rear ranks of our quarry, with fifty paces less than that between us and the start of the bogs. Now there was not a man among the enemy who did not know we were behind them. The increasing pressure from the rear transmitted itself visibly along the column, which was not less than six men deep by about five hundred long. All space between the marchers disappeared, and those at the very front broke and ran from the press, heading for the apparent safety of another open valley at the crest of the tunnel-road through the trees ahead. The entire column was running by the time I pulled my horsemen to a halt just short of the bogs. We sat there and watched the shock wave recoil as the men in front crested the hill to find themselves confronted by two Roman cohorts drawn up in maniple formation, waiting to receive them. As they bunched together in fatal hesitation, our concealed men hit them from both sides.

Militarily, I suppose it was a great success. The slaughter was appalling, for as the men we had hidden in the woods moved in for the kill, the enemy packed on the road itself were unable to fight back. We, the cavalry, had served our purpose. All we had to do now was watch and wait for any attempt at retreat that came our way.

At first there were about a dozen, perhaps a score of men who fled back from the tunnel of death that awful road had become. They stopped when they saw us waiting for them. While they were in no immediate danger, their numbers grew until there were perhaps two hundred of them in a great knot on the road, half-way between the woods and us. After a time, the fugitives from the tunnel grew fewer, until the flow ceased completely. At first, rather than face us, a number of them tried desperately to escape through the bogs on either side of the road, but the man who travelled furthest made less than a hundred steps before he fell for the last time. He had been wearing garish red and green, but he was no more than a black blob by the time he vanished. I turned to Achmed Cato, my lieutenant.

"How many, do you think?"

"Two hundred, perhaps three? Hard to count, Commander."

"Say three hundred. Out of three thousand." I watched them, remembering Publius Varrus. "Are you a Christian, Cato?"

"Aye, Commander, in Camulod."

"What do you mean?" I looked at him. "Not here?"

He grinned, embarrassed. "Mithras is the soldier's god, Commander. He has not let me down in battle yet."

"I know what you mean. Christianity can be uncomfortable when it comes to killing. Sometimes I think the Druids have the right of it. Their gods are not so prickly. They seem older, somehow, easier to live with." I remembered Uncle Varrus's description of his own dilemma as he faced three bound Hibernians on a stony beach. They were defenceless, but vicious and dangerous. To kill them would be murder, according to his Christian faith, but if he released them they would surely murder others, and he could not take them with him. I faced three hundred now, and I had no archers poised on the cliffs above me to relieve me from the responsibility of making a choice. I spoke again to Cato. "I wonder if the Christian Church will ever breed soldiers among its ranks?" He looked at me as if I had gone mad. He had no idea of what was in my mind. "Cato," I went on, "these men are going to come to us. I don't want to kill them, but we cannot take three hundred prisoners."

"Then let them fight, Commander."

"They may have no fight left in them. They don't look too belligerent right now."

"Take them as slaves, then."

"To Camulod? We have no slaves, and no need of them. Slaves are a sickness. Have the trumpeters get me attention." Murder is a sickness, too, my mind was telling me, and killing these men would be murder. Even if they chose to fight, they were dead before they started. I wondered how many had got out on the other side of the woods and how they were faring.

A single trumpet blast gave me every man's attention. I raised my voice. "On the next signal, you will form up on me and make a circle, open on the bogs. These men will enter the circle. I want it one man deep. If they choose to fight, every second man from my left and right will immediately form up in three arrowhead formations, one behind me, one behind Lieutenant Cato and one behind Lieutenant Maripo. Those men will identify themselves now." Amid the stir of interest as the troopers counted themselves off from my left and right, I turned my horse around, telling Cato and Maripo to come with me, and rode back until I was a good seventy paces from the point where the road emerged from the bog onto firm ground. I nodded to the trumpeter and another blast started my men forming around me as I had ordered.

"Maripo," I said, "I want you over to my right there, half-way from me to the end of the line. Take position thirty paces back from the circle. Cato, you do the same on my left." I nodded to the trumpeter again and another blast brought all attention back to me. I raised my voice again. "Once the arrowheads have formed, two more blasts will be the signal for those still left in the circle to break to the rear immediately and form up behind my arrow. I want a block formation there, four ranks of fifty. Once the block is formed, I will move my formation to the right, clearing the ground, is that clear?" I saw heads nodding. They understood me. I raised my voice even higher. "I want to intimidate these people, but not to fight them unless we have to. If any of them try to attack a section of the circle while the arrowheads are being formed, that section will fall back and try to avoid them without allowing them to escape. Remember they are on foot. They will have to run to you.

"We will wait here for them. No talking. No movement. Let them see our discipline." I turned to the trooper who sat behind me on my right, bearing my new standard. "Come with me." I kicked my horse forward into the forefront of the circle and sat there, waiting, for I could see activity among the group at the head of the knot of men on the roadway. Eventually an enormous man who, I could see from even this far away, towered head and shoulders above his fellows, stepped forward and began to advance purposefully towards me. His companions fell in behind him and I sat there and watched them approach.

The rogue walked proudly, and as he drew closer I could see that he was clean-shaven, which surprised me, for those of his people I had encountered before had all worn full beards or luxuriant moustaches. As he drew nearer still, however, I was shocked to see the reason for his lack of facial hair. He was only a boy! A huge boy, but still a mere stripling in age. He had a barbaric splendour about him, too, in a tunic of yellow, bordered with red, a breastplate of bronze on his massive chest and fur leggings tied around his thick calves. He wore an armlet of beaten gold on his left arm above the wrist, and the gold tore of a Celtic chief about his neck. A longish sword hung from a belt slung crosswise from his right shoulder.

When he reached the edge of the bog between the furthest points of the horns of my ring of men, he stopped and looked around the ring from left to right, all the way, before allowing his eyes to return to me. His face held no expression. The men behind him had stopped when he did. None of them moved a muscle. To my right a horse snorted loudly and stomped, fly-bitten. The silence stretched, and then he reached behind him and unslung a battle axe. He swung it gently in his right hand and caught the shaft in his left, just behind the head. He moved forward again, stopping about twelve paces in front of me while his men fanned out behind him, forming a solid half-circle facing my own. He had obviously issued his orders before approaching. His eyes had not left mine.

"So," he said. "It is time for us all to die, it seems." His eyes were filled with scorn as he looked from me around the circle of my men. "You'll find us not too shy about taking company with us."

I realized with surprise that he spoke in his own tongue and that I understood him easily. Some of his words were pronounced differently, the intonation was different, but the basic language was the same as that of Uric's people. I chose my next words carefully and spoke back to him in his own tongue. "If you wish to die, we can accommodate you quickly," I said. "But ask yourself first if it is really necessary."

His jaw dropped in astonishment. It was obvious that he had been talking to himself before.

"How does a Roman turd like you come to speak the Tongue of Kings?"

"The Tongue of Kings? The Romans call it the tongue of the Outlanders, that I know. But we are not Romans."

His brow creased momentarily and his eyes flickered uncertainly over my armour and trappings. "Not Romans? What does that mean? You dress like Romans. You act like Romans. Who are you, then, if you are not Romans?"

I gripped the shaft of my long spear and reined my horse in tightly as it tried to move in protest at being bitten by a fly. "We are the owners of this land," I said. "And you are raiders. We may dress like Romans and we certainly fight like Romans, but we are Britons, concerned only with defending our homes, our people and our lands against the likes of you, invaders from beyond the seas."

He threw his head up haughtily. "Invaders, is it?"

I shrugged. "Invaders, pirates, raiders—it makes no difference. You do not belong here and you come in war so, as you said, it is time for you to die."

He fell into a crouch and his men tensed behind him. "Come and kill us then, if you can."

I smiled down at him. "Oh, we can. Be in no doubt of that." I started to raise my arm to give the signal to engage, but he stopped me.

"Wait!"

I dropped my arm. "Well?"

He licked his lips and looked around my men again. All of their eyes were on me. "Take us as prisoners!"

In spite of myself I had to grin, admiring the fellow's gall. "Prisoners? Three hundred of you? You can't be serious! What would we do with three hundred prisoners? Spend the rest of our lives looking after you and waiting for you to rise up and attempt escape?" I shook my head. "No, that won't do at all, I think—"

He broke in, "You will not have to keep us long. King Lot will buy us free."

Now I laughed aloud. "Lot? *King* Lot? Has the caterpillar sprouted beauteous wings? King Lot!" I stopped laughing and shook my head. "You are twice mad, my giant fellow. Mad to think that animal would care whether you live or die, and mad again to think we'd sell you to him to let him use you against us a second time."

When next the young man spoke, there was urgency and conviction in his words. "He will buy us free, I swear it! He has to! He has no other choice."

That gave me pause. I gentled my horse again and looked the giant straight in the eye. "You intrigue me. Lot, from the little I know of him, will always have other choices. But speak on. Tell me what you mean."

He licked his lips again and let the head of his battle axe fall to the ground, straightening from his crouch as he did so. "I am Donuil, High Prince of the people the Romans call the *Scotii*. My father Athol is *Ard Righ*, the High King. My sister Ygraine is to be wife to Lot of Cornwall, and alliance has been made between Lot and my father: he aids us in our wars; we aid him in his. This has been our first fight on his behalf."

"You didn't do too well, did you?" I raised my arm and our circle broke apart as I had ordered, leaving a ring of mounted men behind which three large arrowhead formations formed, their points facing inward. He watched my people carry out their orders like machines, his face losing some of its high colour. Three single trumpet blasts told me the manoeuvre had been completed and I raised my arm again. The remainder of the circle broke and formed one massive square formation behind my arrowhead. The young giant in front of me returned his gaze to mine, his face gaunt.

"It is time to die, my friend," I said. "We cannot afford to keep you alive, and besides, with any luck, my cousin Uther has already killed *King* Lot. Fight well, and farewell." Again I started to raise my arm and again he stopped me.

"Your cousin Uther? That means you must be Merlyn."

I bowed my head slightly in acknowledgement. "I am. So?"

"They say you are a man of sense and honour."

"Do they?" I felt a wry smile on my face and a tug of regret that I had to kill this man. "And who are they? Lot of Cornwall knows nothing of sense or honour, and I would be surprised to hear any ally of his profess to know of them."

"I have heard the Druids speak of you."

I was becoming impatient and ill at ease with this. I had no wish to personalize an enemy before killing him.

"What is your point, man?" My voice reflected my impatience.

"I will make a bargain with you, Merlyn." His eyes were desperate and I felt a formless stirring of distaste.

"What kind of bargain do I need to make with the likes of you?" I asked with half a sneer forming unbidden on my lips.

"Life! Lives . . . Your men and mine."

Now what? "Go on," I said, "I'm listening."

He swallowed hard and looked at the men crowded behind him. Their faces were grim, but I took it as a sign of respect for their king's son that their silence remained absolute. He spoke again to me.

"Enough have died. My people will never recover from this loss. We are beaten." He drew a great, shuddering breath. "If we have to die now we will, but we will take a lot of your men with us."

"So? That is a soldier's risk." I pursed my lips. "I'm still waiting for you to make your point."

"It is this: You fight me, man to man, on foot. If I win, let my men and I go free, back to our boats and home. You have my word of honour that you will hear no more from us."

I raised an eyebrow. "And if I win?"

He shrugged. "Then my people withdraw, leaving their weapons here."

"And go home anyway? You call that a bargain? You win both ways."

He shook his head, a short, violent shake. "No! You do. All of your men remain alive too, but they keep their weapons either way. If my men go home without theirs they will be disgraced forever."

"Disgraced forever? Why?"

He shrugged his huge shoulders. "It is the way of our people. Cowardice is unforgivable."

"So why would you even suggest such a solution?"

He looked me straight in the eye and I saw truth in his gaze. "I think I can beat you. But even if I lose, they will still be alive. They will continue my race."

I decided quite suddenly that I liked this young man. He had a dignity about him that reminded me of my great-uncle Ullic. I considered his bargain and my mind leaped ahead of it. He was big and strong enough to beat me, but that did not worry me. If we fought, I felt that I would have the victory, but then I remembered my father's recent rebuke after my foolish confrontation with the bear. In the fight the young Celt was proposing, one of us must die, and the odds were even that it might be I who fell. It would be irresponsible to take that risk in front of my own troops. I shook my head.

"No," I said. "But I have an alternative offer. Surrender yourself, alone, to me personally, as my prisoner. If you do so, I'll escort your men back to their boats and send them home, with their weapons. You will be hostage for their good behaviour."

He frowned at me. "Without a fight?"

"You've had your fight." I nodded to the road behind him. "You lost, remember?"

He shrugged his shoulders again and looked down at the axe in his hands. "I have no choice, have I? How long will you keep me prisoner?"

I had not even considered that. I did so now. "Five years," I told him. "If at the end of that time we have had no more trouble with your people, I will release you."

"Five years?" He was aghast. "Five years of bondage? Chained up like a bear?"

I shook my head slightly. "I made no mention of chaining you up. You will be my prisoner. You gave me your word that your men would leave and stay away as part of your initial bargain. You did so in a manner that made me believe I might trust that word. I would be prepared to trust it still if you promised not to attempt escape, but to serve your time with me."

"*Serving* you?"

"Serving *with* me."

Our eyes locked and his narrowed as if trying to see beyond mine, into my head. Then he gave a curt nod. "Agreed. But let my people go."

"I will. Did any escape from the far side of the woods?"

"I don't know." His eyes were bleak.

"Well," I said, "we will find out. If there are survivors there with my father's troops, will they be bound by your bargain, too?"

His eyes narrowed again. "They will. They are my father's people."

"Good, then we had better go and find out if any of them are still alive. Tell your people what is happening. I'll tell mine." I turned to my standard-bearer and spoke in my own language. "Bring Achmed Cato and Lieutenant Maripo here to me." When they arrived I told them what I had arranged. Maripo said nothing, but Cato looked worried.

"Commander, can you trust a man like this? A pirate?"

I nodded. "I think I can, Cato. He is no pirate in the ordinary sense. He's an envoy of his father, the king of the *Scotii*. Anyway, time will prove me either right or wrong, and in the meantime we have saved ourselves from losing men needlessly. I want to send an escort of two hundred back with them to the coast. You will lead them. I don't expect you to have any trouble on the way, but if you do, I expect you to conduct yourself accordingly. If they break faith with you, wipe them out. We'll disarm them before they leave and keep their weapons under guard. See them loaded into their boats and under way, then make your own way directly back to the Colony."

"Are we allowing them to keep their weapons? Really?" His eyes showed his surprise.

"Aye." I gave a small smile. "When the men are aboard, let them have their weapons back."

He still looked dubious, but he did not demur, merely shrugging his shoulders. "You're the commander, Commander," was all he said.

My smile grew wider. I instructed him to hold the prisoners there pending other arrivals and further orders, then I returned to my young prisoner, who had finished talking to his own men. "Did you tell them they would be allowed to keep their weapons?" I asked him.

"Aye. I told them they would have them back once aboard ship."

"That is correct. I have instructed the commander of the escort that will accompany them back to their boats. They are aware of the terms of your hostage status?"

"Aye. They are aware."

"Good. I hope they hold you in high esteem. Ask them now to throw down their weapons, all of them in a pile, and move away from them. My men will load them on to one of our commissary wagons later. Do you ride?"

"No."

"Then I hope you can walk quickly. We are going to check the extent of the slaughter up ahead there, in the woods. You will have to come with me. It will not be a pleasant passage, but if there are any of your people left alive on the other side of the woods, we should try to get there before someone decides to execute them all. Let's go."

"What in the name of God possessed you to enter into such a stupid bargain with a bare-arsed savage?" My father had ridden hard to the top of a knoll and drawn his horse up there to wait for me, greeting me thus before I had reined to a halt, but I was ready for him.

"Perhaps the very name of God itself, Father."

His horse pranced uneasily, dancing sideways to keep clear of mine.

"What's that supposed to mean?" He was almost snarling at me. "Spare me your fancy words, Caius. This is no time for sophistry."

"There's none intended, Father. I meant what I said." I turned and looked down over my shoulder to where his own prisoners stood huddled in misery, surrounded by vigilant troopers. At a glance, I estimated their number as at least equal to that of my own captives—perhaps a few score more. I looked back at my father and shrugged. "Two thousand and more men went into that wooded road and to my eyes, only three hundred came back out. I did not know how many had come through on your side, but I did know that more than a thousand died there in that trap."

"So?" He had no patience with this line of reasoning. "Well? What are you saying? Is there something strange about that? They were soldiers, Caius. Soldiers expect to die."

"Not so, sir. Not soldiers. They were men. Ours were the soldiers, and they struck from hiding, in stealth."

My father was completely baffled, thinking I had lost my sanity. "And?" he demanded in disbelief. "Would you rather *they* had died? Our men?"

"No! You misunderstand me. Give me at least a chance to try to make you understand." I undid my chin strap and removed my helmet for the first time that day. "Will you hear me out?"

"Do you doubt it?"

"No, Father, I don't. Forgive me." I clawed at my hair, matted and soaked with sweat from the heat of my helmet. "I know what I want to say, but I don't know where to start." I dismounted and sat on the grass and my father did the same, leaving me time to collect my thoughts. Finally, I began to talk. "I knew they had lost more than a thousand men, perhaps two thousand, in what seemed like moments. And I did not like the thought of killing three hundred more.

"We are Christians, Father, are we not? We are told to love our enemy, to turn the other cheek. We cannot do it, of course, in life. But surely we can try? We cannot claim to be Christians if we condone senseless and unnecessary slaughter. You are the one who

taught me about taking personal responsibility for my own actions."
I broke off, and thought again about what I wanted to say. "I suppose what I mean is that I did not choose to be responsible for
what I saw as the needless deaths of three hundred beaten men
plus those of my own men who would have died in the killing of
them." I looked at him, fully expecting him to interrupt me there,
but he said nothing and I continued. "I suspect you were having
precisely the same kind of thoughts when I arrived. Am I correct?
Or would you have had your troopers kill these people out of hand,
in cold blood?" He frowned and his lips thinned, but I hurried on
before he could respond. "That's rhetorical, of course. Had you
intended that, you'd never have taken them as prisoners in the first
place. In any case, young Donuil offered a way out. His life, in servitude, as hostage for the absence of his people from our lands. It
seemed to me to be a fair solution."

"From what viewpoint?" My father's voice was calmer now.

I plucked a long stem of grass and nibbled on the soft end of
it. "From the viewpoint of history, I suppose. Our own history.
Rome herself set the example centuries ago, and has continued to
do so ever since. Better, I thought, to let them leave with their lives
and be responsible for the life of their own prince than to extermi-
nate them and await reprisals."

He was biting at the skin of his lip, his eyes fixed on mine. "And
you would trust this prince, this Donuil, to keep his own word?"

"Yes, Father. I would trust this Donuil."

He twisted sideways and fumbled with his swordbelt, trying
to make it lie more comfortably beneath him. He was only partially successful, and ended up drawing his dagger from its sheath
and gazing at the point of it.

"Vortigern," he said.

"I beg your pardon?"

"Vortigern. It's a man's name. He's a warlord in the north-east.
Have you heard of him?"

I shook my head. "No. Never. Should I have heard of him?
Who is he?"

My father stabbed his dagger into the ground, hard, and then drew it out again, the gritty, alien sound of the earth scraping against the iron blade setting my teeth on edge. "Vortigern is doing what you're doing," he said. "He is putting his life and the lives of his people into jeopardy by trusting an alien people who have no conception of what trust means. Reason tells me that the idea of trust, as we understand it, must be a truly alien concept to them." He stopped and looked at me and then, seeing my incomprehension, wiped the blade on the hem of his tunic and went on to explain.

"Vortigern's lands are up on the north-east coast, in the area that has been getting the heaviest raids and the roughest treatment from invading Saxons. He and his people fought them well enough for years, but there were more fresh raiders coming in each year, while Vortigern's best people were being killed off steadily. Finally, he made an arrangement with a man called Hengist, one of the Saxon chiefs who came back year after year. He would give the Saxons land, he told them, land for them to farm and live on, if they would agree to help him defend his own land and theirs from other raiders."

"And?" I finally had to ask him. "Did they agree?"

For a long time I thought he wasn't going to answer me at all, but then he shrugged and sighed deeply. "Aye, they agreed."

"Why, that's marvellous," I said, full of enthusiasm.

My father looked at me with a strange expression, part pity, part impatience. "Is it now? And what happens tomorrow, or next year, or the year after that, when the Saxons he has invited to live with him want to go home and bring back their wives and children and brothers and families? And what happens when all their friends and families come here and there isn't enough land for them to farm?"

I blinked. "They'll clear more land and farm that."

"Aye, Caius, that they will. And they'll need more and more as their numbers grow, and one day they will decide that there isn't room for Vortigern and his people there any longer, because by that time it will be their land, and they'll throw Vortigern and his descendants out, alive if they're lucky." His voice had been rising as he spoke and now he paused and gathered his patience again, lowering his tone. "Vortigern is playing a suicidal game, Caius. He is not merely welcoming strangers to his lands. He is allowing uncontested entry to an alien race, an alien culture, an uncivilized and savage people who are intrinsically inimical to Vortigern's traditions and way of life. He will lose everything, sooner or later. It's inevitable." He paused. "Inevitable. You do see that, don't you?"

I nodded. "Yes, Father, I do, now that you explain it so graphically. But I can't see how it affects my own decision regarding this young Celtic chieftain. I am not inviting him to come here and farm my land. I can't find it in me to think that I have made the wrong decision."

My father squeezed his face between his palms and rose to his feet, his decision made. "Very well, Caius. You are my son and a soldier. More than that, you are your own man, with the right to make your own judgments. I have my doubts, but I will not say I told you so if you are wrong. I'll only hope you learn from your mistake—if you have indeed made one. How do you intend to proceed now?"

I tried hard not to allow my relief to show in any way, but got to my feet as casually as I could and replaced my helmet on my head. My father could still make me feel like a small boy. "I will have Donuil speak to your prisoners and explain the situation to them. I expect no trouble, since they have no choice. They are barbarian, but I think they do not lack honour. I will escort all of them back to the coast and send them home. Then we'll return to Camulod. We should be no more than three days behind you."

"How many are we freeing altogether?"

"Six hundred here, five hundred at the coast, guarding their ships."

"Eleven hundred men . . ." He shook his head again. "I hope you have the right of it, Caius, for if you are wrong they will eat you alive."

"I know that, Father. I believe I'm right."

He nodded. "Well, don't be longer than three days behind me or I'll pronounce you dead."

I smiled. "No need of that, Commander. By the way, what were our losses on the road?"

"Less than a hundred," he said, looking around him. "We lost one for ten. Not a bad exchange, under the circumstances."

"No," I said. "I suppose not."

He glanced at me, sharp-eyed. "What's the matter?"

"Oh, nothing. This is my first major battle, in terms of the numbers of men involved. I suppose I'm still trying to adjust to the thought of eleven or twelve hundred lives being snuffed out like lamps within the space of an hour. Eleven hundred. That's a lot of corpses. They'll breed a lot of maggots."

He frowned slightly. "It's half as many as it would have been without your bargain! But you're right. That road will be unpleasant to travel for the next few months. I don't think, however, that you have lost sight of what would have happened at Camulod had we let them get through this valley unscathed."

I nodded agreement. "It had to be done, I'm aware of that, but it doesn't make it any the less sickening." I put my foot into the stirrup and swung myself up onto my horse. "As long as people like the *Scotii* and the Picts, and the Saxons for that matter, see us as weak, helpless victims in a leaderless land, this kind of carnage will go on. But it galls me that Lot of Cornwall should stoop so low as to bring in invaders to help him."

My father cleared his throat derisively and I marvelled again, for the first time in ages, at how clear his speaking voice had become. "Well, my son, I can guarantee you that Lot would not describe himself as stooping low to achieve his ends. That one is aiming high. He seeks dominion. Lot of Cornwall sees himself as High King of Britain, I fear." He mounted his own horse.

"High King of Britain? Lot of Cornwall? You jest, surely, Father?"

But there was no humour in my father's grim face. He grunted and spat, clearing his mouth before he spoke again. "No, by the

ancient gods, I mean it. I have ill reports of him. He looks to conquer all of us."

"Then his ambition will kill him, for he has to reckon with
Uther, myself and you, and he's not man enough for any of us. I
wonder how Uther is faring right now?"

My father hitched around in his saddle, peering backward to
where his army awaited him. "We'll find out soon enough," he said,
abstractedly. "Go you and see your prisoners out to sea. And don't
take too long about it. We'll be waiting for you in Camulod."

XIV

I n the event, we were no more than one day behind my father
in reaching Camulod. I took Prince Donuil to meet his surviving men immediately upon leaving my father, and the joy
with which they greeted the young man was worth beholding. He
explained to them the terms under which he had bought their lives
and extracted a pledge from all of them to honour his commitment. There was little argument.

The next day we reached the coast where they had beached
their fleet. Seven hundred *Scotii*, as it turned out, escorted by my
four hundred mounted men. Donuil himself went forward to speak
to the guards he had left behind and I allowed him to do so without an escort. He was gone for more than an hour and returned
with a grizzled veteran almost as big as he himself. When they
came in sight of us they stopped and I rode out to meet them. The
big man with Donuil was the first to speak.

"My nephew here has told me of the terms he has reached
with you, Merlyn Britannicus, and I have no choice but to abide by
his terms and yours." He stopped and I waited for him to continue,
which he did after clearing his throat and spitting. "Understand that
had we known we were facing Romans, we would have behaved
very differently!"

I could not let him get away with that, for his bearing implied
that by behaving differently they could have beaten us. "What does
that mean? You lost more than a thousand men. You marched into
an alien land without sending out scouts. You are lucky to be still
alive, and luckier still to be sailing home with your weapons and
your honour intact."

The big man flushed. "I know that. I had no thought of demeaning you. What I meant was that we were marching to join King Lot. By his tale your people are nought but a nest of bandits who threaten the existence of his kingdom. He told us that you are a rabble."

I grunted. "Well, if rabble we are, we are a well-disciplined rabble."

"Aye, and a strangely honourable one. I am Fergus, brother to King Athol and uncle to Donuil. My nephew has told me of your behaviour and of your treatment of him. I will take back your conditions to my brother Athol, and I am here to swear my solemn pledge that you will hear no more of us for five years from this date." I nodded my head, accepting his pledge, and he went on, "At that time, five years from now, we will return to this spot to claim our prince. If he is well and alive, we will take him and leave."

"He will be."

"He had better be, noble Roman! Take good care of him, for if he is not here on the due date, you will have war with every man on our island, and not all your Roman wiles will win that war for you."

I looked him straight in the eye. "I hear you. If your prince abides by his sworn word he will come to no ill at my hands, nor at the hands of any of my people."

The big man did not take his eyes away from mine. "Make you sure that he takes no ill at the hand of any, be he friend or enemy."

I allowed a smile to soften my next words. "Will you threaten me forever, or shall we take our leave of each other now?"

He nodded. "So be it. He is in your hands."

Donuil still had not spoken, but now he turned to his uncle and embraced him, and we withdrew to watch from a hillside as they embarked and put to sea, each boat towing an empty one behind it. When they had shrunk to the size of toys on the horizon, I turned to look at my young prisoner. He stood erect, straight as a spear, his eyes fixed on the distant fleet, his face giving not the slightest indication of what thoughts were going through his head. I felt for him, imagining what my own feelings would have been had our situations been reversed.

"Prince Donuil," I said. "It is time. We must return to Camulod. You may ride behind one of my men."

He looked at me with empty, emotionless eyes. "I will walk."

"So be it." I gave the signal to my waiting troops and we began the long journey home.

He walked every step of the way, his pace tireless and unflagging, at the left side of my horse. On one occasion, when we were crossing boggy ground, I told him to take hold of my stirrup, but he merely looked at me and kept his hands by his sides. We did not speak further. When we stopped to camp on the first and second nights, he accepted food wordlessly and then lay down to sleep in the spot I indicated to him, and I had no doubt that he slept soundly, for we had been pushing our horses at a hard walk, which meant brutal speed for a man on foot.

As soon as we reached Camulod, I handed over my prisoner into the keeping of a centurion with orders that he be confined, unchained, in one of the cells that we kept for our own petty offenders, and there I left him for twenty-four hours, giving him time to consider close confinement while I looked after the affairs that had accumulated during my absence.

Uther had not returned from his foray against Lot, although he had sent back the legates Titus and Flavius with two hundred of the four hundred men they commanded. Frustrated by their failure to find Lot on our lands, Titus told me, Uther had decided to pursue him all the way back to Cornwall if he had to, but could not justify depriving Camulod of three of its senior commanders for a task he felt could be handled effectively by one. He had taken half of their troops in addition to his own and had penetrated the south-western peninsula with a force of five hundred, since which time no word had been heard of him. My father was worried. On his return, after speaking to the two legates, he had called an immediate meeting of the Council to discuss all that had happened since our departure, and to assess the state of readiness of the fort and of the colonists themselves. By the time I arrived with my cavalry, he had everything in order. He was in the midst of redeploying his infantry, who had had twenty-four hours' rest and were ready for anything, and I was happy to discover that there was almost nothing for me to do. The few minor duties that fell to me were quickly taken care of, and I was free to make my way to my hidden valley and Cassandra. I left word with my father and rode out of the fort just as the shadows began to stretch out in the late afternoon.

Despite the lateness of the hour, the sun was still hot and I sweated freely as I rode, the beads springing from my forehead beneath the headband of my helmet and running down to burn the corners of my eyes while others bedevilled me with the tickling of their progress down the valleys of my back and chest under my heavy armour. I found nothing strange, however, in riding to a lovers' tryst fully armed and armoured, and had the thought occurred to me then, I would have been hard pressed to recall a time when I went anywhere, even within Camulod itself, without my heavy and ungainly impedimenta. My armour, from helmet to boots, was as customary to me as my skin, so that I was aware of it—and uncomfortable—only when I removed any part of it.

Evening was approaching as my horse emerged from the narrow path through the bushes into the tranquillity of Avalon. I saw Cassandra immediately, standing with her back to me, staring into the waters of the pool at her feet. Some instinct must have warned her that she was being watched, for she turned and saw me there. Even in the gathering dusk I saw the pleasure in her eyes at the sight of me. She came running across the short, green turf towards me, her teeth gleaming in a smile of welcome, and I sat there on my horse and watched her approach, feeling my own cheeks bunching in a smile. She stopped right in front of me and her hands bade me welcome, and invited me to step down from my saddle.

As soon as my feet were on the ground she took me by the hand and began tugging me in the direction of the hut. I let her pull me and led my horse behind us, dropping the reins as we approached the door so that he began to graze immediately.

The room was filled with flowers. Vases and bowls of blossoms bedecked every available surface and the scent of them hung sweet and heavy in the air. A small fire burned brightly in the fireplace, but the room was free of smoke, and I was grateful once again to my uncle for teaching me the secret of building a flue. She stopped me in the middle of the floor and took hold of both my hands, holding me at arm's length and running her eyes over me from head to foot. I did the same to her and wondered again how I could ever have thought her ugly. Then her hands were undoing the fastening of my helmet and removing it from my head. When she had laid it on the table, she undid my new cloak, running her fingers admiringly over the great silver bear embroidered on it before she folded it and placed it beside the helmet. Next, she took off my swordbelt and armoured kirtle of leather, so that I wore only my knee-length tunic. She had never done this before, and I stood there like an ox, grinning with pleasure and making no move to help her as she ministered to me.

When she had stripped me completely of my armour she grinned at me, poked me in the stomach, skipped nimbly to the door, and ran outside. Smiling, and wondering what she was about, I followed her slowly, only to find that she had already run more than half-way to the entrance of the path down which I had so recently arrived. Evidently, I was supposed to follow her. I drew a deep breath and took off in pursuit, thinking to overtake her easily, but by the time I began to experience my first shortness of breath, less than half-way up the steep, narrow path, it had begun to dawn on me that this young woman had no intention of being lightly overtaken; not only did she remain out of sight ahead of me, but I could hear no sound of her progress. I accepted the challenge, lengthened my stride and began conscientiously to control my breathing, sensing that victory in this chase might not come quickly.

I was breathing hard, almost gasping for breath, by the time I reached the summit of the path and broke into the clear ground at the top of the hill. Cassandra was waiting, grinning merrily, a hundred paces from me at the opposite end of the rolling hilltop. As soon as she knew that I had seen her, she turned and disappeared downhill again. I stifled the urge to curse, paused for the space of several heartbeats to catch my breath again, and followed her.

In the course of the hour that followed, I received a humbling lesson in physical fitness and self-sufficiency, and came within reach of her no more than twice, each time only because she allowed me to. On the first of these, when I had paused again for breath, wondering where she had gone, she dropped onto my shoulders from a tree above me, her weight knocking me off my feet and down a grassy bank. Her arms hugged me tightly to her as we rolled together and my nostrils were filled with the warm scent of her, hair and sweat and wild blossoms, all mixed with the sharp tang of crushed grass and dry, pungent, crumbling earth. We came to rest at the bottom of the slope, me lying flat on my back with the wind knocked out of me, and she sitting astride my chest, grinning down at me, her smooth, firm, bare thigh beneath my hand. Before I could move to collect myself or utter a sound, she chuckled softly in her throat, ruffled my hair and was up and away again, and I realized that she had not even been breathing hard! A short time later, she dived from beneath a bush and wrapped her arms around my knees, bringing me crashing to the ground again, but this time she did not even pause to savour her victory or feast on my discomfiture before dashing away again.

At that point, in a last, desperate attempt to safeguard the few pitiful shreds of dignity I could muster, I abandoned the chase and began to retrace my steps, willing myself to run smoothly back towards the valley and, within moments, it seemed, she was running easily by my side, her eyes fixed on the path ahead. Accepting the futility of any attempt to reason, or even communicate with her on my terms, I ran on without looking at her, but during the gentle journey back to the hut, I was conscious of the weariness and frustration and anger draining steadily from my body, so that I arrived at our journey's end rejuvenated and only pleasantly tired. She stopped by the edge of the lake and looked up at me, her eyes shining and her skin rosy and slick with perspiration. She turned aside and ran into the lake, struggling against the pull of the water at her knees until it was deep enough for her to throw herself full length and swim. I was mere moments behind her, and the water felt wonderful.

Later, when we had emerged shivering and run into the hut, she produced two blankets for us, then took my hands and pulled me to the wooden chair beside the fire, tugging and pushing at me until I sat down. Then she knelt, swathed in her blanket, and began poking and prodding at the fire, stirring up the flames until they blazed and adding dry, thick logs. That done, she lit a taper from the fire and used it to light three oil lamps, and all the while I was content to sit and shiver and watch her, drinking in her every movement, catching glimpses of the way the single, wet tunic she wore clung to the lines of her body beneath the blanket, and itching to take her around the waist and kiss her marvel of a mouth with its wide, full lips.

In the face of her now obvious delight in my presence, the only things that restrained me from laying hands on her were the warning of Daffyd and the memory of what had been done to her. Although her body was healed, those wounds were still too fresh in her mind. I contented myself with looking at her, wondering if the tumultuous feelings I was undergoing were merely unrequited lust, stirred and aggravated by the exercise she had put me through earlier, or the magic that I had heard men talk of as love. I had thought myself familiar with both, for I had lusted for years and had love for many people—mainly men, with Luceiia a notable exception. What I now felt in mind and body, however, bore little resemblance to my love for my great-aunt.

The heat from the fire soon dried us off, and as the dusk deepened outside, the combined light of the lamps and the fire grew stronger, casting dancing shadows on the walls of the hut. It was a simple, crude building in the light of day, but now, in this darkening evening, it took on a warmth and air of comfort that were soothing, almost magical.

As soon as the lamps were burning clearly, Cassandra laid aside the blanket that had covered her and went to move the pile of my

outer clothes and armour from the table into a corner. It made an
awkward burden, and I started to stand up to help her, but she
saw the move and shook her head, frowning and waving her hand
to make me stay where I was, so I relaxed again and continued
watching her.

Once the table was clear, she went to a row of boxes on a shelf
and produced bread, cheese, apples and wine, laying them out on
the table before me. I felt saliva spurt under my tongue and realized I had eaten nothing since dawn. She herself ate little, but she
watched me closely as I wolfed down my food, her eyes moving
from my plate to my mouth with every bite I took. I offered to
share my food with her, but she smiled and shook her head, content, apparently, to watch me eat. Eventually, I had had enough and
pushed my plate away. She refilled my wine cup, then cleared away
the remaining bread and cheese, returning it to the storage bins on
the shelf. It was dark outside now. The firelight had faded again.

"Listen," I said, as a nightingale began to sing outside.

She paid no attention, either to my words or to the bird's song,
and I was once again smitten with a stark reminder of all the beauty
of the world that was lost to her. I had known that she was deaf,
and had accepted it, but it had not struck me until that moment
that she could never enjoy the song of a bird. I felt a great lump in
my throat and my eyes blurred, and then she was standing before
me, her eyes wide with alarm and concern at the sight of my tears.
I shook my head violently and started to wipe them away with my
wrist, but she stopped me and wiped my cheeks dry with her own
soft fingertips. I could see the question in her face, *Why are you
weeping, Caius Merlyn?*

I forced back the pain and tried to smile at her. It was not difficult. What I did find difficult, however, was to reconcile the difference I perceived between the boyish hoyden who had outrun
and humiliated me that afternoon and the demure and gentle person who was now so evidently content to share her home and fire
with me. She took me by the hand again and led me to the chair
by the fire, and this time, when I was seated, she sat at my feet,

holding the fingers of my right hand in her own and resting her cheek against the back of my hand as she stared into the fire. I could feel the softness of her face against my hand with every nerve end in my body, and I dared to move the tip of one finger minutely, entranced with the smoothness of her skin. Tiny though the movement was, she turned and smiled up at me, squeezing my hand and ending the freedom of that finger.

I have no idea how long we sat thus, silent and motionless, but eventually the heat of the fire made me drowsy and I startled both of us by awakening with a jerk as my neck muscles relaxed and allowed my head to drop forward. I blinked myself wide awake and with great reluctance rose to go, hating the thought of leaving to ride back to Camulod alone.

She watched me intently as I rose and crossed to the corner where my armour lay, and then she got up and came to me, holding out her hands to help me with my harness. I was in the act of strapping my armoured kirtle around my waist, and she took the buckle in one hand and the end of the strap in the other, frowning gently up at me. I grinned at her and sucked in my waist, and she pulled tight on both ends of the belt, but without making any effort to feed the end through the buckle. Instead, she shook her head, a questioning look on her face. I assumed that she was asking me if I had to go so soon, and I pantomimed tiredness and the need to sleep, pointing to the door and, by association, towards Camulod. In answer, she turned her head towards the pile of furs that was her bed, her hands still pulling the straps of my kirtle tight. But I knew that I could not sleep there. I wasn't that strong. I shook my head and smiled again, and she let go of the belted kirtle so that it fell at my feet. There was a determined look about her that surprised me. I watched her as she returned quickly to the fireplace and threw some fresh wood onto the embers. This done, she came back to where I stood, stooped to retrieve my belt and then straightened up to look directly at me. Deliberately, as though defying me to stop her, she threw the skirt of armoured straps back into the corner and took me firmly by both hands, drawing me, not

altogether unwillingly, towards her bed, where she tugged at me
until I sat down.

As soon as I was down, she put one hand on my chest and
pushed me back onto the furs and began to undo the thongs of
my sandals. I relaxed and let her do it, enjoying myself immensely
and fighting hard to keep the pleasure of looking at her and enjoying her ministrations separate from the sexual anticipation that
was urging me to seize her and bear her down with me into the
intimacy of the soft furs. The former was permissible; the latter
was simply not.

Her head was bowed as she concentrated on untying the knot
that held my left sandal in place and I propped myself up on my
elbows, the better to enjoy the sight of her beauty in the leaping
firelight. I decided that on my next journey I would bring her something richer and softer to wear than the plain cloth tunic she wore
now. The knot came loose and she pulled the sandal off, leaving
me free to wiggle my toes, and as I did so she laughed aloud. The
sound shocked me, for it was the first time I had heard it, and I was
astonished to realize that she laughed like any ordinary woman, in
a gurgle of clear, liquid notes of great purity and beauty.

"Cassandra!" I said, but of course she paid no attention. I touched
her on the head and she looked at me in inquiry, the laugh still
radiant on her face. "You laughed!" She saw my lips move and
tilted her head to one side like a puppy dog and again I was smitten with pain at the impossibility of communicating with her. The
smile lingered on her face and I made myself smile back at her as I
shook my head to indicate that it was not important. She reached
for my hands again and tugged me to a kneeling position. I offered
no resistance, allowing myself to be positioned as she wanted.
When she had me kneeling upright, she made a strange gesture
which had me completely at a loss. She read the incomprehension
in my face and repeated the gesture, crossing her arms in front of
her and drawing her hands up her sides, and I realized that she
was telling me to remove my tunic. All at once I was overcome
with embarrassment. I shook my head firmly. This time, her tiny

headshake and slightly puzzled frown said *Why not?* as clearly as though she had spoken the words aloud. I could only shrug helplessly. Very deliberately, she tilted her head again, this time to the other side, and scanned my face intently, then she rose to her feet and slowly drew her own shift over her head, not taking her eyes from mine for a second in the process. I stared in wonder at her beauty. She had gained weight and lost all signs of her injuries since the time when I had gazed in horror at the damage that had been done to her. Then, her lacerated body had seemed thin and undernourished; now, it seemed as though I was looking at a different woman. Her breasts, though not large, were full and rounded, her belly smooth and flat and unblemished. She stood with her feet slightly apart and only a blind man would have been unaware of the thick profusion of hair between her firm, round thighs. I knew my mouth had fallen open, rapt as I was in the splendour of the sight before me. And then she stooped, quick as a wink, seized the top fur of the pile and was underneath it almost before I saw her move, pulling it up to her chin so that only her perfect face with its huge eyes and mouth remained exposed to my gaze, and still I did not move, though the blood was hammering in my ears.

Slowly, lying on her back, her gaze fixed on mine, she raised the covering in a plain request for me to join her. Eventually I moved to do so, reaching for the edge of the covering, but she dropped it immediately and shook her head and pointed her chin explicitly at my tunic. I removed it, feeling strange—not foolish, but unsure of myself, for I could hear Daffyd's exhortations against doing anything that might hurt her either physically or in her mind. I moved again to join her, now wearing nothing but my breech clout, and again she stopped me with an upraised palm and three distinct, pointing jabs of her finger. I nodded my understanding and rose to extinguish the lamps, after which I returned to find her holding up the covering to allow me to climb in beside her.

The furs smelled of wild lavender and roses and I wondered how she had managed to achieve that effect as I lowered myself cautiously to rest beside her. We had soft bedclothes at home in

Camulod, but still used skins on campaign. My own campaign bed skins still smelled feral after years of use. I could see her face quite clearly in the flickering firelight, although my face must have been in shadow to her. As I came to rest facing her, lying on my left side, she moved slightly towards me and I felt the warmth of the soft underside of her thigh against my bent knee. I held my breath, not daring to believe that this was actually happening. I lay there unmoving, drinking in the beauty of her, my knee, our sole point of contact, feeling as though it was being burned with exquisite fire. We lay like that for long moments until my breathing steadied and my smile became less like a rictus, and then I felt her thigh withdraw from my knee and knew bitter disappointment until I realized what she was doing. She pulled herself up on her right elbow above me and undid the fastening of her hair with her left hand, allowing it to fall in a loose cascade across her face. The action exposed her breasts to my view from a distance of less than a handspan and I gazed at the tension of the firm skin and the pointed pinkness of her tiny nipples. She reached her free hand towards me and traced the outline of my cheek in a feather-like caress. I felt a lump of pure tenderness swell in my throat. Goose-flesh broke out all over my body as her fingertips dropped from my chin to my neck and moved down almost weightlessly to trace the length of my breastbone. She saw my hissed intake of breath and felt the involuntary stiffening of my whole body, for she smiled again and increased the pressure of her index finger by a hair's weight, continuing her movement until her fingertip rested gently in my navel. My stomach was as tight as a drum as her hand retraced its delicious journey until her palm and fingers gently cupped my right shoulder and pushed until I was lying flat on my back. I closed my eyes and felt a shudder pass through my body with the pressure of her breast against my chest and the soft, moist, unbelievable warmth of her glorious mouth covering my own, and I realized that all of the kisses I had ever experienced had been waiting for this.

I am an old man, now, recalling this night across the abyss of fifty years and more, but the memory of that kiss still stirs the hairs on my arms and causes nightingales to sing in my memory. In all of his writings, save for those in which he dealt with his friend Equus's sister Phoebe and with Scilla Titens and a few intimate recollections of his marriage, Publius Varrus kept his private thoughts of his women to himself, as did my grandfather Caius. My father spoke to me of love and lust on a few occasions, straightforwardly as a soldier will, but I, for my part, spoke to no man of love. I was regarded as a celibate, which indeed I became. But I have known a love that transformed my life and shaped the man I was to become, and I feel no constraint in writing of that love today. The awakening of it that night, when I was reborn into a world of brilliant colours and amazing textures, changed my life and reshaped the foundations of my manhood.

It was the most wondrous night of my whole life, and I passed through it as one would a wonderland of purest fantasy, willing the falling sands of time to float like thistledown in summer zephyrs and struggling mightily now and again, flaring in silent rebellion, each time an errant thought of Camulod and that other, lesser life teased at the edges of my consciousness to remind of me of things undone and duties unfulfilled. The hours stretched slowly, filled with wondrous, rippling darkness and unearthly joys the like of which I had never imagined.

I avoided the hour of reckoning—of wakening—as resolutely as I could. Eventually, however, I could procrastinate no longer. Camulod and my duties were waiting and I had to go to them. Cassandra helped me to dress and walked with me, her arm around my waist, to where my horse stood grazing. I felt a stab of guilt that I had left the poor beast there all night wearing his saddle. I tightened the girth and turned to bid my love farewell, but she was gone. I looked all around me, scanning the entire valley with my eyes. She was nowhere to be seen, yet I knew she was watching me, unwilling to display the tears that this leaving must bring.

I stepped up into the saddle and walked my horse away, back into the world of men and their cares and woes.

XV

The door of my father's office stood open and the sentry on duty there saluted smartly as I approached. I returned the salute and stepped into the doorway, rapping my knuckles lightly on the door post as I saw my father in his usual position at his table, his head bent over an unfinished report. He looked up under his brows and grunted at me.

"Ah! You're back, good. Have a seat. I'll be with you in a moment."

I took off my helmet and made myself comfortable, looking around at the Spartan austerity of this tiny cubicle where General Picus Britannicus spent so much of his working life. The room measured less than four good paces long by the same in width and held nothing but my father's work table, two chairs, two wooden chests bound with iron, and his own stool. Along the back wall ran a double shelf that held some bound books, a pile of reports and some rolled maps. His swordbelt, helmet and cloak hung from wooden pegs in the wall beside the door, and a large leather bucket by his feet served as a receptacle for anything he did not want to keep lying around. I looked long at the battered table on which he was writing; it was as much a part of my father as anything else he owned. Long and narrow, it formed a partitioned box two hands-breadths deep and sat on two collapsible trestles that fitted into slots fashioned to hold them on the underside of the table. It could be locked with a spring-loaded tumbler lock, and it went with him everywhere he went, loaded upon the commissary wagon. On campaign, it held the same place in his tent that it held here within his office.

On the wall at his back, above the double shelves, hung a simple wooden cross, a gift from his old friend Bishop Alaric, and I wondered again, as I did each time I came here, at the strength of the faith of men that had turned this symbol of shame and degradation into a symbol of triumph and love.

There had never been anything admirable about a cross in Roman eyes. Since the beginnings of time it has stood for the direst punishment a criminal could suffer. Death on the cross meant death by slow degrees of consummate agony as the force of gravity dragged inexorably at the victim's body, tearing the bones from their sockets, ripping joints and sinews, searing his brain with pain that dragged on with no respite until death, which came more often from thirst and starvation than from any other cause, and thirst and starvation are slow ways to die.

The Christ, they said, had died in three short hours, nailed to his cross. If that were true, he had been fortunate and had barely known the pain of crucifixion—some men screamed for days up there. He had been fortunate, or he had had help. The spearpoint that pierced his side might have been premature, and might have been heavily handled. It should have been a mere test to see if blood still flowed in the veins of the condemned man, for while blood flowed, life remained, and while life remained the body stayed on the cross. I have heard people swear it was the nails that killed him. That is flat untrue. Nails through the wrists and ankles will cripple and maim, but they will not cause death. That would have been too merciful a death for someone sentenced to the cross. Others said the flogging he received had caused his death. That might have some truth in it, especially if the man was already weak, but this man was the Son of God. How could he, then, be weak within Himself? Besides, I knew about the skill of Roman floggers. They had centuries of tradition behind their art and knew precisely how far they could go without causing fatal damage. My father's voice broke in upon my thoughts.

"How is your foundling?"

I snapped back to the present. "Cassandra? Oh, she's well." I tried to keep my voice casual and betray none of the emotions that filled me, but I was unsuccessful, for his eyebrow rose immediately.

"She is . . . well, is she? It pleases me to hear that. When will she be well enough to visit us here in Camulod?"

"I . . . I do not know, Father." I made my face as grave as I could, wishing him to think I still had grave reservations about her overall health. "I could not guess with any confidence. She is still . . . weak, in some ways."

"Aye. And quite strong in others, I can see." His voice was heavy with irony and I felt my face flush.

"You sent for me, sir."

"Aye. I did. For several reasons, the first of which is the least important in real terms. This barbarian, the Scot. What do you intend to do with him?"

"Do with him?" The question caught me unprepared. "What do you mean?"

He looked at me, wide-eyed, his face reflecting an uncharacteristic bewilderment as he admitted, "I don't know what I mean. I was hoping you would help me define what I mean. You have managed to saddle us with a useless mouth to feed and a responsibility to guard this man for years. I only hope you have some idea of what's involved here. Have you thought about it?" In spite of his bewilderment, his frown indicated that here was matter for serious consideration.

I nodded. "Of course I have."

"And?"

I shrugged, trying to put conviction into my tone. "I have decided to offer him the opportunity to pass his time here usefully."

"How, in God's name? The man's an Outlander and an enemy!" That was almost a bark.

I shrugged again, recognizing the repetition and attempting unsuccessfully to stifle the movement before it was complete. "I don't know yet."

"Not as a soldier, then?"

"No . . . I don't know. Perhaps, or perhaps as a servant of some kind."

"A *servant?* Caius, the man is a warrior and a king's son, and a

Scot, to boot. Trying to make a servant out of him would be akin to training a grown wolf to act as guard dog to a child! It is not in his nature to be a servant. He will never submit to that."

"Well, perhaps a soldier, then."

"Trained to our ways?" I almost flinched at the scorn in his voice. "The way the Romans taught *their* enemies to overwhelm them? I tell you, lad, you teach this man to fight the way we do, and he'll go home and teach his kinsmen how to beat us."

I shook my head at him. "No, Father, that he won't. I would not be so stupid as to raise a viper in my bosom. I intend to talk with him today. I locked him up as soon as he arrived to let him think about imprisonment. I hope he will see reason and decide that he has more to gain by working with us than by mouldering in a cell. We will see. I'll inform you later how the meeting goes. What else did you want to talk about?"

"Uther," he growled. "There's still no word from him. I'm starting to worry."

"Why?" I had not even begun to grow concerned. "No news is good news, in this case. If Uther had been killed or defeated, we would know of it by now. Lot's forces would be everywhere, drunk with victory."

My father looked unconvinced. "Well, you may be right," he growled.

"Father, you know I am. Uther has turned them back and, being Uther, he is worrying at their heels like a dog baiting a bear. He'll drive them home to Cornwall and then he'll come back for more men to keep them there, confined in their wooden stronghold. You'll see. I'd be prepared to wager on it." That earned me a glowering glance and a sharp warning.

"That is exactly what you're doing, boy."

"Well," I said, changing the subject, "time will tell. What else is there?"

"This!" He indicated the parchment in front of him with a gesture of disgust and I knew we had come to the crux of this meeting. "Victorex has been dead how long? Ten years now? Since he died, no one has been able to give me a concise report on our strength of horses. No one. I have four 'reports' here. Four separate responses to the same demands: How many head of stock do we possess in all and how is our breeding program progressing? The answers are all different, not even close to each other. The two furthest apart involve a difference of six hundred and twenty head. Six hundred and twenty! When I arrived back in Britain with Stilicho there were not that many horses in the Colony. Now we can misplace that number without even noticing, according to my own horsemasters!"

"Which do you believe to be most accurate?" I asked him. "Do we have so many that six hundred could be overlooked?"

He shook his head in frustration. "Caius, I have no way of knowing! That's what makes me so angry. I have no idea, and no one else has, either."

A progression of images flitted through my mind, pictures of the herds of horses that now seemed to be everywhere on our estates. "Surely there must be something we can do to remedy that, Father?"

He thumped his fist on the desk top. "There is. I want you, personally, to take a census of our livestock, starting immediately. I want an itemized head count of every animal on the Colony, particularly horses, but cattle as well. As far as the horses are concerned, I have to know how many battle mounts we have, as opposed to workhorses, and then I require information on our stud farms: how many stallions, mares and fillies; how many geldings; how many colts and foals; everything you can find. And I want it presented in a written report, detailing our entire resources, right down to the number of mares in foal." He pointed a rigid finger at me, underlining the importance of what he was about to say next. "This is not a task for delegation, Cay, it's far too important. I must have trustworthy numbers. That is why you are to do it in person. Your presence and authority will give this census an aura of official importance, which is exactly how I wish it to be perceived. It *is* vitally important. I want results as soon as possible. How long do you think you'll need?"

I stood up, shrugging my shoulders. "As long as it takes, I suppose. Certainly not less than a week and probably closer to two, by the time we visit all of the outlying farms and check the stock on each of them. It may take even longer than that. We do have a lot of horses nowadays."

"Talk to me of accurate numbers, Cay, not of lots. So be it. Start today, with the horses at hand here in the fort and stables. And be thorough, Caius. I want every head accounted for."

I nodded, saluted him, and left to go to the Armoury to collect my thoughts and make my plans. Two hours later I summoned a secretary and gave him the announcement I had prepared, instructing him to make twenty copies for my seal. It was a simple announcement to the commanders of each camp in the Colony, and to the masters of each farm, to gather all of their livestock in preparation for a visit of inspection by myself within a given period of days. When the secretary had gone about his business I relaxed and yawned, allowing myself to think about the pleasures I had enjoyed the previous night and savouring the image of Cassandra that burned clearly behind my eyes. In the course of my day-dreaming, I remembered my resolve to bring her something fine to wear and I sprang to my feet and made my way directly to my Aunt Luceiia's home.

The old lady was so happy to see me that I felt my usual guilt at spending so little time with her. She fussed over me, sending a servant to bring me wine, and seating me on her most comfortable chair. She chattered happily for some time about the affairs of her household before turning to my reasons for being there. As soon as she did that, I realized that she had known from the moment I walked in, with that infuriating percipience so often possessed by the elderly, that I had come to ask a favour. I know now it was ingenuous of me not to recognize that she must have determined my purpose immediately. From the very diffidence of my bearing, when I arrived, it would have required no great mental effort to conjecture that there was a woman involved.

She played for a while at guessing who it might be. She knew I had no trouble attracting any of the available women in the

Colony, and once I had assured her that I was not in trouble with a jealous husband or paying my attentions to too young a girl, she became quite perplexed. I was on the point of confessing the truth when she suddenly spoke up.

"Wait! I have it!" Her face lit up. "The girl. What's her name! The mysterious one who disappeared from the guarded room after being ravaged and beaten so savagely. What *was* her name? Cassandra! That was it. You have her, don't you?"

I nodded, smiling with rueful admiration yet again at her perspicacity, and then I began haltingly to explain the entire circumstances of Cassandra's disappearance to my beloved great-aunt. I concealed nothing, telling her of my suspicions about Uther, even though it was an appalling admission in the face of her steadfast love for her grandson. She listened impassively, and when I had finished she sat silent, neither judging Uther nor condemning me for my lack of trust in my own family, although she seemed to have less difficulty than I did with my father's philosophy on the benefit of the doubt.

"Tell me," she asked eventually. "How do you feel about Uther? Do you have anger towards him in your heart?"

I shook my head slowly. "I don't think so, Auntie. Not anger. Confusion, more than anything. Your suspicion of the priest Remus makes far more sense to me than my suspicion of Uther's guilt. I wish we could have found that man, but we did not, and so the doubt remains. I will have to bring Uther and Cassandra face to face one of these days. That's the only way I'm going to know for sure, and the thought of doing it appals me."

I had one more confession to make, and that was my love for Cassandra. That stumbling admission melted my great-aunt's heart while turning my face redder than a berry. Aunt Luceiia's expression was deeply serious and sympathetic. Did I wish to bring Cassandra to Camulod to live with her? She would be delighted to have her. I explained my reservations on that score, claiming expediency and the ease of safeguarding Cassandra in secrecy, rather than my own selfishness and my too rational fear of losing her, and Aunt Luceiia accepted them.

"Well, if you don't seek shelter for her, what did you come to ask me for?"

I cleared my throat. "Clothing. She has only one garment, Auntie, and it is a poor, rough thing. I had hoped you might be willing to let her have something old of your own, which would surely fit her."

She smiled gently, a look of mild disbelief crossing her face. "Clothing? Is that all? Well, I can see your point. If she is to winter out of doors she'll need more than one shift. Come with me. Give me your arm, and we'll see if I have any rags lying around that she can have."

I supported her by the arm, feeling the fragile weight of her, and she led me into her dressing room, where she uncovered chest upon chest of women's clothing.

"What colour are her eyes?"

"Grey."

"And her hair?"

"Fair."

"Fair! Is that the best you can do?"

"I think so. It's not yellow, nor is it golden. It is fair."

She sorted swiftly through the contents of her chests, throwing the occasional garment at me until my arms were full. Finally she stopped.

"There," she said. "That ought to do her for a while."

"All of these? Aunt Luceiia, these are beautiful! They're far—"

She cut me short. "Too fine? Is that what you were going to say?" I nodded, suddenly uncomfortable. "Shame on you, Caius Britannicus. You would have me believe you love this girl, and then tell me these things are too fine for her? If she has what it takes to enthral you, Nephew, dressed in only a simple shift, then these things are not good enough for her."

She paused, eyeing me with her head to one side, and then she sniffed and turned quickly away, but not before I had seen the twinkle of amusement in her eyes. "I shall have to meet this young woman," she said, over her shoulder. "If she won't come to me, then I shall find a way to go to her. Now, those are all light things. She will need some heavy woollens for cold weather, and I have just the thing." She crossed the room and began to sort through another wealth of clothing, all of these heavier than the ones I held, and the pile in my arms grew cumbersome. She finished it off with a magnificent, heavy, hooded cloak of thick, white wool that would shut out a winter storm completely. Finally, she was satisfied. "Good. Bring all of these back into the family room. Ludella will pack them in a chest and you can send a soldier for it in an hour or so. It should sit on your horse's rump, so you'll have no problem transporting it. Now. Is there anything else she needs?"

I could think of nothing else, and thanked her profusely, but she waved my thanks away.

"Now give me a kiss and let me get about my business. I have company coming."

I grinned at her. "A secret assignation?"

"No. A priest."

"More priests, Auntie? Haven't you got enough of those?"

"Don't be impertinent. Kiss me and go."

I did as she bade me, feeling much better than I had in coming.

Back at my quarters I called in the guard on duty and told him to have my prisoner brought to me under escort and to send the Legate Titus to me immediately. By the time I heard the approach of marching feet, I had signed the copies of my orders on the horse census and was finishing my instructions to Titus, who glanced curiously at the giant young Scot, saluted me smartly and left to begin the count of the livestock in the fort. I looked up at my prisoner.

He stood erect, a portrait of pride and indifference, staring at a spot somewhere above my head. His escorts flanked him, standing stiffly at attention.

"Thank you," I said to them, "you can wait outside." They withdrew, closing the doors behind them. I let young Donuil stand there as I returned to the documents in front of me, giving them one more unnecessary reading. Finally, I sat back and crossed my legs. "Well, Prince Donuil, what do you think of Camulod so far?"

He did not answer, so I rose and crossed to the window, turning my back on him deliberately, fully aware of the sword I had left lying on the table top within his reach. The shutters were open and I looked for some moments at the life going on outside. There was no sound of movement from behind me. I turned back and faced him. He had not moved a muscle. I crossed my arms in front of me and spoke to him again, weighting my voice only slightly with an edge of ill humour.

"Are you being sullen just to bait me? Or do you regret your bargain already? Your presence here spared the lives of more than a thousand men. Do you intend to celebrate that by spending five years in silence? And in a cell?" Still no response. I went back to my seat and sat there, staring at him in silence, fully prepared to wait him out. I had nothing to lose but time and it was on my side. The silence stretched and grew until it approached the point where stubbornness became a matter of pride, but I was prepared for that. Just before I judged that time to have arrived, I picked up a small wooden hammer and rang the brass gong on my table top. The door opened immediately and the guard stepped into the room.

"Commander?"

"Ask the centurion of the guard to send a messenger to me at once."

The guard left and we returned to the waiting game, and this time I busied myself with one of my uncle's codexes until I heard a knock at the door.

"Come!"

A trooper stepped into the room. "Centurion Tertius sent me, Commander."

"Good. Please go at once to the quarters of my aunt, Luceiia Varrus, and collect a chest that she has there for me. If it is not ready, wait for it and take it to my sleeping quarters. You will be expected."

"Yes, Commander." He, too, left and I spoke again to Prince Donuil.

"Obviously you have nothing to say. Do you wish to return to your cell?" No flicker of reaction, so I went on, "I had thought to have offered you better quarters, but since you seem to have no interest in being civil I can only assume you are comfortable enough where you are presently lodged. You surprise me. Five years can be a long time, behind bars." That reached him. He frowned and glanced sidelong at me.

"What kind of better quarters?"

I resisted an impulse to smile at him. "Open ones, for a start. Not quite fit for a prince, but comfortable enough for a princely prisoner."

"What would I have to do?" His voice was heavy with suspicion, wondering what price I would exact of him for any relaxation of vigilance. "If I were to accept these better quarters, what would you expect of me?"

I shrugged one shoulder. "Little more than you have already promised. I have your word that you won't attempt escape. Now, in return for your co-operation, I could permit you a room of your own, with privacy."

"Co-operation?" I could tell from his voice he knew I was about to name my price. "What would this co-operation consist of?"

"An end to this sullenness of yours, for one thing. There is no need for it, and it simply breeds suspicion and dislike." He blinked and was silent for a moment, obviously confused and trying to hide it.

"And? What else?"

"A willingness to contribute to the life of this Colony while you are part of it."

"Contribute? What form of contribution?"

"Work of some kind, not necessarily menial. We all contribute, every one of us, each according to his abilities."

He looked sceptical. "Even you?"

"Of course!" I laughed. "Even my father, the General. There are no parasites in Camulod."

I could not identify the tone that now coloured his voice. "What does your father do?"

"He is Administrator and Commander-in-Chief of our forces. He heads the Council of Governors of the Colony."

"And you, what do you do?"

"I assist my father. I keep records. I command a regiment. And I count horses."

His face went blank with surprise. "You what?"

"Count horses. I have just been charged with taking a census of all the horses that the Colony owns."

"You have that many horses?" His eyes showed wonderment. "How long will that take?"

I made a face to show my ignorance of that answer. "I do not know. In truth, I have no idea. A week, perhaps two, if nothing unexpected happens, like another raid, to interrupt the task."

His face creased into a frown. "What could I do? I have no training in any kind of work such as you describe, and I will not work with my hands like a bondsman."

"I didn't think you would, nor would I ask you to, but there must be something you can do. Do you have skills with iron?"

"You mean making it? No."

"Can you write and read?"

"No."

"Can you relax?" He blinked at me and I signalled towards the chair in front of him. "Sit down, you are too tall to gaze up at constantly." He sat down slowly and I picked up the sword that lay on the table and unsheathed it, laying it before him. "Look at it," I said. "This sword was made by my own great-uncle, Publius Varrus, a master smith. He was a soldier and a founder of this Colony, but he worked with his hands in metal all his life and saw no shame in it." I slipped the blade back into the sheath. "Every man has skills that are all his own, Donuil. Here, in our Colony, we ask that each man use his skills for the benefit of everyone, earning in return the right to live here, sharing in the Colony's prosperity. By making your own contribution you would be earning your keep—no more, no less. You will be asked to do nothing that could embarrass you or cause you to feel guilt in any way. You will not be asked, for example, to fight against your people, should they raid our lands again, although such an event would itself place you in a bad position, since your presence here means that we are at peace with Hibernia for five years."

"No! That's not true." There was urgency in his voice and he shook his head tersely. "You are at peace with my people, but not with all my countrymen. We have many kings on our island and few of them are friends. The fact that you hold me as hostage will mean nothing to the other kings. They have no love for me or for my people. They war with us as much as they do with Britain."

"Hmm!" I gnawed at my lower lip as though this had not occurred to me. "That could be awkward. How will we know that any future raiders are not of your people?"

The young man held his head high. "My father's standard is a black galley set on a field of gold. All of our ships carry it. My people will stay clear of you and your lands."

"Good." I nodded to him. "I believe you. But we have lost our track. Would you be willing to consider taking part in some way in the life of Camulod?"

He looked me in the eye. "Aye, Caius Merlyn, but there is a problem."

"What is that?"

"I do not have your Roman-British tongue. You are the only man I've met so far that I can talk to."

"Then you will have to work with me, somehow, until you learn our language. Will that gall you?" His face broke out slowly, but not reluctantly, into a smile.

"No, I think not."

"Good, then there is no problem. How old are you?"

"Seventeen. Almost eighteen."

I whistled my surprise. "You're a big lad for your age. Think about this. Consider what you might do that you can see as being of help to me and we will talk again tomorrow." As I said this, my door burst open and my father strode into the room, his face like thunder. He stopped short when he saw that I had company and looked from Donuil to me, making no sign of greeting to either one of us.

"Caius. When you are free, come to my quarters." He left as suddenly as he had come, closing the door behind him and I wondered what had upset him so. As soon as he had gone I turned back to my prisoner.

"So be it. Think on what I have said until tomorrow. In the meantime, I will have Legate Titus assign you to a room of your own. As of this moment, you are free to move about the fort, but be careful. Remember your own point about the language problem. In fact, it might be better not to wander off on your own until I have had time to show you around. I will do that tomorrow, too. Now I have to go and meet with my father and find out what has upset him. Come with me. I'll take you to Titus on the way and have him fix you up." I stepped to the door and held it open, and as he passed in front of me to leave, I stopped him with my free hand on his arm. "Welcome to Camulod," I told him, smiling. "I think you may like it here, once you get used to it." I offered him my hand and saw no reluctance in his face as he shook it.

XVI

It took me almost half an hour to find Titus and instruct him on what I wanted him to do with Donuil, so that as I approached my father's office I found myself thinking that he would, by this time, have had a chance to simmer down and be more objective about whatever it had been that infuriated him. I was wrong. He was still black-faced and grim.

"Where have you been?" he snapped as I stepped across his threshold. I blinked at him in surprise.

"Pardon me. I have been making arrangements for the suitable quartering of my prisoner."

"What quartering? He should be in a cell. We have more to be concerned with than the comfort of an alien raider."

I decided not to pursue that one. "What's the matter, Father? I've never seen you so upset."

"Upset? I am not upset! I am disturbed and uneasy and running short of patience with fools, but I am *not* upset!"

"Oh! Very well, then, what's worrying and disturbing you?" I had not bothered to close the door behind me as I entered, mainly because his temper had taken me so much by surprise. Normally the most imperturbable of men, my father was by nature cool and judicious, although in his infrequent fits of anger he could be implacable. He walked past me and closed the door himself. I turned to watch him as he did so, noting the effort he made to calm himself before turning back to me.

"Sit down, Caius. This has nothing to do with you. I need your advice. You are far more equable than I am in these matters." I felt my eyebrows rising. What, in God's name, could have affected him this way? I was glad to know it had nothing to do with me, for that left Cassandra free of his anger, too, and I felt a surge of relief. I sat down and watched him cross back in front of me to stand behind his big, wooden armchair. He leaned forward slightly and gripped the arms with his hands. "Priests!" he said, almost spitting the word out. "Tell me about priests, Caius."

I was bemused. "What can I tell you, Father? I know almost nothing about them. They live to preach the word of God to men."

"Yes, but what are they? What kind of beings?"

"What do you mean, beings, Father? They are priests! Men!"

He cut me off abruptly, with a hard slash of the edge of his hand. "No! No, Caius, that will not do. I will not accept that. They are not men. Not as you and I think of men. That crippled bastard Remus—the one you were unable to find after the affair of the beaten girl—was he a man? I think not!"

By this time I was totally mystified, and I held up my hands with what I hoped was a disarming smile on my face. "Whoa, Father, you're not making sense. I have no idea what you're talking about. Please! Start at the beginning and tell me what's been going on that I have been so ignorant of."

He moved around and sat in his chair, where he scrubbed his face with the palms of his hands as though washing it. That done, he blinked hugely, stretching the skin around his eyes as though struggling to remain awake. "You're right, Caius, you're right, I'm being irrational. Forgive me. This thing sprang out on me full grown. I should have been aware of it much sooner, but I chose to ignore the signals."

I waited, leaving him to collect his thoughts, and eventually his agitated features began to relax and a contemplative look came into his eyes. And still I waited, although it was becoming clear that he was immersed in his thoughts so deeply that he had momentarily forgotten I was there. Eventually, I cleared my throat quietly and spoke. "The priests, Father?"

"What? Oh yes, the priests. They deal in power, Cay. They deal in power."

"Of course they do," I agreed. "The power of God."

He threw me a glance filled with what was almost pity. "God has little to do with it, Caius. Power is power. It exists of and for itself. And the power to sway men's minds is the greatest and most lethal power of all. Why do you think these people exist at all?" I shook my head slightly and he went on. "You don't know? Let me ask another question, then. When did you last meet someone who had spoken directly with God? Not *to* Him, but *with* Him?"

"Never." I heard the incredulity in my own voice.

"Why not?"

"Because God doesn't speak to men directly."

My father slammed his clenched fist on the table in triumph. "That's right, Caius! Never directly! Only through priests. And whether the god is called Baal or Moloch or Jupiter or Helios, he has his priests to make clear his will to men. We may be talking of false gods and false priests, but there has never *been* a god *without* priests. The priests accept the sacrifices on the god's behalf, and they shape the minds of worshippers the way *they* wish them to be shaped. I've never really been aware of it before, but I always think of priests with their hands out, either demanding sacrifice or pointing in accusation."

I frowned at him. "What are you saying, Father?"

"I am saying that priests—all priests—are power-mongers. They deal in exploitation, and they exploit the minds of men."

I shook my head in disagreement. "No, that may have been true in olden times, Father, but it's hardly true today. I cannot think of Bishop Alaric as an exploiter."

"No more can I, nor was he. But he may have been the single exception that proves the rule. I have met no other like him, ever." He stopped talking for a space, obviously thinking about Alaric and what he had just said. When he resumed, his voice was more controlled—no less angry, but tightly reined. "There is a new breed of priests abroad in the world today, Caius, and they are multiplying like maggots. They call themselves Christian, but I think they have little in common with the Christian faith I hold. According to their dictates, men like old Bishop Alaric were heretics and unbelievers, misguided sinners who led their flocks astray, to use the shepherd image they are so fond of."

I heard the scorn in my voice. "That is ridiculous! Bishop Alaric was the most devout and holy man I ever knew!"

"Aye, he was. No doubt of it." My father's agreement with me was heartfelt. "But the savage-eyed zealots who rule the roost in Rome now say Alaric was a sinner. He and all his ilk. Followers of Pelagius!"

"What?" I was astounded. "But that would mean half the bishops in Britain!"

"More than half." I was floundering by this time, trying in vain to make sense out of what I was hearing. My father's voice was flat and emotionless as he went on, "Apparently, things have progressed quickly over the past few years among the Christians in Rome. We here in Britain have had little contact with the Church hierarchy since Honorius told us to look after our own affairs eighteen years ago. Since the revolt of the Burgundians in Gaul a few years after that, and the wholesale slaughter of priests then, there has been almost no contact between our bishops here and those in Rome. Burgundians eat Christian priests, it seems. And things have changed."

I felt myself frowning. "What things? How?"

My father grunted deep in his throat. "I'll give you three names: Paul, the Saint of Tarsus; Pelagius, the lawyer of Britain; Augustine, the Bishop of Hippo. That is all you need. Three men, and among the three of them they have bred what may be the biggest power struggle in human history, eclipsing the politics of all the Emperors combined."

"Pelagius?" I was surprised. "I don't see the connection. Pelagius is no priest. He's a lawyer, as you said, and a friend of yours. I've heard you talk of him often."

My father's headshake was brief. "Hardly a friend. But I met him once and spent some time with him. He impressed me greatly."

"I know," I said. "I read Uncle Varrus's account of the conversation you and he had when you came back to Britain twenty years ago. Pelagius and Augustine were at odds with each other even then, according to that account."

"That's right. They were. And the conflict continued. Augustine, it seems, denounced Pelagius to the Bishop of Rome—who now calls himself the Pope, incidentally, claiming primacy over all other bishops—and demanded his excommunication for heresy. The case went back and forth for several years, but Augustine won. Pelagius was excommunicated and all of his teachings, theories and beliefs were declared to be heretical . . . I remember that conversation I had with Varrus, but I did not know he had written it down. I'd like to read it. Do you still have it?"

I nodded, my mind skipping immediately to where the book in question lay safely stored. "Of course. I'll bring it to you this evening. It's in one of his codexes in the Armoury. But when did all of this happen, Father? When did the excommunication take place? And what has all of this to do with Paul of Tarsus?"

"Nothing—and everything. Paul's teachings are being used as a means to an end, and we'll discuss that later. What is important to us now, here in the Colony—to you, to me, to all of us—is that Pelagius is outlawed, declared a heretic and all his teachings categorized as heresy. That means that all of us who follow his beliefs are barred from salvation. Almost the entire population of this island we live on!"

I shook my head. "I am a soldier, Father, not a theologian. I cannot see what is so sinful or awful in Pelagius's theories."

"You think I am any different? But I can see the fault for which he was condemned. He dared to stand up against Augustine of Hippo. Pelagius is a humanist, Caius. He believes in the dignity of man, in personal responsibility, in freedom of choice and freedom of will! He stands condemned out of his own mouth, because his teachings undermine the priests themselves. Give a man the right to talk to God on his own terms, to bear God in his own heart and deal with Him in justice on his own behalf, and you negate the need for priests! That's why Pelagius is excommunicate!

"Bishop Alaric and his people have taught the way of Christ

to us in Britain. They preach love and infinite mercy, and that nothing—no sin—is unforgivable. But now the men of God in Rome have ruled that *Pelagius* is unforgivable. They have damned him for daring to differ with their views. That is politics, Caius; there is no love of God involved here. In their lust for power over men, these bishops have condemned much of the populace of the entire world to eternal damnation, unless the world repents and does things the way these bishops want them to be done. That involves *changing their beliefs!* It may not sound like much when said aloud like that, but when I start to think of what's involved here, it frightens me to the depths of my soul." His voice tailed off into silence.

"But can they do this, Father? Are these bishops that powerful?"

"Who is to gainsay them? They call themselves the Fathers of the Church. They speak, they claim, with the full authority of God Himself and of His Holy Saints."

"Including Paul of Tarsus?"

"Including Paul of Tarsus."

"There's more to this than meets the eye, Father—my eye, at least. What is so important about Paul?"

"Women." My father spoke the word with hard emphasis. "Of all evangelists, Paul is the misogynist, the woman hater. Now, it seems there is a move afoot—not just afoot, but far advanced—to lend far greater credence to his words than in the past."

"How can that be done? What do you mean?"

He drew in a sharp breath. "It has become the style among the churchmen in Rome, it seems, to denigrate women in general. It's a fashion that has been growing since the pederasts and homosexuals achieved their vaunted equality under the Caesars, and it grew even more strongly after some of the Roman women of the great families began speculating in company stocks and in real estate development. But it has grown beyond belief recently. Women are being perceived nowadays in Rome, mainly through the machinations of these churchmen, as the Devil's spawn and servants, dedicated to the damnation of men."

I had never heard my father speak so eloquently or forcefully about a non-military subject. I was astounded. "You must be joking, Father! You are, aren't you?"

He looked directly at me. "No, Cay, I am not. The current mode among the new breed of churchmen is to condemn women, more and more virulently."

"But why?"

"How would I know that? Because they are convenient, I suppose. The Church in Rome has been predominantly a male hierarchy since the earliest times. Women have never prospered in the Church. Perhaps the Elders now seek to crystallize their hegemony. I don't know the underlying reasons, Caius, but that is the way it is." He paused, piercing me with his eyes. "You don't really believe what I am telling you, do you?"

I had to shake my head, for in truth I could not bring myself to believe that he was right. That he was serious and believed himself to have the right of it, I had no doubt, but my sanity demanded that he be mistaken.

"Shake your head all you like, Caius, but disabuse yourself. It is the truth. These things are happening, and they have come to Camulod. That disgraceful debacle in the dining hall last night was proof of it."

"What debacle? What are you talking about?"

"How can you not know? We almost had a riot here last night over this question. How could you be unaware of it?"

"I was away last night. I returned this morning, met with you and have been on the run ever since. What is going on?"

"Good God, Cay! You have to stay more aware of what's going on. I spent *three hours* this afternoon talking with priests of both factions—our British ones and their Roman ones—Pelagian and orthodox, as these zealots would have it! They have, among them, issued me—and all of us—with an ultimatum: salvation or damnation, on the terms of the Church in Rome, without any recourse to trial. That is what's going on!"

I was bewildered and admitted it. "I'm sorry, Father. I had no idea. Have we a choice?"

He snapped open his mouth to shout at me, I could see it in his face, and then subsided, looking down at the table top in front of him.

I continued speaking. "I mean, what are we to do? It sounds as though the battle lines between these two schools of thought are clearly drawn. Are we in a position to debate them?"

He sighed, a long-drawn and distressing sound. "I don't know, Cay. I simply do not know. The only thing I do know with any certainty is that this whole question has sprung up suddenly, although it has been fermenting for years. I believe it is the biggest and the most vexatious question any of us will face in our lifetime, or in the lifetimes of our children. How are we to proceed from this day on in the way we live our lives and worship our God?" He was silent again for a short space, and then continued, "I wish my father were still alive. His was a mind fashioned for abstractions like this. Mine is not. How can I take this question to the Council? It would tie all of us up in argument for years. If we accept the dictates of the Pope in Rome and the Bishop of Hippo, we must—and I have to emphasize the imperative—we *must* abandon completely all of the rules we have been taught to live by until now. That involves the certain condemnation of Bishop Alaric and his kind, who adopted the teachings of Pelagius in good faith. But on a far more subtle level, it involves the surrender of our will to the dictates of the men in Rome, and *that* is what Pelagius was against from the beginning. His contention and his fear were that the so-called men of God were taking unto themselves the attributes of God. They were taking the teachings of the Christ Himself and interpreting them to suit their own requirements. And Pelagius was *right*, Cay! He was *right!* And they have proved him right by excommunicating him. They have condemned him to eternity without salvation. The Christ whose faith they follow would never condone such extreme punishment. Yet these men, who live in Rome in luxury, I'm told, have taken to themselves the power to tell all others how to live, and to condemn them to perdition if they do not obey." He stopped, and drew another deep breath.

"Pelagius was simple in his teachings. There is nothing anti-Christ in him. He teaches us that we must choose between the laws of God and the ways of licentiousness. He says it rests in us to choose to follow the Christ or to spurn him. He tells us we are made in God's image, with the *innate* ability to aspire to joining God's heavenly host. That innate ability is at the centre of this controversy. Our will is free, as was the will of him we call Satan. The temptations we face are the same as Lucifer's. But Pelagius gives us hope in ourselves, and dignity, and a sense of worth."

I was fascinated by this new view of my father. I listened, spellbound, as he went on.

"The followers of Augustine of Hippo, on the other hand, deny us that sense of worth. We are born in sin, they say, already doomed to our fate, unless we subjugate ourselves to their ways, begging *their* intercession with the Divine to give us grace." He was waxing angry again, outrage swelling in his face. He slammed his hand down on the table top and drew himself to his full height. "Do you have anything of great importance to look to now?"

I shrugged my shoulders. "No, nothing that will not wait until tomorrow."

"Good. Let's get out of here and go for a ride. I want to shout and rave and vent my bile, and there's no profit to be gained by doing it where I can be overheard. Do you mind?"

"Not at all, lead on."

While we walked to the stables in silence and saddled our horses, I thought about all my father had said and about the conflict that had so suddenly consumed him. I knew it was important then, but I had no idea that the past hour and the hour to come were to affect me so strongly that they would influence the evolution of an entire country in the course of coming years.

On leaving the fort we took the new road to the villa, but left it at the bottom of the hill and struck south towards the forest's edge. We rode in silence, each of us with his own thoughts, until the silence of the forest cloaked us and all sounds from Camulod were long lost behind us. We rode through a series of dense thickets, which had kept us both busy trying to stay in the saddle, and emerged from the last of them to find ourselves in a beautiful, gladed area with wide expanses of open grassland, from which sprang magnificent beech trees. The thought occurred to me that this must be a holy place to the Druids, and that brought the question of excommunication back into my mind. Most of my Druid friends were not Christian, so they had no worries about salvation or eternal life. Some of them, however, had become converted to Christianity in recent years and yet lived a life that was little altered from their traditional ways. This new direction from Rome, I felt, could be ominous to these people, whose conversion had come directly from the compatibility of the humanity of Pelagius's beliefs and the mellow benignity of the Druidic ways. Some of these men might have been in the fort the previous night, and I wondered if they had been affected by what my father had described as a riot. Finally, when I had gone over everything my father had said for about the tenth time, I could stand his silence no longer.

"Father?" He turned to me. "What happened last night? You said there was almost a riot. What caused it? Who was involved?"

"Priests caused it, Christian priests fighting with Christian priests. I wasn't there. I ate in my quarters with Titus and Flavius. We were disturbed at our meal by a messenger sent to us by your friend Ludo. The common dining hall was crowded, as it always is at that time of night, and an argument broke out when a group of priests who had just arrived that afternoon refused to be seated at the same table as two of your Druid friends. Popilius, the senior centurion, was in the hall. He offered to reseat them at another table at which some other priests were already seated. They refused to sit with these people, either, and one of them started shouting about damnation and anathema. Popilius tried to shut him up, but one word led to another and these two groups of priests actually came to blows! Can you imagine?

"Well, by the time poor Popilius had gathered his wits enough to call up the guard, the whole place had degenerated into an armed camp. Can't blame Popilius. He simply did not anticipate violence from churchmen, especially among themselves. It got out of hand too quickly for him. But that Ludo's a bright one. As soon as he saw which way the wind was blowing, he sent word to me. By the time I got there, the guard had all of them under restraint."

"So what did you do?"

"Confined the lot of them under guard for the night."

"In the *cells?*" I was aghast at the thought, but my father dismissed my concern brusquely.

"Where should I have put them? In my own quarters?"

"Good God! I can't imagine priests coming to blows with each other."

"I couldn't either, until I saw it. But I told you I spent three hours with those people today. I have no trouble imagining it now. It was the first such occurrence, to the best of my knowledge, but I fear it will not be the last. Not by any measure."

My father reined in his horse, so that I had to do the same to mine, and when he spoke next, his voice was low and vibrant with urgency. "Caius, hear this. This new band of priests, seven of them in number, provoked the entire disgraceful debacle deliberately. Today they turned the rough edges of their tongues and their intolerance on me. On me! They came into my fort—and it is mine, for all intents and purposes—*demanded* my hospitality, abused it flagrantly and arrogantly, and treated *me* like a criminal for having dared to lock them up, and like an excommunicate heathen for daring to differ with their opinions and beliefs. They told me that I should clean out Camulod; get rid of all the women in the fort; and close the doors of Camulod to all priests who will not swear to the apostasy of Pelagius and his teachings. And that I should accept the error of my ways with *humility* and *beg their pardon* for my sins!" His voice was shaking now with outrage. "And!" he went on, "*And* once I had applied for and received their forgiveness, and had been reaccorded the right to salvation, I should begin a series of . . . *inquiries* into the beliefs of each of our colonists, doing all in my power to ensure that they conform to the new doctrines! All in my power, you understand, includes expelling people from the Colony."

I was hearing far more than I had bargained for.

"What was your reaction to all of this?"

"My reaction? I had to sit on my reaction. I cannot remember ever having felt so powerless in my life. I could have taken them and flogged the flesh from their bones, Cay, but it would not have made one jot of difference to their attitude. I had no power to *change them.* These men are convinced that they are right, and that the rest of the world is wrong. There is no *giving* in them, no compromise, no gentleness, no humanity. They are zealots. Fanatics. They are a new breed of priests altogether, and they frighten me, not for myself but for the world they seek to rule and change and conquer. And they call themselves Christian." He sighed, noisily, a mixture of anger and indignation.

"Four hundred years have wrought a lot of changes in the Word of the Christ. Do you remember the story of Jesus on the mountainside, when he preached the blessedness of the humble, the peacemakers, the seekers after justice? Well, that story and its sentiments sit strangely with the way these men of God behave today. The Son of the Carpenter is being lost sight of, Caius. His words are being reinterpreted and 'improved upon.' Jesus, the Christus, talked of love and of peace. Now there are factions warring within his Church, condemning each other with sheer hatred and intolerance. Love is out of favour."

"So you said *nothing* to them when they railed at you?"

He threw me a look that spoke loudly, and I saw Picus the Legate as well as Picus my father in his eyes. "No, I didn't mean that. But I said nothing rash, nothing in anger. I told them that I would consider their words, think about them, and give them an answer soon. And in the meantime, I sent them back to the cells under guard, with strict instructions that they not be allowed to speak to anyone until I have reached my decision."

"And?"

"And what?"

"Have you reached a decision?"

"Yes, I have reached a decision." He kicked his heels into his mount's flanks and we began to move forward again. "But only within the past few moments, in talking it over with you." His voice died away, and I saw no profit in commenting upon the worth of my contribution to the discussion to date. We rode side by side in silence for a spell and then he started talking again.

"One of them told me about a new lifestyle being followed in the Church today. It is called monasticism. It involves a complete withdrawal from public life. Its adherents live in *monasteries*—enclosed communities of men only, who dedicate themselves entirely to penitence. These people mortify their own flesh, Cay. They abase themselves constantly before their God, who is a contradiction in terms: a Christian God as stern and unyielding as they are. Worldly pleasure of any kind is anathema to them. Women are instruments of the Devil himself, used by Satan to ensnare all men and draw them from the path of salvation. What do you think of that?"

I had to smile. "Aunt Luceiia will be impressed."

He barked his abrupt laugh, his sense of humour reasserting itself briefly. "Aye, she will. I tell you, Caius, the arrogance of these men astounds me. From where I look at it, everything they are doing flies in the face of the gentle, humane Christ that I was taught to worship and revere."

"Aye." I cleared my throat. "So what have you decided, Father?"

He looked at me sidelong, angling his mount closer to mine.

"I believe that the decision I made years ago to follow the ideas of Pelagius was the correct decision. These zealots make Pelagianism sound like Onanism. I see it as the only sane and decent way a responsible, proud man can live his life . . . with free will and the integrity of his personal belief. If I am wrong, then I will bear the consequences when I die. In the meantime, I shall live my life according to the dictates of my conscience, and I will suffer no person under my jurisdiction to be maligned, harassed or victimized for his—or her!—beliefs.

"These seven priests will leave our lands tomorrow under escort. I will not threaten them. If they come back, they will be made to leave again. And again, until they grow old and tired." He sighed. "I have lived more than fifty years to be told I am condemned as a heretic. And I am told this by a ragged, unwashed man who offends my nostrils and my sensibilities ... I choose to live the way I have always lived—perhaps as a heretic, perhaps not. But I can at least stand the smell of myself. If it is mortally sinful to bathe, to laugh, to enjoy life in moderation and to honour women, then I fear I must continue to live in what is seen as sin. I am too old to change."

I felt a surge of pride and love for this man who had sired me.

"These priests are misguided. But they are also dangerous. There is a massive struggle going on for dominance in this world, Caius. These people are the proselytes of the power-mongers. If the newly named Pope comes here from Rome in person to convince me I am wrong, I will listen to him, but he must bring more reasonable arguments than his minions bring. Let's go home. I have some priests to talk to."

It never crossed my mind, then or at any other time, that my father might be wrong. My grandfather and Publius Varrus had lived their lives as they did, models of probity both, in natural nobility and dignity, and they had trained my father. And so it came about that when the boy who was to be my charge came under my influence, I taught him in the old ways of Ancient Rome, Republican Rome, and in the ways of old Bishop Alaric and Pelagius, and in the ways of my father's and his father's Camulod, which was not the way of new Rome. The boy I taught learned cleanliness, simple Godliness, discipline and the life of a warrior. He learned to enjoy the goodness of life, to enjoy and appreciate the goodness and the strength of woman, and to take for granted the inherent nobility and goodness of man.

XVII

At the tenth hour of the following morning, I witnessed what was probably the most portentous event that ever occurred in the Great Council Hall of Camulod, an occasion that, to my mind at least, unquestionably dwarfed all of the glories to come in the days of Arthur's reign, and indubitably influenced all of them. It was a gathering—almost a ceremonial—that, though small in itself, was to influence the course of life in the province of Britain for ever.

My father had summoned a plenary meeting of the Council and augmented the company with the full officer complement of the garrison, including the ten senior members of the *Centuria*, the warrant officers. All military personnel were instructed to attend in full parade uniform, so it was a brilliant and colourful assembly. Extra seating had been brought into the Council Hall to accommodate the unusual number of people in attendance, and the circle of fifty or so men took up almost the entire circumference of the Hall, leaving the centre empty, with an open segment at the back of the circle to allow the group of priests to enter.

Everyone was punctual. My father began by outlining the situation for the benefit of the partially informed and the totally uninformed, of whom there were very few. He followed his outline with the announcement that he had arrived at a unilateral decision on what to do, and that his decision would be binding upon everyone in the Colony for the ensuing twenty-four-hour period, at the end of which he would be prepared to listen to arguments and to accommodate compromise in response to intelligent and informed opposition. Until that time, however, his decision and the enforcement of it would be absolute.

He had invited their attendance here today, he went on, to witness the delivery of his decision to the visiting priests so that no one, whether in the Council or on the staff of the garrison, could claim to have been unaware of developments. Having said all of this, he ordered the priests to be brought into the assembly under escort.

There was a loud murmur of comment and speculation at this order, which my father chose to ignore, and the noise grew and was sustained during the interval that followed. I noticed that my father took care in the meantime to allow no eye contact between himself and any member of the assembly. Someone called his name, but he ignored the summons, turning and beckoning me. I walked across and leant towards him.

"I only regret that Uther has not returned. Of all the people here, he is the one with the greatest right to have been consulted in this matter."

"Don't let his absence concern you too much, Father," I said with a small smile. "We both know Uther well enough to know that he will have no quarrel with your findings, unless it be on the grounds of too much restraint. Had he been here and subjected to the abuse you had to face, these priests might have been sorry men today."

As I returned to my seat, there came a sudden hush, spreading inward from the entrance to the hall, and we looked up to see the seven priests being brought forward into the open circle. Centurion Popilius himself advanced ahead of the six-man escort party who herded the priests to the centre of the circle and then came to a halt. The silence in the room was absolute and my father, who, like everyone else in the Hall, was seated, remained sitting as he spoke into it.

"Thank you, Centurion Popilius. You may dismiss your men, but ask them to remain outside. You yourself may join us. There is a seat for you." Popilius saluted and did the General's bidding, instructing his soldiers to remain within hail. While the escort were leaving the hall I gazed in frank curiosity at the priests who stood before us.

They were all young, and all were dressed in ragged, dirty black cassocks bound at the waist with plain rope. It was to this fact that I at first attributed the strange aura of uniformity I sensed about them. It took me some time to redefine that initial reaction. There was a sameness, certainly, but it had nothing to do with what they wore; it was in their eyes, and it was almost indescribable. The word that first occurred to me was wildness, but as this confrontation continued I replaced that with arrogance, then disdain, then intolerance, and finally fanaticism—although I had never heard the expression prior to my father's use of it the day before.

Whatever that expression in their eyes signified, I found it disconcerting to the point of being almost frightening. Then I remembered the name of the Hebrew fanatics of biblical times, the followers of Simon Zelotes, the Zealots, the men who would gladly die for their own, steeped-in-blood beliefs. You could tell simply by looking at these men that they believed, deep in their souls, that they were the masters here and we were all their inferiors. There was no deference or civility apparent in the demeanour of any of them. They looked around them at the assembly with sneers of defiance on their faces, and then their leader took one long step forward and addressed my father in a loud, hectoring tone that no one in the assembly hall could fail to hear.

"I assume, Picus Britannicus, from the numbers you have assembled here, that you have decided to make public your renouncement of the heretic Pelagius and his misguided teachings and to seek the forgiveness of Holy Mother Church!" Someone seated in the circle of the hall drew in his breath with an audible hiss, but the priest continued, "It is only fair to advise you, however, that in the light of your treatment of myself and these of my brethren who have shared your prison with me, the clemency you seek might be slower in being granted than it might otherwise have been. To lay hands on, or to offer insult to, the envoys of the Holy Father in Rome is not the best way to seek the favour of the Church."

The speaker, a tall and emaciated man who could have been any age from twenty-five to thirty-five, had a voice that grated on the ears. His face was so thin as to appear cadaverous and I knew his breath would be rancid and foul. My father swept him with his eyes from the hem of his garment to the top of his head and then spoke as though the priest had never opened his mouth.

"I have assembled these people here to witness the delivery of the decision I promised you when we last spoke." He paused, seeming to weigh his words. "I am Commander here—Commander-in-Chief of this Colony. In terms of years, I am an old man, although by the grace of God, I am still young enough and healthy—"

"I warn you, Britannicus! You stand excommunicate! Speak not of the grace of God in terms of yourself. You blaspheme!"

This outburst produced a shocked reaction from the assembly. My father gestured for silence, then drew a deep, deep breath and held it until his face began to grow red, at which point he released the pent-up air steadily and audibly. I, who knew all the signs, had never seen him so angry. The tall priest, however, stood his ground boldly, his face a mask of arrogant intransigence.

Finally, my father spoke, his words slow and sibilant, his voice pitched ominously low. "Priest, hear me clearly and without distortion. I dislike threats, either given or received. And I dislike hasty judgments. Most of all, however, I dislike bad manners. You are here to hear my decision on a matter of great import, and by the crucified Christ, Son of the Living God, you will hear it in courteous silence *if I have to have you stifled and bound hand and foot!*"

Again he quelled an outburst, this time of approval, with a glance of implacable anger, so that the spontaneous support subsided immediately. He returned his eyes to the priests. "Hear me, now! I suffered your abuse and your scandalous tongue in silence for hours yesterday ... That was yesterday. Today, it is my turn to speak, and not only will any interruption be unwelcome, it will not be tolerated! I will, as I have said, stifle you and bind you if you force me to. The choice is yours." He paused, awaiting a reaction, and receiving none, continued.

"I am a soldier. As a young soldier, I had no time for religious pursuits. As I have grown older, however, I have made some study of the Christian doctrine, particularly the spread of it in Britain. It has been, by and large, a Roman religion, spread, over the years, through Roman settlement and Roman civilization. The people of Britain are not, or have not been until recently, predominantly Christian. In the past few years, since the withdrawal of Rome, they have had other things to occupy them. Survival, for example . . . The people of this land are beset on every side by invaders. North, south, east and west, they have to contend with Picts, Saxons, Angles, Jutes, Franks and Scots. All of these come to kill, to conquer and despoil, to pillage and destroy. None of them have the slightest regard for the *people* of Britain other than as sacrificial sheep.

"If you travel elsewhere in Britain you will find temples to the old gods, still in use. The foothold of the Christian Church in this land is tenuous, at best. That it exists at all is due to the efforts of the bishops here in Britain, men like our own Bishop Alaric, whose saintly piety and caring gave hope to the people who knew him. When a man, or a woman, can have no hope of being able to keep anything he or she owns for any length of time, then that person's sense of personal dignity and worth, his own integrity, becomes special to him. Bishop Alaric and his fellows worked hard to keep the people of this land free from despair. They taught them love, charity and the belief in the merciful omnipotence of God and His Son, Jesus . . . They offered people the hope of happiness beyond this squalid and vexatious life on earth, and they adopted the tenets of Pelagius, because they believed his teachings and beliefs to be righteous and wholesome in the eyes of God." He paused again and such was the power of his delivery that none attempted to interrupt him. Eventually he continued.

"Let me repeat that. Alaric and his fellow bishops believed that the ways and the teachings of Pelagius were righteous and whole-some in the eyes of God. By direct association, Alaric and his like saw no dichotomy between the tenets of Pelagius and the word of the Christ Himself." The tall priest made as if to speak but he was cut off by the savage, chopping motion of my father's hand. "And now," my father went on, his voice level and temperate, his delivery slow and considered, "now, in the space of three short days, we are ordered—not requested—to accept the allegation—not the fact—that Pelagius is apostate, that his teachings are sinful, and that our beloved friend and mentor, Bishop Alaric of Verulamium, was a sinful man, misguided and inept, irresponsible and incompetent ...

"We are commanded to recant our allegedly profane beliefs; to accept your unsubstantiated assurance that our entire way of life is in error; to admit, under pain of eternal damnation, that *your* way of worshipping our God is the right way and the only way; and to sue for your clemency. We are required to review our entire social structure and to relegate our own womenfolk to an inferior status that is entirely alien to us as Celts and Romans in the first place, and to the entire social mores of the people of Britain thereafter."

Picus's voice was the only sound audible in the room. He paused once more to let all he had said sink home to his listeners, then continued. "All of this you made abundantly clear to me yesterday. You made it painfully clear. And I told you then that I would consider your words and your message and arrive at a decision on how life in this Colony is to proceed from this day forth. In the meantime, you have been kept apart from my people. Imprisoned, as you choose to describe it. Let me point out to you that the laws of hospitality in this Colony and in this land are sacrosanct, and mutually binding upon host and visitor ... It was you who forced my hand in the matter of your detention, by causing unnecessary, unwarranted and unprecedented strife beneath my roof. I chose to extend that detention after my interview with you yesterday, because your intolerant zeal alarmed me when I considered the effect it might have among these people of ours, who are simple people, unused to sophistry, oratory and semantics.

"It is with my mind attentive to the needs and the general welfare of the people of our Colony that I have deliberated upon your words and made my decision. I have said I am a soldier. I am no philosopher, nor am I a theologist, but for better or worse, I have a responsibility for the welfare of this Colony, and I believe in fulfilling one's responsibilities. It is therefore my responsibility,

I believe, to learn more of these sweeping changes of which you bring word, and to seek assurance from the highest level of authority to which I can gain access that such changes come as the result of careful consideration and debate, and are not foisted upon us simply at the whim of a mere man or even a group of men seeking to further their own aims. It would be *irresponsible* of me to accept your assertions at face value: they are too sweeping, too extreme and too important to be taken lightly. That is my *administrative* decision, as Commander-in-Chief of this Colony. Take it with you back to Rome . . . We are not obdurate, but neither are we prepared to risk endangering our immortal souls without prudent investigation of the circumstances governing this signal change of posture within the Church." He paused again, and again the silence held until he resumed.

"On the other hand, as a man and a soldier, I find that I have no sympathy for your point of view. I find this idea of Monasticism both odious and offensive. It seems unnatural. Had Jesus wished his followers to behave in this fashion, He would have clearly stated so, or so it seems to me. He was an articulate speaker on all other things. I hear no misogyny in the Words of Jesus. Was it not He who said: Let he who is without sin cast the first stone? . . . That, sir priest, tells me that the Christ Himself recognized man's right to responsibility and self-determination. I will embrace the tenets of Pelagius personally, until someone more wholesome and more reasonable than you convinces me that I am wrong."

The priest could bear his own silence no longer. "You are accursed!" he cried out. "You are blasted with the sin of Lucifer, gross pride! And you will burn in Hades!"

My father's patience finally snapped and his voice became brittle with disgust. "Get these people out of my sight! Popilius, see to it they are given food and drink and have them taken under *heavy* escort to the borders of our land and *forbidden* re-entry." He had to shout to make himself heard above the imprecations of the priests who were now all shouting, creating pandemonium. Popilius's men must have been waiting directly outside, for they appeared immediately and began herding the shouting zealots out of the hall, and even after they had left, their shouting continued. "Popilius!" My father's voice had risen to a roar.

"General?"

"A *heavy* escort. I want those people out of here quickly and I want them out *now*. Put them in a wagon. Gag them if you have to."

Popilius left and my father sat down again, ashen-faced. For a long time nobody in the Hall moved or spoke. The shouting outside died away into silence. Then Julius Terrix, leader of the Council and the son of one of the first Colonists, rose to his feet.

"Picus Britannicus. You have said that your decision is to be inviolable for twenty-four hours, and you have taken upon yourself an awesome responsibility in behaving as you have this day." I felt tension knotting in the pit of my stomach anew, but he went on, "I have no right to speak for any other here, since we have not acted as a Council in this matter, but I, personally, endorse your stance, your decision, and the thoughtfulness with which you presented it. On behalf of myself and my wife, I thank you."

Everyone in the room must have been holding his breath, as I was, waiting for Julius Terrix to make his pronouncement, for as soon as his thanks were uttered the entire circle of men were on their feet, cheering my father in a way that I had never heard before. I crossed to his side, my heart swelling with pride and affection, and offered him my hand, and only the steely pressure of his fingers on my arm betrayed how relieved he was by the general approval of his actions. I nodded to him and would have left him to his congratulations, but he retained his hold on my arm and pulled me aside.

"Well," he grunted. "That's one burden out of the way."

I grinned at him. "Aye, and well out of the way."

He frowned. "It will come back, believe me. We have not heard the last of this affair."

I blinked at him. "You said 'one burden,' Father. Are there others?"

"Aye. One other, but now it's yours."

I stared at him, wordless, and he continued, speaking in a low voice and glancing around to make sure no one could overhear him.

"They've turned me into an Administrator, Cay, and tied me to this Council Chamber. My soldiering days are over." He held up a peremptory hand to cut off my protest. "No, hear me, boy, and listen well. I am not unhappy about what I am saying. Nor is this any sudden whim or hasty decision. The matter has been in my mind for long months now. It's time for you to take command, formally, of our fighting forces." He paused, eyeing me keenly, one brow high on his forehead. "I'm not saying I'm too old, boy, so don't look at me that way. What I am saying is that you are ready for command and I have other matters, some of them vital, demanding more of my attention. I will still ride out to battle as and when the need arises, but time is pouring through my fingers like sand and there is too much to be done here in Camulod. That is my decision and there is no alternative, no recourse. You command. Uther will answer to you, and you will still answer to me in all but military decisions. There the last word is yours from this time on. Are we agreed?"

"Yes," I said, finally, bereft of words and fighting an urge to stammer, "but—"

"No buts. I shall inform the others—everyone—this evening. You have earned this position, my son. Now live with it." He gripped me, briefly and hard by the upper arm, nodding and smiling. "I look forward to serving under you, Caius Britannicus."

He spun on his heel and went to join his well-wishers without looking back, leaving me with my chaotic thoughts. Finally I collected myself and made my way out of the hall and back to my quarters in order to rid myself of my cumbersome finery before the noon meal.

I was surprised and pleased to find young Prince Donuil waiting for me in my rooms. He rose as I entered and nodded to me in a gracious, not unfriendly manner. I grinned at him and threw my cloak across the table that served as my desk.

"Good morning. I hope you have not been waiting too long? There was a Council meeting."

"I know. I found one of your soldiers who speaks my tongue. He told me there was great excitement. Then I heard all the shouting and commotion in the yard. I thought about going to see what was happening, but there was anger in the voices, so I came here instead."

"A wise move. Yes, there was anger in the voices, beyond a doubt."

"What is going on? Or can you not tell me?"

"Why not?" As I changed into my lighter uniform I told him what had been happening and how my father had resolved it.

He listened in silence until I had finished and then said, quite simply, "Your father seems to be a man of principle. He and my own father would get along."

"You think so? That's interesting. But you are right, my father is a man of principle. Are you a Christian?"

He shook his head. "No. We've had priests working in our lands for some years now. They are harmless enough, and they have won some followers here and there, but not many, not in our lands, at least. Some of the other kings encourage them, though. One bishop in the West, a man called Patrick, is building a great following. There are wondrous tales about him. I think it will take more than tales, though, to make me give up the old ways."

"You mean you would rather play than pray?"

"I would rather fight."

I grinned at him. "Aye, I'm sure you would. Let's go and find some food. Have you thought about what you might like to do while you are here with us?"

"I have."

"And?" I waited.

"I'm half starved. Could we find the food first? I think I might find it easier to say what I have to say on a full stomach, and you yourself might not suffer in the listening, with a good foundation."

I was intrigued. I could see that whatever it was he had decided upon had not come to him easily, but there was no truculence or resentment in his demeanour, so I led him across to the refectory by the kitchens and watched in amazement as he wolfed down three times the amount of food I ate. The place was quiet for the time of day, with only a few junior officers near us and one knot of off-duty troopers at the far end of the big room. Eventually my prisoner consumed the last of his bread and cheese and pushed his empty platter away with a contented grunt.

"I can see now why you are so big," I said, smiling. "Is this part of a plan of yours? To eat us out of provenance and starve us into submission?" A few of the young officers turned in surprise at the sound of my Celtic words. I ignored them and continued to smile at my prisoner, who gazed back at me for several moments, searching my comment for hidden meanings before his own face creased in a half smile.

"It is in my mind that you and your people here would not submit to starvation."

"I will not argue with you on that. What else is in your mind?"

"It is in my mind, too, that I know Lot of Cornwall no better than I know you, having met the man only twice and briefly each time."

"And?"

"I believe that my people would have a more beneficial alliance with you, than with Lot."

"How so?"

He made to respond immediately but then paused and considered his words so that his face grew speculative before he said, "I am not sure. Something of honour, I think. You have honour and understand the need for it. The King of Cornwall deals little with it, from what I have learned."

"How can you know that, Donuil, if you don't know the man?"

He shrugged his huge shoulders. "How do I know if the sun is shining before I leave my hut in the morning? There are signs and sounds that announce it. There are signs that make it clear to me, also, that we of the *Scotii* would be better allied with your Colony."

"But our Colony needs no allies. Especially in another land beyond the sea."

"Perhaps not, Caius Merlyn, but ask yourself how great your need of enemies is, across the same sea?"

"A good point, Prince Donuil!" I nodded in agreement. "If our enemies have allies across the sea, then we have enemies across the sea and should bestir ourselves to seek alliance there with others who could keep those enemies at home." He nodded, and I went on, "But that becomes complicated, even in the telling, and we have already solved the problem. Your presence here has cut the string from Lot's alliance. Your people are no threat to us, for now."

"Not for five years, at least, you mean."

"Not for five years, at least."

"And after that? What do you think will happen when my time with you is up?"

It was my turn to shrug. "Who knows? Much can happen in five years. The worst that could happen is that your people could war against us again. But by that time we would have made our preparations to receive them. It would not be pleasant, but we would be forearmed and ready for them." I looked directly at him and his eyes were wide and frank, looking straight into my own. "But we are not here to discuss a war that may or may not happen in five years. We are here to discuss your thoughts on how you might profitably spend those five years, with an eye to your own good and comfort, and a non-traitorous benefit to the community that will be your host during that time."

He smiled. "Nicely phrased, Caius Merlyn."

"Well," I smiled back since he had caught my intention so clearly. "What have you decided? It's taking you a long while to come to your point."

"Aye, I suppose it is, from your viewpoint. From my own, however, I can't see the need for rushing brashly into any deep commitment. My father always taught me that nothing important should ever be put in danger by too quick an approach."

We were interrupted at this point by the approach of Titus who, tactful as ever, greeted me formally in front of my prisoner and made apologies for interrupting us. I stood up and waved away his apologies.

"What is it, Titus?"

"I thought you'd like to know immediately, Cay. We've just received word from the outposts that Uther and his men are on their way in. They should be here within the hour."

"Is Uther well?" My heart felt lightened within me, for ever since my father's admission of concern over Uther's continued absence, I had been worried like everyone else by misgivings about what might have happened to him.

"Apparently. He's riding at the head of his men."

"Thank you, Titus. That's good news. I'll be on hand to greet him at the gates. Tell my father."

Titus glanced at Donuil, saluted me formally again and left, and Donuil followed him with his eyes until he left the refectory. Titus and I had been speaking in Latin, so Donuil could have understood nothing of what was said.

"Who is he, that man? What does he do?"

"He is Titus, my father's adjutant."

"Adjutant? What's an adjutant?"

I had to think about that. What *was* an adjutant? "Assistant, I suppose, would be as good a word as any, although he serves as the administrator for my father, too, in many things, so he is far more than a mere assistant. He holds a position of unassailable trust."

"I see. Has he been with your father long?"

"Aye. More than twenty years. Why?"

He shook his head. "It was just in my mind that he seems a bit long in the tooth to be still a runner."

"A runner? What do you mean?"

"You know, a fetcher."

I felt my face freeze in disapproval. "I think you had better be careful what you imply, Prince Donuil. That man is the closest friend my father has. The position he holds within this fort and within the governing body of this Colony is second to no one save the General himself. There is nothing servile about Titus or his function, and there's not a man in the place, except yourself, who speak from ignorance, who does not hold him in the highest regard."

Before I had finished this retort, stung as I was by the slight I had interpreted from his remarks, he was holding both hands up, palms towards me, his teeth flashing in a wide grin. "Hold! Hold! I meant no offence! Easy, now!"

I bit my words off and tried to moderate my tone. "What *did* you mean, then?"

"Well now, Commander, I've been watching the adjutant, noting what he does, and trying to define his purpose here. I told you that I found one of your men who speaks my tongue. I asked him about the man's position last night, and all the information that I got was most informative. He is a man of many parts, your Titus. Many parts and many skills; many talents and much worth." He was smiling still, but there was no mockery. "But you'll admit, when all is said and done, that what he does, in everything he does, is serve your father, although you might prefer the word *assist*—no matter what your father's needs may be. Is that not so?"

"Aye. That is so. That's what he does. He serves my father, his General. Better than any other here."

"And he takes no ill by such service?"

"How should he?"

"I do not know, Caius Merlyn! Among my people, I think, it would be impossible to ever show that kind of servitude to another man without losing your independence."

I was still nettled. "You think we lack for pride?"

"No, no, not at all!" The lad was at pains not to give offence, as he had said. "There's simply a difference in the kind of pride, that's all. Among us, I think it can be a weakness, for we are too fierce in our pride. Each man among us fears to seem dependent on another. That is a weakness, because shared strength and shared responsibility, as they are practised here, breed solidarity. I can see that, even after only days in your company. But I never noticed it before, until I found myself here, observing you people.

"No," he went on, "you do not lack for pride. You carry it away beyond our ken. Your kind of pride extends to others, to the people around you, and you have no fear of being judged dependent. That has to be a strength." Donuil paused, then continued, "Your father is no longer young. When he is dead, will you command?"

"Aye. Here in the Colony, I will."

"And will Titus then become your adjutant?"

"If he is still alive, then I suppose he will. Why do you ask?"

"Curiosity, that's all. You have no adjutant of your own?"

"No, I have no need of one." His tone was making me curious. "Anyway, we are off the track again. When Titus came in, you were just about to tell me what you would choose to do here in Camulod."

"Aye, I was. That's what I'd like to do." I blinked in incomprehension. "Him. The adjutant, Titus. That's what I'd like to do."

"You mean, be an adjutant?" I was bewildered.

"Aye," he nodded. "Your adjutant."

"*My* adjutant?" I could not have been more at a loss. "But . . . But . . . that's not possible!"

"How so?"

I was floundering. "Well . . . You know nothing! You know nothing of our ways. You have no training! You can't even ride. You don't speak the language. You're a *hostage*, for God's sake!"

"What has that to do with it? I am a hostage now, but I will not always be one. I am not suggesting I would start today. But I could start learning."

"How?" I was totally bemused, resisting the urge to laugh, knowing it would offend him.

"The same way I learned to walk and talk—by working at it! I can learn to speak your Latin tongue. I would learn to ride. And I would serve you honourably and with dignity!"

This last sobered me and I saw, in spite of the many objections that instantly came to mind, that the lad was serious. I began to feel uncomfortable, for I really had no wish to offend or insult him. I shook my head, and began to speak in a low voice, hoping that he would hear in my tone the honest regret with which I had to refuse him.

"Donuil," I said. "You are a prince of your people and you are here as a hostage for their behaviour. When I asked you to give thought to how you would choose to spend your time with us, it never even occurred to me that such a proposal would occur to you. Surely you must see the impossibility of it? In five years' time, you will go home, and in the course of time you will claim your kingdom. If, when that comes to pass, we can be friends, I'll be well pleased, but in the meantime, you are an enemy, by definition." I stopped and gave my head a shake. "I am honoured, boy, that you would even think of this, but . . ." I ran out of words.

He was staring straight at me. "May I speak?"

"Speak. Go ahead, but—"

"And will you hear me out?"

I sighed. "I'll hear you out, but you're wasting your time if you think you can change my mind."

"What should I call you?"

"You mean in conversation? Call me Commander Merlyn. Everyone else does."

"Commander Merlyn. Very well. Commander Merlyn. First, you should know that I am not a boy. I underwent the rites of manhood three years ago. I am a man, here and at home among my father's people." He paused and I waited, determined not to interrupt him again. "There is not the slightest chance that I will ever claim my kingdom, as you put it. It is not mine and never will be. I am the second youngest of eight sons. The highest rank I can ever hold at home is that of a small chieftain, and I would hold that rank only by the grace of my six elder brothers, four of whom have no use for me. It is my father's pride that will stand by me in my time as hostage here. If he should die before my time is up, my brothers will make nonsense of our pact with not a thought for me. This you should know. I thought about it in your cells on my first night here and the truth of it has shaped my thinking in this matter.

"I have one brother, Connor, whom I admire. You look like him, but Connor is a cripple. He lost the use of his legs when he was wounded fighting a bear single-handed. He will not be king, either. His goodness is great, but his physical disability is greater.

"It was in my mind that I could enjoy serving you—serving *with* you, as you put it yourself on that first day. I don't know how I could do it best, I only know I could." I moved as if to speak, but he forestalled me, raising a hand. "This language thing: I could learn Latin fast enough, if I needed to. But it occurred to me you might find it truly worthwhile to have someone to talk to at times, one you could trust, without another knowing what you said." He paused again, frowning to himself. "It is in my mind that being an adjutant is much like being a trusted friend. Trusted and valued. I would find no disgrace in earning your trust and value, and it seems to me that you should find no disgrace in my suggesting that it would be to your benefit, too.

"If there is one thing that my father taught me well, Commander Merlyn, it is the evaluation of men. I look at you and see the way you deal with men, from your father to your servants and your soldiers. You have their respect, and you do not fear to show yours for them. More important, though, you have their liking, their admiration, because of *what* you are, ahead of *who* you are. Those two, respect and liking, do not always go together. I know that everyone here, yourself included, sees me as a barbarous pirate. Well, barbarous I may be, according to your values, but I am no pirate and I am not stupid. I know my own worth. And I know what it could be worth to you, Caius Merlyn Britannicus."

By this time, I was listening in amazement, hearing far more intellect and maturity than I would have expected in this young man, who continued to speak, presenting his thoughts in flawless order. "Right now, I don't know how to ride, but I can learn to take care of your horses and their trappings, and in learning that, I'll teach myself to ride. I don't know your weapons, but I would make it my business to take care of yours, to clean them and maintain them, and in the cleaning and maintenance of them, I'd learn the handling and the use of them. The same goes for your armour and your clothes. As soon as I've learned to speak your Latin tongue, I'll be your personal messenger." He smiled here. "In the meantime, I'll act as your bodyguard. I have the size and strength for that, at least.

"I have five years to spend here, Commander. If, in that five years, I cannot perform the tasks you find for me, I'll step aside. If, on the other hand, you find me suitable and we work well together, I'll stay here with you, of my own free will, having earned the right to make my home right here in Camulod. That is all I have to say."

I had been sitting with my head down for several minutes, squeezing the ridges of my eyebrows between thumb and middle finger to mask my expression from his gaze. Now I held my position and let the silence stretch as I strove to accommodate the outrageous thoughts that were going through my mind. At length I sighed and looked up to find his wide eyes fixed on me in an unblinking stare. I shook my head slightly, still bemused at my thoughts. Everything in me was urging me to take him at his word.

"What am I to say? You honour me, Donuil. Of that I have no doubt. And you have met my reservations and dealt with each of them in a way that makes them seem petty. I must admit, the idea no longer seems as outlandish as it did at first. As you say, you have five years. The suggestion has much to recommend it, but what do you have to gain from such a bargain?"

He grinned. "A place in Camulod, your Colony. The right to ride with you and follow your ways. I would have no complaints."

I shook my head again. "My father would have an apoplexy."

"Why?" Again he grinned, his teeth flashing. "He stands to gain great strength, too. A loyal Scot in his household."

It was my turn to grin. "He'd rather have a hundred in his cells. But I will think about it. Quite honestly, the idea intrigues me, and the more I think about it, the more it appeals to me. I'll sleep on it and let you know what I decide tomorrow."

"Very well, Commander. I can wait."

"I'm pleased to hear that. In the meantime, my cousin Uther is expected any minute. That is what the Legate Titus came to tell me. He has been having dealings with your former ally, the self-styled King of Cornwall. It will be interesting to hear what he has to report. Come with me to the gates to watch them enter. Uther is always worth watching."

He rose to his feet, towering above me. "Uther Pendragon. I'm looking forward to seeing him. I've heard much about him."

"In Hibernia?"

"Where? Oh, you mean in Eire. Hibernia? That's an ugly name. Aye, but that's where I heard of Upstart Uther and Cowardly Cay. That's what Lot's people call the two of you."

I felt a flush of anger. "Some day, if I ever meet him, I shall be sure to take issue with him on that."

XVIII

U ther rode into Camulod in style, in spite of the fact that the column of riders behind him numbered less than four hundred of the original five hundred men he had led into Cornwall, and in spite of the fact that more than a few of those bore evidence of wounds. As we watched him approach, it occurred to me that he and his party looked extremely fresh for a returning raiding party, and I wondered if he had taken the time to clean himself and his men up before approaching Camulod. The thought was malicious, almost vindictive, and it shamed me. I glanced sideways to where my father stood less than three paces away with Titus by his side, and as I did so, I heard him remark, "Now there, Titus, rides a commander who has an eye for morale—not only among his men, but in the Garrison. He must have had his men stop and police themselves so as to make the best impression on the watchers here. Good thinking, that, good for discipline!"

My father's comment made me feel petty, but it also made me aware of the reason for my pettiness—my own uncertainties on how to deal with Uther and the problems he presented me. I knew I was not prepared to act as though nothing were wrong between us, even though Uther himself might be totally unaware of anything. It had been several months since the attack on Cassandra, and we had not spoken to each other in all that time.

I knew that Uther would be happy to see me, and my stomach roiled at the hypocrisy of embracing him with all of my doubts unsettled in my mind. I could not face him, I decided, and turned to leave, but as I did so I was confronted by young Donuil on my left, watching the approaching column, and I also became acutely aware of everyone else who was standing nearby. If I were to leave like this, abruptly and without reason, they would all wonder why, with the possible exception of my father, who harboured his own doubts, yet was prepared to extend the benefit of those doubts to Uther. I bit down hard and stayed where I was, watching the approach of Uther's cavalcade.

A pair of standard-bearers flanked him, right and left, each bearing a massive banner, one of which depicted the red dragon of his family, the Pendragon, and the other the great golden dragon that was Uther's new personal standard. Riding abreast behind these three came Uther's four senior squadron commanders, followed in their turn by a glittering troop of Uther's own squadron, his Dragons, as he called them. Directly behind these, at a distance of about fifteen paces, rode a quartet of strangers whom I identified as Cornish by the differences in their clothing, and behind them came the remainder of Uther's troop in a column eight ranks wide.

My attention was fastened immediately on the strangers, my first thought being that they were prisoners. I dismissed that thought immediately, however, because of the confidence in their bearing and the condition of their dress, which was too fine to indicate any privation or struggle. Then I saw that they were in fact riding in pairs, masters and servitors, for the front pair rode unencumbered while the horses and the bodies of their followers were laden with baggage. They had to be high-ranking hostages, I decided, or else ambassadors of some kind from Lot himself, although why a victorious leader should return with ambassadors from a defeated enemy, and a treacherous one at that, was beyond me. Defeated armies did not dictate terms or sue for special conditions or treaties of peace; they submitted, and that was that.

"An embassage of some description, obviously," my father murmured beside me, "although the reasoning behind it baffles me. Why should Lot think we would be interested in talking to his minions? If I were in his shoes, I'd be afraid my servants might be executed out of hand as retribution for my perfidy!"

"You are not Lot, Father. From what I know of him, he would not lose a moment's sleep over such an outcome. He's buying something by this move. Perhaps time. Anyway, we'll soon find out."

The cheers of the onlookers were deafening now as Uther's troops approached the gates, and we withdrew to the reviewing rostrum to allow them room to assemble in the courtyard. Eventually, they were all ranged before us and silence fell at a blast from the trumpets.

Uther drew himself erect and saluted my father formally. "General, Hail! I have the honour to report the successful completion of this expedition. We bring reports of victory against the enemies of the Colony, and we bring also ambassadors"—there was the merest trace of irony in Uther's tone—"from Lot of Cornwall, whose representations will be made to you and to our Council at the time of your choosing. In the meantime, I have only to report that an additional thirty men are left behind us at the borders of our lands, receiving medical aid from our physician there and awaiting wheeled transport back to Camulod."

My father nodded formally on hearing this and ran his eye appreciatively over the newly returned men, ignoring the "ambassadors" completely for the time being, until he could form a clearer idea of their purposes.

"Soldiers of Camulod!" His voice was not raised particularly high, but it carried clearly across the courtyard. "Welcome to your home. You have done well. Each of you will have forty-eight hours relieved of duty."

Uther saluted again on behalf of his men. "Our thanks, General. Permission to dismiss?"

"Granted."

Uther signalled to his senior centurion, and the ranks wheeled and filed out of the courtyard, heading for the stables, leaving only Uther and Lot's "ambassadors" still before us. The onlookers, for the most part family and friends of the returned troops, left with them, following them to the stables to await their men's release. Uther flicked a glance sideways at his ambassadors and swung himself out of his saddle to the ground, crossing towards me with his arms flung wide, his great grin threatening to split his face in two.

"Cay, you whoreson! We haven't been drunk together in years, it seems to me!" His arms closed around me in a bone-crushing hug and I could not help but respond in kind to his warmth and obvious pleasure in seeing me. He stank of sweat, his own and his horse's, even though he was clean shaved and recently washed. I hugged him back, relieved to discover that my own pleasure was utterly genuine.

"You stink!" I said. "Even worse than I remember. Welcome home. We were beginning to think, from your silence, that you had met your inevitable end at the hands of some jealous husband or lover. But I'd forgotten how, smelling like that, it would be impossible for you to get near a woman."

"You ought to know better than to worry about me, Cay. I'm too fast to catch, too dangerous to fight, and too good for any woman to complain of me to any lover! I am unkillable! Uncle Picus!" He released me and threw his arms around my father, and I could detect no reservation in the affection with which my father greeted him. I looked around me for young Donuil, but he was nowhere to be seen, so I gave my attention to the four strangers, who remained mounted and looked around dispassionately at their first view of the interior of Camulod. Two of them were servitors, as I had thought. The other two were clearly of high station. All four rode bareback. I sized up the two spokesmen, neither of whom seemed aware of my scrutiny.

Both of them were of a kind, black-haired and swarthy-skinned, and their clothing had much in common with the dress of other Celtic peoples I knew, although those men of Cornwall claimed lineage from the tribe that Caesar's men had called the *Ordoviceii*. They seemed to be of a height, too, except that the one closer to me seemed somehow disproportionate. This puzzled me for a moment and I looked for an explanation, and found one. Their horses were of different sizes. The closer man rode a far smaller horse than his companion, and yet his head was on a level with the other's. I realized that he had an inordinately long spine, and saw that his legs were short and squat. His face was long and bony, and his eyes were deep set and far too close together for the width of his face. His mouth was hidden from my eyes by a long, drooping moustache. He was narrow of shoulder and his long, oiled hair curled down between his shoulder-blades. I took an instant dislike to him and turned my attention to his companion.

There was nothing unusual about this fellow except his eyes, and they were extremely unusual, being bulbous and of different colours. His right eye was so dark brown that it was almost black, the iris barely discernible. His left eye, however, was a brilliant and startling blue. It was a face to frighten children, for it looked as though his skull had been formed without eye sockets, and the eyes had been affixed to the front of his face later, so that they bulged hideously. I wondered what men called him behind his back, for his clothes were rich enough to ensure that very few would dare demean him to his face.

My father turned towards Uther. "Commander Uther! A word with you." There was nothing in the tone of his voice to indicate any kind of discomfort or impatience. Uther left Titus and Flavius and made his way across to us.

"Uncle? What are you two hatching?"

"These men, Uther. Why are they here? Are they on an embassage or are they prisoners? It might be a good idea if you were to share your thoughts on the matter with us. Don't look at them."

Uther grinned. "I've no intention of looking at them, Uncle. They approached my camp one night, claiming the protection of the Christian Church, and requested that I escort them here to you to discuss matters of great import—equal import to the master of Camulod and the master of Cornwall."

"What is this weighty matter?"

"I've no idea, but they had a bishop with them who begged me with terror in his eyes to accede to their requests, although there was more of demand than request in them. My first thought was to send them packing, minus their clothes and servants, but there was something about that bishop's terror that changed my mind."

"Priests again! Where is the bishop now?"

"He returned to the fort. I had a strong feeling he would rather have stayed with us, but he was under some kind of constraint."

"He went back alone?"

"Aye, and unwillingly, I thought."

My father raised an eyebrow at me.

"Cay? What's your reaction?"

"It sounds . . . interesting. When do you expect to speak to them?"

"Uther? What do you think?"

"I wouldn't recognize their damned existence at all if it were left to me, but I suppose you ought to receive them tomorrow, or the day after."

"Not tonight?"

"Absolutely not, Uncle. They're Lot's men and Lot is an evil and vicious whoreson. Let them cool their heels for a few days. It will do no harm. Receive them, quarter them, feed them and let them wait."

I was suddenly acutely uncomfortable. "No," I said. "Wait a moment. There's something out of kilter here, something I don't like." They both looked at me questioningly and I shook my head. "It doesn't make sense. Lot may be everything you say he is, Cousin, but he's also bold, and he's cunning. He must have some plan in mind to send these people here, and whatever they are in truth, I'll wager they are far from ambassadors. They could be spies, but to what purpose?" A sudden, errant thought clicked into place. "Time!" I said. "He might be trying to buy time." They frowned at me in puzzlement, clearly not understanding. I could only shake my head. "I don't know why, but the idea simply occurred to me that we might be doing exactly what he wants if we keep these men waiting."

"You might be right, at that, Cousin Longhead." Uther was still frowning, but more thoughtfully now. "But even if you are, we'll achieve nothing by meeting with them tonight. I won't be of any use to you, that much I can warrant. I'm standing here and talking, but I am dead on my feet, and yet I want to be there to hear what they have to say."

"So be it." My father had made his decision. "We will talk with them in the morning. For now we'll leave them here in your care and we two will take no heed of them. See to their quartering yourself, Uther, but then come to my quarters before you do anything else. Cay and I will be waiting for you." He clapped Uther on the shoulder and pushed me forward with his other arm, and we walked away together, leaving Uther with his guests.

We headed directly for my father's quarters, and as we approached the main door of the building in which he was housed, I saw young Donuil trying to attract my attention. My father saw him, too, and left no doubt in my mind as to how he felt. "Now, by the Cross of Christ, here comes your tame heathen. Get rid of him, Cay. We have more important things to do than waste time with him!"

I stopped and Donuil hurried towards me, nodding uncertainly to my father who strode on without acknowledgement. I held up my hand to stem the young man's words before he could utter them. "Donuil, I have no time to talk to you now. My father has called me into conference and has no time to waste."

"But—"

"No buts, Donuil! I am commanded, and if you are to work with me, you'll have to learn what that means. I'll seek you out as soon as I am free, I promise. For now, however, I must go." I walked on and he stepped aside with a crestfallen, worried look.

As I entered my father's quarters, I met one of the troopers hurrying out. I was still looking over my shoulder at him as I stepped into the room.

"I sent him for wine. Uther will have a thirst on him, I suspect, and talking is dry work."

"Aye. So is listening. You look worried, Father. What do you suspect?"

He had removed his cloak and helmet and now he shrugged out of his swordbelt and sprawled in a comfortable chair. "Sit down. I don't know why, but I don't like this. Not one little bit of it. I want to question Uther more closely on the circumstances of this 'request' from the bishop. Lot is an animal and a cunning one. This thing stinks of some pending perfidy."

I had been removing my own outer garments and now I settled into a chair across from him.

"I've been thinking," I said, straightening my tunic beneath me. "Uther said the bishop went back to the fort. That must mean that Uther was encamped close by, perhaps in front of its very gates. That would mean he had been able, with only five hundred men, of whom he lost almost a hundred, to drive Lot's entire army within the gates."

"You're guessing, lad." My father's voice was sceptical. "I can't see any way that Uther could defeat Lot's army with only five hundred men. But you're right about one thing. It seems strange that he could be that close to Lot's stronghold and still feel safe enough to make a camp."

As he finished speaking, Uther came in, unfastening his cloak, closely followed by the trooper bearing a tray with a flagon and cups. "Ah! Mother's milk!" he said, eyeing the jug. "Pour me a large one, trooper. I have half the dust of the south-west on the roof of my mouth." The soldier poured and passed the cups around, leaving as we drank to the safe return of the hero. Uther drained his cup and refilled it before perching comfortably on the table's edge. "God! That tastes good! Uncle Picus, you're obviously waiting to hear something. What is it?"

"The news of your campaign."

"I told you. We were victorious."

"You lost a hundred men."

Uther's face grew serious. "Aye. I lost a hundred. Thirty will have a chance to ride again, but the other seventy are gone."

"How?"

"Mainly in one bad trap, along the coast of Cornwall."

"What happened?"

"I learned an expensive lesson. We rode into a trap in broad daylight, and were cut down."

"Tell me."

Uther heaved a sigh. "I've never seen the like of it," he said. "We had not sighted the enemy in three days, but we were following their trail, which was plain to see. We had come on the scene of a skirmish. There must have been sixty corpses, obviously killed in battle, and a group of ten who had been executed. They were all stripped of clothes and weapons."

"Who were they? Have you any idea?"

Uther shook his head. "None at all. I only know they weren't mine. Anyway, the tracks leading away from the spot were plain to see, so we followed them."

"For three days?"

"That's right."

"And you saw nothing of the enemy?"

"We didn't even know if this *was* the enemy. Not Lot's men, at least, although anyone we met there would be an enemy."

"Wait a moment. What about the party you rode out to meet? The ones who overran our outpost?"

"Saw neither hide nor hair of them. We found signs of their passage, headed away from here to the south-west, and we followed them, but we lost the trail as soon as we hit hard ground. After that, we were searching for shadows."

"You saw no one at all?"

"That's right, Uncle. Not a soul. The land was empty."

"Until you found these corpses?" Uther nodded solemnly. "And after that you followed more tracks for three days until you rode into a trap." Another nod. "Didn't you have scouts out?" Uther merely raised an eyebrow at that, not even deigning to answer the question. "Well? Did you have scouts out?"

"Of course we did."

"Then how in the name of Christ's Cross could you ride into a trap?"

"Without the slightest difficulty, Uncle. Our scouts rode right through it without even suspecting its existence and I followed them in a similar frame of mind."

My father snorted. "I suppose you *will* tell us about it?" His heavy sarcasm was completely lost on Uther.

"Certainly, if you'll allow me to." I ducked my head to hide an involuntary smile. I would not have dared to tweak my father's nose in such a fashion. Uther, however, went on imperturbably. "We came to the coast, eventually. It is very rocky in those parts, and the tracks we were following kept close to the top of the cliffs. We had the cliffs and the sea on our right, and the land rose slowly and gradually on our left. There were no trees to speak of, and our scouts kept high on the hills, where they could see for miles. I had them ranging for three miles ahead of us and three out on our left flank. There was nothing, no one. And then the enemy hit us." He paused and we were content to let him take his time. "We had been on rolling terrain for more than a day— unchanging, open grassland along the top of the cliffs. The land higher up was knee-deep in gorse and bracken—nothing tall enough to hide even a man lying down, but thorny and painful enough to make our horses' lives miserable, so we kept below it, on the open grass."

"And that's where they hit you from!" My father could stand it no longer. "They took you from the gorse!"

Uther narrowed his eyes at him and pursed his lips, saying nothing for several moments. Then, "No, Uncle, I told you it wasn't thick enough or tall enough to hide even a prostrate man. They took us from the grass. From out of the ground!"

"That's impossible! Am I to believe in magic, now?"

"That's exactly what I wondered when I saw them appear. I thought, 'That's impossible!' and then I thought, 'It's magic.' Let me admit, it put the fear of death into me in more ways than one. But it wasn't impossible, and it wasn't magic. It was brilliant strategy. And I remembered that you had used it yourself, years ago.

"We were down in a dip—a hollow between two headlands, that must have been half a mile from crest to crest. I discovered later that some upheaval in the past—God knows how long ago— had torn a great crack in the earth that stretched for almost the full half-mile. It was as though the whole cliff there had leaned side-ways, towards the sea. In some spots the crack dropped seemingly for miles, but for most of the way it was filled with rubble, and even had grass growing on the bottom.

"The thing—this ambush—had been long in the planning. The gorse and bracken grew down to the upper edge of the crack, but the entire length of the chasm was completely covered by a long, narrow, tightly meshed net on top of which they had spread turf and sunk gorse and bracken plants. Then they merely climbed down beneath their net, completely hidden, and waited for us to come to them."

My father's face was grim. "How many of them were there?"

"More than two hundred."

"How did they fight?"

"Effectively, and from a distance. They were all bowmen."

"What did you do?"

"What could I do? After the initial surprise I led a charge up the hill."

"And?"

"They broke and ran. To left and right. In alternating squads, each half laying down fire to cover the others in withdrawal. They were deadly. We were lucky we lost as few as we did."

"You mean they beat you completely? How many of them did you get?"

"Four."

"Four! Out of two hundred?"

"Yes, Uncle. I had other things to occupy me and I decided to call off the chase."

"Other things? What other things?"

"The screams of my men and horses."

There was silence for a few moments.

"Uther, you are not making sense. What screams? Why should screams be of any import in the pursuit of a fleeing enemy?"

Uther leaned over and refilled his cup, his face expressionless. When he had finished, he took a sip and then resettled himself on the table's edge, where he remained, silent for a while, gazing into his cup. Finally he spoke, and his words chilled us. "Uncle Picus, every man, and every horse, who was as much as scratched by one of those arrows, died screaming as though being burned alive. They died in mortal agony, their muscles locked in spasm. There were no exceptions."

"Good God!" This was my father. I could find no words.

Uther continued speaking. "I knew quickly that there was something wrong with what was happening. There are always screams in battle, particularly when horses are injured, but there was an aura of dementia about the tenor and the volume of this screaming. So even at the charge, I looked to see the cause, and there was a trooper, a stolid man I have known for years, screaming like a ravished girl and shaking a bleeding hand as though trying to tear it off his arm. And beside him, kicking and screaming on the ground, lay another, with an arrow clean through the fleshy part of his upper arm. It was a flesh wound. There was no cause for reactions such as I was seeing. Only a very few men lay dead, Uncle, but the others were all going mad. I had my trumpeter sound the recall, but even after we had stopped the hunt, the whoresons kept on firing as they ran, and every time an arrow found a mark, the screaming grew." He shook his head in disgust. "I lost sixty-three men and seventy-two horses. All dead. All wounds were fatal. No one recovered. That's why I say we were lucky to have lost no more. Even after I had called off the pursuit, they could have returned to the slaughter."

"Why didn't they?"

Uther took another pull at his drink, then answered, "Because they had been too eager. They ran out of arrows. They knew at the outset that, thanks to the venom on their barbs, they had no need to shoot to kill, so they were letting fly at random, hoping to do the maximum damage in the shortest possible time. They overshot, that's all."

"And you did not pursue them?"

"Not immediately. As I told you, I had other things to concern me. I didn't know then that every wounded man was going to die the way they did. We were concerned with trying to help them. It was only later we realized how useless our efforts were. By that time, the assassins were gone. They had galleys concealed below the overhang of the cliffs ahead of us and behind us."

"What kind of galleys?" My father's voice was sharp with interest.

"Big ones. Biremes."

"What about the thirty casualties you reported having left at our perimeter? Why didn't they die, too?"

"They were wounded honestly, in fair battle."

My father got up and walked about the room, thinking over what he had heard. "This Lot has much to answer for, when he and I come face to face."

Uther shook his head, a wry look on his face. "Apparently not, Uncle. His two crows outside deny any knowledge of venomed arrows. They claim that our attackers were not Lot's men."

"How can that be? It was Lot's land, was it not? And they were waiting for you."

"Aye, that they were. But Lot claims to have lost sixty men in battle against sea raiders. And these bowmen left by sea."

"Pshaw! Do you believe him?"

"No. I don't. But that proves nothing." Uther finished his wine and placed the cup on the table beside his left hip.

I spoke for the first time. "Then who were the men you found dead? And who were the ten others you found executed?"

Uther grunted his disdain. "As far as I'm concerned, they could all have been Lot's own men. He's a cold-blooded beast. It wouldn't be beyond him to bait his trap by killing some of his own, especially if they were enemies from his jails, or malcontents. Dead like that, they would be useful to him. Alive, they'd be a nuisance."

"You really think he'd do that?" I asked.

Uther's look of wry amazement was eloquent. "Don't be ingenuous, Caius. Of course he would! He used those poisoned arrows, didn't he? His trap worked, didn't it? I tell you, it had been long in the planning. The swine would use anything to gain his ends."

"And what are his ends, Uther?" My father's voice was low. "What is this self-styled King of Cornwall really after?"

"You want me to hazard a guess?" Uther pushed himself erect, away from the table. "I would say dominion."

"Over what?"

"Over this whole land, starting with Camulod, and over every person living in it."

My father received this in silence, resuming his seat and steepling his fingertips beneath the end of his nose. I shifted in my chair, saying nothing, waiting, as was Uther, for him to resume. Finally he straightened and sniffed audibly, looking at me.

"Dominion . . . to conquer all of us. Does that sound familiar?"

I nodded, recalling him saying those very words. But he was already speaking to Uther.

"These ambassadors. Tell us more about them."

"There's not much more to tell. We rode on to Lot's main camp—it's a log-walled fort, primitive but well-sited—and met only token resistance along the way. When we arrived, we found the fort sealed and everyone inside. We drew up outside the walls and a party came out to parley with us. They asked us why we had invaded their domain. They had given us no provocation. I demanded to speak with Lot, but he would not honour us with his presence. We made camp within a mile of the fort. That night, these fellows came out to us with the bishop, and what they had to say convinced me that there was little to be gained, for the time being, in simply sitting there. The place can be supplied by sea. I decided to come home and regroup, after reporting and having the benefit of your advice.

"We started back the following day. Two days ago we surprised a small army of Saxons—real ones. That's where we took our other casualties. We lost three killed and the rest were wounded. We smashed the Saxons. They fought to the death. We obliged them. That's all I have to tell."

"You had thirty wounded in that fight?"

"No. About twenty. Twenty-two, in fact. The others were hurt during the token resistance I mentioned earlier. The fighting along the road to Lot's fort."

"Wait now, Uther. Let me understand this fully. You reached Lot's fort, his main camp, with almost no difficulty, apart from that one encounter with the bowmen. You arrived to find the place closed up against you, with everyone inside. Is that correct?"

Uther nodded.

"There was nobody outside at all?"

"Not a soul."

"So you could have besieged them?"

"Aye, we could have. But what was the point, and where my justification? I had no proof that he had moved against us, none at all. I felt as though we were the invaders, the unprovoked aggressors, on *his* land. He has some able negotiators in his pay. In any case, I had only four hundred men. I had no way of knowing how many he could field against us. The sea was at his back, too. If those galleys we'd seen were really his, they could make nonsense of any attempt at siege. His fort is built right above the shore, on the cliffs there."

My father was pacing the floor by this time, his eyes fixed on Uther so that his head swivelled as he traversed the room. "So. Lot presented you to yourself as the aggressor. He made no overtly hostile moves. He disclaimed knowledge of this disgusting thing with the poisoned arrows, and he dispatched these two 'ambassadors' to talk to us." His gaze swung to me. "Caius, you are the thinker. What's he trying to achieve here? He's up to something."

"Clearly," I admitted, "although I fear we'll find out nothing until we hear this embassy. Uther, did he make any reference at all to the attack from the north by the Hibernians?"

He shook his head. "None at all."

My father snapped his thumb and forefingers. "You're right, Caius! He is attempting to buy time. But to what purpose?"

"The apparent purpose doesn't matter, Father. It's the time itself that is important, I'm convinced of that, and I think I know how and why, but I must ask you both to bear with me and what might seem like foolish questions. By sending his people back with you, Uther, he was sure of gaining both time and information. Had we lost to the Hibernians, or been mauled by them, you would have ridden home to a very different reception than the one you received. His 'ambassadors' would have been able to report the situation from their own, personal observation. They will still be able to do that, since Lot has no idea that we know of his alliance with the Hibernians."

"What are you saying?" Uther's face had grown dark at this new information. "There was no coincidence in the double attack? Lot has allied himself with Outlanders?"

"Aye," I answered him. "He and his people have been busy. They have made friends among the Scots in Hibernia. Friends, it now appears, who could aid him militarily on land, and also keep him well supplied by sea in the event of a siege of his own stronghold."

"How did you find out about this?"

"By accident," Father intervened. "Cay made a bargain with a prince among the enemy. Kept him as hostage in return for sparing the lives of about a thousand of his men."

Uther turned to me at this, his eyebrows raised.

"It worked out well," I said, forestalling his question. "I trust the man. His word will hold, and that means that his father's people will make no move against us while we have him. Five years. He was the one who told us of the alliance." Uther looked confused. "Don't you see it yet, Uther?" I pressed him. "Lot can have no idea that things turned out the way they did. As far as he is concerned, we believe we have been attacked by raiders from Hibernia, that's all. If we drive them off, it will be at cost to us—the higher the better, from his viewpoint. In the meantime, he makes a diversionary move against us, timed to coincide with their attack, to force us to split our troops. Having achieved that, he withdraws ahead of us without provoking us, making you appear the aggressor. Then he *does* attack you, mauls your men and your morale significantly, but goes to great lengths to maintain an appearance of innocence. He must have been sadly disappointed by the small scale of your losses.

"In any event, as the innocent, offended party he has the right to send back messengers with his aggrieved complaints about our invasion of his territories. These spies, armed in their innocent appearances, will quickly bring him information on the success of his allies' incursion against us. Whichever way the affair turns out, he has gained time and intelligence about our condition and our state of readiness against further attack. Best of all, however, in the aftermath of such sustained action by us on two fronts, his spies will be able to form an intelligent estimate of our real strength in men and horses."

During this summation my father had been nodding in grim-faced agreement. When Uther finally spoke, there was a tone of unwilling admiration in his words.

"That whoreson! What a devious, treacherous, unprincipled—"

"Aye, all of those and more, Uther," I said, interrupting him. "But include brilliant, and painstaking. If he were on our side, he'd be one of our master strategists. The flaw in his planning has been accidental. We turned the tables on his allies and arranged the truce we did, and we came out of it with more information from a first-hand source than Lot could possibly have anticipated."

"So be it, Caius," said my father. "You may have entered the mind of our antagonist far better than either Uther or I could have done. I for one can find no fault in your logic, or your deductions. But I confess your reference to buying time still leaves me grasping for meaning. Why should he need time? For what? What can we expect next?"

"He may have bought it already . . . I'm guessing now." They nodded, their eyes intent, and I took a few extra seconds to prepare my next thoughts. "I think Lot is here, close by us now. I think he'll attack us soon with everything he has, as soon as he can, before we are ready for anything. Uther, did you receive any indication at all of the strength he had concealed within his walls?"

A brief headshake. "Absolutely none. It could have been empty, or he could have had men piled in there, row on row, like logs. I have no idea."

"That's what I thought. Very well, visualize this, and bear in mind the type of man we have to deal with here. Uther might have come home to face one of three situations: The first, and most desirable from Lot's point of view, would be that we had been completely beaten by the Scots invaders, and Uther would thus be riding into a deathtrap. The second would be that we had come home victorious, to whatever extent we might have been able to salvage a victory—I honestly do not believe Lot could have imagined such a complete victory as we have won, since God was clearly on our side and fighting with us, and Lot has little to do with any God. In this event, Uther would return to find us licking our wounds and recuperating from our exertions. The third possibility is that we might still be engaged in campaigning against the invaders, so Uther would find only a holding garrison in Camulod.

"Any one of these three possibilities would work to Lot's advantage. Remember, his spies ride with you, Uther, and you are supposedly convinced of Lot's blamelessness, despite any personal hatred you might have for him. Are you both with me thus far?" They nodded, still listening intently.

"Now, if I were as devious as Lot, I would attribute to us sufficient malice to keep these two men waiting to deliver their messages. A day, at least, two days or three if my luck was working for me. If the Scots have been victorious, then Lot has no problems. If we have won, then we need time to lick our wounds and regroup, and we should be relieved to get Uther's reassurance—in spite of any personal misgivings—that the trouble in the south-west was without substance." I was confident in my logic, but its conclusions were startling, even to me. I took a deep breath before delivering my next statement.

"Father, Uther, I am prepared to wager that Lot followed hard on Uther's heels, and is now less than two days' march from here, in full force, waiting for his two spies to come back. If they do not arrive within two days, he will know that we were not defeated in the north. If we hear his envoys and send them back immediately, tomorrow, then he'll know within three days and still be closer to us than we would suspect. On the other hand, if we keep them waiting for two days, three days, he will have all the time he needs to deploy his armies and hit us from every direction, when we least expect it. He'll either use the departure of his spies as the signal for attack, or he'll move against us while they are still here."

"Would he sacrifice his friends that callously?" My father was still thinking of Lot in terms of normal human decency.

"The man has no friends, Father. He wouldn't think twice about it. I believe Lot of Cornwall intends to initiate all-out war against us, no less than three days from today, and no more than five. So let's say four days, but be prepared for three. And he'll be right here at our gates."

The silence that followed this assertion seemed to last forever. It was my father, clutching at straws, who broke it. "Cay, I'm not disputing your logic, but there's one flaw in it. Our own people are out there, throughout our lands. If Lot's army were to attempt to approach us, no matter how carefully, we would have word of it."

Even as he was speaking, I shook my head, denying him that avenue, which I had already considered. "Would we, Father? Don't forget his two hundred bowmen with their arrows that can kill with a scratch. Those people could move in a circle around us on a mile-wide front and kill every living soul. Especially if they did it in stealth. We haven't got that many people out there, and those who do live on the farms tend to congregate, after working all day. There would be no survivors to escape with warnings. The same applies to our sentries and outposts. Poisoned arrows! All it takes is a scratch. Uther, how long does it take a man to die?"

"All of the men I lost were dead within half an hour. Less than half that time for most of them." He was looking at my father, who listened, pale-faced.

"Father," I said, my voice as gentle as I could make it, "we have to assume that the people in and around Camulod itself, the people we can hear and see, are the only people left alive in the entire countryside who are not our enemies."

"That is monstrous!"

"Monstrous and evil. But it is typical of Lot of Cornwall, who is an evil monster."

He was convinced. "So be it! What do you suggest we do?" He was himself again. I changed my tone.

"We move. Immediately. Uther, not much rest for you tonight, Cousin. We'd better get Titus and Flavius in here, Father. We're going to need them."

He struck the small gong on his table and instructed the soldier who came at its summons.

Uther sighed and stretched himself. "What have you got in mind, Cay?"

"Your envoys. I don't want them to suspect that we are mobilizing. They must know nothing. The only thing I want them to think is that we are as stupid and unsuspecting as they assume us to be. Fortunately, if my suspicions are right, they'll take our treatment of them at face value. I want an unobtrusive guard placed over them, but I want them to know it's there. Keep them away from any place or any person that might make them suspicious of what we are doing. In the meantime, I've already sent word to the stewards of our breeding farms to assemble all our animals for a census. We made those arrangements by sheer chance, before we knew anything of this, but it means our horses will all be gathered right where we need them.

"Lot already knows that Uther had his four hundred horsemen with him, so he'll be expecting to find them here. That's good. They'll be here, but what I'm thinking of is that difference you mentioned, Father, of over six hundred horses. We know we're stronger than anyone else suspects. I'll be surprised if we have less than seven thousand souls living in the Colony, scattered throughout our camps and farms?" It was a question, but neither of them reacted.

"Do you agree? About seven thousand, counting women and children?"

My father nodded. "Aye, that many at least. Our numbers have been growing steadily for years. We have more than two thousand here in Camulod itself, within and around the walls. We've always concentrated on our strength—our ability to defend ourselves—but in the past few years, what with one thing and another, we seem to have lost sight of numbers."

"What about the records?"

"The fact is no one has checked very closely for some time. The last count I remember placed our numbers around four thousand, but that was some years ago."

"How many years ago?"

"Four, perhaps five. Our main priority at the time was to grow enough food to feed everyone. We cleared more land and recultivated several of the abandoned farms around our perimeter. If you remember, you were worried at the time about the extra patrolling that would be involved."

"I recall it well," I said. "But I think you'll be surprised, when you check our rolls again, at just how much we have grown."

Uther interrupted me. "You've sidetracked yourself, Cay. You were talking about my four hundred cavalry. What was the point you were going to make?"

"That they should stay here, to defend the fort. In the meantime, I'd like to send another thousand horsemen secretly out of the Colony."

"A thousand?"

I shrugged. "They may not all be astride cavalry mounts, but I'll wager we have the horses, and we have the men to ride them. The men won't all be fully equipped, either, but they'll be able to sit on a horse and hold a spear and they'll frighten the spirit out of Lot's army when they appear unexpectedly at their back!" They were both looking at me, their eyes begging to be convinced. "Uther. Where are your four hundred billeted now?"

"Victorex's old place. But we dismissed them for forty-eight hours, remember?"

"Damnation! Well, that's acceptable. They'll stay and be recalled here on duty when their leave is over. Damnation! They are our best. I had hoped to replace them with other, lesser troops, but no matter. When it comes time for them to strike with us they'll be invaluable. Please see that they are back on duty here tomorrow night. I'll raise our extra thousand from the other camps and farms.

"I want a column of a thousand mounted men on the move to the north-east by noon tomorrow. More, if we can manage it. The commissariat will have to be instructed as soon as possible to prepare rations for ten days for at least that many men. We'll have to disperse them in a fan. I don't want the tracks of a thousand horsemen to be visible. I don't care how that's done, but it's essential. If I'm right, Lot's people will come in from the south and west. Ours will have a chance to get out to the north and east if they move quickly, but if they leave visible evidence of their passing, Lot will know they're out there.

"In addition to that, I want to recall every man from every outpost on our borders. That will seem suspicious to Lot, I know, but we'll declare a festival of some kind. I don't care. I just want them back here, within walking distance of the safety of the walls. Remember, we're supposed to think the danger's over for a while. We can relax our vigilance."

Another thought occurred to me. "How are our stores? Can we sustain a siege, Father?"

"Yes, for at least a month."

"Good. We won't need that long, with any good fortune. The stores and supplies down in the villa buildings should be loaded up during the next few days, ready to move up here to the fort at the first sign of trouble. Have I missed anything?"

Uther spoke up. "What about our people? The colonists here in the fort? Shouldn't we warn them?"

I considered that briefly and vetoed it with a terse shake of my head. "Can't afford to, Uther. It's too dangerous. They have to behave normally, for the benefit of the watchers. All we can do is bring as many of them in close as we can. Of course, if we declare a holiday, a celebration of our victories and your safe return, then that will get them here. That could be done tomorrow, too. We've never done anything like that before."

"Not so suddenly, at any rate," said my father.

"All the better, then." I had that good feeling that comes of recognition of a right idea. "So this is unprecedented. A spontaneous holiday. Let everyone believe the feasting will start tomorrow night and continue the following day. Father, you'll have to make your invitation sound genuine, and yet peremptory. Everyone is to attend. You'll have to inform the Council of what's afoot, too."

"I'll have to do that, anyway."

"Then do it early, as soon as possible, but send the word out first. We need our people safely here as soon as possible. If worst comes to worst, how many people can we hold in Camulod?"

"More than we have. Far more. No problem there."

"Good. Our colonists have been training for this for years. Now we can only hope the training has been adequate."

Titus announced his arrival at that point with a soft cough from the open door, and Flavius came up behind him.

"Come in, both of you," my father said, "and close the door at your back. Pull up that chair, Titus. Flavius, you'll find an extra one in the other room. We have an emergency situation on our hands."

It was approaching midnight by the time we got out of there. Everyone knew what had to be done, and his part in the operation, and each of us was aware of the need for speed and unobtrusiveness. We were launched on a major campaign, and the very existence of our Colony depended on the speed and the efficiency with which we handled it.

My own initial part was simple and straightforward. I had to alert Ludo and the commissariat to the urgency of the unexpected requirements we were placing on them. It was also my responsibility to make all the arrangements for the removal of extra stores and supplies to the fortress on the following day. This I could handle without raising any suspicions. Since I had already made arrangements to conduct my census, the people at all our depots were expecting me. No one would be surprised by my arrival.

Over everything else in my mind, however, hung a shadow I had placed there with my own words earlier in the evening, when

I declared that only those we could see or hear could be presumed to be still alive. Cassandra's safety haunted me. I knew that her refuge was well hidden and far removed from the beaten track. Lot's marauders would not be seeking signs of life on her hilltop. But the image of the faint track down through the valley to her hiding-place terrified me, and I knew I could have no peace of mind until I had assured myself that there were no visible signs of my entry or egress there. Although I knew I had always taken the greatest pains to leave no sign of my movements there, I determined to be there with her before daybreak, to check her safe concealment again.

I left my father's quarters and went straight to the kitchens, where I found Ludo still active. As I entered, I met one of my own men emerging. It was his misfortune to be in the wrong place at the wrong time. I sent him down to the villa with a message to Strato, our masseur, to have the fires banked and the steam room ready, and to be prepared to give me a complete working over within the next two hours. I also told him to have my horse saddled and waiting for me with the guards at the main gate.

Ludo was surprised to see me at that hour. He had been supervising a general clean-up of his kitchens and was just on his way to bed when I arrived. The refectory was empty. I sat him down and told him what I required of him and his face wrinkled wryly as he realized that he was likely to be more busy than he had anticipated over the course of the next few days. I left him taking a renewed interest in his inventory, and went to visit Questus, our senior quartermaster, to tell him the story. He at least had managed to sleep for several hours prior to my disruption of his schedule, and he accepted the situation philosophically, recognizing the urgency involved and moving immediately to accommodate it.

My next stop was at the quarters of Lucanus, our chief medical officer. Since the affair of Cassandra's disappearance, he and I had been on terms of mutually respectful civility, but we would never be friends, I thought, or more than formally cordial in our dealings with each other. He, too, had been asleep for hours, but his discipline had accustomed him to being called upon at any time, so he was alert and already thinking ahead as I brought him up to date. I could see him mentally taking stock of bandages, splints, medications and the like as I spoke. To him, as to each of the others, I was careful to emphasize the necessity of concealing all preparations from the eyes of the visiting envoys.

It was the darkest part of the night by the time I left him, and I was twice challenged by sentries as I made my way to the main gate, carrying a torch that was beginning to burn low. I had completely forgotten my promise to talk to Donuil the Hibernian. My horse was saddled and waiting for me as I had ordered, and I could see the speculation in the eyes of the guards as I approached.

"Did the trooper I sent out get back yet?"

"Yes, Commander. About an hour ago."

"Good. He'll be asleep by now. Lucky man. And my masseur down at the villa will be cursing my sleeplessness, which is now his. How long till dawn?"

They glanced at each other, and the one who had spoken before replied, "About two and a half hours, Commander."

"Good. By that time I'll be bathed, oiled, rubbed down and wide awake, though my name will be unkindly mentioned by the people I'll be inspecting at such an ungodly hour. Take this, will you?" I handed him my guttering torch, and pulled myself up into the saddle. "One thing about being prepared for a nasty, unpopular job is that nobody else ever is. Good night to you!" I kicked my horse forward as they opened the great gates for me, and left them looking at each other, no doubt in agreement that all officers were insane and bloody-minded tyrants.

The moon had set, but the skies were clear, and as my eyes adjusted to the starlight I discovered that I could see more than adequately for the journey down the road to the villa, where lights were burning in the bath house.

XIX

In less than two hours, I was riding again in the direction of Cassandra and Avalon. I had steamed and bathed and dozed, and I had been oiled and perfumed and scraped and pummelled until my body tingled. I felt good, and my mind was attuned to the problems facing us, and to the steps we would take to solve them. I arrived on the hilltop before the first hint of dawn appeared in the sky, having left my horse tethered below, safely out of sight, and I sat on the summit and watched the eastern sky give birth to the new day, as I thought my own thoughts about the young woman who slept soundly in the valley below me.

As soon as there was enough light to see by, I went to the entrance to the pathway and scoured the ground for signs of human passage. There were none. Nothing at all to indicate that anyone had passed this way in years. I had taken great care to avoid leaving any marks in the past, and the path, though clearly enough a path, was freshly overgrown with grass and undisturbed. I had to be content with that, since it would have been impossible to hide the pathway entirely. My examination complete, I tried to think of anything I had missed—anything that might in any way betray Cassandra's refuge to a casual passer-by, but I could think of nothing, although all at once, it seemed, there were more than a dozen good reasons in my mind for going down to her. I should check that she had enough food and fuel, for one thing. I should make sure that her hut was warm enough, now that the nights were growing colder, and I realized that I had not brought the clothes with me that I had scrounged from Aunt Luceiia. I cursed myself for my thoughtlessness, but was able to console myself that I would have good reason to return with them later. My mind turned to its real reason for wanting to see her, and I felt my belly tighten at the thought of climbing into her warm bed and feeling her taut young muscles clench against me. Tonight, I promised myself, and began to make my way back to my horse.

At the very top of the rim of the hollow hill, however, I stopped dead in my tracks, my flesh crawling in horror as the aroma of wood-smoke gently drifted into my nostrils. Her fire! She must just have lit it or rekindled it from embers, piling new twigs and branches to feed it, and if I could smell it from here, so would anyone else who came within smelling distance. I turned on my heel and headed back the way I had come, wondering already how I was going to persuade her that she would have to live without fire for at least a week. I had to convince her of the danger of her fire without reawakening a fear of rape and mutilation in her mind.

I had no doubt of the welcome with which she saw me entering her little valley. She climbed all over me, her warm mouth covering my face with kisses that I was happy to return. But eventually I took a firm grip on myself and pushed her gently away, holding her firmly by the wrists until she stood looking at me expectantly. When I was sure I had her attention, I pointed to the fire and made a show of sniffing the smoke. She frowned at me at first, and then her face cleared and she smiled, tugging at the fabric of her tunic, trying to hold it up to me with one hand and beckoning me to approach with the other. Wondering what in Hades was in her mind, I approached her and let her pull my unresisting head down to her tunic. It smelled of wood-smoke! She had understood me.

Encouraged, I smiled and nodded at her and went back to the fire, where I traced the path of the smoke upwards with my open hands, pointing to where it was drifting into and over the trees. She followed with her eyes and nodded again to me, her smile now a little more uncertain. I kept my face solemn as I mimed the way the smoke drifted, and how I, or anyone else, smelled it in passing. My nostrils twitching like a rabbit, I feigned surprise, identification, then a search among the bushes, sniffing all the time, and then discovery of her fire.

She understood, watching me closely. Convinced now that nothing I did would escape her, I crossed to the pile of wood beside the fire and selected small, dry sticks that would burn with a minimum of smoke. I carried these a little way from the fire and lit them with a branch from the existing fire. When they were burning brightly, I indicated that there was no smoke, or very little. Quickly then, I crossed to the nearest bush and tore off a green twig which I threw on the big fire. It began to smoke immediately, and I pulled it off and stamped it out. I then took my helmet off, filled it with water from the lake, and doused the large fire, leaving the small one burning clearly.

When I looked at her again she nodded her head firmly to show she understood and then pointed to the shrivelled green bough I had stamped out. She waved her arms to indicate smoke and shook her head in a determined negative. No more smoke. I breathed a sigh of relief and gratitude for her obvious intelligence, but her next series of movements worried me again. She moved close to me and took the helmet from my hands, holding it upright, and then laid her hand flat against my bronze breastplate, after which she drew the sword from the scabbard by my side, bracing the helmet against the sheath for purchase. I made no move to stop her. She looked at the sword and then at me and then she gestured up at the hills around us, swinging the sword, and sniffed, looking around her for the source of the smell, which meant, *You are wearing armour, dressed for war, and you mean that there are others up there, enemies, who might smell my fire, don't you?*

I nodded slowly and emphatically, and she returned my nod. Then she replaced the sword in its scabbard, returned to the lake to refill my helmet with water, and doused the remaining fire. She was perfectly calm and self-possessed, and I knew there would be no smoke coming from the valley until I returned. I reached out and grasped her gently by the upper arms and watched her great eyes watching my lips.

"Woman," I told her, smiling, "beautiful, wondrous woman, you have me bewitched!" She watched my lips move, and cocked her head slightly to the side in that enchanting way of hers, before moving close to me and slipping her arms around me, armour and all. Time passed as we stood there hugging each other, I know not how long, and then I became aware again of where and who I was, and of what remained for me to do. She felt me tense as the awareness came to me, and leaned backwards in my arms, raising an inquiring eyebrow and a pointed finger towards the path.

I kissed and released her, hating time and the way it sped. As I picked up my helmet, I pointed again to the fireplace, with a warning shake of my head which she repeated. She would not forget. One more hasty kiss, and I was on my way back to the outside world. My horse whickered in recognition as he came to meet me and I heaved myself up into the saddle with a great sigh of regret.

As soon as I was mounted, I set him at a gallop on the road for the nearest stock farm, leaving him to pick his own way as I looked around me in every direction for signs of life. I was far from sociable as I clattered into Terrix's farm and summoned the senior officer. I tersely explained the situation, and the need to start his men moving out immediately, in small groups, to the north and east. He listened without comment as I emphasized the danger of leaving any recognizable trail or signs that a large number of men and horses had left the area. When I had finished speaking, I asked him if he had any questions.

"Just one, Commander. Where are they going? I know *how* you want my men to go, but not *where?*" There was a nuance in the tone of his voice that I couldn't define, but it made me realize that I was being unfair to this man, who had done nothing to justify my shortness with him. In an effort to moderate my harshness, I summoned a smile.

"Your pardon. My mind is taken up with so many details that I tend to lose sight of the major objectives. Years ago, before we drew in our borders, we had established a camp far to the northeast, towards Aquae Sulis. Do you remember it?"

He nodded, smiling. "Aye, Commander Merlyn, I remember it well. I was second in command there, just before we abandoned."

"Good. Then you know the place. That's our marshalling point. Have your men assemble there and wait with the contingents from the other farms for Commander Uther and myself to join you. We will be there before noon on the third day from now. You should be set to march when we arrive."

"To march back here, you mean?"

"Aye, or wherever. It depends on where the enemy appears. But there's one thing more. Have your people load up every extra piece of supply material you have. Have them do it today and move it all to Camulod as soon as they can. I want nothing left out here that Lot's people might be able to use."

"What about livestock?"

"To the fort. The stables might be crowded for a while, but that's too bad. Now you had better get busy, my friend. I have five more farms to visit by mid-morning. And be sure to keep your men aware of the importance of this whole thing. We are dealing here with a treachery that threatens our very survival. See to it."

"Don't worry about us, Commander Merlyn. We'll do our duty."

"Good man."

By noon, I was back in Camulod, my rounds completed, and for the next hour or two I checked on the progress of the arrangements I had made the night before. I was congratulating myself on how everything was going according to plan when I heard my name whispered urgently, and looked to my left to see young Donuil beckoning to me from the entrance to his quarters. I remembered only then that I had promised to speak with him the night before, and I felt a momentary twinge of guilt that was very quickly lost in my curiosity over why he was being so furtive. I moved towards him and he ducked back inside. I stopped at the threshold, leaning against the door frame.

"Donuil? What's wrong, man? Are you in hiding? What have you done?"

"Come inside, Caius Merlyn, and close the door. I have to talk with you!"

I stepped inside and pulled the door closed behind me. His

quarters were much like my own but smaller and darker, with a tiny window that let in a minimum of light. He was sitting on the edge of his bed in deep shadow and I had a sudden, uncomfortable feeling that something was far from right with him. I stood there and looked at him for a long time, waiting for him to speak, until I began to grow impatient.

"What's going on, Donuil? Why all the secrecy? What is this?"

"You should have come to me last night, Commander Merlyn. You promised that you would. I waited all night."

I found myself laughing in mild embarrassment. He sounded almost like a jilted lover. "I'm sorry. I intended to, but we had an emergency to deal with, and your request slipped my mind. I forgot."

"What kind of emergency makes a man like you forget a promise? Had it to do with Lot's men?"

I shrugged. "It could have had, I suppose, but not—" I broke off, realizing what he had asked me. "How did you know they were Lot's men?"

"Because I know them. That's what I had to talk to you about. And that's why I'm staying here in my room. I don't want them to know I'm here."

"Why? Are you afraid of them?"

His eyes flashed at me from the shadows. "I am, and I have reason to be. So do you. They are men to fear, those two."

"How so? Why should I be afraid of them? They are here on a peaceful embassy."

"Disabuse yourself of that thought, Commander. Those two are incapable of anything to do with peace. They are assassins. The best that King Lot has, or the worst, depending on the point of view."

I crossed to the single chair in the room and put my foot up on the seat. "How do you know this, Donuil? Have you met them?"

"Aye. Once, in my father's hall. It was the one with the different eyes that I heard call you Caius the Coward."

"Oh? That's interesting. Tell me more about them, and about why the sight of them can keep you hiding here."

"They're magicians. Warlocks."

"Oh come, Donuil! There's no such thing as magic."

He looked at me, unimpressed by my scoffing. "You tell that to your soldiers, Commander. Don't waste your breath on me or any of my people. These men are evil. They are in league with Darkness. And they are *never* what they seem to be. Death walks at their side and lays his hand on everyone they deal with."

I grunted in disgust and sat down. "Very well, I'll believe you. They are magicians. Now tell me something about them I can deal with. They are men, too, I presume?"

He ignored my sarcasm. "Aye, they are men, after a fashion, but they have none of the needs or the desires of ordinary men. They live only to serve their master, Lot. It is as though they are mindless, otherwise. I hid from them, not wanting them to know I am here, for if they know that, they'll be warned."

"Warned about what?"

"About whatever it is they are here for. If they see me here, free, they'll know I'll tell you what I know of them, if they don't kill me first."

"Come now, Donuil, you're being ridiculous."

"Aye. So you say. I've seen them kill a man who was in a locked and guarded room, just for the sport of it. Just to prove they could do it."

"Prove it to whom?"

"To my father, and to the rest of us. They told us to pick a man at random, which we did, and to lock him up, under guard, anywhere we pleased. We chose one of their men, and the poor fellow went white with the terror that was in him. We took him to a strong hut, all of us. There must have been twenty men there, and the tall one, the one they call Caspar, ordered us to tie the man hand and foot and put a stifle in his mouth. When that was done, he had us all gather round and watch as he sat staring at the man for a long time. The fellow grew deathly still and lost consciousness, although Caspar never touched him. Finally, the big fellow got up and told us to cut the man loose. We cut him loose, removed the binding from his mouth, and he came back to life and started screaming. Caspar and the other one just laughed at him and walked away.

"We locked the fellow up and put guards all around the hut and we all went back into my father's hall, where Memnon, the creature with the funny eyes, began to entertain us in a way of which I've never seen the like. He could make things disappear and reappear somewhere else. We were all amazed and more than a bit afraid, until Caspar interrupts and says, 'The man is dead.' I was sent to look, with two of my brothers. Our own men were still on guard. Nobody had come near the place, they swore. The fellow inside had stopped his howling. My brother opened the door and we went in. The man was dead. Not a mark on him. Not a cut or a bruise or a stain. He was just dead, his face twisted up in terror and his mouth open wide in a scream."

"Donuil, that's just not possible."

"I know, Commander, and if I hadn't been the one to find him, I'd never have believed it myself."

"How old were you at the time?"

"As old as I am now! It was not three months ago." His voice was emotionless and I was impressed in spite of myself.

"So. Why do you think Lot would have sent these two here?"

"To cause death. Why else? It's what they do. It's all they do. I talked with some of their own men about the two of them. Do you know, even their own soldiers hate them and are deathly afraid of them? One fellow told me that they learned their heathen crafts in foreign lands far to the east, beyond the Saxon wildernesses. They know the secrets—all the secrets—of murder. They have poisons, they say, that can kill in a hundred different ways. They can burn a man to death without fire, just by cutting his skin!"

That one brought me erect. "Say that again?"

"I said, they can burn a man to death without fire, just by cutting his skin."

"What does that mean?" He heard the strain in my voice.

"I don't know, Commander. That's just what I've been told." I felt a grim determination settle over me as I thought about what

Donuil had told me, but I kept silent as he continued. "I don't know what reason they've given you for being here, either, but it's a lie, whatever they told you. Lot keeps these two only to spread terror. Be sure of that, Commander. They are here to kill, and to spread fear." My mind was filled with imagined screams, and I saw Uther's soldiers writhing in agony. The faces of the two men grew vivid in my mind's eye as the voice in my head put names to each of them: Caspar and Memnon. I was barely aware of Donuil's next words. "They're not from Britain, you know, Commander? They're from some place called Egypt, beyond the seas."

Memnon and Caspar! My decision was there in my head almost before I was aware of it. I rose quickly to my feet. "Where are they quartered? Do you know?"

He shook his head.

"Stay here. I'll come back for you later." I went directly in search of Uther. One of the guards in the courtyard told me that he had seen Uther pass just a short time before, headed for the refectory with his two "guests." I made my way directly to the guard-house just inside the main gates. Curio, the sergeant of the guard, saluted me as I approached.

"Centurion, I need a squad of twelve. Assemble them here immediately in full kit. Jump to it. I'll be back shortly." I spent that time looking for my father, but wherever he was, I couldn't find him. Curio had the men assembled when I returned, and the sound of our marching feet turned many heads as we approached the refectory.

Uther looked at me quizzically as I approached their table. Every eye in the room was watching.

"Cay? Something wrong?"

"Yes, Commander. Very wrong. Your company."

Both of them stared insolently at me, neither making a move to rise.

"What about my company, Commander?"

"I'm placing them under close arrest."

"On whose authority?" For a moment, I had the feeling he was going to dispute me.

"My own."

He smiled and turned to his companions. "Gentlemen, my cousin here, Commander Caius Britannicus, has the responsibility for maintaining discipline and order within these walls. I'm afraid I have to yield you to his care."

They were both frowning now. Caspar looked at my troopers with disdain, and then at me. "You take a lot upon yourself, Commander. Since when has it become usual to treat ambassadors with such hostility?" I could hear the foreign tenor in his voice—not strongly, but it was there.

"Since I discovered who and what you are! Centurion! Search these two carefully. Strip them naked. Make sure that they have nothing left to them that could become a weapon. Keep their clothing, and issue them tunics to keep them warm. Then lock them up and hold them under guard." I looked each of them in the eye. "You can go now, on foot, with these men, or you can be carried. The choice is yours. Take them away."

They left, closely surrounded by their twelve guards. Uther had remained seated through the whole thing. When they were gone, he whistled softly to himself.

"All right, tell me. What was all that about?"

I seated myself across from him, feeling the tension ebbing slowly. "I've just been told, by a stranger who knew nothing of your story, that those two whoresons are Egyptian magicians, masters of poison, who can burn a man to death without fire, simply by cutting his skin. Does that remind you of anything?"

"By the Christ! Those poisoned arrows!"

"That's what I thought you'd say."

"Who told you this?"

"Donuil, my young Hibernian hostage. He saw these two in action, when they came to his father's hall, less than three months ago. He recognized them yesterday and hid from them, afraid that they would see him and kill him. He has a very healthy respect for their killing power. Did you find out their names?"

"Yes. They're called—"

I cut him off. "Caspar and Memnon?"

"Caspar and Memnon, that's right."

"Then that proves it. Those names are Egyptian, but more than that, they're the names Donuil gave me."

"How do you know?"

"I told you. He knows them."

"No, not that. I mean how do you know they're Egyptian names?"

"I read a lot, remember?"

Uther made a wry face and jerked his head to indicate he would never understand me. "Now what? Does Uncle Picus know about this?"

"Not yet. I couldn't find him. Once I knew who those fellows really were, I didn't want them running loose in the fort."

"Yes, I could see that." His smile was back in place. "Where's this Hibernian of yours?"

"In his quarters. Come on, I'll introduce you to him. You can hear for yourself what he told me."

"Lead on, Commander. I'm in a fever of impatience."

"There's one more thing to do. Their servants have to be arrested, too. Where are they?"

"In the barracks with the common herd. I'll have them picked up."

"Pick up their baggage, too, and have it sent to my father's quarters. It will be interesting to see what's inside it."

Uther summoned a trooper from another table and issued his orders, and as he was doing so it occurred to me that there was no longer any need to keep our preparations secret. As Uther turned back to me, I told him so. "This changes matters, Cousin. We can start moving the extra supplies into the fort openly now. I'd better get the word out."

"What if Lot has spies out on the hills watching us? Won't that warn him that we've guessed what he's up to?"

"I no longer care. We'll start moving the stuff in first thing tomorrow morning. Our column started moving out this morning. They'll be far to the north-east tomorrow. All that will be left for

Lot's people to see will be the recall of our infantry and the gathering of our people and supplies. Even if he guesses we are ready for him, he'll never guess that we've already spirited an army out from under his nose."

He threw his arm over my shoulder. "Cay, my honoured Cousin, your shrewdness and your intelligence never fail to impress me. We'd better let Uncle Picus and the others know you've changed all their plans. They're going to be very pleased with you!"

In spite of my cousin's friendly sarcasm, my father and the others *were* pleased, after they had time to assimilate the changes and the reasons behind them. It took an hour to assemble my father, Titus, Flavius, Uther, myself and Donuil in the Armoury. Uther and I had thoroughly searched the baggage of the "ambassadors" before the others arrived, but it yielded nothing sinister or exotic. When everyone was assembled, I had Donuil repeat his story, prompting him myself on the points I wanted made clear. Uther supplied the translation into Latin for the others. When he had finished, my father and Titus directed a few questions at him, and then we let him go back to his own quarters. He stopped at the door, however, and looked at me.

"Commander Merlyn? Could I speak to you for a moment? Alone?"

I excused myself and followed him outside, where he stopped and turned to face me, his face troubled.

"What's wrong?" I asked him, in his own tongue.

"Their baggage. It should have contained more than it evidently did."

"What d'you mean?"

"I don't really know, Commander." He shrugged in frustration. "But there should have been more to find. These men go nowhere without the tools of their trade, for their traffic in death."

"What tools, Donuil? What are you driving at?"

"Their baggage should have contained things that were strange to your people, things that would cause comment. Did they search the iron-bound boxes?"

"I don't know." It was my turn to admit ignorance. "What iron-bound boxes are you talking about?"

"The two they never let out of their sight. One of them is slightly bigger than the other, and both are heavy."

I sniffed. "I'll check. But I think you are concerned about nothing."

"I hope I am, Commander." He did not sound convinced.

"Anyway—" I clapped him on the shoulder—"I'll look for myself and let you know what I find. Now get to bed."

I went back into my father's room. There was no discussion of the initiatives I had taken after hearing Donuil's story the first time. Everyone agreed that I had acted correctly. My orders were in place and would be carried out the next day, beginning at daybreak. In the meantime, we had little to do but wait. The logistical details of storage, supplies, allocation of space and food rationing were in the hands of Titus and his quartermasters. Uther and I would get a good night's sleep and leave for the north-east before dawn, travelling alone and unobtrusively to the rendezvous with our cavalry.

My next stop after leaving the Armoury was back at Donuil's quarters. He was still there, stretched out on his bed.

"Hey!" I said from the doorway. "Are you going to lie there for the next five years?" He sat up and blinked at me.

"What was the name of the soldier you found who speaks your heathen language?"

"Rufio."

"Big, burly man with a bright red beard?"

"Yes, Commander."

"I know him. Good! Let's go and find him." I had a centurion find him for me and order him to my quarters, where Donuil and I were waiting for him. He turned up a short time later, looking apprehensive and doubtless worrying over which of his misde-meanours I could have discovered. When he saw Donuil standing beside me, his apprehension deepened.

"You sent for me, Commander?"

"Yes, Trooper Rufio. I understand you speak our guest's language?"

He swallowed. "Yes, Commander."

"Good thing, since he doesn't speak ours. I'm putting you under special orders from this time on. Who's your centurion?"

"Phideas, Commander. 'C' Squadron."

"Phideas. That's right. He had you up in front of me on charges not too long ago. Brawling, wasn't it?"

"Yes, Commander."

"And insubordination, if my memory still works."

Again the swallow. "Yes, Commander."

"You and your friend—what was his name? Strato?—the two of you took on almost the whole of 'A' Squadron over some woman or other, and one of you was unwise enough to knock a decurion unconscious when he tried to stop the slaughter."

"Yes, Commander. I didn't see who he was until I hit him."

"Mmm! Well, any insubordination from now on will be to me, personally, since I am claiming your body for my own purposes. I'll instruct Centurion Phideas to that effect. In the meantime, I'm making you personally responsible for the welfare of our young friend here. You understand? He needs an interpreter, and he needs someone who knows his way around both this fort and a cavalry camp, who can show him the ropes. I'm making him one of my junior officers, one of my *Optiones*. I want you to make that clear to everyone concerned.

"You will treat him well, look after his butt, and teach him as much of our language as you can. Shouldn't be difficult. He's a bright lad and he's eager to learn. Most importantly, however, I want you to make a cavalryman out of him. Teach him about horses: how to care for them, how to groom and feed them, how to equip them, and how to ride. He's a complete tyro, so I'm making you a nursemaid. But you'd better teach him well, because he's going to be my personal attendant. That means he'll also have to learn the use, care and maintenance of weapons, armour and personal gear, all of my campaign equipment. Can you handle all of that, d'you think?"

He had been staring at me wide-eyed, his face a mask as he absorbed everything I was throwing at him. When I asked him this last question he blinked once and cleared his throat.

"Yes, Commander. Er . . . how much time do I have, sir?"

"How much do you think you'll need?" He glanced sideways at his new charge who was watching us, not understanding a word.

"Er, for the basics? Everything? A month?"

"A month you have. From tomorrow. Thirty days to turn a heathen prince into a Camulodian trooper. Don't worry about his officer's duties. That's my post. Just keep him out of trouble with your mates until he learns to handle himself. I'm assigning both of you to my personal squadron. You will hold the rank of acting centurion, with privileges. Hold it carefully. If you do this job properly, the rank will be permanent. Let me down and you'll be a bare-arsed trooper in Phideas's squadron again so fast, the speed of it will make you dizzy. Understood?"

His face broke into a wide smile. "Yes, Commander!"

"You will both need new uniforms. My troop wear black and silver, with the bear emblem. See Popilius. He'll set you up with whoever you need to deal with. Oh, and you'll need this." I sat down and stamped my seal onto a wax tablet, and over it I inscribed, "Centurion Rufio acts for me in the matter of the junior tribune, Donuil.—C. Merlyn."

"Take care of this, and use it only if you have to. I'm leaving tomorrow for a few days, so I won't be able to supervise your transfer. With that, you can handle it yourself. Talk to the Legate Titus.

"Now you'd better go and release yourself from 'C' Squadron. I'm sure Phideas will be heartbroken to see you leave, and as a centurion, too! I'll explain matters to the new junior tribune here and you can start him on his training tomorrow."

"Yes, Commander, and thank you." He saluted me and then he saluted Donuil and left.

Donuil turned to me, his eyebrows raised in curiosity at the salute, and I went over the whole thing again with him in his own language. By the time I had finished he was grinning from ear to ear, and he stood to attention and saluted me too. I had to smile.

"Thank you, Tribune Donuil," I said. "Please remember to tell Centurion Rufio to teach you to salute, too!"

As soon as I had got rid of him, I stretched out on my bunk and fell asleep, after taking the precaution of telling a guard to wake me up at nightfall, in three hours time. He did so, and under the friendly cover of darkness I left the fort and travelled back to Avalon with Cassandra's new clothes.

When she had overcome her awe and delight at the abundance of riches I had brought her, I spent two pleasant, satisfying hours in her arms and was back in my own bed shortly after midnight.

XX

I was in the stables when the messenger found me.

"Your pardon, Commander Merlyn, but Commander Uther requests that you join him in his quarters for a few moments."

I looked at the trooper in surprise. "He's supposed to be here already. I'm almost ready to leave."

"The Commander is ready, sir. His horses are tethered by the main gate."

I told him to tell Uther I would be along directly and continued tightening the girth on my saddle. My pack-horse, which was really an extra charger, was already loaded up with the few supplies I needed. It was still only the third hour of the morning. I guessed that Uther had gone to bed early and been up for hours.

I found him in his rooms, leaning against the whitewashed wall, putting an edge on a dagger with a small stone by the light of a couple of oil lamps.

"Good morning, Uther. All ready? What's up?"

"Good morning, Cousin." He grinned at me and nodded towards his bunk. Curious, I stepped to his bed and looked down at the device that lay there on top of the blanket.

"What is it?"

"Pick it up, then you tell me what it is."

I looked at it more closely before touching it: a weapon of some kind. A short, thick handle, covered in leather with a strong-looking leather loop at one end. The other end was sheathed in iron and attached to a short length of heavy chain links and on the other end of the chain, a ball about as big as a clenched fist.

"Is that iron?"

"Pick it up."

I did, and the ball, which *was* iron, remained on the bed as the chain extended with a series of clinks. I pulled it towards me and the ball fell from the bed, hitting the floor with a solid thud. The overall length of the thing was slightly shorter than my arm. I hoisted the ball clear of the floor. It was heavy.

"Very well, Uther. What is it?"

"Oh, come on, Merlyn! How many times have I had to listen to the tale of how you discovered the use of the saddle and stirrups? Can't you imagine what that thing would do to a man on foot if you swung it round your head?"

I hefted it tentatively, and suddenly I had no trouble in seeing what it was. "It would impress him."

"It would indeed—helmet, skull and all."

"Where did you get the idea?"

"You remember Vegetius Sulla's whistling stone? Partly from that. Partly from Grandfather Varrus's old story of you and the club. It's been lying around in my head for a long time now. I decided to have one made last time I was home. It worked, but the chain was too long, so was the handle, so we cut the length of the handle and reduced the chain to fourteen links, and there you are. I had one made for each of us. Yours is black, mine is red, see?" He bent and scooped another one from the floor by his feet. "Wrap the loop around your wrist and you can't lose it, even if you let go of the handle."

"Very impressive! But why did you make me come all the way here to get it? Couldn't you have brought it to me?"

"Are you mad, man? Those things are heavy! I would not even try to lug two of them all the way to the stables! I'd look like Vulcan himself, dragging those things across the courtyard."

I laughed in spite of myself and hoisted the ball up, catching it in my left hand. It *was* heavy. "Come on," I said, "We'd better be moving. Thank you for this. I promise not to hit you with mine if you don't hit me with yours."

"Done! Now let's get out of here. We have about two hours of darkness left."

By the time the first pale hints of dawn began to appear in the sky, we were far to the north-east and making good time, each of us leading an extra horse. We had ridden in silence, our ears straining to pick up alien sounds in the darkness around us, for it was in both our minds that Lot's bowmen with their poisoned arrows could be anywhere, but we met no one and heard nothing to alarm us, and soon the darkness had leached away sufficiently for us to discern the swelling bulk of the Mendip Hills on our right. We rode on into one of those magical mornings whose beauty remains in the mind long after the day it gives birth to has been forgotten. The entire landscape was veiled in a grey, low-lying mist that swirled around our horses' hooves, and every leaf, every blade of grass, hung heavy with dew, so that as the warmth of the sun dispersed the mist it seemed that we rode through a land encrusted with glittering, multi-coloured jewels. Single trees stood out from their neighbours as though burnished in pale greenish gold, and the world was filled with the singing of uncountable birds.

We were riding side by side, our knees almost touching, when we breasted a low rise and saw the strange markings on the valley floor in front of us. For my part, although I saw the thing in front of us immediately, I was slow in recognizing it. Not so Uther, who drew in his breath with an abrupt, hissing sound.

"You were right, Cay. They're on the move."

It was the trail left in long, wet grass by a large party of men who had crossed our path very recently. Their passage had flattened a broad swath of grass, dislodging the dew, so that the rays of the morning sun showed their tracks as a broad highway of darkened grass, black-green against the sea of sparkling dewdrops to either side.

"Where did they come from, Uther? Which way?"

"From the east, heading west. You can see that from the way the light hits the flattened grass. They must have been riding north, like us, hugging the flank of the hills, then swung left to get to the hills on the other side."

I glanced along the broad path stretching to our left. "You think they might be your poisonous bowmen?"

"Not a question of might be . . . I'd wager on it. Lucky we weren't here ten minutes ago."

"You think they passed that recently?"

"Not much more than that. The birds are singing, so they're not close by, but the dew only fell in the last hour or so and they went through after that."

"So what do we do now?"

"Exactly what we are doing, Cousin, but faster. There's nothing we can do about these people. We are only two against God knows how many of them. Let's head on, collect our own people, get back to Camulod as quickly as we can, and hope for the opportunity to provide a very nasty surprise for our visitors."

He kicked his horse forward and I followed him across the pathway of Lot's assassins, breaking into a canter as we traversed the open meadow between us and the unbroken line of trees ahead. As we reached the forest's edge, we both turned to look behind us at the unmistakable path our own horses had created in crossing the grass. It was now broad daylight and the sun was visible. Uther kneed his horse around towards the trees. "An hour at the most and the tracks will be gone. Let's just hope none of them head back this way too soon."

"Why should they? They're heading west and they have a long way to go."

"So do we, Cousin, and this forest doesn't look hospitable. Let's go."

Uther was right. Far from being hospitable, the stretch of forest we now faced was almost impenetrable, and there were times when we had to dismount and lead our horses through narrow gaps between thickets of ferocious undergrowth that simply refused to yield a passage. We struggled for well over an hour before the growth began to thin, but it seemed we had successfully negotiated the worst part of our journey, and we were able to mount again and ride through the remainder of the forest.

Finally, when the sun was almost directly overhead, we came into a meadowed clearing dominated by one massive old oak tree that stood on the bank of a clear, fast-flowing brook, and by tacit consent we dismounted and unsaddled our horses. Sometime later, the comfort of our mounts attended to, we sat on the bank of the stream, chewing on some of the cold venison and fresh bread we had brought with us from Ludo's kitchen.

"How far do we have to go, do you think?" I asked.

Uther shrugged and bent over to scoop up some water from the stream. "Should be there by nightfall, if we can make better time for the rest of the day." He drew himself erect again, wiping drops of water from his chin. "You know, Cousin, I never have remembered to congratulate you on your new rank . . . Supreme Commander of Camulod."

I was instantly on edge and distinctly uncomfortable, although not from his tone. I glanced at him quickly, but there was nothing to see in his eyes. His face was almost expressionless, with merely the hint of an ironic smile tugging at the corner of his mouth. I bent to the water and drank, too, more to conceal my sudden insecurity than anything else, then straightened up and waited, but he said nothing more.

"Thank you," I said eventually, moving back to sit beside him, then waited again. Uther, however, merely sighed and lay down, making himself comfortable on the grassy bank, leaving it for me to continue the conversation. "When did you find out?"

"What? About your promotion? When I returned last time. I meant to say something, but by then it was old tidings, and I forgot. But I'm glad for you. You earned it."

"You don't mind?"

"Mind?" He laughed aloud, and raised his head from the ground to gaze at me in surprise. "Why should I mind? Did you think I would be envious?"

I shrugged my shoulders. "Not really, although I must admit the possibility had come into my mind."

He propped himself up on one elbow and shook his head, as though in wonder at my silliness. "Tell me, Cay, will you be envious of me when I am King of Pendragon?"

I felt my eyes grow wide. "Of course not."

"Then why ask such a question of me?"

"I don't know, Uther. Forgive me." I felt foolish and petty, but he had already changed the subject.

"But there's one other thing I never did ask you. The girl, Cassandra . . . how did you get her out of that guarded room?"

Coming as it did, this question, too, caught me off guard. I felt a wave of resentment wash over me and all of my doubt and distrust came flooding back. I bit back the hostile response that sprang to my tongue and turned my face away to mask my feelings, hiding my agitation by answering his question with one of my own. "What makes you think I had anything to do with it?"

He barked his short, ferocious laugh. "Come on, Cay, this is me! Uther! Either you spirited her away, or I have to start believing in magic. Of course it was you! But how in the name of your Druid mystics did you do it? And why did you do it?"

"She was in danger."

"From whom?"

"From whoever it was who tried to kill her in the first place."

He sat erect now and looked at me in surprise, an expression of genuine puzzlement that made me wonder if he truly was a remarkable actor. "Why would anyone try to kill her?" he asked. "She was raped and beaten, from what I understand. Badly it seems, but why would anyone try to kill her? And if they had, why wouldn't they have done the job properly in the first place? She was no better than a slave girl. No one would have paid much heed."

My anger boiled over. "To murder? In Camulod? My father makes no secret of the fact that the price for rape and murder in his command is death! You seem to take it very lightly, Cousin, but that's the way it is! Death. My hope was that she might identify her attacker, or attackers, if there were more than one of them, which I doubt!"

His eyebrow had gone up at the strength of my outburst and now when he spoke, his voice was low. "Why would you doubt it?"

"I have my reasons."

"I'm sure you do." His voice was much quieter now. "Do you mind my asking what they are?"

"Ask yourself, Uther!"

"Ask myself?" He frowned slightly and shook his head abruptly. "So why would it be so important to you—because it very obviously is—that this girl should be able to identify her attacker? *That* is what I'm asking myself, Cay. Why? You went to a great deal of trouble to protect her. Why? She was a stranger."

"Not to everyone! She was no stranger to you!"

"To me? What does that mean? I wasn't even in Camulod!"

"Oh yes you were, Uther!"

Now his frown was deep and angry. "Are you suggesting . . ." His voice tailed away to silence and I watched the muscles in his face as they reflected the thoughts going through his mind. If he was dissembling, he was performing masterfully. "It was that night, wasn't it? The night I left?"

"Yes. The night you left in a rage, swearing to teach her a lesson she would not soon forget. They found her in the stables next morning. She had been beaten almost to death. And you were gone. No one had seen you go. No one knew where you had gone."

"I see." He was not looking at me. His eyes were fixed on a rock in the stream bed and on the water that spumed around it. "So you, quite naturally, assumed that I had done this thing." His eyes flicked up to hold my gaze. "It was a very brutal beating, wasn't it?" I did not respond. "And you thought me capable of that kind of bestiality?" I simply stared at him. "You still think so?"

"I don't know, Uther."

"You wanted her to recover and identify me?"

That, and the way he said it, made me pause. "No, I wanted her to recover and identify her attacker. I did not want it to be you." He was looking directly at me. "I was afraid it might be, but I was hoping she would prove me wrong."

"So why did you arrange for her to disappear? You could have kept her there until I came back."

"I could have, but by keeping her there I was putting her life in danger."

"How, in God's name? I was nowhere near!"

"Are you admitting guilt?"

"No, of course not, but you suspected me."

I got to my feet and looked down at him. "That's trust, in a strange way, I suppose. I suspected you, but I had no proof and I could have been wrong. I wanted desperately to believe I was wrong. And if I were wrong, then her true attacker could have been any man in Camulod. It could have been one or even more of the men guarding her—any of them. And any of them could have killed her. That would have proved you innocent, but she would have died in the proving of it."

He considered that for some time, then jerked his head in a brief gesture of acceptance. "So how did you get her out?"

"By trickery. She was gone before I ever mounted a guard over her."

"No. Her guards saw her."

"They saw a boy who took her place. He ran out of the building while the guards were waiting for someone to try to get in."

Uther shook his head, a slow smile of wonder stealing over his face. "You are quite a man, Cousin. Where did you take her to?"

"A safe place. Why do you ask?"

"Curiosity."

I shrugged again. "She is . . . safe."

"Good. Then I hope I'll have the pleasure of meeting her again some day and putting your mind at rest, one way or the other."

I had to ask my question. "Was it you, Uther? Did you do it?"

He was silent for a long time, holding my gaze, a strange look on his face that I had not seen before. "You saw me as I left, that night. You obviously thought I was angry enough to do it. Then I disappeared, which could be taken as an indication of guilt." He paused, evidently remembering. "The four wenches we had that night. They must have said something. What happened to them?"

"They never knew. I sent them away early the next morning, before they had a chance to hear about it. They went under close escort—some trusted men of Titus's—ostensibly to set up a house for us in Glevum. The news had not yet spread, and they knew nothing of what happened."

He thought about that for a short time. "My thanks, Cousin, for that. You evidently had at least some doubts in your head about my guilt."

"Some." I nodded. "Enough to convince me to take steps to protect you from gossip. I was angry and confused, but I wanted to conduct my own inquiries uninfluenced by hearsay."

He stood up. "Well, Cousin Cay, I'm in a bad situation here. I could claim innocence, but it wouldn't put your doubts to rest. I know the truth of it, but you are going to have to live with your doubts, I'm afraid—for a while, at least. Can you continue to do that?"

"Why not? I've been doing it for months."

"And you can still ride with me?"

"Aye, Uther, and fight with you, and hope I've been mistaken. I have strong doubts about your guilt and your innocence, both, and I have no proof of either. On the other hand, I've known you all my life and no man is dearer to me."

There was a half smile on his lips. "So you would forgive me for one lapse?"

I shook my head, seeing Cassandra's battered body in my mind. "No, Uther, I would not, not for that one. That was inhuman, unforgivable. I simply hope it wasn't you who did it, and until the day when I know for certain, one way or the other, I will treat you as Uther Pendragon, cousin and friend untarnished."

He was no longer smiling. "Caius," he said, "I tell you truthfully that I can see your reasons for doubting me. Were I in your shoes, thinking these doubts of you, I do not know if I could hold myself to be as magnanimous as you are now. Thank you for that." And then the devil flickered in his eyes again, and he added, "But do try to remember that most human men, being only men, cannot stand too much magnanimity in others. It smacks of sanctimoniousness."

He rose to his feet before I could frame a response. "Come, we had better be on our way. Time is not waiting for us and our troopers are."

We made good time for the remainder of the day, but it was after sunset before we arrived at the abandoned farm where our forces awaited us. Uther spoke for both of us, issuing orders that we would break camp at dawn and march back immediately. We would encamp the following night and finish our return journey by sunrise, so that, providing the enemy was in place, we would arrive at his back before noon.

We held a short council of war for the benefit of our junior officers and then Uther and I retired to our leather campaign tents, exhausted by the day's journey, and hoping against hope that we had built our campaign around the correct supposition: that Lot could not know our true strength, since we ourselves did not know it, having had no opportunity to conduct our census. If we were wrong somehow, if Lot had assessed our true strength accurately, then we would be riding back to Camulod without the advantage of surprise.

We headed back towards Camulod the following morning by a longer, more circuitous route than the one Uther and I had taken on the way out, making no attempt to hurry. It was essential that we arrive no sooner than Lot, and our best estimates indicated that he would strike against the fort either the following day, the third of our schedule, or the one after that. Uther wanted to have our forces within striking distance of the Colony by dawn on the fourth day. I would have preferred to wait one day longer, to allow Lot the time to assess his position and commit himself to a course of action that we could then disrupt.

As it turned out, however, neither of us had a choice. We had miscalculated by one entire day in Lot's favour, for he had arrived with his army on the plains of Camulod midway through the afternoon of the day we left, and as we made our leisurely way southward, his forces were battering brutally at the fort itself.

His unexpected arrival took my father and his defenders totally by surprise. A large number of infantry, almost a full cohort, were

busily at work throwing up a defensive breastwork and ditch at
the bottom of the hill. Popilius himself, our senior warrant officer,
was commanding them, and faced with a decision either to abandon the incomplete breastworks or remain there to defend them, he
chose the latter. Approximately a mile to the north of his position,
to his left, another large party of troops was involved in removing
everything useful from the buildings of the villa farm. The officer in
charge of this operation was a young man, but a wise one. By the
time he was apprised of the rapid approach of Lot's advance parties,
it was already too late for him to retire to the fort in safety with his
men, so he took immediate steps to strengthen the main building
of the villa to the best of his ability. By overturning the wagons
they had been loading and using them as barricades, he and his
men were able to construct a defensible perimeter, and there they
remained, a potential thorn in the side of Lot's advancing army.

The fighting on that first afternoon was savage. Lot's army
was largely undisciplined, each unit paying heed only to the most
basic orders of its local commanders. His soldiers, if they could be
called such, were all unruly individuals, and their first assault on
the villa's defenders turned into a disorganized brawl, quickly and
effectively won by the defenders, who fought as a unit and drove
their attackers off to lick their wounds as darkness began to fall.
Instead of allowing his men time to relax after beating off their
assailants, however, the young officer in charge took advantage of
the weakness he had perceived in the enemy's lack of discipline and
led his men through the darkness, in a hard and bitter fight, to join
Popilius's cohort a mile away. Hearing the noise of the fighting,
and guessing what was happening, the veteran Popilius flung out
his men on his left flank along the hillside, until they made contact
with the fighters from the villa and enabled them to gain the comparative safety of the unfinished breastworks.

In the meantime, under cover of the darkness, the opportunity
arose for Popilius to withdraw his men completely from their unfinished camp and get them up the hill in safety to the fort. Instead,
he sent a courier up the hill to inform my father that he intended

to hold his position and defend it against Lot's rabble. His major problem, he pointed out, would be the danger of being outflanked and infiltrated by Lot's people, who might attempt to climb the hillside on either side of his position, and start shooting arrows into his men from above and behind. My father sent out two squadrons of bowmen to guard his flanks, and at the same time he sent out three of his best riders to break through Lot's cordon and find us, warning us to get back sooner than we had planned.

These messengers were to tell us that Picus himself would be holding back his own cavalry. The brunt of the initial defence would fall on the shoulders of Popilius and his infantry. As soon as we put in an appearance, my father would loose his own seven hundred cavalry in a frontal attack, down the road and into the centre of the enemy.

One of these three messengers found us just after noon the following day and we immediately began a forced march, cursing the caution that had sent us so far north needlessly. My father had estimated the strength of Lot's army at around four thousand, a number that surprised me and added greatly to my sense of having erred badly. The urgency of a quick return had become immediately and devastatingly obvious.

Late in the afternoon, heavy grey clouds began piling up in the west, and we could see lightning flickering among them. The heat grew more and more oppressive as the storm drew closer, so that I found myself anticipating the chill of the rain that was sweeping towards us. My pleasure was short-lived. The downpour was awful, blowing against us in torrents, soaking everyone and everything completely and almost instantly, and turning the soft earth under the hooves of our thousand horses into a bog, so that headway was almost impossible. I had never seen such heavy rain, and it showed no signs of abating. The clouds were so thick that they blocked the sun completely, so it seemed we rode at night, although we knew there were still several hours of daylight left. We had no option of resting to wait it out, however; we had to keep moving as quickly as possible, and what had started as a leisurely march quickly

degenerated into a nightmare ride, with horses slipping and falling everywhere, terrified by the savagery of the storm, the glare of
the lightning and the chaotic noise of thunder, wind, rain and battering hailstones.

The freak storm lasted for almost three hours, and by the time
the clouds finally began to break, our force was totally demoralized.
It had been impossible even to shout to each other during that
time, and every man had been immured in his own private hell,
suffering the agony of cold, wet clothing and armour, exhausted by
the relentless struggle to keep his horse upright, moving and sane.
The first break in the clouds showed us the pink and purple high
sky of the setting sun, which took with it our only opportunity of
finding warmth and dryness that night, for all the wood in the
land lay soaked. We settled our minds to the prospect of a long,
miserable night.

Uther made his way to my side. "What do you think?"

"About what? I don't think I'm capable of thought. It's a mess."

"We all know that, Caius." There was a measure of asperity in
his voice. "I didn't come to you to hear you crying! I want your
opinion as an officer. Is it better to stop here and rest or to ride on?
We've still got a long way to go and it's getting dark."

I made myself think, and it turned out to be easier than I
expected, for a memory of Uncle Varrus sprang into my mind
unbidden. I took a long look around me, as far as I could see. We
were in the bottom of a shallow valley and as the land rose to my
right it flattened out slightly before rising again to a heavily treed
hillside. A picture emerged in my mind of a boat burning.

"Who's our quartermaster?" I asked Uther.

"We have three. Why?"

"Send them to me. We'll stay here tonight. The rain's gone.
We'll move up to the high ground there and see what we can do
about getting dry. Pass the word for one man in every two to start
gathering wood. Enough for four large fires, big enough to dry us
all off."

"Are you mad?" Uther's voice sounded shocked. "Fires? Everything's soaked! How in the name of Hephaestus are you going to light them?"

"Publius Varrus's way. That's why I want our quartermasters."

He looked at me in silence for a while, then shrugged his shoulders and rode away, signalling to a centurion. Very soon thereafter, everyone was out of the valley and up on the high ground. Within half an hour four large piles of wet wood had begun to take shape and I had spoken with the quartermasters in charge of our commissary supplies. They, too, thought I was mad, or at least profligate, but they produced the oil from our rations, poured it over the sodden wood and set it alight, and in what seemed like no time at all, our entire force was clustered around four massive conflagrations. I had no fears at all that these fires might be seen by unfriendly eyes. We were still a long, long way from home. The effect on our men was magical as the chill slowly thawed from their bones and their clothes began to steam. After a while, smaller fires began to appear apart from the larger ones, and the commissary staff began doling out food. The night was warm, too, and most of the men were almost naked as they waited for their wet clothing to dry. Leather legionary tents sprang up like mushrooms and out of chaos and demoralization came order, new resolve and comfortable rest. I was determined to make the most of this mood of renewed optimism, and I kept the men moving in relays to gather fresh supplies of wood, giving the roaring bonfires no chance to die down.

It must have been close to midnight when Uther approached me again, an excited look on his face. I was surprised to see him still awake and told him so, but he just shook his head briefly in that characteristic way of his, managing to convey the triviality of my thought in one gesture. "We're blind, Cay. Stone blind and foolish."

"Why? And how?"

"I've been racking my brain trying to think of the quickest way back to Camulod come daylight. I imagine you have too?" I nodded and he went on, "Well it suddenly hit me! Where are we and why are we here?"

"You mean here and now?"

"Yes, I mean right here and right now, and don't even bother trying to think about the answer, because I'm going to tell you. We are in the middle of nowhere, travelling a confused route from the camp to Camulod because we have to remain hidden, correct?"

"Correct. So? What's your point?"

"My point, Cousin, is that we are behaving like idiots. There is no need for secrecy now. Lot is at Camulod and all we have to do is get there as quickly as possible ... And there's a road less than seven miles to the east of us that will take us within five miles of Camulod! We can mount a forced march down an open road now. No need to go on blundering through this damned forest."

I had jumped to my feet as he was speaking. "By the Christ! You're right, Uther! I am a fool!"

"Well, you're hardly lacking for company."

"Seven miles to the road, you say?"

"At the most. Perhaps half that far. I don't know. I've never been so far off the road in these parts. I know the last villa the Atribatus brothers bought is somewhere to the south-west of us— that was the last new property the Colony acquired—but exactly how far away it is—again, I don't know, perhaps ten miles. But from there, it's only eight miles to the road. We've been swinging in an arc. We must be close to the road right now."

I headed for my horse. "I'm going to find it right now."

"In the dark?"

"You're fire blind. It's a clear, moonlit night."

"Wait then. I'm coming with you."

So we rode together and once away from the firelight it was easy to find our way between the clumps of trees that dotted the landscape. The road was less than two miles from our starting point, stretching black and straight and open from north to south. We rode straight up onto the roadway and sat there laughing at each other, until Uther spoke.

"Well, what do you think?"

"No need to think. I know. If we roust out our column now, we can be within a few miles of Camulod by dawn."

"My thoughts exactly. What are we waiting for?"

We galloped back to our camp like a pair of excited boys and roused everyone. The fires and the heat of the summer night had undone the damage of the storm and all of the men had managed to obtain some rest. There was some alarm and panic when we clattered in, but soon every man in the place was gathered around us as we sat there on our horses. Uther held up his hands for silence, and when he had it he looked at me in inquiry.

"Go ahead," I told him. "It's your show."

He grinned and raised his voice. "Hear me!" The silence grew more attentive. "You all heard the news today. Lot is at the gates of Camulod. The storm last night delayed us badly, and we will be hard put to come to Camulod before tomorrow night, taking this route. And if we do not come, our friends and families will die." Nobody moved or spoke. Uther looked at me again and then continued. "We have been blind, soldiers of Camulod. The road the Romans built is less than two miles from where we stand. If we go now, we can be close to Camulod by dawn. What say you?" The roar of surprised approval raised goose-flesh on my body. "So be it. Leave your supplies and tents here and mount up. Bring only what you need for fighting. The commissary wagons will stay here and follow later. We have a lesson to teach the usurper from Cornwall. We leave within the quarter-hour!"

We arrived back at Camulod in the heavy darkness before dawn and immediately deployed our men within the fringes of the forest that framed the great military practice plain at the foot of the hill. Uther had sent out some of his Celts earlier to range ahead of us and try to determine what had happened during our absence, but to a major and alarming extent we could see for ourselves.

Camulod was burning with a lurid, awe-inspiring glare that lit up the entire top of the hill, and we could hear the noises of a continuing battle at the bottom of the hill, around the hastily improvised fortifications that Popilius had been building when Lot's army arrived. On our right, to the north, fires still burned sullenly in the wreckage of the villa. Even from more than two miles away, the scene resembled a madman's vision of Hades and bitter, acrid smoke blown on the breeze caught at the throat.

"Well?" Uther's voice was rough and abrupt in my ear. "What's our move?"

I shook my head, my mind in a turmoil from the evidence of destruction in front of us. I was fighting against tears of anger and frustration and had to swallow hard several times before I could trust my voice to answer him. "I don't know, Uther, I don't know. It's too dark. If we attack now we will have only the firelight to guide us. There could be any number of men out there, hidden in the darkness."

"Aye, there could be." His voice was taut and rough with his own rage. "But the whoresons will never expect to find a thousand of us smashing at their ears. Let's hit them now."

I was strongly tempted to agree with him, but then I remembered we had scouts out there in the darkness and became freshly aware of the silent army at our backs. They had been warned under pain of court martial to make no noise that might betray our presence. I realized that throwing our men into a night attack would be wasteful for several reasons. I jerked my head in a negative. "No, Uther. If we move against them now, we lose our initiative. They won't see our strength, and I want them to see us—a thousand fresh horsemen. Fresh to this fight, at least. Fresh to them. We have to wait for daylight and for our scouts to come back."

"Come back? They may all be dead, Cay! That's Camulod burning up there! Your father is up there, so is my grandmother."

"Uther, I know that." I wanted to scream at him, but managed to keep my voice low and urgent. "Do you think me blind and a fool? But the choice is simple: either we attack now in anger, in darkness, as a blind rabble, and risk achieving nothing, or we wait for an hour and attack in daylight when our strength can be seen by Lot's people and by our own. Lot obviously thinks he has the battle in his hand, or he would not have his men fighting through the night. He is trying to wear our people down, but he is wearing his own down, too. Come daylight, they will not be ready to withstand the sight of a fresh army of cavalry at their backs. Our people, on the other hand, will take new heart at the sight of us."

He was unconvinced. "But what about the fort? It's burning, Cay. They must be fighting up there, too."

"I hope not," I responded, showing my own uncertainty. "But if they are, there is nothing we can do to help them. There are two armies between us and them."

"Damnation," he exploded. "There must be something we can do!"

I reached across and grasped his shoulder forcefully, trying to make him accept the truth of my words. "Nothing right now, Uther! Accept it. Nothing useful. Not before daylight. In the meantime, we can try to draw up a plan of attack." As I said this I heard the sound of a low-pitched challenge, answered immediately, off to my right, and then a small group of figures came towards us out of the stifling blackness. All were on foot and all save one were ours. The exception was a young squadron leader who had remained in Camulod with my father and Titus when we left. Uther and I swung down from our horses and went to meet him, Uther reaching him a fraction ahead of me and greeting him with the question that had sprung into my own mind. "How did you find us? How did you come here?"

The young man saluted both of us. "Commander Uther, Commander Merlyn, the Legate Titus sent me out of the camp at nightfall to wait for you here. I had to make my way along the side of the hill towards the villa and then circle the enemy to get here."

"Alone?" I interrupted him. "You came alone? What if you had missed us in the dark?"

"No, Commander," he interrupted me without being aware of it, "not alone. There were three of us. One stayed to the north of the villa to await you there in case you had not already passed. A second stayed half-way between there and here, and I came on alone. The Legate had no knowledge of the time of your arrival, but we all hoped that it would be tonight."

"Where is the Legate now?" This was Uther. "What happened up at the fort?"

The messenger shook his head. "I have no idea, Commander. I was with the force the Legate brought down the hill to reinforce the camp on the plain yesterday, but whatever is going on up there only began tonight, after we left to look for you. There was nothing amiss before that."

"How strong is the camp on the plain?" I asked, only too aware of how little we knew of the true state of things. "Can they hold out?"

His answer was immediate and positive. "Yes, Commander. We have over a thousand men there now, perhaps closer to fifteen hundred. They are well supplied and under the command of the Legate Titus and Popilius, the *primus pilus*. They can hold out for one more day at least, although they have been under constant attack since early yesterday. The Legate's reinforcements had to fight their way through."

I snapped my fingers impatiently, seething with frustration. "What can you tell us of the enemy? How many? How strong? Do they have cavalry? How are they disposed? Are they using poisoned arrows?"

He forestalled me by raising a hand, palm towards me, and I subsided in surprise. "Please, Commander Merlyn," he said, "I have all that."

"Good," barked Uther, smothering a laugh. "Spit it out, then."

The soldier turned towards Camulod, placing himself between Uther on his right and me on his left, and gestured with his left hand towards the south. "The enemy's main camp lies over there at the base of the hill, about two miles from where we stand. The fires are all out, otherwise we could see them from here. We have estimated their full strength as somewhere between five and eight thousand men, although it has been difficult to judge because of the constant stream of new arrivals, always from the south-west. Many of them are on horseback, but they hardly qualify as cavalry. They show no sign of discipline or training. We saw no evidence of organized manoeuvring. They are mounted, but most of their beasts are mountain ponies." He paused, and then went on, "On our way out here earlier, my companions and I tried to gauge the number of campfires. We estimated half, perhaps more, of the enemy are in their main camp, asleep. The remainder are attacking our camp on the plain, trying to wear our people out and, we think, trying to distract their attention from whatever is happening above in the fort. And no, Commander Merlyn, no poisoned arrows have been used as far as we know."

He stopped again, to let us digest what he had told us, but it was clear that he had more to say. Uther and I said nothing, waiting for him to resume. When he began to speak again his voice was different, dropping, now that he had finished speculating, into the trained, familiar monotone of the soldier repeating a dispatch.

"The Legate Titus will be prepared to bring his men out from behind the wall at daybreak, but he will not emerge until you have shown yourselves to the enemy and distracted them enough to allow him to attempt a safe and disciplined exit. He suggests that you might wish to launch your attack along a staggered front, committing your left in strength first. The Legate has observed that the enemy's main camp effectively blocks the exit from the plain to the south. His suggestion is that your opening attack, with your left, will begin to force the enemy northward in strength. By reserving your strength and committing it in staggered waves, the Legate feels that you could compress that northward movement into a rout, since he and his infantry will leave our camp by the south and east entrances and attack the enemy from the side and rear as you complete your advance, effectively cutting them off from their camp completely.

"Once their northward movement has started, the Legate suggests that our combined forces work together to increase its momentum. He suggests further that you withhold your extreme right in deep concealment in the forest to the northeast until the time comes to commit it. As the press of the enemy begins to clear the north-east corner of our camp, a third contingent of our troops, a cohort strong, will issue from the north gate in a new flank attack, supported from your side by the last squadron you have that is visible and uncommitted, charging them directly from the east, their right. No great need for discipline here, the Legate feels, merely timing. Then, at the correct moment, which will be signalled to you by a charge from the fort itself by the Legate Flavius and his four hundred cavalry, you will produce your uncommitted reserves on the right, in strength, out of their concealment to the north-east."

He stopped again, and smiled grimly before ending the proposed plan. "In the meantime, as soon as the final battle is committed, your left wing, at the rear of the rout, will disengage, turn about and capture the enemy encampment, leaving our infantry to follow up on the retreating enemy."

We had been listening to him in motionless concentration, visualizing the entire battle as he laid it out, seeing the stark, pristine simplicity of it and growing increasingly conscious of how important timing would be for the entire enterprise. When he had done, there was silence for several seconds before Uther spoke.

"Whose plan is this?"

"General Picus's, Commander."

"I thought so." He turned to me. "It will work, Merlyn. What side do you want, right or left?"

I shrugged. "Makes no difference. Your choice. But we are running out of time and we have much to do."

"Good, I'll take the left and go in first. How many men will I have?"

I was already estimating our forces. "Three hundred, but you have to move them quickly. To gain effect, you have to launch your charge from behind their camp, almost directly south of them, so you have to move now."

"I'm gone already. But what else should I know?"

My mind was racing. I spoke to the young messenger. "You command a squadron?" He nodded. "Then today you command our centre, with four hundred men. Choose a subordinate to lead two hundred, south of a median from here to the fort, to strengthen Commander Uther's thrust once he has achieved his surprise. You yourself choose the time to commit your own two hundred to the charge, when the enemy has cleared the north-east corner of our camp. I will stay hidden with our remaining three hundred and await Flavius's sortie from the fort. Now, let's move."

Uther was watching me closely. "Merlyn," he said, "you look displeased. What's wrong?"

"Nothing. But I would like to know what's going on up at the fort. Flavius may not be able to bring out his cavalry."

"Then he'll be dead. That's the only thing that will stop him."

"I know," I concurred, "but as I said, we don't know what's going on up there. If Flavius does not come out, my three hundred will not make much of a difference."

Uther barked his strange laugh again. "By that time, if that happens, it will not matter, Cousin. We'll be in the hands of Mithras. Anyway, I will keep watch. If Flavius does not come out, I'll turn my own men and come to help you rather than capturing their camp. One way or another it will be an ending, have no fears."

I grinned at him in the greying darkness. "I have no fear, Uther. I'm too terrified for fear!"

He laughed again and punched me in the shoulder. "See you later, Cousin."

I can take no credit for the conduct of the battle or for the successful unfolding of the plan. I can say only that it worked perfectly when it did unfold. We had the better part of an hour to make our troop dispositions before daylight revealed our presence to the enemy. By then I had my own three hundred men well hidden, far to the right of Uther's launching point, with time on my hands to worry over whether he would make it to his own position in time to begin his attack with surprise on his side. I had nothing else to do but wait for the sounds of his charge, but I waited and waited and the sky grew bright. Finally, when I could wait no longer without seeing for myself what was afoot, I went back alone towards the forest's edge and found a spot where I could see through the screen of trees. There was no sign of Uther's force on the plain to my left. He had not yet moved his men out of hiding.

I can recall my initial reaction of anger clearly as I wondered why he would have delayed so long, and I leaped from my horse and went forward on foot. Ahead of me, on the very fringe of the tree line, stood a mighty oak tree, and I climbed high into its branches and looked out over the *campus* that stretched unbroken from its base to the hill of Camulod. The citadel on the hilltop was obscured by drifting smoke, but as I looked a wind sprang up from the east and began blowing the roiling clouds away from the walls. I could see no flames, but I was far away. And it was only then that I perceived the reason for Uther's delay in launching his attack.

The enemy was on the move, in massed, seemingly disciplined ranks, towards our camp at the bottom of the hill. As they moved, I guessed their numbers at around five thousand, with a leading assault force of some three hundred war chariots. I stared at these in disbelief, not having known until that time that war chariots still

existed in Britain. To my knowledge, none had been used in battle
for decades, and then only in the far north. They moved with pomp
and purpose, and as they neared our embattled camp their brethren
who had been attacking it, some two to three thousand strong, fell
back to give them access.

As these retiring fighters streamed away, their numbers mingled with and crossed through the confident, advancing army, so
that for a space all semblance of disciplined movement disappeared,
and it was then that Uther committed his forces from the south,
behind them, his brazen trumpets neighing loud and clear. His surprise was absolute. Lot's melding armies, advancing and withdrawing through each other, wavered in confusion for a fatal interval as
their commanders sought to assimilate and respond to this unexpected apparition. By the time their ranks started to wheel in some
semblance of formation, Uther's three hundred cavalry, charging in
five tight-knit, invincible wedge-shaped squadrons, each with three
individual twenty-man wedge formations, had halved the distance
separating them. I watched spellbound in admiration, clearly seeing Uther's great dragon standard at the apex of the central squadron. This was the formation manoeuvre we had spent month after
month preparing but had not used in battle until now.

Then, a half minute before the opening clash of battle, another
rally sounded to my left as the first half of our centre, two hundred
horse, broke into their charge, their formations emerging as they
built up speed, advancing to hit the enemy on the now-open flank.
I glanced back towards Uther's charge and, in the moments that
remained before the action joined, I saw the morning light reflect
from massed spearpoints as Titus sent his infantry out through the
southern and the eastern gates in maniples of one hundred and
twenty men each.

Caught up in the excitement of the scene, I almost lost sight of
my own role in the events that were unfolding. Lot's people came
to pillage, I exulted. They had not known what they would really
face. They had not expected Roman tactics combined with the
strategies of Alexander! Then I threw myself down from the tree,

leaping from limb to limb, castigating myself for my doubts, but already beginning to anticipate the launching of my own three hundred men. I swung myself back onto my horse and rejoined my troops, signalling them to stand fast, then I sent one of Uther's Celts up into the tree where I had been, bidding him pass the word to me when the enemy had passed the northeast corner of our camp and the final assault of our centre had begun.

It seemed to take hours for that to happen, and in the meantime we sat and waited, seeing the battle only through the eyes of the man up in the tree although, from his shouted commentary, it soon became clear that all was unfolding as planned. I experienced again the agonies of waiting and wondering, and in my agitation I found myself fidgeting with the weapon that Uther had made for me, the iron ball on the length of chain. I untied it from where it hung by my saddle and slipped the loop over my wrist, gripping the thick, wooden handle and enjoying the substantial, solid weight of the apparatus. I was standing in my stirrups, vainly trying to see through the screen of leaves ahead of me when the cry came from the man in the tree above: the gates of the fort were open and our cavalry coming out. I swung the iron ball around my head, shouted to the men ranked behind me, sat back in the saddle and kicked my horse hard, seeing the man in the tree coming down almost as fast as I had, and then we were out in the open and driving hard across the path of Lot's demoralized army, trumpets blaring, lost in the growing thunder of our hooves as our mounts increased their speed with every stride, moving into the tight, arrowhead formations that were designed to slice through any mass of foot-soldiers. And as the distance closed between us and the enemy, I raised my eyes again and again to the summit of the hill in front of us and heard my own voice soaring in exultation as I watched my father's cavalry swarming out from the curtain wall and pouring down the hill to join us for the killing.

In the heat of the battle, Uther's new weapon impressed me more than anything else. It felt feather light in my grasp and yet each time that swinging iron ball hit someone, it threw the man bodily aside like a child's doll of cloth and straw. At one point I felt a heavy blow on my chest and then a pain in my wrist and briefly saw a spent arrow fall down by the side of my horse. I ignored it and killed another man on the ground, caving his helmet and skull with my swinging ball before the realization hit me that I might be dying from one of Lot's envenomed arrows. I felt a wave of panic sweep upwards from my gut and I reined in my horse violently, oblivious of the fighting around me, my eyes fastened to the small, shallow cut on my left wrist. And then my proud horse went to its knees with a stricken grunt of pain and I found myself standing on the ground, my feet still in my stirrups as the horse heaved under me in its death agony. Even as I regained my senses I saw the broad blade of a spear directed at my chest and I threw myself to the side, vainly trying to kick my feet free of the stirrups. One of them came free, and luckily it was the one I needed free to save my life. The spearhead hissed along my side, beneath my arm, and then the man holding it crashed into me, throwing me backwards and driving the breath out of me. Through eyes suddenly awash with tears I saw him come to his knees above me, shortening his grip on the spear, and then he was gone, smashed backwards himself by a swiping sword across the face. A second later there was a horse directly above me, rearing to keep from trampling me, and I heard a voice yelling my name.

"Commander! Merlyn! Can you rise?"

It was Catius, one of my own officers. I nodded to him, scrambling to my feet, even then admiring the way he controlled his mount, circling it on its hind legs, keeping an army at bay. I grasped the handle of my ball and chain in both hands and began flailing it around my head, dropping three men and clearing a space around me, and as I did so, I remember thinking that the noise and confusion was far worse here on the ground than it ever appeared from the back of a horse. It also occurred to me that I was obviously not poisoned. Then I heard Catius again, screaming at me to climb up behind him. I glanced around and saw the carcass of my own horse not three paces away, with only two of the enemy between it and myself. I swung my new weapon aloft with a roar and charged at them, catching the first full in the breast with the lethal iron ball, seeing his companion slip and fall at the same time in the bloody grass. I continued the momentum of my swing, spinning on my feet like a wild man, to shatter the second man's skull at the full swing, my arms fully extended. The effort almost toppled me, but it brought me alongside my dead horse, facing Catius who was close by me, his right arm extended towards me. I jumped up onto the dead animal's flank and hooked elbows with Catius as he passed, swinging myself high over his horse's rump just in time to go flying onwards as the beast took a spear full in the neck and went down instantly. Catius and I landed still linked together by our elbows, although this time my feet were beneath me, so that I staggered and fell backwards again, seeing Catius disappear beneath a giant brute of a man who held a short-sword like a dagger. I had lost my grip on my flail, but I could still feel the weight of it on the thong around my wrist. I scrambled up to crouch on all fours like a bear, just in time to see the giant fall away, skewered by a spear. Catius did not move. And then I felt the killing rage break loose inside me, and heard my own voice roaring in my ears as I stood erect and regained a grip on my terrible iron flail.

From that time on I remember nothing, until I found myself facing another giant Celt, with the chain of my flail somehow wrapped around the shaft of his axe, and the knowledge clear in my head that I no longer possessed the strength to pull it free. I was too tired. I released my grip and pulled my wrist free of the retaining loop and saw the flash of triumph in his eyes as he swung his axe high, letting my flail fall unheeded to the ground. But I was only tired. I was not yet dead, or even beaten. Before his axe had reached the apex of its swing, I had unsheathed my short-sword and buried it to the hilt beneath the fool's breastbone. Then I stood there, too tired to move again, and watched death blossom in his eyes before he fell. I made no attempt to pull my sword free. Slowly, in a stupor, I bent down and slipped the thong of the flail around my wrist again and then I sat down, not because I wanted to, but because I was completely spent. The flood of the battle had moved away from me and I was alone and alive in a sea of dead and maimed men.

I do not know how long I sat there, but eventually my breath and some of my strength came back to me and I rose to my feet and gazed at the carnage that surrounded me. A black and silver draped corpse caught my eye and I moved towards it, thinking it was Catius, but it was one of my troopers. So were the next eight I looked at before I found poor, courageous Catius, who had died trying to save me. The sight of his staring, lifeless eyes finally sobered me completely and I leaned over him, trying in vain to close his lids, before straightening to look more objectively about the field. As far as I could gauge, Lot's dead outnumbered ours by ten to one, but I could see far too many of my own men huddled in death. I saw my own dead horse nearby and beside it the body of Catius's mount, and at the sight of them my eyes swam with tears. I found nothing strange in grieving for horses amid so many dead men. In truth, the human dead were too numerous to allow for any pity; the mind could not absorb them. But the horses were innocent. I removed my helmet and wept, head down, for the pain and the folly and the outrage caused by one man's treachery. And then I replaced my helmet, fastened it securely, reclaimed my short-sword from the corpse of the last man I had killed, and went to search for Lot of Cornwall, striding across that field of death, hearing only now, and still only faintly, the screams and moans of the wounded who lay everywhere. As I walked, my eyes were fastened on the still-struggling masses in the distance. I held the shaft of my flail in my right hand with the chain over my shoulder and the ball dangling at my back, and as I went I prayed that Lot was not yet dead, because I had a lust to teach him the brute power of my new weapon.

Camulod still burned, and the sight of it smoking there upon its hilltop hardened everything within me. I remembered Daffyd the Druid talking of Lot's fortress in the west, and how it was said to be impregnable, and I swore an oath to send it tumbling, logs and stones and men, into the sea.

I found myself becoming more aware of the life and the pain yet present in many of the men about me. Their screams and moans and pleas for help seemed to grow louder all the time, until my head was filled with the chaos of them, but I ignored them all, friend and foe alike. And then I saw a horse, alive and well it seemed, standing head down, about two hundred paces from where I was. I approached it with caution, having no wish to frighten it again, but it stood calmly and let me take it by the bridle. It was almost exhausted, its flanks and withers scummed with sweat and blood. I hoisted myself up on its back and began to walk it towards our camp, realizing from its stirrups and the length of them that its previous rider had been one of our men with legs far shorter than my own. Having been afoot for so long, I was surprised by how much I could see from the height of a horse's back. The entire battlefield now took on a familiar perspective and, relieved of the need to walk, I began to look around me more carefully.

About three hundred paces short of the armed camp Popilius had built, I came across another of my men, this one alive. He was Polidor, a centurion in my own troop, and his left arm was bound up in a tourniquet above the elbow. I brought my horse sidling up to another dead animal and clumsily helped Polidor to climb up behind me. Not a word passed between us until he was mounted and clutching me with his good arm.

"How bad is it, your arm?" I asked him.

He answered me through clenched teeth, his voice harsh and sibilant, "Bad enough, Commander, bad enough."

"Well, if this horse can hold us both up for a few moments longer, we will make it back to the camp there. Where did our army go?"

"Don't know, Commander. Probably chasing Lot back to Cornwall."

"I hope not! The last I saw of them, they were heading north."

The poor horse was staggering by the time we were seen from the walls. The camp was not fully manned, obviously, but there was a garrison of sorts and some of them came running to meet us.

Above us, Camulod smoked sullenly. I helped Polidor down to outstretched arms as gently as I could, and saw him safely laid on a bier made of a shield slung between two spears. Then I kicked my exhausted horse to a walk again, in through the north gate, where willing hands were waiting to help me down and remove my battered armour.

XXII

"Did you know you had this, Commander?" I looked tiredly at the arrow one of the men was holding out to me. "No, where was it?"

"Lodged in your armour, sir, at the shoulder."

"In the back?"

"Yes, Commander, between the joints."

I shook my head. "Didn't feel it. Careful, it might be poisoned."

The trooper held it up to the light and then his face registered amazement. "By the gods, Commander, I think it is! There's a coating of some kind on the iron."

I felt the goose-flesh of horror stirring on my neck again. "Let me see that. Give it here." I held it up to the light as he had done and saw what looked like a residue of silvery-green crystals on the iron tip. They resembled nothing I had ever seen before. I shuddered in loathing and threw the thing from me. "It might well be. The very thought of it sickens me. Be careful of it!"

The trooper who had handed it to me had moved to retrieve it. He picked it up, holding it very carefully, and peered again at the discoloured tip. "Well," he said, almost to himself, "we'll soon find out."

"And how will you do that, Trooper? Do you intend to try it out?" My voice sounded slurred to my own ears, so tired was I.

"Yes, Commander. On one of those whoresons over there." He nodded to a huddle of prisoners I had not noticed.

"You will do no such thing!"

"Why not, Commander?" His look was one of hurt innocence. "I will simply scratch one of them. If it's not poisoned, then there's no harm done. If it is, then we will know who used them last time."

I blinked at him, remembering the harmless arrow that had nicked my wrist, and remembering that this arrow, the one he held so cautiously, had lodged within a fraction of a finger's breadth from my neck. I nodded. "Go ahead, then."

He crossed directly to the group of prisoners, seized one of them by the arm, pulled him out of the group and scratched him deeply with the arrowhead. The prisoner gazed at the wound, dull-eyed, for several moments and then raised his eyes to me, his injured arm held stiffly, so that the small, bleeding wound inside his elbow joint was plain to see. His face was empty of any expression.

I turned away to the centurion beside me. "Water. I need to wash some of this mess off."

"I have already ordered it, Commander."

I saw two soldiers approaching, bearing jugs of water, and then I heard a strangled moan from behind me and whipped my head around to look. The prisoner's face was no longer vacuous; it was a rictus of pain and terror as he held his injured arm out stiffly in front of him. Even as my mind accepted what we had done to him, his moan changed to a high, gurgling scream and he threw himself to the ground, writhing in agony, tearing at his arm and jerking it as though trying to wrench it from his body. I opened my mouth to shout, but nothing emerged, and we stood there, horrified beyond expression, watching the fellow go into paroxysms, arching his back clear of the ground so that he was supported only by his head and his heels until he toppled sideways, scissoring and writhing. It was the most awful spectacle any of us had ever seen. My mind was screaming, *That should have been me! That should have been me!* until one of the centurions suddenly regained his senses and put the suffering man out of his misery with a swift, merciful, chopping arc of his short-sword. Yet even after the man's head was severed, the body continued kicking and convulsing, spraying great gouts of blood around the yard.

I swallowed the bile in my throat with a great effort and looked for the man who had scratched the prisoner. He stood transfixed, his face as white as death, the arrow lying at his feet where it had fallen from his nerveless fingers.

"You were correct," I heard myself say. "Pick up the arrow and keep it safe for me. Treat it with care to protect its coating. I will have need of it later." I turned then to the ashen-faced soldiers who had brought my water. "Bring that into the tent there. I will wash now."

I washed myself in a haze of cold detachment, dousing my whole head in the water that remained, and then I dressed again in my armour and the tattered remnants of my great, black cloak. My body felt refreshed, I remember, but my mind seemed numb, and I was conscious only of what I had to do next. When I emerged from the tent I found Popilius himself awaiting me, and the camp filling up with dusty, bloodied and weary soldiers.

"Commander Merlyn." Popilius's voice was full of concern. "Are you unhurt? We had thought you dead."

I reassured him mechanically and asked him what had happened in the fort above. His face immediately became troubled but he could tell me nothing other than that whatever had occurred had taken place after nightfall. Since then he had had neither the time nor the opportunity to learn of conditions there.

"So be it," I said, "I shall discover for myself. I am going up there now. What about Lot? Where is his army?"

"Scattered, Commander, what is left of it. Destroyed."

"And Lot?"

Popilius shrugged his big shoulders. "No one seems to know, Commander. He may be among the dead."

"No." I heard the disgust in my voice. "Not that serpent. His kind seldom die that way, with honour. He must have run."

Popilius sounded dubious. "If he did, then he did it quickly, Commander. Uther's men were in his camp within minutes of their first charge."

"Oh, Popilius, he did it quickly, rest assured of that. But he cannot run far enough. Britain is no longer big enough to hide that man from me." I glanced towards the hilltop. "Form up your men, Popilius, and let's go see what waits for us in Camulod."

He cleared his throat, as though apologizing for his next words. "It cannot be too bad, Commander. The cavalry came out. They would not have done that had they been hard pressed."

"True enough, but did my father lead them?"

"I don't know, Commander."

"Well, let's go up and find out how bad the damage is. It worries me that no one has come out yet."

He was determined to be sanguine. "They'll all be fighting the fires."

"Aye, and glad of our help."

Popilius was right. Every able-bodied person in the fort was fighting the fires, most of which appeared to be under control by the time we arrived. It was only as I entered the gate into the smoke-filled yard and saw the extent of the damage that I thought of the Armoury and the treasure that lay hidden beneath its wooden floor, and my heart leaped into my mouth. The courtyard was chaotic, criss-crossed with lines of firefighters swinging leather and wooden buckets from hand to hand from the great reservoir tanks by the west wall. The yard was awash in filthy, soot-scummed water. I left Popilius deploying his men to the bucket lines and made my way as quickly as I could to the west wall, against which Uncle Varrus had built his house and Armoury. Miraculously, I found the building intact, but surrounded by a phalanx of Uther's Celtic bowmen. The thatch had been fired in places, but the flames had not had time to take proper hold before being doused with water from the nearby tanks. As I approached the bowmen I heard my name being called and Donuil came towards me, accompanied by his guardian, Centurion Rufio. Both men were black with soot from head to foot, but they were the first faces I had recognized since my arrival.

"Donuil," I snapped, one eye on the bowmen, "What has been happening here? What is going on?"

He drew a great, gulping breath, trying to suck fresh air into his lungs when there was none. "It was the wizards, Merlyn, Caspar and Memnon. They escaped from their cells in the middle of the night and opened the gate in the rear wall. There were men waiting outside. They had come up the cliffs at the back."

I was stunned. "They escaped? How? That should not have been possible. They were heavily guarded, were they not?" Both men nodded in assent. "Then how could they escape?" I saw the troubled look in both men's eyes and pounced on it. "You know. Tell me. How could they escape?"

Donuil's low voice contained a hint of truculence. "I told you, Merlyn Britannicus, before you left, when first they came. These men are necromancers—wizards, magicians, servants of death. They have powers that ordinary men lack."

"Rubbish! This was treachery. They must have suborned a guard."

"No, Merlyn!" The big Scot's tone was categorical. "That is not the way of it. They killed all the guards. It was magic of some kind. I woke in the night and went to check on them, for I fear them, as you know. Rufio came with me. When we arrived, the cells were open and the guards all dead. Not violently dead, mark you. We thought at first they were asleep."

"Damnation, Donuil, what you tell me is impossible! How could chained men kill their guards from inside a locked cell?"

"It is not impossible! The men were dead and the prisoners gone. I know not how they did it, but they did it! We raised the alarm immediately, but were not in time to stop them from opening the gate at the back. We managed to close it again, but a large number of men got in."

"How many?" There was something wrong here, but for the moment it eluded me.

The two men looked at each other and guessed, "Fifty? Perhaps sixty."

"And fifty men did all this?" I waved my arm at the desolation around us.

"They had fire arrows. They fired the thatch."

"How many are left? I presume they are in there?" I indicated my uncle's house.

"We don't know, Commander. Perhaps ten or twelve. They . . . they have hostages."

I felt my skin crawl again, as it had over the poisoned arrow. "Who?" But I already knew.

It was Rufio who answered me. "Your aunt, Commander, the Lady Luceiia. Her women. Some others."

"My father," I said, unable not to say it. "Where is my father?" Silence. "Where is he?"

"Dead, Commander."

The silence stretched on for an eternity, and finally I heard Rufio speak again, his voice sounding distant. "They killed him in his bed before they opened the gate." His voice rang in my ears like a brazen bell. My knees gave way and I felt Donuil grasp me and hold me up. I hung there, letting him support my whole weight until my head cleared.

Finally I whispered, "Where is he now?"

"Still in his bed, where we found him."

"Wait here." I left them and made my way to my father's sleeping quarters, oblivious to my surroundings, uncaring where I stepped.

It was as they had said. My father, General Picus Britannicus, had died in his bed. But not asleep. The bedclothes tangled around his bare legs told me of a struggle and an image flashed into my mind of an earlier struggle from which he had emerged alive. His body hung backwards, his head and shoulders between the edge of his cot and the floor, so that I could not see his face. There was blood everywhere. I looked up at the light streaming in through the tiny, sooty window above his bed and my soul felt empty. I walked around the bottom of his cot and tried to lift him onto it, to arrange him with more dignity than his killers had left him, but he was rigid and cold. The gaping wound in his throat had completed the work begun by a Pictish arrow so many years before.

I abandoned my futile attempts to move him and sat on the edge of his cot for a long time, careless of the blood that lay congealed beneath me, remembering the roughness of his voice that I would hear no more, and staring at the massive hand that stretched stiff and clawlike at the end of his rigid arm as though still clutching at life. And as I stared, my resolution hardened.

By the time I emerged once more into the courtyard, I was fully in control of myself again. Somewhere close by a baby was wailing and the sound prompted the thought in me that I might never weep again. Donuil and Rufio were still where I had left them, facing towards me, waiting for me to come back. The ring of bowmen still faced inward, towards the Armoury. The fragrance of cooking food caught at my nostrils. Either the kitchens were undamaged or Ludo was improvising. The noise in the courtyard was appalling. There was smoke everywhere, swirling and eddying among the buildings. I was conscious of all of these things, affected by none of them.

My mind was focused totally on the problem of getting the magicians and their hostages out of the Armoury. I knew in the coldness of my soul that had they not held my Aunt Luceiia there, I would have stormed the place and sacrificed the other hostages. But Luceiia was there, and I could take no risks with her safety—the more so since she was now the last survivor of the original Colonists of Camulod. One clear thought kept returning to my mind, to be suppressed time and again, until I could no longer deny the rightness of it and was forced to admit that it represented the only route open to me, even though the risk that it entailed was petrifying.

I spoke to Donuil and Rufio. "Wait for me here, I have some arrangements to make. Let no one make a move against those people in there until I return, is that clear?" They both saluted me and I left to make my preparations.

I returned within the half hour and went straight to Donuil. "Have these magicians seen you?"

"What do you mean, Commander?"

"I mean have they seen you here? Do they know you are here willingly?"

He frowned, thinking. "No, Commander. I have been careful to avoid them."

"Did they see you in your father's hall?" He nodded, frowning. "And do they know of your father's high regard for you?"

He nodded again. "Aye, they do. I heard them speak of me as my father's favourite son, even though I was not firstborn."

"Good." I reached out and grasped his forearm. "How would you like to earn your freedom today?" The measure of my need of his assistance was implicit in my offer and he was astute enough to realize that immediately. His eyes narrowed.

"My freedom?"

"Yes, today. Immediate release from your bond."

He seemed about to scowl at me. "How would I do that?"

"By performing a service for me."

"A service." His expression was difficult to read. "What kind of service?"

"A pretence of being what you are, a prisoner, but an unwilling one."

"Pretence?" Now he frowned. "I do not understand."

"It's not difficult," I told him. "These people—these magicians, as you call them—hold my aunt hostage. She is one of the two people in the world I hold most dear. The only way I can think to save her life is to put it at risk in an exchange of hostages."

He was silent for the space of a few heartbeats, then, "You mean me, in exchange for her?"

"Yes."

He frowned again and shook his head. "It won't work, Commander. These men care nothing for me."

"No, but Lot does, or he will, as soon as he comes to realize that he can increase his influence over your father and impress your sister by producing you safely from captivity. He would see you as a political tool of great power—a means of fortifying his alliance with your father and his people."

The young Scot was far from stupid. He saw the flaw immediately. "But Lot is gone, Commander. As soon as he reaches his home he will see the truth of things, that our army was broken. Our forces would be useless to him now."

"I disagree, but that is not important here. The point is that
these people don't know the truth of it. They will seek to make the
exchange for the advantage of handing you over to Lot. They will
see a golden advantage to themselves in that. Which of them is the
stronger?"

He shrugged. "Neither is stronger than—"

I cut him off impatiently. "Nonsense. In any and every partner-
ship there is a dominant and a subservient partner. That is human
nature. Think! Which of them makes the decisions?"

He paused, but only for a heartbeat. "Caspar. Memnon is the
follower."

"That's what I thought. I will release you to Memnon, who will
also have my aunt with him. I will keep Caspar. We will all go from
here to an open place where there can be no chance of trickery on
my part. Once we are there, Memnon will release my aunt to walk
back to me. When she has reached me, I will release Caspar."

Donuil's face clouded. "That's a simple exchange. It would
work without me, Commander Merlyn."

"Aye," I nodded. "It is true, it might, but I doubt it. They have
more advantage now than such an arrangement would give them.
There's too much risk for themselves involved as things stand. The
advantage of gaining you might make the difference in their thinking." I paused, thinking, then shrugged. "At any rate, I can think of
nothing better. But even so, I would trust neither of these creatures.
If Memnon should think to rule his magic kingdom alone, he might
destroy my aunt and leave Caspar to me. That will be your service to
me—to kill the animal if you so much as think he dreams of harming her. I will provide you with a knife, hidden in your clothes."

"I see." His brow had cleared, but the frown returned immediately. "But what then? What if your exchange should work, without treachery? I have no wish to share Lot's hospitality."

"Why not? He would send you home."

He looked at me in silence for a moment and then nodded.
"So be it. I will help you."

"Good. But you will have to be produced in chains. It would

not look convincing otherwise." He shrugged and I addressed his guardian. "Centurion Rufio, take Donuil to the cells and shackle him securely—and don't be too gentle, he has to look the part he will play. Give him back his own clothes, too."

When they had gone, I approached the doors to the Armoury, waving the bowmen away, and hammered on the panel with the hilt of my sword. There was silence for a few moments and then a voice shouted from behind the door, asking me what I wanted. I demanded to speak to either Caspar or Memnon and told them who I was. More time passed, and then the doors opened slightly and the deep voice of Caspar, the swarthy, short-legged swine, asked me what I wanted. I spoke to the crack between the doors.

"First, hear what I do not want. I have no wish to waste time haggling with you. You have the mistress of this house there among your hostages. She is very old. If she is already dead, then so are you and everyone else within those walls, hostages or no. If she is still alive, show her to me and I may let you buy your worthless lives in return for hers."

I heard a hurried, whispered conversation, then, "This woman. What is she to you?"

I gritted my teeth. "She is my father's aunt."

Silence, then, "Your father's aunt? But your father is dead, Caius Merlyn." My heart thudded in my chest and I thought, *I know that, and so are you, you stinking lump of Egyptian dung.* "But you are still alive," the voice continued, "And so is your aunt."

I swallowed hard. "Prove that. Show her to me."

Again, a whispered conversation, then, "Wait. You shall see her. But any tricks and we all die, the old woman first."

I waited.

Eventually the doors swung slowly open and there, in the middle of the hallway, held firmly by a man who stood behind her with a knife at her throat, stood Luceiia. She had blood on her face from a cut on her forehead, her hair hung down in rat tails and her clothing was in tatters, but her eyes were open and she stood erect and defiant. I called to her, asking if she was unhurt, and she answered in a remarkably strong voice, "Kill them all, Cay! Don't—" Her captor's hand clamped over her mouth and the doors slammed shut.

Moments later they opened again, very slightly.

"Well," the voice said, "As you see, she is alive. Now what was that about selling us our lives?"

"Come outside, damn you," I barked. "I will not converse through a closed door! No one will harm you as long as that lady is in your power. Her life and safety are worth more than all of yours combined." I turned deliberately and walked away to stand in plain view in the courtyard with my back to the door.

About five minutes passed before the doors swung open again and Caspar and Memnon emerged together and stood blinking in the smoky afternoon light. I stood unmoving, forcing them to approach me. Caspar stepped out boldly, a sneering smile on his face. Memnon, the more timid of the pair, looked around him nervously as they approached. They stopped about two paces short of me and I faced them with loathing seething inside me. Caspar, naturally, was the first one to speak.

"Our lives. What are they worth to you?"

"Not a pile of pig droppings."

"Then let me rephrase my question. Your aunt's life—what is that worth to you?"

"Your lives."

"That's better. There are fourteen of us, in all."

"No, there are two of you. The others are already dead."

"You must be mad, Caius Merlyn. Why should we surrender our bodyguard, when we have the old woman? She is obviously worth more to you than all of this." Caspar gestured disdainfully at the smoking ruins that surrounded us.

"Be careful, animal," I hissed at him. "My father's blood is still wet on your stinking hands, so do not push me too far. My aunt has had a long and useful life and would be the last to blame me for sacrificing the short time she has left for the privilege of crucifying you!"

That penetrated his reptilian armour. He blinked like a lizard and cleared his throat, accepting my resolve. "You cannot really expect me to sacrifice my men to you with no advantage?"

"No advantage? You call life no advantage?"

"You quibble, Merlyn. Our lives we have, as long as we hold the woman and you hold your rage in check. But that latter part concerns me. Your rage, I mean. I would be a fool to trust a man who burns so visibly with hatred of me. Therefore, I will keep my men for the safety they offer me against your blood lust."

"No!" I was practically spitting at him, yet fighting hard to keep my hatred under control. "I have said I will not bicker with you. Give me the woman and you two go free and there's an end of it. You have my word."

"Your word?" There was no trace of a smile or sneer on his face now. "I trust in no man's word. You will have to do better than that."

"Then what do you want? I want my aunt alive and safe, and free to live until she dies naturally. She has earned that. In return, I am prepared to forgo the pleasure of killing you two with my own hands, or even of having you die by someone else's. So, if you will not accept my word, what will you accept? Name your terms. If they are within reason I will grant them. I can say no more."

Caspar paused before answering. Then, "What we require is some way to ensure that there could be no treachery." He cut me short before I could vent my outrage. "You know what I am saying. Neither of us will ever trust the other. Memnon and I would like to leave this place alive, with our companions—"

"No! They die."

"No, they do not!" His voice was low. "We have need of them— a need to bring them home safe to Lot of Cornwall."

I made my voice as flat as possible. "Lot is dead. He was killed on the plain below."

Caspar laughed in my face. "Lot? Fool! Lot never left Cornwall. He sits in his stronghold there, awaiting news of his campaign. He sent another in his place, to wear his armour and inspire his army. No, Merlyn. Lot is too clever to be killed by the likes of you."

I heard the truth in his voice and my heart hardened even more against this "king" in Cornwall. When I responded, my own voice was pitched as low as his.

"There is nothing more loathsome than a cowardly commander who skulks in safety while others do his fighting for him. And this is your lord? The master you must appease by bringing your sneaking killers safely home?"

"Aye, Caius Merlyn." He was smiling that hateful smile again. "Such is the way of the servants of kings and princes."

My heart leaped in my chest, but I spat on the ground and made to turn away in disgust, before pausing as though a thought had just occurred to me. I turned back slowly, squinting at him speculatively and seeing a flicker in his eyes that told me his mind was racing, trying to anticipate what I had in mind. "What do you know of Hibernia?"

"Hibernia?" His face remained expressionless, but he was powerless to control the jerk of Memnon's head. "Nothing. What do you mean?" He turned his head slightly and directed a glance of such cold venom at his partner that I would not have been surprised to see Memnon fall on the spot. Then his cold, lizard's eye swung back to me. "What of Hibernia?"

"A prince of Hibernia," I said. "You spoke of kings and princes. I have one in my cells."

"A prince of Hibernia? Why should that interest me?"

I let him analyse my expression as I pretended to think my next words through. "We took him captive more than two weeks ago. He had landed with an army in the north, just as we were attacked from the south-west . . . The incident that led to your presence here. It occurs to me now that your noble master may have had a hand in both events, since treachery and duplicity seem to be his stock in trade." I had his entire attention. I gave him time to think.

"How do you know this captive is a prince?"

"He is a prince. He wears the golden tore. We hold him hostage against the good behaviour of his people."

"What is his name, this prince?"

"Donuil, son of Athol."

"Where do you hold him?"

I raised an eyebrow as though amused. "In chains, in my cells, in the building beside the one where I held you and should have killed you."

"Has he been tortured?"

Now I allowed myself a small frown of bemusement. "Why should that interest you, who claim to know nothing of Hibernia?"

"I lied." His eyes bored directly into mine. "Has he been tortured?"

It was my turn to sneer. "No, he has not been tortured. He is my prisoner, not yours. We hold him, that is enough. We have no need to torture or maltreat him. He is a freeborn Celt and his chains are torture enough."

Caspar licked his lips, his expression, for all his discipline, that of a merchant who sniffs a bargain. "What is he worth to you?"

"Less than he might be to you, I think." I made no effort to hide my contempt. "Now that your king's army is smashed and running home with its tail between its legs, he is worth nothing. We destroyed his father's army first and then yours. Any value that he might have had to me is ended. But I thought he might be of value to you, to take home to Lot. Give us my aunt and you can have him."

"Ha!" The scorn in his voice was grand. "You think me mad? No, Caius Merlyn, not for your aunt, for then you would be free— and glad—to kill us all. But you can have all the other hostages in return for him."

I looked at him in disgust, shaking my head slowly. "You have not seen the truth yet, have you?" I said. "Does it not sink into that reptilian skull of yours that the old woman is all I care about? The others, all of them, mean nothing to me. If you had taken only them you would be dead by now and they with you. Weighed against the life of my father, they have no significance."

He believed me implicitly because I was voicing thoughts with which he could identify completely. I watched him biting the inside of his cheek, making evaluations, reaching a decision.

"Very well," he said, his accents short and clipped. "You can have my twelve men. In return for this Scot."

"Did I say he was a Scot? I said only that he was Hibernian. You are correct, of course; he is a Scot. But why, I wonder, would you want him so badly? Would he be worth that much to your pus-filled king? I would hate to think he is, but I don't really care." I hesitated for half a breath. "Your killers, and the other hostages, and you can have the Hibernian. That will leave you two, him, and my aunt. We can arrange her release under any terms you wish. I'm sure your twisted mind will come up with something serpentine enough to gull your men and ensure your own safety. Go away and think about it. When you are ready to talk again, just open the door and come out. One of my men will come for me."

I turned on my heel and walked away from them, holding my head high until I passed from their sight. Then I leaned against the nearest wall and vomited up my hatred and disgust.

XXIII

I spent the next hour touring the fort, assessing the damage and making arrangements to move our colonists out, while we cleaned up the mess and made the fort fit for living in again. There was food available, but I had no stomach for it. I was in the grip of a force that kept me functioning and thinking clearly about every problem brought to my attention, but there was a constant, distant buzzing in my head that separated me from everything else going on around me, so that I seemed able to concentrate only upon individual matters, one at a time, without being distracted.

I called Popilius to me and walked with him to the main entrance of the fort, where we stood looking down in silence at the confusion on the plain below. Directly below us, looking like a boy's unfinished model, lay the fortified camp that Popilius and his men had been building at the time of the attack. Further away on our right, to the west, the scattered detritus of Lot's encampment lay strewn across the countryside. The rest of the plain, the entire length and breadth of it, was littered with bodies, tiny stick men and horses thrown carelessly in every attitude of death and abandonment. Far to our left, around the shoulder of the hill, smoke still drifted sullenly from the villa. The wind had dropped.

Popilius's voice broke through my thoughts. "That has to be cleaned up. It will take time."

"Aye, but we have time. How many prisoners did we take?"

He shrugged. "About three hundred, at the last count I heard of, but there may be more as our people come back."

"What were our losses?"

"Not as heavy as I expected." He stopped talking and worked to undo the chin strap of his helmet, finally pulling the heavy helm from his head and wiping sweat from his brow with the crook of his elbow. "Your cavalry arrived just at the right time. Head count isn't complete yet, but I know of three hundred infantry dead, and sixteen hundred wounded, two hundred of those serious."

"Those are large numbers, Popilius."

"Aye, but smaller than they might have been had you not guessed Lot's plans."

"I guessed wrong."

"Only by one day, Commander. If you had not guessed at all, we would have been taken completely by surprise and slaughtered."

"Aye, Popilius, perhaps." I sighed and then nodded towards his armed camp below. "That was a good idea. I commend you on the speed of your reactions."

He shook his head abruptly. "It was your father's idea, not mine. We had hoped to bring all the colonists inside the walls and have a garrison down there to hinder Lot, supported from up here."

"We can still use it," I told him. "Split your men in two—half to double the size of the camp down there and finish it, the other half to start collecting the dead for burial. Set the prisoners to work digging pits, deep pits and large, and keep them at it until the job is done. Lot's carrion we will bury on the right, there, where he camped. Our own dead will lie on the far left, towards the villa. See that both batches are buried well, Popilius. The stink of rotting friends is as foul as that of foes. As soon as that is done and the camp enlargement is under way, start moving everyone out of the fort. We will all live down there on the plain for a time. The interior of the fort will have to be gutted, cleansed and rebuilt. I want every sign of fire, every charred piece of wood, every last hint of stink removed and buried or otherwise disposed of. Take the debris out through the small back gate and burn as much of it as you can on the hilltop there. And that reminds me, we have to find a way that will ensure we are never surprised from the rear like that again. Any suggestions?"

"Aye." Popilius nodded his grizzled pate. "One."

"Well?"

"Set up a permanent camp out there, behind the walls on the top of the hill."

I stared at him. "That's it! Do it. Eventually, we'll extend the walls of the fort itself to cover the whole hilltop." I stopped and turned to look behind me at the fort, my eyes searching for I knew not what. "Now," I asked myself aloud, "Have I missed anything? Yes, the refurbishing." I turned back to Popilius. "Every mason, every carpenter, every craftsman we have will work full-time inside the fort until it is done. All labour to be supplied by the prisoners. Feed them adequately. Keep them healthy, strong enough to work hard and long, but kill any of them at the first sign of recalcitrance. They caused this carnage; they will rectify it."

"And afterwards?"

"After what?"

"When the work is done? What then?"

"Then they will work in the fields, replacing the men they killed."

"All of them?"

"As many as remain alive, yes."

"But where will we keep them, Caius?"

I shrugged. "Let them build their own prison camp on the hill behind the fort, in the space normally reserved for stables. They can build cages for themselves." I looked back down to the plain below. "Collect all the officers' bodies in one spot, Popilius. We will bury them in a single grave there, in the middle of the *campus*."

He coughed, clearing his throat. "Your father too, Commander?"

I looked at him. "No, Popilius. My father will be buried here in the fort, beside his own father and Publius Varrus."

"Aye, Imperator!" He saluted me with the formal title of Imperial Commander.

"Don't call me that, Popilius. It is a Roman title, foreign now, and we have no need of it here in Camulod. Now, can you think of anything else I have missed?"

He cleared his throat and answered, "Aye, yourself, Commander Merlyn. The fires are under control and nearly all out, and everything is in hand. I will set the rest in motion, and as our people come back, things will return more or less to normal, or as close as they can be. You still have to deal with those whoresons in your uncle's house. Your quarters are intact, untouched. You would feel better for a wash and a change of clothing."

I was staring again at the scene laid out below, watching the tiny figures of our soldiers moving in the field, counting the dead, identifying the fallen, searching for wounded. I nodded in agreement. "That is logical, Popilius, and probably true." My voice sounded dead and distant, ringing in my head. "I'll take you at your word. When they come looking for me, tell them where I am." I left him and made my way back to my quarters. On the way I met Ludo coming from the kitchens. He looked at me solicitously and asked me when I had last eaten. I shook my head and waved him away without an answer, my concentration now focused on reaching my quarters without collapsing.

There was a soldier on guard outside my door, and I was grateful for his assistance as I stripped out of my filthy clothes and washed the grime of the battlefield away. By the time I had dried myself and changed into fresh clothes, Ludo had found me again, and had brought a huge bowl of meat and vegetable broth, "drinking temperature," he told me, and insisted on standing there while I drank it. It was delicious and invigorating and by the time I had finished it, I felt like a man again.

I thanked both of them for their trouble and went looking for Popilius. I found him in the centre of the main yard, supervising the clean-up crews. All the fires were thoroughly doused by now and there was little smoke left, although the entire fort stank like a charnel house. As I approached him, however, and before I could speak, a runner arrived looking for me, with word that Caspar and Memnon had come out to speak with me again. I had time only to learn from Popilius that there was still no sign of our cavalry returning, and that our death toll had now climbed above the seven-hundred mark. As I turned to leave Popilius, I noticed the ruins of the Council Hall for the first time. Nothing remained of it but the walls, and the sight of it triggered a thought. "Tiles, Popilius," I said.

"Commander?"

"Tiles, clay roofing tiles like the ones on the villa. Make sure we use them in future on all our roofs. No more thatch within the fort. Will you see to that?"

"Aye, Commander."

The two grotesques, Caspar and Memnon, were lounging in front of my uncle's doorway, awaiting my return. The sight of them stirred up the sour sickness in my belly again. They straightened up as I approached, looking me over from head to foot and I was glad I had washed and changed. The sneering smile was back on Caspar's face.

"Commander Britannicus. I am honoured that you should feel obliged to dress for us."

I cut him short immediately. "Shut your evil mouth for everything but our business," I snapped at him. "I have neither time nor patience to waste on you. You live or you die by the end of this conversation. There will be no further talk after that."

He smiled again at that, but his voice dropped low. "We will all live. Except, of course, our twelve unfortunate companions whom you have sworn to kill. Memnon and I have put our minds to work as you suggested, seeking a means of ensuring that our lives will not depend entirely on your personal goodwill. We believe we have a solution." He stopped talking, evidently waiting for some kind of response from me.

"Go on, I'm listening."

"Well, we have two problems. The first of these is caused by our companions, those same twelve men. We do not believe, Memnon and I, that they will trust us fully in disposing of their lives and welfare. Had they remained in ignorance of your aunt's importance in your eyes, our task would have been far simpler. You, however, brought her to their attention, so we can hardly be expected to persuade them to relinquish her to our particular care. They see salvation in her now."

"What's your second problem?"

"Ah, yes, the second problem. That concerns the release of your aunt and our unhindered departure from your lands. That one, we feel, can be resolved to everyone's satisfaction. The first is far more pressing."

"How many hostages do you hold?" The question had been burning in my mind for hours.

"Eleven, plus your aunt. Nine women, two men—all servants."

"Have they been harmed?"

He made a face, indicating a lack of both knowledge and concern. "The men have been subdued; the women, used. In war that happens."

I said nothing. I was unsurprised and unconcerned. I knew my aunt's serving women. They could survive the humiliation of mere carnal abuse. It would be unpleasant but none of them would die from it. I was thinking furiously about how to separate the twelve men from the others, and the more I thought about it, the more insoluble the problem appeared. It was unthinkable that these men would be foolish enough to separate themselves voluntarily from Aunt Luceiia, whose value was now known to them. I felt anger and frustration building up in me, and cursed myself for not having seen the futility of trying to bargain my way out of this situation. There seemed to be no way out. I would have to release all of them, and still rely on Caspar and Memnon for Aunt Luceiia's safety. The realization sickened me. But then my frustrated silence gained me an unexpected reprieve. Caspar himself presented me with the only possible solution.

"How badly do you want these men of mine? Alive, I mean."

"Explain yourself," I answered, trying to school my face to show nothing even while my interest quickened. "What do you mean?"

"Exactly what I said," he responded. "If you want them alive, you will never have them. Dead . . ." He wiggled his fingers fastidiously. "That might be . . . achievable."

"How? My men could never get close enough to surprise them."

"No, but Memnon and I could."

"Twelve of them?" I heard the scorn in my own voice. "Twelve men who don't trust you in the first place?"

A small frown appeared briefly between Caspar's brows and he hastened to correct me. "When I said that, I meant simply that they would not trust us to deal with you for their lives. They are not depraved enough to think that we might kill them ourselves. These are simple men, Commander."

I felt my skin break out in goose-flesh at the calmness of his voice. I swallowed hard and fought to keep the loathing out of my voice as I continued speaking. "How could you do that? Physically, I mean? How would it be possible?"

Caspar smiled. "That is our business and you may leave it to us. Our bargain was that you would trade the Hibernian prince for the twelve men and the other hostages, was it not?" I nodded in assent. "Well then, I have merely to return and say I suspect you of planning something to undo our efforts, and to suggest that we separate the hostages, one to each man, except for myself and Memnon. Any one of them, at random, may guard your aunt. Then we will move them into separate rooms for strategic safety. It will be done. They will believe me, since one of them will have the old woman. Once they are . . . separated, Memnon and I will remove them, one or two at a time . . . Efficiently."

I shuddered in spite of myself and tried to turn it into an angry shrug. "No," I snapped, "I will not allow that. It is too dangerous. My aunt could be killed."

"She will not be harmed, believe me. Memnon and I have means at our disposal for the silent dispersal of death . . . means of which you could never conceive . . . All we require is time. When we are done, we will open the doors again and you can count the bodies as we throw them out. After that, you will release your captive to us and we will send out the hostages."

"No! Hostages first, and then you get the Scot."

"Commander!" Caspar's voice seemed filled with genuine pain. "You must show a little faith. The Scot is our passport home to Lot. The other hostages mean little or nothing to you, you have said as much. We will still have the old woman. What difference can it make at this point?"

I gnawed on my lip, but I was prepared to concede on this point. "Probably none," I admitted finally. "Very well. That's how we'll do it. How long will it take you to get rid of the twelve men?"

"Two hours, perhaps more. It will have to be done cautiously."

"Aye, I believe you. So be it. Get about your work. I have no wish to discuss the how of it with you now or later." I watched him walk away, hearing Donuil's words in my head: "These people deal only in death." A wave of faintness and nausea swept over me and I stood there gritting my teeth until it wore off, after which I signalled a centurion who had been standing behind me, out of earshot, watching everything that went on. He came smartly to my side and I indicated Uric's bowmen who still held their watch in a semicircle around the yard.

"Centurion, I want you to relieve the bowmen here. They've been standing guard for hours. Replace them with our own soldiers. They are to stand watch vigilantly, but make no move towards the house. Inform me immediately if any noise is heard from within. If the silence holds, I expect the doors to be opened again in a matter of hours. Send runners to find me when that happens. Is that clear?"

"Yes, Commander." He repeated my instructions verbatim and I left him to carry them out as the first drops of rain started falling from the afternoon sky, which had turned leaden without my noticing. I glanced up and saw that the clouds were heavy and unbroken. Rain would provide a mixed benison. It would settle the flying ash and douse the last of the smouldering timbers within the fort, but it would also make life unpleasant for the men on burial duty and for the soldiers working to enlarge the camp on the plain below.

I made another tour of Camulod, this time seeing far more than I had taken in on my previous circuit. The damage did not seem as extensive as I had feared earlier, although it was bad. The Council Hall was completely destroyed, of course, and so was the larger part of the stables. Most of the storage buildings were intact, however, and so were the bath houses, the kitchens and the large dining hall. The officers' quarters and the sick bay had escaped entirely, which I already knew, and the major portion of the common barracks seemed unscathed, although the entire section of buildings against the north wall—mainly barracks, tanneries, and barrel-makers' cooperages—had been gutted. The large building that housed the centurions had been badly damaged—again the northern part, which was the cavalry centurions' quarters. The huddle of buildings in the centre of the fort seemed to have burned in places and survived in others, with no apparent pattern to the damage. The potter's shed and warehouse were untouched, as were the two main forges, but the wheelwright's shop was gone from between the forges and the ale-maker's store behind the potter's warehouse had been burned out.

I saw Popilius by the main gate and crossed to him, and as I did so the heavens opened. The noise of the torrential rain striking my helmet was deafening, and we had to shout into each other's ears to make ourselves heard. He had a final report on the casualties, up to the flight of Lot's army. In all, we had lost close to nine hundred dead. Of that number, two hundred and thirty-nine were colonists and non-belligerents: old men, women and children. Another hundred and ninety-two were cavalry casualties, and the rest, some four hundred and sixty men, were infantry. In addition to these losses, he informed me, we had another hundred or so seriously wounded who were not expected to survive, and there were more than three hundred dead horses on the field below. As soon as I heard this last item, I realized that I had made no provision for the burial of horses, but he had already taken care of the oversight and there were teams hauling them away even now.

The numbers apalled me. Nine hundred dead and another hundred marked to die! That, added to the other casualties we had sustained over the previous few weeks, meant that our overall strength had been severely depleted. I added the numbers quickly in my head: more than fifteen hundred men in all; almost one-third of our total fighting strength gone within a month! Popilius was still shouting in my ear, talking about enemy dead, but I had missed the gist of what he was saying, except for the number. I stopped him and asked him to repeat Lot's total losses. Almost four thousand. Good, but not enough.

Suddenly, as quickly as it had begun, the cloudburst died away and the sensation was as though a fog had sundered. I had been staring towards the main entrance gate, seeing nothing through the driving rain for long moments, and then I found myself gaping in almost superstitious awe at the apparition that confronted me in the open gateway. Two gaunt, dark, ravaged figures stood there, leaning on staves, looking like the very harbingers of death, until I recognized the taller of them as the leader of the zealot priests my father had banished from our lands months earlier. As I watched him, still powerless to move or say anything, this priest looked all around the littered yard and raised his staff high in his claw-like hand, pointing it to the sky. His shout broke on my ears like the screech of a rusted hinge.

"This chaos is heaven's judgment on Godless men!" The vigour of his shout stopped all men who were within the sound of his voice. People on all sides stopped whatever they were doing and looked around to see who was making this disturbance, and the priest knew they were listening and his voice grew even louder. "Look on the power of the Lord of Hosts and be ashamed and walk in terror! They that mock His word will be cast down ..."

I heard no more, for I was running, fumbling for the sword beneath my water-sodden cloak. My feet felt like lead and I seemed to be running through high, wet grass that tugged at me and hampered me, slowing me down to a dreamlike, struggling crawl. The priest's companion saw me coming and tried to step between us, his eyes wide with alarm and fright, but I picked him up like a baby and threw him aside as though he were weightless, and then my hands closed around the scrawny throat of the still-screaming zealot. I drove him back, hard, against the wall on one side of the gate and still he shouted and spat, his adam's apple wobbling beneath my thumbs. I smashed my right knee hard into his groin and threw him sideways and he fell and lay face down, buttocks in the air, one hand clutching his testicles, his neck stretched, dirty grey and inviting like a duck's neck on a chopping block. My sword came easily into my hand now and I swung it high and brought it hissing down as someone's shoulder crashed into my ribs and dashed me backwards into darkness.

XXIV

I awoke to the sound of a door opening, and I heard Popilius say, "How is he?"

Another voice, this one belonging to the medic, Lucanus, answered him. "Still asleep."

"Will he be well when he wakes?"

"I think so. He was exhausted. His father's death was hard for him to take."

"So was that whoreson priest. I should have let Merlyn kill him."

"No, Popilius, you did the right thing. He will thank you when he wakes up."

"Hah! You think so? I doubt it. Few men earn thanks by felling their Commanders, especially when they knock them cold in front of their troops."

"Nonsense, this was a special case. Commander Merlyn was not himself."

"Aye, perhaps. We'll see. What was that stuff you made him drink? He's been asleep for more than ten hours."

I heard Lucanus rise to his feet as he answered, "A potion to bring on sleep. He needed it."

I opened my eyes. I was on my cot in my own quarters and they were standing by my table, looking at me in the light of a flickering lamp. Lucanus spoke to me before I could move. "Don't try to move, Commander Merlyn. It might hurt."

I blinked at him and tried to speak, but my tongue was clogged. I swallowed, thickly, thinking that I could feel no pain. I tried again. My voice sounded rusty. "Why should it hurt?"

"Because I drugged you. Your head might be sore. Your body

will ache too, because of all the bruising you sustained yesterday, one way and another."

I closed my eyes again. "Internal bleeding," I said. "You said that is what causes bruises, didn't you?"

"Yes, I did." I could hear surprise in his voice that I should remember.

"What news of Uther? Has he returned?"

"No, not yet." Lucanus turned away from me, picking up a jug from beside the bed. "There's been no word of him at all, but you know Uther better than I do. He will not come back until he has decided there is no further profit in following the enemy." That was true, and I accepted it.

"Popilius," I said, "When you attacked me, as I was about to kill the priest, I was awaiting a summons from my uncle's house. What did you do about it?"

"Nothing, Commander. I didn't have to. It has not come yet. The house has been silent since you left. The watch has changed twice and is about to change again."

I lay motionless, my mind racing as I tried to imagine what might have happened in the house where the hostages were held. I gave up. "The watch is about to change again? What hour of night is it?"

"The last. An hour before dawn."

I swallowed again and Lucanus brought me some wine mixed with water, which eased the pain in my throat. "Why did you stop me from killing the priest, Popilius?"

He did not answer for several moments, then, "The man is mad, Commander. It would have been murder, and you would have regretted it, I thought, no matter what the provocation."

I absorbed that. I had been mad myself for a short time there in the rain.

"You had time to think all that?" I asked him.

"Well, no, Commander. I didn't have time to think it, not in words. I just knew."

I took a deep breath and could sense Popilius holding his breath. "Well, your instinct was sound, my friend," I said. "What you did was correct. I would have regretted the killing, surely. We will speak no more of it, you and I. Forget it happened, but accept my thanks."

I raised my head cautiously without ill effect and brought myself gently to a sitting position before lowering my feet carefully to the floor. Both men watched me carefully; neither moved. I took a deep breath.

"How do you feel?" Lucanus asked.

"A few twinges here and there," I answered. "Popilius is a large man."

"It was not only Popilius. You had some imperial purple bruises when they brought you here."

I grinned, tentatively, stretching gently as I did so. "Yes," I said, remembering the battle on the plain. "I rolled around quite a lot yesterday. Have you two been awake all night?"

Lucanus's face actually broke into a smile. "No, Commander. We have both had some sleep, though not as much as you."

"Good." I moved a shoulder joint exploratively. "I could use a steam. The bath house wasn't burned. Does it still work?"

"Aye, Commander." Popilius was smiling too, relieved that I bore him no grudge.

"Then I'll try it, if the furnaces are hot. If I am summoned, that's where you'll find me. By the way, where is the priest now?"

"Far away, Commander. I had him tied back to back with his companion, threw them in a wagon and had them escorted from the Colony."

"Excellent! You have an aptitude for doing exactly the right thing on your own initiative, Popilius. Some day it will get you into terrible trouble. Now, where are my clothes?"

I wrapped myself very slowly and carefully in some heavy woolen sheets, trying in vain to move without causing myself pain, and made my way through the darkness to the bath house, where I spent a blissful hour in steam and hot water, floating in the dark like an infant in its mother's womb, and thinking deeply.

It was almost full daylight as I approached Uncle Varrus's house again, and I arrived there in time to meet a soldier who was setting out to look for me. I presented myself to the centurion in charge of the guard, who pointed wordlessly to the open doors of the house.

"When did that happen?"

"A few moments ago, Commander. One moment they were closed, the next they were open."

"Did you see anyone? Hear anything?"

"No sir, nothing at all, except the open doors."

"I see. Well, we'll wait." As I said the words I saw movement in the shadows beyond the open doorway and the body of a man fell out into the courtyard. I felt the centurion stiffen and start to react and I caught him by the arm. "Wait, Centurion. I expected this. There's more to come."

There were. Eleven more bodies soon sprawled in a pile. I stepped forward and approached the doors. There was no further movement from within.

"Caspar! Are you listening?"

"I am."

"I will send a centurion to bring the Hibernian prisoner. While he is doing that, I will also have my men approach in pairs and remove these bodies. After that is done, we will make final arrangements for the release of my aunt. As soon as you have the Hibernian, I expect immediate release of the other hostages."

"As you wish."

I called the centurion of the guard to me and issued him his instructions. He saluted and set off, and I turned to follow him. Caspar's voice stopped me.

"Merlyn!"

I turned back towards him.

"You have a reputation for trickery," he said, and I could hear a warning in his tone. "You also have one for honesty, but I have no wish to expose myself to that any more than is necessary. From now on we will keep this door between us when we talk."

"Why, Caspar? Do you fear for your safety while you still hold my aunt?"

"No, but I fear your wiles. I would rather be sure than dead."

I put iron into my voice. "Caspar, I guarantee you, personally, that you will come to no ill before these negotiations are over."

"I choose to disbelieve you, Caius Merlyn."

"Then so be it. That is your misfortune. The liar's tragedy is that he can never believe anyone else. I'll be back shortly. Hide as much as you want, wherever you wish to. You are safe for now, but I swear to you, Caspar, that for the murder of my father your life will end at my hands eventually."

I walked back to the courtyard, passing the first pair of my men on their way to collect a corpse from the front of the house. By the time all twelve corpses had been removed, the centurion had returned with Donuil, who had been festooned with chains the day before. I did not dare acknowledge him, for Caspar and Memnon would undoubtedly be watching from the shadowed interior of the open doorway. I spoke to the centurion, telling him to strike off the young giant's chains. He dispatched a man at the run for a chisel and maul and I stood there, ignoring Donuil until the man returned. When the chains were off, I drew my sword and waved Donuil towards the front of the house. He played his part well, looking suspicious and confused as his eyes went from me to the darkened house and then back again. "Go!" I barked at him, and he went, unwillingly and suspiciously, holding his body tense as though to flee at every step.

He stopped in the doorway for a space, then disappeared inside. Within moments, the other hostages began to emerge, blinking in the daylight, which was growing brighter as the sun rose higher. I grasped the first girl, Eunice, by the wrist and asked her about my aunt. She told me that Luceiia was well, only lightly bound and unharmed. When the hostages had all passed by, most of them in tears, I approached the doorway again.

"Now we can end this," I called into the emptiness beyond the doorway. "You are but three men, defended by your threats against the woman you hold. Tell me what you want, quickly. I want you far from my sight and smell."

To my surprise, Caspar stepped into the open doorway and stood there looking at me with his usual sneer. "We wish to leave here quickly and safely. That is all. In that, you and I are almost in agreement. Have you no wish to ask me how the twelve men died?"

Again I felt surprise, this time at the vanity that prompted this question. "None at all," I answered.

"That surprises me, but I am going to tell you anyway. You see this?" He held something up, pinched between his thumb and forefinger. I squinted, but the distance between us was too great and I could see nothing. His smile grew wider. "Small, is it not? It is a thorn, Merlyn, an ordinary thorn that has been steeped in a poison distilled from the venom of a variety of snakes. It will kill a strong man in moments, if the thorn is skillfully placed. Memnon and I are expert in the placing of them. Each of the twelve was pricked by one of these." I said nothing and he went on, "Your aunt has several of these in her clothes. She does not know they are there, let alone where they are. A scratch from any one of them will end her—unpleasantly. A well-placed blow from either Memnon or myself will drive a thorn home. An embrace of any kind, for example from a would-be rescuer attempting to snatch her away from danger, would be almost equally certain to produce death. What I am saying, Caius Merlyn, is that if you have plans to rid yourself of us in any drastic and final fashion, you must be sure that we are far removed from the old woman before you do anything, lest we should fall on her."

The calm, dispassionate tone of his voice as he spoke these words made me grit my teeth and I closed my eyes to mask my anger. Opening them again, I saw Donuil, his hands upraised in a double fist, directly behind Caspar. The Egyptian's reactions were lightning fast. The instant he saw the change of expression in my eyes, for I could not hide it, he threw himself into motion. But he was too late. Donuil's blow took him between the shoulders, knocking him towards me. I stepped to meet him, noting his fingers spread wide as he fell, and kicked him with all of my strength beneath the arch of his ribs, driving the breath from him in an explosion of agony. He wrapped his arms around my leg, trying to drag me down, but there was no strength in him and I avoided him easily, leaving him squirming on the ground as I leaped towards the doorway and Donuil.

"Where is Memnon?"

"Over there, by the wall." He pointed towards the huddled shape of the other magician, adding unnecessarily, "He is dead."

"Aunt Luceiia," I called, trying to condense all the urgency in the world into my voice. "Don't move! Stand where you are! Stand absolutely still!" I could hear the running footsteps of soldiers outside, coming towards the doors, and in the gloomy interior I could see my aunt, standing against a wall on my right. Her arms were bound and she stood motionless.

"Caius," she said, "I could not move even if I wished to."

"Thank God!" I crossed to her and stood in front of her. "Auntie, there are thorns among your clothes, thorns steeped in venom. The slightest scratch from one of them could kill you, so please try not to move at all until I have one of your women come here and disrobe you."

She shook her head in the briefest disagreement. "Don't be silly, Cay, there are no thorns. The ugly one was just about to put them among my clothes when that giant young man killed him."

I turned to Donuil, who stood beside me. "Is that true?"

"Aye. You told me to protect her if I saw her threatened, did you not?"

"I did." A wave of relief rippled over me. "I did indeed. I'm glad you remembered. You will not regret it." I drew my sword and cut my aunt free. She seemed completely unflustered by the whole situation.

"Thank you, Nephew," she said. "These people have converted my house into a sty for swine. Please send my servants home quickly. They have work to do."

I watched her in amazement as she bustled away towards her family room at the back of the house. When I looked at Donuil, he was grinning at me.

"What are you grinning at?"

"Your face. Have you lived this long and not learned that old women are the strongest creatures in this world? Besides, I am a free man, am I not? I have a right to smile."

I sighed and smiled back at him. "Aye, that you are, and that you do. I owe you far more than freedom, Donuil."

"I am glad."

"What do you mean?"

"That you owe me more than my freedom."

"How so? Why?"

His grin widened. "Because now I call the debt. I want to stay here in Camulod and be your adjutant, as we discussed. Now that you are in debt to me, you cannot refuse me."

I gazed at him in some amazement. "You wish to stay here? Of your own free will?"

"I do, and you can use me, too. Your colony has lost a lot of good men recently."

"Fine," I said. "Wonderful! So be it. We will discuss the terms of your service later, when there is more time for such things. Right now there is a sorcerer to attend to." I started to look around me. "Where was Memnon when you killed him?"

Donuil pointed to my right. "Over there, by the wall, he stood just behind your aunt."

"What happened to the thorns?"

The big Celt shrugged. "I don't know, I didn't see any thorns, but I wasn't looking for anything. I thought he was going to use his hands to hurt her. If he was holding anything, he probably dropped it right there."

I bent over and looked at the floor and there was a small strip of cloth, folded over on itself. I picked it up carefully and opened it to see that it contained a row of black thorns, each about an inch long, stitched through the cloth about a quarter of an inch apart. I counted twenty-five of the deadly slivers and looked up to find Donuil staring at the thing in my hand.

"That's a lot of death," I said.

"A lot of danger," was his low-voiced response. "Those things ought not to be left lying around. Someone could stand on them."

I folded the cloth up and tucked it carefully into my scrip. "I will look after these," I said. "Don't worry, Donuil, no one else will be exposed to them."

We walked out into the courtyard together to find Caspar on his knees, his arms tied around a spear thrust across his back and in front of his elbows. Four soldiers guarded him. I stopped in front of him and looked directly into his face. There was no sneer on it now.

"You will be tried, publicly, by military tribunal, in front of the Council Hall at noon today," I told him. "Expect no mercy. You will be executed. I myself will execute you." I spoke to the guard commander. "Take him away and hold him well. Let no one approach him. I want four men with spears around him at all times. And keep him in the courtyard, tied to a stake. If he gives trouble, knock him down, but do not kill him before noon."

Five hours later, at noon, I nodded to the trumpeters and silence fell on the packed courtyard as the brazen tones of the military horns rang out. I stood above the man and detailed the catalogue of his crimes in utter silence. He took it well. His face betrayed no expression. When I had finished reading, I turned to the officers who stood behind me, and then faced the crowd again and raised my voice so that they could all hear me.

"In the matter of execution, our law is simple. Once judgment has been passed there will be no delay and death will be brought about by the means decreed, as soon as possible. Some crimes must merit death by hanging, some by decapitation, and some by crucifixion, although that method has not been used in Britain for more than a hundred years." I paused in my delivery to look again at the prisoner, then continued. "This man's crimes are not dealt with by our laws, however, for he has committed a crime more heinous than our lawmakers could foresee." I turned and held out my hand to a centurion nearby, who handed me an arrow. I held the arrow high above my head.

"This is a poisoned arrow. One scratch from it will bring an agonizing death within minutes. But some men can last for thirty minutes before they die . . . Very strong men. Some of our own soldiers lasted thirty minutes against the venom. Some were luckier and died more quickly. This man, this . . . sorcerer, is the poisoner. The secrets of the ingredients of the poison are contained within his mind. My judgment is that they should be cauterized and sealed therein forever." I turned and leaned forward quickly, before anyone could divine my intention, and scored the arrowhead twice across Caspar's brow, forward and back, cutting two lines that gaped and then began to bleed. His eyes went wide with horror and he screamed. I broke the arrow across my knee and handed it back to the man who had given it to me. "Burn this. Immediately." He saluted and spun on his heel to carry out my order, disappearing in the direction of the furnace that fed the bath house.

The rest of us stood there in the bright noon sun and watched Caspar die—all of us, appalled and sickened by his screaming agony.

Finally, when his legs had ceased their frenetic dance and the corpse lay still, I looked up at his guards. "Bury him in the mass grave on the plain, with the rest of Lot's filth." His death had not been quick.

I turned and left the courtyard, looking at no one, and made my way directly to the Armoury, hoping no one would try to follow me. No one did, and as I entered I locked the big, bronzed doors behind me before checking, very belatedly, the safety of Excalibur.

After I had retrieved the wondrous sword from its hiding-place beneath the floor, I sat alone in the shadows of the great room for hours, struggling against my emotions and feeling very unsure of my own strength, all the while polishing the sword with the silken shawl in which it was wrapped and wondering where I could hide it again to be absolutely sure of its safety. There were four great treasures in my life, and it seemed to me I had done well by none of them. The greatest of these, my beloved Cassandra, was safe, I could only hope, in Avalon, blissfully unaware of the chaos that reigned outside her tiny world. I dared not allow myself to imagine

otherwise. The second greatest, this sword Excalibur that was my
sacred trust, was safe and undamaged, but through no grace of
mine. Had the building been fired, the sword could have been lost,
damaged, or even found and stolen. My stewardship had been badly
lacking in that area. The third was my father, Picus Britannicus,
murdered in his sleep while I was absent. And the fourth, Aunt
Luceiia, had almost been killed while I was present!

My mind in a chaos, and trying vainly not to panic over my
fears for Cassandra, telling myself frantically that there was nothing I could have done differently and that she would be well until
I reached her, I went over and over in my mind everything that had
happened in the previous few days up to the death of my father,
and once I had faced that incontrovertible truth—the fact of his
death—I stood vigil for him, there in Uncle Varrus's treasure room,
for more than two hours, standing erect and at attention, holding
Excalibur and paying my own, personal, private tribute to the man
who had sired me. I would probably have remained there throughout the day and well into the following night had I not been forced
unwillingly into activity by the sheer volume of work that I knew
remained to be done.

The effort and concentration demanded by my long immobil-
ity forced me to think more and more clearly of my responsibilities,
and I became increasingly aware, although with great reluctance,
that I had little time to indulge myself. Finally, my mind aswarm
with chores that demanded my attention, I replaced Excalibur in
its case and returned it carefully to its hiding place beneath the
floor boards. Kneeling there on the floor, I thought of Cassandra in
her valley just a few miles away and prayed that she had been in
less danger than the sword. And I swore to myself that, come what
may, I would hold her before this day was over.

XXV

I had heard no one approach along the passageway outside, but suddenly the handle of the door was tried, and then came a knock.

"Commander Britannicus?"

Recognizing the voice of Lucanus immediately, I stiffened, and then told myself that nothing further could have gone wrong, else I would have heard more noise.

"Yes, I am here. What is it?"

There was a pause, then, "May I speak with you, Commander?"

I felt a surge of anger at his intrusion and fought it down. "Is it important?" I asked, keeping my impatience from my tone.

"I believe so, Commander."

I rose to my feet and made my way to the doors, unlocking them and opening them to reveal the physician standing, shadowed, in the hallway outside, his hands behind his back and his dark, sardonic face twisted in an unreadable expression. He had bathed and changed since I last saw him and was now wearing a long, pale blue tunic fringed with dark green fabric.

"Well, Lucanus? What is so important that it must be discussed now?"

"A matter of procedure, Commander. Your aunt, the Lady Luceiia, asked me to bring you to her family room."

For some reason, his words displeased me even more than his interruption had. "Did she indeed?" I snapped. "And since when have either you or my aunt had anything to say in matters of procedure?" I was conscious of being rude to the point of boorishness to a man who had given me no real reason, but Lucanus took no offence, merely shrugging his shoulders and nodding in acquiescence. "You are correct, of course. Nevertheless . . ."

"Yes, nevertheless. Very well, I'll come with you." I pulled the doors closed behind me and accompanied him along the passageway to my aunt's private suite of rooms.

As we entered her main living room, I was conscious, as always, of the feeling of well-being it brought me, in spite of all the pains now afflicting me. A fire burned brightly in the hearth, its flames reflected in the polished surfaces of brass and bronze ornaments scattered throughout the room. My aunt was not there. Lucanus crossed to stand by the fire, and I threw myself into my favourite chair, the great, overstuffed seat that had belonged to Uncle Varrus.

"Beautiful room." Lucanus was looking around him admiringly.

"Aye," I grunted, "but it has known better times. Where is my aunt?"

"I've no idea," he answered with a shrug, and moved to the table that held wine and green glass cups. He picked up the silver ewer beaded with moisture and began to pour as he spoke. "She may be resting. It took me more than an hour to find you. Never occurred to me that you might be here in the house. Here." He handed me a cup of wine. "I am not making free with the Lady's hospitality. She bade me pour you a drink if she were not here when we arrived."

"Thank you." I sipped, and then gulped the ice-cold wine thirstily. "God, that's good!" I whispered, feeling the delicious pain of iciness in my throat. I waited until it passed, and then took another sip before adding, "I had no idea you were an intimate of my aunt, Lucanus."

"I'm not," he answered, smiling, "but we spoke at length today."

"On procedural matters."

His answering look to that was as sardonic as my tone had been. "Yes."

"Which particular procedures were you discussing?"

It was his turn to drink before answering. At length he put down his cup and looked straight at me. "Your father's burial."

Pain flared in me anew. I had not seen my father since I had tried to lift him back onto his bed. I cleared my throat, trying to swallow the lump there and control my voice, but I was unable to return Lucanus's direct look. "Where is he now?"

"Here in the house. I have bathed and changed him, and he is laid out in dignity in Publius Varrus's bedchamber."

"How? He was rigid. I tried to move him, but couldn't."

Lucanus nodded. "No longer. The rigor has worn off. I was able to cover and conceal his wounds. He looks . . . asleep, no more."

I gulped and nodded. "Thank you for that."

"No need, Commander. He was my Legate and my friend."

"Thank you, anyway. My thanks, as his son."

Lucanus inclined his head. "It was my pleasure, painful as it was. More wine." It was not a question, and I held out my cup for him to fill it. Watching him as he did so, it occurred to me that there was far more to this senior physician than I had ever been aware of. He reinforced that conclusion immediately, straightening up and asking me, "How had you thought to dispose of his remains?"

"Dispose of . . . ?" I blinked, shaking my head. "I . . . I hadn't . . ." I hadn't thought of it at all, was what I started to say, but I changed the words as they sprang to my tongue, "I hadn't really seen any need to dwell on it. He will be buried beside his father and Publius Varrus. Here in the fort."

"Naturally, and very properly, Commander, but may I make a suggestion? With all due respect?"

"You would have something different?"

"In a measure, yes. Not completely different, but signally different."

I drew a deep breath, feeling a resurgence of the impatience I had felt earlier. "You are talking in riddles, and I am talking about my father's funeral. Make sense, Lucanus."

"I will, if you will hear me."

"I'm listening."

"We are burying men by the thousands, down on the plain."

"So? What does that have to do with the Legate Picus Britannicus?"

"Nothing, and everything." He moved to the fire and stirred the logs with the toe of his boot. "Every man being buried down there died, directly or indirectly, because Picus Britannicus was in command of this fortress, is that not so?"

"In a manner of speaking, of course. What of it?" I was sitting erect now, wondering where this conversation was headed.

"Then is it not fitting that the manner of Picus's passing, the occasion of his death and the events surrounding it, should be markedly different from those thousands of others?"

"For a certainty! But they will lie in mass graves. He will lie here in the fortress."

He pursed his lips and moved from the fire to sit on a high-backed couch across from me, sitting well back and raising his arm to rest his cup against the arm before responding. "Then let his *ashes* lie here in the fortress, Caius! Beside his father and his uncle."

"What?" I heard the amazement in my own tone, but his voice drove on over my objections before I could form them.

"Cremate him as a Legate. Burn his body, Commander! In a grand conflagration. In the style of the old Legions, who honoured their dead Legates with the purifying flames of Mithras." I subsided into my chair now, slouched, as he leaned forward and continued, "I know burial is the Christian way, Commander, but the people—our people!—need a symbol, a rallying point. What is one more burial among all these thousands, no matter where it takes place? Our army has been battered and savaged, and our home almost burned to the ground, but we survive!" He paused and then swigged savagely at his wine before going on, "The people of this Colony are stunned. There's hardly a soul left alive who has not lost someone in this carnage. Everyone is devastated, and life holds little meaning right now. The soul seems to have gone out of all of us, including you. Titus and Flavius are now the senior officers of the garrison, next to you and Uther, when he is here. Both of them are excellent men. You know that and I know it. But they are lost,

Caius, lost without your father, who has been their father, too, in a very real sense for more than twenty years."

"I hear what you are saying, Lucanus, and I understand what moves you, but this cannot be! We are Christians, as you said, and the Church teaches us that men must be buried whole, to rise again on the Day of Judgment."

"Balls! We are soldiers, Caius Britannicus, and we still pray to Mithras—who is still the god of soldiers—when we march into battle. The gentle Christ had little time for soldiers."

"But—"

He cut me off. "No buts, Commander. You were there when your father dealt with those noxious priests! Have you forgotten the logic he brought to bear on them? Have you forgotten all we were taught that led to that confrontation?

"We believe—and for our beliefs we are labelled Pelagians and not Christians—that God created man in his own image with the divine spark that makes man godly in and of himself! That spark is his immortal soul . . . Immortal! . . . It cannot be destroyed. It cannot be defaced, or broken, or rent apart. It is a man's soul that will stand before God at Judgment time. The body falls to dust, and so do the bones that shape it." He broke off, eyeing me strangely. "Or do you think all that has changed? Do you believe Bishop Alaric lies in the ground intact, as on the day he died? Or your grandfather? Or Publius Varrus? Need we dig them up to see?" He shook his head, denying me the comfort of that thought. "Eight years, perhaps ten. That's as long as a human body lasts, once it's been buried. After that, there's nothing but loose bones for animals to dig up. There is no wholeness, or wholesomeness, after death. That is medical—and natural—fact, and the churchmen cannot change it by merely issuing edicts."

I was gazing at him now, wide-eyed. "What kind of physician are you, Lucanus?"

His head jerked at the unexpectedness of my question, but it did not distract him from his path. "Physician? What kind of physician am I?" He paused, as though considering his answer, and then continued with a gentle, slightly bitter smile. "I am not a physician at all. A physician deals in herbs and potions; in the diagnosis of sickness and the distillation of cures; in the cure of ulcers and lesions and the application of leeches." He placed his cup gently on the table and then looked up at me from his half-bent position, that small smile still in place. "What I really am, Caius Britannicus, is a surgeon, a healer of bodies broken internally and externally." Now he straightened and I heard the pride in his voice. "And I am one of the best in the world, because I am a product of the Medical Corps of the Roman Army. Physicians, even the best of them, work mostly on faith, bolstered by observation of the ailments that beset even the healthiest of people. Surgeons, on the other hand, operate securely in the faith that they have learned through study of the human body and the bones and organs that sustain it. The Army Medical Corps, composed almost wholly of surgeons, is the only corps that has grown in stature and ability as the Legions declined. It has carried medicine, and the repair of broken human bodies, to a level never known on this earth until now.

"As a surgeon, I soldiered with your father on his last four campaigns, he with his sword, and I with my caduceus, my bandages, my splints and my knives and surgeon's tools. I staunched the blood and gave the wounded opium to kill their pain. I cut off limbs, set fractured bones, sewed up cuts and cauterized veins and arteries, and I saved lives almost as quickly and effectively as my companions took them. I am a sworn enemy of death in all its forms, and I will not sit still and countenance the death I see threatening all that I love today."

He had risen again and was pacing the room, gesticulating with both hands, yet not spilling a drop of wine. He swung back to face me, his back to the fire. "I have a hospital full of wounded and dying men, and I have more bodies than I have room for. I have a staff of five young trainees and two competent surgeons who are working even now, as we speak, up to their buttocks in blood and guts and pain. And we have no opium. Have had none for years. But what I really fear, Commander, the thing that turns my guts to water, is the aftermath of this struggle we have just come through. Camulod was almost destroyed! Its Commander was killed in his bed! When the pain of each person's individual, personal losses wears off, tomorrow, or next week, or next month, or next year, all that's going to be left, unless we do something about it, is hopelessness. Disillusionment. And that damnable state, Commander, is a bigger killer than war. Disillusionment kills ideas, and it kills ideals."

He had finished, for the time being, and a silence hung and stretched between us. I stared into the fire and thought about all he had said.

"So," I resumed eventually, keeping my voice reasonable, "you would have me burn my father, not bury him. What then? What purpose would be served?"

Lucanus was ready for the question. He spoke without hesitation and I knew he had been waiting for me to ask precisely that. "A sacrificial one. An honourable one. We would create a martyr, light a fire to the memory of Caius Picus Britannicus that would stiffen the sinews and the resolution of everyone who watched. And everyone would watch. A funeral pyre is a memorable tribute to greatness, Commander, as well as a call to vengeance."

"It would be blasphemous."

"Balls, Commander! To permit, or even to encourage by inaction, the demoralization of these colonists and the eventual destruction of all that Picus and your grandfather and the others that have gone before have worked for—that would be blasphemous. That would call down the wrath of heaven on all our heads."

I recognized the conviction in his tone and knew I had been wrong, and my decision was made in that instant. I stood up, smiling as though he had soothed away all my pains, which to a degree he had.

"You seem remarkably fond of balls, Lucanus."

"Not unduly." His smile matched my own. "I've seen enough of them and removed too many of them to be overly impressed by them. But they do connote a certain urgency."

"They do indeed." I offered him my hand and we shook as friends. "Lucanus," I said, "I have misjudged you, and disliked you without cause. I regret that deeply."

He grinned at me. "Forget it, Commander. You knew me as a stern and disapproving physician, and even *I* found me unimpressive in that guise. It's only as a surgeon that I shine."

"Then shine, Surgeon, from now on." I stopped, remembering. "But where's my aunt?"

"Oh, she'll come when I send for her. In truth, she chose not to be present for this meeting."

"Good, then go you to her now and make your report. I'll go and talk to Titus, Flavius and Popilius and get them started on the arrangements for the funeral. When do you think would be the best time to do it?"

He frowned, deep in thought. "The day after tomorrow probably, just before sunset, for the funeral pyre. Then the following afternoon for the interment of his ashes. That should be long enough for the embers to cool, I think. Everyone in the Colony should attend both services, and you should give much thought to who will speak, and what they will say."

I nodded and turned to leave, but his next question stopped me in mid step. "By the way, how is the girl, Cassandra? Have you checked on her safety since your return?"

I turned slowly to face him. "No, I have not, so I can't answer your question."

"It was not my question; it was your aunt's. She thinks, and I agree, that you will not be able to rest easy until you have settled that." He spoke in the quiet, confident tones of his profession. "Make your arrangements with the others, and then go to her. You need not be back until noon tomorrow. I will cover for you, as your *physician.*"

Amazed, and humbled in some strange way, I nodded my thanks and left him smiling there, not even wondering if he knew where I was going.

I went directly to the room where my father lay on the great bed of Publius Varrus. Lucanus had spoken the truth and I stood in wonder at the evidence of his skills. My father, whom I had last seen strained in the agony of violent death, now seemed to be sleeping peacefully, reclining in full armour, helmeted, and draped in his great black cloak as though snatching a quick nap before setting off on a campaign. He was pale, but there was no trace of blood to be seen on him, and the chinstrap of his ceremonial helmet covered the gash in his throat. My own throat filled with hurt and pride and my eyes blurred with tears that spilled over and down my face. Caius Picus Britannicus was at rest, and nobly so, and I left him there.

XXVI

I f there is a more unpleasant or unforgettable taste than copper in this world, I have never experienced it. Once, when I was a very small boy, I held a copper coin in my hand for a long time on a hot summer's day. My hand grew moist and sticky with sweat and that small copper coin, a humble *as*, seemed permanently stuck to my skin. I can remember Uncle Varrus shouting at me to stand back and stay clear of the cart he was driving that day, and as the great, noisy vehicle passed me, its solid wooden wheels dwarfing and deafening me, a sawn log fell from the back of it and rolled a little way towards me. I remember thinking that I was strong enough to carry that log to where my uncle had been stacking them all day long, but I needed two hands free to lift it and so I popped the warm, sweaty coin into my mouth. I am sure it was the shock of that violent, outrageous taste that stamped the details of that incident into my young mind for ever.

I think of that every time I grow deeply, stirringly afraid, for there is something about gut-churning fear that generates an illusion of that bitter taste. The same taste filled my mouth that evening as I approached the little valley in the hills. I had ridden my horse hard, all tiredness forgotten, since leaving the fort on my usual roundabout route. Now, as I neared the end of my journey, the shapeless fears that I had refused to acknowledge for the past several days got the better of me and I knew abject terror. What would I do if Cassandra were not there when I arrived? What would I do if she were there, but had been found and harmed, perhaps even killed? I almost killed my poor horse, flogging it mercilessly over the last three miles, but then at the start of the steep, narrow entrance to the valley, I had to dismount and walk, leading the unfortunate animal by the reins.

The first thing that struck me as I entered the bottom of the valley was the utter stillness of the place, and my heart swelled with an unbearable fear that disappeared in a wave of relief and joy as Cassandra came dashing from the bushes, her face ablaze with welcome. I had been gone from her for five days, and in the isolation of her silent world she could have had no conception of what I had been doing or what had been occurring within miles of her, for which I thanked God. Nevertheless, from the welcome she gave me, an observer would have thought she had not seen me in months.

Neither the fire in her hut nor the one in the clearing had been lit since I had taught her the lesson of the smoke, so I lit the interior fire now, as the late afternoon shadows changed to evening shades, and set out to gather more firewood while there was still enough light to find it by, thinking to myself that I was lucky to have arrived no later than I had, and that the daylight hours here in Avalon were very short.

That thought led me back to Cassandra's welcome and to an uncomfortable consideration of the means Cassandra must use to pass the time she spent alone between my visits. And that in turn gave rise to a series of questions that troubled me increasingly as I wandered far from the clearing in search of wood to burn. How *did* she spend her time? Living in a world of total silence as she did, how could she amuse herself? What did she do all day alone? And all night, on those long, dark evenings? Sunny days and fine evenings were one thing, I thought, but cold, stormy, dank and cloudy times must be quite another. Even this search for wood, I realized, would be a killing task on a wet, miserable day. In the past, fuel had always been plentiful here. No one had ever stayed in the valley long enough to consume the firewood that lay readily to hand. Now, however, with two fires burning night and day, every day, fuel was becoming hard to find. It had to be sought out, further and further from the clearing, and then carried, or dragged, back through the underbrush. And in my absence, Cassandra must do it by herself.

We made love in the firelight that night until I fell into an exhausted sleep from which I awoke twice with the image of my father's corpse in my mind.

It was late in the morning when I left to return to Camulod for the funeral rites, and the parting was more difficult for me than it had ever been before. My heart ached to leave her alone there by the little lake, and anxiety over my newly awakened recognition of her solitude plagued me all the way home. I knew the day would come soon when, one way or another, despite my own fears, I must bring her back to civilization and the company of others.

I found Titus and Flavius talking together in my father's day-room, Titus seated behind the desk, on my father's stool, and Flavius perched on one of the other chairs as they reviewed the arrangements they had made. Everything was well in hand, they told me. News of the funeral service had been circulated to everyone, and the event was scheduled for the third hour of the afternoon, which left me two hours, during which I had nothing to do but change into my ceremonial uniform and try to empty my mind of my concern over Cassandra while I prepared for the occasion, an unprecedented event for Camulod.

When I had last spoken with Titus, Flavius and Popilius, before leaving for Avalon the previous day, I had outlined my wishes for the ceremony. I had admitted freely that I was improvising, never having seen or experienced a military cremation. In the interim, however, Lucanus, who had followed the Eagles longer than any other officer now alive in the Colony, had produced several documents on the subject of military funerals in ancient times, and in my absence the four of them had decided to adhere to the procedures outlined in these records.

Flavius now informed me that Popilius, as *primus pilus*, would officiate at the ceremony, since this was a military occasion and not a religious one. The entire garrison of the Colony, excepting only a

skeleton crew of guards, would be on parade in full dress uniform.
Titus, as titular Legate and acting Commanding Officer, would
inspect the troops, while Lucanus, as Senior Surgeon and now the
senior serving officer surviving, would deliver the eulogy. Popilius
would head the Centuriate, as was his right, and would supervise
the order of the ceremonies, direct the honour guard, and attend to
the lighting of the fire that would consume the corpse.

The pyre itself, Flavius assured me, would burn well and quickly.
It had been built upon an iron grid mounted on an altar of stones
to ensure strong, clean ventilation, and its timbers were solid, seasoned and dry—massive, hand-hewn beams torn from the interior
of the Council Hall and drenched in pitch to make them burn
the hotter. Gratified and impressed by the thoroughness of their
planning, yet depressed by the prospect ahead of all of us, I thanked
them for their efforts and left them, making my way out into the
main courtyard. The work of cleaning up was almost complete
already, and I could see where reconstruction had begun in several
places, although no one was working there this afternoon. The grim
pyre that would consume my father's body dominated the entire
area, standing alone in the centre of the great yard. This was the
first such pyre I had seen, and I could only presume that Lucanus's
documents had contained some details on the building of such
things. Fascinated, I approached it and gazed into its heart.

It was a massive, five-layer bed of square-cut timbers, each two
handspans thick. Three of these layers, forming the top, bottom
and middle strata of the bed, were made of beams cut four paces
long. The two remaining layers, laid crosswise between the three
long ones, were shorter—only three paces long. The beams were
spaced evenly on all five levels, leaving a latticed pattern of air vents
to feed the flames. Every beam had been soaked in pitch, and the
smell of it caught at my throat. Above this bed, our carpenters had
built a box, an oven, of the same materials, open at one end to
receive the iron box that would contain my father's body. The roof
of this box, too, was three layers thick, the timbers arranged the
same way as those in the bed beneath. The heat generated by this

pyre would be intolerable. My father's flesh and bones would melt and dry into dust long before the flames burned down and the ferocious embers settled into ash.

Pensive and disturbed afresh, I left the place and walked out through the main gate, nodding in passing to Marcus, the centurion of the guard. Below me lay the new camp built by Popilius and his men. To my right, far off in the southern distance, I could see the enormous pit dug by our Cornish prisoners to hold their dead. The pit on my far left, much smaller, though still enormous, would hold our own dead thousand. The smallest pit, almost directly below me, on the northern side of the new camp, would hold our officers. Nothing moved on the plain, and I realised that Popilius must have kept his burial parties working through the night, for there were no bodies to be seen, and the pits themselves seemed to be almost filled.

Donuil joined me as I stood there musing, and waited beside me patiently until I spoke to him. He had come to ask my permission to attend my father's funeral, and I was both surprised and touched that he should wish to do so. My father had shown him little tolerance in the brief time they had known each other. I told him I would be glad to see him there, and again we stood in silence for a time.

It was only as I turned to re-enter the fort that I noticed he was frowning, mulling something over as he gazed into the distance, looking at nothing. I asked him what was troubling him and he began, hesitantly at first, but then with increasing confidence and conviction, to tell me about his continuing concern that we had missed something vitally important in our dealings with the two dead warlocks. Their baggage, according to Donuil, should have contained a cornucopia of black arts. I assured him again that all of their possessions had been searched thoroughly and nothing sinister had been found, but he was unconvinced. He asked me whether their iron-bound chests had been found, and when I told him there had been no such chests he shook his head in emphatic denial. He had seen those chests with his own eyes, he swore, in his father's Hall, and they were the most precious things the warlocks owned. Caspar had told his father, in Donuil's hearing, that they went nowhere without them. If the boxes had not been brought into Camulod, then the warlocks must have hidden them before their arrival. They must have stopped somewhere on the road.

I looked at him in irritation when he said that, my patience with this superstitious blather rapidly deserting me. "They did," I replied. "You were there when my father mentioned it. Uther stopped his men to allow them to clean up before riding into Camulod." He looked at me then and shook his head wryly before reminding me that my father had spoken in Latin, which was incomprehensible to him.

We walked together as far as my quarters, and as we walked I mulled over what he had said, wondering how much of it was fact and how much Celtic fancy. Those chests would be valuable, indeed, if they existed and if we could locate them. I decided I would speak to Uther about that stop on the road, if I ever saw him again. And then I wondered again where he was, knowing how he would mourn my father's death and regret missing the funeral.

I found Lucanus waiting for me in my quarters. He glanced at me critically and asked me how I was feeling. When I told him I was well, but not looking forward to the proceedings of the next few hours, he looked relieved.

"None of us are," he said. "Titus asked me to come by and speak to you. He forgot to mention one last suggestion when you spoke together earlier. He thinks it might be fitting if you were to wait with the Lady Luceiia at her house, and bring her to join the proceedings when everyone else is assembled. He will send an honour guard to escort the two of you as chief mourners."

I agreed to do that, thanked him for his courtesy and set about dressing.

I can remember almost nothing of my father's funeral, apart from scattered impressions that struck me at the time and stayed locked in my mind: the silent presence of the dense-packed crowd, bearing their own grief over lost loved ones and their palpable aura of bereavement; the heavy sound of iron-shod feet marching in slow cadence to the throb of martial drums; the brazen fanfare of horns and bugles as the funerary bearers, eight senior centurions, slid the riveted iron coffin into the nest prepared for it among the pitch-glazed timbers; the creak of Popilius's heavy, polished-leather, ceremonial armour, as he stood at attention by my side; the spitting noise of the pitch-soaked torch as he stepped forward to light the pyre; and then the solid, roiling tower of smoke that ascended in yellow, grey and purple belches while its base was devoured and displaced by the searing, furious heat of the flames that glazed our eyes and beat against us even where we stood, behind the circle of the honour guard, twenty-five paces distant. And I remember the noise, the all-embracing, all-consuming, demented sound of the roaring, hissing flames that ate my father.

I know rain threatened, yet the sun shone throughout, but I remember nothing of that. I know, too, because he told me later, that Uther arrived back during the funeral, and, seeing the pall of smoke from afar, led his exhausted men at the charge against the attackers he immediately assumed were there. When they divined the true reason for the billowing column of smoke, he and his men approached quietly, leaving their mounts outside, and stood unnoticed at the rear of the crowd, which was already starting to disperse.

When it was over, I walked home in silence with Aunt Luceiia, then returned to my own quarters, where I removed my armour and slept for hours, awakening only after dark, refreshed and hungry.

I was surprised to find Uther in the refectory, eating alone. We greeted each other soberly. He told me how sorry he was about my father, but I merely nodded—there was nothing to say—and went to help myself to some food. I cut a thick chunk of mutton from a still-warm carcass on a spit over the glowing embers of a fire, and a substantial slab of bread to rest it on. The remains of some kind of vegetable stew, cooked in a meaty broth, were congealing in a pan by the fire. It looked unappetizing, but I spooned some of the lukewarm broth over my bread and mutton and took it back to where Uther sat. He pushed his platter away as I sat down, but stayed while I ate my own food, and as I ate, he talked, telling me of his pursuit of the fleeing remnants of Lot's army. He and his men had been merciless, killing every one of Lot's people they caught—he estimated the numbers they had slain in the course of two full days' pursuit in the hundreds. Finally, however, he had called in his forces and abandoned the chase when he learned from a dying Cornishman that Lot had never left the south-west.

He had heard the story of the sorcerers and their hostages since his return, and his mention of it reminded me of Donuil's concern. I pushed away the remnants of my own food and sat back, looking around for a wine jug. There was one on a neighbouring table, and when I checked it I found it still half full. I took two cups, swilled them out, and poured for both of us. Uther held his high.

"Here's to your father, my Uncle Picus," he said, in a low voice. "He was a man among men. There are not many left of his kind. I wish I had come home two hours sooner." I joined him in the libation and we sat in silence for a while, until he asked me, "What are you thinking?"

"About the sorcerers." I had been sitting staring into my cup. "Caspar and Memnon. And their master, the spider, Lot. That whoreson will die at my hands. I have sworn it by my father's death."

"Then we had better ride together, Cousin, and it will be a race, for I've sworn the same oath."

I looked at him and we smiled together. "Then he's already a dead man," I said. "How had you planned to kill him?"

"Slowly, with any means at my disposal. Slowly and painfully. I want him to know at his end that he is dying, to know it is by my hand, and to beg me for the deliverance of death. And I'll refuse the whoreson."

I laughed for the first time in days, but I was far from amused. "You're almost as bad as he is!"

"No, Cousin, I am not. Lot is a pestilence who should not be alive." There was no sign of humour in his eyes. "Perhaps I was exaggerating about the manner of his death, but not about the certainty of it. This world will be a better place rid of his filth." He wrinkled his nose. "But you were thinking of the warlocks. Why? They are already dead. What profit dwelling on them?"

"Did you guard them closely on the journey here from Cornwall?"

"Guard them?" He raised his eyebrows in surprise at the question. "Well, yes and no. I detailed a man to keep an eye on them because I didn't like or trust them, but I didn't exactly chain them up. They were, after all, supposed to be ambassadors of some kind."

"Aye, they were that, indeed. Ambassadors of death."

"I had no way of knowing that at the time."

"No, you did not, nor could you. I'm not blaming you. But you did keep them under watch?"

He responded with a tiny shrug of one shoulder. "To a degree, yes. But they gave us no trouble, and we were on the move all the time. There was no real need to watch them closely."

"What about when you stopped?"

He looked at me warily, his curiosity stirring. "We stopped only to eat and sleep. What are you digging at, Cay?"

"Their baggage. Did you notice how much they had?"

"No. I could not have cared less about them, let alone their baggage. I had other things to worry about. They had their two servants, and two extra pack horses. Four men and six horses in all. My only concern was that they kept moving and didn't interfere with our progress. They did. Why? Did I miss something?"

"You may have. Young Donuil swears those two went nowhere without two particular, iron-bound, chained and locked boxes. Do you remember seeing anything like that?"

He shook his head, sticking out his lower lip. "No, but I told you, I paid no attention. What was in these boxes?"

"I don't know. They didn't bring them into Camulod. Donuil swears they contained the secret tools for their black arts."

"You mean magic?" Uther's tone was openly sceptical.

"Of a kind. The magic of venom for arrows, certainly, and God knows what else besides."

"Shit and corruption!" The scepticism had vanished.

"You stopped that morning before coming into the fort. Can you remember exactly where that was?"

"Of course. At the crossroads by the big, shattered ash tree, about five miles out on the east road, where the forest thins out for a space. I let my men clean themselves up in the brook there."

"Then that's where they must have hidden the boxes. Who was the man you detailed to watch them?"

"Gareth, one of my own men. But they couldn't have hidden anything, Cay. They didn't have time. We didn't stop for long enough."

"Long enough to defecate?"

"Yes, of course. Some did, but—"

"Then that was long enough. I didn't say they buried the boxes, Uther, only that they concealed them. You can be sure they had planned their move, probably in their own heathen tongue, long before the opportunity arose."

Uther was frowning suddenly. "Wait a moment, wait a moment . . . There was a disturbance of some kind, now that I think about it . . . Something to do with the horses. I didn't pay much attention to it at the time, because it was over quickly. That might have been when they did it. There was something about redistributing the loads." He shook his head. "I'm sorry, Cay, I can't remember."

"Your man Gareth should remember. Where can we find him?"

Uther gazed into his cup and swallowed a draught before answering, "We can't. He's in the common grave, down on the plain. He was one of the first of my men to go down."

"Damnation! Anyway, I know the place. I'm going to go and look around there tomorrow. I'll take Donuil with me."

"I'll come too." He stood up. "I know exactly where they were, and where the disturbance occurred. If they did hide anything, it must have been near there. If the boxes exist, we'll find them. But now I'm going back to sleep. I had a few hours earlier, but I haven't had a decent sleep in days. What about you?"

I yawned. "I don't know. I'm yawning, but I don't feel sleepy, and yet I'm bone tired, does that make sense? I think I'll take a walk to digest this meal, and then get some more sleep myself."

"Good. Hammer on my door when you get up. We'll break fast together, find your young heathen and be on the road early. We should be able to find those things, if they are there, and be back here by noon. Good night to you. Sleep well, Cousin."

I bade him good night and walked outside to the main court-yard. An honour guard detachment still ringed my father's pyre, which now smouldered angrily, glowing bright red and blue in the blackness of the night. I walked through their circle and stood close to the fire, even now feeling its fearsome strength tighten the skin of my cheekbones and bare legs as I peered into its heart, seek-ing the iron coffin that contained the remains of the man who had sired and shaped me. I knew it was there, but I could not see it in the incandescent brightness. I offered up a prayer for my father's soul and stood there a long time, silently remembering.

Finally I stepped away from the fire and back through the ring of guards into the darkness, but I carried its heat with me for some time as I walked in the coolness of the night. At length, however, the heat wore off and the chill of the darkness reminded me that I was lightly dressed for night-time walking. I made my way back to my quarters and climbed into bed, where I slept dreamlessly.

We found the warlocks' boxes the following day, with almost no need to search. Uther led us directly to the spot where the dis-turbance with the horses had occurred, and we struck into the woods immediately. Donuil, who had been driving Uncle Varrus's sprung, two-wheeled cart, left it on the road to follow us on foot. We found the boxes less than twenty paces from the road, hidden in a small gully cut by a streamlet. Donuil jumped down into the gully immediately, catching his clothes on the wild brambles that filled the place and cursing at the thorns that clawed at him. The image chilled me instantly.

"Donuil!" I shouted. "Get out of there!"

He looked at me in amazement, as did Uther, but he turned and climbed back up out of the hole. I slid from my horse and drew my sword, using it to hack away the brambles that choked the hid-ing-place, kicking them aside until the boxes were uncovered.

When I had cleared the space around them completely, I knelt on one knee beside the boxes, peering closely at them, ignoring the heavy chains that bound them and concentrating only on the wooden cases. My presentiment had been right. I looked up to where Donuil stood watching me. "Come down now, carefully, and look at this." When he had joined me, I pointed a finger where I wanted him to look. "Recognize that?"

He shuddered in loathing as he saw and recognized what I had found. "One of *them*," he whispered, staring wide eyed at the sharp, black thorn that was lodged in the woodwork of the case.

"Aye, and there are more. Anyone finding these boxes and trying to remove them would not have lasted long. Uther, come and look at this."

Uther jumped from his horse's back and came down to join us. I pointed again to the thorn. "See that? It's first cousin to your poisoned arrows. A prick from that, and you're a dead man. Those are the thorns that Caspar used to kill his twelve men, one thorn, one man."

He grimaced. "Come on, Cay. Are you serious? That's not possible."

"Try asking those dead men to agree with you. I'm telling you, Uther, these little things are deadly."

He stooped closer to peer at the one I had shown him, prepared to be impressed in spite of himself. "They don't look deadly, do they?"

"That's why they work so well."

His eyes were now moving over the boxes. "How many of them are there?"

"Too many. Eight that I can see, but there's probably a score more of them around all four sides and the top of each box. There wouldn't be any on the bottom."

"How do we get them out?"

"Cautiously," I said. "One at a time."

I used the point of my knife to dislodge the thorns, and I handled each of them with great respect, thrusting them, one at a time,

point first into the packed earth of the stream's bank. Eventually,
the task was complete and the boxes were safe to handle. Uther
wanted to open them immediately, and so did I, but I had doubts.
The care with which the outside of these things had been protected
worried me. Anyone patient enough, and knowledgeable enough,
to work his way through the maze of thorns, chains and locks
around these boxes would be ill advised, it seemed to me, to simply
throw open the lids without further precaution.

We carried the boxes intact to the racing cart and took them
back to Camulod, where, in spite of the curiosity and impatience of
the others to see what they contained, I stored them in my quarters
until such time as I could approach the problem they presented
calmly and examine their contents with an open mind.

XXVII

I waited for two weeks before opening the chests we had recovered, and then spent the following weeks in a state of absolute fascination as I examined, item by item, the contents that lay revealed. Had anyone been watching me, observing my behaviour as I first opened their lids, he might have doubted the soundness of my mind. I had had the chests moved into the main smithy, and had then banished everyone, sealing myself inside with my prize. As soon as I was alone and safe from interruption, I set to work immediately to open them. They were big, and heavy, one slightly larger than the other, perhaps a handsbreadth longer and a span higher.

A maul, a cold chisel and an anvil made short work of the chains, but each box was sealed by a spring lock that required a key. Publius Varrus had been a master lockmaker, and when I was a boy he had explained to me the action of spring locks. I crossed to his old work space by the main forge and opened the battered, much-stained wooden box that he had used to hold his collection of keys. They were all still there, dozens of them, coated with rust. I found only two that seemed as though they might fit the locks on the warlocks' cases. A few moments scraping each with a fine file to remove the rust, a few drops of oil, and the lock of the first box, the larger of the two, clicked open in response to my gentle pressure.

Letting out my breath in a hiss, I turned to the second box and unlocked it, too, with only minor difficulty. Now I drew my sword and, leaning backwards as far as I could, used its point to attempt to raise the lid, knowing that when I did anything might happen. The sword was too short to permit me enough leverage from a safe distance. There was a javelin leaning against the wall, and I used that instead, at arm's length, crouching low as I placed its point against the front flap of the lid and pushed it up and open. Nothing happened, although I flinched at the clatter of the lid as it fell backward. I opened the second box the same way, with the same result. I waited, motionless, while I counted slowly to one hundred and then, finally convinced that no poisonous vapours were to be released, I stepped forward cautiously and looked at what I had uncovered.

The interior of the first box was beautifully made, rimmed by a scored, wooden edge as wide as my hand, with the central portion divided into a grid of twelve square compartments, four long by three deep. Leather thongs lay piled, apparently haphazardly, on top of the contents of the compartments. I leaned forward and probed the thongs cautiously with my fingertip. They seemed to be plain leather, with no sharp points hidden among them. I made to pick them up, and then I realized that they were handles, one attached to each side of each section of the scored wooden frame. The wide, scored border was a series of nested trays, made to fit one into the other, each growing progressively deeper, but each offering complete security and safety to its contents.

As I progressed slowly and with care with my examination of the contents, I put aside some of the more baffling objects for further study. Some of these were, and were to remain forever, mysterious. Others, however, were more easily identified, and still others I was soon able to classify. All of them, I found without great surprise, were dangerous, capable of dealing death in one way or another. I discovered, for example, four oblong clay boxes, glazed inside and out, with fitted, sealed, similarly glazed lids, containing an oily, pungent, greenish paste that turned out to be the venom used on the poisoned arrows. I spread some of it on metal, and as it dried it left a scaly, crystalline residue that I recognized as the same that had coated the arrowhead with which I had executed Caspar.

Other jars and boxes, phials and glass tubes held a wondrous range of substances, all strange to me: crystals and powders; pastes and crushed mixtures of things that had been ground down by mortar and pestle; unguents and oily substances that seemed to have been rendered over fire; bunches and boxes of dried berries, grasses, leaves and even seeds or nuts. The colours of many of these materials were astonishing: bright and dull greens; glowing reds from cinnamon to crimson; rich, startling blues and yellows; one glossy, almost radiant black; and a full range of whites, darkening into pale and dark browns.

All of these I inspected with great care, melting them, if they would melt, to see how they would react; mixing them in water; exposing them to air and fire; testing them in every way I could think of, including feeding them to animals, most of which died, and keeping copious notes on my findings.

One of them astounded me, and although to this day I have no knowledge of what it was, I used it sparingly for long afterwards until I had exhausted it, once I discovered how it worked. I found a box of it, almost full, hidden at the deepest level of the larger chest and tightly bound with twine. It was a blackish, granular powder of no distinction that I proved harmless immediately by feeding small quantities of it to three rabbits with no ill effects. Having determined it was not a poison, I tasted it. It was unremarkable, tasting like charred ashes, save for a saline tang that I could not define. I mixed it in water, stirring it well and watching it to see how it dissolved or altered. It did neither. Discouraged, and on the point of pouring it out, I remembered whence it had come and reasoned again that the Egyptian sorcerers would not have kept it so securely among their clandestine treasures unless it had value of some kind, so rather than pouring it onto the floor to waste, I strained it through a cloth, twisting the fabric tightly until it contained only the original pinch of powder. That done, I spread the moist powder on a piece of tin and held it over a candle flame. It dried out slightly from the heat, but nothing more. Disappointed, and by now losing interest, I shook the residue back into the scrap of cloth through which I had strained it, balled it up carelessly, and threw it into the fire of the forge, where it exploded with a great whoosh of flames and billowing black smoke that caught at my throat and brought me choking to my knees, eyes streaming and heart palpitating in panic.

When I had regained my breath and my composure, I placed another pinch of the powder carefully on the top of the bench and touched it with a burning taper. As soon as the flame touched it, the powder, whatever it was, ignited with a flaring hiss of intense flames, emitting great, rolling clouds of bitter, blinding smoke. Fire powder! Within an hour I had established that it was the most combustible substance I had ever found. No flame was required to ignite it—it reacted with equal violence to the heat of a spark. Amazed and mystified, I packed it away again, safely out of sight, wondering how I would ever find a use for it.

I had been secretive about the boxes and their contents, and Uther had forgotten their existence within days. Donuil did not forget, but he disliked the boxes and avoided them, trusting me to find out what I could about them. No one else knew of their existence. And as I worked with them, fascinated by their contents, it never crossed my mind that the mere possession of them might change men's perception of me, in the years ahead, from soldier to sorcerer.

Towards the end of my third week of study, however, I was forced to lay them aside for other matters. News came from the north-west of another sudden, overland attack, this time on Uric's lands by hostile, unidentified forces from the north-east, reinforced by more of Lot's people from the south who had attempted a seaborne invasion from Lot's north Cornish territories. The invaders, we were told, had been driven back on both fronts after harsh fighting, but Uther's father Uric had fallen, slain by a poisoned arrow.

My cousin Uther was now King of the Pendragon.

He took the news less than well. In fact, he collapsed, hit far harder by grief than I would ever have suspected he could be, and it surprised me deeply to discern that his grief sprang from a deep and obviously genuine love for his father, an affection I had never suspected. This realization astounded me, and forced me to a drastic re-evaluation of my uncle Uric, by whom I had never, frankly, been impressed.

Among all the strong and forceful characters who made up our family—and many of them seemed superhuman—Uric, king though he had been, had seemed one of the least remarkable, over-shadowed, to my mind at least, by almost all his relatives. Yet here was Uther, my wild, unmanageable cousin, weeping openly over the death of his father in a way that I, who had loved my own father deeply, had been unable to. Prompted by guilt, I suppose, and an urge to reexamine the life of this uncle whom I had obviously not known at all, I tried on several occasions to entice Uther to talk to me about his father, but I was almost totally unsuccessful until one afternoon, days after the arrival of the news, when we were alone together in Uncle Varrus's Armoury.

We had been discussing Uther's plans. He was about to leave for his mountain kingdom to claim his inheritance and see that all was in order. After that, he intended to raise some levies and to lead a retaliatory strike against Lot. We had just agreed on a plan to augment his mountain forces with a strong contingent of infantry and cavalry from Camulod. These would march under the nominal command of one of our junior commanders, a brilliant young Celtic cavalryman called Gwynn, until such time as they could join up with Uther.

I was seated at Uncle Varrus's old desk by the open window, and Uther had just stood up from where he had been leaning against the arm of one of the big couches by the wall. He was on his way out, opening the heavy doors, when I made some comment or asked him something about his father. To this day I have no recollection of what it was I said, but Uther swung around to face me, his face black with sudden anger, and for a moment I thought he was going to attack me. He stopped short, however, expending visible effort on biting back the words that had sprung to his tongue, and finally, after an obvious struggle for control of himself, smiled at me strangely—a tight, small, regretful smile—before shaking his head and starting to turn away from me again.

"No!" I snapped. "Stop right there. Let's have this out."

He stopped and turned back to face me, his eyes guarded now, empty of any sign of the sudden hostility that had overtaken him. "Well?" he asked.

I cleared my throat, suddenly at a loss, and then asked him directly. "What was all that about? That display? What were you going to say?"

He stared at me for the space of several heartbeats, blinking his eyes slowly, and then he sighed a sharp, impatient sigh and turned away again, only to check himself and swing back towards me. "No, dammit," he said. "It's time someone told you."

"Told me what?" I asked.

He looked at me and I could see him hesitate as he searched his mind for the proper words to use. Finally, he moved back and sat on the arm of the couch again, his eyes fixed on mine as though pinning me to my place.

"Cay," he said finally, his voice pitched low, but in a tone that suggested he would brook no argument. "You are an amiable fellow. You are a good friend and can be an enjoyable companion when you want to be, but you can also turn my stomach at times.

"You are always so *right*. Are you aware of that, Cay? Aware of how predictable, and ultimately how infuriating that can be? You are always right! You are always so ... so correct, so decorous, so proper, so courteous, and you know all the correct things to say on any occasion, and that's all very well, but there are some things in this world you know nothing about!" He stopped, took a very deliberate breath, ignoring my stunned expression, and continued. "Judgments, for example. Let's talk about judgments for a moment. You're a great judge, Cay ... Or perhaps it would be more accurate to say a great judger! You find it very easy to pass judgment on practically everything and everyone, based on the relevance of that thing or person to your personal values, and its performance according to your criteria."

I stood wide-eyed, stunned by his sudden eloquence, so out of character for a man I knew to be generally only semi-articulate. I felt both my feelings and my pride hurt, although I had not yet had time to absorb Uther's attack on me. The martinet in me told me he was overreacting to something, obviously something I had said. But what had I said? As these thoughts were flashing through my mind, he drove on without pause.

"And that's another thing, of course. You also have set criteria for everything—for every conceivable circumstance under the sun or moon—so you never lack a standard for any of your judgments—" I started to interrupt his diatribe, but he shouted me down, telling me it was time for me to hear some home truths. I subsided as he continued. "I was talking about judgments and I had not finished. You are forever making judgments, Cay, and the frightening thing about that is I don't think you are even aware of it. Everything has to be either black or white in your world. Everything has to fit within a category, and only you are allowed to designate the categories. You did it to me, with that silly child Cassandra, or whatever her name was. Someone thrashed her. You decided I was the one because I had been angry at her, angry and vengeful, so your verdict was guilty!

"And my father. You judged him, too, and found him lacking. You judged him a nonentity. Don't interrupt me!" This last was hissed at me as I moved to speak and, abashed by his vehemence, I subsided again as he went on. "I know my father was no Publius Varrus and certainly no Caius Britannicus . . . He knew it, too. He wasn't even an Ullic Pendragon. But by the Living God, he was a Pendragon and he was a King, and he was a good man, a kind and considerate father who loved his children and was not afraid to show that love, even when the children had grown . . ." His voice faltered and grew quiet.

"I never spent much time with my father, Cay, but the time I did spend with him was among the best I ever spent with anyone. I could talk to my father in a way I could never have with you, or anyone else. Sometimes we didn't even need words. We were happy enough simply being together . . ." His words died away completely, and by this time I had absolutely no thought of stopping him.

Eventually he continued, his anger swelling again. "Look at you! You're astounded that I can show any feelings of grief or love, aren't you? I know you are, because for years you've had me categorized as a profligate, a fighter, a soldier and a savage, with little of your education and few of your refinements. My prime concerns, in your mind, are wine, women, horses and fighting, isn't that so? Of course it is. I know that!" He stopped abruptly and looked at me, soberly.

"Well, hear me, Cousin Caius. I loved my father, Uric the King, Uric Pendragon. And I intend that my sons should say the same of me, when I die. I want them to say, with pride, 'I loved my father, Uther the King!' If I am correct, and your judgment of me has been wrong, take note of that. It will not be the first time your judgment has been wrong in the eyes of others. And yet there is no sin in being wrong, Cousin. As long as we can admit our errors. We learned that long ago, you and I, from old Bishop Alaric. The tendency to error is what makes us all human, but only the capacity for compassion exalts a man beyond the merely human."

He paused and stood there for a few moments before continuing in a more reflective tone, almost as an afterthought, "You have a need for more compassion, Cay, and that means you must try to be more human. Learn to evince a willingness to make more errors—if you can. Perhaps then you might find, deep inside, some tolerance. Try it, Cousin. You will improve by it, believe me."

With that, he spun on his heel and strode from the room, leaving me with much to think about, although in the time that passed immediately after his departure I was unable to think at all. My self-esteem reeled in the wake of such a brutal, unexpected attack. He was distraught, I told myself. His father's death had unhinged him, making him say things he neither meant nor believed. But even as my mind formed the words I saw the lie in them. Uther had said what he said because he believed it. He saw me as a self-righteous prig, disdainful of anything that did not bear my own, personal imprimatur. He believed my attitude towards him and his father was one of condescension, condemnation and disapproval. I stopped, chilled by a tiny, barely identifiable tic of recognition buried somewhere deep down at the back of my consciousness. And as I examined it, the chill grew, raising goose-flesh as I thrilled with the horror of perceiving, and admitting, that my cousin was right.

Having felt that—or perhaps merely suspected it—I could go no further without confronting it fully, and so, in all ignorance, I set about what I later—often ruefully and sometimes even bitterly—had to acknowledge to be one of the biggest follies of a life that has sometimes seemed drowned in folly: I took myself to task without the slightest thought of the enormity of what I was about. I set out to break down whatever it was that made me *myself*—to divide it into segments comprehensible to myself, determined to arrive at a complete knowledge of myself and to discover my own true beliefs and attitudes about the people around me and the life we all shared. I can recall the callow, arrogant ignorance with which I took up this task that day, the foolish boastfulness with which I assumed that I would be able to plumb the depths of my own character in the space of a day or so, and arrive at a means of changing myself completely—for the better and for ever! I was completely unaware that I was throwing myself into a lifetime's task, and a heart-breaking, painful process that, once begun, would become impossible to abandon or even to neglect.

I have heard men otherwise considered wise say that it is impossible for a man to lie to himself. Of all human statements, I think that must rank among the most foolish. We lie to ourselves constantly, trying to live up to our own expectations of ourselves. Self-delusion is probably the most common of all human characteristics.

If I have gained any wisdom in my life, it is the wisdom to thank God for having kept me too busy during those days for time to dwell deeply on this quest for self-knowledge. I must have been insufferable to those around me, because I soon began to discern the amount of work and dedication that would be called for, if this task I had set myself were to be faced properly, and I felt a driving need to discuss it with anyone and everyone who would listen. I saw almost immediately that the temptation towards self-delusion is enormous. I saw also how easy it would have been simply to decide that I had been correct in my own interpretation of myself, because I knew myself better and more profoundly than any other could.

Fortunately Meric, my old Druid teacher and mentor, came to visit us at Camulod around that time. Meric was a lover of argument, polemic and philosophical debate. He and I spent days together, deep in conversation, and everyone around us must have been sad to see him depart after only a few weeks, leaving them vulnerable to me and my agony again. When I saw the glazed look I came to recognize and hate invade the eyes of yet another unwilling listener, I would sometimes sneak away to find my love in her hidden vale, knowing that I could talk to her for hours and hours, should I so wish, and that, no matter what my topic, she would sit in her wordless, soundless world, content simply to have me there beside her.

I did decide that Uther's assessment of me had been correct, and I set out to change myself in a number of ways, including curing myself of my tendency to be judgmental. I thought long and hard, for hours on end, on what my father had had to say just a few months earlier on judgments, and his views on evidence, circumstance, and the value of reasonable doubt. And I decided that I had a duty to come to know everyone around me as well and as thoroughly and genuinely as I possibly could, so that any judgment I might be tempted to make concerning them would at least be based on knowledge and understanding. Again, a massive and intimidating undertaking, and yet one I began to enjoy more and more as I worked at it. For I soon found that the rewards of this new policy far exceeded the hardship involved.

I found that the people I spent such time with became more friendly, more personable and more willing to trust me, once they came to accept that I really was interested in knowing them for who and what they were. And I found that most people were far more admirable than I had suspected they might be, so that I soon came to recognize respect for what I now know it to be—something to which all people are entitled, until they forfeit it personally and wilfully.

I learned much about the *people* of Camulod, and came more and more to think of them as "my" people, but it was to be many,

many months before I had either the opportunity or the courage to face Uther and admit that he had been right, and to ask his forgiveness. When I finally did, he frowned in complete puzzlement, then realized what I was talking about and grinned and squeezed the back of my neck in one great hand, saying he had heard I was changing quickly—and for the better—and that he had high hopes for me.

With Uther gone to his mountain kingdom, I felt free to spend more time, in longer and longer stretches, with my beloved Cassandra. Our chain of command in Camulod by that time was such that, had I so wished, I could easily have stayed away for months on end, secure in the knowledge that everything would progress peacefully and lawfully in the Colony during my absence, and that any emergencies would be dealt with swiftly and competently, without any need of guidance from me. That I chose not to do so was the result of several circumstances, one of them being the new resolve I have just described. Another was the genuine pleasure I found in the training of young Donuil for the duties he was determined to assume in the future, a pleasure leavened by the keen, intuitive insight the young man demonstrated, and reinforced by the genuine need I perceived to advance his education as quickly as possible, with a view to grooming him as an eventual replacement for Titus. Titus had been badly affected by my father's death, and almost overnight I watched him change into an elderly man—he who, like my father himself, had previously seemed impervious to time and its dictates.

In my passion to make changes within myself, I took pains to spend a great deal of time with him, mainly in the evenings, when the daily tasks were completed. I spent long, wonderful evenings talking with him, but primarily listening to him talk about my father and the years they had spent together. On many of these occasions, we were joined by Flavius, the third member of my father's triumvirate, and listening to the two of them reminiscing I learned more about the man who had been my father than I had ever known.

On one such evening, soon after Uther's departure, all three of us mellowed by wine, I told them in detail of young Donuil's idea, and of my own conviction of the strength and soundness of it. When I had finished talking, they both sat silent for a time, digesting what I had told them. Neither was quick to comment. Titus was the first to speak, clearing some phlegm from his throat and turning to Flavius. "What do you think, Flavius?"

Flavius scratched at the tight-curled, wiry, iron-grey hair that covered his scalp and remained silent, thinking his way deliberately through the pros and cons of this unexpected proposal. "I'm surprised," he admitted, eventually, "but I'm not opposed." He continued to scratch, gazing at me, his thoughts and attention turned inward. "He's an impressive young man, so I think you should go with your instincts, Cay. Give the boy his head and see how he performs. He might let you down, and you won't know that until the time comes. But anyone else you choose—and you'll have to choose someone—might let you down, too, even harder. You want to try the lad. Then try him, I say, and good luck to both of you. You're going to need someone. There's no one else qualified to do the job right now, and sooner or later you're going to have to turn us two old war-horses out to pasture."

Titus sat up, as though he were about to dispute that, and then he sighed and slumped in his chair again. "Flavius is right, Cay," he said. "The timing is good. And I believe you are doing the right thing, although the boy has much to learn. Fortunately, he learns quickly and well. That is already obvious from the way he has picked up our language. You should prepare a formal, disciplined schedule of duties for him: so much time with Rufio, learning basic military skills, so much time with you, learning the needs you will have for him, and the remainder with me, learning to understand and control the things that make this Colony function." He moved to a more comfortable position and grinned at me. "I'll be happy to teach him what little I know. I'll even show him how to break and manipulate the rules he himself will have to live by. Have him come to me tomorrow, before noon. I'll try to get to know him better during the coming weeks. That way, I'll be able to gauge the speed and the extent of his future tuition."

Deeply moved by their support and empathy, I thanked them both, and our conversation moved on to other things. But the die was cast for my future adjutant.

XXVIII

A valon became my sanctuary in the days after the loss of my father. The rude hut we had been so glad of in the beginning was no longer quite so rude. Every time I had visited Cassandra, from the earliest days of her sojourn there, I had done some kind of work on the small building, and I usually brought something with me to improve the place, to make it more weatherproof or more comfortable. It was now warm and snug, verging on the luxurious in some respects, although still tiny. Each time I arrived there, I left the world behind me, losing all thought of temporal problems as I descended the steep, twisting pathway to where she waited for me.

I had long since given up making any attempt to entice her to leave the valley and return with me to Camulod. Several times I had tried it, and she had come to recognize the attempts, so that now she would not even venture with me to the pathway leading up the hill. I made no serious effort to convince her that her return was important to me. I was really quite content to keep her there, all to myself, sharing her with no one, knowing that she was there, waiting to comfort me whenever the realities of life at Camulod became overpowering.

For a very long time after the events surrounding the death of my father, however, life around Camulod remained quiet, pleasant and peaceful. The upheavals caused by Lot's invasion, or by Caspar and Memnon's invasion, soon died down and passed into memory, and life regained its normal tenor. Donuil's education in our ways continued with a swiftness that surprised and gratified all of us. He was quickly accepted by the entire garrison—thanks to Centurion Rufio, who also flourished under his new responsibilities—and by the colonists themselves, and the friendship between us grew steadily as we discovered more of each other's character and disposition. Summer faded into autumn, with a fine harvest, which advanced slowly into another mild winter and a brilliant spring. All awareness of threats from outside seemed to have vanished, except that patrols still came and went regularly and there was no lessening of vigilance among the military guardians of the peace.

In the spring, however, Aunt Luceiia's ubiquitous bishops brought news of another kind: tidings from Rome.

I heard the news on my return from one of my frequent three-day visits to Cassandra in the springtime of the new year, when I was summoned to visit Luceiia. I found her in unusually high spirits, even for her. She informed me that, now that spring had arrived, she intended to return with me to Avalon—she herself used the name—to meet my Cassandra and convince her to come back with us and live a civilized life in Camulod, where she and I would be married.

I was nonplussed, and immediately at war within myself. Part of me saw the sense of what she was proposing, but another, possibly stronger part, was unwilling even to consider forsaking the private happiness I had known with Cassandra in our tiny valley. Aunt Luceiia, however, would brook no argument, and when I finally managed to insert a few words into her animated monologue I agreed that it would be wonderful, at least, for her to meet my love. I also asked her, although without much real interest, to be more specific about her "news from Rome," news of which I knew nothing.

Her eyebrows rose slightly in shock. "What do you mean, you know nothing about it? Everyone knows about it!"

I shook my head. "Forgive me, Auntie, but I have no idea what 'it' is."

She blinked at me, still looking slightly astonished. "Why, Germanus of course."

"I beg your pardon?"

"Germanus. Germanus is 'it.'"

"I see. Which Germanus are you talking about?"

Her eyebrows quirked into a fleeting frown of impatience. "General Germanus, your father's friend, the former Legate who served with him in Asia Minor under Stilicho. He is now the Bishop of Auxerre."

I was thoroughly confused and held up my hand, in an appeal for patience. "Please, Auntie, forgive me. I've been away for a time, and all of this has happened in my absence, so be patient with me if I seem confused. General Germanus is the Bishop of Auxerre, in Gaul?"

"That is correct."

I shook my head again, thoroughly confused. "But how can that be? How can a Legate be a bishop?"

My aunt sniffed eloquently. "Easily, it seems. Germanus retired from the Legions, as all men must at some time, and entered the priesthood, which few Legates, or other soldiers, for that matter, ever do. He was always a deep-thinking man, apparently, and he is now the Bishop of Auxerre, and a very highly respected theologian, according to the reports I have received."

"From your own bishops, of course."

"Yes." My aunt was unconscious of any irony.

"I see. So what else have your bishops told you?"

She bridled like a proud pony and answered me with an indignant expression and a condescending tone to her voice as though explaining the obvious to one who was already well informed. "That, in spite of the teachings of Pelagius being condemned as wickedly controversial, we the people here in Britain still cling to them."

"But we always have, Auntie, and we have always known it. What is so new about that?"

Luceiia drew herself upright. "The novelty, Nephew, lies in the fact that there is almost open, holy war among our British bishops. Not all of them are followers of Pelagius. There are many, it seems, who adhere to the teachings of Augustine of Hippo and the hierarchical powers of the churchmen in Rome. Those bishops, the Orthodox Bishops of Britain, as they call themselves, have written to Pope Celestine, begging him to intercede for them here in this country."

She paused for a moment, then went on. "Pelagius is dead. He died last year in Palestine. He died excommunicate."

"How so? Pope Innocent exonerated him!"

"No," she corrected me, "Innocent excommunicated him. It was Pope Zosinus, Innocent's successor, who absolved Pelagius, eleven years ago. That was short-lived, however. Zosinus changed his mind, and his decree, the following year, under pressure from the combined bishops at the Council of Carthage. Pelagius lived his last ten years apostate."

"Thereby proving the validity of his own beliefs. How can such total condemnation be Christian? I understood no sin was too big to be forgiven." Another thought occurred to me. "What of his followers?"

Aunt Luceiia sniffed. "We have all been declared heretics, although we have not yet been actively declared excommunicate. We are being told now that the Church Fathers in Rome consider us to have been misled for many years, seduced from the proper path of the Church's teaching through no fault of our own. They now wish us to submit voluntarily to the will and the teachings of Rome. The Holy Father in Rome, Pope Celestine, is sending Germanus of Auxerre, the warrior bishop, here to Britain to debate the question of Pelagianism—that is the name they are giving to our beliefs versus their 'orthodoxy'—with our own British bishops, in the great theatre at Verulamium."

She had my full attention. This was what my father had called for in his confrontation with the zealot priests. "A debate, you say? A public debate? When, Auntie? When is this to take place?"

She looked me in the eyes shrewdly, assessing the sudden interest in my voice. "In September, six months from now, but why do you ask? You wouldn't be thinking of going to listen, would you?"

Her tone made me smile. "Why not? Would it surprise you very much if I showed that much interest?"

"In matters of the Church? You?" she scoffed. "My dear boy,

whatever hopes I might once have had for your salvation are long dead. You are my nephew, and I love you, but you are a scandalous libertine." She laughed aloud. "I can no more imagine you travelling from here to Verulamium for a debate between bishops than I could imagine my Publius, God rest him, earning his living as a fisherman."

I grinned with her. "Why not, Auntie? Publius Varrus, having decided he must be a fisherman, would have had boats sink beneath him from the weight of his catch." I paused, sobered. "Seriously, Auntie, I think it would be irresponsible of me to miss this debate, if I could possibly arrange to be there."

"Irresponsible, Cay?" She had caught my mood change, and leaned back in her chair to scrutinize me more closely, squinting her eyes slightly as she sought to read my expression. "Why irresponsible? That is a weighty word."

"This is a weighty matter, Auntie."

"Is it indeed? Well, I confess it is. Weighty and profound. I know that, but it surprises me that you should recognize it, too."

I made a wry face. "Am I that predictable? So easy to dismiss as shallow?"

"No, God forgive me if I make you feel that way, Caius. I am merely ... surprised, that is all. You will admit, will you not, that you have never shown any interest in such things before?"

"Freely. But people change, Auntie, and I suppose I am changing ..." I fell silent, and she allowed me time to collect my thoughts. "I've been thinking a great deal about my father, and the things he stood for, and I don't think I have ever in my life seen anything finer, anything more fitting, or more dignified and decorous, than the way he defied and denied those odious priests in Council that day, before he expelled them from the Colony.

"And yet, thinking of that, despite my admiration for my father's stance, and his judicious reasoning, not to mention his restraint—I don't think I could have put up with the abuse he swallowed that day—I've also had to think about the long-term effects of his actions that day. We have not heard the last of that affair, and my father is no longer here to deal with the repercussions. But someone will have to, and I think that someone will be me. Honestly, Auntie, I don't know if I can cope with that task. I haven't got the moral certitude, the scope of experience, the authority or the tempered judgment that my father had." I paused again, breaking new ground here, seeking new words to describe my thinking, and as I did so, I became aware of the expression on my aunt's face.

"What are you thinking? Do I sound arrogant?"

She smiled, shaking her head gently. "No, anything but. I'm entranced, but I don't want to interrupt your train of thought. Go on, Caius, please. Tell me your thoughts, and don't worry about mine."

I was sheepish, admitting my own bafflement. "Please understand, Auntie, that I'm as surprised as you by what I'm saying. I've never voiced these thoughts before today. They have been in my mind, obviously, but I haven't really been aware of them, other than in passing. There has been no urgency to them, if you know what I mean ..." My mind was spinning, thoughts tumbling over each other faster than I could grasp them, and Luceiia remained silent, aware that what I needed was a sympathetic ear to hear my thoughts, rather than words to interrupt them. I floundered on.

"Bishop Alaric was your friend, Auntie. You loved and admired him. So did Grandfather Cay and Uncle Varrus, and everyone else who knew him. I have been raised according to his teachings, and although I never really knew him, I know he was a simple, godly man, that he lived in the love of the Christ, and that his living was beyond reproach.

"All this I know, as I know that his entire being was dedicated to the propagation of the Church, Christ's Church. And yet here we are today, all of us in Britain, condemned and excommunicate because of his teachings and his beliefs, in spite of all his piety. That confounds me. What was his sin? What grievous offence against God was Alaric guilty of? He espoused the cause of Pelagius, whose teachings indicated that men have a God-given, divinely inspired nobility of soul, precisely because they were made in the Image of God!" Frustration threatened to overwhelm me, and I stopped to draw several deep breaths before I could resume. "My eternal salvation may depend upon it, Auntie, but I cannot accept an essential wrongness in that premise. God made man in His own Image and Likeness. Those are the basic tenets of the Church! And if that is so, then there is an element of the Divine in man, in his very nature. But now the men in Rome, the men who rule God's Church, have decided that their way, their definition, their interpretation of God's will, is more correct than the opinions of Pelagius, or Alaric, or any of the other British bishops who admire Pelagius's ideas. And to ensure they will have their way, they threaten all of us—this entire country—with eternal damnation! Faugh! It's disgusting!"

Her face was utterly devoid of expression, revealing neither censure nor endorsement. I plunged ahead. "And so, I think . . . No, I believe, I'm *convinced*, that this debate you speak of will be the most important event of its kind in this country's history. Germanus is a soldier, and to have been both a Legate and a friend of my father, he must be a good one. It follows logically, therefore, that he must be a pragmatist. I can't imagine him as a zealot of the kind we envision when we think of the new Roman clerics. And yet, by the same token, his must be a formidable mind, schooled in logic and theology as well as in military strategy and tactics. He will be a fearsome and ferocious debater, a prosecutor. He would not be coming, otherwise.

"This debate, Auntie, will be the arena in which all of the ideas, and the values, and the worthiness of Bishop Alaric, and Caius Britannicus, and Publius Varrus, and Picus Britannicus, and all their peers, will be either defended and exonerated, or attacked, vilified, condemned and proscribed. The Pelagian British against the Orthodox Romans. Heresy against dogma . . ." I paused, over-whelmed by the import of my own argument. "I have to go, Auntie. To Verulamium. I have to be there, to witness this, because after this event, in this four hundred and twenty-ninth year of Our Lord, no matter what the outcome may be, life in Britain will never be the same again. This entire land of ours, and all the people in it, will be on trial in this debate, not merely for their lives, but for their eternal souls."

When I had finished, the silence between us was long and profound. I slumped in my chair, slack-muscled, as though I had been involved in some strenuous, exhausting physical endeavour. Finally my aunt moved to pick up a small mallet and beat the gong on the table beside her chair. Her housekeeper appeared immediately.

"Martha, bring some wine for my nephew. The cold, sparkling kind from Gaul. Open a new jar from the ice house."

When Martha had gone, I asked, "Why have you no male servants, Auntie? You're no man-hater."

She smiled. "No, I simply prefer to have women around me. I have lived enough of my life in a male-dominated world. Women have different values, Caius, and I find I identify more easily with them, now that I am old." She paused, collecting her thoughts. "I wish your father had been here to listen to you today. He would be very proud."

"You think so? Thank you, Auntie."

"Now be quiet and let me think."

We sat again in companionable silence until Martha returned with my wine, which was delicious and icy. When she had served me and left again, my aunt said, "Of course you must go. I had intended to go myself, but I am too old and it is too far. You will be my deputy. But what about your Cassandra? You will be gone for months."

"I'll take her with me. It will be wonderful for her."

"All that way? And will you go alone? Just the two of you? All across Britain?"

"Well, no, not alone, that would be asking for trouble. But just a small party, strong enough to be secure."

"Against what? An encounter with a boatload of Saxon marauders?"

I frowned at her. "What are you suggesting, Auntie?"

She looked down and fingered a fold in her gown, keeping her gaze downcast as she said, "I may be interfering again in the matters of men, but you yourself said this debate would be—could be—the most important event in the history of Britain, Caius. Do you not think the style and substance of your attendance there, as our emissary from this western region, should be sufficient to substantiate the fact that there is a significant Christian presence here?"

"What? You mean . . . ?" I subsided, letting her unspoken suggestion filter through the clouds in my mind, and finally I had to smile, shaking my head in admiration. "You know, if I tend to forget that you are the sister of Caius Britannicus, and were married to Publius Varrus for decades, you always find a means of reminding me. You're brilliant, Auntie. And correct, needless to say. Camulod should attend this debate in full panoply. I will discuss it with Titus and Flavius, and we will put the matter to the Council immediately."

"Good. I thought you might." She smiled. "As soon, of course, as your male mind came around to it. Now, tomorrow, we will ride out together to your Avalon, just the two of us. The weather is beautiful, and I have need of fresh, spring air. And it's high time I had the chance to evaluate this little priestess of yours."

BOOK FOUR

Kings

XXIX

"The Senior Surgeon, Commander."

I followed Donuil's pointing finger with my eyes, to where Lucanus was climbing the hill towards us. He rode bent forward uncomfortably, his downcast eyes watching his horse's hooves as the beast picked its way cautiously among the stones and boulders littering the sloping hillside. He was still no more than half-way up, making hard going of it, and I smiled at the picture he made, recalling a comment written by Publius Varrus many years before describing his own discomfort on a horse's back. I turned back to Donuil.

"The good Lucanus is a brilliant surgeon and a fine physician, Donuil, but he's no cavalryman. He and you together must be the worst example of our military strength an enemy could see."

Donuil grinned at me, completely unabashed. "Ah, but then, Commander, we are not your military strength. The Surgeon will never have to execute his surgery from the back of a horse, so his skills won't suffer from his lack of comfort when perched on an animal's rump. I, on the other hand, being the naturally spirited creature that I am, am improving daily in spite of—and you yourself will admit this—the direst of circumstances. My very race dictates I have a natural law to overcome. If the gods had meant us Ersemen to ride horses, they would have filled Eire with the things."

I did not answer him. I was too busy scanning the meadow that lay below us. We were about to make our first road camp, and I had climbed this hill to survey the site I had selected, hoping to find it as ideal as it seemed from below. I was more than satisfied. "It's perfect," I said. "Now, I want the camp laid out down there as though we were on the plain in front of Camulod. Four equal areas oriented north and south, one for each squadron, the commissary and supply wagons in the middle, and the extra mounts there in the front, closest to the road. You follow me?" He nodded, and I raised my eyebrow, my only response. He flushed and nodded again, saluting me with his clenched fist.

"Your pardon. Aye, Commander. Four separate areas, as in Camulod, one to each squadron, the commissariat in the middle and the extra horses in front, at the south, between the camp and the road for safety."

"That's better. Please inform the squadron commanders."

He saluted again and rode off cautiously down the hill, although not quite so awkwardly as Lucanus, whom he passed on his way with a quick, distracted nod. I smiled as I watched him go, pleased with the way he was learning. It was against all his Hibernian training and background to submit to the kind of discipline I was exerting on him, but he was coping and coming to terms with it willingly.

Lucanus came up alongside me and reined in his animal, a placid beast specially chosen for him. He loosened his helmet, pulled it off and wiped the sweat from his brow with his bent elbow.

"On my oath, Britannicus, I will never understand why you people insist on wearing armour in weather like this. It's hot enough to melt flesh!"

I smiled, but didn't even bother to answer him. As Senior Surgeon, he, above all others, understood the military requirement for preparedness at all times. He watched me closely, waiting in vain for me to rise to his bait, and then swung his horse around to look down into the valley.

"They look good, don't they?"

"Aye, Lucanus, they do. And so they should. They are good. They're the best. Camulod's best, and that means the world's best, for my money."

On the road below us, our entire contingent was now in view, and they presented a pleasing picture of military correctness. The First Squadron, made up of our most experienced veterans, bore my great black and silver bear standard at their head—where the

Roman Eagle would have been in bygone days—along with their own regalia: a crimson standard featuring a white stag and surmounted by a spread of antlers. They rode in a tight-formation column, with their squadron and troop commanders in the lead, followed immediately by the two standard-bearers, and then the remainder of the squadron, four ranks abreast in files of ten. Fifty paces behind their rear rank came the Second Squadron, in similar formation, followed in turn by the water wagon—a large, pitch-sealed, cylindrical oaken tank, laid on its side and mounted on a wheeled platform, drawn by two horses. After that came the six great commissary wagons—huge, double-axled things with enormous, spoked wheels of hand-carved oak, rimmed with iron tires—each drawn by a team of six massive draft horses. Behind the wagons came the extra mounts, tight-herded by the young men whose only work was with the horses, until the time they earned promotion and began training as troopers. Behind the extra horses, far back from their dust, and protecting them from attack from the rear, came the Third and Fourth Squadrons, equal in size to the First and Second, but made up of less seasoned troops and leavened by older, well-hardened men. One hundred and seventy-five fighting men in all, including officers, and exclusive of the commissary staff and herd boys, who brought the total number to just over two hundred.

We watched in silence as they halted to await Donuil's approach, the commanders of the rearward squadrons riding to the head of the column to meet him. A series of shouted commands rose through the late afternoon air, and the First Squadron wheeled to the left and made their way from the road into the wooded meadow I had chosen as a campsite, crossing directly to the area designated for them. It took some time for the entire train to regroup in their allotted places, but then, at a shouted command, they all dismounted as one, and the open meadow was transformed as they set about making camp on this, the first night of the journey to Verulamium.

"Quite a difference from the old, walled infantry camp, isn't it?" Lucanus murmured.

"No, not really, not when you think about it, Luke," I responded, using the name he had asked me to call him once we became friends. "It's still the same basic design they used in ancient times— four divisions and two cross streets. The only real difference is that walls are unnecessary, and unwanted. The horses are the walls, all by themselves. We simply split the horses up into four or more groups and have their riders stay close by them. And we increase the areas between the squadrons to leave enough room to manoeuvre in the event of an attack. It merely looks different. The new format works the same way as the old one did, and for exactly the same old reason—the one that's seldom recognized, but always honoured."

Lucanus looked at me sidewise, sensing a trap. "Oh really? And what reason is that?"

"Mess call, Luke." I was smiling, but serious nonetheless. "Think about it. It's more than simply Roman discipline. Digging the ditch and building the walls each day on the march was originally a very real precaution against attack, but the routine continued centuries after peace had been established throughout the Empire. There came a time—and it lasted for centuries—when the odds against a Roman camp being attacked must have exceeded ten thousand to one, and yet the discipline persisted."

"Fine," he grunted eventually, when he realized I was waiting for him to ask. "I'll risk it. Why did it persist?"

"Because it had another purpose, rooted in certainty." I could see that he was bracing himself to be the butt of some joke of mine, eyeing me warily and prepared to come up with some quick and witty rejoinder. "No, I'm serious. Bear in mind that the only time a legionary had to himself was at the end of the day. A very large part of the punctilious tradition of Roman camps came from the simple fact that, after a hard day's march, the commissary people needed time to prepare dinner without being harassed by hungry men with nothing to do. So to get around that, the Army made it a rule that the soldiers had to dig a ditch and build a rampart every day, then pitch their tents, before they were released to eat and relax. Gave the cooks time to get dinner ready. Now our troopers have to unsaddle, groom, feed and water their mounts, clean and tend to their harness, pitch their own tents and build their own fires before they can eat. Still gives the cooks time to make dinner. And dinner on the march is the most important part of a soldier's life—infantry or cavalry."

"I suppose it is." Lucanus looked impressed. "It's certainly the most time-honoured. You can't buy that kind of security. And that reminds me," he went on, "speaking of buying, did you bring money?"

I turned to smile at him. "Aye, I brought money. Gold. It's in the quartermaster's wagon. Why?"

"Why not? The rest of the world still uses it, presumably, and we are going to pass through Londinium."

That sobered me. "We are indeed, Lucanus. We are indeed. I wonder what it will be like?"

He looked at me in puzzlement. "What? Londinium? Why should you wonder that? You've been there before, haven't you?"

I shook my head. "No, never. You have, I suppose?"

"Of course I have. I was there with your father, when Publius Varrus was brought there in chains by your grandfather."

"When they met Stilicho, you mean?"

"Yes."

"Luke, that was years before I was born! It has been thirty years since Stilicho went back to Rome."

"So? What does that have to do with anything, other than the compound fact that you're little more than a babe in arms and I'm not as young as I used to be?"

I shrugged. "It seems to me a lot might happen to a city in thirty years, without the Army there to keep order."

He dismissed that out of hand. "Nonsense, Caius. And anyway, the Army was there for at least a decade after Stilicho left. God, man, you're talking about the administrative centre of the Province, not some small hamlet filled with ignorant peasants. The civil authorities would have taken over immediately, when the Armies left. The *curiales* and the local magistracies and the Regional Councils. They were more than capable of maintaining order."

I ducked my head, conceding ignorance. "Well, you may be right, and I hope you are. But I remember what my father said about trying to enforce the law without the strength of the Army to back you up. Anyway, we'll find out in a matter of days. Three days, four at the most, if we can keep up this pace."

We had ridden forty miles that day, heading north from the Colony towards Aquae Sulis, but striking eastward at the intersection of the two main roads some thirty miles south of the town. We would spend the night here, in open meadowland beside a low-walled site that had been a march camp for centuries, and we would reach Sorviodunum, the first town on our route, by mid-afternoon. Our outward journey would take us north-east via Sorviodunum, the town the Celts called Sarum, to Silchester, then to Pontes, and on to Londinium. From there we would head straight north to Verulamium along the oldest road in all of Britain. We would return along a westerly route, by way of Alchester, Corinium and Aquae Sulis, completing a rough circle and showing our presence across the entire interior of South Britain while keeping well clear of the coastal areas where there were rumoured to be heavy concentrations of entrenched Saxons.

Lucanus put his helmet back on his head. "The lads are keen," he said, nodding down to the meadow. "They're in good spirits."

He was right. The camp was already taking shape below us, as the troopers finished stringing their harnessing lines and tethered their horses in rows, leaving enough room between animals for each rider to work unhampered by his neighbours on either side as he unsaddled his mount and looked to the animal's needs.

Some of the herd boys had begun to move among them, carrying bins of oats from one of the commissary wagons, while others were replenishing the water wagon's tank from the nearby brook and preparing to distribute the animals' drinking water. The remainder were attending to the tethering of the spare mounts, in the protected area directly to the south of the central crossway, closest to the road. Each horse carried its own nose-bag and leather water bucket in its saddlebags. The commissariat had been set up in the central space, equidistant from each of the four squadron encampments, with enough space surrounding it for the men to spread out and eat on the grass in comfort, if the weather was fine, or to deploy into formation around it rapidly, in the event of an emergency, without undue confusion.

I remembered the night my father had designed the layout, emphasising the need for both disciplined formality and adaptable elasticity. His original design had been for a camp of four

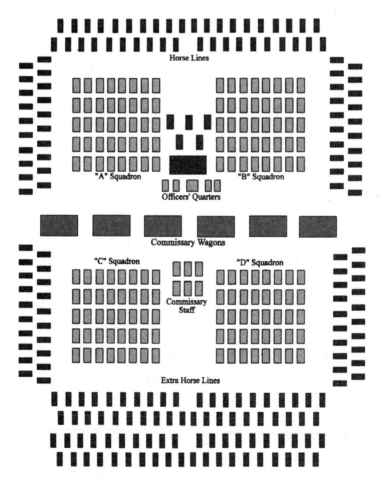

Camulodian Cavalry Encampment

squadrons of forty men and horses. Lesser numbers could be accommodated at individual commanders' discretion, but any force greater than three squadrons in strength could begin to present problems in disposition, dispersal and discipline.

My father's new camp formation permitted expansion to accommodate any number of squadrons, and was based on a checkerboard scheme, with the commanders quartered between the First and Second Squadrons, and the commissary staff between the Third and Fourth. I could see it clearly taking shape in the space beneath our perch on the hilltop, and I can still visualize it today. It was a shape that was famed in this land, but that has not been seen in decades and may never be seen again.

Later that night I lay awake in my cot, listening to the voices of my men, still grouped around their fires, and to the infinitely varied noises of the camp. I was pleasantly tired, but far from sleepy, and as I lay there, enjoying the comfort and the peace, my thoughts drifted through a review of everything that had happened in the past few months since the night my aunt had convinced me that Camulod should attend the Verulamian Debate in grand style.

Once convinced her advice was valid, I had not procrastinated. I thought carefully about what I had to say, and brought the results of my deliberations to the first full meeting of the Council that followed. I had argued my case eloquently, I thought at the time, and had convinced everyone of the merit of Aunt Luceiia's contentions. The vote in favour of my recommendations was unanimous, and we began making preparations immediately.

It was natural, I suppose, that everyone who heard about it, from Councillors to trainee troopers, wanted to join the excursion, but the criteria governing the expedition and its personnel were decreed absolute from the outset: this was to be a military delegation, in all of its aspects. The main objective of the exercise, apart from the obvious one of representing the concerned but cohesive and self-sufficient Christian community in the far west, was to demonstrate our military capabilities to everyone with eyes to see it. For that reason, no civilian supernumeraries would accompany the expedition. I alone would represent Camulod as Commander and spokesman. For exactly the same reason, reinforced by the solid, enlightened thinking of the Legate Titus, every trooper and every officer in the train had to *earn* his place.

Four brand-new, elite cavalry squadrons would be formed from the mass of Camulod's forces, and only the best in their own categories would qualify. That, we decided, was fair, since it provided the opportunity for every man, from the rawest recruit to the most seasoned veteran, to vie for a place of honour in an appropriate squadron. Since competition among officers for the same type of honours would have been *infra dignitatem*, the squadron and troop commanders were selected by lot in Council and announced with much fanfare. Titus, Flavius and I myself saw to it that only the names of the very finest of our commanders were submitted, so we were sure that the chosen officers would be well received.

The competition that began immediately for inclusion in the ranks of the four squadrons did wonders for the flagging morale that had threatened us after Lot's near-capture of the fortress. Old rivalries were revived and new ones came into being overnight. The dust clouds over the great plain below the hill never settled, as squadrons and mounted troopers in twos and threes drilled, wheeled and manoeuvred at all hours until, eventually, the ranks of the new squadrons were filled and the squadron colours decided on and distributed.

I had far less trouble deciding on the composition of our squadrons than I had on the matter of whether or not Cassandra should accompany us to Verulamium. I wanted passionately to take her with me, but the current composition of our party—all men and all soldiers—had presented unforeseen complications to that, and I had not yet made up my mind on the day when, at her own insistence, I led my aunt slowly down the path into our hidden valley, holding her aged but still strong hand all the way, lest she slip and fall.

As on most occasions, Cassandra surprised me by running to meet me, her face a portrait of delight. She stopped short, however,

when she saw my companion, blushing in confusion and embarrassment. Aunt Luceiia, on the other hand, was well prepared for
this encounter. She had evidently given much thought to how she
would behave in order to put Cassandra at her ease, and she went
straight ahead and embraced the girl, motioning me to come and
join them and share the embrace.

Later, while Cassandra was cooking, my aunt said to me, "So,
Nephew, you have impressed me, in spite of myself. I had suspected that this young woman might be more than simply *special*,
in the sense that young lovers use the word, but she is utterly
delightful, far ahead of what I had anticipated. And as for your
stated opinion on her breeding, you are completely wrong. This
child is no peasant, nor were her people. We may never know her
true background, but there is a nobility in the girl. She is far too
good for you, libertine that you are. You still intend to take her
with you to Verulamium?"

Luxuriating in her approval of my love, I was surprised by her
question. "Of course, Auntie. I wouldn't dream of going without
her." My decision was that swift and that simple.

"Hmm. And when will you leave?"

"Late in July—early August at the latest. But you know that."

"Yes, Nephew, I do."

"Then why did you ask?"

She looked me straight in the eye and shook her head in wonderment. "I asked because I cannot believe the obtuseness of men."

"Obtuseness?" My face must have been a picture of bewilderment. "What did I say? How am I being obtuse?"

She shook her head again, but her voice was gentler when
she said, "Your obtuseness, Nephew, lies in your failure to see that
by August, your Cassandra will be within two months of having
your child."

I was thunderstruck! I gaped and spluttered and floundered,
cursing my own blind stupidity. Of course she was pregnant! How
could I not have seen it before this? And through all of these revelations, Cassandra worked away at preparing our meal, unaware

of the consternation behind her back, until I calmed myself eventually and swung her around to kiss her gently, placing my hand on her belly. Then she knew I knew, and her eyes filled with tears of happiness.

Of course, from that point on, there was no question of her accompanying me to Verulamium. There would have been no question of my going either, had Aunt Luceiia not immediately set about convincing me that it was my duty to go. Cassandra would be safe, she promised me, while I was gone. She herself would persuade Cassandra to return with us to Camulod, to marry me legally and to await the birth of our child. By the time I returned from my Verulamium pilgrimage, my wife and child would both be awaiting me, healthy and happy. I believed her, and I returned to Camulod alone.

XXX

Aunt Luceiia remained alone in our valley with Cassandra for a full week. When I returned at the end of that time, I did so in a light, two-wheeled gig that could easily accommodate all three of us plus our baggage and all Cassandra's belongings on the return journey. Quite simply, it had never even occurred to me that my aunt's campaign to win Cassandra back to Camulod might be unsuccessful, since the love and respect they had demonstrated for each other from the outset was total and absolute, and their ability to communicate with each other without words seemed to me little short of magical.

Our entry into Camulod, later that same day, caused a mighty stir. The young woman who sat so calmly erect by my side, between my aunt and me, bore not the remotest resemblance to the half-starved waif who had returned, riding behind Uther, from that distant patrol, and no one recognized her. Nevertheless, the sight of her, the beauty and the strangeness of her, gave rise to an instant seething of speculation and gossip, which neither my aunt nor I relieved in any way. I, for one, had much more on my mind than idle rumours and conjecture.

I had been bracing myself for trouble for two full weeks, ever since I accepted that Cassandra would really be returning to Camulod. Suddenly uncomfortable with my cousin's continuing absence from the fort—a condition that had, until then, been pleasing to me in my ambivalent frame of mind—I had begun willing Uther to return immediately, preparing myself for the inevitable confrontation between him and Cassandra. I was determined to bring them face to face without warning, knowing that only then, in his complete surprise, could I read Uther's guilt or innocence with conviction. As it turned out, however, that resolution was to remain unattainable. Uther was nowhere near Camulod when I brought Cassandra back. To the best of our knowledge, he had not left his Pendragon lands since returning there after his father's death. There had been no news of him since his departure, nor had anyone had any indication when he might return to Camulod. He might, for all we knew, already be campaigning against Lot, far to the south-west in Cornwall.

Irrespective, however, of my readiness to test Uther's response to the sight of Cassandra, I was totally unprepared for Donuil's reaction.

We had been back in my aunt's house for several hours, and I had shared Cassandra's conducted tour of the establishment, enjoying her pleasure and wonder at the richness of the house and its appointments, seeing it myself through her eyes as though for the first time. She had finally retired, ushered by a gaggle of my aunt's serving women, to bathe and change her clothes, and I was banished from their company. I sent a trooper to find Donuil and tell him I was back and to bring me any work that had to be done.

An hour later, I was hard at work, whispering the words to myself as I fretted over the appalling syntax of a report written by one of our Councillors and dealing with the variety and distribution of the crops being grown throughout the Colony's holdings. It was a dreadful and depressing task, and I was schooling myself to be patient, resisting a growing urge to call the writer of this mess into my presence and excoriate him, when an ungodly clatter made me leap like a faun. Donuil had been perched across from me on a high stool, polishing my parade breastplate. Now he was on his feet, stiff as a board, his face waxen, wide eyes staring at some point behind my head, and my best armour rolling noisily on the floor at his feet. I turned to follow his stricken gaze, and saw Cassandra standing by the open doorway behind me, peering backward over her shoulder at something in the hallway behind her. As I looked, too startled yet to speak, she turned back towards me and her eyes fell on Donuil. Her whole face altered instantly into an expression of astounded disbelief, and then splintered into an instant, joyful smile of recognition.

Donuil continued to stand there as though petrified for several more long moments, and then he lurched toward her, walking stiff-legged, his mouth hanging open, a look of awe mixed with fear on his face. When he reached her, he stopped short of touching her and fell heavily to both knees, reaching out his hands to her. Radiant, she gave him both her hands, and he stooped his head to kiss them, but she was already pulling him to his feet, clasping her arms tightly around his neck and kissing him wildly on the face, the eyes and the forehead.

As I watched this astonishing sequence of events, I was aware of an equally astounding rush of conflicting emotions. In a few brief moments I felt fear, suspicion, jealousy and a sudden rage that blanketed all the other feelings and quickly threatened to overpower me. Then all of these left me as suddenly as they had sprung into being, when big, ferocious Donuil turned to me, his eyes running with tears, and whispered in a choking voice, *"Dear dree*, Commander, it's *dear dree."* Then he turned again and fell to his knees a second time, throwing his arms around my beloved's hips and burying his face in her bosom, his shoulders shuddering with sobs.

His words made no sense to me, but his actions, his possessiveness, filled me with a sense of doom. I stood up slowly from my chair and walked towards the two of them, my gaze shifting from Donuil to Cassandra, who was now also in tears. She watched me approach, but made no move to disengage her protective arms from around Donuil's head, hugging him to the soft fullness of her breasts. I felt my anger surging back, stronger than before, but she looked at me and smiled lovingly through her tears, and my flowering rage wilted as my confusion increased.

"Donuil?" I asked, hearing my own voice, low and wondering yet filled with menace. "What is it, Donuil? This *dree?* What is *dear dree?* Do you know this woman?" I can remember thinking that

I had never heard myself sound so foolish. If there were anything certain on the face of the earth, it was this man's knowledge of this woman.

He turned his head to face me again, peering at me through the cradle of her arms, and his voice came to me muffled by her sleeves. This time, however, I understood every word he said. "It's Deirdre, Commander. We thought she was dead. My sister, Deirdre."

My sister, Deirdre! Shocked beyond credence, I literally pulled the two of them apart from each other, holding them at arm's length as I stared from one face into the other, moving my head rapidly from side to side as I compared his big face with her small one, and seeing the resemblance immediately. Brother and sister! I let fall their arms and walked away to the closest couch, where I collapsed, my heart pounding in my ears.

Cassandra was beside me immediately, her eyes filled now with concern for me, her brother abandoned on his knees in the doorway. I touched her cheek, brushing away her tears, and gently took her in my arms, cradling her and warming her with a sudden overflowing of love that was mixed with guilt over my conflicting reactions to what I had seen. Donuil knelt still, staring at us, incomprehension in his eyes.

It took almost an entire day for us to assemble the story into what had to be its truthful form, mainly because the only two of us who could speak were each having trouble accepting and believing the other's explanation of his involvement. Donuil could not accept that I had known his sister for months before I met him, nor could he believe that he could have been so close to his sister for so long without having any inkling of her existence. For my part, I was simply stunned to be faced with the truth about Cassandra, who was Cassandra no longer. I was also amazed to see her conversing fluently and rapidly with Donuil in a silent language of hand-signals that meant nothing and less than nothing to me, apart from the dumfounding truth that Cassandra was an eloquent and fluent conversationalist!

It was only later that I realized they were conversing in Erse, which explained why Cassandra and I had never been able to communicate. Being deaf and mute, she had never heard my Latin language, and so the movements of my lips, framing the sounds I made, were completely alien to her understanding. I, on the other hand, had presupposed her to be from Britain. It had never crossed my mind she might be Hibernian. How could it have? And what difference would that have made? Finally, however, I accepted the truths that had been thrust upon me and, with them, a new understanding of my beloved Cassandra, who had been Deirdre all her life. And I accepted, with intense excitement, the knowledge that I would be able to learn the hand-language she and Donuil used so expertly. I devoured everything Donuil had to tell me about her, and about her early life.

As a child, he told me, she had been known as Deirdre of the Lilac Eyes, the darling and favourite of her father, Athol, High King of the Scots of Hibernia. Her unformed beauty had even then been legendary because of her colouring, and her suitors had been many and wealthy. Her mane of flowing, red-gold hair, her milk-white skin and her startling, lilac-violet eyes had marked her as one blessed by the gods, and that blessing would pass on to the man who became her husband. Even today, in speaking of his sister's beauty, Donuil's voice was so hushed and awestruck that, in spite of my love for his sister and my longing to learn everything of her, I grew embarrassed for him.

Cassandra had been my love for long, golden months. Donuil's Deirdre, on the other hand, held no sway in my heart. And therein lay the cause of my embarrassment: I could see no commonality between my Cassandra and Donuil's Deirdre. The woman I loved was no flaming, red-golden-haired beauty with violet eyes. Her hair was long and lustrous, but it was fair, and no more than that— not golden, and with no trace of red. Nor were her eyes purple, or violet, or even lilac; they were huge and silvery, granite grey, almost completely colourless in any normal sense, yet changing to the palest of blue in certain lights. Eventually, in a mood of great discomfort, I said as much to Donuil.

He stared at me, wide-eyed, and waited for me to say more, but I had no more to say.

"So," he asked, eventually, "what are you saying, Commander?"

"What am I saying?" I put down my cup and looked at him in amazement, wondering how he could ask me anything so obvious. I pointed to his sister, who sat opposite me, her gaze moving from one to the other of us as we spoke. "Donuil, the girl you are describing from your memories bears no resemblance to this woman sitting here. Not the slightest, can't you see that?" He blinked at me, looking confused, and Deirdre leaned forward intently, looking from him to me. Her fingers began to fly, and he gazed at them, deciphering her meaning, and then his face cleared.

"Deirdre says to tell you about the sickness. But, Commander, you know about that! I've been talking about the way she was before the sickness. It was only after that she changed."

"Sickness? What sickness? And what should I know of it? We've had no talk of sickness, Donuil. You're saying a sickness changed her?" I looked intently at Cassandra, who gazed solemnly back at me from great, pale grey eyes. "A sickness changed the colour of her hair and eyes? Donuil, are you talking about magic again?"

"Aye, Commander Merlyn, I am." He nodded and his gaze was as unblinking as his sister's. "And my sister is the living proof of its existence."

I moved across to share Cassandra's couch, drawing her into the bend of my arm and kissing her temple, looking across the top of her head at her brother. "Tell me," I said. The story he told me was a strange and wondrous one, and I believed it, word for word. Whether it told of magic or not, however, is something I cannot say, even to this day.

On Midsummer's Day, in the ninth year of little Deirdre's life, through the freakish anger of some Erse god, the light of high summer had been almost completely eclipsed by the darkness of an enormous storm that uprooted trees and blew down buildings and caused rivers to overflow their banks, flooding fields and houses. Scores of people were killed and hundreds injured, and cattle drowned by the dozens. And in the middle of the confusion, young Deirdre of the Lilac Eyes disappeared.

Her father's men searched for her in the aftermath of the great storm, hunting high and low for three days, at the end of which they pronounced her dead. And as they were preparing her funeral rites, she walked into the middle of them, dazed, with eyes staring.

They dried and cleaned her and put her to bed, and her father's finest healers cared for her, feeding her potions to break the fever that racked her. Watched over and protected by the tribal priests, the child tossed and turned for four days and her fever persisted, burning up her tiny body and ravaging her reserves of strength. Then, on the fifth day after her return, the fever receded and she awoke and described, with crystal clarity, the place where she had been during the storm. She told of a rocky cavern, reached by a passage slanting downward from a cave on the side of a hill, and filled with skeletons and treasures. When questioned as to how she had reached this hillside, who had shown her the place and why she had gone, she would not answer, but she described the route she had taken, and the landmarks that marked the way.

Her father Athol sent a group of warriors immediately to seek this place, and they found it without difficulty, although more miles away than they had thought to look. And they found the skeletons, and the treasure—a hoard of ancient weapons made mostly of bronze, and bars of gold, silver and iron, as well as jewellery.

In the meantime, however, even before the searchers had set out, Deirdre's fever returned, more virulent than ever, and the child fell rapidly towards death. The fever rose and rose, beyond the point where any healer had ever known a fever go without causing death, and then it levelled off and stayed at that pitch for days. The flesh fell, almost visibly, from the child's body until nothing was left but bone and sinew. The priests and healers tried everything to keep the child hydrated. They bathed her constantly. They fed her with water sweetened with honey, administered through tubes of animal intestines fed down her throat. And they waited for her to die.

But she did not die. She hovered on the edge of death for six full weeks, and then she began to recover. She regained her weight and her strength and her smile. But her hair had lost its colour and so, to the horror of everyone who saw it, had her eyes. People began to whisper, and then to say aloud that Deirdre of the Lilac Eyes had died, and had been replaced by a changeling. And the only person who might ever have convinced them that the truth was different—the child herself—made no attempt to do so. She came back from her illness to live an alien life among them. She never responded to their voices and she never spoke again.

In spite of the fact that they had all benefited by the child's experiences and been enriched by the treasures of the cavern she had found, her people grew more and more afraid, as people will, of what they saw as her magical experiences. As time passed and the strangeness of the changes in her became more and more widely known, the word was put about that she had been accursed, and that no good would come to anyone associated with her. The treasure, people whispered, was but the god's replacement fee for having abducted the child. It was obvious, they said, that the child had fallen—or been cast down—from being blessed by the gods. From being a child beloved by all, she became a creature feared without cause and shunned by all but those who loved her most dearly— her father Athol, and her favourite brother, Donuil.

In the aftermath of the illness, unable to understand what had happened to her, but convinced that she was still his beloved sister, Donuil had spent long hours and days with the child, learning again, from the beginning, how to communicate with her. He learned that her mind had emerged unscathed from her illness, that her soul, the essence that made her who she was, had remained intact. And, over the next five years, they had developed the hand-language they used between them. At the end of that time, Deirdre had fallen sick again, although not so seriously. She had developed a fever and had taken to her bed. The following afternoon, while

428   JACK WHYTE

Donuil and his father were hunting, she had disappeared again, unseen by anyone, and this time she had not returned. They had all assumed her dead, until today, five years later. And now I had to sit in silence, seething with impatience, while Donuil learned the story of his sister's disappearance, by watching and translating the messages of her flying fingers.

It was a story that did not take long in the telling, although there were aspects of it that were both confusing and mystifying. In listening to Donuil's translation of what his sister's hands were telling him, I was frustrated by my inability to question her directly. There was far more to her story, I felt, than what she was telling us, but I had no way of asking her for more details, not knowing what details there were to be added.

She remembered nothing of her second illness, nothing at all. She had no memory of leaving her bed or her father's hall. She knew only that she had awakened one bright summer morning among complete strangers who, by their familiar treatment of her, were obviously not strangers at all. These people knew her extremely well, although she had no recollection of ever having seen them before. They knew, for example, that she could neither speak nor hear, and they communicated with her by touch and by broad hand-signals. Their treatment of her was rough, but neither intolerant nor unkind, and yet she was treated as a servant, a menial. Knowing who she was, but not how she had come to be where she was, Deirdre had tried to run away from the encampment that night, but she had been caught without difficulty and put directly to work, performing tasks that were strange to her, but to which her body responded with the ease of long practice.

She had noticed her clothes, too. They were alien and coarse, but they clung comfortably to her body with the ease of long wear and they were very obviously hers. Frightened and confused, she suspected that she was no longer in the land her father ruled, but she had no idea where else she might be. She had never travelled beyond her father's lands.

Days later, she came face to face with her own reflection in a bronze mirror and fainted dead away with terror. She did not recognize the face she had seen. It was a woman's face. Hers had been a girl's. A second, fearful look had convinced her that she had not lost her mind and was not insane, but that somehow, by some evil magic, she had lost much of her self; she had lost years of her life, during which she had grown from being a child to being a woman, with no knowledge of the change or the passing years. And now she lived a life of silence among strangers.

She shared the lives of two particular strangers, a man and a woman who fed her and sheltered her. The man was a pedlar, the woman a herbal healer, and they were constantly travelling, selling his wares and her skills throughout the countryside. Deirdre's main job was to help the woman gather her herbs and simples, although sometimes she would help the man with his goods, carrying burdens like a pack animal. And sometimes, when the mood was upon him, the man would come to her bed and use her sexually, without passion, and she permitted this without thought, because she knew, somehow, it had always been thus.

And then one day, without any warning, the man had fallen sick. The woman came down with the same sickness the following day, and Deirdre had nursed them both until they died, within hours of each other. She had been kneeling by their bodies hours later when Uther and I passed by and found her.

I do not know how long I lay awake in camp that night, remembering. I know only that the camp had quieted without my noticing, and only the occasional whickering of a horse broke the silence before I fell asleep.

XXXI

We set out jauntily on the second day of our march, filled with well-being, and confident of reaching Sorviodunum by mid-afternoon. The sun, too, began its journey across the new day's sky bravely, blinding us as we rode directly into its brilliance, but the sky behind us in the west soon filled with banked clouds that outmarched both us and the sun. By mid-morning the brightness had gone from the day, and by noon we were riding through rain squalls that followed each other like yoked oxen, ever more frequently until the rain fell relentlessly and stayed with us all the way to Sorviodunum.

I do not know what we had expected to find in Sorviodunum, but I remember that the town's dreary dilapidation appalled all of us. It was a town in name alone, in that it was a large concentration of buildings, many of which had been public edifices at one time and more of which had been the homes of townsfolk. Now almost all the buildings were in ruins and the citizens—we used the word reluctantly—ran in terror from our approach. Needless to say, we found no food to purchase. We camped overnight in an overgrown field outside the town and moved on at daybreak.

Fortunately for our spirits, the weather had improved overnight and we were greeted once again by clear skies come daybreak. We made good time from then on, meeting no one on the road, so that, in time, my unease over the deterioration of the once-fine town of Sorviodunum began to dwindle. The weather continued pleasant, with no more of the rain that had fallen on our second day out of Camulod. We skirted the tiny town of Silchester completely, making no attempt to approach it, and eventually came to Pontes, the last remaining town between us and Londinium.

Here we found signs of life aplenty, but they were not signs that I responded to with warmth.

As soon as the townspeople saw us approaching, they withdrew behind their walls and barred their gates, refusing us entry. Seeing that they feared our strength, and respecting their fear, I held our men at a distance and approached the walls alone, seeking to speak with someone in authority. That was useless. No one would speak with me, even from the safety of the walls, in spite of every protestation I could offer them. Eventually, seething with anger and frustration, and controlling a very strong urge to provide them with real reason to fear us, I accepted the futility of the situation and led my people away from there as quickly as I could, riding in a black rage that kept my subordinates intent upon not catching my eye and thereby attracting my displeasure.

Only Donuil and Lucanus had the confidence to impose their presence on my bitter mood. Donuil rode in silence, slightly behind me, his horse's nose level with my right knee, close enough for me to address him should I wish to, yet just far enough removed for me to ignore him, as I chose to. Lucanus, on the other hand, stayed away and allowed me to stew for the space of an hour, but then he cantered forward and demanded my attention.

"Why are you so angry?"

I jerked my head towards him, attempting to wither him with a look, but he would not be intimidated. I looked back at the road ahead and rode on in silence. He spoke again.

"They were afraid."

That was so obvious that I still did not deign to answer him. He tried again.

"You're acting as if those people back there had insulted you personally. Is your pride that fragile?" I glanced sideways at him again, silently consigning him to Hades as a persistent nuisance. "Caius!" He was almost laughing. "In God's name, you'd probably have done the same thing, in their shoes. They're vulnerable—and terrified."

Now the anger spilled from my mouth. "Of what?" I jerked my head backwards, indicating the ranks and files behind us. "Do we look like Saxons? Is this an undisciplined rabble, looking for rape and plunder? Did they take me for a marauder, a raiding thief?" I saw immediately from the shock on his face that this response was totally unexpected. He opened his mouth to respond, but I gave him no opportunity. "Damnation, Luke, that's the third town in four days I've had to bypass! We were supposed to eat there tonight—at the very least, we were supposed to reprovision! Our commissary isn't set up to feed two hundred men and their horses all the way from Camulod to Verulamium. That's why we are carrying money! It was part of our operational planning to purchase rations along the way. There was never any question of having to be entirely self-sufficient! Had I known—or even suspected—that the towns along our route would be in the condition they are in, or that any of them would close their gates to us, I would have done things very differently."

"Ah, I see. You're feeling guilty."

"No! Dammit, why should I feel guilty? There was no way I could have known this would happen."

"Correct, except that, as Commander, it's your responsibility to anticipate things like that. Isn't that so?"

It was one thing for me to berate myself for my shortsighted-ness. It was quite another to have to hear about it from a subordi-nate. I had to bite back a surge of petulance before my good sense reasserted itself and I was able to identify the tone of his voice as being sympathetic. I looked at him again.

"Yes," I answered. "It is."

"Horse turds, Commander." I blinked in surprise and he kneed his mount closer to mine. "You can no more be held responsible for those towns than you can for failing to anticipate the situation in Londinium."

"What situation in Londinium?"

He shrugged. "I don't know, any more than you can be expected to. I haven't been there in thirty years."

I felt the anger swell up in me again, born this time of his apparent frivolity. "Damn you, Luke, this is no matter for foolery. We are seriously short of provisions."

"I'm being completely serious, Caius. We may fare no better at Londinium than we have elsewhere."

"I doubt it," I snapped. "But first we have to reach the place, if we don't all starve first. We'll reprovision there and buy enough to carry us to Verulamium. As you yourself pointed out, it's the administrative centre of Britain!"

Now, however, Lucanus shook his head. "No. That's what I told you the day before yesterday. But I've been thinking since then about everything I said to you that day, and I now admit I was probably talking nonsense. My heart, not my head, was ruling my thoughts. I think now we'll find *you* were the one whose guess was more accurate. Londinium by now will be just a town like any of the others we have seen—bigger, but probably no better off. In spite of what I might like to believe, you were right and the past days have proved it. Britain is no longer an imperial province, Caius, and Londinium's no longer Roman."

I stared at him. "What are you hinting at, Luke?"

"I'm not hinting, I'm simply restating the fact you brought home to me the other day. It has been twenty years since the last Romans left. Londinium will no longer be the Londinium I knew. You've never been there, and I haven't seen it since the armies left, but twenty years can bring a lot of changes.

"The engineers are all gone, long ago, as are the magistrates and governors. Now, as a physician, I have had to ask myself who has been running the water and sewage systems for the past two decades? Who's been collecting taxes to maintain the public works? If I allowed my imagination free rein, I could frighten both of us with thoughts of plague and pestilence." He paused, and when he resumed, his voice was lower, more introspective. "I think both of us may have been expecting great things of Londinium, Caius, in different ways, and I think we are both due for a grievous disappointment."

I heard hoofbeats approaching quickly from the rear. It was a messenger from the First Squadron to remind me that the men had not dismounted in almost four hours. I grunted acknowledgement and sent him back to his commander with word to rest, feed the troops and water the horses.

As the column halted and began to dismount, I nodded to Lucanus to accompany me and rode off the road. The fields surrounding Pontes had been few in number, small and ill maintained, and had petered out within a mile of the town. Since then, we had been riding through dense forest that hemmed us in tightly on both sides. The broad, cleared ditches that had originally protected the roadsides had long since disappeared without trace. Now the space they had occupied was choked with thick shrubs, bushes and mature trees. For the past half-mile, however, the trees had begun to thin out, and now we were flanked on both sides by a large, grassy clearing, strewn with the charred remnants of an old forest fire. I aimed my horse towards a pile of boulders about fifty paces from the roadside, and there we dismounted and climbed up to sit on the rocks.

When Lucanus had made himself comfortable beside me, we shared a drink from my water bottle. I watched him as he drank. "Were you serious about plague?"

He grunted and shook his head, lowering the flask. "No, of course not. I was simply being an alarmist. It's a pessimism born of my profession. We have absolutely no reason to suspect any such thing."

I was disconcerted, nonetheless, and his denial did not reassure me. I cleared my throat, hoping to clear my mind with it, and continued. "Well, let's suppose you're right and Londinium's a mess. What can we do?"

He replaced the stopper in the flask and handed it back to me. "About what? Provisions? Nothing we can do, except try to forage elsewhere. There's still game in the forests and fish in the streams, and the horses can still graze."

"And what about the remainder of our journey? If there's no food available in Londinium, then things might well be the same in Verulamium, too. This whole adventure could be a fiasco. Our objective is to demonstrate our strength and presence. If all the towns are abandoned, or closed to us, our time and effort will be wasted. Should we abort now? Turn around and go home?"

He thought about that for some time, mulling over the pros and cons as I was doing. Finally he shook his head. "I would say no. Bear in mind the word was sent out that the debate would be held in Verulamium. It would seem reasonable that arrangements have been made there to house the people coming from all over to attend." He paused. "In the final analysis, we will know nothing about Londinium until we arrive there."

He dug a small pouch out of the scrip by his side and tipped some shelled hazelnuts into his palm before offering the pouch to me. I shook a few into my hand and began popping them into my mouth, one at a time. The silence between us stretched, each of us engrossed in his own thoughts. I looked at the troopers who had dismounted all around us. They had filled every inch of space in the clearing, it seemed, and were sitting, lying or walking around, according to preference, all trying to rid themselves of saddle sore-ness. Most of them were very young. If I were leading them into a wasteland . . . if Lucanus were correct and Londinium lay empty or, God forbid, filled with pestilence, many of them might not return home, and the responsibility would be mine. Luke had dropped the thought of plague into my head, and now I could not ignore it. I had recognized his reference to public works and the difficulty of maintaining them; stagnant waters, particularly in congested urban areas, bred plague and pestilence. My mind conjured a vision of bleak, lightless streets littered with swollen corpses. Committing my men to die in battle, should the need arise, would cost me not a moment's discomfort. But the thought of leading them like sheep into a filthy, plague-ridden town, to die in agony and filth and squalor, with no more dignity than rabid rats, appalled me. And suddenly my mind was made up.

"Can we bypass Londinium and go directly to Verulamium?"

Lucanus shook his head briefly. "No. Not easily."

"Why not?"

He shrugged his shoulders. "Our horses, and the river, the Thamis. We crossed it two days ago, when it was narrow. Now we're on the wrong side of it and it's too broad to swim and too deep to ford. We have to bridge it and the only bridge is at Londinium."

"What about a ferry?"

He shook his head again. "I doubt we'd find one big enough. We have two hundred men and two hundred horses, and wagons. That's a big river, Caius, probably bigger than you've ever seen."

"Damnation!" I rose to my feet. "Very well, here's my decision." I looked around me again, at the trees that hemmed us in. "As soon as we get out of this forest, if we ever do, I want to get off the road. We'll travel overland. That will allow us to hunt as we travel, so we can feed the men. If we come across any farms that look even remotely prosperous, we'll buy grain for the horses, otherwise they can graze as we move.

"When we approach Londinium, we will stop and make camp. Then I myself will go into the town—"

"With a suitably armed escort."

"Right, with a small party, to check conditions for myself before we lead the men in. I'll try to find out what's happening in Verulamium—somebody should know—and when I think the way is clear, I'll send word back for you to bring in the remainder of the party. We'll get to the other side of the river as quickly as possible, and strike north immediately for Verulamium."

He stared at me for several moments and then nodded agreement save for one minor proviso: he would ride with me into Londinium. He would not trust me, he said, to recognize a rampant plague even if the stench of it overpowered me.

About ten miles further on, we emerged from the forest. We had been on a gradual but definite gradient for five miles by that point, and the trees petered out quite abruptly, giving way to high, rolling moorland. We had not seen another living soul since leaving Pontes. I gave the signal to leave the road, and we swung north-east, making good time over hard, grassy ground for the rest of the day.

We stopped late in the afternoon and made camp in a lush, grass-filled meadow by the side of a clear, fast-flowing brook. I had sent out a hunting party earlier to range ahead of us, and they had fared well, bringing back three fair-sized deer and a huge wild pig.

The commissary people set about their business immediately, and soon the smells of roasting meat filled the air and set everyone's stomach juices churning in anticipation of the feast.

The following morning, the weather held fine, sunny with only occasional showers, and again we made good progress. Donuil was a huddled clump of misery as he was each morning, his long body still unused to riding great distances every day. He swayed wordlessly on his horse's back as he followed close behind me, and I took care to require no errands of him before noon, knowing that as the day progressed, he would regain control of his loosening muscles and begin to improve visibly. It happened every day, and each day the recuperative process took up slightly less time.

By early afternoon he was talking again, his usual, cheerful banter, and I had started to believe there might be a real chance of making a horseman of him after all. We were riding together at the head of the column, enjoying an unusually long spell of sunshine between squalls, when Donuil, whose eyes were far keener than anyone else's in the group, picked up a movement on the ridge far ahead of us.

"Someone coming, Commander." He nodded towards the movement he had seen. "Straight ahead. Must be some of our scouts."

"How many?" I could see nothing but I did not doubt him.

He screwed up his eyes, concentrating, and it was several moments before he answered, "One. It's Orvic."

I glanced at him, irrationally irritated by this evidence of his amazing visual superiority.

"Damnation, Donuil, how can you know that? I can't even see him moving yet!"

He smiled, his eyes still on the approaching figure. "It is Orvic, Commander, and his hounds. That's why I thought at first there might be more than one man."

I saw them then, the tall, long-haired, long-legged Cambrian Celt with his golden torc around his neck, and his three great wolfhounds ranging around him. He was a distant kinsman of mine, a nephew of my grandfather, Ullic Pendragon. Orvic was a man unique even among his unique clan, for he was renowned as both fighter and hunter, yet even more famed for his skills as a bard and as a breeder of wolfhounds. He had decided that he would ride with us to Verulamium to attend the debate. He was no Christian and had no interest in the theology to be debated, but he had never visited that part of the country and he had thought it fitting that we should allow him to escort us.

When he rode up, we exchanged greetings and then waited for him to tell us why he had come back. I had long since accepted the futility of trying to rush Orvic in anything, but he came to the point with surprising swiftness, speaking directly to me. "Where are you going?"

I raised my eyebrows at his tone, but answered him directly. "To Londinium, to see what's happening. Why?"

"Forget it. You have no need to see what's happening there."

I frowned. "How can you know that?"

His frown matched mine. "Because I've been there. Believe what I tell you."

I glanced around me at my five companions. They were all watching Orvic closely, no suggestion of doubt visible on any of their faces. I turned back to the big Celt. "What's wrong there? Is it inhabited?"

"Inhabited? Aye, it's inhabited, course it is, but it's no place for you or your people."

"Why not?"

"Pestilence of some kind. It's not what I'd call rampant yet, but it's there. There doesn't seem to be wholesale death, but whatever it is, it's created chaos in the town. There's fighting everywhere, and nobody seems to know who's in charge, or who's fighting who. There seem to be four, perhaps five separate factions and there's more corpses in the streets from the violence than from the sickness. The forum's a slaughterhouse and the basilica's on fire, along with a good portion of the rest of the town."

"How did you find all this information? Were you inside the town itself?"

"Aye, and outside it, looking in."

Lucanus spoke up. "Then you may be carrying the sickness."

Orvic looked at him, then back to me. I could have sworn he was on the point of smiling. "Aye, I might. But I doubt it. I didn't get close enough to anyone to catch anything except words, except for one fellow, and he was outside the town."

"And?"

"And that's all. He was healthy as a horse and bleeding like a sow. He was a mercenary, from my part of the country, if you can believe it. I didn't know him, though. He'd fallen off the wall—been thrown off, really. I sewed up a gash in his thigh and splinted the bone, and he was happy to talk to me. Told me he started out years ago working for the Grain Merchants Guild, but that's long gone, ten years ago or more, and he ended up with a gang of ex-soldiers who looked after their own interests and nobody else's. There's no organized authority in the town. Basilica's been deserted for years, except for squatters. Town council stopped functioning more than five years ago and the so-called better class of citizens are all either dead or they've moved away. I told you, it's chaos—a rats' nest. A good place to stay well clear of."

My horse reared at a fly bite, taking me by surprise and almost throwing me, and I wrestled him back under control, sawing on the bit and venting some of my frustration on the poor beast. By the time I spoke again, I had my feelings as tightly under control as the horse.

"We have no choice." My voice was stony. "We have to go in to cross the bridge."

"Find another way, Merlyn." He looked me straight in the eye. "There's nothing but heartache in there for you."

"Nonsense! We have two hundred men. We'll carve our way through if we have to."

Orvic hawked and spat, an eloquent statement of disdain. "You might take them in, but you won't take 'em all out again. You've got wagons, provisions and horses, and all of them make you fine targets. Streets are narrow and the roofs are high. It's less than a mile from the north wall to the river and the bridge, but you'll never make the transit. As soon as you approach the gates, even before you enter, all those warring bastards in there will unite against you. They'll block every street junction, then line every rooftop and cut you to pieces from above. Your men will have no room to manoeuvre, or even to dodge the missiles. And then they'll barricade the entrance to the bridge against you. Believe me, Caius Merlyn, the bridge is not available to you for crossing the river."

"Damnation! Then what do you suggest? Should we sprout wings and fly?"

"Aye, if you can." He grinned as he said the words, but there was no trace of humour in his eyes. "But it might be more realistic to skirt the city to the east, upriver, and find a ferry or a ford."

"And what if we find neither? Do you know where there are any?"

He jerked his head. "No, but you'll find one or the other, sooner or later. People do cross over without having to go through Londinium. What will it cost you? A day? Two days at the most, and you'll keep your troops alive and healthy. Increase your speed and your daily travel for the next two days after that and you'll make up the time you've lost."

What he said made sense. There had to be either a ford or a ferry not too far upstream. I decided to accept his evaluation of the Londinium situation, and signalled the dismount, giving my men the chance to relax and stretch their legs. Then, with Orvic's assistance, we spent the next hour discussing ways and means of circumventing the town and its dangerous bridge.

That night, after our plans had all been made, I wondered at myself. I have never been good at taking advice. An analyst of advice I was, certainly, in that I always took pains to consider—and occasionally defer to—the opinions and viewpoints of those around me. I usually chose, however, to cleave to my own judgment, trusting my own instinctual responses to the responsibilities I alone bore. That, I had learned from my father. His credo on leadership had been simple: a leader—any leader—bears full and final responsibility for the welfare of the people he leads. In success, he might be magnanimous in the sharing of credit, but in failure, the fault, the responsibility and the consequences are his alone to bear. On that phase of our expedition, however, I had accepted advice twice, from two subordinates, without any reservations, on two consecutive days. On each occasion that advice had run contrary to what I myself would normally have chosen to do, and upon it I had based decisions that I would not normally have made. In the light of what happened afterward, and aided by years of hindsight, I find it impossible not to believe I was under the influence—mystical or supernatural—of powers over which I had no control.

Publius Varrus wrote prolifically towards the end of his life, setting down his recollections of all that had happened to him since he met my grandfather, Caius Britannicus. It used to amuse me that, each time he was faced with the task of describing some event or occurrence that he did not fully understand, Uncle Varrus would resort to the assertion that he was not a superstitious man, but . . .

At this point in my tale, I understand fully, for the first time, how Publius Varrus felt at such times. I, too, am not a superstitious man, but I believe that journey to Verulamium was fated to take place. And I also believe that the only reason it took place was to bring about a series of meetings that would not—could not—otherwise have occurred.

Orvic had been right about the cross-river traffic upstream from Londinium. Less than a day's march upriver from the town— a progress greatly hampered by our wagons and the lack of a road—we arrived, unsighted and unchallenged, at a regular crossing point. A deeply rutted track led us alongside the great river to where the thick growth of willows and scrub lining the bank had been cleared to accommodate a primitive ferry. This device, no more than a large, floating platform, was anchored and operated by a system of ropes and pulleys, all firmly fastened to two massive oak trees, one on each side of the river. When we arrived, the ferry lay on the opposite side from us, untended, and it had obviously been there for some time, for the river had receded in the hot weather and the craft lay high and dry on the mud of the riverbank. We couldn't move it at all, from where we were, although we put as many men on the pulley ropes as we could. The river itself was wide and muddy at the crossing, flowing slowly and placidly with no visible eddies and no indication of strong currents. One of our younger squadron leaders, claiming the ability to swim like a fish, volunteered to swim across and test the current and the depth of the stream. He came to his feet in midstream, with his head clear of the water, and called to us that there was no current to speak of.

A dozen men and horses followed him to prise the ferry free of its muddy berth, and in less than two hours, our entire force had crossed over safely and easily, the wagons on the ferry and the troopers on horseback. We camped that night close by the river-bank, screened from the other side by the fringe of thick willows.

The following day, we set out eastward again, following the track leading from the ferry. The track soon petered out, however, completely overgrown, and after that our pace slowed to a crawl as we travelled through heavily forested, trackless land. The trees were mainly great oaks, ash and beeches, so that there was little under-growth to hamper our passage, and we would have been able to make good time had it not been for our heavy wagons. Their huge wheels sank into the soft forest floor almost to the axles, and their immense width made them difficult to manoeuvre among the trees, while the dead trees and boughs that littered the ground often blocked their passage completely, so that our troopers spent as much time on foot as they did on horseback, labouring like slaves to remove the worst of the obstacles and free the wheels.

Late in the afternoon, towards sunset, we emerged without warning on the verge of the great Roman road leading north-westward from Londinium to Verulamium. There was no fresh meat for our fires that night. The noise of two hundred horsemen and heavy wagons crashing through the forest had banished all the wildlife for miles around. The trees that lined the road closely on both sides were much younger than the forest giants beneath which we had been travelling all day. They were tall and thin, much faster growing than the huge, stately oak, elm and beech trees of the deeper woods, but their outflung branches had already met far overhead, turning the road into a green, leaf-roofed tunnel.

The first milestone we came to told us we were thirteen miles north-west of Londinium. Two miles further on, just as I was beginning to worry about finding a suitable campsite, we emerged into an open meadow with a clear, gurgling stream and a covering of new saplings growing among the charred remnants of another old forest fire. The sun set minutes before we reached the spot, and by the time we had set up our encampment it was almost fully dark, thanks to the high trees on all sides of us.

We ate by the light of the cooking fires, and I decided to allow the men to rest the following day, while I myself went hunting with our Celtic bowmen.

XXXII

It was a long shot—perhaps too long, I thought—but the stag made a perfect target, silhouetted against the cloudless sky, and since mine was the most powerful bow, Orvic indicated with a nod that the shot was mine. I raised Publius Varrus's huge bow and sighted carefully, drawing the taut, thrumming string back all the way to my ear, feeling the power of the mighty weapon and visualizing the flight of the arrow it would hurl into the teeth of the light wind. The stag stood on the skyline at the crest of a hill, about two hundred paces directly ahead, but separated from us by a narrow, deep, brush-choked gully. We had been stalking him and his two consort does for two hours, and this was as close as we were likely to come to him, thanks to the depth of the ravine between us. In the space of the few heartbeats between my full draw and release, I found time to admire him as he stood poised between two trees, his head raised so that his massive antlers lay along his spine, his gaze fastened on something that had alerted him on the far side of his crest. He was completely unaware of us, masked as we were from his sight by a thin screen of leaves and from his keen nose by the wind that blew directly from him to where we stood.

I exhaled slowly through my nose, and released the arrow, feeling it launch straight and true, and as I did so the stag disappeared. So abrupt was the transition from stationary target to empty skyline that I felt a superstitious shock at what seemed like magic.

"Shit!" The voice was Orvic's, and as I heard the exclamation I saw the stag again, bounding down the side of the ravine straight towards us, closely pursued by the two does. Even as I saw him, he leaped to his right and was lost among the rank brush that filled the gully. Only then did I lower my bow and turn to the others.

"What happened?"

Orvic's face was filled with disgust. "Something scared him. Something on the other side, something he saw or heard."

I glanced at Donuil and Curwin, neither of whom had spoken. "Either of you hear or see anything?" They shook their heads. "Well," I went on, "we might as well move on. We won't get another shot at—"

"Quiet," Orvic hissed. "Listen!"

We listened, but there was nothing to be heard above the whisper of the leaves in the wind. Orvic was frozen in place, a picture of absolute concentration.

"What—?"

He cut my question short with a savage gesture and I held my breath, straining to hear whatever it was he seemed to have heard. Again, however, I heard only the wind. After a few more moments he relaxed, his body losing the angular tension that had briefly intimidated the three of us who watched him.

He turned to face me. "What were you going to say, Caius Merlyn?"

I shrugged with one shoulder, slinging my bow across my back. "No more than the obvious. We might as well move on. Those three deer are far gone and we won't find them again. What did you hear?"

"I don't know. May have been nothing, but I thought I heard shouting." It did not cross my mind to doubt him. Orvic's powers of sight and hearing were legendary. He continued speaking, almost to himself, frowning at his own thoughts, his eyes narrowed. "Something set them off." His eyes widened, aware of me again. "Go you and collect your horses. I'm going over there to the crest." He moved to the edge of the gully and looked down. "It's not bad here, I'll be able to get down and up easily, but you won't, not with horses." He looked off to his right, to where the gully petered out about half a mile away. "Best bring your horses round that way, then follow me down into the valley on the other side. If there's nothing there, we'll keep hunting. May be pigs or bear down in the valley there. Be quick." He stepped to the edge of the drop, still holding his big bow in his left hand, and let himself drop over, vanishing as quickly as had the stag.

I had taken no ill at his assumption of command. In a situation like this, Orvic was far more capable than I. I turned to my two companions. "Let's go."

Half an hour later, out of breath from running to Orvic's summons, I reached out and laid my hand on the bark of a tree that leaned drunkenly out and away from me. Beneath me was a sheer precipice, falling almost straight down for what must have been at least fifty paces to a great pile of rubble and scree containing the skeletons of other trees that had obviously fallen from the edge where we stood. It took no great imagination to see that the face of the cliff had been flaking away since time began. Beyond the rubble at its foot, the ground was grassy and fell more gradually, but still steeply, for almost half a mile further before it began to level out towards the valley bottom. I was on the very edge of a long, forest-crowned escarpment, which rose higher to my right as the ground sloped steeply upwards, and from somewhere up there a stream swept outward over the edge and fell, glittering and splendid in the strong sunshine, to dash itself to foam on the rocks below before swirling on down to join the river in the valley bottom.

We had no eyes for any of the beauty surrounding us. We were aware only of the fight in progress directly below where we stood, less than a mile from us.

"Foreigners. They're all Outlanders." The words were little more than a growl in Orvic's throat. I glanced at him, taking in the fierceness of his scowl and the heavy displeasure in his eyes.

"The attackers are, anyway," I agreed. "They look like Saxons."

"Aye, they are, of some kind. But the others are Outlanders, too. They're not from Britain, least not any region I've been in."

"Can you be that sure from up here?" I squinted against the sunlight that was beating on us from almost directly in front, trying vainly to see details that Orvic had obviously seen. "I can't see them well enough to notice a damn thing odd about them. What do you think, Curwin?"

"No use asking me. I'm as blind as you are, but if Orvic says they're Outlanders, then they are. He's the one with the hawk's eyes."

I glanced behind me to where Donuil, the fourth member of our party, stood looking out over my shoulder.

"What about you? Can you tell who they are?"

Donuil shrugged, shaking his head. "No," he said, "but they're well dressed and well organized. They know what they're doing, but they're too badly outnumbered to survive much longer."

His final words had echoed my own thoughts. I looked back down, cursing the distance and the impossibility of getting closer. There seemed to be about eighty to a hundred in the attacking party, who were easy to identify as Saxons by their large, round shields. The group opposing them looked to be between twenty and thirty strong, and had occupied a ruined farmstead in the valley bottom, making use of the tumbled walls and outhouses to defend themselves.

"Must be bowmen." This was Orvic again. "Look, you can see how the other whoresons are hanging back, hiding. And there's a few of them lying out there in the grass, see? Some dead, some alive. Have to be bowmen down there, keeping them pinned. Otherwise there'd be nothing to stop them from just running in and killing the lot, three to one . . ." He grunted to himself again, sounding surprised. "You know, I think them others are Romans."

"What?" His words surprised me. "What d'you mean?"

He looked at me as if I were soft in the head. "Romans, you know? From Rome. They're wearing white, most of 'em. Whiter white than I've seen in many a day."

"By God, you're right, they are." My mind was racing. "How well do you know this part of the country, Orvic?"

His answer was gruff. "Not very well, but enough. Why?"

"How far are we from our camp?"

He looked around him, seeming to sniff at the windless air. "Less than a mile, if we could fly. Closer to three by the path. We've been moving in a great circle. What's in your mind?"

My half-formed idea had evaporated before he finished speaking. I shrugged my shoulders and nodded downward, feeling oppressed and helpless. "Oh, not much of use. If those *are* Romans, and now I think you're right, then they are here for the same purpose we are. They're headed for Verulamium. I was trying to think of some way to help them. My first thought was to bring our cavalry, but there's no time, and anyway, I was grasping at straws. I forgot about this cliff for a moment."

He grinned and nodded towards our left. "No, your horses couldn't jump down that, not here they couldn't. But they might, if they was to come round to the north over there, about a mile further down."

"What? How?"

"By the road. It comes down on the far side of the old farm, there." He turned his head, looking up along the cliff to the south. "You see that waterfall? That's the same stream you're camped beside. It runs under the road, through a culvert. You remember?" I nodded, waiting. "If you was to send your man Donuil up there, to run along the stream bed, he could be at the camp in no time, being the runner he is. Then he could bring your horsemen round by the road and have 'em in place almost by the time we get there."

"Get where?"

Orvic turned back towards the valley and pointed. "Down there, boyo. That's as nice a place as I've seen for a bit of target shootin'."

As I looked at the spot he was indicating, Curwin stepped to my side, handed Orvic his bow, then unslung his quiver from around his shoulders and handed that over, too. Then he turned without a word and began striding off into the forest behind us.

"Where are you going, Curwin?"

"Arrows. I'll catch up."

I turned back to Orvic, who was shrugging the second quiver over his shoulders to lie alongside his own, but before I could speak he nodded to Donuil.

"Can you do it, boyo? Run along the stream up there to your

camp and fetch the others?" Donuil glanced at me, then nodded. "Then go, fast as you can! We'll be down there when you get there, and there's trouble we may have, so waste no time on the road. Get you gone."

As soon as we were alone, Orvic drew two short pieces of leather thong from the scrip at his side and began binding his own bow and Curwin's together. I watched as he finished by slinging the double bow across his shoulders, the staves to the front and the strings across his broad back. Then he leaned outwards, scanning the cliff face below.

"Where did Curwin go?"

Orvic looked back at me, a tiny frown of impatience on his face. "He told you. To get arrows."

"But he had arrows. He gave them to you. Where will he get more?"

"Saddlebags. Didn't you see 'em?"

I shook my head. He knelt on one knee, placed his hands on the rim of the precipice, and leaned over further before looking up at me again. I drew a deep breath and squinted towards the spot he had pointed out earlier, then moved forward and looked down from the edge. "You think we can get down there?"

He hawked and spat out into space. "Oh aye, no trick to that. Trick is to do it alive, and at our pace."

I filled my lungs, held the air, then released it through pursed lips. "Fine then. You go first, and I'll follow. But what about Curwin?"

Orvic was already on his belly, his legs over the edge. "What about him? He'll come after us. We'll wait for 'im at the bottom, then he can lower the extra arrows down to us." He lowered himself gradually until his head disappeared below the edge, and as his fingers followed, his voice came back up to me. "It's not as bad as it looks, once you've your face to the rocks. Just come slow now. I'll guide your feet the first few steps until you get the hang of it."

He was right. It wasn't as bad as it looked—not quite. But it took us almost half an hour to climb down the fifty or so paces to the rock-strewn ground beneath the cliff's face. Orvic could have made the descent far more quickly had I not been there, and as it was, Curwin had almost caught up to us by the time we got down, and he had travelled a mile in each direction, to and from the clearing where we had left our horses, since I had lowered myself over the rim. But both of them were mountain reared and used to playing around on vertical surfaces. I was more accustomed to horizontal movement.

Safe at the bottom, I regained my breath while we waited for Curwin to slide down the last few yards to join us. He was not even panting. He threw me a look that was eloquent without words, sniffed audibly and turned to Orvic.

"Sent the boy back to camp wi' the horses. Told 'im to bring 'em on down with the others." He shrugged off the burden he had been carrying: two very large, densely packed quivers of arrows, one over each shoulder, with the straps crossed in front of him.

"Good." Orvic had already separated the two bows he had brought down the cliff and had shrugged off Curwin's quiver, placing it beside his bow on the ground. He and Curwin immediately began sharing the arrows from the extra quivers, cramming them into their own and handing a large double handful to me to stuff my own quiver until it was packed to capacity. As I set about the task, my curiosity was uncontainable.

"You had these on your horse, Curwin?"

"Aye."

I could not hide my amazement. "You always carry so many arrows?"

"Aye. Best get moving, Orvic."

"But why, Curwin?"

He did not even glance at me. We started moving downhill and I fell into place behind him.

"Ask my brother." His voice came back to me over his shoulder.

"What brother? I didn't know you had one." I was watching the ground at my feet, stepping carefully.

"I don't, not any longer. He ran out of arrows, hunting one day, arguing with some others over who had killed a deer. They had more arrows than him. Used them to kill him." He paused in mid step and looked back at me as though expecting me to be smiling. "I'd rather be laughed at and well armed than be shot at and not be able to shoot back."

That was the last word on the topic.

Orvic began leading us diagonally across the steep hillside, angling downward towards the promontory he had pointed out from the clifftop. As we went, Curwin rolled up the quiver that had been emptied and tucked it securely beneath his belt. The second, still a good two-thirds full, he slung over his shoulder again. Orvic pointed to the gully ahead of us that had been cut by the stream falling from the cliff above.

"Once we get down in there, we should be able to move all the way down without being seen." He began to trot and Curwin and I followed him, leaning into the hillside for balance, until we jumped down between the banks of the stream.

"Right," Orvic grunted. "Nobody saw us. Now, here's what I see. There's some bushes further down there along the bank, and they'll get thicker and bigger as we go downhill. By the time we get to where we're going, they'll be trees. The stream bed there falls east until it's close to the valley bottom, then veers away to the north, and that's where we climb out and head uphill—south. Another two, three hundred paces, but we'll be well hidden. There's a point there, ending in another cliff, but it's not as high as the one we just came down. Ground falls away on both sides. We'll still be 'bout half a mile, maybe a bit less, from the farm where the Romans are, but we'll be in easy bow shot of the Saxons. Should be able to shoot 'em like rabbits. They won't be able to get to us, not without running uphill towards us and trying to get around us to the sides. We've got enough arrows. By the time we run out of shafts, most of the whoresons should be dead." He paused. "Course, if they come too thick and we let any of them around the sides to get behind us too soon, we'll be the dead ones. You ready?"

A short time later, the three of us stood side by side on the second clifftop, about ten paces above the ground that fell away

again beneath us. The space where we had emerged from the clustered hawthorn trees was large enough to allow us all to stand and
move comfortably. The Saxons were spread out beneath us, the
closest of them less than a hundred paces distant, the mass of them
closer to two hundred. Another two hundred paces or so beyond
the furthest of them lay the ruined walls of the farm that sheltered
the defenders. No one had seen us.

Curwin drew an arrow from his quiver and smoothed the flights
between a spit-wet thumb and fingertip, watching Orvic from
the corner of his eye. "Well?" he grunted. "You've got the best eye.
Want to take the first one?"

Orvic nodded. He already had an arrow nocked, as did I.

"Range finder. Aye." He raised his bow slowly and took his time
sighting, but Curwin interrupted him before he could loose his shot.

"Where're you aiming?"

"There!"

We watched as his arrow flew straight and true towards a cluster of half a score of men some hundred and fifty paces directly
ahead of us, but the angle was deceiving from our height and the
missile shot into the ground just short of the group and disappeared without being noticed.

"Shit! There's nonsense!"

He aimed more judiciously next time and his second arrow took
one of the group in the side of the head, somewhere in the region of
the point of the jaw, and jerked him clean off his feet, hurling him
sideways away from his companions who scattered in confusion,
looking around in vain for the source of the sudden death. None of
them thought to look upward to where we stood on our cliff so far
away. They had never met the Pendragon Longbow before.

"Lovely shot," said Curwin. "They don't know where to start
lookin'. Now, watch this . . . The big whoreson over there on the
left, with the red beard and the green tunic."

He raised his bow quickly, angling his arm in front of me so
that the flight of his arrow bore no comparison to Orvic's line, and
as my eyes sought and found the man he had described, so did

Curwin's shaft. The Saxon had been standing upright behind a tree, his back to the bole, waving his arms wildly as he urged his companions to the attack. Curwin's arrow nailed him there, upright, piercing him completely and penetrating the tree behind him. Orvic fired again before I could launch my own first shot, and then we settled into a lethal routine, selecting our individual targets at random, but keeping each far removed from those that had directly preceded it, and bringing them down one after another until our combined efforts had slaughtered fourteen men. As I took down the fifteenth, someone detected our shooting platform high on the hillside above them, and once we had been seen, the Saxons came boiling towards us in a screaming tide of rage.

From that point on, all three of us drew and fired as quickly as we were able, and my arm and fingers had begun to ache by the time the charging men had halved the distance to us. From the edge of my vision I saw one bare-headed giant running in great strides, ahead of his companions, and I traversed my bow quickly, sighting on his huge chest, but then, as I released my arrow, he fell to his knees and disappeared. I thought at first that one of my companions had killed him, but their bows were bent, arrows unlaunched as their eyes widened. And all along the line of attack, the Saxons vanished, leaving only their large number of dead and wounded in sight.

Orvic cursed. "Gone to ground. There's a bank there that we can't see from up here. Now it gets nasty. They'll be looking for ways to come around us, so keep your eyes wide."

We waited. Somewhere out in front of us a man was screaming. Above us the song of birds filled the skies. The screaming man's voice rose to a shriek and then died away to a gurgling, agonized moaning, and then to silence. Nothing moved. My arm muscles were cramping with the tension of keeping my bow drawn. I released it slowly, keeping my arrow nocked.

"Orvic, should we be thinking of getting out of here?"

"Aye, but there's nowhere to go, boyo. 'Cept back up there where we came from. We try that, they'll run us down. How many did we get?"

I scanned the killing ground in front of us. "Thirty-four, by my count."

"Aye, that's what I see. Not bad for three men, eh?"

It was a phenomenal amount, but I didn't respond. Thirty-four from eighty left forty-six—more than enough to make short work of us, now that our bows were almost useless, and less than forty paces separated us from where they had gone to ground.

"Look yonder." Curwin's voice was close to my shoulder. "We gave them a breathin' space, anyway."

I looked towards the farm wall that had sheltered the besieged party. There were men moving about rapidly, out in front of the defences, bent over, their eyes on the ground.

"Never mind them, Caius Merlyn, keep your eyes on these whoresons close to us!" Orvic's harsh voice jerked my eyes back to the ground below us, but still nothing appeared to be moving. Orvic continued to speak, his eyes sweeping the terrain then flicking a glance towards the farm. "Whoever's in charge over there's no fool. But then the Romans never were, were they? They're collecting spent arrows while the Saxons are involved with us. Now what I'm wondering is whether they'll come out to help us, or whether they'll leave us here to die and take their own chances again when we're done for." He nodded downwards to our left, pointing to where the stream bed we had followed from the ridge above fell steeply away to the north. "You watch that side, I'll take the other, and Curwin, you watch the front here. That ridge they're hiding behind can't be no more than twenty to thirty running steps from the stream bed down there, so be ready for them. First sign of movement, let fly, and don't miss! If they get into yon stream bed, under the bank where we can't see them, or around our flank on the other side, we're dead men."

He moved away to his right, sweeping the branches of the trees back with one arm as he cautiously skirted the very edge of our small cliff. Curwin hawked and spat loudly, and as he did, the giant Saxon I had been aiming at earlier sprang into view again, running hard towards the stream bed, crouched over, followed by a horde of others. I snapped off a quick shot at him and missed, but brought him to his knees with my second arrow, only to watch him being knocked aside by one of his followers who staggered, almost lost his balance then lurched forward and fell over the bank of the stream and out of sight. I saw another fall sprawling, shot by Curwin, and then another as I brought down one more. And then there were no more Saxons in sight.

"Orvic," I yelled. "They got past us, into the stream bed. Six or seven of them."

Curwin was standing by my side. "They can't get up here without coming out of the cut. I'll hold 'em." Then he was gone, vanished into the trees at my back.

I could hear the twanging of Orvic's bowstring on my right as he fired rapidly, and shouts and yells drifting up from below on his side. Nothing moved below me.

"Orvic, do you need help? You want me there?"

"No, damnation, stay where you are. None of these whoresons are going anywhere." A pause, then, "Where's Curwin?"

"Gone to keep them pinned in the stream bed."

Something snapped in front of my face and I jerked my head back in sudden terror, hearing an arrow smack into the bole of the tree beside me. I looked down, but saw no sign of the archer. To my right, Orvic had stopped shooting.

"They've got bows," I yelled.

"I know." His voice startled me, coming from close behind me. I swung round and saw him leaning against a hawthorn tree, his face ashen, his homespun tunic crimson with the blood from where an arrow had pierced him cleanly, angling upward beneath his left collarbone. As I stared at him in shock, his knees folded and he fell forward onto his face, driving the shaft right through his shoulder.

Now I heard shouting from beneath again, and swung back to my watch, drawing my bowstring back as I turned. There were Saxons running again towards the stream, but now they were faltering, turning as they ran, and some were standing, staring backwards. I dropped one of the latter, driving an arrow into the base of his skull, hammering him down the slope. Before I could nock another, however, they were all running back downhill again, away from me, and I looked beyond them to see the Romans who had held the farm charging towards them in a tight, hard knot of clustered horsemen, swinging in hard across the Saxons' rear from my right and herding them northward, down the slope towards another distant band, a much larger band, of advancing cavalry. My own! I dropped my bow and ran to Orvic, pulling my knife. He was unconscious. I cut through the arrow, quickly and without gentleness, just below the flights, and pulled the rest of the shaft out through his wound in the direction it had travelled. He felt nothing, and I ripped part of my tunic and stuffed both sides of the wound, entry and exit, binding the packing in place with both our bowstrings. As I was finishing, Curwin arrived back, crowing with pleasure and relief, but as he saw what I was doing he stopped in his tracks.

"It's not as bad as it looks," I told him. "A clean wound, and shallow, angled upward. Looks like it glanced off his rib-cage and went beneath his collarbone. Nothing vital hit, as far as I can see. He'll mend and pull his bow again with the best of us."

I left the two of them together, Orvic still unconscious, and began to make my way down to where the last movements of the drama below were being played out. From above, I could see that the Saxons were dying hard, expecting no quarter and giving none, each of them evidently prepared to go down fighting. In spite of myself, I felt a surge of admiration for their stubborn, pagan courage. The remnant of the fighting was sweeping away from me as I walked alone through the carnage of the battlefield among maimed and dead men. I stopped and turned around, looking up to the point from which I had so recently been shooting. The cliff below it looked unscalable from here, impregnable, towering above me like the wall of a fortress and backed by the grand sweep of the hillside leading up to the escarpment, the face of which was laced by the silvery cascade from the stream. The point itself looked far more distant and inaccessible from here than it had felt up there. I could see no sign of Curwin or Orvic. I became aware of my own shadow, stretching ahead of me westward, up the hill, and it shocked me to realize the sun had not yet reached its noonday zenith.

I heard my name shouted, and turned back to the valley to see Donuil cantering towards me awkwardly, holding the reins of his horse and my own in one hand and clutching my helmet beneath his other arm as though it could anchor him to his beast's back. Moments later, mounted and helmed and feeling much bigger and more in control of my destiny than I had afoot, I gave Donuil my bowstave and quiver and trotted ahead of him towards the gathering that marked the final outcome of the running fight. Apart from a brief word of thanks, I had said nothing to him and he left me to my thoughts. Moments later, I saw Lucanus and made my way to where he was bending over one of our young troopers. I told him about Orvic up on the point above, and he dispatched two stretcher-bearers to bring the big Celt down to safety, warning them against dropping their burden on the steep slope. That done, he returned his attention to the trooper at his feet, ignoring me completely.

"How many casualties, Lucanus?"

"Too many. Five dead, seven wounded including your friend up on the hill. This one's the worst."

"How bad is he?" The young trooper was unconscious.

"Axe wound to the thigh, as you can see, knife wound in the kidney, and probably a broken skull. He won't recover." He still had not looked up. Sighing, I left him to his work and looked around me.

The centre of activity, now that the fighting was over, was a densely packed group of horsemen, some of them my own, milling together on my right in the grip of the euphoria that always accompanies survival after a fight. At the centre of this eddy, I could clearly see a small group of four or five uniformed officers talking to some of my own officers, all of them set apart by the dignity and calmness of their bearing. I kneed my horse towards them as they moved towards me, making their way with authority through the press surrounding them, and as they came, some of my own troopers recognized me and raised a cry of welcome, bringing all of them surging to surround me in a great circle. In the middle of this circle, I came face to face with the strangers, and a silence fell around us.

"Caius Britannicus?"

The speaker was evidently their leader, and as I nodded, I drank in every detail of the man. He was older than me, considerably older, somewhere in his mid-fifties, I guessed, but he had the unmistakable bearing and authority of a professional soldier and a born leader. His uniform was magnificent: helmet, breastplate, armoured kilt and leggings of rich bronze inlaid with gold, all worn over a tunic so white that it dazzled the eyes. A rolled cloak of magnificent deep blue lay tethered over his horse's withers.

"That is my name."

"Well met, then! We are all greatly in your debt. I know not where you and your men came from, but I thank God you did, when you did." He pointed upwards, towards the point at the top of the cliff behind me. "Had it not been for your arrival and the assistance we received from someone up yonder, I doubt that any of us would have lived to see the sun set today. The heathen had us neatly trapped and would have picked us off one at a time." He glanced back at me and smiled then, his whole face transformed into a glow of warmth, and seemed to shake himself mentally. "But please," he said, pointing towards the ruined farm in the distance. "Allow me to be hospitable. We spent last night among the ruins down there, little thinking we would have unwelcome guests by morning, and we were comfortable for a while. Will you and your men be my guests for today?"

"Happily," I said, already feeling a profound liking for the man. I turned to where my troop leader Cyrus Appius sat listening on my right and told him to collect the men and bring them on down to the farm. The few wounded would be tended by Lucanus and the squad seconded to him for that purpose.

"Forgive my asking, but why did you allow them to hold you trapped you like that?" I was riding beside the leader, conscious of the fact that he had not told me his name. "I mean, you're cavalry. You could have broken out easily."

"Aye, but there are not enough of us. Less than twenty fighters. We could have broken out, but we have priests with us, a large party of them. They would have been easy pickings for the Saxons. Couldn't just leave them there, could I? By the time I broke out, fought through them, regrouped and swung around again to attack, the Saxons would have been inside, behind the walls, and *they* would have been able to keep *us* out. I did not think I could make it work, so I had decided to stay where I was and fight it out. They had us by at least three to one. But where in Hades did you come from? You're not Regular Army, that's obvious, since there is no Regular Army in Britain any more. So who are you? And what are you doing out here in the middle of nowhere with two hundred cavalry? And how did you come upon us?"

My horse had fallen back slightly as the stranger was talking, and now I kneed him forward, coming up alongside the man again. "We're on our way north and, as I said, we were hunting. Some of the towns we've passed seem plague-ridden, so we've avoided them. But because of that, we've been unable to buy food, so I sent out hunting parties this morning. My own party was up on the escarpment there when we heard the noise of your fight. The rest you know."

He swung his head around, looking at me wide-eyed. "That was you, up there? The bowmen, up on the cliff?"

I shrugged and grinned. "Yes, myself and two others. We saw you from the top of the escarpment yonder, up by the falls, and we came down to help. Donuil, here, ran back and roused the others and brought them down by the road over there to the north."

He blinked again, his eyes filled with something like awe. "Well, Commander," he said eventually. "You leave me with nothing to say, but you will forgive me if I regard you for a while as some kind of *deus ex machina*, for your arrival and intercession seem truly supernatural." I shrugged again, suddenly uncomfortable and unsure of how to respond. He changed the subject abruptly. "You're headed north, you say. So are we. To Verulamium."

Now I grinned at him. "I had guessed as much. It's the only reason I could come up with for your being here. I reasoned that you must be escorting priests to hear Germanus the Bishop debate with our bishops." He drew his horse to a halt and turned to look more closely at me, hitching himself sideways to see me better, an expression I took to be one of rueful surprise on his face. I grinned again. "Am I correct?"

His mouth twisted into a small grin, too, and he twitched his head in a gesture that fell only slightly short of acknowledgement.

"Almost," he said. "I am Germanus the Bishop."

XXXIII

My first impressions of Bishop Germanus and his associates were chaotic—a series of disconnected images rendered the more haphazard by the giddiness and excitement of victory, with the milling, undisciplined euphoria it generated, and then further befuddled by my profound shock over Germanus's revelation of his own identity. A warrior bishop was alien to my experience, a complete contradiction in terms to one who had grown to manhood knowing bishops only as gentle, frequently reclusive men of peace and pacifism. I had known, of course, that Germanus had been a soldier, with a long and successful career as an Army Staff Officer, and that he had retired as a full Legate—a General commanding an entire Army Group. But I had given no thought at all to the means by which the transition from general to bishop, from man of war to man of God, had been achieved. Somehow, through sheer indifference, I had allowed myself to accept, without consideration or question, the notion of a nebulous, mystical metamorphosis of the nature of the man involved—from militant to penitent; from chalk to cheese; from one archetype to another. Now that I was shocked into confronting my own malformed expectations, I immediately acknowledged the impossibility involved. It was inconceivable that Germanus the Bishop would react to aggression and physical threat in a way that was fundamentally different from the reaction one would expect of Germanus the Legate. The man before me now was an anomaly unlike any other in my experience: a devout man of God, thoroughly trained and experienced in warfare. It was a radical and unexpected combination.

Germanus must have read my consternation in my eyes, for he laughed suddenly and pulled his mount into a high, prancing turn that left him close to me on my left side, and leant forward to speak for my ears alone.

"Our gentle Master bade us turn the other cheek to those who would defame us, Caius Merlyn, but he seized a whip Himself when He was outraged in the Temple." He nodded towards the Saxon corpses that littered the hillside. "Turn the other cheek to such as these, my friend, and they'll rip off your Christian ears, before they remove your head." He smiled at me then, a warm and friendly smile. "See to your troops. We'll talk back at our camp yonder."

We exchanged nods and I watched him ride off with his followers before I turned to my own men, who were even now assembling their formations. Lucanus, I saw, had already sent the wounded, on a series of litters, down to the camp below and was now riding slowly towards me. I waited until he reached me and then gave the signal to my men to move off, pulling aside with him to watch them ride past. In the distance, behind them, our heavy wagons were trundling slowly down the road from the ridge above.

"Well, Lucanus? How badly did we fare?"

"Six wounded, none seriously now. The seventh died—the one with the axe wound. We were fortunate to escape so lightly. Who was that you were talking to? Their leader?"

"Yes, in more ways than one. That's the man we came to hear. Bishop Germanus."

I watched his eyes widen in amazement, much as my own must have done.

"A *bishop?* Leading cavalry?"

"No," I told him, grinning. "A soldier, doing God's work as best he can."

"That is obscene."

"No it's not, Luke. It's different, I'll grant you, but there's nothing unnatural about it when you consider the man and his life." I stopped and sniffed, scenting my own hypocrisy. "Mind you," I went on, "I must admit I thought as you did, at first—until I'd had time to adjust to the reality of the situation." I told him then what

Germanus had said to me. Lucanus looked around him at the scattered Saxon corpses and sighed.

"Do warrior bishops drink good wine?"

I laughed. "I have no idea, but I hope so. Let's find out."

We followed our men down to the ruined farm.

Our original estimate from the top of the ridge had been quite accurate. There were twenty-eight men in Germanus's retinue, and of those, fourteen were clerics of varying description. Four of them, I discovered later, were bishops like Germanus, from Gaul and Italia. They were a strangely featureless group, these clerics, ranging in age from the late teens to the mid-forties, I guessed, all of them distinguished by their lack of individual distinctiveness. They were dressed alike, for the most part, in long, plain robes of brown, black or grey homespun cloth, and while several of them wore stout leather belts to waist their robes, there were others who wore a plain length of rope as a girdle, reminding me unpleasantly of the zealot priests who had invaded Camulod. I would discover later from Germanus that these symbols of poverty were manifestations of a growing inclination towards austerity among some churchmen, a proclivity being fostered by the adherents of the Monasticism that was now becoming an increasingly prevalent influence among the religious community in Rome, having spread there from Greece and the Eastern Empire.

The remainder of the party, who had formed the wedge of cavalry that had rescued us, were very different, both in character and in appearance. These men were soldiers, with the uniform, bearing, and manner of soldiers, although the latter was restrained out of respect for the piety of the group they were escorting.

Their commander, a tribune called Marius Tribo, was a gregarious young man who treated his two young subalterns, the decurions Plato and Rufus, with strict yet tolerant authority and goodwill. Plato and Rufus, for their part, used a similar approach with their troopers, a nine-man squad who had obviously served together long enough to be the kind of close friends that only serving soldiers can be. Tribo told me, over a cup of excellent wine, that

they had been stationed in Gaul for the past four years, campaigning against the Burgundians, who were threatening to take over the
entire country. They had already done so, for all intents and purposes, he admitted. There was now no more than a corridor along
the north-western coast where Roman forces could feel any degree
of security. He, his two subalterns and nine men were all that
remained of his original force of eighty—two complete cavalry
squadrons. Replacements had stopped reaching them a year before,
and they had been delighted when they were ordered to escort
Bishop Germanus and his four episcopal companions to Britain
to attend the debate in Verulamium. The rest of Germanus's party
would assemble there. The lesser churchmen in the present group
had joined them in Britain, on the road from the south coast.

As Lucanus and I stood talking with Tribo and his two decurions, Germanus himself approached the fireside where we stood
and, taking me by the elbow, nodded pleasantly and made an
excuse for taking me away. I followed him to another fire set apart,
where no one was cooking and none could overhear us. He had
removed his armour and now wore only his simple, white tunic
and leggings.

He seated himself on a stool and waved me to another beside
him. I sat down, feeling his eyes on me but not wishing to give
offence by staring frankly back. It was a beautiful, warm day and I
wondered about the fire. Every other fire in the camp was crowned
with cooking stones, but this appeared to be built for heat alone.

"A cold land you have here, Caius Merlyn, even on a warm day."
Germanus reached out his hands towards the flames. I looked at
him in surprise and he smiled. "I am still unused to being far from
the sun of Africa. My blood is thin. Even in Italia, which is far
warmer than this, I am constantly beset with chills." He was gazing
into the flames as he said this, and I looked at him openly now.

I guessed his age at between forty-five and fifty, and probably
in the upper part of that range. His hair was dark, crisp and curly
and shorn close to his scalp in the Roman military fashion. His skin
was dark, deeply tanned by years of exposure to burning sunlight,

and his deep-set brown eyes were creased around the outlines with wrinkles. It was a strong, good face, and the rest of the man was made to match it. His shoulders were broad and his chest deep, his arms strong and clean-muscled with no sign of advancing age. His legs, the right stretched out towards the fire, were solid and well-shaped. Altogether a formidable man, I thought, for a soldier, let alone a churchman.

He cleared his throat and spoke without looking at me. "Caius Merlyn Britannicus . . . I served at one time with a man called Britannicus . . . Picus Britannicus. Any relation?"

"He was my father, sir."

"Was he indeed?" Now he looked at me. "The golden hair should have told me so without my having to ask. I knew him well, once. He was my friend for many years, under Stilicho." He paused. "When did he die?"

"Some months ago."

"That recently? My condolences. He was a fine man and an inspired cavalryman."

"Thank you, sir. He thought well of you, too. When my great-aunt Luceiia heard your name, she recognized it instantly from my father's letters. It was she who told me who you were . . . are. She was sorry not to be able to come with us, but she is a very old lady now."

Germanus was looking at me thoughtfully, his upper lip caught between his teeth. I lapsed into silence, waiting for him to voice what was in his mind. He did not keep me waiting long.

"Caius? Merlyn? What do your friends call you?"

"Either," I told him, smiling. "But mostly Merlyn."

"Well, Merlyn then . . . an unusual name . . . Is it British?"

"Celtic, from Cambria. Merlyn is one of the Celtic gods."

"I see. Well, Merlyn, I came here to Britain to debate the theories of the Church in Rome and elsewhere with the British . . . adherents—I almost said disciples—of a man who stands condemned for apostasy, if not outright heresy."

I nodded. "I know. Pelagius."

"Yes, Pelagius. I'm surprised you know of him. How *do* you know of him?"

"My father knew him."

"Aah!" Germanus nodded, smiling to himself. "Why would I even ask? Of course your father would have known him. The man came from Britain and made a name for himself. Your father would have sought him out for that alone. Picus was fiercely proud of being from Britain." He paused, frowning now. "But that alters nothing. As I was saying, I came to debate the teachings of Pelagius—his beliefs, which have been proved heretical. But this debate is theological, bishop to bishop. It can have little significance—the form and content of the debate itself, I mean, not the outcome—for ordinary men. And none at all for women, I should think. So tell me, if you please, about this great-aunt of yours . . . Luceiia, you said? How would she have learned of this? And why would she wish to attend? And why," he drove on, "having decided she wanted to attend, would she not then do so, in spite of being hampered by her age? I should have thought that if her mind is clear enough to conceive of the issues involved, and her interest keen enough to discover the date and the place, then her age alone should not have deterred her."

I was nodding my head in agreement before he had finished speaking. "It didn't, but the distance did."

"Distance?" I heard his surprise. "How far have you come?"

"More than a hundred miles."

"Great God! To hear bishops argue?" His amazement was clearly unfeigned. "Why? What possessed you to make such a journey to such an end?"

I hesitated, thinking over the response that trembled on my lips, fully aware that he expected me to be out of my depth amid the technicalities and doctrinal points under debate. Well, I might be, but I would discover that for myself. I emptied my cup at a gulp and threw the lees into the fire.

"I think I came for the correct reasons, Bishop . . ." I hesitated again, then continued, suddenly convinced of the truth of what I would say. "And I think you may be wrong in claiming this debate to be of no interest to ordinary people. You misjudge us here in Britain, I believe, and the quality of our beliefs."

He was staring at me, his expression difficult to interpret, although I detected only interest there and no sign of censure, nor of umbrage at the temerity of my words. A silence grew until he broke it. "Go on. You have not finished, I think." His tone was gentle.

"No, I have not." I stopped again, then coughed to clear my throat before continuing. "But I came to hear you debate the error of Pelagius's teachings as the Church in Rome sees them, not to debate with you, or to talk about my own problems."

"Do you fear to speak of those?"

"No, not at all."

"Then speak on. I'm listening."

Still I held back, rapidly reviewing the arguments and viewpoints I had heard my father formulate and defend. Germanus betrayed no impatience with my silence. A voice nearby rose into a shout of laughter then died away. Birds sang above me. The sound of the flames consuming the wood of the fire seemed very loud. Finally I began to speak, and once I had begun, the words came fluently.

"My father's father had a lifelong friend, a bishop named Alaric, from Verulamium, the site of your debate. I knew him when I was a child, but I can recall little of him now, yet I know much about him. I know about his life, because my grandfather, and then his friend, my great-uncle, both wrote much about him, and I read all of their writings.

"He was a simple, godly man of great faith and deep humanity. He lived his life as an example of Christian piety to all who knew him, or knew of him. He never harmed any man, never behaved with anything less than perfect decorum and perfect charity, never swore a false oath in his life, never abjured his God or his beliefs, and never, ever, dealt in treachery of any kind.

"He died, eighteen years ago, just before my eleventh birthday, leaving this life as he had lived it, borne up by his belief and his trust in God and His perfection."

I stopped again, pausing until Germanus glanced at me. Then, when I held his eyes, I said, "You said Pelagius had been condemned for apostasy, if not outright heresy . . ."

He nodded, and I continued. "I understand apostasy, in the sense of abandonment of established policy or doctrine—and I must tell you that I cannot see how anyone could accuse Pelagius of abandoning Christianity or its teachings—but I don't understand the meaning of heresy. I have heard the term—my aunt Luceiia used it—but I don't know what is involved in it. Apostasy sounds ominous, but heresy must be worse."

Germanus stirred and looked away from me towards the fire, which collapsed upon itself, hurling up pale, barely visible sparks into the bright afternoon air. "It is," he said, sighing deeply. "Much worse. Apostasy, as you correctly define it, is the abandonment of religious faith and principles. Heresy is the adoption, and the teaching, of an opinion that runs directly counter to the orthodox teachings of the Church. It is mortal sin."

"Hmm!" I tucked my hands beneath me, flat on my stool, and leaned forward. "According to whom? That troubles me, Bishop. It troubles me deeply. I have difficulty in imagining how anyone could accuse Pelagius of being unchristian, but this heresy is frightening." He was watching me again as I continued, "It is a mortal sin to hold an opinion that runs counter to the orthodox teachings of the Church. Is that what you are saying?" He nodded, and I shook my head. "That is something new to me. Tell me, if you will, who defines the orthodoxy?"

He was looking concerned now. A deep cleft had appeared between his brows.

"The Church Fathers."

"And who are these fathers?"

"The senior bishops."

"Forgive me, but which senior bishops?"

"The bishops of the Primary Sees: Rome, Antioch, Hippo and several others."

"Hippo. The Bishop Augustine."

"Yes." His eyebrows had shot up. "You know of the holy Augustine?"

"Only by hearsay, and not of his holiness, merely his opinions, though it would seem they bear great weight."

Another frown. "You sound distressed."

"I am!" I rose from my stool and stepped to the far side of the fire, looking down at him and speaking across the flames. "Bishop Alaric, of whom I spoke moments ago, was one of the finest men my grandfather, my great-uncle and my father ever knew. He was truly a holy man. And towards the end of his life, he recognized the teachings of the man Pelagius as being divinely inspired. He saw no grounds in them for questioning the beliefs of any Christian man—no conflict, no transgression, no shame and certainly no sin.

"But the Bishop of Hippo did, most certainly, and now Pelagius stands condemned by Hippo's power. And now you tell me Bishop Alaric died in a condition of mortal sin, because of that conflict? Because his opinion differed from that of Bishop Augustine? And Augustine is a holy man? You leave the rest of us little ground for hope of salvation if such as Alaric may stand condemned to eternal perdition by such a holy man!"

I could see how deeply my outburst was troubling him. His face was wrinkled with concern, but still I saw no anger there, no judgment.

"Merlyn," he said, his words slow and measured, "you do not know Augustine. I do. He is a brilliant and worthy man, gifted by God himself, and has spent his life, since coming to the Church, in contemplation and in penitence, seeking the way of God."

"No, you must pardon me if I offend you, but I cannot accept that. He may be brilliant, as you say, but he is a man, Bishop, as am I, as are you. No man can be God. Whence comes this *orthodoxy?*" I almost spat the word, so great was my disgust, but hurried on, giving him no chance to interrupt me. "Alaric taught us of a loving Christ who came to bring men amity and peace, gentleness and forgiveness, tolerance and charity ... A simple carpenter who spoke in parables and defined beatitudes and died in ignominy that men might be redeemed through infinite mercy. Where has that teaching, that example gone? There is little of it in the Church of the Christus today, it seems, when men—*men*, Bishop—grasp power and abrogate and negate and annul the role of the Saviour, designing and redefining the Words and Will of God to their own ends in the name of *orthodoxy*; and consigning others to eternal damnation because their *opinions* differ!"

I ran out of words and breath and realized that I was glaring at him across the fire, my eyes aware of, yet ignoring, the sting of the smoke. He was staring directly back at me, motionless, his eyes wide. My heart hammered in my breast and I felt the stirring of a formless shame, or dread, in my belly. I knew beyond doubt that his next words, his immediate response to my outburst, would cast a die that would shape my attitudes and my behaviour forever from that moment on.

Germanus evidently perceived the importance of his response as well as I did, for he withheld it. He held up his right hand, palm towards me, in an unmistakable gesture bidding me to remain where I was, and moved away from the fire into the nearest tent. I stood there, watching the entrance where he had disappeared, clenching and unclenching my fists in agitation, willing my heart to slow down and behave normally.

Moments later, he reappeared, carrying two clean goblets and a flask of wine.

"Sit down, Caius Merlyn."

I resumed my stool and he poured the wine wordlessly, handing one cup to me. It was cold, the wine it held a pale yellow colour. I took it and sipped, savouring the taste in spite of my agitation. Germanus replaced the stopper in the flask and sat back down on his own stool, sipping reflectively. The fire crackled, and settled in upon itself again. It would need fuel soon.

"There is nothing to gain in bitterness, Merlyn, and you are bitter. You are also in error." I glanced at him, prepared to question, but he went on, "Your friend Alaric is in God's own hands and has nothing to fear. His error, at the time he made it, was no error, since it had not then been defined as such. So put your mind to rest on that affair."

"But . . ."

He looked at me. "But what?"

I shook my head, baffled. "How can you know that, Bishop? If to hold a particular opinion is mortal sin today, how could holding the same opinion be blameless less than two decades ago? I cannot understand that."

He shrugged his wide shoulders. "I appreciate your dilemma. Nevertheless, that is the way of these things. The Church, in its wisdom, has decided that Pelagius was gravely in error in his teachings."

"But the Church is composed of men, Bishop, ordinary mortals. How can those men decide for all others on matters so portentous?"

"Because they are empowered to do so—to construe the law—and the mass of men must have clear laws to guide their steps."

I shook my head in denial, feeling the frustration building up in me again. "No. Power is more at stake here than is law. You quote a paradox, Bishop. Pelagius defended the law. He was a lawyer. His contention was that the theory of Divine Grace—the need for direct, supernatural intervention in order for mankind to win salvation—denied any requirement for human law, since no one could condemn a criminal who pleaded that God had not given him the Grace to withstand temptation. And now you speak of men's need for laws—the major part being defined by a few men—to condemn such champions of law."

He dismissed my contention with a solemn headshake. "You misconstrue my words. By any rule of judgment, these fathers of the Church are far from ordinary. They are all extraordinary men, of great erudition, piety and worthiness."

"By whose definition?"

Now he appeared to be growing impatient. His mouth pursed, and his tone grew cold.

"By definition of the bishops of the Church in conclave."

"Men, again, pre-empting the words of God."

"Be careful, Caius Merlyn! You may go too far."

"No, Bishop Germanus, I have come this far, and I am here because of the type of men who brought the words of today's Rome—today's Church in Rome—into my father's house and forced him to banish them for their presumption. Men who entitled themselves men of God, and demanded that Picus Britannicus accept them, their intolerance, and their intolerable hubris, upon their word alone."

He was wide-eyed again, astonished by my words. "What? What hubris is this? You say your father banished them? Bishops from Rome? I have heard nothing of this."

"These were not bishops. They called themselves priests. But yes, my father threw them from our lands, under restraint."

"Great God! Tell me about this."

I took another mouthful of delicious wine, and then told him the entire tale of the wild-eyed zealots who enraged my father, and then me. He listened in silence, without interrupting me. When I had finished speaking, he gave a great, deep sigh.

"Zealots," he said, using the word I had not spoken. "I fear they are becoming numerous. And the damage they cause may be irredeemable. I begin now to understand your hostility, not to me, for I sense none of that, but to the Church and its authority." I said nothing, encouraged, nevertheless, by his acceptance of my tale. He sighed again. "And it was this . . . event . . . that caused you to make this journey?"

I nodded.

"I ask you again, to what end?"

I finished my wine and refused his offer of another with a raised palm and a headshake.

"My father told them he might reconsider his decision, if and when he received instructions, or at least some communication, from the Church authorities in Rome. None came, and now my father is dead. Yours is the first mission of any import of which we have heard since that time, and we felt, my aunt and I, that it would be important to hear your message at first hand."

"I see. Well, hear it you will, most certainly. I can assure you of that. But you are a soldier, hence a pragmatist, and here is talk for clerics—theology, semantics and metaphysical theoretics. What will you do if you cannot understand the gist of it?"

I grinned at him, my good humour suddenly returned. "Ask you to explain it to me, Bishop, in words a soldier *can* understand."

He grimaced. "That is simplistic. I am both fish and fowl in one sense, that is true, but never simultaneously. When I assume the one persona, I abandon the other completely. I have to, else I could not subsist in either role." He paused to think, then resumed. "Tell me, Caius Merlyn, if you can, if there were one . . . element, one attribute of this debate for which you would be waiting, searching perhaps . . . what might it be?"

I barely had to think before responding, "Power." I saw his frown of puzzlement and explained. "As I have said, you are the first senior bishop to have come to Britain since the legions left—the first, at least, with any mission of great purpose of which I am aware—and the message you bring with you possesses power, great power, and great potency. Sufficient of each, perhaps, should you convince your peers here in this land, to change the very way our people think and act. That power will be unveiled and exercised in Verulamium. I want to witness it and gauge its temper." I paused, giving him time to respond, but he said nothing.

"By extension of that," I resumed, "should your debate prove inconclusive, or insufficient to convince our own bishops of the rightness of your cause and the stance of these Fathers of the Church of whom you speak, then I, and my people, will continue to live by the rules taught to us by Bishop Alaric and his like. These rules hold that all men and all women are born equal in the sight of God, each with unique strengths, each with a role to fill, and each with the God-given power to recognize and assess both Good and Evil and to assume the burden of choosing between the two. And all Christians accept personal responsibility for their own actions and choices, in the eyes of God and by the exercise of their own free will."

Germanus sat erect throughout this diatribe, gazing at me with narrowed eyes, his chin cupped in one hand, his elbow resting on the back of the other arm across his middle. When I had finished, he looked away, into the heart of the dying fire. Then he sighed again.

"You should have been an advocate."

"No, sir," I responded, "I am a soldier. Pelagius is advocate enough for me, and for my people."

"Hmm. You know he is dead?"

I nodded, saying nothing.

Germanus rose to his feet. "Merlyn, I could respond to what you have said, but I will not, not now. Your words, and the simplicity with which you state them, seem irrefutable, I know, and I will not condemn your evident faith in the truth of them." Again he sighed, a gusty, heaving sound of breath drawn, it appeared to me, from the soles of his feet. "But there is more to it than you can know. Which is, of course, why I am sent here."

He smiled at me and held out his hand. "Again, Caius Merlyn, let me thank you for your assistance today. Without it, we might never have seen Verulamium, and there would be no debate for several more years. I must go now and become the bishop again, discarding arms and armour and praying for humility to arm me in grace against the task ahead." He hesitated for an instant. "We will talk more on this, I promise you."

I stood by the fire and watched him enter the tent that was obviously his, and from that moment on I saw no more of Germanus the Legate. We rode thereafter in escort of Germanus the Cleric.

XXXIV

The experience of being in Verulamium disturbed me deeply. I had the same feeling of alien wonder and dread I experienced much later in my life, at my first Celtic funeral gathering in Hibernia, surrounded by masses of people making merry, eating and drinking and celebrating the humanity of the deceased, while the corpse lay stark and grim-faced among them. In a gruesome parody of life in death, Verulamium was a town whose passing was being celebrated—largely unconsciously, I was quite sure, by the majority of the celebrants. It was a ghostly, moribund place, dilapidated and run-down, experiencing one last glimpse of bustling, urban life, thanks to the crowds that had descended upon it and around it, attracted by Germanus and his visiting bishops and the importance of the occasion.

The first incongruity I noticed lay in the buildings. Some were inhabited, but most were no more than shells, looking fine enough on the outside, but empty, gutted and ravaged within, offering no spark of warmth or comfort. I had thought I knew this town well from my readings, and I had visualized it all my life as the home of Bishop Alaric. In my mind, I had always seen Verulamium as a lovely, stately place, wealthy, yet bucolic and well tended, with a healthy, prosperous populace. In reality, it was a ruined wasteland, and I met very few who lived there. Only within the original Roman walls, a tiny enclave the size of a fortified encampment—which it had originally been—were there any signs of permanent, ongoing habitation.

The throngs of people who jammed the streets by day camped by night, for the most part, in the fields surrounding the town. The public basilica and baths had been hastily renovated to accommodate the influx of delegates to the debate, but they were woefully inadequate to serve the multitude that materialized, drawn by the promise of momentous developments, and the empty buildings quickly became public latrines, the stench of which did not take long to permeate the air in all directions.

The Great Debate itself was to be held in the large amphitheatre outside the town, which, as I knew from Uncle Varrus's tales, could house upward of seven thousand seated people, but by the time our party arrived, three days in advance of the opening of the proceedings, there were already more than twice that number of people in and around the town. There were clerics in abundance, of course. Every bishop in Britain who could attend was there in person, and more than a few of them had brought staff with them. At first it amused me—later it upset me—to see how widely the various groups and sub-groups of clerics varied in their appearance. Some were dressed plainly and with dignity, as befitted their calling, but many more—far more—deported themselves as men of wealth and substance, wearing rich robes and bearing jewelled crosses and gold vessels.

And then there were the crowds. Many were sober, decent folk, the people of Britain come, as had we, to hear and see their destiny debated and decided. Others, however, and there seemed more of these than any other kind, were the type that are always attracted to large gatherings, looking to fatten themselves off the gullibility of fools. There were hawkers and peddlars and thieves and cutpurses, harlots and harpies and whores, musicians and tellers of tales, actors and singers and tellers of fortune. There were sellers of wines and beer and mead and food of all descriptions.

Nowhere were there any keepers of order. And the result was chaos.

I had hardly spoken ten words to Bishop Germanus since the day of our first meeting. For the duration of our journey northward together, he had kept to himself, a bishop again, spending his time in prayer and contemplation, preparing his mind for the debate that lay ahead. We had parted company on the outskirts of the town on the morning we arrived, he and his companions heading inward to meet with the rest of his retinue while my party swung eastward in search of a space large enough to allow us to encamp and still be within easy reach of the town and the amphitheatre.

That evening, however, a short time after sunset, as our encampment was settling down after the evening meal and I was enjoying a flask of mead by my own fireside with Lucanus, Germanus came to visit us, in his capacity as bishop, complete with long robe and pastoral shepherd's staff, accompanied by another.

Greatly surprised, for I had not really expected to meet with him again, let alone speak with him, I made him and his companion welcome and called for Donuil to serve them some mead. Lucanus made to excuse himself immediately, but Germanus invited him to remain, apologizing for the interruption. He turned then to me, indicating the man he had brought with him.

"Caius Merlyn, you have not met Bishop Patricius of Verulamium, although he knows your aunt, the Lady Luceiia."

I remembered immediately. This was the bishop who had first brought the mad priest Remus to Camulod, although he could hardly be held to blame for Remus's madness. I shook his hand and told him I had heard my aunt speak of him, though I refrained from telling him she thought him not half the man his predecessor had been. He was a big, old man, self-satisfied and well-fed in appearance, but gentle-voiced and inoffensive of manner. I introduced them to Lucanus, who had met Germanus before but had never spoken with him, and asked them to be seated on the two extra folding stools Donuil had placed between ours. When they were comfortable by the fire and we had shared a friendly toast to the forthcoming event, I asked the purpose of their visit.

I had been aware since their arrival that Germanus looked ill at ease, but I had no means of divining the reason. Now he frowned and sucked in his lips as though clearing his mouth of an unpleasant taste, and when he spoke, his words were unequivocal.

"Our purpose here, Caius Merlyn," he said, "is both presumptuous and indefensible."

I flicked a glance at Lucanus who was already looking at me, an expression of quizzical surprise in his eyes. I looked back to Germanus.

"Well, Bishop, that assures you, at least, of my complete attention."

"Hmm! Have you been in the town?"

I shook my head. "No, not yet. We've been setting up camp since we arrived."

"Any of your men there?"

"No, not until tomorrow. Why? What's wrong?"

He jerked his head, a gesture of disgust. "The place is in a state of anarchy ... chaos ... Thousands of people, of all descriptions, many of them lawless, and no means of maintaining order, no means at all."

I stared at him in surprise. "Is there that much need of it?"

He blinked at me in incredulity. "Need of it? Of order? How can you even ask such a question? There are thousands more people here than anyone had dreamed might come, and they lack both accommodation and latrines. Latrines, Merlyn, the bane of all commanders in the field. The filth has already started to pile up everywhere, and filth breeds pestilence, as you well know. Far worse than that, however, for the moment, is the lack of food. There have been no arrangements made by anyone to feed these thousands of people, who have been arriving here in multitudes for days. Some have been here for weeks. Most brought some provisions with them, but those have already been consumed, since most people also thought to buy food here, and there is none, or very little. What little there is has been appropriated by a group of brigands—"

"Appropriated? How so? Did no one try to prevent them?" Even as I asked, I knew how silly was my question. Germanus's expression and his next words proved it.

"Merlyn, they are well organized, and therefore dangerous and powerful. Verulamium, on the other hand, is home today to four hundred souls. One man, an honest fellow called Michelus, functions as an *aedile*, or mayor. He has four others, townspeople, who help him keep the peace in normal times. Now that abnormal times have come to Verulamium, he and his four, even augmented by my own escort, are rendered useless. I said these thieves are organized, and they are apparently disciplined, to some degree at least. From what I can gather, they are a loose-knit band of ruffians, numbering more than fifty, probably mercenaries or worse, who were attracted here by news of our gathering. They arrived some days ago, assessed the situation, saw their opportunity and took control of the available food supply using force and intimidation.

"There is trouble brewing as we speak. Not all the people who are gathered here are sheep. A corps of resistance has emerged, although belatedly, and a violent confrontation seems inevitable. The entire town could be in flames before dawn. People will die there tonight, Merlyn, and as time goes on and the numbers grow, things will deteriorate further and more quickly." He paused and cleared his throat, clearly embarrassed. "I came to ask if you would use your men to assert control in the town. As I've said, I have my own escort, but they are not enough. I will put them at your disposal."

I could hardly believe what I had heard, although I did not doubt one word of it. Nor did I doubt that my own men were crucial to the well-being of everyone in Verulamium. The doubt that crashed down upon me immediately concerned my right to plunge my men into a confrontation that was, in reality, none of their affair—a confrontation that would almost certainly be violent and bloodily brutal if it took place, as it undoubtedly would, in the streets of the town . . . particularly if those same streets were filled with civilian rioters. I looked to Lucanus for support, but he had his head down, staring into the fire. My gaze moved to Bishop Patricius. He sat gazing stolidly at me, his face betraying nothing but concern, whether for my plight or the town's, I could not guess. Germanus stared levelly into my eyes.

"Damnation, Bishop," I said, fighting my feelings of rising panic. "I can't order my men into the town. I have no right, no authority for that. They are here with me on an embassy, no more; to demonstrate a presence on behalf of our Colony. I have no right to endanger their lives in a situation such as this."

"You endangered them to help us."

"That was different. You were being attacked by Saxon raiders, Outlanders. The people in that town are Britons." I shook my head, hating myself. "No, I cannot order my people to do this."

He nodded. "I understand your reluctance." A long pause, then: "You could ask them, however."

I looked at him. "What d'you mean, ask them? To volunteer?"

"Yes."

"And what if they refuse, as they ought to?"

"Then they refuse."

I sat in silence for several long moments, staring sightlessly into the flames of the fireplace, my mind spinning with possibilities. By the time I looked up again, my eyes dazzled by the firelight, I had decided. I called for Donuil and sent him to assemble my officers here at my tent. I said nothing further to the others and we waited together in silence for the time it took for the men I had summoned to arrive and stand in a knot just beyond the firelight. When all thirteen of them were there I called them forward, introduced Germanus, whom they knew, and Patricius, whom they did not, and then told them what had transpired. They listened in silence, and when I had finished speaking, they, too, considered in silence what I had said. I had made no effort to hide my own misgivings over Germanus's request, and I had gone out of my way to emphasize that I held them under no obligation. When I thought they had had sufficient time to think it over, I asked them for their opinions on what we should do. Pellus, my Chief of Scouts, spoke up immediately.

"No need for discussion, Commander. We should go in. Not tonight, if we can avoid it ... not without taking a good look around ... but there's a job to be done, and we can't just sit back and let this kind of thing go on. Let these whoresons get away with this here, and they'll be somewhere else next week, or next month." He turned to look at Cyrus Appius, the leader of the First Squadron. "What do you say, Cyrus?"

Appius nodded. "Absolutely correct, sir," he agreed, his eyes on mine. "It's not something we expected, but we can't ignore it. We really have no choice but to go in there and put things to rights. We should organize some food foraging parties, too."

I looked at the others. "Does anyone disagree? Anyone want to bring anything else up for discussion?" No one moved or spoke.

"Very well, then," I continued. "But the criteria that I applied to you must also apply to your men. There can be no coercion. This is an affair for volunteers only. Summon your people. I'll speak to them as soon as they're assembled in the commissary area."

As the officers dispersed I turned back to Germanus. "Well, you have it, it seems. With their officers in favour, I expect half of the men will go along."

He shook his head and smiled. "No, Merlyn, all of them will, and I am grateful . . . We are grateful." Bishop Patricius nodded in agreement.

My mind was already grappling with logistics. "I can have your twelve Romans?"

"Of course."

"Good, then here's what we'll do. Pellus, my Chief Scout, is going to want to go into town now to look around and gauge the temper of things. I shall go with him, but not in uniform. That would be incendiary, I think. As has also been made clear, we don't want to send our people in there tonight if it can be avoided. We'll put them on alert at once, just in case, but we'll have them ready to move in at dawn, when most people will be asleep. That way, we'll be *in situ* before anyone can object, and after that it will be easier. In the meantime, please arrange for your Roman escort, who have already been seen by everyone, to be prepared to come inside tonight and extract us in the event of trouble. Can you arrange that?" He nodded. "I shall also need to meet with this *aedile*, Michelus, and his people. Have them meet with us at the tenth hour by the main entrance to the basilica. And the others you spoke of, the ones organizing the resistance to these thieves, can you bring me to them?" He nodded again, betraying no sign of rancour at my assumption of the role of Legate. I was thinking quickly, trying to remember anything else that might be important. Finally I shook my head. "That's all I can think of, for the moment. The troops should be assembled soon." They were gathering as I spoke. "As soon as they are ready, I'll speak to them and ask for volunteers. As soon as that's done, they will have to start preparing for whatever comes. At that point, there will be nothing to keep you here, Bishop Germanus. You may then go and look after the things I have requested, and we'll meet your people inside, by the basilica, at the time arranged. By then I will have had time to walk around the town and assess it for myself."

When our troopers volunteered to a man, Germanus squeezed my arm, thanked me again and left our camp.

That turned out to be a long night. After making my way into town at the time arranged, accompanied by a well-armed but discreet escort, I met with Germanus and his contingent of local leaders in the darkened courtyard of the town basilica. The bishop had been correct. Violent death was already loose in the streets of Verulamium: we had found several corpses casually strewn in the streets and alleys we traversed. There was an almost palpable air of tension surrounding the furtive group that awaited me in the light of the guttering flames of six matched pairs of cressets, and looking at their shadowed faces I had not the slightest doubt that what had already occurred would be as nothing once the spark ignited among the volatile tinder evident in the bearing of these men.

Introductions were brief and the meeting began with bad news. The thieves, aware of the danger they now faced from the organizers of the resistance, had immured themselves in a strong house against the town walls. One of them had been captured earlier, however, and had volunteered the information, before carelessly falling to his death from a rooftop, that a messenger had already been sent out the previous day to summon reinforcement from the renegades' base camp some thirty miles away. At least another hundred of these wastrels were on their way to Verulamium, panting in the expectation of riches, and were expected to arrive before daybreak.

That news, unwelcome though it was, when coupled with the surprising numbers of the men commanded by Germanus's small group of leaders, relieved me of the dilemma that had been plaguing me. My cavalry would have been useless in a street fight, but they could smash these oncoming reinforcements in the darkness within sound of the town walls. That would take much of the fighting spirit out of the band waiting to be strengthened here in Verulamium, particularly if they could be prevented from making any kind of sortie to join the newcomers.

Linus, the most formidable of the men Germanus had brought to meet me, assured me that he had close to three hundred men, locals and visitors, willing to fight with him to regain the food stores held by the outsiders. He assured me that his people could contain the brigands while we rode out, simply by turning their fortified house into a prison by sealing the exits. I went with him to satisfy myself that he had the necessary numbers and that they could, in fact, do as he promised they would. That done, I made my way back to camp and immediately began making my own arrangements and instructing my troop commanders.

Six short hours after the meeting at the basilica, dawn was starting to make itself apparent in the eastern sky and there was still no sign of the expected reinforcements for the thieves. My stomach was churning with unease since, with the dawn, I would have to take my men into the town, leaving the enemy at my back. Knowing well the dangers of delay and the growing need for incisiveness, my officers had assembled around me, awaiting my decision. They sat their horses in silence.

We were less than a mile from Verulamium, on the northeast approach, where the road dipped down into a valley at the end of the final straight stretch to the east gates. My men were spread out on both sides of the road, facing north-east. In the darkness, in unknown territory, our choice of terrain had been severely limited, but this was to have been a night action and the enemy would have been massed on the road. Now, with a cloudless sky, my soldiers would be blinded when the sun came up. I heard hoofbeats on grass, approaching fast, and young Yerka, one of my decurions, came at a gallop, pulling his horse to a rearing halt beside me.

"They're coming, Commander, but they're still a long way off, more than two miles up the road and all afoot. Pellus sent word as soon as his men made contact."

I grunted, my mind made up for me by the news. There was no point in our remaining here on the hilltop facing an open valley. The newcomers would turn and disperse the moment they saw us in the gathering light. I turned to my commanders.

"We've nothing to gain by remaining here. The valley there is almost a mile wide. We'll go down into it and move across it, at the walk. By the time we reach the other side, it should be full light, and the enemy should be within a quarter mile of us. We'll charge up the hill and over, half our force on each side of the road, and our surprise should be complete. They won't outrun us from there, and we'll have them. We'll spread out and overtake them on both sides, ride around them, then turn and take them from the rear, with the sun at our backs. Then we'll chase them down here into the valley and make sure that none of them gets out again. As soon as it's over, we will regroup and return to Verulamium. Move out now."

I rode down into the small valley—which looked for all the world like the dried-up bed of a river far more massive than the tiny stream that flowed there now—keeping to the road, between our two groups, and gave the signal to halt when we were less than two hundred paces from the northern rim of the valley. I checked right and left, making sure my lines were ready, then signalled the advance. The sound of our horses' hooves swelled like thunder as we built up speed, and then we were surging up the side of the valley and breasting the swell of the slope.

My estimate had been correct. The forces opposing us were less than a quarter of a mile from the rim of the valley when we rose into their astonished view, and the far sides of my formations had already extended into their enveloping sweep before I fully became aware of what was happening ahead of us.

In the first place, I had expected to see a rabble of about a hundred ruffians who could be relied upon to halt immediately and then scatter in panic. What I saw in fact, was a force almost equal to my own, but of infantry. And instead of panicking, they were already beginning to deploy into two tight, diamond-shaped defensive formations bristling with long, wicked-looking spears. Everything developed very quickly, almost too quickly, and I barely had time to shout to my trumpeter before it was too late. I saw his astonished face as he heard my order and raised his trumpet to his lips, dragging his horse to a halt. I reined in my own mount, signalling to all who could see me to do likewise, and as the brazen call rang out, loud and clear, I watched my men's fine, dashing charge falter and die.

Less than fifty paces remained between me and the forces now drawn up against us. I held my mount still, watching and waiting as my troopers reorganized themselves, pulling their horses in and around and then converging silently around the enemy force until my own position became merely one point in a circle. There were horsemen among the enemy formations, four that I could see. For a long time, no one moved at all, and an unnatural silence stretched throughout and around the circle. Finally I kicked my horse and moved forward, aware of Donuil and someone else, probably the centurion Rufio, moving behind me. I walked my horse forward until half the distance separated me from the other ranks, and there I stopped and waited. The defensive ranks eddied, then parted, and the four mounted men came forward to meet me. As they came, I studied them, picking out their leader immediately. He was a well-made, handsome man with a great, drooping moustache in the Celtic fashion. I guessed him to be about ten years older than me, in his late thirties. He wore a conical metal helmet with no face guard and leather armour studded with bronze plates, and he rode straight-backed, his head held high to expose the thick, gold chieftain's tore that circled his neck. The other three rode slightly behind him, one of them an enormous man, fully as big as me. He wore a helmet in the Roman fashion, with a tall, horsetail crest and bronze side-flaps that obscured most of his face, but I could see that he was younger than his companions, blue-eyed and clean-shaven. The other two wore full beards.

The leader stopped a horse's length in front of me, and his eyes swept over the men ranged on either side of me. He had evidently appraised my appearance as I had his. When he spoke, in Latin, his voice was deep and pleasant.

"Who are you? Romans?"

I shook my head. "No, we are Britons, from the west."

One eyebrow rose. "Where in the west?"

"A place called Camulod."

He shook his head, slowly. "I have not heard of it."

I nodded, accepting the truth of that. "You will."

"Who are you?"

"My name is Britannicus. Caius Merlyn Britannicus. Who are you, and whence come you?"

He smiled. "I am Vortigern, King of Northumbria. In the north-east." As he spoke, one of his three companions advanced to sit beside him. I ignored this one, keeping my eyes on Vortigern. This was the man of whom my father had spoken disparagingly. The king from the north-east who had made a suicidal pact of some kind with the Outlanders.

I kept my voice pleasant. "And why does the King of Northumbria ride through South Britain with an army?"

He gave a great, barking laugh, and I felt a liking for him, in spite of my misgivings over this meeting. "Army?" he scoffed. "This is not an army. It is an escort, and not even mine. I have it by the good grace of my friend, here, Jacob of Lindum." He indicated the grizzled man who sat beside him. I looked at Jacob of Lindum and nodded. He returned the gesture soberly.

"That answers only half my question, Sir King," I continued. "You have not said what brings you to South Britain."

"No, I have not. Nor have you told me why you attacked me, or almost did."

I shrugged. "The attack was planned, but not against you. We were expecting . . . a different force."

"What kind of force?"

"A rabble, come to swell the ranks of a band of thieves who have fortified themselves in the town behind us."

He turned on his horse's back and looked at the men behind him, and some kind of signal passed among them. I felt myself grow tense, but he turned back and put my mind at ease. "I believe then we have saved you the trouble. We met them yesterday, late in the afternoon. They attempted to take advantage of our advance party, not realizing we were close behind. We chastised them and sent away those that remained to lick their wounds."

I felt a great sense of relief, and it showed in my next words. "Then we are well met here. Where are you bound?"

"To Verulamium, to hear the bishops debate."

Now I laughed aloud. "Then welcome, King Vortigern, and all your friends, to Verulamium. Now, if you will stand your men down, I will arrange for mine to escort yours, and we will enter Verulamium together, where I will introduce you to Bishop Germanus, sent from Rome, who is awaiting our return with some anxiety, I have no doubt."

Between there and the town, I explained to Vortigern and Jacob of Lindum what had been happening, and from the moment our combined forces arrived within sight of the town, the unrest was over. Faced with the menace of our combined forces, and outnumbered more than six to one, the brigands surrendered immediately to Bishop Germanus—they would speak with no one else—claiming sanctuary and bargaining for their lives with the promise of returning the stolen supplies unspoiled. The alternative they offered, and I for one had no difficulty believing them, desperate as they were, was that they would set fire to everything and die fighting. In spite of the discontent voiced by Linus's auxiliaries, frustrated now through losing their chance to spill blood, their terms were accepted and they were banished under fear of death. The stolen food supplies were then restored to their rightful owners, and regular hunting and foraging parties were dispatched to search for and procure sufficient food for all comers.

It was not until much later that day that we all came together again, the crises resolved, and this time there was ample opportunity for talk and relaxation. Vortigern's men, or rather Jacob of Lindum's, were encamped close by my own, and at Vortigern's request, I had gone with my officers into his camp, where he regaled us with fine food and wine.

At one point in the early evening, I found myself alone with Bishop Patricius, and took the opportunity to question him about the priest called Remus. Patricius remembered the man clearly enough, but did not know him well. They had merely travelled together, he said, as far as Camulod, which was the furthest west Patricius had ever been. He had met the priest while on his own way north after a visit to a brother bishop in the now almost derelict town of Isca Dumnoniorum in the south-west, having decided to visit Camulod solely to meet my aunt, since he had heard so much about her from his peers, who knew of her from Bishop Alaric's time. Remus had accompanied him after a chance meeting along the way. He then went on to tell me, however, that only weeks before our present meeting he had learned, in a letter from his friend in Isca, that a priest called Remus had been killed in that town after being caught beating a young woman to death. Still visibly upset over such behaviour and such a death for a priest, he wondered to me whether or not it might be the same man. For my part, stunned by the import of his story, I told him the entire tale of Cassandra's ordeal, and he promised to pray for both of them.

I left him after that and walked away to be alone, feeling my heart bounding within my breast. Remus had repeated his crime, it seemed, and died for it, which meant that Uther was innocent, absolved, and I was freed from doubts and agonizing. Given, of course, that this dead priest was the same Remus! I resolved to inquire of the bishop in Isca as soon as I got home. There surely could not be two priests called Remus who walked with the aid of a stick!

XXXV

Later that evening I went looking for Lucanus, to share with him the tidings from Patricius, but before I could find him I felt myself being watched. That is a strange sensation, and one almost impossible to describe, but when you feel it, when you *feel* someone's eyes on you, there is no mistaking it. I froze in mid step, trying to place the emanations that assaulted me, then I turned slowly round and looked to where a figure stood in shadow, observing me.

I squinted, peering in vain to penetrate the shadows and identify more than the black shape I saw. "Who's there?" I called. "Who is that? Come out, where I can see you!"

The figure stepped forward into the light and I felt my heart give a mighty throb as my breath caught in my throat, threatening to choke me. I was looking, in astounded disbelief, at myself! And "myself" was staring back at me, wild eyed. Wordless, lost in mutual disbelief and amazement, we moved slowly towards each other. The apparition facing me was differently dressed, but of a height, build and colouring that matched me perfectly.

I was the first to speak. "Who are you, in God's name?"

He stared back at me, as though considering whether or not he ought to answer me. "Ambrose. Ambrose of Lindum. Who are you?"

"Merlyn Britannicus."

"So it was you! We met this morning. I ride with Vortigern."

He began to move sideways, around me, looking me over from head to foot, and I did the same, so that for a spell we circled each other like wrestlers. My mind was racing, for I recognized him now as the tall, helmeted warrior who had ridden behind Jacob.

"Ambrose of Lindum?" I was searching my mind for some explanation of his startling appearance, telling myself that such coincidences—such astounding resemblances between total strangers—must, and do occur. But all I could see in my mind was the stocky squatness, the short, bowed legs and the square, grizzled, red-hued face of the only other man I had ever met from Lindum. "Are you the son of Jacob of Lindum?"

He shook his head. "No. He is my uncle."

"Your father's brother?"

"No." Another headshake. He was almost squinting at me as he continued, "Jacob is husband to my mother's sister. My father was a Roman. He died before I was born. His name was Ambrosianus . . . Mar–"

"*Marcus Aurelius Ambrosianus!*" The name exploded in my mind and from my lips like a lightning bolt as the answer came to me and I knew with complete certainty to whom I was speaking.

His eyes flew wide with shock. "How could you know that?"

I turned my back on him, clutching my head in my hands as a storm of conflicting emotions caught me unawares; despair mixed with exaltation, and other feelings too new and sudden to analyse or define, threatened to overwhelm me. He was my brother! My half-brother! My father had had another son! And had died without knowing it! Reeling with the sudden knowledge, I felt my senses desert me and I fell to one knee, incapable of remaining upright. In a moment, he was kneeling facing me, clutching my shoulder, his eyes wide with concern.

"Are you ill? What's the matter? Here, let me help you up."

I took hold of his arm, feeling, even in my confusion, the strength of the muscles there, and climbed back to my feet, fighting to keep from swaying and falling down again. My brother! And out of nowhere, unheralded, unthought of and unsought . . . yet not, I knew with absolute, startling clarity, unlonged for. But now what was I to do? What could I say to him? How could I tell him what he had found, whom he had confronted? How does a man tell another man such a truth as I had to tell him? Certainly not abruptly, that much I knew ... I could have no thought of blurting it out in the open without any kind of preparation. Faced with the sudden, certain knowledge of his own mother's infidelity, a man might kill—and justifiably—the bearer of the tidings. I also knew beyond question that I had to distance myself from Ambrose of Lindum immediately, at least for long enough to grapple with my own thoughts, and come to some kind of arrangement with myself, some plan for informing him, welcoming him without being too precipitate or causing more than necessary pain. Nor was the irony of such a "welcome" lost on me—he would not thank me for it, not at first. Such welcoming might be the most unwelcome of all his life. It did not cross my mind for a moment, nevertheless, that I should not tell him, nor did any feeling of animosity towards him exist in my mind or heart. I simply knew I had to remove myself from his presence for the time being, and the further the better.

I thanked him for his assistance and begged his pardon, pleading a sudden nausea from something I had eaten, and left him standing there, gazing after me in perplexity, as I sought the cloaking anonymity of the darkness beyond the campfires.

The night was cool but pleasant, and I walked quickly once my eyes had adjusted to the dark, pacing with great strides that stretched my legs and made me concentrate on watching where I trod while I allowed the tumultuous thoughts inside my head to riot, swirling and tumbling as they willed, seeking their own level in the way of floodwaters, roiling and turbulent, clashing in violence and only slowly, gradually, inevitably lessening and gentling to a point where I could begin to make some order from their chaos. I recalled the tale my father told, and the tragic incompleteness of his knowledge: his lifelong ignorance that his illicit, nocturnal communion with the "dream-woman" who had used him and almost repaid him with death had resulted in a son who was the image of his unknown sire, a soldier—as witnessed by his place at Vortigern's side—whose very bearing would, I suspected, have brought a swell of pride into my father's—his own father's—chest.

As these thoughts were passing through my mind, however, I found time to wonder at my own reactions to this Ambrose, telling myself ruefully that I had no reason for endowing him with the attributes that sprang so readily into my imagination. I knew nothing of him, beyond our one all-too-brief encounter, and I well knew the folly of placing too much trust, too soon, in any man. And yet I also knew I could trust my own instinctive assessment of men, even complete strangers. My life had depended on that ability too many times in the past for me to doubt it now. Ambrose, I believed, would be all that he appeared to be, and I felt sure, deeply and strongly within myself, that the day would come when he and I would be brothers in every sense of the word.

By the time I stopped walking, I had passed far beyond the confines of the camp into an open meadow, and I stood there for a long time, staring up at the myriad swirling, spiralling stars in the cloudless sky, allowing my mind to empty itself, and then recalling how, one night in the time of my grandfather's father, one of these same stars had crashed to earth, bringing the Skystone and Excalibur into the world of men.

He called himself Ambrose, Ambrose Ambrosianus, proud of his Roman blood, but he was in error and in ignorance. His real name was Britannicus, Ambrose Britannicus, son of Picus Britannicus, son of Caius Britannicus, latest in a long line of Eagles. He was, or ought to be, as much as I, a Prince of Camulod, equal with me and with Uther. My body stirred with goose-flesh. Perhaps here was the man to wield Excalibur! Perhaps this was the one whom, according to Uncle Varrus, I would know above and among all others—the Champion whose coming had been dreamed. He bore the blood of Caius Britannicus; perhaps he had the vision, too.

Fighting to contain my excitement, I swung round and gazed back towards the lights of the campfires, too far away to see who moved there, but thrilled to my bones with the knowledge that one of them, one of those moving forms, was my own brother, Ambrose Britannicus. The Great Debate, I realized gradually, had become almost insignificant to me now, usurped by the most urgent imperative in my life: the need to sequester, to inform, to embrace and to come to know my sibling. Calm once more, my heartbeat safely harnessed, I set out back to the encampment to find him and draw him aside to where I could tell him all that he must know.

On my return, however, Ambrose was nowhere to be found. Vortigern's camp was filled with the noises of comradeship and celebration, but my brother sat in none of the gathered groups. Eventually, after my second fruitless circuit of the fires, I approached the central gathering again, the noisy, relaxed group of officers and clerics lounging informally among a cluster of large fires in the space in front of Vortigern's own large tent. Few of them paid any attention to my arrival and I made my way directly to the group that held Vortigern himself, with Lucanus, Pellus, Cyrus Appius, Jacob of Lindum and several others unknown to me. The sight of Jacob gave me pause and I changed direction to avoid being seen by him, moving around the group until I stood behind him, out of the direct light of the fire. He, like Ambrose, had seen me only in my armour, anonymous beneath my heavy helmet. The sight of my yellow hair and my uncanny resemblance to his "nephew" might shock him and give rise prematurely to the kind of speculation I knew I had to avoid until I had had occasion to speak to Ambrose.

Pellus had been saying something as I approached, and now Jacob himself was answering, his voice urgent as he sought to acknowledge and yet refute whatever it was that Pellus had been saying. Every eye in the group, including Vortigern's, was on Jacob, and as I scanned the faces of those seated opposite, failing to find Ambrose among them, I was listening with half an ear to what was being said.

"... the same at first, when I first heard of it. My reaction was exactly the same as yours. *Foolish*, I thought. *Stupid and dangerous and irresponsible.* Those were my first responses. But that was more than ten years ago, before I met Vortigern, and before I met the people he'd brought in. Since then I've changed my mind. I know them now, all of them, and I can accept what's happening ... I'm not completely comfortable with it, even now, I must admit, but in comparison with the alternative, there's not much I could say with confidence to prove he's wrong. I mean—"

"But he has to be wrong!" This was Pellus again, turning to Vortigern even as he spoke. "Will you not admit, King Vortigern, there's room for grievous error in your thinking? These are barbarians, when all's said and done . . . Outlanders just like the people against whom, through them, you seek protection. Their background, their mores, their very way of thinking is alien to our own way of life."

Vortigern was staring directly at Pellus, the hint of a frown marring his handsome face, and knowing now what they were discussing, I sat down unobtrusively on the end of a log, safely obscured from the general view by the broad back of the man in front of me. Earlier in the day I had clearly recalled my father talking of King Vortigern: of how he was tempting fate by allowing foreign mercenaries to settle in his lands, paying them for protection with holdings of their own and thereby granting them a foothold and a promised future in Britain. Acceptable enough, he had pointed out, if only one could somehow guarantee that these same barbarians would not wish, at some time in the future, to share their new-found freedom, wealth and bounty with their friends and families, relatives and neighbours still struggling for survival beyond the sea. Someday, my father had foretold, these newcomers would arise in power and stretch themselves, claiming the land as theirs, and in so doing dispossess their hosts.

Silently, with the others, I watched Vortigern's face and waited for him to speak, admiring the effort with which he restrained his understandable wish to savage Pellus. Finally he cleared his throat and spoke, his voice clear, almost a monotone in its lack of emphasis, the hint of a gracious smile quirking his lips.

"There may indeed be room for error in my thinking, Master Pellus, but Jacob, here, spoke of alternative considerations and I would ask you to consider the alternative to my having any thoughts at all in this matter . . ." He allowed that to hang there, vibrating in the silence for a moment, before he continued, "Would it be better not to think at all, and therefore to do nothing? To wait, and sit back, and see my lands and my people savaged and laid waste by an endless plague of raiders from all directions?" He shook his head, still calm. "No. I can assure you, that is what would have happened before now—years ago—had I done nothing. Because we, my people and I by ourselves, were powerless in the face of the onslaught that threatened us even before the legions left."

In spite of my own misgivings, I found myself applauding Vortigern's dignity, his decorum and his complete lack of anger. He continued to speak, looking around at all the faces watching him.

"You must understand, all of you, that these people I have ... brought in ... came at my invitation. They were not invaders; not pirates or savages. I sought them out, in their own land, and asked them to come here. Their fleets have made the seas around us safe again and their strength on land bars our territories to the invaders from the north. Their leader Hengist was my friend during my boyhood. He is my friend now. I know him well, him and his people, and I respect them. I also employ them in a manner that benefits both parties. We have given them land in return for their fighting skills and their assistance in protecting what is ours. I know they are alien and Outlanders, but our common interest in protecting what we hold together will lead to prosperity for both our peoples. There is a Greek word—*symbiosis*—that describes the situation. It involves two different species, with completely differing needs, coexisting in harmony and to mutual benefit. That is what we have achieved in Northumbria, and it is working well."

There was silence after this surprising speech as Vortigern's listeners took time to assimilate what he had said. Finally Pellus shook his head. "Well, King Vortigern," he said, "I've never heard of your *symbiosis*, but I know what makes sense to me and what does not. This with the Outlanders seems to me like sleeping with an adder in your bed. Better your bed than mine." He cleared his throat, shaking his head again. "I have no wish to offend you. I have shared your fire and your food and your drink and will not fight you with words you have no wish to hear. Your Outlanders are your affair and your lands lie far to the north-east, while ours are to the south-west. I pray your venture will work out for you, but hope never to see your 'allies' near to Camulod."

Vortigern smiled and stood up, bringing his people to their feet with him. "You never will, friend Pellus, but a time may come when you and yours might be glad to follow our example. For now, I will leave you with your discomfort, and free to speak your mind without fear of offending me. Good night."

He turned and made his way into his tent, and his going was the signal for the dissolution of the group around his fires. I rose quickly and left before anyone could notice that I had been sitting there in the shadows, and as I walked through the encampment towards another fire, I saw Ambrose ahead of me, crossing to my left. I called his name and waved so that he stopped and waited for me to approach him, that same look of slightly bewildered, almost hostile curiosity on his face. I stopped almost within arm's reach of him.

"You and I need to talk. Will you walk with me?" He nodded, wordlessly, and walked beside me as I led him through the lines of tents and out into the field where I had walked before. Once away from the dazzle of the campfires, our eyes adjusted to the darkness and the illumination from the gibbous moon in the cloudless sky was more than adequate to light our way until we approached a clump of large boulders that lay far enough from anywhere to be safe from casual listeners. There I stopped.

"This is far enough."

"Far enough for what?" There was caution in his voice, and curiosity, and a hint of latent hostility.

"For us to talk without being overheard."

He shook his head, a tightly controlled, tense flick, as though dislodging a fly or a buzzing insect. "Why should we fear, or should *you* fear being overheard?"

"Because I have things to say for your ears alone."

He looked around, leaned back against a boulder and crossed his arms in front of him. "Well?"

I turned slightly away from him, glancing back towards the distant fires. These next few moments were going to be very important. "Tell me about your mother," I said. "What is her name?"

"Boudicca," he said, and nothing more. The name surprised me. "Boudicca? The same as the Warrior Queen?"

"The same." There was no hint of levity about him. "My mother traced her descent directly from Boudicca, the Queen of the *Iceni*."

"Through three hundred years?"

He gazed at me, one eyebrow raised in the way my father had, and the way his father had before him, and for a time I thought he was not going to answer me. Then he said, "Yes, through three hundred years. You find that strange? Our blood is pure, unmixed and undiluted."

I frowned. "Your father was Roman, you said."

He nodded. "An exception to the rule. There have been others, but on the whole, not many. The *Iceni* of today are still the *Iceni* Caesar's legions fought. The same who burned the town of Camulodunum and almost took this country back from Rome."

"But you don't call yourselves *Iceni* today."

He shook his head, the start of a small smile on his face. "Nor did we then. It was the Romans who called us by that name."

"Of course," I said, matching his smile. "Where is your mother today?"

His face set into a mask. "Why would you wish to know that?"

I shrugged. "Mere curiosity. Is she in Lindum?"

"No." The negative was abrupt, accompanied by another jerk of his head. "I don't know where she is. I never knew my mother. I was raised by her sister, Gwilla, and by Jacob, her husband." He clearly had no more to say than that, but I could not settle for incomplete knowledge.

"You say you don't know where she is, not that she is dead. Is she in fact alive?"

"I told you, I don't know. No one does. She left me with her sister when I was a child and she disappeared. She hasn't been seen again."

"I see. And your father died before you were born?"

"Yes."

"And you are, what, twenty-eight?"

He frowned again. "How do you know that with such authority?"

I smiled. "Because you are six months younger than I am, and I'm twenty-nine." As he started to speak, I held up my hand to silence him. "Ambrose," I continued, "I have a story to tell you, and it is one that you may not enjoy, but you will be able to judge its truth for yourself, in the listening. All that I ask is that you let me tell it without interruption, for if you interrupt, with questions or denials, we'll be distracted and the whole story might not come out. Will you listen? And not interrupt, even though I promise you it will not be easy?"

He straightened up from his slouch and pressed his hands together, breathing deeply and finally emitting an explosive sigh. "You make it sound ominous, but yes, I will listen without interrupting you, even if what you tell me makes me want to kill you."

"I hope it won't," I said, and then I began. I told him the entire tale of Picus Britannicus and the wound he had taken, and the manner in which he had killed his host, Marcus Aurelius Ambrosianus. It took a long time, and before I was half-way through he had turned his back on me, leaning his weight against the stone behind him and staring off into the darkness so that I could not see his face. When I had finished speaking, a long silence stretched between us. I made no attempt to break it, knowing instinctively that he had heard enough of my voice and my words and that, whatever was going on in his mind now, he would take his own time in reacting to my message and the turmoil it had brought into his life. Finally, after a long stretch of utter stillness, he spoke without turning towards me, his voice drifting backward to me over his shoulder.

"So be it," he said. "I accept and believe your story. My mother was a whore and my father an ineffectual fool and a murderer, and your father—who is suddenly my father—killed him. Killed them both, in fact."

I waited, but he said no more, and I realized with mounting disbelief that he had dismissed the major part of what I had told him; had failed, in fact, to consider any part of it other than that sole aspect upon which he had seized. Stung to anger in spite of my resolve to accept whatever he might have said, I snapped, "I made no judgment on your mother! I did not know her, nor did you, so neither of us may presume to know her mind or to impugn her motives. And her husband, your father as you call him, was an old man, driven by an old man's despair to save his honour."

That brought him swinging round to face me, his eyes blazing, even in the moonlight. "What honour? My mother and your father combined to deprive him of all honour!"

I bit back my own angry retort, forcing myself to take a deep breath and hold it before speaking again. Then I chose my words carefully, wishing to give him no cause to fight me, and willing my voice to sound calm and reasonable.

"Ambrose, we have no cause to believe that . . . and the evidence would seem to indicate that it's untrue, in any case."

"Evidence!" His voice shook with scorn and wounded fury. "What evidence? What need is there of evidence? It is *evident—sublimely* evident—that my mother was depraved. Her own actions condemn her to anyone with ears to listen to the story of her infamy. . . ."

He subsided into silence and I drew another deep breath, and now when I resumed he did not attempt to interrupt me.

"Listen to me," I went on in a much gentler voice. "I have been thinking deeply about that since I first saw you and realized what must have happened . . ." I paused, aching with the need to help him. "You have said you believe my tale. Well, if you do, then you must believe all of it. It's not good enough simply to hear the parts you want to hear. The whole deserves examination, not merely the parts."

"That's ridiculous." His voice was the distillation of bitterness. "What is there to examine? To hear it is to believe it at first draught. The woman—my . . . my mother—was a faithless wanton. Without her faithlessness, there would have been no tale to tell."

"No, Ambrose, you are wrong. That is not so." My heartbeat had surged suddenly, for I had seen his error, and its incongruity, even as he spoke the words, and now I hurried on, trying to articulate the thought that had leaped into my mind. "Without my father's *recognition* of her—by sheer blind *chance*—in that market-place on his way to embark for Italia, *there would have been no tale!* My father believed until that point he had merely been dreaming, and there is no sin or guilt in dreams. He would have thought no more of his dreams, and the cause of your father's attack upon him while he slept would have remained a mystery, unfortunate and inexplicable. Only that single sight of the woman, by mischance, changed everything for ever. And had that not occurred, your life would not have changed."

"What . . . what do you mean?" His expression now was one of uncertainty, triggered perhaps by the arrangement of my words. I held up my hand in an appeal for time to complete what I was thinking, for I was using words now that had not occurred to me before this moment.

"We will never know the exact truth of what your mother thought, or what motivated her to act as she did," I said. "But consider this, if you will. . . ." My thoughts were outstripping my abilities to voice them. "Suppose . . . just let us suppose, ludicrous though the thought might seem at this moment, that your mother had a deep and genuine love for the old man. He had no son. Is that not so? Only a single daughter in her teens. You were his only son?" He nodded, his face twisted in perplexity. "Then let us suppose also that his age made it impossible for him to father a son. Not to attempt the feat, you understand, but to achieve it. For all we know, he and his wife could have been trying for years. Will you agree to that?"

He nodded, yet I could see he was baffled and still angry. I rushed on with my thought before he could speak. "Now, consider this. A virile, healthy soldier of noble birth, dreadfully wounded in the neck and face but otherwise complete and whole, comes to live in their house. This man is in constant pain from his injuries and his face is heavily bandaged. For much of the time, he is effectively blind, deaf and mute, and is heavily drugged against his pain at all times. He never sees, and seems unaware of, anyone in the household, but is under constant surveillance by physicians, the household staff, the daughter of the house—we know that because my father spoke of her—and therefore, it would seem probable, also by the mistress of the house.

"Now suppose again that somehow, perhaps by overhearing the physicians speaking among themselves about their charge, she learns that the soldier is sexually healthy, purging himself of seed in dreams at night as strong men will in celibacy. Might she not see that, somehow, as a cause for regret, a waste? I mean this seriously, Ambrose, and who can ever tell what thoughts go through the mind of another? And might she not then think of it for long weeks, during which the soldier's strength increased although his wounds did not improve . . . and might she not devise, in her love, or in her desperation, a means of using—borrowing, one might say—the natural, outflowing strength of one man, all unknown to him since he is drugged at all times, to benefit the flagging strength of another whom she loves?"

Now he did interrupt me. "Wait! Are you implying that my mother might have done what she did out of love for my *father*?"

I nodded my head. "Yes, I am."

"That is obscene! I've never heard the like—"

"No more have I, but it makes as much sense as the other! Think about it, man! This was no ordinary lust. There was nothing *personal* in what my father dreamed. It was a vision remembered, nothing more! The hazy recollection of a nocturnal image. To believe your mother capable of such mechanical impersonality, such mindless, self-destructive and aggressive lust, would be to brand her truly monstrous, and I doubt that she was anything like that."

"This is insane! I've heard enough. Thank you for your attempt to salvage my mother's worthlessness, although I know not what you hoped to achieve."

"No, damnation! Listen to me, for this is as new to me as to you and I don't know, either, what it means, but it seems reasonable to me. Ask yourself what I have to gain from this. Your mother means nothing and less than nothing to me. Why should I try to improve your memories of her?"

"Aye, *there's* the truth!" His voice was grating. "The woman you are trying to describe would have been capable of great love, is that not so? Great enough to abandon a baby? The fruit of her perfidy and infidelity!"

"Or the reminder of her failure!" His face froze. "Can't you see it?" I asked. "Can't you see what it would have meant to her? *Think*, man! The woman seeks to impregnate herself, using an available source that offers no threat. And she does it from a deep and self-less love . . . otherwise she would not be able to do as she did and retain any claim to humanity. She knows that her pregnancy will exalt her husband, who knows how much she loves him, and trusts her implicitly. And then something goes wrong. Her husband finds out what she is about, but not the reason for it . . . not the truth. He suspects the worst—conspiracy and seduction within his own household. In his agony, and sense of betrayal, he seeks to destroy the wrongdoer . . . but in his eyes, Ambrose, *the wrongdoer is not his wife!* He could have killed her with impunity for adultery, had he so wished, under Roman law. He chose not to. Unstable as he evidently was to attempt a murder in his own home, he did not try to kill his wife. He chose the innocent party, instead, not realizing that *there was no guilt* other than that born of his wife's love for *him*. And in the attempt, he died, leaving his pregnant, grieving wife to bear both her guilt and the child who had brought about his death. You. Remember, she fled the household directly upon his death. My father never saw her, did not know her . . ." I allowed that thought to hang there, between us, and then I closed my argument.

"So she abandoned you, but not completely . . . not completely, Ambrose. She did not drop you to die by the roadside somewhere, as she might have. She left you with her sister. With her own family, knowing they would accept you as part of their family. And she allowed them to believe her husband had fathered you. Only then did she disappear, probably in despair and with no wish to continue living. And has never been seen since . . . Now can you tell me why she might have done such a thing as to abandon you like that, rather than simply leaving you to die elsewhere?"

He shook his head, silent now, his face almost in repose, and I finished what I had to say, knowing in my heart that what I had said—this explanation that had come to me from the depths of my mind—was correct.

"Simply because she could not bear to live with you, even though you were innocent of any wrong. This was a wondrous woman, Ambrose, if my reasoning is sound, and I believe it is. Think of her with pity, if you can, and with affection. Out of love for an aged man, and driven by well-intentioned desperation, she might have undertaken a course fraught with great risk, one that could have given her little pleasure. And out of all these benevolent efforts came tragedy. Her husband, for love of whom she had done all this, was ignominiously killed, believing her treacherous and breaking his own sacrosanct Roman law of hospitality. And she was left with you, the daily reminder of her culpability. Marcus Aurelius Ambrosianus was your mother's husband, Ambrose, but he was not your father. And every time she looked at you she would have seen that, along with the fact that your true father—no more than an instrument to her—meant less than nothing to her and did not even know she, or you, existed. You and he were merely the progenitors of her guilt, the tools she had foolishly used to procure the unlooked-for death of her husband. Thank God she let you live. Many another would have killed you in the womb."

In silence, bereft of words, he turned away from me again, back to his perusal of the darkness beyond the rocks, but not before I had seen the glint of moonlight on the tears that spilled down his cheeks. I waited, but I knew he had no more to say, and after a time I stepped forward and laid my hand gently on his shoulder, feeling the tension in him.

"Listen," I told him. "It is late, and you have no need of company, so I will leave you now. Think of what I have said. You are my brother, my father's son, and you have a home in my home in

Camulod should you choose to accept it. We will speak more tomorrow, but I'll make no move to impose upon you. Seek me out when you are ready. Good night."

I left him there alone, standing among the boulders, and made my way to my own tent where I lay awake for a long time.

XXXVI

B y mid-morning I had heard nothing from Ambrose, although I had stayed close to my tent since rising, delegating my normal duties to Cyrus Appius. I had said nothing to Donuil or to anyone else about my encounter with my brother the previous night, and I could feel Donuil watching me solicitously whenever he felt I was unaware of him. In the meantime, I was content to wait. Ambrose might come looking for me at any time. I felt sure he would have passed a sleepless night with so much on his mind and had probably remained abed this morning.

It was a fine, early autumn morning, the air snapping for the first time with a hint of the winter lying in wait not far away, and the camp was almost deserted, one-third of our number on patrol duty within the town and most of the remainder at the debate itself. As I sat idly by the fire listening to the sharp, abrasive sound of the whetstone Donuil was using on the edge of my sword, a shadow fell across me and I turned to see Lucanus looking down at me, his back against the sun.

"Good day to you," he greeted me. "What's wrong?"

"Wrong? Nothing in the world that I know of." I beckoned him to join me. He approached, but remained standing. "Where have you been all morning?"

He shrugged. "Walking, and working. One of our troopers fell and broke a leg last night, badly. I set and splinted it last night, but had to set it again this morning."

"What happened? Was he drunk?"

"No, he fell down some stairs, but he was sober." He dismissed that with a wave of his hand and went on, "I'm more concerned with you. What's wrong with you? You have done nothing today but hang around here. That's not like you."

"Isn't it?" I smiled. "I'm thinking, that's all, and waiting."

"Waiting for what? Caius Merlyn Britannicus waits for nothing and no man . . . at least, the one I know does not. So what's afoot?"

I laughed. "Nothing's afoot, at least nothing to concern anyone. I looked for you last night. I had some news to tell you about Uther, after I had been speaking to Bishop Patricius."

"You mean about the priest, Remus?" He nodded. "I heard. I spoke to Patricius, too, after you. He told me what you had discussed." He paused, his eyes searching mine. "It must have been a great relief to know that your suspicions were unfounded." His tone made a question of the statement.

"It was. I slept well, last night. I have more news for you, too, on another matter, but it will have to wait for a while. Where are you going now?"

"To the debate. I hoped you might come with me. The formal commencement was this morning and I missed it, as did you. We did, after all, travel a long way to be here and to witness the proceedings."

I nodded. "Yes, we . . ." My voice died away as I saw him look beyond me and I knew, from the way his eyes widened and his jaw fell agape, what he had seen. I turned in my seat to see Ambrose standing by the side of my tent and could sympathize with Luke's shock. In darkness, Ambrose had resembled me amazingly. In broad daylight the effect was emphasized. He could have been my twin.

"Ah, Ambrose!" I rose quickly to my feet. "Welcome. Let me introduce you to a friend of mine, Lucanus, our superb physician, who thinks of himself as a surgeon." Luke's eyes were still glazed as I continued, "Lucanus, this is Ambrose . . . of Lindum." I could say no more until I knew the route that Ambrose would elect to follow.

Ambrose stepped forward and bowed slightly to Lucanus, a formal, yet courteous and friendly gesture. "Master Lucanus. Caius Merlyn misleads you, but out of courtesy, and I can see you see that for yourself. My name is Britannicus . . . Ambrose Britannicus."

I heaved a great sigh of relief. "Donuil," I called into the tent, "come out and meet my brother."

A period of confusion and wonderment ensued, as Donuil and Lucanus attempted to come to grips with the reality of this confrontation, but I cut it short, promising to explain fully later. I had seen from Ambrose's expression that he was not yet fully comfortable in his new role. I asked the others to permit us some time alone, and they left immediately. I led Ambrose into my tent and waved him to a seat. We sat in silence for a spell, simply looking at each other, savouring the likeness between us.

"Would you like something to drink?" I felt a sudden need to put him at his ease, but he shook his head and then seemed to relax, clearing his throat.

"Last night . . . Last night you said I should thank God my mother permitted me to live . . ." He made an attempt to smile and, shaky though the result was, I felt far better than I had in many hours. "I came this morning to tell you I agree with you . . . and I thank God, indeed." I could see tears welling in his eyes, and when he spoke again his voice shook, although only very slightly. "Merlyn, I spent the night thinking of all you said, and I believe now that what you told me—knowing and considering your own uncertainty—must be the truth. It seems against all reason on the one hand, but on the other it reeks of truth. We will never know for certain, as you said. I know that, and I regret it, but it *feels* like the truth, in *here!*" He pounded his chest with his clenched fist. "My thanks to you," he went on, fighting to control his emotions. "You have given me back my mother."

I swallowed hard. "I've given you more than that, my friend, and it benefits me as much as you, for I now have a brother almost like a twin, while you inherit another life: a noble father you never knew you had, plus a whole clan of kinsmen and a Colony like no other in this land . . . Not to mention Uther Pendragon, unknown to you at present, who will howl with mirth and outrage when he sets eyes on you. But we'll have plenty of opportunity to talk, now that you've begun to adjust. For the moment, I was about to leave for the debate with Lucanus. Will you join us?"

He shook his head with regret, rising to his feet. "I cannot, much as I would like to. I have things to do, and I have been lazy this morning, although I have told my uncle everything you told me, and he agrees with your reconstruction of events. Will you dine with me tonight?"

I felt my eyebrow go up at the mention of Jacob of Lindum's concurrence with my theory, but felt it best to say nothing about it then. Instead, I smiled at him. "With whom else should I even think of dining? Of course I will. Shall you come here?"

He nodded. "When the debate is over for the day."

We embraced for the first time as brothers, and went our separate ways, he to his affairs, and I towards the amphitheatre and the Great Debate.

After a long search of the large and strangely festive crowd who filled the amphitheatre, I found Lucanus seated among a group of single men, some of whom I recognized. They seemed to be the only people within the great place who actually appeared to be listening to the debate going on in the arena. Lucanus saw me and made room for me between himself and his neighbour who was, I noted with surprise, none other than King Vortigern, though there was nothing particularly regal about him today as he sat swathed in a huge, grey cloak, attentive to the events going on before him.

Vortigern glanced at me and nodded as I sat down. "Merlyn." He spoke softly. "Cold, out of the sun."

His eyes and ears returned to the debate and I nudged Lucanus. "What's happening?"

"You'll know as much as I, before you're much older." He did not look at me but spoke out of the corner of his mouth. "This fellow has just begun to speak, and already he has lost me. I've no idea who he is . . . one of Germanus's new bunch who were here where we arrived. The old fellow who spoke before him was going on about the findings of the Council at Nicaea convened by Constantine a hundred years ago . . . Something about Arianism and the Divinity of the Christus ... I think he was defending himself against some earlier allegation, before I arrived, of Arianism, but I cannot be sure. It's quite difficult to hear clearly. These men are clerics, not trained actors."

He was correct in that. The present speaker had a thin, querulous voice that would have been indistinct from the other side of a dining-room table. From where we sat, some twenty paces from him and hemmed in by people, he was almost impossible to hear, even with total concentration. For some time I listened hard to the whine of his voice, trying in vain to decipher his words, but eventually my mind drifted to Ambrose and the changes to my life his life would bring.

When I snapped out of my reverie and returned my attention to the proceedings, another man was speaking. I had not even been aware of the change, and I found no great difference. My buttocks were sore. I shifted in my seat, searching for comfort, and the movement attracted the attention of King Vortigern, who looked at me sidelong, the hint of a smile on his handsome face.

"Are you enlightened, Master Merlyn?"

"No, Sir King." I grinned at him ruefully. "I am bored, and lost, and beginning to regret the long journey that I faced with such high hopes. I cannot hear the half of what they say, and more than the half of what I can hear flies over my head."

"You'll hear better tomorrow." Lucanus spoke from my other side and Vortigern and I both turned to him.

"How so?" Vortigern asked, and drew another grin, this time from Luke.

"Because tomorrow there will be no one here except the bishops. Look, this is the first day of the proceedings and already more than half the people have gone off to other things. The noise is dying down even as we speak. I don't know what they all expected, but it is lacking here, whatever it was. No spectacle, no pomp, no entertainment ... merely a gathering of clerics, discussing abstractions." He glanced at me. "That is what we came to hear, is it not? Clerics discussing abstractions?"

I had to smile, serious as the matter underlying his question was. "It was, Lucanus," I responded, "but we did not foresee, I think, quite such abstract surroundings for the abstractions."

"Hmm! You would prefer distraction, I perceive."

"No," I demurred with a laugh, "not so. But I *would* prefer more concrete in the mix."

"Ooh!" He wrinkled his nose in disgust at my bad pun, but Vortigern laughed aloud.

Other people were turning around to look at us now, wondering what the cause of our hilarity might be, and Vortigern stood up, bringing all of his people to their feet with him. "Enough of this," he said, "I, too, am bored. I shall ask Germanus tonight to tell us what went on. For now, I feel like a pleasant ride in the countryside." He nodded a courteous farewell and left with his courtiers. A few moments later, Lucanus and I followed him, leaving the bishops to their polemics.

To no one's surprise, Lucanus's prediction was accurate. After the first day's dreary, arcane argument, few if any of the common people went again to the scene of the debate. I attended every day, for at least an hour or two, during the first week, but thereafter, as my disappointment with my own inability to comprehend the gist of the debated matters grew, my daily attendance dwindled accordingly. And not for two weeks, until the eve of the final day, did I have an opportunity to speak again with Germanus.

The weather had grown gradually colder, day by day, so that men spoke of snow, notwithstanding that the trees were all still green, their leaves only beginning to show faint signs of russet. Drawn in search of warmth from the unseasonable chill of the evenings, by the start of the second week people had begun to gather in the temporary taverns that had been set up in several of the larger abandoned houses. The streets and alleys were all well patrolled by my men and by Vortigern's, so none of these places were in any way troublesome. On the contrary, they were warm, bright and cheerful for all their recent birth and temporary nature, all selling simple—and sometimes not so simple—nourishing food as well as ale and mead, and causing more than one visitor to shake his head in admiration at men's ability to turn any circumstance into profit.

Vortigern, Jacob, Lucanus and Ambrose and I, along with several others including Pellus, Cyrus Appius and some of Vortigern's circle, had formed a loose-knit caucus, gathering on most evenings, those of us who had no other duties, in one such place, which we had named the *Carpe Diem*, in recognition of the brevity of its existence—past and future—and of its owner's opportunism. As frequently happens in such instances, our presence attracted other soldiers but repelled most civilians, so that in a matter of days the *Carpe Diem* had become acknowledged as a soldiers' haunt.

On this particular evening, however, I had fallen victim to my conscience and remained in camp to show my face among our troopers and to bring my daily journal up to date, a task I loathed but one that had a long tradition in Camulod. The custom had begun with my grandfather, whose insistence upon keeping such a record had been the only thing that had saved the lives of all his men, as well as himself and my great-uncle Publius from charges of desertion and sedition. From that day forward, every expedition led by my grandfather or any of his family or descendants had been carefully chronicled from day to day. In my case, I was literate enough, and facile enough, to have perfected the art of keeping concise notations on each day's events. From time to time, however, normally once every third day, I would review these notes and amplify them into the form of a journal.

Such was my task this evening. Feeling the cold in my fingertips, I had asked Donuil to light a brazier in my tent, and had swung around my father's old campaign desk so that my back and my right side could enjoy the heat from the glowing fire. It was late, long since dark, but the proximity of so many clerics had produced a beneficial glut of splendid wax candles, fifteen of which burned steadily and luxuriously in three tripod-mounted holders around the back and sides of the desk, allowing me to write in unaccustomed brightness and comfort.

I was enjoying my task for once, writing down fully and completely my recollections and impressions of the events that had taken place and of the wealth of new friends we had encountered. I had already dealt with Ambrose and the unexpected resolution of the mystery of my father's convalescence and the attempt on his life. I was outlining my thoughts *pro* and *contra* Vortigern's employment of Saxon mercenaries in Northumbria and the entire matter of self-protection in the face of invasion, when I heard the sound of voices outside my tent, where Donuil was still moving around, attending to his own duties. Moments later, I heard the flaps of my tent being pulled apart and I swung around to see Bishop Germanus leaning in.

"Merlyn? May I disturb you?"

"Of course!" I rose quickly to my feet to welcome him, making no attempt to hide my surprise and pleasure. "Come in, please, Bishop. You are not disturbing me at all. I was just finishing off here and thinking about having a cup of wine or mead."

"Think no more." He produced a flask from behind his back with a flourish. "I bring an offering in return for my impertinence in thrusting myself upon you. They told me at the *Carpe Diem* you were here, labouring alone, so I sought you out."

"The *Carpe Diem*? You went there?"

He heard the surprise in my voice and grinned at me as he stepped into the tent. "I did. A minor sin of intolerance leading to another of self-indulgence. I could not stand the thought of any more learned debate this night, so chose to seek the company of soldiers." He was looking around the tent, enjoying the warmth and brightness. "You are well set up, here, for working late at least." His eyes crinkled in raillery. "Are you sure you have enough light?"

I laughed. "Aye, thanks to the excellence of your clerics' supplies. From now on, when I hear mention of the light of learning carried by the Church, I'll know what it means. Please, sit down." I unfolded a stool for him by the fire and found two cups while he withdrew the stopper from his flask and poured for both of us.

For a time we talked of inconsequential things as we enjoyed the comfort of the glowing brazier and the luxury of his excellent honeyed mead, each of us glad to idle away some pleasant time without any urgency imposing itself on us. When we ran out of trivialities, we talked of the condition of the town of Verulamium and of the similar fate that seemed to be settling upon all the towns of Britain now that Rome, with its urban influences, was no longer part of the life of the country. Germanus was convinced that all towns would eventually fall completely into disuse, an idea that sat uncomfortably with me. He pointed out that, without a unifying, centralizing force such as the Army, and lacking the necessary volume of road traffic moving from region to region in organized trading ventures, there could be no real need or use for townships in the sense in which they had grown up. Not all towns would die out, however, he opined. There would always be points of natural confluence at which colonies would cluster, much as our own Camulod had grown out of our need to defend our farms, but he convinced me that the civically governed towns of Britain, as we knew them now, would continue to decline swiftly until such times as regular commerce and traffic re-emerged on a large scale. When I asked him for an opinion as to when that might be, he shook his head and looked grim. He had no hopes that it would be soon, he said, or even within the lifetime of anyone now living. He had seen the homelands of the Saxons who were now raiding Britain so regularly, and nothing he had seen there encouraged him to think the raids would lessen. The Saxons, in his opinion, looked upon Britain much as the ancient Israelites had looked upon Canaan: as a land flowing with milk and honey, containing all the blessings that their own lands lacked. He could see no hope of freedom from invasion for this land of ours. The raiding would continue, he believed, and would escalate until God Himself saw fit to bring an ending.

That disheartening observation led us on to talk of the organization of defences against the peril, and he spoke now as Germanus the Legate as we discussed the matter of Vortigern. From there, looking for brighter skies, we talked of my new-found brother, and

then of dreams and symbolism. His views on the latter surprised
me, for I had believed—somewhat foolishly, I soon realized—that
both as a professional soldier and as a bishop he would have little
patience with either of these insubstantial, almost superstitious
notions. He disabused me quickly, pointing out that, as a bishop at
least, he dealt with and made use of symbolism constantly. The
Christian Cross was, after all, the symbol of our Faith. I could not
argue with that, but we discussed the Cross and the emerging use
of the crucifix at length. The two were not the same, Germanus told
me. The crucifix, with its pain-racked victim, symbolized crucifixion, as it was meant to, glorifying the horrifying fate of the Divine
Saviour at the hands of man. The Cross, however, was a different
entity. He assured me that it was a much older symbol of light and
revelation, revered in ancient Egypt and even earlier in Babylon.
The Cross was also one of the distinguishing symbols of Mithras,
the god of light, whose cult had worshipped in secrecy. Mithras
had also been for centuries the Roman soldiers' god of militancy,
masculinity and the manly virtues. I had known these things, but I
listened to him in silence, unsure of what to make of it all—coming, as it did, from a Christian bishop.

One thing was certain, he summed up, making me feel much
better: an emblem, some form of simple, immediately recognizable
symbol—a signet of belonging, of conformity, of identity—was
essential to the success of any great popular movement. I listened
and nodded my head wisely, feeling the mead making my head
spin, and completely unaware that Germanus, bishop militant of
God's Church in Rome, was implanting a seed in my consciousness that was to grow and influence an entire people.

More than two hours had passed before we allowed the conversation to turn towards the debate that had filled the past two
weeks, and even then we approached it cautiously, he graciously
avoiding the temptation to talk in terms of polemics and theology.

"Well," he asked me, "as a soldier, what did you think?"

I made a face. "As a soldier? I thought the same as I thought as a
man. I was totally lost from the first day. Hardly understood a word,

let alone the ideas that were being thrown around so strenuously."

He smiled, gently. "Yes, I noticed your presence became harder to detect from day to day. I warned you, however, the first time we met."

"True, Bishop, you did." I thought about that, remembering my reaction to his surprise that I should wish to be here at all. "But I wanted to be there, as I told you at the time, to witness this, because of its importance to us all. I tell you frankly, though, there were times I wanted to jump to my feet and scream for someone to say something in plain language, something a man might have a hope of understanding. Finally I lost hope, trusting instead that somehow I might have a chance to talk to you, to ask you what had happened, what had been decided."

"Well, I'm here. Ask me."

I looked at him, seeing the man and not the cleric. We had done serious damage to the contents of his flask since he arrived, and he was relaxed and comfortable. Donuil had replenished the brazier some time earlier, before he went to bed, graciously refusing our invitation to join us. Now the coals glowed at their peak, throwing out an hospitable, smokeless warmth that had lulled both of us into a condition of perfect equanimity. I smiled at him, enjoying the mood.

"Bishop, I don't know where to begin . . . I don't know what to ask."

He sniffed, and reached for the flask again, pouring the few remaining drops into his own cup after I had waved it away from mine. "Well then," he murmured, "let me help you, since I know what you need to know but may be loath to ask." He sipped, sighed and placed his cup by his feet. "In the matter of excommunication for past sins, I issued no decrees. I had taken to heart, you see, your eloquent observation that, in the absence of formal guidance from outside, from Rome, you and your people were and are honour bound to live by the teachings of your bishops and your early faith. No man could find fault with that, Merlyn; its truth is self-evident." He paused, mulling over his next words, then continued. "The benefit of the doubt, therefore—that sophisticated wisdom propounded by your father and so ably transmitted by you to me—must be applied to all in like case. So there have been no major . . ." He sought the correct word, ". . . proscriptions ordained. And yet heresy is heresy and cannot be countenanced." He stopped again, eyeing me shrewdly.

"I know how your soldier's mind works, I believe. I know you have no patience with sophistry, so I'll speak plainly." He hitched himself erect and the pleasant mellowness faded visibly from his features. "As a soldier and an officer, you have high regard for the law. You must have; it goes with the responsibility . . . It is the law itself I speak of now; the Church's law, with all the awesome responsibility that entails. Apart and aside from all of the polemical and theological discussions that have unfolded here in Verulamium these past two weeks, one truth has been brought home, I believe, to the bishops assembled here from all over Britain: without law there is chaos. We saw the truth of that on our arrival here. That truth loses nothing of verity in the governance of God's affairs on earth. Somehow, somewhere, there must exist a central core of ratified, accepted truth—of dogma, if you like—if existence is to continue sanely. The confrontation of philosophies between Pelagius and Augustine of Hippo resulted in an impasse that had to be resolved. A reasoning, educated man can see much apparent truth, much plausibility, on either side of the debate. But those differences are merely philosophical, Merlyn, and therefore human. They are not, at bottom, theological. Within that difference lies the ordinary man's inability to comprehend the nature, and the seriousness, of the dispute." He paused again, watching me to see how I was responding to his words. I schooled my face to impassivity, however, and he eventually resumed.

"The law requires the existence of judges—arbitrators—learned men who, by virtue of their wisdom, are considered capable of assessing and assimilating all the materials relevant to the situation under dispute and arriving thereafter at a just, compassionate and humane resolution. The bishops of the Roman Conclave, and of those of Antioch and the other major Sees, perform the same function and, in their wisdom, they have chosen to decide this issue as they have. Pelagius stands apostate, and his philosophy and teachings are condemned. You, as one man, may rail against the judgment, but you must, perforce, accept it. There is no other recourse. The case has been considered at great length, over many years and by many people, and judgment has been passed." He sighed. "The bishops of Britain have now been informed, formally, by me, of how matters stand. They may choose hereafter to ignore my message, but if they do, they will do so in full and conscious knowledge that they proceed thenceforth in defiance of the verdict of the Church at large. They will thus proceed in sin, and *ipso facto* under pain of excommunication and damnation ... No man, however, bishop or other, will stand excommunicate for how he has believed or behaved prior to this time." He paused again, his forehead wrinkled in a frown.

"Merlyn," he said at last, "I cannot utter words of condemnation to you personally. You will live, as you must, according to your conscience. You are a good man and I see no wickedness in you. When you go to Judgment, God will know how to deal with you, and He is merciful where mercy is warranted. Bishops, however, are another matter altogether. They are the teachers, the exemplars, and their lives are subject to intense scrutiny by God and His Angels. I have decreed the establishment of schools—theological schools dedicated to the teaching of orthodox doctrine to the bishops of Britain now and in the future. The teachings of Pelagius will be heard no more in Britain's Christian instruction ... That is what has been achieved here, and I believe, with all my heart and soul, that the achievement is significant and good."

There was not much I could say after that. He had put my mind at ease and absolved me of concern about Bishop Alaric and his eternal fate, and had as much as promised that, if I continued to live as I had in the past, without falling into evil behaviour, I might approach my God with rectitude and confidence. Peculiarly Pelagian attitudes from the champion of orthodoxy.

The mead was gone and we seemed to be the two last people left alive in the whole encampment. It was very late when I walked with Germanus to the edge of our camp and saw him escorted safely on his way to his own quarters.

XXXVII

The Great Debate ended in an atmosphere very different from the one that had surrounded its beginnings two short weeks before. The vast crowds of revellers had dispersed in the preceding days, and at the end there remained only the clerics and the military presence supplied by ourselves and by Jacob of Lindum's people. The town of Verulamium, so briefly resurrected, had already fallen back into emptiness and decay, it seemed, and Michelus and his lawkeepers were once again empowered to maintain the peace in their small village within the original walls. Outside the town, the great amphitheatre sat empty again, its ranked and tiered seats and empty stage awaiting a future performance that might never occur.

On the day of our departure, after a late breakfast and a last round of farewells, we took our separate paths homeward. Vortigern and Jacob's party, including Ambrose, rode off first, heading east to join the great road north that ran the length of Britain. Saddened as I was to part from my new-found sibling, I took pleasure in the knowledge that we would meet again soon, when he came west, as promised, to Camulod. Germanus and his retinue, with their cavalry escort, rode south towards Londinium, whence they would travel south-westward to the coast, avoiding the new Saxon coastal settlements in the south-east, and thence to Gaul. We of Camulod struck out directly west, as we had planned, for Alchester and Corinium, where we would swing south through Aquae Sulis and home.

It was cold when we set out, and it grew colder as we proceeded. We were less than a day's ride from Verulamium, on a featureless road that climbed steadily through a fog of trailing, water-laden clouds, when heavy snow began to fall in thick, large flakes that swirled in a treacherous, bone-chilling wind and cut visibility to a few dozen paces. Our men reacted to snow this early in the year with shock and anger, despite the warning cold of the previous week. It was not yet full autumn, and the trees, though browning steadily, were still in leaf! I called my squadron commanders together and issued orders that we would encamp immediately and wait for this untimely storm to blow itself out. We made a cold and miserable bivouac and remained there for three long, wintry days, during which the unseasonable storm alternated between calm, silent periods of dense, thick-falling snow and lengthy periods of Hadean savagery when the shrieking, icy wind drove pellets of frozen snow before it like lethal weapons. Its fury finally abated, however, and we were able to ride on eventually through a now alien landscape, labouring heavily through deep drifts of snow beneath a sky still thickly shrouded with heavy, sullen clouds, and belaboured by a wind that had lost little of its malignity. We were high up, so the few trees we passed were small and hardy, but their leaves had been frozen by the snow and icy winds and now hung dead and crumpled, many of them fallen from their branches while yet green, their fruit unripe, their seeds stillborn and blasted. We were too high and too far from habitation for cropped fields, but I wondered uneasily how the harvest would fare if this unusual weather was widespread.

By noon the following day, nevertheless, we were well along on the road again and the air was warming rapidly, the cloud cover breaking up and scattering to allow weak sunlight to fall through so that the spirits of our men brightened visibly. I rode in a pensive frame of mind, once again mulling over the conversation I had had with Bishop Patricius regarding the fate of the priest Remus. I pulled my mount around at one point and rode back towards the tail of our column looking for Lucanus, feeling a sudden need to talk with him, but I found him talking earnestly with Cyrus Appius, his concentration wholly taken up with their conversation and his efforts to keep up with Appius's superb horsemanship. I turned back before I reached them, suddenly unwilling to interrupt their colloquy simply to allay my own boredom. At the head of the column once more, I cleared my mind of my previous thoughts, straightened my shoulders and increased the pace slightly, smiling to myself as I did so, feeling a small, malicious pleasure in knowing that poor Luke would have to work harder than ever now to keep his mind on the two matters demanding his attention. The sun shone fully on my shoulders, warm and pleasant, and I felt better than I had in days.

Later that afternoon, breasting a hill crest, I saw a green, unbroken meadow falling gently away before me with no sign of snow anywhere and, acting purely on impulse, I reined in my horse and waited until the head of the column caught up to me. Cyrus Appius approached me, a question on his face, and I grinned at him.

"Our horses need a run, Cyrus, and we need to blow away some cobwebs. There's an empty valley below us, on a long, easy slope. Deploy your men in squadrons. We're going to attack it." I turned to Donuil. "Take my standard to Rufio and tell him to ride with it until he is half-way up the opposite slope yonder. When our men reach the valley bottom, he is free to go where he will. The first man to reach him and claim the standard wins a flask of my own best wine for each of his squad mates tonight when we make camp. But tell Rufio I don't want him easily caught." I spoke again to Cyrus Appius. "It's about two miles, plus whatever Rufio can gain. What do you think?" He grinned at me, saluted, and swung away to issue his orders.

I rode with them, exulting in the exhilaration of the charge and trying to be at the finish when Rufio was finally run down, but I was a hundred paces distant, my big horse faltering, when one of Cyrus's own squadron claimed the prize amid cheers and jeers and groans of disappointment. By the time the confusion and merriment had worn itself out and some kind of order had been restored, the sun was beginning to sink low and I called for my officers to set up camp again. It was a happy camp that night, and I went to sleep well pleased with myself and my men.

Two days later, we sat, stunned, at the top of another hill, gazing at the smouldering ruins of what had been the little town of Alchester. Pellus had brought the news personally, and we had ridden hard for three hours to arrive here, although we knew we were far too late to be of any assistance to anyone. His scouts had found only smouldering ruins early that morning, which meant that the conflagration had occurred at least the day before, since they would have seen the flames had they burned at night. In the tiny forum in front of the town hall lay a heaped pile of bodies, more than seventy of them, and another thirty charred, hideous, doll-like obscenities had been found within the basilica itself. Most of the corpses in the square were men, boys and infants of both sexes. Only four ancient, withered female corpses were counted. The remains in the basilica could have been anything.

Pellus had ridden to consult with one of his scouts as soon as we breasted the hill and now he came galloping back up towards us.

"They came from the west, along the main road." Pellus was a gruff-spoken man who had no time for titles or military courtesies, and I had long since grown used to his ways. "A big party, well over a hundred strong, but we already knew that. My men tell me they headed back the same way they came. Left lots of signs, and spilled off the road surface into the soft ground on each side. Big party. Don't know who they are, but they're not Saxons; we're too far from the sea, and they've got horses."

I glared at him. "These are cavalry?"

He shook his head. "Didn't say that. Said they had horses. Probably wagons, too. But there's a lot of them on foot. Took what booty they could find, though there couldn't have been much here worth having, and all the women. My man Paulo reckons they're a day, a day and a half ahead of us, taking their time. Won't be expecting any opposition. Damn sure won't expect us to be running up behind them."

"Their misfortune," I snapped, turning to Cyrus Appius. "Forced pace from here on out. Issue dry rations to all ranks as we move; we'll eat on horseback. Quarter-hour rest every ten miles. I want

to catch these people by this time tomorrow. Tell your people." I
turned back to Pellus. "I want you and all your men far out in
front, in a narrow arc. Don't worry about our flanks. These people
don't know we're coming. Tell your people to find them as quickly
as they can, then keep them in sight, but to stay out of sight themselves. They know what to do, and you know what to tell them.
Move out now."

We rode far into the night, stopping to sleep for only four hours,
then rising and saddling up long before dawn, so that by the time
the skies began to lighten behind us in the east, we had already covered ten miles along the solid Roman road, and it was there that a
returning scout met us with the news that the enemy was less than
three miles ahead, still in camp. Pellus had estimated their numbers
at something less than three hundred, of whom less than one hundred were mounted. The most puzzling part of the scout's report,
however, was the indication—and it was only an indication, since no
one had been able to get close enough for absolute confirmation—
that there were no non-combatants among the enemy. No women
and no prisoners. Surprised, but not unduly concerned, I concluded
that the women had either been killed or—a more likely alternative since we had found no corpses, and women might be considered
a valuable commodity in terms of slave prices—they had been
detached and sent off by some other route to await eventual collection and disposal. I decided to attack the sleeping camp immediately.

We charged out of the rising sun and surprised the strangers in
a short, hard, bitter fight. It was a complete rout, and our trumpeters had to blow long and hard to recall our blood-hungry troopers
from their pursuit of the fleeing remnants of the raiding party. We
lost twenty-three dead and twice that number wounded, as opposed
to one hundred and eighty-one enemy dead and no prisoners. I
estimated that about a hundred of them had escaped, but the news
brought to me by Centurion Rufio dispelled any thought of giving
chase to them. Rufio had fought and killed one of their leaders, and
before the man died he had damned Rufio, telling him that Gulrhys
Lot of Cornwall would take revenge for this.

The news appalled me. If Lot was on the rampage again, and this far north—more than a hundred miles above and to the east of our Colony—then my place was in Camulod, and I had no time to waste in getting there. Now, however, thanks to this latest episode, I had more than forty disabled men with injuries ranging from slight cuts to serious wounds, and only a hundred and thirty-some sound fighters remaining, which meant that I could not reasonably split my forces and drive on to Camulod in the cause of urgency. To leave our wounded behind, even with a strong escort, in territory that might be swarming with hostile forces, would be to condemn them to death. The corollary was that my own remaining troops, minus the escort for the wounded, would be depleted to the point of dangerous folly in the event that we encountered serious opposition on our route south. I cursed myself for having tied my men, through what I could only define as my own culpable ignorance and irresponsibility, to the pace at which the most seriously wounded could travel—a snail's crawl.

A quick conference with my officers confirmed my assessment. There was no safe means by which we could split our party now that we suspected—and had to believe—that what we had assumed to be a self-sufficient band of marauders might in fact be but one element of a much larger force: an invading army.

I sent Lucanus to distribute the fifteen most seriously wounded men among three of our huge wagons, redistributing their remaining cargo among the others. Then I detached a forty-man squadron to augment Pellus's scouts, first making them change out of their uniforms, enabling Pellus to throw a wider and more mobile protective screen around us as we moved. Those arrangements in place, we struck out again for Camulod, driving on as quickly as we could without seriously threatening our wounded and, for that same reason, keeping to the main road as the most level and direct route, knowing that it was also the most visible and therefore the most vulnerable.

The full truth began to assert itself within hours. Large as it was, the group of "raiders" that we had inadvertently come upon was as I had now begun to fear, no more than a skirmishing force, a single faction of a wide-ranging but rapidly coalescing army that must number in the thousands. As returning scouts began to come galloping from all directions with news of hostile sightings, a picture of the emerging situation formed quickly in my mind. Large groups of soldiers—I had no choice but to consider them soldiers, undisciplined and ungovernable as they might be—were converging, mainly on foot, upon some prearranged meeting point that seemed to lie to the south and west of our present position. According to our scouts, there were horsemen and even a few old-style chariots among these groups, but no evidence of organized cavalry. We had reports of sightings to the north-west and west, and to the east and south-east. I had early sent an extra detachment of fast riders directly to the north, behind us, to see if we were being followed from that direction. We were. A large concentration of mounted men was massed some fifteen miles behind us, using the road as we had. The scout who brought this report had managed to range fairly close to these newcomers, spying upon them from a fringe of trees close by the road, which curved in a wide loop there, winding between two hills. He had then cut across country, avoiding the loop and regaining the firm surface of the road in time to be safely out of sight on his return journey before the large group re-emerged from the hill pass. He was adamant that these people, too, were mere horsemen, undisciplined and formless, definitely not cavalry.

My mind finally made a connection that had been eluding me. Our scouts were passing freely to this point among the various armed groups on which they were reporting simply *because* there were so many people crossing and criss-crossing the country around us. It was evident that none of the insurgents expected to be challenged or accosted. None suspected that we, or any other forces inimical to their own, were among them. I realized that that state of affairs would continue only until the moment somebody recognized us as being uniformed. That awareness came to me as we descended into a small, wooded valley, which offered us protection for as long as it took us to halt, shed or conceal our uniform armour, and make ourselves look as motley as we could. Although few of us carried any clothes that were not regulation uniform and colours, we did what we could, most of us contriving to disguise our soldierliness, of which we had been so proud until then, under wrappings of torn horse-blankets. There was little we could do about our helmets. They were all of a kind, and we could not very well remove them, for we would have looked even more conspicuous riding to war bare-headed. I broke up that uniformity, however, by having one man in three remove his helmet and carry it at his saddle-bow. They were all short-haired, which endows men with another unmistakable military uniformity, but I hoped that distance would disguise that from casual view. Fortunately, many of our men had acquired heavy, external clothing of one kind or another in Verulamium because of the unseasonably cold weather, and I had seen fit to allow them to do so, more out of necessity than any willingness to allow their appearance to deteriorate.

Before we saddled up again, I explained my thoughts to all of them and impressed them with the need to disguise ourselves even more thoroughly; I ordered all of them to be aware, from now until we could no longer disguise ourselves; of the urgent need to avoid anything and everything that could be recognized as military formality or discipline. Having spent years learning to ride as a unit, I told them, their lives now depended on appearing to be a rabble.

We emerged from the little, wooded valley around noon, looking nothing at all like the squadrons who had entered it, and over the course of the next four miles I harangued my men continuously, forcing them to spread out into a straggling, sloppy, widely dispersed train, riding in groups of no more than five together, the majority of them ranging far out on both sides of the roadway whenever the encroaching woods would allow them to do so, thereby creating the impression, I hoped, that no more than forty or so belonged to the party closest to, and presumably escorting, the five wagons we had left in our train. Within one of those wagons, folded and concealed, lay my great black bear standard and all the outward paraphernalia that had previously marked us so clearly as a force to be reckoned with.

A few miles further on, after passing through a long stretch of heavy woodlands, we encountered our first "hostiles." The road emerged from the woods into open grassland, bare of snow now, although the wind was still cold enough to make a mockery of the bright sunlight, and as we straggled out into the glare of the sun, we were confronted by a group of about twenty horsemen approaching the road from our right. They drew rein as they saw us, and sat watching us with suspicion but no outright hostility. Clearly they were prepared to accept us, but were curious as to who and what we were. The suddenness of the meeting crystallized some of the thoughts that had been going through my mind and I acted on impulse, forcing myself to turn casually in the saddle and speak to my companions without betraying any of the chaotic reactions that leaped in my breast.

"Cyrus, spread the word among the men, but do it without being obvious. We are from Northumbria, detached from Verulamium by Vortigern as his ambassadors to other kings. Donuil, come with me. I'm going to speak with these people. The rest of you remain calm and take your lead from me."

I kneed my horse sideways and approached the newcomers as though I had been expecting to meet them. Their obvious leader was an enormous man, bearded, wild-looking and heavily muscled, whose immense frame dwarfed the large horse on which he was mounted. He was armoured in layered thicknesses of toughened bull hide reinforced with plates of bronze, and he carried a large, round shield slung across his back. He sat calmly, reins loose on his horse's neck, and watched me impassively as I advanced, his face betraying nothing of his thoughts. I addressed him in the mixture of Latin and Celtic that I had used with Vortigern's people.

"Well met," I called out when some twenty paces separated us. "I am Ambrose of Lindum, nephew to Jacob, Councillor of Lindum, and the bearer of greetings from King Vortigern of Northumbria to King Lot of Cornwall. This is our first time so far south, and we are without guidance. Can you tell us how far we have to go to the meeting place?"

I was prepared for a challenge and swift action, because the only reference I had had to any meeting place came from my own assessment of the intelligence brought to me by our scouts, but my question provoked no suspicion and no response. By this time I had stopped almost within sword's length of him, and I allowed my gaze to move idly over his companions. They were an unsightly crew, all heavily armed and armoured like their leader, and all unkempt, with long hair, beards and moustaches. Their leader continued to look at me in silence, considering my words, and then his eyes moved to Donuil, taking in the size of the young man.

"Who are you?" he asked him.

Donuil shrugged his broad shoulders and looked defiantly back at the big man. "Cormac," he said.

"Cormac? What kind of a name is that? Are you one of Vortigern's tame Saxons?"

I was gratified by this signal of acceptance, but concerned at the same time that Vortigern's affairs, and his folly, were so widely known. Donuil spoke on.

"It is Erse, and noble. I, too, ride with Vortigern—by choice."

"A mercenary." The leader dismissed Donuil and looked back at me, indicating my dress with a disapproving scowl. "You look Roman." He made it sound like an insult. I took no offence, keeping my voice pleasant.

"My father was. My full name is Ambrose Ambrosianus. And our armour is Roman because it works well for us. The Romans understood such things."

He scowled again and snorted through his nose. "Derek," he said then, "from the north-west coast, Ravenglass. It was a Roman town, once, before we threw them out."

"I have heard of it," I responded, ignoring the obvious boast, and indeed I had, from Vortigern himself, less than a week earlier. "The Romans had a fort near there, once, a place called Mediocogdum."

His eyes widened slightly in surprise. "Huh," he grunted. "It's still there, empty and abandoned, above the road through the high pass. How would you know that?"

I shook my head, indicating that it was unimportant. "I have a memory for insignificant things. Somebody mentioned it, a long time ago, I know not who or when, but I recall something about it being the most westerly fort along the Wall."

"There's no wall there." His voice was scornful. "The Fells are walls enough. It's a grim and cheerless place, haunted by spirits and shunned by wise men. We will ride with you. We should reach the appointed ground by late tomorrow."

I eyed his men, deciding to take no chances and knowing that I had to assert my own authority immediately with this man. "If you wish, so be it, but tell your men to keep apart from mine. We have come a long way and my men are tired and impatient of the road. You'll notice some of them have wounds. We've already encountered unfriendly strangers and I want no more such stupid, wasteful nonsense. We are on an embassage, and I have no wish to spoil it through petty squabbling with every bad-tempered stranger we meet." I waited for his response, but when it came, it surprised me.

"No more have I. My people will keep their peace, so be sure yours do not provoke them."

And so it came about that we rode in company with our enemies for several hours, during which I learned much of Lot and his affairs and what he had been about since his last attack upon Camulod. I was surprised—and yet, upon reflection, not so—to find that Lot, like his father Emrys before him, was master of a large fleet of galleys permanently engaged in piracy. He had a stronghold now, with its own natural fortifications: a high-cliffed, sea-girt island on the north coast of Cornwall, which guaranteed his pirates a safe base, and Lot grew ever richer from his levy on the flow of booty they generated. Those riches he had amassed carefully, then used to purchase armed support from all directions, gathering a massive army with large payments of gold and the promise of enormous riches to be garnered from the conquest of

the wealthy area around Glevum, Aquae Sulis—and, by association, Camulod.

Derek, a king in his own right, had been recruited by one of
Lot's sea-going chieftains, who bought his services with gold and
promises of more to be won. Derek had taken the gold, and then
he and his twenty mounted men had ridden southward on their
own from their mountainous land to join Lot's gathering host. The
remainder of his men, a force of perhaps two hundred, had been
ferried south by Lot's galleys and would join the riders at the meeting place, thirty miles north of Aquae Sulis and approximately
twenty miles south-west of our present position. I listened to all of
this and said little in response.

As we rode and talked, the road had been descending gently but
steadily, so that we were now riding through dense, high trees again,
and I knew that the forest would stretch ever thicker and unbroken
from here to the gathering place of Lot's army. If we were to avoid
being trapped there, we would have to turn around, and soon, and
make our way back to the high ground, free of trees, whence we
would have some hope of circling around the meeting place and
escaping to the south and Camulod. I glanced up at the small patch
of sky I could see between the tops of the trees that pressed in on
the road. It was growing late and my mind was seething with the
urgency of our rapidly worsening situation. The closer we drew to
Lot's gathering point, the greater would become the concentration
of hostile troops converging on the meeting place, and sooner or
later—if we had not already passed it—we would arrive at a point
where discovery of our true identity would become inevitable.

Derek of Ravenglass, for all his roughness and his uncouth ways,
had turned out to be a pleasant enough travelling companion,
but now I found myself thinking seriously about ways and means
of killing him and his men without creating too much noise and
attracting unwelcome attention. The time was fast approaching
when our new companion would expect to stop for the night, and
that was unthinkable. Were we in fact to remain in his company
until morning, my men and I would have no hope of escaping the

trap in which we had found ourselves and which was tightening more surely around us with every moment that passed.

I reined my horse in a tight turn and rode back towards the wagons, leaving Derek and Donuil together at the point with three of Derek's senior men, then I pulled off to the side of the road, among the bushes, and looked at the wagons as they rumbled past, a mixed group of my own men and Derek's riding among and around them. I saw no signs of hostility between them; they were all soldiers together, apparently, and content to share the warrior's burden of boredom between dangers. A few nodded to me in passing but, miraculously, none snapped me the customary, punctilious salute. I saw no sign of Lucanus and presumed he was inside one of the wagons, with some of the wounded men. As the final group approached me, I saw Pellus riding in last place. He drew rein as he reached me and together we waited until we were far enough behind the others for our conversation to go unheard.

"What are you doing back here?" I asked him eventually.

"Waiting for you. Knew you'd come back sooner or later. What's in your mind?"

"Concerning what?"

He threw me a look filled with irony, tacitly begging me to spare him my word games. "There's a party of dead men riding here, Merlyn, and I don't know if it's us or them. It's your decision, but you're running out of time to make it." I did not respond to that, so he continued. "The rest of our troopers are riding behind us, five hundred paces back. They'll be along any time now. I've got a pair of my own men leading them, making sure they remain out of sight of the main party, while the road's winding like this. God knows what'll happen if it ever straightens out again to be a proper Roman road. I've called in all my people long since. Nothing to be gained by keeping them out there ... too dangerous. We know Lot's people are everywhere, so there's nothing else to discover."

Even as he spoke, I heard the sound of our approaching troops. The wagon group had already vanished around a turn. I looked back at him.

"What about the large mounted group behind us?"

"Still there, fifteen miles back. But the road between us and them is full of others now. They all headed for the roadway as soon as the forest started to thicken. Might be Outlanders, but they're not stupid. We have to get off this road."

"How?" I looked at the thick undergrowth behind me. "We'd have to cut our way through that. It's impenetrable."

"Nah! It's not bad." Pellus hawked to clear his throat, then spat noisily. "Hundred paces, no more. After that, it's deep forest. Big trees, no undergrowth, easy going. But we have to get rid of your friends before we leave . . . and we have to be quiet about it. How many are there all together?"

"Twenty-one."

"Then that's almost ten to one. We'll take them tonight, shall we? After dark? Then we can head out through the woods, lead our horses until we can see well enough to ride."

It was my turn now to return his look of irony. "And what about the corpses? You think the people behind us will simply pass by twenty-one bodies without wondering who killed them, and why? Or without wondering why there's signs of two hundred horsemen leaving the road and heading off through the bushes? And have you an answer for me to the question of what we do with our wagons? Or should we simply abandon them and the fifteen wounded men in them?"

He blinked at me, his expression indicating clearly that he had given no thought to this last point. "Shit," he said, at last. "That's it, then. We're stuck here. We can't get off this road, so we're dead men."

Something in his words triggered a thought, and I felt my heart begin to pound. "No." I held up my hand to silence him. The front rank of our main body had now almost reached us. "No, there may be a way to get us off the road legitimately and leave the wagons safely. Let me think for a moment." We drew aside again as our men began to pass us, riding in formation again, now that there was no one to see them. I watched them as a stranger might, my concentration focused on the thoughts teeming in my mind.

Finally I had it. I remembered Derek's scornful remark to Donuil about being a tame Saxon. "Yes!"

Pellus watched me closely, waiting. I grasped him by the arm. "Do you have a man who has not been seen by any of these people?" He nodded. "Good. We're going to need him. Now you and I will find Lucanus, and Lucanus will write you a letter. He will also refuse to abandon his charges. I'll leave you with him to await the letter, and I'll return to the point and start getting my people settled for the night. In the meantime, as quickly as possible, as soon as he has the letter, send your man looking for me as though he were a stranger, newly arrived. It's important that he pretends not to recognize me. My name is Ambrose Ambrosianus; be sure he knows that. The 'dispatch' he carries will be from Vortigern, who is having troubles with his tame Saxons and has summoned me to return to the northeast immediately. I will leave our wagons—along with a fistful of gold for his trouble—with Derek of Ravenglass and his people. They'll see that Lucanus and his charges come to no harm, and because they're all badly wounded, Lucanus will be able to escort them through and beyond Lot's assembly point, and from there home. Your part, as soon as you've seen your 'messenger' safely on his way to me, will be to start bleeding your men away into the woods, here, in small groups, so they'll be safely ahead of my party before we set out. They should be able to move unchallenged in the darkness, and to make good time once they are out of the forest. There's a full moon tonight. We will reassemble tomorrow morning at the site of this morning's fight—we should be well behind the enemy by then—and from there we'll strike out southeast as a unit again, and loop around this meeting place and south of Glevum until we hit the high road again to Aquae Sulis and Camulod. Let's find Lucanus."

The following morning found us safely reassembled, one hundred and twenty strong, riding again beneath the banners of Camulod. My hastily improvised plan had worked in every detail, and Lucanus, with a small group of volunteer wounded, had been left in comparative safety under the protection of Derek of

Ravenglass who, in return for a heavy bag of the gold coins we had never been required to spend, had promised me to see my wounded companions safely through Lot's gathering and put them on their way to a place where they could be tended. Lucanus, for his part, knew the cover story I had invented on meeting Derek. He could claim safely to have been on his way to Lot, accompanying me, as an envoy from Vortigern. His men had been wounded in a fight with others we had met along the way. It would be up to me to find a way of salving my own conscience for deserting my friend in such a manner, although my duty dearly lay in reaching Camulod as quickly as possible.

It was a fine, clear day, betraying no hint of the alien, wintry weather of the previous weeks. The sun shone brightly and warmly, and we drove ourselves hard, angling south-eastward and keeping our scouts ranging far ahead of us, on the alert for more enemy formations. The relative inactivity of the preceding weeks had worked both for us and against us. Our horses were well rested and healthy, but our own bodies had grown slack, so that more than a few men reeled in the saddle with unaccustomed aches and pains by the time we swung south and west to bypass the area where Lot's army was converging.

I missed Lucanus on that ride and so, it was plain, did Donuil. He rode in silence, his face grim as he struggled to keep his seat on the big animal that surged beneath him. Donuil would never be a confident horseman. Our order of march was simple and progressive: walk, trot, canter, gallop, canter, trot, walk; one mile of each, in three parallel, close-formation columns of six abreast, permitting our horses to conserve their energy while covering distance effectively and quickly.

By mid-morning of the second day of hard, relentless riding, we were on our home ground, tired but jubilant to recognize our own Mendip Hills in the distance. We had seen few signs of the enemy since the previous forenoon—a few distant formations, too far away to concern us, and all of those now heading north. We would be in time, it seemed, to warn our people. I was tempted to relax our pace, but resisted and instead urged my people on to greater speed. The miles fell away beneath our steady rhythm, and as the afternoon shadows began to lengthen, the Mendips rose around us and we swung directly towards Camulod.

At one point, crossing a high, expansive area of open grassland that rose to a narrow pass between two low hills, I led my column forward, listening to the muffled thunder of our drumming hoof-beats as the others fell into place behind me. The blood was singing in my veins as we climbed at a steady canter, and I was reviewing the events of the past few weeks, the threat of Lot and his assembling army temporarily forgotten now that we were so close to home. I had met and befriended Germanus the Bishop, Vortigern the King, and Jacob, the Chief of Lindum, and I had found a brother in Ambrose—not merely a brother in spirit, but in fact; a sibling! I had also learned the tenor of the discussions at the great debate and could report that Alaric's immortal soul was safe and we were in no danger of being excommunicate. And now I was returning home to my Cassandra, who was Donuil's sister Deirdre, and to our child. Filled with the joy of anticipation by this last thought, I sank my spurs into my horse's flanks and surged ahead of my men as we approached the crest. Beyond it, the valley that lay ahead of me was tiny, covered in short, green turf and rising steeply to another, more pronounced crest. Hearing the riders behind me speed up in response to my surge, I put my heels to my horse again and leaned forward, bracing myself in my stirrups, and whispering into his ear for more speed, so that he bounded to the top of the crest and charged over it into the slight depression that lay beyond, where he screamed in terror and reared violently, throwing me from his back as he tried, vainly, to avoid the grisly pile of human bodies that lay concealed by the last few feet of the crest. And even as I fell heavily, I heard him crash onto his side, and the sound of arrows hissing through the air around me.

The fall hammered the breath from me, and I lay gasping in agony and out of my senses for a time, whooping and sucking in terror-stricken panic for air that would not come, while chaos blossomed around me. By the time my breathing began to return to normal, I had recognized Pellus's staring, lifeless eyes gazing into my own and had realized that the piled bodies belonged to our scouts, for Orvic lay sprawled beside Pellus; the new-healed scar from the last arrow that had sought him gleamed livid. I had little doubt that all our scouts were in this pile of dead, for there must have been a dozen corpses, and Pellus had had few more than that. How they had died, how they could have been surprised so completely, would remain forever a mystery to me. Pellus had been the best, the most experienced scout I had ever known, and Orvic had been more animal than man in sensing danger. His instincts and his ability to scent trouble had astounded me on many occasions over the years I had known him. And now both were dead, Pellus's throat transfixed by one arrow and a second buried in his heart, while Orvic's back was arched unnaturally, as though attempting to dislodge the shaft buried between his shoulder-blades.

The sounds of conflict came back into my consciousness—all the noise of battle, the screams of men and horses, the muffled thunder of hooves, the clash and clang of weapons, and throughout all this, the lethal, whipping hiss of hard-shot arrows. Fully conscious by this time and preparing to rise to my feet, I realized that no one seemed to be shooting at me. I raised my head cautiously and looked around me. I was alone, except for my horse, which stood nearby, head down as he cropped the short grass, ignoring the carnage close by. My head was pounding painfully and I reached up to rub it, feeling instead the smooth, sun-warmed metal of my helmet. And then I heard a new sound, an onrush of fresh horsemen, and I struggled to my feet just in time to see a wedge-shaped formation of mounted men sweeping down from the hillside above to crash into the seething ranks of my own troops. To my right and left, the hillside was alive with bowmen, most of whom were now throwing their bows aside. They could not shoot, now that their own men were in the way. As they cast away their weapons, they drew swords and rushed down to join the struggle below.

I walked slowly to my horse, feeling a sensation of dizziness which faded rapidly as my strength returned. My iron-balled flail hung from my saddle bow, unused since the first confrontation with Lot's army when my father died. I raised one foot to the stirrup and pulled myself up onto the horse's back, noting as I did so that my troops were faring very badly. Many—far too many—men and horses lay strewn on the ground. The bodies bristled with arrows. Those who remained alive were packed into a dense, milling throng, dismounted survivors among them. I loosened my flail, swung it around my head, and spurred my horse towards the fighting.

I had not even had time to spur my horse to a gallop before yet another wave of horsemen came sweeping down from above, and I felt myself groan with despair and a blossoming rage that changed to incredulity as I saw the great red and gold dragon standard of Uther Pendragon at the head of the newcomers. I screamed a welcome and urged my mount forward faster, and sometime in the course of the fight, I found myself riding knee to knee with my wild, grinning cousin, sweeping all before us until we were separated by the swirling tide of the fight.

Sometime later, my great horse went to its knees beneath me, stabbed or hamstrung, and I fell forward onto the grass, losing my grip on my flail. As I lay there, winded, Uther saw me on the ground and leaped down from his horse to stand astride me, clearing a space around us with his own whirling flail and I knew that if I could only rise to my feet, the two of us together could vanquish all who stood against us. But I could not rise, with Uther straddling me. Moments later, he grunted and sprawled forward, off balance, propelled by a spear thrust to the middle of his metal backplate. I scrambled to rise to my feet, and as I did so I felt someone grasp my dangling flail and pull it, tearing the restraining thong from my wrist as I pushed myself to my knees, and then I saw my assailant, a dirty, bearded, broken-toothed, grinning madman, whirling the ball around his head, his battle-crazed eyes fixed on mine as I knelt, off balance, at his feet. I threw myself forward again, too slowly to evade the swinging ball, and the world ended.

XXXVIII

I opened my eyes in a new world, one in which I was a total stranger, a world in which I was to exist for almost two whole years.

When I opened my eyes the first time, this new world consisted of a single, white-painted room, containing four other people. I knew I was in a room. I did not know where. I knew I was in a bed. I knew that the people watching me were wearing coloured clothes: orange and green and blue and white. At least I think I knew that then. I might have simply learned it later and not remembered doing so. I did not know the people. I watched them look at me, and lean over me. I watched their mouths move. I did not know they were speaking. I did not know I was not hearing them. I did know I felt pain, I knew my head and my body were both filled with pain. Soon I closed my eyes again.

Sometime later, I was aware that the people in the room were different. Two were the same, a man and an old woman, but two were much younger. I knew none of them.

On another occasion the man, thin and dark-faced, leaned close to me, looking into my eyes. His hair was receding at the temples leaving a pointed peak, and as I looked at him I saw tiny holes high above his forehead where hair had once grown. Then his face wavered and became two faces, alternately overlapping then drifting apart. Pain pounded behind my eyes. I closed them again.

There came a time when I heard sounds before I opened my eyes. When my lids rose, I was looking at the ceiling of the white room, and the same thin, dark-faced man hovered above me, looking down. His mouth moved and I heard the sound of his voice. I knew it was his voice, but the sounds meant nothing. I became aware of movement to one side of me, but when I tried to look in that direction I could not move my head. It was fixed. Immobile.

I was aware of long passages of time, and of the pain either lessening or simply becoming more bearable.

Once I heard a bird singing somewhere and the sound of a heavy tread approaching me. I opened my eyes and found I could move my head as a large, dark-haired, broad-shouldered, heavily moustached man with blue eyes came to a stop beside me, looking down at me with a frown on his face.

"Merlyn," he said. "Caius Merlyn Britannicus, are you in there?"

I felt my throat swell and wanted to weep. I had understood what he said! He remained there watching me for some time, and I made no effort to communicate with him. I did not know that I could. Eventually he left, and as he passed from my sight, I continued to wonder what he had been trying to say. Who was Merlyn Caius Merlyn Britannicus? And who was I? The sudden knowledge that I could not answer that question in my own mind filled me with a terror that was all the more frightening because I could not remember ever having felt that way before.

I learned very soon afterwards that *I* was Caius Merlyn Britannicus. The old woman told me, the woman in blue who was always nearby. I watched her as she passed my bed one day, and she saw me watching her. She stopped in her tracks, motionless, and looked at me for a long time, and then she approached me and picked up one of my hands, holding it between her own.

"Caius?" she whispered. I looked at her more closely than I ever had before, taking in the whiteness of her hair, the smoothness of the skin stretched over her high cheekbones, and the deep blue of her lovely eyes. I felt her hand squeezing my own.

"Caius, can you hear me?" I gazed at her.

"Caius, can you *understand* me?" There was a different tone to her voice now. "I know you can see me, and I know you can hear me, so if you understand my words, squeeze my hand the way I am squeezing yours." Again I felt the pressure of her hands. "Squeeze my hand, Cay." I tried, and she felt it, and her eyes filled with tears. She moved even closer to me, sitting on the edge of my bed.

"You *can* understand. I knew you could!" She smiled now, and such was the warmth of that smile, the love and the tolerance in it, that I felt my own face respond and my lips move to form an answering smile. Her face grew radiant.

"Do you know me? Do you know where you are?" No response. I didn't know how to respond. Undeterred, she went on, "If you do know me, or if you know where you are, squeeze my hand again." She waited until she was sure that I was not responding, then she tried again. "Very well, if you do *not* know me, squeeze my hand." I squeezed, and she sat back with a short cry, but only for a moment. Then she was leaning forward again.

"Now listen to me, Cay. I am your aunt. My name is Luceiia. Can you say that?" Again, I understood her words and knew what she wanted, but I did not know what she wanted me to do. She moved again, so that she sat with her hip against me, her body twisted so she could look directly into my face. She moved her mouth slowly, speaking clearly: "Lu-cei-ia. Loo-chee-ya. Say that, Cay."

I felt my tongue move but my lips were gummed together. They would not open. She was watching my mouth closely now and she rose and moved away quickly, returning with a moist cloth which she used to clean my lips, running her cloth-wrapped finger end into my mouth and around my gums. It felt wonderful. She tried again, and this time I repeated what she had said. "Luceiia." It meant nothing to me, but it was obviously very important to her. I had learned my first word.

I learned very quickly after that, as a child does and, like a clever child, I had many willing teachers. The thin, dark-faced man told me that his name was Lucanus and that he and I had once been friends, but that I had lost my memory. He told me that my memory loss was complete, that I was an empty vessel, but that I might one day remember everything. In the meantime, he said, I could relearn all that I had forgotten. He was encouraged in this belief, he told me, because I was not a completely empty vessel. I could still speak and understand what was being said to me, which meant that, somehow, the damage done to me had not been unlimited. I remember that today, his way of phrasing that. He did not say the damage had been limited; it had not been unlimited. Even though that subtlety escaped me at the time, I also remember that I wondered what he meant, and asked him. He blinked at me, then paused for a time before saying, "You were hit very hard on the head with a large metal ball . . . a club with a swinging head." That meant nothing to me, so he continued, watching my eyes closely all the time. "We thought you had been killed. Uther found you being guarded by young Donuil, your tame Celt."

"Uther?" I searched my empty mind, seeking for a meaning. "Who is Uther?"

"Uther is your cousin and your closest friend. He has been here several times to visit you. A big, dark-haired fellow with blue eyes and a long moustache." I smiled, remembering: *Merlyn Caius Merlyn Britannicus.* That had been Uther.

"Anyway, Uther had been tracking the invaders who ambushed you up in the hills, but he had not expected you or anyone else to come along, so you surprised him as much as your attackers surprised you. He had been plotting a trap of his own when you and your troopers sprung the trap in which you were hurt. By the time he was able to organize his forces and attempt a rescue, it was almost too late. He and his men drove off your attackers and brought you back here to Camulod. Do you remember Camulod?"

I shook my head, only then becoming conscious of the extent of things I could not remember. Thinking back to that time now, I see many things that I failed to grasp, let alone remember. When Lucanus told me, for example, of how he had bored a hole in my skull with an auger to relieve the pressure of blood built up in there and pressing on my brain, all the while fearing the attempt might kill me but knowing that I would inevitably die if he did not do something, I listened without surprise or disbelief, utterly oblivious that such things were not supposed to happen. *Haematoma,* he had called the pressure. He had relieved me of a *haematoma* by drilling a hole into my head while I lay unconscious, and the operation had been successful.

I spent many hours talking to Lucanus, and to many others throughout the years that have lapsed since then, about the phenomenon known to physicians as amnesia, although no one has known more about it than he did. I learned that it is a surprisingly common occurrence, stemming from a wide variety of causes, but that its very commonness of occurrence is the only common thing about it. No two cases that he had ever encountered, Lucanus told me long afterward, had ever been the same, or even comparable, apart from the single common point of memory loss. Some people lost only parts of their memories and never regained them. Others lost all memory, then regained it in a very short time. Some people's memories returned to them slowly, over years, while others regained theirs in their entirety within moments. Some amnesiacs retained familiarity with their surroundings but lost all knowledge of their own identities; still others knew perfectly well who and what they were but lost all awareness of limited periods in their past. Mine was the most drastic case Lucanus had ever encountered. I had lost everything, including self-awareness, and had become *tabula rasa*, as he termed it: an empty slate.

As time progressed, I found out everything about myself. I met all my old friends and renewed many friendships. Their assistance and the good will they accorded me made the process easy. And yet it was never complete, because the relationships, old as they might be, had no personal significance to me beyond the point at which they began again. I identified with whatever it was that had occasioned these friendships originally, but I recalled nothing and no one. They brought the young Erse prince Donuil to see me and he spoke to me in his Celtic tongue and I understood him. He talked of the fight and how he had thought me dead after seeing me felled by my own flail. The man who swung it had been set to hit me again when Donuil killed him. I listened, responded politely in the young prince's own tongue and invited him to visit me again, but I did not remember him. They told me of my father, Picus Britannicus, and I had no recollection of him. They showed me my grandfather's books, and my great-uncle Varrus's books, but to me they were meaningless, because, although I could speak my own Latin language and the Celtic tongue, I could no longer read and the names of the writers meant nothing to me.

They told me that Cassandra was dead, with her unborn child, killed by persons unknown while on a visit to her secret home, and I accepted the information without comment since it had no relevance to me, even when they told me she had been my wife and the unborn child was mine. I was not callous; I was unknowing. My mind was empty of knowledge of her name, her face or her appearance. I relearned the facts, but I could not resurrect the emotional involvements.

Finally I moved out of my sick room and into the life of the fort they called Camulod. Uther, who should have been my teacher, I was told, was away on campaign in the south somewhere, fighting an extended war against King Lot of Cornwall—another meaningless name, although I understood its implicit menace. In his stead, therefore, Donuil the Hibernian prince and the Legates Flavius and Titus began to teach me to ride again and to handle weapons. I took to these activities immediately and instinctively, mastering each of the tasks I was set as quickly as they were presented, but none of them occasioned any further or deeper awareness. I simply had a natural aptitude for such things.

The spring of the second year of my new life arrived and lengthened into a summer that was followed lazily by an autumn in which I was plagued with formless, gradually worsening headaches. Then, after the onset of an early winter, Uther finally returned to Camulod. I had been anticipating his return, because apart from the recurring headaches, of which I had informed no one, by this time I was almost wholly back to being the man I had been before, according to everyone who knew me, and there were many who believed that meeting Uther would be the final step in my regaining my sense of self.

He arrived at nightfall on the second to last night of November, and I remember how glad he was to see me waiting for him with the others in the great courtyard. He leaped from his horse and ran to me, his face split in a great, joyful grin, and swung me off my feet in an enormous hug. I smiled back at him and returned his embrace, but inside myself, where I had learned to conceal my confusion, I felt devastated. The sight of him brought no memories, and my head began to ache again.

I had made two solid, honest friends since my homecoming, starting afresh with each, although they both assured me we had been friends before. These were Lucanus and young Donuil. They accepted me now as I had become, not as I had formerly been, and I loved them both for that. Almost everyone else treated me as they did because of what, or who, I had been. I could see through that pretence instantly and no one was ever able to fool me. Only with these two did I feel whole, because neither made any attempt, ever, to prod me back towards being the Caius Merlyn everyone else was seeking. Their friendship, abetted by the wholehearted and unequivocal love of my great-aunt Luceiia, enabled me to survive a long and brutal winter with a degree of equanimity, enjoying what I had, rather than pining uselessly for whatever it was that I had lost.

Uther, however, laboured hard at accepting me as I was now. His treatment of me was at all times straightforward, open and considerate—sometimes, I felt, too much so. He was scrupulous in his efforts to treat me as his equal and his lifelong friend, but I could sense an awkwardness in him. It came to a head on a sunny morning in March the following year when, during a hard-fought bout with me, he suddenly sprang away from me and grounded the point of his sword. I grounded mine, too, but watched him narrowly; this cousin of mine was a doughty and crafty opponent. He wiped the sweat from his brow with the sleeve of his tunic, his breath heaving in his chest from the exertions we had been sharing, and I was astonished to see tears standing in his eyes.

"By God, Cay, I can't stand this! You're you, and yet you are not. It's like playing with a ghost. You are complete sometimes, and

I love the fight in you, and you were ever thus, and yet ... and yet, much of the time now you are too different. My boyhood friend Cay simply is not here."

I felt a lump swell in my own throat at the sight of the tears in his fierce eyes, and I stepped forward, arms spread wide to embrace him. Our breastplates clashed together as our arms went round each other and he snorted into my ear, half laugh, half sob, before pushing me away to arm's length and looking me in the eye.

"I leave tomorrow, Cay. Back to the south. Lot is still alive and fighting fit in spite of all my prayers to the ancient gods to blast his benighted soul to smoke and ashes, and I won't rest until I've cut the head, with my own sword, from his stinking neck. I wish you could come with me, but I doubt it would be wise. You are too gentle nowadays, Cousin. Stay here, and train, and try to find yourself. I hope when I return you will know me again."

Four days later, missing him already and knowing I was unfit company for any of my friends, I mounted my horse and rode off alone, taking care to avoid being seen by Donuil, who dogged me everywhere, to the little valley my aunt told me I had called Avalon. There, I stood by the banks of the tiny lake, close to the wall of the small stone hut, looking down at the grave that they told me held my lost love and my unborn child. I had come here several times— once with Luceiia and once with Donuil; other times alone. And each time I came I felt guilt, crushing and hopeless, over my inability to grieve for what must once have been most dear to me.

Today my head ached abominably, throbbing so fiercely that I almost felt as though it moved rhythmically in time to the surging of my blood. I knelt by the foot of the grave and began the prayers I had been taught for the souls of the two people beneath me. How long I knelt there I have no idea, but the pain in my head swelled unbearably, and I eventually rose to my feet with great effort, knowing that the time had come to seek out Lucanus and tell him what had been happening to me. As I stood, my head seemed to spin and a dark, reddish mist swirled in front of my eyes. I thought I turned towards my horse, but instead I found myself facing the front of the hut, with its hanging, ruined door. My knees gave way and I felt myself pitch forward, seeing the edge of the door rushing towards my face.

I did not lose consciousness, and as I lay there with my face in the cool grass the excruciating pain inside my skull began to recede, to be replaced by a different, external pain. Eventually I was able to get up again, and then I discovered the source of my new pain. In falling, I had grazed my forehead against the door's edge and gouged a cut that was slowly leaking blood down my face and stinging painfully. Moving with great caution lest I renew the agony in my head, I went to the water's edge and knelt among the reeds there, scooping up the cold water to wash the blood from my face. The water felt wonderful, almost icy, and my head quickly began to clear, so to aid the process I leant forward gracelessly, bracing myself on my bent arms, and ducked my head completely beneath the surface, enjoying the sudden shock as the enveloping coldness chilled my scalp instantly and snatched my breath away. Feeling much better, I knelt erect again and began to flick the excess water from my short hair with my hands, and as I did so, I remember, I froze, motionless, my heart filling up with some enormous, nameless dread, my eyes dazzled by the brightness of the sunlight shimmering upon the waters ahead of me. I heard a drumbeat echoing somewhere, and only after long moments recognized it as the beating of my own heart. The sensations that swirled through me now were different from those caused by my aching head. These held the nausea of terror and the fear of turning my head to look at what I had no wish to see. I heard a ghostly, whooshing sound, the sound of ravens' wings, and then my mind filled with the surging image of a prancing shadow horse, its death-grey, shrouded rider standing in the stirrups, swinging a weapon round his head, splitting the air with the same sound of wings until he swung it at me, hurling me, shattered, into the waters of the mere.

Donuil, my faithful hound, rescued me before I could drown. He had followed me, of course, but knowing I wished to be alone, he had remained hidden, content to watch me, concerned as ever for my welfare and safety. Almost recovered I might be, but to him I was far from myself and therefore I bore watching at all times. He pulled me out, lifted me across my horse and bore me back to Camulod unconscious.

Lucanus took one look at me, it seems, and drilled his hole into my skull again, quickly this time, since the original aperture was plugged only with beeswax. Once again I awoke to find myself immobilized and bound to my bed for months.

This time, however, no further damage had been done. No *tabula rasa* greeted them on my awakening. My memory was as it had been—complete but incomplete. I mended quickly, but had to swear an oath to Lucanus that I would inform him immediately in future of any aches or pains within my head. Even when I had promised him, he looked gravely concerned and warned me that he had only ever performed his *haematoma* surgery once on anyone. He had never heard, he said, of the procedure being conducted twice on the same person. He was obdurate in refusing to allow me from my bed before he was convinced that I was, in fact, healing normally. It took six more weeks to convince him of that, and each day and night of those six weeks I was haunted by the death-grey vision that had assailed me by the lakeside. In vain I told myself it had been caused by the deep-seated pressure in my skull, but I could not rid myself of the conviction that something important had occurred there.

Within two weeks of being allowed to leave my bed, Lucanus permitted me to mount a horse, and from that moment on I fretted impatiently, waiting for Donuil to ride off on an errand to some neighbouring farm. As soon as he did so, I made my way directly to the valley again, dreading what I might find, but fearing even more the burden I would bear if I allowed my fear to stop me from going back.

Nothing had changed. The tiny grave was there, grown over now with weeds, since Donuil had been held in Camulod, tending to me. I walked to the water's edge and found the spot where I had knelt that day, and I knelt there again, waiting to be assailed afresh, but nothing happened. I gazed across the surface of the tiny lake and saw only the trees on the other bank. My logic had been correct, I realized; the phantasms that had plagued me had sprung from the pressures in my head.

I became aware of the anomaly before I actually looked at it. It was merely *there*, present, a strangeness that attracted me by its very difference. Even when I focused on it, I could not see what it was. It lay just out of reach, a stick of some description, short and thick and absolutely straight, hanging vertically in the clear water between two clumps of reeds. I looked more closely, then realized it was too short. It did not reach all the way to the bottom but merely hung there vertically, waterlogged in some strange fashion. Idly, I splashed my hand towards it, trying to make it move. The water churned around it, but it hung there almost motionless, as though anchored. And then I saw the loop, floating almost invisibly just below the surface. I stood up and stepped into the water, sinking almost to the knees in the muddy bottom as I reached out and grasped the thing. It was slick and greasy in my grip, covered in algae, but it came to me easily as I pulled and lifted it. It was a man-made shaft, not a stick, and it ended in a fitted iron butt from which depended a length of chain and a heavy iron ball, rusted to the colour of the mud on the bottom. My flail! And yet I knew immediately it could not be, for mine was lying somewhere up in the Mendip Hills, wrapped around the skeletal wrist of the man who had last swung it.

If you don't hit me with yours . . . The words rang clearly in my head and the voice was mine, but to whom had I said that? I looked at the dripping weapon in my hand and heard more words.

Can't you imagine what that thing would do to a man on foot if you swung it round your head?

It would impress him.

Aye, helmet, skull and all . . .

I promise not to hit you with mine if you don't hit me with yours.

Uther! The other voice was Uther's! But when had we said those words? *I promise not to hit you with mine if you don't hit me with yours . . .* And then it came to me. It had been the morning of the day we set out against Lot's first invasion, the last time I saw my father alive. And suddenly my father's face was there in my mind, twisted in death as he sprawled in rigor mortis across his bed, and I felt a stab of agony as I remembered, not yet aware that I was remembering. Then, incongruously, I heard Aunt Luceiia's voice: *Her injuries were awful, as though she had been battered to death, her skull completely crushed . . .* Then Uther's voice again: *The bitch! I'll find her later and teach her a lesson she won't soon forget . . .*

The voice I heard screaming then was my own, as all the agony and grief, the sudden realization of my lost love, crashed down on me at once and I staggered round to look at—and this time really to see—the piteous, weed-strewn little grave that contained my beloved, my dreams and my life.

Publius Varrus remarked several times in his writings, and I have always agreed with him, that words, the strongest tool men have for communicating ideas, are hopelessly inadequate for the tasks we sometimes ask of them. This is most particularly, and inevitably, true when we find ourselves struggling to describe the most basic and fundamental human emotions: love and happiness; hate and bitterness; grief and anguish. I have no recollection of kneeling there by that graveside or of what thoughts passed through my mind. I only know that when I became aware again of the world around me, night was falling quickly, my thighs were quivering with exhaustion, and the grave before me had been plucked clean of weeds, its edges smoothed and its surface, bearing multiple imprints of my palms, patted flat. My mind was also filled with a decision made, and my breast was filled with a cold and reasoned, emotionless placidity that entailed an utter and complete knowledge of what I had to do.

Sometime later, still filled with that unutterable calm, I opened the door to Luceiia's family room and stopped short on the threshold, stunned by the sight of her in the lamplight and suddenly aware, from a completely new perspective, of another dimension to all I had lost through my illness. She was no different from when

I had last seen her earlier that day, but now I remembered the beloved Luceiia Britannicus who had ridden with me to meet Cassandra just two years before, and this was a different person. Those two years had wrought enormous changes in my aunt. She had shrunk, and looked tiny and fragile. And yet the same lively wit and beauty sparkled from those great, indomitable blue eyes as she turned to look at me.

She recognized the change in me immediately.

"You remember!"

I nodded, mute, still standing in the doorway, and she moved to me quickly, drawing me into the room, her eyes already awash with tears.

"Thank God, Caius, thank God! What happened? How? Have you told Lucanus? Does anyone else know?"

I shook my head, still wordless, answering all her questions with one gesture, my throat completely choked by a great, swelling lump of grief and misery. And then the dam broke and I was riven by a violent, wrenching sob and gave way completely to the pain inside, allowing it to overwhelm me. I felt my aunt's arms go around my waist and I enfolded her in my own, feeling the smallness of her and the love and sadness that frailty brought me as I cradled her gently and allowed my tears to fall unchecked into her silver hair. When the paroxysm had subsided, she led me to a chair and pressed me down into it, then sat close to me and watched me until I had mastered myself again. She made no attempt to speak, waiting in wisdom for me to begin. I was in no hurry. I sat there, empty now, my eyes closed, and waited until I felt the resolute calmness I had previously felt reentering my body and filling me to the point where I could speak again. Finally I opened my eyes and looked at her. Her own eyes were filled with love and concern.

"Auntie, when exactly did Cassandra . . . when was she killed?"

She gazed at me. "You have been there again? To the grave?"

I nodded. "That's where I remembered. When, Auntie?"

She shook her head, a troubled frown on her brow. "We don't know exactly, but it was soon after you left for Verulamium. She left here to return to your little valley ten days after your own departure. She was happy there, and lonely here. She was heavy with the child, of course, but she was healthy and blooming and still well short of her term, so I saw no reason to keep her here . . . not when her heart was so obviously there . . ." Her voice faded, then resumed. "I expected her to return within the week, but even when the week passed with no sign of her I was not concerned. The weather was clement, better than it had been all summer, and she had taken the little two-wheeled cart, so she was well stocked with provisions. It was only after ten days that I began to wonder, and so when Daffyd arrived that same day, I asked him to go and visit her, just to be sure."

"Daffyd? It was Daffyd who found her?"

My aunt nodded, miserably. "She had been dead for some time by then. More than a week, Daffyd thought. Poor Daffyd. He found her, and he cleaned her, and he buried her. Then he came back and told us."

I swallowed hard. "What about the baby?"

She looked me straight in the eyes and shook her head. "It was still inside her, if that's what you are asking. They died together, intact."

"Was she . . . Did he find her in the water?"

She nodded her head, her face drawn with concern. "Yes, yes he did. He told me at the time, but I had forgotten. The poor child was dead. Where he had found her made no difference to me. How did you know? Did Daffyd tell you?"

I shook my head, mute, recalling with horror how a human corpse could look after days of submersion in water. My dear aunt could have no idea of such atrocities. My next question was difficult, my voice almost defying me to make it utter the words. I had to draw a deep breath and hold it before asking, "Was Uther in Camulod then?"

She nodded. "Yes, he was. As a matter of fact, he had arrived on the morning of the day Cassandra left-" She bit off her words and looked at me in dismay. "Caius! Why did you ask me that?"

"Because I want to know, Auntie. When did he leave?"

Her eyes widening in horror, she shook her head in denial of what I was implying. "I . . . I . . . Caius, you can't be—"

"When did he leave, Auntie?"

"Within a few days. You know Uther. He comes and he goes, always riding somewhere."

"He was gone, then, before Daffyd came?"

"Yes, days before! But I can't allow you to think what you are thinking, Caius. It is unjust, infamous! You suspected Uther before, but you know it was Remus the priest who committed that crime."

"Remus is dead, Auntie, long since . . . and far from here, long before this crime was committed."

"No, Caius!" The anguish in her voice was as keen-edged as my own.

"No," I whispered, aware of how much I was hurting her. "Perhaps not. But I have to know, Auntie. I have to *know!*" Inside my heart, however, I did know. I spoke purely to soothe this woman I loved more than any other now alive. I drew another deep breath and changed the subject.

"Auntie, did anyone ever tell you about my brother Ambrose?"

Her expression changed to one of wonderment and she nodded. "Yes. Lucanus told me about him, although he knew few details. He said you were like twins. I would have sent for him, but I did not know where to look, or what to say to him." She shook her head in slow, tacit acknowledgement of how little any of us know of others. "Twins . . . Of course, that could not be. He must be older than you, sired before Picus met Enid. Theirs was a hurried courtship, and I cannot believe your father capable of infidelity so soon after his marriage to your mother."

Realizing only then that she knew nothing of the truth of what had happened, I told her the entire story as I had heard it originally from my father, and as I had reconstructed the later events for myself. She listened in silence and when I was finished she was smiling again, her concern over me and her grandson Uther forgotten for the moment.

"I must meet this Ambrose, and soon. I thought I only had one great-nephew."

I stood up. "You will, Auntie. I am sending Donuil tomorrow to bring him here. I must leave Camulod immediately, and I don't know when I will return."

She stared at me for the space of several heartbeats, her eyes wide with renewed alarm.

"You are leaving Camulod? But why, Cay, to what end? Where will you go?"

I shook my head, unwilling to lie to her but driven to prevaricate for her peace of mind. "I don't know, Auntie. Wherever my path leads me. But I must go. I cannot remain here. I need . . . time . . . Time to be alone with myself and to untwist my mind. I have lost years. I knew that yesterday, but today I see the import of what I have lost."

She gazed at me without speaking as I continued. "My new-found brother Ambrose—if he will come, and I believe he will—should be here in my place. Camulod is as much his home as it is mine. I know you'll teach him all he has to know. And he's a warrior. Vortigern the King holds him in high regard and his own men of Lindum are proud to soldier with him. He is strong and bold, and the reports I have heard of him hold him to be just and fair-minded, clever and responsible. He will replace me more than adequately, I am sure, and Camulod has need of him, stranger though he may be at first. Titus and Flavius are too old to govern by themselves now, but aided by you and Lucanus, they can train Ambrose to take his rightful place here and await my return."

My aunt accepted all I said, but still did everything in her power to dissuade me from leaving, and to influence my thinking in the matter of her grandson. We talked for a long time, but I was adamant. My path lay clearly before me. I took my leave of her at last and went in search of Lucanus.

It was raining heavily enough to have doused the torches on the walls as I made my way across the pitch blackness of the parade ground to Lucanus's quarters, but I found him where I had expected to, not yet abed, writing in his sick bay surrounded by lit tapers. I paused before entering, struggling with myself and with my rage against Uther. Lucanus, I was determined, should have not the slightest hint of my renewed suspicions. This interview was crucial to my plans, central to my ability to walk away from Camulod and my responsibilities. Luke would fight me, I knew, if he suspected me of harbouring new doubts about my cousin. I reviewed the course I wished this conversation to take, then stepped into the sick bay.

Lucanus glanced up as I entered and nodded briefly. He held up a hand to indicate that he would be with me in a moment and waved me to a chair as I shrugged out of my rain-damp cloak, and I sat waiting in the shadows until he had finished writing. Finally he put down his pen and turned to me. "Well," he began. "I haven't seen you all day and did not expect to see you so late tonight. What's on your mind?"

I plunged straight in. "How did you get back to Camulod after we left you on the road with the northern king . . . what was his name?"

He made a face of surprise then rueful dismissal. "Derek. Derek of Ravenglass. We returned quickly and directly, but not without trickery. As I've told you before, your friend Derek was a mixed benison. He escorted us to the meeting place, but then abandoned us in the middle of Lot's army, which was short of wagons for transporting their supplies. He had to meet his two hundred men. I was glad, yet strangely sad, to part from him. I found him offensive, but his men protected us. After he left, I thought we would lose the wagons."

"He was supposed to escort you through and past Lot's army. That's what the gold was for."

Lucanus shrugged. "I know, but he changed the terms-" He broke off, his features sharpening as he gazed keenly into the shadows, trying to see my face. "Who told you about the gold? You and I have not discussed that."

I nodded, acknowledging his acuity. "No one told me. I remembered."

He was on his feet instantly, moving towards me, all of his physician's instincts on full alert. For a while we sparred verbally, he trying to question me on every aspect of my recovery, and I to avoid being diverted from my purpose. I gave up eventually, realizing that I would make no progress until he was at least partially satisfied with my recovery and the cause of it. I told him of recovering my memory while kneeling by Cassandra's grave, a minor lie, but one that was necessary to avoid approaching the matter of Uther's guilt. He threw a thousand questions at me, and I attempted to answer all of them until I reached the point where I could take no more.

"Enough, Luke," I told him finally. "I am fully recovered and that's that. And not only do I recall everything that happened before I was struck down, but I recall everything that has happened since. There are no holes in my mind now, so leave off with your infernal, snooping, physician's questions."

"Surgeon's questions." He was grinning at me and I grinned back.

"As you wish. Surgeon's ... but I have some questions of my own that require answers." I stopped, remembering. "You mentioned trickery a while ago. You said you came here directly but not without trickery. What did you mean?"

He grinned. "Deceit. I remembered the towns we passed on the way to Verulamium and our fear of plague. So I put it about that the men in our wagons were sick of some pestilence, not wounded. Derek's people had gone by then, so there were none who knew anything different, and suddenly our wagons were undesirable. We cut straight through Lot's army and moved ahead of them and safely back to Camulod."

"I see. Inventive of you. And where was I when you arrived?"

"Abed and dying. In your aunt's house. You had been there for several days. You were barely alive. As soon as I saw you, and the state of your head, I knew what had to be done, although I thought I might have come too late."

"So you drilled a hole in my head."

"I did, and let some of the air out." He smiled again. "It was only a small hole, but I was amazed by the blood that came out of it. I have to tell you again, however, that I am still deeply concerned by the recurrence of that *haematoma*. I'll be watching you closely from now on, since I can't trust you to report your pain."

"You can. I've promised you. I owe you my life now twice over, obviously."

Lucanus shrugged, his smile still in place. "No more than you owe it to Donuil or Uther. Between us, in our different ways, we've managed to salvage you. How will you reward us, I wonder?"

The irony of his question made my heart leap in my breast as a voice in my head said clearly: *Painfully, my friend.*

To escape my sudden confusion, I stood up and moved forward into the light, pausing by his desk to run my fingertips across the papyrus on which he had been writing. "Tell me what happened to the army we encountered north of Aquae Sulis that time. They were poised to take Glevum, then Aquae, then Camulod. Obviously they didn't, but why not? I must have heard at the time, but I was not myself and since then I've forgotten, until now."

He smiled and grunted. "They killed their own threat, with no trouble to us. It was a small army, no more than four thousand men, it seems. They struck Aquae Sulis, but found nothing there worth having, so they demolished what little remained of the temple of Sulis Minerva, then marched north against Glevum. Lot, as usual, was not among them, and the 'general' he had sent to marshal them was killed in a squabble in Aquae, leaving them leaderless. Anyway, Glevum brought them less than Aquae had, and so they struck west, into Cambria, seeking the gold-mines at Dolocauthi. We heard no more of them."

"I see. It seems God was on our side then. We were in poor condition to repel their attack, had it come." Lucanus nodded in agreement, looking up at where I stood above him. I perched on the edge of his table. "I intend to send Donuil tomorrow at first light to carry a message to my brother Ambrose in Lindum, or in the kingdom of Vortigern if that's where he is now. I am convinced he should come here. God knows, we have need of him. I would also like you to welcome him for me when he arrives and make him feel this is his home. May I rely on you for that?"

"Of course, you know that." A tiny frown of curiosity ticked between his brows. "Where will you be?"

I shrugged. "Away. I'm leaving for a while. As I've already told the Lady Luceiia, I need to spend some time alone. There are too many memories here right now, and they are all too fresh, too new . . . too sudden."

"Aye, I can understand that." His voice was pitched low and filled with sympathy. "Where will you go? Do you have any idea?"

Loathing myself for the direct lie to my best friend, but fortified by that same, icy calm that had been in me all evening, I forced my face to remain expressionless. "No," I answered, shaking my head to emphasize the unimportance of that. "Perhaps south, perhaps east. I'll follow my nose. But it's important that Ambrose be made welcome here, and that he involve himself to some extent in the destiny of this place. His grandfather and his father built it, so it is his legacy. And he has martial skills that we can and must use in any way we may. I've no fears of his not prospering here, and loving it, and Uther will like him." Then, with the barest pause, as though the thought had just occurred to me, I went on. "Where was Uther headed, by the way? Do we know?"

"God knows!" Lucanus yawned and stretched. "To the best of my knowledge, or anyone else's for that matter, he marched south and presumably to the west of us. It's been months now, as you know, since we saw hide or hair of any Cornish forces in this region, and your belligerent cousin spoke only the day before he left of carrying the war to its last stage and burning out the nest of rats Lot calls a fortress."

"Aye. What did he call the place?"

"Nothing, as I recall. I doubt it even has a name. Most people refer to it simply as Lot's Nest."

"Lot's Nest, rats' nest, there's no difference, but it might take a deal of burning. How many men went with Uther?"

"Enough. Two full thousand, half horse, half foot. But you're right. It could prove difficult to burn, and Lot might not even be there."

"How so?" A note in his voice had struck my ear strangely. He returned my gaze evenly, allowing a short silence to stretch between us. "What do you mean?" I pressed the point.

Lucanus continued to stare at me for several more moments, then he shrugged his shoulders. "Simply what I said. When Uther came home at the start of the winter, when it grew too cold and treacherous for campaigning, you may recall he cursed Lot and his wealth very effectively. *Do* you remember?" At that moment I was able to identify the reason behind the peculiar look in his eyes. The physician was still looking for gaps in my memory. I nodded, as casually as I could, and he went on, apparently satisfied. "Well then, you'll recall that Uther's concern—and he was convinced, for whatever reasons, that he was right to be concerned—was that Lot would use the winter rest period this year to reinforce and strengthen his armies. He has the wealth to do it, if we are to believe what we have heard about his pirates, and the winter months when the snows blocked the hill passes gave him the time."

I nodded again, remembering, and he continued, "Lot has that kind of wealth, and the mercenaries out there in Hibernia, and even in Gaul, know of it. By this time, for all we know, the entire peninsula down there could be jammed with new levies, primed for battle. With water on three sides, it's easily supplied by sea with stores or men. Uther marched south—that's all we know. He took the great road. He could have left it at any point and struck inland, to east or west, depending on what his outriders found before them." He yawned and stretched hugely before concluding, "You know that as well as I do, if you would but think about it."

I nodded. "I agree. He could be anywhere. I won't keep you longer from your work or from your bed, my friend. I only wanted to say goodbye, since I intend to leave with the dawn, and to ask for your support in this matter of my brother Ambrose."

He smiled. "You know you didn't have to ask that, Cay, but

I'm glad you told me of your intentions. But don't leave yet. I am not tired, and I've finished what I was doing. I have some excellent wine here."

"Can't, Lucanus. I still have to find Donuil and instruct him on what I wish him to do. It is imperative that he leave in the morning. And besides, you yawn like a man deprived of sleep for days."

"Nonsense! And why the urgency? Let Donuil rest. He'll be deep asleep by now. Tell him in the morning."

"Sick with an aching head?" I grinned at him again. "No, really. I told you I intend to leave at first light and I meant it. I also intend to leave clear-headed, so accept my thanks for the offer and my regrets. I agree with you about disturbing Donuil, however. I have to write a letter to my brother, and Donuil may as well sleep until I've done it. Good night, Lucanus. Sleep well."

I had no sleep that night, listening to the thrashing rain, and the second hour before dawn found me walking, fully dressed save for my boots and cloak, through the darkened house towards the room that housed Publius Varrus's treasures and his books. There, by the light of my solitary lamp, I toured the walls slowly, looking at the ancient weapons that hung there and remembering my great-uncle and the way he had loved and treasured these antique symbols of man's dexterity and ingenuity. Reaching his great African bow, layered of wood and horn and sinew, I took it down from the pegs that held it and tested its spring in my outstretched hands. It was as supple and mighty as ever. Donuil had replaced it here after bringing me back to Camulod from the Mendip Hills, two years before. It had not been oiled or polished, I could see, in at least half that time, but it had evidently not suffered from the neglect. A quiver full of long, carefully fletched arrows hung beside it, and I took that down as well. A small drawer in the table directly beneath, against the wall, held a supply of bowstrings made from stretched sinew, each wrapped and tied with care. I took all eight of them, dropping them into my scrip, then crossed the room again to lean the bow stave and quiver by the doors, where I could pick them up on my way out.

Finally, unable to postpone the moment longer, I took down the wooden hammer keys and used them to uncover the long, polished case that lay hidden, coated with dust, beneath the floorboards. Moments later, Excalibur sat firmly in my grasp, thrilling me with its power. I sat there on the floor, my legs dangling in the hole at my feet, and raised the sword above my head, watching the light from my lamp reflected in its glittering silver blade, and turning it this way and that to catch the ripples of refraction along its planes. Every detail of that magic, long-gone day, the first time I had seen this wonder, passed through my mind. I drew the hilt close to my eyes and examined again the perfect symmetry of the huge gold cockle-shell that was its pommel, and I flexed my fingers around the wire-latticed grip, made from the belly skin of a great shark. With the tip of my finger I traced the Celtic scrollwork on the broad cross hilt, trying in vain to detect the edges of the silver leaf covering that coated the bronze. And I heard again the voice of Publius Varrus from his death bed, instructing me in my duties concerning this wondrous weapon, which he had made with his own hands. As I listened to those words, whispered from the depths of my soul and my memory, so newly returned to me, the exhilaration I had felt seeped out of me to be replaced by a creeping nausea. I might never look upon this wondrous sword again. With the approaching dawn, I would ride out in search of vengeance, hunting the grandson of the man who had made it. Only one of us, and perhaps neither one, would return alive. But if I died, Excalibur, my sworn and sacred trust, would remain here, concealed from all eyes and therefore useless forever. That could not, must not be so.

Today I can find some tiny cause for pride—a very tiny cause, insignificant against the monstrous anger that consumed me at the time—that it did not occur to me to take the sword with me. I could not even then, in my swamping bitterness, conceive of using the sword Publius Varrus had made to kill the son of the child Publius Varrus had fathered. No matter how obscene I considered Uther's sins to be—knew them to be—I would never have thought to kill him with Excalibur.

Slowly, and sick with the knowledge of what I had to do, I laid the gleaming blade gently in its sculpted bed, then closed the lid, hiding the sword from my eyes again for what I felt might be the last time, and carefully wiped off the dust from the polished lid. That done, I lowered the case carefully back into its hiding-place and resealed it beneath the floor-boards. Then I crossed to my great-uncle's writing desk, where I used my lamp to light more tapers, after which I found pens, ink and parchment and began to write. By the time I had finished, although it was still darkest night, my fingers ached from the unaccustomed effort of holding the pen.

I wakened Donuil in the pre-dawn blackness, when there was still no sign of light in the sky to the east. He was surprised to see me up and about before him and I did not bother to explain. I placed my lamp on the table by the door of his sleeping chamber and perched on the edge of his bed, where I repeated the now familiar story of my coming odyssey in search of myself. I repeated the explanation of how I perceived the need for Camulod and Ambrose to be brought together, and explained to him why I wished him to go in search of Ambrose, wherever he was to be found. I also told him in detail the message I wished him to relay to my half-brother, and then listened while he repeated it back to me. I instructed him to take two companions with him, the centurion Rufio and Curwin the bowman, and to be careful on the road. I myself, I told him, would probably be gone for no more than a week or two, after which I must return to Camulod and to my duties. His search for Ambrose, on the other hand, might take months.

Finally, when I was convinced he knew what I required of him, I gave Donuil the letter I had written and with it my instructions, taking pains to make it clear to him that I was merely taking precautions against a premonition I had dreamed of, and no more than that. He would give the letter to my aunt in the morning, bidding her keep it sealed and safe. In the highly unlikely event that I had not returned to Camulod within a year from this date, she was to give the letter to Ambrose and remain with him while he read it. And if, for any reason, Ambrose had not come to Camulod, she was to do the same with Uther; failing Uther, with Titus or Flavius or the senior officer in command at that time.

Donuil was mystified by my instructions, but I did not enlighten him. In my own mind, I had done all I could do, and I had no options. My responsibility was clear. If Uther were here two years from now and I were not, then I would be dead and Excalibur, for better or for worse, would be rightfully his. If neither of us returned, this way at least the weapon would remain in Camulod and might, some day, fulfill its original purpose. I watched as Donuil locked the letter safely in his chest, then I made my way to the stables, where I took time to ensure that my various possessions, including Publius Varrus's great bow, were securely stowed, fastened and wrapped against the elements.

In recognition of the foulness of the weather, I lashed a thin, tightly rolled, straw-filled palliasse behind my saddle, having wrapped it in a firmly bound length of the same material from which my foul-weather cloak was woven: dense-fibred brown wool, thick and springy, with a waterproof texture that was strengthened by a scraping of rendered wax. My great black war cloak with the embroidered bear on the back was folded in a pannier on the pack-horse, protected by a covering of the same waxed wool and safe from rain, damp and mildew. Finally satisfied that everything I could do had been done, I mounted the big black that had once been my father's, and as I clattered over the cobblestones and through the main gates leading the pack-horse and an extra mount, two lonely, chilled, wet sentries were the only ones to mark my passing.

XXXIX

On leaving Camulod, I rode directly east along our own well-used roadway until it intersected the great north-east to south-west road built four hundred years earlier by the soldiers of Julius Agricola. From there I headed directly south-west. Uther had led out his two thousand men by the same route, although all signs of their passing had been blotted out months earlier, long before the fury unleashed by the lashing rain that had begun the day before I left and poured without respite for the next three days. As night was falling, I approached the tiny town the native Celts were now calling Ilchester. Apart from its unmistakable layout, nowadays the town bore little resemblance to anything Roman, and the original fortifications were almost completely obliterated already. It was a dismal, squalid little place where nothing ever happened, and yet no one I asked there showed any awareness of Uther's having passed through three months earlier, which led me to infer that he had skirted the town, preferring to keep his movements secret from the citizenry. I spent the night there, despite the threat of verminous bedding, determined to enjoy the dryness of a roof over my head for what might well be the last time for several nights. I pressed south again in the morning, making only slow headway, however, against the driving rain.

I slept beneath the dripping trees the second night, no more than twenty miles south-west of Ilchester, having given up all hope of reaching Isca that day, and was surprised to find I slept quite well, wrapped more or less warmly in my blanket-like cloak, which was lined with softer wool than the coarse nap that formed its exterior. Everything was wet, however, even far in from the road in the depths of the forest, and I had no hope of lighting a fire. As

I rode on the following day, the unrelenting cold finally began to penetrate the warmth of my heavy, weatherproof clothing and I felt myself becoming chilled, bone deep, until I began to shiver uncontrollably. I knew I had to find shelter, a dry place where I could light a fire and dry out my damp, cold clothes. The rain blew endlessly into my face in icy spikes, chilled by a blustery wind that swirled around me and my horse as though determined to obliterate us, the last two living creatures in this grey, sodden world. I had not met a living soul on the road since leaving Camulod—only mad people and soldiers on urgent duty would brave weather like this without dire need.

By mid-afternoon, my self-absorbed misery had become so all-encompassing that I nearly passed by an old, dilapidated road house, set so far back from the roadside that I had almost not seen it. I reined in my horse and peered at the place through the curtain of driving rain that obscured it. It looked unprepossessing; neither clean nor friendly, and normally I would not have considered stopping there, but I was cold, wet and miserable, and I told myself that the dismal weather would have made even Camulod look dingy and uninviting.

I tethered my horse in the yard, removed my bow, quiver and pack roll, and entered the building without seeing one person. The *mansio* was small. Its atrium had been roofed over, creating a central hall two storeys high, with covered stairs leading to the second floor where a passageway protected by a waist-high wooden wall ran around the sides of the enclosure, giving access to a number of rooms that were presumably for the guests. The large, roofed space was warm and dry at least, if very dark, and from the ground floor area passages and doorways radiated in all directions. A countered space against the west wall was obviously intended to serve as some kind of porter's or receiver's station, but it was untenanted, although it was lit by two small tripods, each holding the dwindling, messy stubs of four fat, sputtering tallow candles.

I called for attention and eventually the proprietor came striding from the rear of the place to greet me, appearing surprised that anyone should be travelling on such a night. He was a heavy-set, red-faced fellow with a wispy beard and a truculent, ill-tempered look about him.

"Good day to you. I need a room. One with a warm bed and a door that locks."

He eyed me, taking me in from the top of my dripping head to the soles of my chilled feet, and nodded. "Aye," he grunted, "you do, and towels and a large fire and hot food. I'll have my wife prepare them for you. How long will you stay with us?"

I grinned at him through chattering teeth, relieved by the warmth of his greeting, which his initial expression had not led me to expect. "Perhaps forever; at least until I'm warm again and the rain abates, but probably only until tomorrow."

He nodded and, beckoning me to follow him, led me directly upstairs to a pleasant, clean-smelling room where, during the next quarter-hour, I unpacked my belongings and spread them out to air, having carried all of them in from the yard in three journeys, leaving my horses in the care of a groom who seemed to know what he was doing.

Later, I went downstairs to eat a simple but large and nourishing meal that I had been savouring for some time thanks to the delicious smells of roasting meat that drifted up from the kitchens towards my room on the second level. Since I was the only guest in the hostelry, my host and his wife, whom I discovered were named Lars and Brunna, invited me to eat with them, making a fourth with Brunna's brother Eric. I was glad to accept their invitation and the warmth of their company. The food was excellent, and accompanied by a delicious, full-bodied red wine, and I found myself thoroughly enjoying the companionship of these strangers whose comportment bore little of the normal attitude of *mansio* keepers towards their guests. When the meal was over, there was still wine in the great jug, so we lingered at the table, comfortable and friendly in the ample light of a dozen candles and a huge, roaring fire, while the deluge continued outside with an energy that kept the sound of water pouring from the roof a constant accompaniment to our talk.

Brunna's brother Eric, I discovered, was a trader who travelled the length and breadth of the southern region, operating from his home close to the town of Isca. He was a droll fellow who kept all of us entertained with tales of his adventures on the roads. I asked him eventually whether the growing Saxon presence in the south-east was injuring his ventures, and he looked at me and laughed.

"Injuring them? From what viewpoint, my friend?"

I was perplexed by both his answer and his humour. "From the point of view of interfering with your livelihood, I suppose," was the only response I could summon. And at that he laughed again, even more loudly than he had at first.

"Interfering with it? May the god of travellers protect you, friend, they *are* my livelihood."

I was astounded. "What do you mean?" I asked him, spluttering in my confusion. "They are Outlanders, savages. They come here with no purpose other than to kill and plunder and pillage. How can you trade with them and hope to continue living? They are alien, without honour."

The smile disappeared from his face at my words. "No, sir, they are none of those things to me. I have never received any ill at their hands. In the communities they have set up along the Saxon Shore they live as well, and as peacefully, as any in this land—more so, indeed, than most. They are mere people—men and women like any others—who have come here seeking a place to live and prosper, and they have need of my goods, so I trade with them as I would with anyone else who has the wherewithal to trade."

Neither his sister nor her husband spoke at this, and I looked at them for support against his ravings. They sat content, however, not put out at all, and Lars looked at me and shrugged and smiled as if to say, "I agree with him. How can I then gainsay him?"

I sat there in amazement, pondering Eric's words and the reactions of his kinfolk, and realizing I had nothing more to say. Upon hearing his opinion stated so simply, I had no other choice than to believe him, although my training would not permit that.

"Nonsense," I continued eventually, trying to keep my voice

even. "What you say is self-serving, Eric. Admit that, at least. You are fortunate in that they need what you have, otherwise you would not be here this night. These people are invaders. The most vicious of their kind in all the Western Empire. They have been terrorizing the whole country for decades."

He shook his head, completely unabashed by my words, and as I listened to his response I felt myself grudgingly acknowledging the truth of what he had to say, although I found it unpalatable.

"No, friend Merlyn, you are selecting your truth to make your own point. You said it yourself. They have been coming here for decades, but for how many decades? How long has the Saxon Shore been called the Saxon Shore? A hundred years? More? Are we to believe these people, these Saxons, have been coming and going constantly through all that time, raiding and leaving?" He smiled and shook his head again. "I know Saxon settlements not fifty miles from here, to the eastward, where there are children being born to Saxons who were born right there.

"They fought when they first came. Of course they did. They were unwelcome, and the land was disputed. But now the land is theirs, and they maintain it better, in most cases, than the people who were there before them did. The Romans fought when first they came here, too. They came as conquerors, remember. Only after all the fighting was done did this land of ours settle down to prosperity."

His eloquence in front of me, a stranger, was probably due, I decided, to the quality and quantity of the wine we had been drinking, but I was unhappy with the way he had demolished my objections.

"The Romans came here for a purpose," I said, hearing the wine and truculence in my own voice. "And they were good for Britain. I myself am of Roman descent."

Eric was grinning widely now, his eyes dancing with mischief. "Of course the Romans came here for a purpose. They came to conquer and to pillage. They came in search of tin and gold and precious treasures. And then they stayed." He shrugged his shoulders, spreading his palms. "But that was centuries ago. I am not decrying them—neither them nor your Roman blood, Merlyn—but who is to say the Roman purpose was more noble than the Saxons' is? Is it impossible that some of your future children may bear the blood of Saxons mingled with your Roman blood?"

"By God, I hope it is!"

Lars cleared his throat loudly, drawing my eyes to him. He had decided it was time to change the subject. I watched him now looking at my clothing, noting the style of it. "You're Roman, you say? Forgive me if you think I'm being inquisitive, but Merlyn sounds like no Roman name I've ever come across."

I felt a smile tugging at my lips in the face of his obvious desire to lead our conversation into quieter paths. "That's true. I am half Celt, and Merlyn marks me, but my name is Britannicus—Caius Merlyn Britannicus."

"Britannicus?" His expression quickened. "Are you from up Aquae Sulis way?"

"Close by. About thirty-five miles south-west of there. Why?"

"It's an unusual name. A friend of my father's had a friend from Aquae Sulis called Britannicus, a long time ago. He went to live there. Name of Varrus. He was a smith, walked with a limp. Why are you smiling?"

My smile had become a huge grin and I leaned towards him now, across the table. "Because I can hardly credit what I'm hearing. *Varrus!* The friend you speak of was my grandfather, Caius Britannicus. Publius Varrus married his sister, my great-aunt Luceiia."

"Get away! Well I'm damned!" He was staring at me, wide-eyed. "Did you ever know his friend Equus? That was my father."

I could hardly contain my astonishment and delight. "Equus was your father? I knew him well, when I was a small boy. He lived with us. But why don't I know you? I've known your brothers from my infancy."

"Joseph and Carol. Well I'm damned!" He reached across the table and picked up the wine jug to give himself time to absorb what he was hearing, pouring another cup for all of us. "You knew

Joseph and Carol? I was the eldest. Ran away and joined the legions when I was just a younker living in Colchester. Didn't want to waste my life in a dirty old smithy. Wasted it in the dirty old army, instead. Got back years later to find they'd all moved away to the west somewhere. So you knew Joseph and Carol? Well I'm damned."

"Knew? Lars, I still know them! They're in Camulod, our colony. They operate our smithies nowadays."

He looked at me strangely and I sensed a sudden stillness in the others who had been hanging on our every word. "Camulod? Uther Pendragon's place? They live there? *You* live there?"

I was taken aback. His tone said quite clearly, unmistakably, that he had thought only monsters and outlaws lived in Camulod.

"Well, yes, they live there, and so do I, but I would hardly call it 'Uther Pendragon's place.' Uther lives there, part of the time, and commands our forces for the time being, in the war against Lot of Cornwall, but his kingdom—his 'place' as you call it—is in the mountains of Cambria, several days' ride to the north-west. Believe me, Camulod is far from being Uther Pendragon's place, or anyone else's. It's a thriving community, held and maintained by its colonists. You've obviously never been there."

He made a derisive sound in his throat and shook his head in a brief, abrupt negative. I frowned, unable to believe what I was hearing.

"Why not?" I continued. "It's not that far from here, no more than fifty miles." I was even more disconcerted now to see hostility and fear in his face and I glanced at the others, to see it mirrored in theirs. I rushed on, eager to find the source of it. "Good God, Lars, you all look as though you're afraid of the place and all it contains! Why? Your two brothers are there, and I live there, and it was founded and built by people like your own father and his friends. Why should anyone—and you of all people—be afraid of the very name of it?" It was evident that he was not going to answer me, and I had a sudden revelation. "Or is it Uther Pendragon you fear?"

His face darkened, rigid with hostility at the very mention of Uther's name, and I knew I was correct. "Why, Lars?" I was insistent. "Why should you fear Uther Pendragon? Tell me."

He cleared his throat. "Ask Eric. And Brunna."

I turned to them, to include them in what had suddenly become a very personal matter.

An hour later, I had heard more than I ever sought to hear. Lars and his wife Brunna, and their extensive family in and around Isca and the surrounding villages and hamlets, were the ordinary people of this region. In their minds there was no difference between Uther of Camulod—how that name galled me!—and Lot of Cornwall. They thought of both men as demons incarnate. The armies of both had ravaged this entire countryside over the past three years, looting and killing and raping as they pleased. The local people had far less fear of Saxons than they had of their own kind.

Lars told me he had returned from his service with the legions almost twenty years earlier and had met and wed Brunna shortly after that. He had fought with Magnus Maximus, and then with Stilicho's legions after Magnus was killed. When the Emperor Honorius killed Stilicho, his own deputy and former Regent, Lars deserted and made for home, and the journey as a fugitive, ending finally in the quiet backwater of Isca, had taken him three years. Brunna's family had been merchants of some stature in Isca, and her father had set them up fifteen years ago in this hostelry. They had prospered for twelve years, until Lot of Cornwall decided to extend his territories by conquest.

The previous year, while I had been relearning how to live, both of their sons, aged fourteen and twelve, had been taken in a sweep by Uther's soldiers and hanged out of hand along with twenty other men suspected of giving aid and sustenance to the enemy. Two months after that, at harvest time, Brunna's youngest sister, a fifteen-year-old girl, had been ravished and killed, with three of her friends, by a party of Lot's people. The father and brother of the girl whose home they had been visiting were butchered while attempting to protect the girls.

The picture these simple people drew for me was clear. The "enemy," in their eyes, was anyone who was armed and rode a horse or marched carrying weapons. Uther Pendragon and Gulrhys Lot were monsters, and any trees beneath which they rode were likely to bear dangling, human fruit. Their very names carried with them the stench of rotting flesh and burning homesteads, and evoked chaos, screams of despair, and long, starving winters.

Their story drove the wine-fed euphoria from my head and I slept heavily that night. The following morning, I was on the road again, driving my horses hard along the road to and beyond Isca to the south-west. Lars and all his family would make their way as quickly as they could now to Camulod, bearing a letter from me to my aunt that would place them under my official protection. In the meantime, I rode hard, with my gaze focused on the road ahead of me, and on the confrontation with my cousin that lay at the end of it. I rode seething with a fury so great that it had almost displaced my personal grudge against Uther. To hear the name of Camulod spoken in fear and loathing had outraged all within me and made me rage at my own former, self-inflicted blindness. We had heard tales in Camulod of atrocities and vicious acts of terror being committed by our own, but had discounted them, choosing, in what I could now identify with ease as smug complacency, to attribute such tales to the lies and rumour-mongering of Lot and his creatures—fictitious calumnies concocted for the purpose of turning the people of our own lands against us. Now, shaken by the revelations of the previous night, I saw the Dream of Caius Britannicus and Publius Varrus reduced to smoking cinders in the terror of the people of this land around me. Where had the vision of my people gone? What had happened to their ideals of freedom and justice and dignity and worth; of free men, living and working in freedom, having the right to bear arms to protect that freedom against all usurpation, even by their own kind? I cursed the fate that had left me senseless of what was happening around me for two crucial years, and spurred my mount harder.

And as I rode further and further west after leaving the great road, I began to see signs of depredation all around me: burned farmsteads; charred and shattered houses; dangling, withered corpses in the trees; meadows strewn with the skeletal remains of soldiers and horses. And no people. None at all. The land lay empty and devastated, and my anger grew, feeding upon itself.

And then, on a morning bright with sun and the song of larks, I breasted a hill and found fresh corpses sprawled in the autumn grass in my path. I reined in immediately, scanning ahead for possible danger, but whatever peril there might have been earlier had moved on.

Satisfied that the dead and I were alone, I dismounted and went to examine them more closely. They were strangers all, but very newly dead, their flesh still warm, their blood yet liquid, and I left them where they lay.

A short time later, seen only by a pair of eagles circling high above, I stopped by the side of a small, swift-running freshet, stripped and bathed, shivering with the cold, and then allowed the sun's warmth to dry me. I pulled on a fresh, light, clean tunic, then unpacked and shrugged into the ring armour I had adapted from the Saxon devices of the same kind. Mine was designed for a horseman—a heavy coat with a wide-skirted tail ample enough to spread when I was mounted to cover my own and my horse's haunches, and long, loose-legged trousers. The suit was made from well-worked, supple, black-dyed leather and covered with many thousands of tiny, overlapping rings of iron, brass and copper wire that would stop a hard-swung sword, a thrown spear, or an arrow fired from any but a long, Celtic bow. It covered me from neck to ankle and, while it was cumbersome to wear afoot, it served its purpose magnificently when I was mounted.

When I was fully armoured, my long surcoat securely buckled down the side, I repacked and restowed all my gear, then donned my great black cloak with its emblazoned silver bear. I still wore my silvered Roman helmet with its black plume and full cheek-plates—I had not yet been able to improve on that design—and now I strung the great, horned African bow of Publius Varrus and slung it across my shoulders with a full quiver of long arrows. The black war cloak was heavy on such a hot day—it drew the heat of the sun into itself immediately—but I wanted Uther to know who was coming long before I reached him; and the discomfort involved in wearing it was unimportant. By my right knee, slung through three rings attached to a long, flat piece of toughened leather hide, hung my cross-hilted cavalry sword. On the other side, the hook attached to hold my iron flail glittered, unused. I dug in my spurs and my big black surged forward, leading its consorts.

I had crossed the highest ground in Cornwall, it appeared, for from that point onward the land fell away beneath me, each successive hilltop lower than the one that had preceded it, until eventually I approached the sea coast, seeing from afar the sunlight glittering on the sparkling surface of the waters that stretched beyond the horizon. There, in the valley bottom beneath the last upsurge of coastal hillside, I found the massive track of a passing army, coming from the highlands to my right and proceeding westward, along the coastline. The debris they had left behind lay scattered everywhere and the scene of their passing was a broad riverbed of bruised and flattened grass the width of the valley bottom, winding away from sight to disappear into the south-eastern hills. They had passed by perhaps the day before, no more than that. The grass, I knew, would show little sign of their passing by this time tomorrow.

Without pausing, I put the spurs to the black's flank, heading downhill and cross-slope to find and follow the broad swath. My way was clearly marked and my apprehension grew with every mile. I found the first corpses within four miles of joining the wide track. There had been a skirmish, probably a rearguard action, and Uther's people had not been victorious. All of the dead wore Uther's red dragon blazon, and there was a heap of them, some twenty in number, who lay piled together without weapons. They had been wounded earlier, dragged together, and killed out of hand. All their throats were cut.

From that point onward, I was seldom out of sight of death in one form or another. Several of the bodies I found wore the black boar of Cornwall, but the great majority wore the red Pendragon mark, and too many wore the armour of Camulod. I stopped counting when I had reached several hundred. After that, I simply rode and looked, goading my horses to move more and more quickly through a landscape littered with slain men who had died fighting, and hanged men who had not, and butchered men who had been bound and then casually slaughtered, and among and around all of them were the carrion crows and other loathsome creatures that far outnumbered their silent hosts and feasted on the fruits of men's hatred of one another.

And then I found a living man, who caught my eye by moving. He was above me on a steep hillside, and I pulled my horse up sharply, dropping the reins and whipping my bow into readiness and taking aim before I realized he wore my own uniform: the black and silver Roman-styled armour of Caius Merlyn Britannicus of Camulod. I lowered my weapon and started up the hillside towards him as he began to walk downhill, lurching and staggering. When less than thirty paces separated us, he fell forward onto his face and rolled down almost beneath my horse's feet. Even as he fell I recognized the face beneath the crusted blood that obscured it. It was young Marcus Bassus, one of my most promising junior commanders and the fourth consecutive member of his family to serve loyally in the forces of our Colony.

I was off my horse before Bassus stopped rolling down the hillside, and I cradled him as gently as I could while I looked around for some spot where I could lodge him without further danger. I thought at first he was already dead, but he was only deeply unconscious and I took advantage of that to drag him across the slope to a spot that was grassy and almost flat. There I undid his breastplate, cutting the blood-slick leather straps, and examined his wounds, seeing at once that he was far, far gone. An arrow had pierced deeply beneath his armpit, striking downward from behind and freakishly finding a path between his ribs and deep into his chest. He must have had his arm extended above his head when he was shot. The arrow had broken off at some time—I could not remember having seen it as he approached me—and only a broken stub, less than the length of my thumb, projected from the wound, greasy with partially congealed blood and crusted with dirt. The jagged end of it had torn the inside of his arm, ripping the muscles there and leaving a gristly mess. I had time to bathe his face and pad the inside of his arm against the splintered arrow-stem with a piece of cloth before his eyelids fluttered open.

He knew me, and he was in control of his senses, and in the quarter-hour before I left him there he told me, speaking in a thin, pain-filled voice and breathing in fast, agonizing but shallow gasps, something of what had happened in the previous few days.

Uther, he said, had blundered badly, miscalculating several elements like a man under a curse. He had a spy within Lot's camp, it appeared, who had provided him with a detailed report convincing him that Lot's main force had been committed in the south-east, prior to Uther's arrival in the west, against the incursion of a large Saxon army. Lot had as usual, the story went, sent his army off without him, and had immured himself to await reinforcements in one of his northern strongholds. Once told of this, and believing his source implicitly, Uther had determined to march northward quickly to the coast, there finally to bring Lot to battle before his expected allies could arrive. Thus determined, Uther had refused to listen to the advice of his senior officers, basing everything on the gamble that Lot's main army was safely committed in the south-east against the Saxons and would await Lot's arrival. In the meantime, Uther believed he had the advantage of surprise, with Lot safely bottled up in a minor stronghold that would not be able to withstand a siege. He had ignored the misgivings of his advisers, who had urged him to protect his back against attack from the north-west where, according to other rumours they had heard, a new army of Hibernian Scots mercenaries, the ferocious warriors who were becoming known as *galloglas*, was on its way to join Lot's summer war.

Uther had chosen to believe otherwise. If the *galloglas* came, he said, they would come by sea, to anchor at the closest point to Lot's stronghold. Should that come to pass before his business with Lot was complete, he believed he could withhold their advance from the coast by using his bowmen to decimate the Ersemen as they attempted to scale the Cornish cliffs.

What he could not have known, however, was the degree of error in his expectations. He had invested Lot's ditched and dyked stronghold according to plan, but even before his engineers could start constructing their siege engines, word had come with the dawn from his unknown spy that the southern army was returning, having failed to bring the Saxons to battle.

That word was followed within hours by a belated warning that a fleet had landed to the north two days earlier, spilling an army that was short of food and was now thrusting southward to join Lot, replenishing its larders as it came. And then, early that same afternoon, another fleet of more than a hundred galleys had come into view from the north-west, converging on the single stretch of beach, not far from Uther's camp, that was not begirt by towering cliffs.

In the space of a few short hours, although through no real fault of his own, Uther had been outnumbered and out-manoeuvred. Immediately upon sighting the relieving fleet, he had summoned his bowmen back from the cliffs and called an immediate council of war, drawing up quick plans to strike south and surprise Lot's main army on the road along the coast, leaving Cornwall's deplorable king safe for the moment in the hands of his rescuers.

They had struck out for the south immediately, and Bassus had drawn the honour of commanding the rearguard. It was one of his own scouts, ranging far behind to spy on the enemy's progress, who had brought Bassus the news of the final blow to Uther's plans. This man, at great risk to himself, had approached Lot's stronghold again and remained hidden among the rocks on the hillside far above, to watch what might develop in the aftermath of Uther's departure. He had seen Lot ride to meet his new reinforcements from the sea, to join them and make off around the coast southward at great speed, the massive Erse galleys surging along under full oar power and sails spread to a following wind, forewarned and fully aware of Uther's strength and his line of march.

Shortly after receiving this information, and before the messenger could eat and ride on to warn Uther, Bassus's rearguard had been attacked and overrun by a heavy, fast-moving concentration of Hibernians. The news of Lot's escape by sea had gone no further. The scout had been killed along with everyone else save Bassus, who had fallen apart from the main slaughter and had been left for dead.

He had lain unconscious all night long, and had struggled in and out of awareness for most of the following day. Only a short time before my arrival had he managed to pull himself out of the hollow where he lay and to attempt to find someone to help him. He had seen me coming, and had recognized me, but had been unable to call to me. Fortunately I had noticed him moving, and now he had passed on the warning, making it my responsibility: Uther Pendragon was headed blindly southward, through rough and roadless terrain that made for heavy, slow going, into a confrontation that he thought would give him the advantage of surprise. Instead, he would find Lot waiting for him with two armies and the sea at his back, while a third army followed hot on Uther's own heels. Uther and his entire force would be annihilated.

Even as I listened, hearing the tortured frailty of his voice and the shallowness of his breathing, I was deciding that I would have to leave young Bassus there alone. He was dying, and rapidly—of that I had not the slightest doubt. But I had to be on my way immediately. I could not afford the luxury of waiting with him even for a short time, and both of us knew that. He would die, and I would— I must—leave him to handle it alone. My personal feelings for Uther were of no importance now, beside the imperative need to find him in time to warn him to turn his army and the men of Camulod around and away from the fate that awaited them.

Bassus finished speaking and fell backward, his eyes closed. I knelt above him, the fingers of one hand grasping his wrist, feeling the still-beating pulse. Sighing, and feeling wretched, I began to rise to my feet and as I did so a cloud of fluttering, fighting crows and gulls swept along the hillside, their jarring voices tearing at my ears. The eyes beneath me snapped open and the dying man followed the flight of the birds with wide, horror-filled eyes. I bent forward and laid my hand on his forehead. It was cold and clammy. I felt his head move in a negative, his eyes still staring. He tried to say something else and I bent closer to hear. And then, in a voice so weak that I could barely make it out, he told me to go, but begged me to kill him first, not to let the crows at him while he still lived. A chilling rush of fear and revulsion swept over me. How could I kill him? He was my friend and had given me nothing but loyalty and obedience. How could I reward him by killing him?

And then, of course, the answer came to me in terms that I could not refute. I could not save him, nor could I remain with him until he died. The lives of too many others depended upon my speed and every moment was too precious now. But neither could I abandon him, leaving him to await, in terror, the arrival of the first filthy carrion crow to alight on his face and pluck out an eye while he was still alive. I wrestled with the truth of that for what seemed an eternity before I nodded silently to him. He read my expression correctly, nodding his own thanks in return. I stood erect, telling him to close his eyes. He did so, and I drew my long cavalry sword, placing its point carefully beneath the arch of his ribs, angling it upward. He drew one last, deep breath and held it, and I dropped, throwing my full weight onto the hilt of the sword, driving it deep into his heart. He convulsed, his legs kicked wildly once and then he was still.

I turned him on his face to hide his brown eyes from the crows, and then I piled what rocks I could find around him in a symbolic gesture of burial. Only then did I clean my blade, before transferring my saddle to my spare mount and riding off quickly without looking back, leading the black and the pack-horse. It was mid-afternoon.

Towards nightfall, I almost rode into disaster, coming upon a group of five mounted men riding towards me. Fortune dictated I should be almost completely screened from their sight at first, however, hidden by a fringe of branches on the last trees of a small copse of stunted hawthorn through which I had been riding, following a narrow, well-worn path. They were approaching the copse, talking among themselves and clearly expecting to meet no one. All five wore brown tunics with a black boar painted or embroidered on their chests. I knew after only the quickest glance around me that I had no chance of hiding from them. There *was* nowhere to hide, and if I tried to run they would hear me. They were close enough to see me plainly already, if they had but looked. I had no choice.

The first man was flung from his horse's back by the force of my arrow before his closest companion realized anything had happened. Stunned by the suddenness of his friend's death, the fellow made the mistake of turning in his saddle to see what had happened to him. My second arrow struck him in the neck, piercing the stretched skin beneath the point of his backward-craning jaw and knocking him, too, over his horse's rump. I killed a third man before the two remaining cursed and broke apart, to right and left, only one of them having seen me, finally, among the branches ahead of them. I snapped a shot at him but missed, and then they were away from me, galloping their horses at top speed. I swung my own mount around and headed back the way I had come, pulling off the path eventually and heading deeper into the copse, to my right. I heard voices behind me, and then a horn blowing. They would be close behind me, I knew, for one of them had seen, even in his fright, that I was alone.

They chased me for hours, higher and higher into the low hills, and only when night fell did I feel safe enough to dismount in a bush-filled hollow and feed my beasts before trying to snatch some sleep, rolling myself in my cloak and stretching out almost under the hooves of my three horses.

I had lost my pursuers. The following morning, creeping cautiously through the mists of early dawn on the hillside, straining my eyes and ears, I could see or hear no signs of them. I saddled up and moved out slowly, taking care to move in silence and to stay well clear of higher ground where I might be seen from below. Towards mid-morning I headed downhill again and angled my search once more in the direction of the broad path trampled by the armies moving ahead of me. All that day and the next I rode, seeing signs of death all around me, but hearing no human voice and seeing no signs of life.

Then, towards the middle of the afternoon of the third day after my encounter with the Cornishmen, I came on the aftermath of an extensive battle and rode slowly into a landscape that threatened to shrivel the mind. The killing ground was an enormous meadow, scattered with stunted trees and spread out at the base of a hollow formed by the sides of four shallow hills. Bodies lay everywhere, strewn in windrows and stacked in formations, scattered at random and heaped in piles, men and animals together. The fighting was over, but it had ended only very shortly before my arrival. The screams and moans of wounded men and horses were deafening, and the stink of blood and offal was a tangible presence. Hundreds of men and women moved through the chaos, drawn from I knew not where. Many of them were helping the wounded, although I knew that many others were plundering friend and foe, living and dead alike. Others, soldiers of both armies, were killing wounded horses, silencing their awful screams. No one approached me or sought to hinder me as I rode through the madness. Here and there I could see pairs of men, running in tandem, carrying stretchers. Other pairs moved more slowly, their stretchers loaded with wounded. I traced the centre of their activity and made my way to where they gathered, recognizing first one and then several of our own medics as I approached.

Mucius Quinto was in charge of the assembly ground. He was a grey-haired veteran almost as old as Lucanus, to whom he was second in command. I found him, flanked by two strong young soldiers, kneeling beside a young man whose breast was thick with blood. Quinto and his people had cleared an area on the eastern side of the great field, and had assembled rows and rows of wounded and dying men from both armies, dozens of rows and hundreds of men, more being brought in all the time. His helpers were our own soldiers, for the most part, although I saw many wearing the brown and black tunics of Lot's Cornishmen. There were no soldiers here in this field now, no enemies; only tired and grateful survivors. There were Druids there, too, moving among the wounded, and a scattering of women here and there, camp followers, I supposed, too stunned to really care. No matter who they were, they were working to appease the pain of the men who had been soldiers and were now men again, broken and bleeding.

Quinto did not even look up at me when I drew rein beside him. I climbed down from my saddle and stood watching as the young man at his knees, no more than a boy in truth, shuddered, convulsed and died, his blank and empty eyes staring up into mine. Quinto paused, his hand outstretched where it had frozen at the sound of the boy's death rattle, then his shoulders seemed to slump and his hand moved again, changing direction to close the staring eyes gently. He paused again, as though collecting himself, and then he was up and moving to the next man, while his two companions picked up the dead youth by the wrists and ankles and carried him away to make room for another. Before they had moved out of his sight Quinto was leaning over the new man, checking for a pulse, then flipping the man's tunic up to cover his dead face. He moved on again as two other men removed that body, and I moved with him. He still had not looked at me.

An ear-shattering scream erupted suddenly from a nearby knot of men clustered tightly around a table, all of them soaked in blood and hunched in a tense struggle to restrain someone beneath them, and I heard the distinctive rasp of a saw going through living bone. Quinto glanced towards the sounds, half checked his step, and then moved on to examine the next man in line. I stepped close to him.

"Quinto."

He turned on me, prepared to savage me for my interruption, then gaped in recognition and I saw his eyes move wonderingly the length of my clean, unbloodied, armoured body.

"Merlyn." His voice was lifeless, belying the surprise in his eyes. "Where did you come from? A rescue? You're too late."

I shook my head, holding his gaze. "No, Quinto, I'm alone. What happened?"

"What happened?" His face twitched into an abrupt laugh that was chilling in its bitterness. "What happened? Can't you see? We had a war. A whole war in the space of two or three hours, and we lost." He looked away from me, his voice dropping as his eyes moved around the ranks of dead and dying. "God, how we lost! And what we've lost! A generation, Merlyn ... an entire generation. . . . There'll be no quick recovery from this . . ." His voice died away completely, then resumed, his tone now hard and angry. "We weren't vanquished, Merlyn. We were utterly and completely crushed . . . shattered and scattered . . . There must have been ten of them for every one of us. Outlanders, mostly. Ersemen. We didn't have a chance, and Uther led us in here blindly to this . . . this slaughter ground."

"How, Quinto? What happened? And where's Uther now?"

Quinto sniffed and wiped his nose wearily with his sleeve. "I haven't got time to talk. There's too much to do and I should be cutting. Some of my assistants are very young, and untrained— untrained for carnage on this scale, at any rate." He moved away and I followed him and three of the next four men he looked at were already dead. The fourth, a Cornishman, had a shattered leg. Quinto sent him to the cutting table. The next man, one of our own, was also dead, his chest crushed into a large, ball-shaped depression. Quinto shook his head.

"Your cousin's toy," Quinto grunted. "I wonder if he ever thought, when he came up with that bright idea, to see it used against his own people? And look at this." He had stooped to kneel beside another man, whose entire jaw had been shattered and torn away from his upper face. "Tell me, Caius Merlyn, what in the face of the sweet Christ's mercy can ever justify this kind of savagery by one man to another? Or any of this madness?" I barely heard what he said. My mind was still on the wound the previous man had borne, made by what Quinto had called my cousin's toy.

"Quinto, what did you mean by my cousin's toy?"

He didn't look at me as he answered, intent as he was on attempting to repair the shattered face beneath him. "Just what I said . . ." He shook his head. "This is hopeless. Nothing I can do. At least he's not conscious . . ." Now he looked up at me and began rising to his feet again. "Your cousin Uther's toy. The flail he made; the ball on a chain. It's been—what—three years since then? Now the damn things are everywhere. I suppose you just can't keep a good idea secret."

My head was reeling. What was he telling me? He had moved on again and I had to step quickly to catch up to him, clutching at his sleeve.

"What do you mean, they're everywhere? I haven't seen any."

He frowned, angry at such trivial talk in the face of so much need. "Then you must be blind. What else do you think could make a wound like that, crushing bones to jelly?" He jerked his thumb savagely towards the man with the crushed chest. "Half the men in Camulod have them, and more than half the men in Lot's damned army, it appears. Now leave me alone. I've got work to do."

But I had not been blind. I had been oblivious and without memory. I still clutched his sleeve, recognizing his impatience. "I'll leave you alone, I promise, but I must know. Where is Uther? And where is Lot of Cornwall?"

He wrenched his arm free, turning away from me, then stopped and looked back at me with a grunting sigh.

"They're together, wherever they are. Where else would they be? When he saw we were beaten, Uther escaped with his reserves to the south—there, between those two hills. I saw them go. So did Lot. He was up on that hill, over there to the east. We had been in a running fight with an army of Ersemen who'd been chewing at our heels for days. I was with Uther and the leading party when we came out into this valley and he saw a chance to turn and fight them. He led us up there, onto the flank of that hill, and as we began to climb it, getting ready to turn and face the enemy, Lot led an army over the top above us, and another entire army, thousands of men, came through the two passes on either side of us. We were trapped from the outset. They'd been waiting for us to do exactly what we did. From then on, it was pure slaughter. Uther managed to cut his way sideways, across the hill and down across the field here and up the eastern flank, but he had less than a thousand men with him. Once there, there was nothing he could do to help anyone. It was all over too quickly. Lot had the advantage from the outset and it kicked the guts out of our men. And when some of our people tried to surrender, they were cut down anyway, so the rest of us prepared to die fighting.

"That's when Uther decided to run . . ." A long pause. "Uther's no coward. I know why he ran. He knew that if he escaped, with the women, Lot would follow him forever and the rest of us left here might have a chance."

"With the women? What women?"

He looked at me as though I should have no need to ask such a simple question. "Lot's women. The queen and her people . . . Anyway, that's what happened. Lot and his savages took off after Uther's group and left us fighting. But all his people followed him, even the ones who were engaged with us. When they saw the others leave, they left us and followed them, and the fighting was over. That was about three hours ago. The rest you know."

"How did Uther come by Lot's queen?"

He shook his head, dismissing my question as trivial. "I can't tell you that, Commander. I do not enjoy your cousin's confidence. I only know that we collected her in passing from one of Lot's strongholds, after we started our march south."

I did not know what to make of this information, but I dismissed it as unimportant beside the urgency of my pursuit of Uther.

"I have to find them."

"Then God go with you, Caius Merlyn. You'll need His help."

"Which way should I go from here?"

He nodded towards the south. "They left by that southern valley. Be cautious, Merlyn."

"I will, my friend. Farewell."

I left him to his work and remounted my horse, closing my eyes and ears to the miserable sights and sounds around me, and for the next quarter-hour I picked my way carefully through that awful field.

I had almost won clear of the battlefield when I heard my
name being called. I drew rein and looked in the direction of the
voice, and there was Popilius, our senior centurion, sitting against
the bole of a small tree less than thirty paces from me. I was
shocked at almost failing to recognize him at first glance. Popilius
had always been my exemplar of miltary propriety, polished and
shorn and brightly armoured, upright and solid and thoroughly
dependable in every circumstance. The man at whom I found
myself gaping now was different from the image I carried of him
in almost every respect.

He was without armour, for one thing, and his right thigh was
swathed in bandages crusted with dried blood and dirt. His left
arm was cradled in a sling made of coarse, grey woollen cloth torn
from a blanket, and the fingers of the hand that protruded from its
cradle were curled and clawlike, also wrapped in blood-stained
bandages. The entire left side of his face was bruised into a blackened mass, and his hair, which I suddenly noticed for the first time
was long and white, hung unkempt and matted over his forehead,
which bore the striations of pain like horizontal bars above his
eyes. His chin was coated in grizzled, grey-white stubble. Popilius
had grown old, very suddenly.

I leaped from my horse and made my way to where he lay
sprawled, almost supine, against his tree trunk. An empty wineskin
lay beside him and I smelled its harsh, sour *vinum* on his clothes
and on his breath. He was lucid, however, and his forehead was
cool to my touch, and I quickly assured myself that his injuries
were not life threatening. He told me he had taken a sword slash to
the thigh and an arrow through the forearm in the running fight
the day before they blundered into Lot's trap. He had been a non-
combatant this day, helpless to influence anything, watching the
entire, catastrophic battle in frustrated rage from the deck of a
wagon Quinto's people had been using to transport the wounded.
No one had paid him any attention, either during or after the battle. He had not eaten anything since the night before, and had
drunk all his wine, finishing it gluttonously hours earlier in hope of

finding oblivion from the horror that surrounded him. He had thought he was dreaming when he recognized me riding by, a vision in my cleanliness and wholeness.

I could not simply leave him there as I had found him. He was Popilius Cirro, one of the last of my father's most trusted friends, and he deserved some show of care from me. Forcing myself to stifle my restlessness and the urging that prompted me to rush on callously in my pursuit of Uther, I fed him from my own supplies and spent some time changing the dressings on his wounds, using strips torn from a spare, clean tunic from my saddle bags. That done, I found some water on a nearby wagon, probably the one he had occupied, and washed him as well as I could, before helping him to move and arranging him as comfortably as possible on a grassy knoll.

I had done as much as I could for him, and it was time for me to move on. I told him so, and he nodded, accepting that, but then he asked me about regaining my memory and we talked for some time of that, and how it had affected me. I told him also about finding young Bassus, and how I had had to kill him. He listened in silence, fingering the stubble on his chin. When I had finished he sighed.

"I'd give anything in this world, Commander, to undo the last three years; to be back in Camulod, with your father alive and the world unfolding peacefully about us. But of course, that's non-sense—women's wishes. You'd best be on your way, if you're to find Uther, though I don't know what you'll be able to do to change anything."

I had nodded and risen to my feet, prepared to leave, when something in his voice, in the tone of it, alerted me. I could not identify what I had heard, but for some reason it made me think of what Quinto had said about Lot's women. I stopped and cleared my throat, looking down at him. "Tell me about the women, Popilius, about Lot's queen. What's going on? How did Uther capture her?"

He, too, cleared his throat, but he looked away, avoiding my eyes. "The Lady Ygraine."

"Sweet Jesus!" As he uttered it, the name flashed across my mind like Publius Varrus's Skystone blazing across the sky. Ygraine! The daughter of the Erse king who was Donuil's father! I remembered Donuil telling me the first time we met that his father and Lot were to be allied by marriage. His sister Ygraine had been betrothed to Lot mere months before. But that meant—and this thought was crushingly, overwhelmingly new to me—that she was also Deirdre's sister ... my Cassandra's sister ... The bitter, tragic irony of it almost buckled my knees, and I had to turn my back and walk away from Popilius to master my thoughts before he read the despair in my eyes.

My mind was screaming at me. Uther could have no idea, of course, who Ygraine truly was. He had killed her sister, bringing me after him, ravening for vengeance, and now when I found him he would be with yet another of this strange Erse family to which, it seemed, I was inextricably bound. I had a flashing image of Cassandra biting down on his swollen manhood and I felt my sanity withdrawing from me like a whirling wind. I pushed my fist, hard, into my mouth and bit down on my own knuckles. The sudden pain enabled me to regain control of my thoughts and force myself to remain rational. When I thought I had myself under control again I turned back to Popilius, clutching my bitten knuckles in my other hand. He was staring at me, wide-eyed, obviously wondering what my next reaction might be. I made myself walk back to him, and when I spoke, my voice sounded calm and reasonable even to me.

"When did this happen? What *has* happened? Tell me now, and leave nothing out."

One moment longer he hesitated, and then he began to speak in a flat, rough monotone. Much of what he would tell me, he was careful to point out at the start, was conjecture, but it was based solidly upon his own observations and upon comments made—or tactfully omitted—by other officers who were closer to the source of the truth than he was. In matters of fieldcraft, discipline, training, deployment and logistics, Uther consulted Popilius before committing himself or his forces to anything. Otherwise, Uther kept his own counsel and Popilius was normally content to have it that way. On this campaign, however, the veteran Popilius had been gravely troubled. His prime responsibility, as he saw it, was the defence and welfare of our Colony. If those twin priorities entailed a pre-emptive expedition into territories beyond our own, he would prosecute that campaign without question or pause, but his primary motivation was always to achieve the objective, deal with the threat and danger, and then withdraw homeward without delay. For more than a year now, he told me, that imperative had been neglected.

In the late summer of my first year of convalescence, Uther's advance party, with Uther himself in command, had surprised and captured a heavily escorted supply train on its way to the south coast, where the supplies were to be loaded onto ships and taken around by sea to Lot's stronghold on the northern coast of the long, Cornish peninsula. Among the personnel accompanying that train been a contingent of high-born ladies.

Uther, ever the dashing, dazzling heroic figure, had never warred on women and was at pains to point this out to his gentle prisoners. He had commiserated with them about the deaths of their escort and companions—the fortunes of war, over which he could have no control other than by ensuring victory for his own men. That done, and all courteously explained, he had entertained them lavishly as honoured guests for three days, during which his army had consolidated their own security and spirited the stolen spoils of the supply train into their own safe custody. Then, when he was sure that their reports could do nothing to hinder either his progress or his safety, he had released the women, sending them southward to their original destination under heavy guard.

No time had been lost on that occasion, Popilius assured me. Little had been risked, and a valuable prize had been gained. It was only months later that Popilius had begun to suspect that Uther himself had gained a valuable prize that day, quite apart from the captured supplies. Prior to that, Popilius had neither known nor

cared about the identities of the women. He had found out only by
accident one night, around the campfire with some of Uther's young
staff officers who had drunk a little too much wine, that one of the
women—the loveliest, of course—had been Lot's queen, Ygraine.

His soldier's mind had been outraged by this information, for
here had been a legitimate spoil of war, a hostage and a bargaining
tool of great power. Why, then, had Uther, who must have been
well aware of who she was and what she would have been worth
in the war against her husband, allowed the woman to go free? As
I listened to his recounting of his misgivings, I was wondering the
same thing myself. She was Lot's queen. She should never have
been released!

Had she been anyone else, however, no matter who, Popilius's
report would neither have bothered nor surprised me. I would have
expected nothing less from my charming and mercurial cousin.
But why in God's name would he have released Ygraine the queen?
It made no sense at all, even had he been besotted by her, for merely
by holding her prisoner he could have pursued his own designs
and seduced her at his leisure, and with pleasure, knowing whose
wife she was. And then it did make sense, in a bizarre, illogical way
over which I had no control. The answer sprang into my mind
completely formed and I accepted it immediately and instinctively
as being true.

All that I knew of Lot, although I had not set eyes on him
since that one time in boyhood, indicated that he was in many
ways abnormal, almost inhuman, in his tastes and desires. Not that
I had any cause to suspect him of being deviate or homosexual; far
from it, his heterosexual lusts were notorious, as was his cruelty. It
simply came to me that the man must be incapable of love—ordinary, human love—and it followed inevitably that his wife, as a
bargaining piece in enemy hands, would have been less than useless to that enemy.

As a spy, however, angry in her Celtic pride and her sense of
betrayal and abandonment by the man to whom she had been given
like a sacrificial cow, she could be recruited to the cause of his

enemies, would become an invaluable asset to them, even if her regal husband never shared a thought with her. From the way my heart swelled with excitement, I knew I was right. Ygraine was Uther's spy, the one of whom I had already heard! She and Uther had met, had quickly become enamoured of each other, and had conspired somehow, in the brief space of three short days, to undo Lot.

In the moments it took for all of this to explode in my mind, Popilius had continued speaking. Nothing had come of the events surrounding the supply train incident, he said, and apart from his outrage and puzzlement over the release of the woman, the whole thing had faded from his mind until about a year after the original encounter. Popilius had been personally inspecting the guards around a night camp when an exhausted rider had come in—a stranger wearing the blazon of the boar of Cornwall, Lot's own emblem—bearing urgent word for Uther.

Within the hour, Uther had ridden out, accompanied by only two of his closest circle, leaving his army under the control of Popilius. Nothing untoward had occurred and Popilius had not been unduly concerned at first. Only when the second consecutive day of Uther's absence dawned had Popilius begun to grow concerned. His concern mushroomed when he made specific inquiries and discovered that no one, including the remaining members of Uther's inner circle, knew where the king had gone. Even his Celts had no idea of Uther's whereabouts, but they at least were unconcerned. To them, their king was inviolable and invincible. He would come back safely.

As it transpired, Popilius had been forced to sit in agonized inactivity for two more days before Uther returned late in the afternoon, just before nightfall, galloping into camp as though he had not a care in the world. He had called a meeting of his senior officers immediately, and told them they would be moving out at dawn. Few slept for more than an hour that night, because long before dawn began to lighten the sky the camp had been broken down and stowed, and the troops were in formation, ready to ride out. They had marched for a day and a half, and then prepared an elaborate ambush above a narrow, mile-long gorge, where the only road ran narrow and serpentine alongside a fast-flowing stream. Every trooper had been turned to work lining the lip of the gorge with massive boulders, assembling an avalanche of rocks that would decimate the forces caught below. Uther's bowmen, in the meantime, were busy digging themselves in on the peat-covered hillsides on the exit side of the gorge, where the emerging road turned left to pass along the bottom of a gentle slope.

In the fight that ensued, Popilius experienced for the first time the destructive power of massed Celtic longbows as used by Uther's people. He had fought several times with contingents of Celts using the bows, but nothing he had ever seen had prepared him for what transpired that day. They had dug themselves four pairs of trenches ascending the hillside, and there were fifty men in each trench. Now, responding to voice signals from a leader in each trench, they began to fire in volleys; fifty long, lethal, deadly accurate arrows aimed and launched at a time from either side of the slope, and each flight followed so quickly by another that each rank had barely time to re-nock and pull before its time came round again. It looked, Popilius whispered, as though it were raining arrows.

Each man, he told me, fired ten arrows into a dense-packed target area that was so close it was impossible to miss. Four thousand arrows aimed at fewer than one thousand close-packed men who had nowhere to run in search of cover. It was over in almost less time than it takes to describe. Not one cavalryman went forward to meet an enemy that morning.

When Popilius had finished speaking, I allowed his silence to hang in the air for long moments before I broke it. "Where did Uther's information come from?"

"You tell me."

"Ygraine."

"That's my guess, too." He sighed deeply. "But it's still only a guess, Commander."

"No, it had to be Ygraine. There's no other explanation."

Popilius nodded. "I agree. That first messenger who came that night I was inspecting the guards, the one who wore Lot's boar . . . he was her man, sent to fetch Uther. I have seen him since, and he was with her when she joined us four days ago."

"She came willingly?"

He grunted. "Aye, and quickly. She had a child with her, too, new born. Lot thinks it's his, apparently, so she must have lain with him at least once in the past year."

"Is it?"

Again came the shake of his white head and a grunt of discomfort as he sought to ease his position. "Your guess is as good as mine. But Uther walks with an extra spring in his step nowadays, it seems to me."

I scrubbed my face with my hands, as though to wash away the need for sleep, although what I was trying to dislodge was a growing need to scream out my outrage. "You've given me much to think about, old friend," I told Popilius, fighting to keep my voice level. "I feel I've slept away two important years and I've much to do to catch up with all that has happened."

He smiled, a brief, wintry grin. "Well, at least you're back, Commander. 'Thank God,' is all I can say. What will you do now?"

"Find Uther immediately. In the meantime, you have your duty to attend to, and it consists of recovering and returning safe to Camulod. We need you, Popilius Cirro. Try to sleep for an hour or so and then send someone to report your presence to Mucius Quinto over on the far side of the field. No point in doing it now, your wounds are dressed and he's too busy to attend to you. As quickly as you can thereafter, get you home again, and don't let Quinto stop until you get there. I have to leave now, but I'll see you back in Camulod."

He grunted again and nodded, looking at me with fondness. "Watch yourself, Commander. Be careful. There's whole armies of dangerous people out there."

I grinned at him. "Didn't anyone ever tell you how dangerous Caius Merlyn Britannicus can be?" I clapped him on the shoulder. "Sleep a while, old friend. Then make enough noise to draw yourself to the attention of our surgeon. Farewell."

XL

The following day, I found Gulrhys Lot, King of Cornwall, hanging from a tree, his hands and feet severed at the wrists and ankles and stuffed into a bag that was tied around his waist. The bag was made of gold brocade and bore the embroidered crimson emblem of Pendragon. The ring finger of his severed right hand still bore his signet: a massive golden ring set with the black boar of Cornwall and proof that the monster was dead.

Ignoring the mystery of my find, I cut the body down and burned it, but I kept the golden signet. I never discovered the truth of how Lot came to die, hanged ignominiously and left to dangle alone and unmourned in a forest glade, his royal seal intact upon his finger in a bag of meat.

I slept that night within a mile of where his ashes smouldered. The smell of his burning was in my clothes and in my hair, and I dreamed dreadful dreams. Sections of armies, bands of fighting men, mounted and afoot, swept and swirled around me in awful silence, though their mouths were wide with screams and their faces harrowed with agony. I saw Lot of Cornwall, mounted on a silver horse, being hit and borne down into a press of bodies, which scattered suddenly to show me Uther, naked and bloodied, his manhood erect with lust, holding Lot's severed, dripping head above his own and laughing in dementia, weeping blood-red tears while I ran towards him, a dagger in my hand, my eyes fixed on the bloodied flail that dangled from his wrist. And suddenly the severed head above Uther was Deirdre's—my Cassandra's—and it was screaming at me, wide-eyed and wide-mouthed, to stay away, to beware, beware, beware; and then came a clanging, echoing blow to my head, a stabbing, crushing pain in my back beneath my ribs and a hideous tearing wrench that started me awake in terror, my heart thudding in my chest. It was morning and the sun was already high.

I lay awake for a long time, unmoving, my mind reeling with the reality of my terror and the unreality of my dream. My back ached agonizingly, just where the dream-blow had struck me, and I knew I had slept upon a surfaced root. Presently, when my heart had slowed down and my breathing returned to normal, I rolled away from it and sat up, rubbing my aching spine. As I rose painfully to my feet, I looked ruefully for the cause of my discomfort, ashamed of myself for having made a boy's mistake in lying down in such a spot. But there was nothing there. The turf on which I had lain was thick and springy. I knelt again and dug in the grass with my fingertips, clearly seeing the imprint of my body. There was nothing: no root, no stone, no projection of any kind. The mossy turf was smooth and soft and yielding. I stood up hastily, aware of a stirring of superstitious fear, and set about saddling my spare mount, leaving the big black unburdened.

I ate as I travelled, on horseback, chewing dried nuts and chopped, dried apples mixed with roasted grain, and as I progressed the pain in my body receded palpably, drawing back slowly from a point beneath my ribs in front, until it seemed to exit from its starting point low in my back. Within an hour of leaving my campsite, it had vanished completely.

Sometime later, when I dismounted to drink from a swift-flowing stream, I saw my own reflection in a sheltered eddy beneath the bank. The sun was high behind me as I stooped to the surface of the water, its light diffused through my long, yellow hair, and I thought again, with a chill of horror, of Deirdre's severed head in my dream. Uther had held it by the hair, but the hair had been red-gold, and Deirdre's eyes had not been hers but the bright green eyes of someone else. Not Deirdre of the Violet Eyes, for green was never violet, and as Donuil had told me, her hair in girlhood had been deep red, the red of day-old chestnuts, not the golden hue I had seen in my dream. When I knew her, as Cassandra,

she had been fair-haired and grey-eyed. This was the stuff of
dreams, but the hairs along my spine stiffened in awe. I scooped up
some water quickly and was about to drink when something struck
me as *wrong*. I looked more closely, and saw the discoloration. It
looked muddy. *Silt in the water*, I told myself, but I had seen such
mud before, too many times.

Less than twenty paces upstream, I found five of my own men
of Camulod starting to bloat in the stream bed. I vomited up the
thought of what I had almost drunk, and when I had recovered, I
went in and pulled them out, laying them side by side along the
bank. I knew all five of them and it was all I could do for them.

Throughout the remainder of that morning, I became inured to
the sight of my own men lying dead. They had taken many of the
enemy with them, but I ignored those completely, my eyes attracted
only to the colours of Camulod and the red dragon of Pendragon.
My route lay directly to the south, to the sea, and I knew I would
wade through the debris of a running fight for the entire journey. I
met five living men of Uther's force, all wounded badly, none able to
tell me anything coherent. I left each of them with food and drink
and moved on. I also found eight of Lot's men alive, five of them
dying. The other three tried to unhorse me all at once, but I had
seen the one crouched in the tree above me and was forewarned. I
killed him as he leaped at me, catching him on my sword point and
thrusting him away and down so that he almost tore the weapon
from my grasp. One of the others seized me by the ankle, but my
horse turned on him, striking him with its shoulder, and he fell
away as I slashed at him, catching him high on the side of the head.
The third man fled and I did not have the heart to follow him.

I stopped to eat and change horses at noon in an open meadow
that seemed miraculously free of corpses and signs of conflict, and
less than half an hour after that I came across a scene that harrowed me far more than the carnage of battle through which I had
been riding all morning.

I emerged from a small valley between two low, swelling hills
to find myself in a devastated farmstead. The farmhouse itself had

been no more than a hovel, but it had been burned and its walls had collapsed upon themselves. The bodies of the farmer and three children, one of them a newborn child, lay sprawled in a pathetic, huddled group close by the gutted building. Beside them knelt the mother, alive and, as far as I could tell, unharmed. She knelt erect, her dry eyes staring into the surrounding hills with the haunted blankness of dementia. I dismounted and approached her with the idea of offering to help in some way, but she was unaware of me or my existence. Even when I took her hand she offered no response, but when I stooped towards the slaughtered baby at her knees she turned on me like a wild thing and tried to bite me. I withdrew hastily and she subsided immediately, ignoring me thereafter, resuming her empty-eyed watch over her dead family and I stood there uncomfortably, my stomach roiling with unwarranted guilt and sickness, until I convinced myself that I could do nothing for her. I backed away in silence and left her there with her grief. Moments later, I found the sea.

Because of the angle from which I had made my unwitting approach, it took me some time to realize at first that the slope I was ascending had an unnatural-looking edge against the sky, but as I drew closer, it became plain that there was no more land ahead of me, that I was ascending a hill that had been sheared off at some time. I ended my ascent on the edge of a cliff that dropped straight down to a rock-strewn beach far below. The tide was out, exposing a long, narrow belt of steeply shelving sand beyond which the sea stretched empty and endless, but after the first wondering glance at the enormity of the vista, my eyes were drawn to a broad swath of hoofprints churned into the wet sand far below and disappearing into the distance to my right. A large party of horsemen had passed below this point only a short time before. Their passage was plain, but the evidence of it in the sand was chaotic, and I was too far away to discern with any certainty the direction in which they had travelled. Individual tracks flanked the main body of the passage on both sides, and I could clearly see in these where flying hooves had thrown scatterings of sand behind them as they went, but it was equally clear that these individual riders, whoever they were, had ridden hard in both directions. I could see for several miles westward, and there was nothing except the broad path dwindling into the distance. I felt instinctively that the signs led east, to my left, but my view in that direction was blocked by the swell of the next headland, and beyond that I could see the crest of another, this one set back so that its top rose above the flank of the one between us. The coastline obviously curved inland to form a bay, and as the coast receded the height of the cliffs dwindled drastically.

I cast one last glance westward, seeing nothing there but the empty shoreline, then I touched my spurs to the big black and rode downhill, angling my descent to take the straightest line to the eastern inlet.

As I regained the edge of the escarpment by the sea I saw bright colours in the far distance, three or more miles away on the beach on the far side of the sweeping bay that now came into view. A band of horsemen—I estimated about a score at first glance—milled in confusion there, almost at the water's edge. The cliff below me was still perilous, although not one-quarter as high as it had been before, and my view to the left was still obstructed by the lie of the land, but the ground was shelving rapidly downhill to my left, the terrain changing from rocky cliffs to enormous, grass-crowned dunes, and I saw that I would soon find a way down. I swung left again, this time keeping to the edge of the clifftop, and as I rode the scene below unfolded. A second party of riders, half again as large as the first and hidden from me previously, now streamed into view, from beneath the cliffs that had hidden them from me. They made their way ponderously through the yielding sand, struggling inexorably towards the first party. Uther's great red war cloak with its blazoned dragon was unmistakable at the head of this second group, even from this distance. Pursuers and pursued.

My heart in my mouth from the excitement of my discovery, I reined in briefly to consider my options. My horse was still fresh—I had not been aboard him for an hour and he had not been exerted. I could see even from where I was that Uther's horses were exhausted. He and his men were only now beginning to approach the first curve of the bay's end. Slightly more than a mile, I guessed, separated them from their quarry across the water, but they would have to ride more than twice that far to reach them. And now I could see that the far party were fighting to drag a boat to the water's edge. It was a big, cumbersome vessel and the ebb tide had left it stranded high on the sand. They seemed to be making little headway.

Again I looked to Uther's group. Their progress, too, was painfully slow. The sand where they were now was deep and dry. I was a good mile behind them. I could descend to the beach soon, but the yielding sand would hamper me, too, whereas the ground here, above the beach, was firm. By staying high, I could make far better time, but would have further to ride to catch up. I let go the lead reins of my two extra horses and sank my spurs into the big black, keeping him on the high ground and letting him find his own way at his own speed. He was ready to run, and his great hooves devoured the distance along the clifftop. As I overhauled Uther's party and passed them on my right, my mind was working frantically, trying to determine who the people in the other group might be. From the bright colours of their clothes, I already suspected that some of them might be women, although many of the Celts I had seen, especially the Hibernian Scots, loved bright, patterned clothing. But if there were women among this group, who were they? Lot was dead, and his wife was Uther's mistress, so she would not be attempting to escape him.

I had arrived, very quickly I thought, at the point beyond which geometry negated speed. Riding further on my present path would take me further away from my target with every stride, so I swung hard to the right and my horse slithered and slid its way to the bottom of the cliff, which was now no more than a steep, sandy shelf above the beach. Now I found myself galloping between high dunes of sand that hid the activity ahead of me, but grateful that the ground was still firm enough to present no problem to my wonderful horse.

It seemed to take me an age to emerge from the dunes by the water's edge, and long before I arrived there I had heard the sound of baying voices announcing the beginnings of a fight. The deepest point of the bay now lay to my right and I was still more than a mile from the brawl ahead of me. I saw a scattering of riderless horses that told me immediately how the struggle would go. The heavy boat lay abandoned at the end of a deep score in the sand, its bows awash, but the men who had been struggling to launch it had been caught before they could either free the boat or remount to meet their attackers. Now Uther's men swirled around them, some of their horses actually in the water so that light flashed from the splashes they made and from their sweeping blades as they hacked and slashed at their quarry.

And yet the fight was far from over. The men afoot were fighting well although barely holding their own. Armed with the bravery of desperation they had formed a line of defence in front of the brightly clothed members of the group who, as I had suspected, were women, and were now huddled in and around the boat. A new core of resistance formed even as I watched, however, and it was an amazing sight to my distant eyes. Half a score of men, seeing the inevitable failure of their efforts to launch the boat, had scattered and apparently fled from the main action, but only to reform in a tight group, ranked in a close formation on the side of a low dune. Now, armed with what looked to me to be Pendragon bows, this group began pouring a concerted, lethal stream of well-aimed volleys into Uther's mounted troops, smashing them from their horses like straw mannikins.

What nonsense was this? And where were Uther's own bowmen? As these questions sprang into my mind I felt my great horse falter and check beneath me and I knew he could not continue much longer at this speed, fetlock-deep in yielding, clogging sand. And even as I leaned forward to encourage him, everything changed in the fight in front of me.

In response to a summons from Uther, many of his men broke away from their individual struggles and reformed into a solid wall of horses that they used to smash their way through the defenders, trampling them underfoot, to reach the women in and around the boat. In moments after that each mounted man had hauled a struggling, fighting woman up in front of him, holding her close around the waist or the neck and using her as a living shield against the bowmen. As soon as the last woman—there were eight of them—had been subdued, Uther himself led the group in a concerted charge against the bowmen on the dune. I watched in disbelief, seeing all of this unfolding the way a sleeping man watches a scene of horror engulf him in a nightmare, powerless to change a detail of his dream and knowing that it will only grow worse as it progresses. My horse was barely moving now, and I was still four hundred paces from the boat, five hundred from the dune. I screamed Uther's name, feeling my voice break at the peak, but no one heard me.

The bowmen on the dune had stopped shooting now. It takes a certain kind of inhumanity to commit callous murder on a living, helpless woman, even when she embodies your own death. Frozen, the bowmen stood and watched, arrows nocked, as Uther's men swept towards them. And then finally, when less than fifty paces separated the two groups, one aimed and fired and drew and fired again and one rider went down, his shield and he both dead. Three more aimed and fired and Uther's group was cut to half its size, but Uther was almost at the foot of the dune by then and the bowmen broke and scattered, casting aside their useless weapons and drawing their swords. Uther threw his helpless shield to the ground and charged after one of the disarmed bowmen. I watched the slaughter in agony, still approaching. I could feel the strength draining away from my body like water pouring from a broken vase, and despair threatened to overwhelm me. I did not know what was happening here, or who these victims were, but I had seen more callous slaughter from my cousin here than I would ever have believed him capable of.

I reined in my mount and sat there, staring. Apart from Uther and his three remaining riders by the dune, there was barely a movement on the beach. One of the women thrown from the backs of the horses got up slowly and stood swaying for a time, then began moving among the others, checking each of them for signs of life. She stooped quickly and helped another to her feet, this one swathed in an enveloping yellow garment that covered her completely except for her arms and one long, slender leg that shone from a large tear in the fabric. The two women clung to each other. Three more of Uther's men were still alive, and now mounted their horses again and began to converge, with Uther and the others, upon the two women. No one had seen me yet, sitting my horse some two hundred paces distant. Now I urged my mount forward again, but even as it began to walk, I reined in and waited.

Uther had dismounted and was approaching the women, who stood side by side, facing him. I waited for him to remove his helmet, but he did not. He merely stopped a few paces from them and stooped quickly to grasp a handful of cloth adorning one of the dead women lying by his feet. He wiped the blood from his sword blade on the cloth and straightened up, slipping the sword back into its sheath. He then flipped the edges of his cloak back across his shoulders. Puzzled, I watched him fumbling at the front of his clothing. I realized his purpose at the same time the women did, for they both turned to run. He closed the distance between them in one leap and grasped the yellow-clad woman by the shoulder, spinning and pushing her so that she fell heavily. The other woman attacked him immediately, and he thrust her aside, throwing her as casually and as easily as if she had no substance. Then he grasped the woman on the ground and, with a great heave, ripped the yellow covering from her body, tumbling her through the air so that I saw naked flesh and long, red hair as the other woman attacked him yet again, leaping this time on to his back. Now I kicked my horse into movement, and as I did so I saw Uther bend and heave and dislodge his assailant, throwing her over his shoulder so that she fell in front of him. He held her with one hand around her wrist and then pulled her erect before jerking her close to him. I knew from the way she stiffened, rigid, that he had stabbed her, pulling her onto a dagger, and I watched her sink to her knees and then fall away to the side. And now Uther was tugging at his clothes again, loosening his belt and tearing at his trousers to expose his loins. I watched him fall to his knees and drag the red-haired woman towards him, grasping her and pulling at her so that he held one of her knees in the crook of each elbow. I was very close, little more than a hundred paces away, still moving like a man in a dream. All eyes were on Uther and his sport. My mind was reciting a litany . . .

Deirdre of the Violet Eyes. Cassandra of the Valley. Deirdre of the Weeping Sighs. Cassandra in the Valley. Deep the grave where Deirdre lies. Cassandra, Merlyn's Folly . . .

I had been unaware of unslinging Publius Varrus's great bow from where it lay across my back; unaware of fitting an arrow; unaware of anything except my own criminally irresponsible naivety. All the pathetic human weakness and frailty of my doubts and agonizing over Uther's capacity to sink to the level of brutality involved in the savage beating and the murder of my beloved now writhed in my scornful awareness. How could I ever have doubted it? I had always known that Uther had a blackness in him I could never plumb. And today, here, I had seen more of it than I had suspected in thirty years of knowing him intimately. And now I found my voice again.

His head jerked up at the sound of my shout, and the six men behind him immediately broke from their admiring huddle and began to spread out, moving towards me. I ignored them.

Uther disengaged himself almost casually from the woman's body and stood up, his male organ gleaming wetly as he stuffed it into his clothing and began to rebuckle his belt. I knew I could kill him from where I sat, but I lusted to confront him, to tell him why he was dying by my hand. Instead, I shot the man closest to me, driving my first arrow through his head, between his eyes, and stringing a second arrow almost before the first struck home. As the dead man's companions began to react, and to spur their horses, I shot a second and then a third, aiming almost casually and without either compunction or excitement. They were merely an annoyance, coming as they did between me and my task that day. Two of the surviving three made the mistake of trying to break away and flee; the third kept coming at me. Had they come together, they would have had me, but as it was, I shot the man approaching me through the breastplate of his armour when he was less than ten paces from me. With the hollow but solid, slightly metallic *thunk* of his death loud in my ears, I turned after his two companions. One I brought down at the edge of the water. He fell into the waves of the returning tide. The last of them, far off by now, presented the first challenge I had yet had. I sighted carefully, leading him as he rode across my left side, and loosed my arrow. It arced and hummed in a perfect trajectory and he watched it seek him, throwing up an arm as though to fend it off, so that it sank to the feathers into his exposed armpit.

My cousin had mounted his horse by this time and sat watching me, waiting. The body of the red-haired woman lay almost beneath his horse's feet. I leaned from the saddle and gently dropped my bow to the sand, and then shrugged the quiver strap over my shoulder and let that fall, too. That done, I nudged my horse slowly towards him. He sat motionless, his helmeted head cocked to one side, watching me and waiting for my next move. When only ten paces separated us, I halted and stared at him. When I spoke, I was amazed at the calmness of my own voice, for I wanted to scream.

"Bloody business, killing women, Cousin." I nodded at the woman's body. "But not your first time, eh?"

I began counting my heartbeats during the silence that followed. At twelve, he said, "*'Cousin?'* Who are you?" I felt as though I had been struck, and I actually felt myself reel. This was not Uther! "Are you deaf? Who are you?"

Slowly, my hand shaking, I reached up and undid the chin strap of my helmet. He sat watching as I took it off and held it in the crook of my left arm and now I saw him react, although his reaction stunned me more than his first words had. I saw his eyes narrow beneath the front plate of his helmet as he stiffened with surprise, and then he spoke again, hesitantly on the first word, and then with complete conviction.

"Ambrose ... Ambrose of Lindum! I thought you went home."

Now it was he who undid his helmet and removed it to show me a face I had not thought ever to see again. He was Derek, the king from Ravenglass, whom I had met and befriended briefly on the road two years before.

"You're with us," he said. "At least you were . . . with Lot. Why did you kill my men?"

I ignored the question. "Where's Uther?"

"Uther?" I could hear the mystification in his voice. "How would I know?"

"You're wearing his armour."

"Oh, him!" He stopped and looked at me wonderingly. "That was Uther Pendragon?"

I nodded. "It was. You killed him?"

"Well, yes, but I didn't know who he was. Never seen him before, not that it would have made a difference."

"Personally? You yourself?"

"Personally. Me myself. I killed him." He seemed to be challenging me to do something about it.

"When?" My voice was no more than a croak and my heart was thundering in my ears as I asked this question, for I suddenly dreaded to hear the answer.

"This morning." The words I was hearing echoed in my head as though emerging from a deep well. "Just before daybreak. We'd been chasing them for days and caught them just as they were breaking camp. Knew it was Uther's army, but they were all scattered and chewed up. Didn't know it was Uther himself."

"Why did you take his armour?" I asked the question knowing it was a vain attempt to avoid what was to follow.

He looked at me as though I were crazed. "Why wouldn't I? He didn't need it any more. I haven't been home in more than two years. He was the only man I've met in months—years, because the last one was you—whose armour was big enough to fit me. Even his helmet fits me."

"How . . . exactly how did you kill him?" It was a question I had to ask, to quell my own sudden certainty.

He shook his head in wonder at my stubborn pertinacity. "What does it matter? With this, same as I kill most men I fight against." He reached down and produced a fearsome weapon from where it hung at his saddle bow. It looked like a reaper's hook fixed to the handle of a battle axe. It had a broad blade three handspans long, both sharpened edges of which were wickedly serrated. The sight of it chilled my gut and brought a cataract of teeming memories.

"In the back. You caught him low in the back ... here." I pointed to where I had felt the agony.

He nodded, his brow wrinkled in puzzlement. "That's right, just below the edge of his backplate. He was trying to mount his horse when I reached him ... one foot in the stirrup, but the horse was shying. Couldn't get a clear swing at his head or neck because of his helmet, tried twice, but couldn't, so I took him low, backhanded. How did you know that?"

"I dreamed it, twice. I felt it this morning, when it happened." His eyes grew wide as he stared at me.

"What are you talking about?"

I shook my head, bemused, trying to shake off the feelings that assaulted me, but he kept talking.

"What d'you mean you felt it? Felt what? What madness is this?"

"Your weapon ... that thing you have there. Did you have it with you when last we met?"

"No." He shook his head. "No, I took it from a Saxon in the north about a year ago. Best thing I ever came across for swinging from a saddle. Why?"

"I saw it in a dream, the night after I first met you. I saw you standing over a dead man ... someone I couldn't see ... but I was saddened by his death. And in my dream you turned on me, with that ... thing in your hand."

He drew himself erect, settling himself in his saddle and blowing out his breath with an explosive sound. "What are you, some kind of sorcerer?"

I was asking myself the same question, for I could no longer deny, as I had been denying all my life, the strangeness of the power that sometimes stirred within me, frightening me with its potency. In a grim, silent parade of mockery, the memories of all the dreams of all the times before passed before my mind's new and all-seeing eye: a hundred and more shadowy events, but prime among them the death of my father; my vision of Ambrose before we met; and the death of Uther at the hands of Derek of Ravenglass. I knew the word for what I had conceived. It was pre-science, but prescience was sorcery, and I had abjured all things magical throughout my life, discrediting their existence unless they involved human, manipulative trickery and the underlying wish to win power, to whatever degree, over men's minds. If what were there within me lay beyond my knowledge, let alone my control . . . I could not face the consequences of that line of thought and so I banished it, turning elsewhere for salvation.

I looked down again at the woman. "Who is she?"

Derek of Ravenglass shrugged. "Lot's whore. I'd heard tell she was fornicating with one of the Camulod bastards. When I saw her with them, I knew it was true."

"But you still didn't know it was Uther?"

"No." He was vehement. "How could I know that? I've been up in the north-west for the past two years. Only came back south this spring, three weeks ago."

"Why did you permit her to escape from Uther's camp?"

He gave a wolfish grin full of sharp canines. "No one 'permitted' her. They closed ranks against us and fought to the last man to give her and her escort time to get away. We've been after them ever since."

I felt a vast calm flowing through me. "What do you know of Camulod?"

He grunted. "Nothing, except that they're hard bastards. They fight hard and they die hard. Why d'you ask that?"

"Because I'm one of them. Now you're going to have to kill me, too, before I kill you."

He settled back in his saddle, his eyes narrowing, hefting his fearsome, hooked weapon, and I heard him sigh before putting his, Uther's, helmet back on his head again.

"You said you were from Lindum, in the north," he said, sounding disappointed. "I believed you. I even liked you."

I nodded. "I can be likable enough, I'm told. But I lied to you. We were caught unawares on the road that day, among Lot's gathering army. We had to lie our way out. I am Merlyn Britannicus, of Camulod. Uther's grandmother and my grandfather were brother and sister." I would fight and kill this man, I knew, or be killed by him, but in spite of all I had seen, I could find no anger in my soul against him. I searched for more fuel. "Why rape the woman and kill the others?"

He was genuinely surprised by my question. "What? Why not, by all the gods? We're at war. Spoils to the victor, death to the vanquished. That's the way life is."

He was right. I unsheathed my long cavalry sword. He looked at it, and then back into my eyes. "You think you can kill me, Merlyn Britannicus?" I did not respond and he went on, "Tell me, you said you dreamed of how I killed Pendragon?"

I nodded. "I awoke with the pain through my bowels, but I didn't know what had caused it until I saw your hook there. That reminded me."

"What time was this?"

"Just at daybreak."

"When I killed him."

"Apparently."

He shook his head in apparent wonderment, clearly at a loss as to what to make of me and my behaviour, then sighed again, a deep, dull, barking sound, and pulled back hard on his reins, dancing his horse around to face me on its other side. "Look, I don't want to fight you, man, but I will if I have to, whether you be Ambrose of Lindum or Merlyn of Camulod. In either case, I have no fear of you, sorcerer though it seems you may be, but neither have I any wish to kill you. So why don't we both simply ride away from here? I'll tell you where your cousin is and you can bury him."

His words did not surprise me. Perhaps they should have, but I barely heard them. I was too busy looking at his saddle bow, at the red-leather-handled, iron-balled flail that hung there, suspended by a leather loop on the side his horse had exposed to me in turning. His eyes followed my gaze and he looked down to where the weapon hung.

"What are you looking at?"

"That flail, is it yours?"

"Aye, mine by possession. It was hanging there when I claimed the horse."

I kneed my own mount towards him. "Then it was my cousin's. May I have it?"

He looked askance at me, one eyebrow raised high, then, seeing that I still held my helmet cradled in my arm, he sighed a third time, dropped his reins on his horse's neck and shifted his hooked weapon to his other hand. I leaned towards him and took Uther's flail when he held it towards me, feeling the familiar weight of it tug at my shoulder.

"My thanks." I raised it high in my right hand, pointing the junction of the chain and handle skyward until the ball dangled before my eyes. Was it the one Uther had made so long ago, or was it another, made to replace the first after that one had been thrown into the mere in my small valley? I knew that I would never know, but now I found myself grateful for the doubt that had again replaced my former certainty. I blinked away the sudden tears that had filled my eyes and hung the weapon gently from my own saddle bow. The northern king had watched me in silence throughout all of this. I looked at him again. "Where will you go now?"

He shrugged. "Find Lot, perhaps, or go home. All my men are gone. Some home, most dead."

"Lot is dead, too. I found his body hanging from a tree." I reached into my scrip and drew out the ring. "See? I took his boar seal."

Derek of Ravenglass sniffed. "Hmm! That's that, then. I'm going home. I've a desire to see my children again."

"Where will I find Uther?"

He shrugged and hung his hook axe again on the side of his saddle, plainly convinced that we had no fight with each other. "Back the way we came. Follow our tracks along the beach. It must be twelve miles or more. You'll see where our tracks enter along a wide stream bed with a great, white gleaming boulder standing in the middle of it. Can't miss it, it's huge and bright white. Your cousin and his people are lying in a clearing three more miles upstream. A lot of mine are lying there too."

We sat gazing at each other in silence for several moments longer, then Derek of Ravenglass cleared his throat. "Well then," he growled, "I wish you well, Ambrose called Merlyn. We were never friends, but we've never really been enemies, either, have we? We've got a saying among our people that only those touched by the gods feel the pain of others. Me, I've never believed in the gods, any of 'em, but there's not a doubt in my mind that you felt your cousin's death. So I think you really might be touched by the gods in spite of what I've always thought. That's why I have no wish to fight you. Farewell."

He spun his horse and moved away and I watched him silently until he disappeared among the distant dunes. Neither of us had considered sharing the company of the other and that was as it should be. When he had gone from view, I looked again at the naked woman lying by my horse's feet and as I did so, she coughed weakly.

Only when I was kneeling by her side, cradling her in my bent arm, did I become aware of how familiar she appeared, and then I knew beyond a doubt that this was Ygraine, sister to Donuil and Deirdre. The resemblance to both of them was there, unmistakable, in her face, and when she opened her great, green eyes, I knew her as the woman from my dreams of the previous night and my skin chilled again with goose bumps. She was unaware of me, or of herself or where she was. Uther's was the first name that sprang to her lips, and then she repeated it, this time less distinctly, slurring the vowels so that it sounded like "Ather."

As I knelt there beside her, a wavelet rippled up the beach and soaked my knee. The tide was flowing fast now, and I thought to move her, but as soon as I began to lift her I stopped again. She was dying and my entire sleeve was soaked with blood. When I looked, I saw that the back of her head was matted with blood that welled slowly, but far too freely to staunch, and her head was crushed. I knew without looking further that she had been kicked by Derek's horse, probably while he was mounting to face my approach.

Presently her eyes focused on my face and she seemed to know me as she asked, "Where is my baby?"

"Baby, Lady? There is no baby here."

"Yes, my baby. My baby bear. I promised Uther I would keep him safe and take him . . ."

"Take him where, Lady?"

"To Camulod! My baby! To Uther in Camulod."

"Ygraine," I whispered, "Uther is gone."

"Uther? Ather . . . My son is Arthur. Pendragon's baby bear, his father call—" Her eyes went wide, startled, and she stiffened in my arms. "Uther?" she cried, and slumped dead.

I laid her gently on the sand and closed her eyes, seeing in my mind the eyes of her sister and her brother. How long I knelt there, my fingers on her eyelids, I have no idea, but I was grieving for her and for all of us who lived in this sad land of Britain. And then I heard, from behind me, clear and distinct as a cockerel's crow, the sound of a baby crying. Incredulous, I swung around to find myself kneeling almost in the sea and hearing the wailing of a baby coming from the great, clumsy, heavy boat that now rode gracefully upon the waves.

Starting to my feet, I flung myself towards it, feeling the water tugging at my armoured legs as I progressed. Deeper and deeper the water grew as the boat bobbed just beyond my reach, until I knew that one more step would take me under. Then, drawing a mighty breath, I launched myself with all my strength and felt the fingers of my right hand grasp the tailboard of the vessel. I scrambled and clawed and soon had both hands firmly in place, knowing that if I let go now I would drown, sinking straight to the bottom in all my armour. I waited and drew several deep breaths, gathering my strength, and then heaved myself up, swinging my right leg up and around to hook my heel over the side. It lodged on the wrong side, hampered by the spur on my heel, and it took great effort to twist it sidewise and inboard so the spur hooked instead on the safe side, holding me firmly. Moments later I had dragged myself up and fallen gasping into the safety of the boat, coughing and spewing bitter salt water, but enjoying the sheer pleasure of lying still, warm and wet, but safe.

I found the baby lying against the single mast, swathed in, and tied into, a black bear skin. A beautiful boy, no more than eight or nine weeks old, his tiny, chubby face was wrinkled in rage, eyes tightly closed as he protested against the hunger he was feeling.

I have never been able, nor am I able now, to describe the emotions that swept over me in those first moments of looking at the child who was to be my ward and this land's too brief-lived glory. I recall the feeling akin to reverence that filled me as I undid the bindings around the bear skin and peeled it away to look at him. He was swaddled in a long, white cloth that was stained and wet with the signs of his discomfort, and as I picked him up and loosened it his howls of outrage grew louder. Shortly thereafter, I held him naked, save for a soiled loincloth, and marvelled at the sturdy strength of him. This tiny, squalling mite was Uther's son, the fact attested to not by his red-gold hair, but by the red dragon crest of Pendragon on the signet ring fastened by a gold chain around his tiny neck. This was my nephew of a kind, blood nephew of my dear, dead wife Cassandra and nephew equally of my faithful friend Donuil, and in his veins, surging in virile potency, ran the pure Roman blood of the families of Publius Varrus and of my own grandfather Caius Britannicus, mingled with the royal Celtic blood of Ullic Pendragon, and of Athol, High King of the *Scotii*, the Scots of Hibernia. Here, in these minuscule, clenched fists, red face and squalling lungs, was a potential giant, distilled of a truly powerful concoction. A Leader, perhaps, to weld together the strongest elements of the people of this land of Britain. A King, perhaps, to wield Excalibur. In my mind, I clearly heard again the words Publius Varrus had spoken to me upon his deathbed: *You'll know the day, and you'll know the man. If he hasn't come before you die, pass the Sword on to someone you can trust. Your own son. You'll know. You've been well taught. And you have learned well. You found the secret of the Lady, Cay, and then the secret of the saddle. You'll find the secret of the King, someday. You'll know him as soon as you set eyes on him.* I looked at this small prince and I knew him and I shivered with foreknowledge, recalling another dream of a shining, silver sword piercing a stone.

As though conscious of my awe, the child stopped screaming and looked directly up at me with wide eyes and my breath caught in my throat. He was well haired, his skull covered with thick, red, curling locks, the kind of curling hair that reminded me of my great-uncle Publius Varrus. But it was his eyes that gave me pause. I had never seen anything like them, yet I had read of them in Varrus's books. They were the deep, golden eyes of a raptor, a mighty bird of prey, an eagle. I had never heard of or seen a baby with golden eyes, but I knew that this baby's great-grand-uncle Caius Britannicus had had such eyes. I drew him close to me, smelling the baby smells of him and knowing I would have to clean him soon, knowing also that I knew not how. And then I raised my eyes for the first time since boarding this craft, and looked towards the shore.

There, shockingly distant and far to my right, I saw my black horse standing on the beach, watching me, his head tilted to one side as though he wondered where I was going. He was the only living thing on all that long stretch of sand, and behind him the land rose rapidly to form a line of cliffs against the sky. We had already drifted almost to the mouth of the bay, and the broad, deep stretch of water between the boat and the beach told me that we would not be returning there today. The breeze that had sprung up, blowing from the land, was gentle on my face, but it was strong enough to drive our boat further from the land with every heartbeat. For a long, long time I knelt there, holding the now quiet child protectively against my breast as we drifted out to sea. Together we watched the shores of South Britain fall further and further behind us.

THE END

JACK WHYTE was born and raised in Scotland and has lived in Canada since 1967. He has been an actor, orator, singer, and poet at various stages of his life, and was awarded an honorary doctorate of letters for his contribution to Canadian popular fiction. Whyte is the author, most recently, of *The Burning Stone*, a prequel to his internationally bestselling *Dream of Eagles* series, as well as the *Templar* trilogy, and the *Guardians* trilogy. He lives in Kelowna, British Columbia, with his wife, Beverley.

Also available from the master
of the sweeping epic
JACK WHYTE

A Dream of Eagles

jackwhyte.com
penguinrandomhouse.ca